American Tumbleweed

By the author of Pain Magnet
available at Booksurge
www.booksurge.com
1-866-308-6235

This novel is a work of fiction.
Names, characters, places,
and incidents are either
the product of the author's
imagination or are used fictitiously,
and any resemblance
to actual persons, living or dead,
events, or locales
is entirely coincidental.

Moylanmedia Edition

All Rights Reserved

Moylanmedia

92 Chandler St

Nashua, NH 03064

www.moylanmedia.com

American Tumbleweed / Jeff Moylan

Visit www.booksurge.com to order additional copies.

Visit www.booksurge.com to order additional copies.

JEFF MOYLAN

AMERICAN TUMBLEWEED

2007

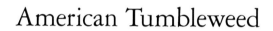

American Tumbleweed

Dedicated To My Father,
Joe Moylan,
Who Provided Me With
The Moral Compass
With Which To Navigate
Even A Fictional World
Of Drug Dealers
And Gun Smugglers.

CHAPTER 1

Tweed could think of any number of places he'd prefer to be right now. But LaGloria had insisted that he accompany her brothers on this miserable night and witness the deed that she had painstakingly arranged for them to do. Frankie sat in the back with Tweed, giving him those sidelong sly dog glances every once in a while.

"You cool, dude?"

"I'm just gonna sit in the car, man. You're the one who has to be cool."

"'Bout you, Nil?"

No response from the driver; no glimmer from the dark eyes that gazed abstractedly from under a brow that was heavy not with care or expression but with bone like a simian ridge, and lined with thin hair that matched his ratty mustache. Although he occupied the driver's seat, Nilvan drove with the least regard for what he was doing, and with the minimum effort. He slouched over the wheel, his right arm resting at twelve o'clock, his fingers draped over the dashboard like a pianist awaiting inspiration for an attack chord. With his other elbow crooked into the door's armrest he propped his head with his left hand, his fingers splayed out around his chin and gripping his beard.

Simply watching Nilvan irritated Tweed. He hated assholes like him who drove sitting off center, arm resting on the wheel, not paying attention. It made him tense enough to be aware of them when he was driving his own car, but now he was a passenger with one of them.

Seeing that they had almost arrived at their destination, Tweed wondered about the set up. He had never liked Frankie or Nilvan, not least of all because they were such fucking idiots, and furthermore he didn't like the idea of being within ten miles of any of their half-assed gigs. Even if LaGloria had planned this one, they were still pulling it off, which meant that something was going to go wrong.

In the back of his mind, he knew that it was the likelihood that they were going to fuck it up that had made him go along with the plan in the first place. But then he hadn't anticipated being along for the ride.

"Hey, Nil-Ban! You awake, Man?"

Nilvan. What a fucking name. How did Mr. McManus ever go along with Nilvan? Of course it was Mrs. McManus, a rare Hispanic beauty of some sort, Tweed guessed South American, who probably named the kids. There was Francisco, who acted like a spic but looked like any other kid; Nilvan, who looked like a spic but acted like a psychopath; and LaGloria, who possessed a gorgeous combination of Irish and Spanish genes, and who was Tweed's girlfriend.

He shoved Nil's seat from behind.

"Fa-KOFF!" snarled Nil, through his fingers.

South St skirted a park on the right and a swamp bordering the commuter rail bed on the left, winding like a switchback. Arbs Park, as it was known locally, was an urban oasis of trees, ponds, and walking trails laid out over 300 vastly irregular acres. It was the only isolated place in the area where 80 thousand residents lived packed in 12 thousand to a mile along the grid of main and side streets abutting the tracks.

Nil pulled in alongside a low wall opposite a modest knoll and nestled the car under an overhang of grapevines. Now Tweed knew why they had picked this spot. Their target would be waiting in a car at the park's entrance gate that was just around the bend in the road. From here they could scale the fence, split up and hike through the brush, and ambush the car from two directions at once. When they finished the hit they could bolt back to their car and blast out of here.

Nil opened the trunk and banged around, opening and slamming boxes. He swore and grunted, and then closed the trunk. The car rocked and the passenger compartment momentarily smelled of gasoline and mildew.

Tweed saw the brothers scramble through a hole in the rusty chain-link fence that ran atop the wall. They kicked up the hillside before disappearing past forsythia and rhododendron bushes.

Now it was quiet on the abandoned street. Rainy weather kept dog-walkers away and since it was after dusk the park was officially closed. The knoll on his right was standing in silhouette against the rose-gray sky with a motley tangle of scrub trees standing on its crest like an unruly cowlick.

Just then he noticed the figures of two men emerging from the profile of the hill. They were armed, camouflaged and hustling down the hillside, undoubtedly heading toward the gate. So this was how it was going to be.

LaGloria had wanted him to witness the setup, to see how she lured Des Kelley to the South St gate by informing him that Bricky would be there waiting for pick up, to be brought to a safe house in Mission Hill. She boasted that she would bring Des down, and that after her brothers did the dirty work, she would let Tweed share in the power and the spoils.

LaGloria could be persuasive, and though he was not convinced that her plan would succeed, he saw no choice but to go along with it. Besides, he was confident that his old man could handle a couple of shit-heads like Frankie and Nilvan. If he did, then he would do Tweed a favor by getting rid of them for him.

It was tempting to get out of the car to follow his father's men to see how they approached the situation. He was familiar with the entrance to the park: the seven-foot-tall cast-iron gates were set between four massive granite pillars. Not an ideal barrier from which to launch a covert assault, due to the poor lines of sight.

Perhaps the McManus brothers expected Des to cross the threshold into the shadows of the park. After all, Bricky was a wanted cop killer, and he wouldn't loiter out on the street. Then as soon as he entered they would open up a barrage on him, taking advantage of the bastion-like enfilade.

How much faith did the old man have in his backup? Their presence made it clear that he was aware of the ambush. If he exposed himself he might reveal the position of the shooters or draw them out. Then again he might simply send his men in to take the boys on directly.

Upside- the element of surprise. Downside- his men would be going in blind, hoping to out-shoot the fuckers. Worst case- if he lost either or both of his men he might still have to take on the boys by himself.

What would Frankie be carrying? Tweed didn't quite see it as he ran off. A long rifle for confidence? Awkward, though. Maybe a .357 revolver. Power as opposed to precision. Nil probably had a shotgun. Enough to blow away an unsuspecting middle-aged man, but was it sufficient firepower to take on two pros with automatic weapons?

Tweed had to get closer. He was in the park and running up a steep hillside before he realized that he didn't remember deciding to leave the car or hop the fence in the first place. His mind leaped ahead to the events about to take place down at the gate below, filling in brief vivid cinematic scenarios like alternate endings to an action adventure flick. Would Des even be in the car? The boys would want to make sure that it was him before firing, rather than face the wrath of LaGloria if they got it wrong.

2

Shards of loose shale scattered over the surface of the slope, shed from the cliffs above. Tweed scrambled with hands, knees, and toes through the black scree toward the base of the rocky prominence from whence he would be able to gain a vantage point. Sweat burst from his pores as he reached a steep cleft in the rock and began shimmying up. He put his back into the vee, and pressing his hands and feet against the smooth rock on either side, he ascended steadily while panting heavily and looking out at the mist and the pine trees.

At the base of the hill a culvert ran between the road and the gate. The sound of the water rushing and tossing in its bed and the drippy sound of rain on the trees combined to place a blanket of calm indifference between Tweed and the action below.

His arms were quivering, and his hands black from the climb as he pulled himself up out of the neat wedge and found a small flat granite shelf upon which to rest and get his perspective. A moment of vertigo swept over Tweed as he peered over the edge to the rocky slope thirty feet below and then to the stream, another fifty yards down at the base of the hill.

The gate was in plain view, illuminated in the clearing at the South St entrance. After a few moments he had spotted Frankie, but he could not see Nilvan, or the other armed men, or a car at the gate, for that matter. But his view of the far side of the gate was obstructed and most of the area immediately beyond the road was lost in trees, brush and shadows.

A sweep of headlights from an approaching car cut a swath of light through the park, and left sintered after-images of rocks, shrubs and raindrops hanging in the space in front of Tweed's eyes until he readjusted to the darkness. As he crouched on the damp ledge, his senses were stretching to encompass the tableau, to have simultaneous awareness of all events occurring in the vicinity. His fingertips were pressed lightly to the granite; the mist condensed in beads on his eyelashes; occasionally an assault squadron of rain droplets jumped from leaves overhead and struck his back and neck. The moisture held down most odors, and Tweed's nose was dripping, but he was aware of a floral musk rising from the woods, like heaps of rotting blossoms, and the smell of his own boots and perspiration.

Frankie was signaling- he had the advance position and would scan the road for oncoming vehicles. There- Tweed saw it now, something stopping at the gate- headlights, blinking out one by one as someone ran quickly in front of them. Frankie crouched in a firing position- suddenly wheeled about- and fired to his flank, as if aiming off into the woods. He was hit, and he dropped his rifle. Then strangely out of sync, delayed by the fog, the report of the shots reached Tweed, with Frankie's muffled cry. He was down but apparently only wounded, as Tweed saw him crawling toward his gun. A number of shots rang out, seemingly just below, near the stream; crisp, loud barks of a high-caliber automatic, interspersed with flatulent booms of a shotgun. Tweed recoiled in horror, pressed back against the rock, hoping to stay silent and invisible up there. And down in the road inside the gate, as Frankie feebly tried to gain a defensible position sitting on his ass in his own blood, a man walked toward him with a handgun leveled at arm's length, and shot him in the head. Des Kelley had taken the coup de grace.

In moments the camouflaged pair joined him in the road where they appeared to speak together briefly. One pointed back over his shoulder and at a nod from Des, sprinted off into the woods. The other man accompanied Des back to his car.

With relief Tweed heard car doors slam and he saw the vehicle lurch away from the gate. Then he noticed the sound of moaning coming from below, at the base of the hill. His legs felt cold and he breathed convulsively as he imagined Nil, mortally wounded, lying in the mud near the culvert. Only the hint of an impulse crossed his mind to check on Nil's condition, to try to get him out of there. Instead a surging desire for flight and self-preservation took hold, and Tweed began looking for a way over the top instead of back down the way he had come. As he stood up, a gust of chill wind took him by the shoulder and he impulsively grabbed the rock-face. One natural handhold led to another and in a matter of minutes he had climbed to the top of the cliff. The bare crag peak exposed the night sky decked in battle grays flying heroically from west to east. A few stars were visible and their obstinate fixation provided movement by contrast to the storm-tossed clouds, the gossamer banks of mist, and even the weary moon.

Running to the opposite side of the summit he sought an alternate descent path and then struck off randomly into the trees that grew on the precipitous slope. Soon he was falling forward, and trying to slow his descent by digging his heels into the soft humus and colliding bodily with the trunks of the thickly overgrown trees on the hillside. Velocity was checked but hardly impeded before he broke free of the tree line, and then he had to pump his legs to catch up with the momentum of his body. The fence was just ahead, about twenty yards away, coming in a rush. Forced to ditch, he tossed himself headlong. He rolled in a heap like he had been pushed from a speeding truck, trying to keep his arms close to his head, brutally beaten for the effort. When the world stopped spinning he was at rest in damp grass at the base of the wall, somewhere on the road where the McManus brothers had parked the car.

Clothing in tatters, bruised and battered, bleeding from the hands, knees and elbows, Tweed climbed the fence and dropped out of the park, leaving what little was left of his coat caught on the top wire.

OK, now to walk to the car, and return to LaGloria to give her the news.

Perhaps it was the ringing in his ears, or the throbbing agony of trudging up the road that distracted him, but it wasn't until he was within fifty yards of the car that he realized someone was standing beside it. Fairly certain that they were facing the other way when he approached, Tweed quickly reversed direction and hustled back along the fence toward a rise in the road. If he could make it over that rise then he could escape unseen. His heart pounded in his ears as he shuffled as fast as he could; he drew rapid, shallow breaths and felt as if he was moving too slowly. Halfway now, when he heard a distinct whoosh. The moment he realized that the car had exploded he felt a blast of heat on his back and saw the whole area lit up like daylight. Half-turning, he saw the fireball and the death-throes of a car in flames.

His left ankle sent searing lances of pain up to his crotch as he hobbled quickly across the street to the low fieldstone wall that served as a visual buffer between the road and the swamp. He vaulted the wall in a dead-man's roll and lay in wet leaves on the other side, gambling that Des would pick up his other comrade before fleeing the scene. Then he would be relatively safe leaving in the direction from which the men had come. He would head past the knoll, through the swamp and on to the rail bed where he could follow the tracks.

With pain that brought tears to his eyes, he drew his leg up and attempted to unlace his boot in order to inspect the damage to his ankle.

It was no use dealing with it now; the foot was already swollen and discolored. Later the boot would probably have to be cut away to free his ankle for treatment. For now it would serve as a splint.

The car's horn lit off abruptly, startling Tweed as he prepared himself for the walk. He stared, fascinated, as the vehicle burned, for it seemed to rally as it was consumed, as if trying to shake off the damage and injury. The horn was blowing and then the headlights came on, and suddenly the motor started. It sat idling, burning and sending vast columns of black smoke into the dark drizzle. One by one the tires blew out in tremendous explosions, the windows began to rise and fall, and from within the maelstrom Tweed could hear the radio booming through the massive amplifier and crossfaders. The windshield erupted in a shower of fragments as if someone had struck it with a sledgehammer from within the car, and the other windows in the car followed in turn, blowing outward in a symmetric spray of safety glass. To Tweed's wincing, smoke-stung eyes it looked like a star going nova and expelling its accretion.

Why did they burn the car? For spite? A last sign of disrespect? It would present a forensic puzzle for anyone investigating. Normally a burned car would be chalked up to theft or insurance fraud. But the discovery of the bodies of the owner and his brother nearby within the gate, clearly the losers in a fight against unknown assailants, would result in a major crime scene investigation. Then again, thought Tweed as he limped away, the car would have been a clue one way or the other and maybe it was better for him that it was gone after all.

He would like to have a ride though, because now Des would be looking for LaGloria, and she was his alibi. He should not, of course, incur suspicion, but it was better that he have a ready answer when his father asked him where he was tonight. And he and LaGloria had agreed to cover each other, should the need arise. The closest phone was a quarter mile away, a tough stretch under the circumstances, but the formation of a goal in his mind gave Tweed a boost and he stumbled ahead.

An impulsive chuckle caught in his chest, brought on by the realization that Nilvan and Frankie were dead, but he coughed instead, guiltily suppressing his satisfaction. There would be dark days ahead, marked by funerals and mourning, and many questions.

Whose jurisdiction was this area anyway? Tweed would need some quiet intel, to keep an eye on the investigation. But he couldn't call his usual sources in the local or state police, because that would tip them off that he might have been involved. Whatever consideration they gave him in his regular illegal activities, however well compensated they were for it, would be far outweighed by a murder rap.

Best first step would be to check with Mrs. Columkille, who was seeing a district judge. Her connections had helped on many occasions in the past; indeed, especially the first shooting incident in which Tweed was ever involved. Jimmy Columkille, her son, otherwise known as Jimmy C, Jimmy C-kill (his preference) or Jimmy Col, (Tweed's preference) was Tweed's age and they were buddies from about age 13 on.

When Col was 16 he got his first car, an Olds Cutlass 442, and he and Tweed spent that summer souping it up with a Holly quad carb and raised manifold, dual glass-pack exhaust, Cragar wheels with 50s, his and Hurst shifter…the works; all banged out, mudded up, and topped off with 36 coats of candy-apple red paint.

One weekend just before the school year started Jimmy and Tweed took a spin by the parking lots along the river to look for girls. The car had a down-throttle purr that you felt in the pit of your stomach like a warm sip of brandy. The girls were drawn involuntarily toward the glossy quarter sprinter and soon the boys were in hoodsie heaven. However after a few moments all that bliss was interrupted when some of the local butts, who were pissed off to see all the chicks hanging around the 442, came over and started hassling. Jimmy was belligerent, however Tweed counseled restraint, seeing that they were outnumbered there at least 6 to 1. But when one of the idiots poured his beer on the roof of the car, Col calmly peeled out of the parking lot on a controlled slab of burning rubber, his face burning red and his jaw clenched.

The trip to the house for the guns and back took about seven minutes, and to the kids at the lot it hardly seemed like any time had elapsed at all. They were milling around by the river, in awkward groups of drunken boys and bored girls, mingling and sometimes pairing off.

Jimmy cruised slowly along the parked cars, aiming his 30-30 rifle out his window as he drove; frustrated by the lack of attention this show of power and audacity was receiving. Then one of the boys in the group raised a hand with a beer in it and pointed at the car with a smiling comment to his pals. Col aimed for the bottle and fired, and his aim was pretty good, but the tumbling slug took off three of the kid's fingers along with the bottle. Suddenly the crowd looked like the little plastic pieces on a vibrating action football game as the electric buzz of panic scattered them. Jimmy and Tweed took turns firing, alternating as the car came about at the end of the row. In all, thirteen shots were fired, according to the tally arrived at by the police when they had finished taking testimony and digging the slugs out of tree trunks and park benches. They had pulled Jimmy over about a mile and a half from the scene, finding two polite kids in the hot-rod with a hot smoking gun on the seat between them.

Tweed wasn't sure if Mrs. Columkille and the judge were lovers at that time, but in any event her influence changed the nature of the proceedings against the boys. She saw to it that the cases were handled separately, that all of the most serious charges, including attempted murder, were levied against Jimmy alone, and most importantly, that Tweed's parents never found out.

After they were arrested the boys spent a night in lock-up, from which Mrs. Col retrieved them in the morning. Subsequently, Tweed never served a day for the crime, and Jimmy's sentence was a mere six weekends in juvenile detention. Somehow the community's initial furor and outrage over the drive-by sniping incident quickly melted into the suppressed and forgotten annoyances of the past. And Mrs. Col's clever manipulation of the system resolved the case of the two rejected teen-agers who had maimed another boy into a simple boys-will-be-boys misdemeanor conviction, clearable upon reaching majority.

...So LaGloria's plan to knock off Tweed's father had failed. Going into it he had felt coerced and intrigued by the romantic logic of her arguments. Accepting that the McManuses would go ahead and try the plan with or without him, he had agreed to it without compunction.

This was a time of tattered illusions, wild surprises, and radical changes. What had bothered him was the difference between the way he and LaGloria responded to those changes. She saw threats and opportunities, consolidations and alliances, where Tweed saw rivals, connections, businessmen. He took the easy-going, organic, cooperative route to success, where she saw a mad scramble over the bodies of the vanquished as the only way. He had built a profitable enterprise with years of diligent care and effort, whereas she had come in as an observer, initially turned on by his willingness to listen to her ideas, later considering herself a consultant and partner.

They had met when he started dealing with Nilvan and Frankie, who were once one of Tweed's only sources for Colombian and Jamaican dope. At the time they were very protective of their little sister as well, flaring into macho displays of hostility whenever Tweed so much as looked at her. But eventually the futility of standing in the way must have become apparent to them, just as the ardor between Tweed and LaGloria was apparent to everyone who saw them together.

But the story of her love for him was counter balanced by the story of her growing hatred for his father. Looking back, Tweed had hated her brothers, too, but he never planned to execute them. Now here he was limping home to her in the rain, and the fruit of her hatred was that his father was still alive, while her brothers were surely dead.

A rancid gassy odor permeated the air well before Tweed reached the edge of the swamp. Skunk cabbage and milkweed grew along the path he followed and the ground was becoming increasingly slick and muddy. When he used to dump hot-boxes along here he had found a way to cut through the fens to the rail bed, but in the dark, without a good walking stick he would be lucky not to end up wading in the oil-slick water up to his waist. Each tentative step prodded unseen critters at his feet to leap into the water beside him, so by poking ahead and listening for splashes he was able to avoid a soaking until he was approximately two-thirds of the way across the swamp.

When he did slip into the shit he was amazed to pull himself out with the aid of an abandoned shopping cart that was submerged in the muck. Where did this thing come from? Dropped from an airplane? He knew there were automobiles at the bottom of the swamp all around him, he had put them there himself. But who would push a shopping cart through here? Neither the mud of the swamp nor the gravel of the rail bed was conducive to the progress of little pivoting solid rubber cart wheels. The local neighborhood kids must have carried the thing and placed it on the rails just to see the commuter train blast it out of the way like a mechanized game of kick-the-can. If so, it had flown pretty far.

Finally, he reached the berm of coal dust and crushed granite that made up the railroad track bed, and there he sat to rest. A mile or so to his right there was a trestle where the commuter rail merged with the main trunk of commercial tracks for the final approach to the city some ten miles distant. As a young child, eight or ten years old, he would leap from one track to the other atop that trestle, thrilling himself with the risk of the forty-foot drop to the pavement below if he should misstep or lose his balance. The sight of youngsters courting danger on the trestle gave chest pains to the engineers running the passing trains. But it wasn't until his own father happened to be passing underneath one day in his car when he looked up and saw his boy in mid-air, foolishly springing a death-defying stunt, that the play came to a halt. When Tweed came home that day so long ago with a bright smile on his flushed face, he walked into a scolding, a spanking, bed without supper and repeated warnings forbidding him to go near the rails.

In the other direction, a mile or so to his left was the broad bend in the track where when he was older and ignoring his parent's warnings he would jump deadhead trains in the evenings for rumbling rides out of town. Tweed remembered running at full speed beside the train, arms outstretched, trying to grab the fleeting chrome handrail bars that were mounted next to the steps at the ends of the passenger cars. It was a one-shot dash along the inside curve of the track, pacing himself to the hammering clatter, drawn along like the litter and dust in the wake of the massive cars. If he had tripped or his hand had slipped he might have perished beneath the wheels or taken a high-speed tumble in crushed stone, rail ties and rusty spikes.

Although the train moved at its slowest at the bend, it felt like it would rip his arms free of his shoulders when he seized the bar. His legs would fly out behind him and in the instant before he pulled himself aboard he'd see the ground whipping by treacherously below.

That was before Tweed started driving; when he knew every short cut, alleyway, backyard, and dead-end in the town. Neighborhoods were different then, however. Nowadays every house had a fence and a snarling Doberman or Rottweiler patrolled every yard.

…A map rolled out before his mind's eye, over which he laid tentative routes, like trying a pencil maze in a puzzle book. He would be wise to stay off the streets.

Sirens were wailing in brisk cascading glissandos above the ostinato growl of the fire engines as they charged through the light evening traffic toward the Arbs Park fire. It was lucky for them that the car was parked outside the gates. Tweed knew from long experience how difficult it could be to locate and extinguish a burning car inside the park. Placing those stolen cars and igniting them was once a favorite pastime, a game he played with the fire department. Tonight the engines would only be the first of many emergency vehicles called to that scene. Soon they'd all be there, from cops to coroners. At the rate he was moving he'd be hearing sirens all night.

CHAPTER 2

In the center of the cheerfully maintained block of businesses on the north side of the town common, the spot that would naturally be occupied by a florist or an ice-cream shop, stood the biz club. It was like a grease-spot on the colorfully fluttering awnings and tasteful ordinance-compliant signage that adorned its neighbors; though some would say that its minor red brick façade and crimson-splashed door provided balance and a note of contrast to the otherwise conventional row of storefronts.

The principal proponents of the Rossie Businessman's Club were its regulars, for whom it was a daily haven. They arrived in the afternoon and entered the place from which no light shone and no music could be heard, sometimes not to emerge until 2AM. Among the regulars was Des Kelley, who usually stopped in to talk politics with councilman Dapper Ferguson, or to debate about the deteriorating social fabric of the town with his good friends, police Detectives Billy Storer and Jimmy Rima.

On this occasion however he was re-grouping and collecting his thoughts over a tepid beer after a strenuous outing at the park. With him at his usual table were his comrades Simon Fecteau and Harris Toole, whose brother Joe was the managing bartender of the club. They were heartily wolfing matching platters of marinated steak tips and cheese on bulkie rolls. Lacking grill or kitchen facilities in his own place, Joe had ordered the food from the bistro that shared a rear alley with the club. It was an equitable arrangement for both establishments, since the bistro could do without the biz club's clientèle, and the club regulars were uncomfortable drinking anywhere that lacked the club's peculiar dank pall.

"So it was the McManus brothers," said Des, looking away.

Simon replied, "Yeah, well I wouldn't have recognized them before and I sure wouldn't recognize them now."

"I looked him right in the eye- it was McManus."

"That's what I mean…"

"Hmmm?"

"After you 'looked him in the eye' not even his own mother could recognize him."

Harris spoke up. "Alright then, this is a preliminary review, not a blasted comedy revue."

Simon: "Review? Two up, two down, enough said!"

Harris proceeded like a patient insurance claims processor ticking off a client's possessions: "Mine had a shotgun, pump action…Fired twice when he heard me coming…Left his weapon at the scene."

Des still had a distant look in his eyes.

"The other asshole had a rifle, military surplus or something."

Simon said, "Yeah, he got off one round in my direction."

Harris: "And we all agree there were no witnesses- no one saw us at the bridge, or at the gate?"

Simon hesitated. "There was one guy. When I was at the car I saw someone, maybe a drunk, walking up the road towards me. When he saw me he turned around, crossed the street and booked it."

Suddenly Des turned his attention to Simon and asked, in a voice that implied that he shouldn't have to, "Well, did you get a look at him?"

"No, it was too dark, the car was already burning by then, and I would have had to chase him down the street to see what he looked like."

Des stared at him for a moment.

Harris said, "You did the right thing, Simon, staying in the shadows. OK, one witness to the car, possibly a bum."

"Alright then. Alibis. We might as well stick to the truth. We met here at the biz club, then we left together for a time, only to return later for a meal."

"Why?" asked Harris. "Why did we leave?"

"OK. We went to pick somebody up," said Des, improvising.

"It takes three guys to pick somebody up? What, were we carrying him or something?"

"So we were visiting somebody."

"Who?"

"Let's say...Tweed. He's usually home anyway."

"So you're going to call him?"

"Yeah, when we get out of here," said Des, before killing his beer. He wiped the sheen of condensation off the bottle and rubbed the moisture between his palms as he thought. It was important to have this review. Yet there'd be a thorough investigation soon enough, when AD Makepeace got involved and convened a hearing into the matter. One benefit of his affiliation with the Paras was their experience in handling affairs like these. Even if the scrutiny was uncomfortable he'd have to defer to Makepeace and organization policy.

Of all things that might have happened, he could never have imagined becoming the target of an assassination attempt. He never saw the McManus brothers as a threat, for that matter. What were they after? Did they act independently? Did someone hire them? All of the events in his life suddenly seemed to be interrelated in new ways. Trouble with his wife Christine. Trouble with Caroline, his girlfriend. His son Tweed's lack of enthusiasm about the cause. The recent arrest of trusted associate Paul Connors. Tweed's girlfriend LaGloria.

It would be tough enough looking into it on his own without having Makepeace digging into his life. Then there was Detective Storer, usually one of his best sources of information. Now he would have to be very careful about what he said around Storer and Rima in order to avoid providing any hints about his connection to the killings at the park tonight.

Suddenly feeling tired, Des passed his hands through his hair, then placed them on the rough, unfinished tabletop in front of him as if to help push himself up from the seat. He paused a moment because the table felt good, real to the touch; and even though a thousand sweaty arms had rested there, and a thousand panther piss beers had spilled there, and a thousand scum soaked bar rags had swiped it, he needed an anchor before moving on.

Harris nudged him, and the three arose and left the bar, without a word, and barely a nod to Joe as they passed.

CHAPTER 3

There is a time when you worry because you're being silly; your expectations are too high. You think people are going to show up on time and they always show up late. Then sometimes you worry because an allowance for reasonable delay has already passed, and then another hour or so elapses. It is justifiable to worry under these circumstances. They should have been here by now. An escalating progression of imagined horrible images illustrated the possible reasons for the delay. Mudslide, car crash, toxic rail car derailment. Arrest, dismemberment, death.

LaGloria paced in her apartment, alternately turning on her radio and shutting it off. The phone was useless; there was no one to call. The television was irritating.

How could something so simple take so long? They left here well over…almost two hours ago, and the round trip should have taken an hour at most. Were they off celebrating? Doesn't Tweed know enough to call? She might expect her stupid brothers to be inconsiderate.

A cup of tea should help stave off the panic. As she filled the kettle with water she felt an overwhelming urge to make phone calls, for information, for help, for a calm voice. But LaGloria was tough, and she mustn't let her nervous emotions get to her. The boys would return at any moment.

She seized the phone. How about Griffin? He always has his eye on the street. Maybe he'd seen Tweed out there somewhere. He's no friend of hers, but what the heck? It took a few seconds to pull Tweed's black book out of his biker jacket and then to unscramble the list code.

He picked up on the second ring.

"Hey, Eddie! LaGloria!"

"LaGloria? Weed's LaGloria?" Eddie sounded puzzled.

"You know any other LaGlorias? Listen, I'm looking for Weed. You seen him around?"

"No, but if he's hanging out he's probably headed over to the Arbs. There's something big going down over there- ambulances, fire trucks, everything."

No shit? You're right- if there's a fire at the Arbs, he's there. K- thanks."

Well, the deal went down anyway. So where the fuck were they?

Suddenly the kettle's whistle sounded and startled the shit out of her. She took a deep breath as she poured the water.

Man, this was not part of the plan, but she had to make another call.

"Sharlae"

"Hey, babe! What's up?"

"You free? I need a ride."

"Ummm, OK, just give me about fifteen minutes to get there. Where're we going?"

"Look for Tweed."

CHAPTER 4

Tweed's swollen ankle was screaming that it was time to stop. Not that he was making much progress anyway. It was difficult under the best of circumstances to walk quickly beside the train tracks owing to the uneven beds of stone, and walking on the ties was awkward due to their irregular placement under the rails. They were a little too close together to walk on them from one to the next, and a little too far apart to skip one. Walking on the rails themselves could be tiring unless you can get into some kind of Zen balancing trance. If you do you're likely to zone out and ignore oncoming trains, and then you end up like the animal that Tweed was seeing bits of here and there as he walked. It was probably a dog, a stray now strewn over sixty yards of track. Had it tried chasing the train, barking and nipping at the wheels until it got sucked in and chewed up? Or had it become transfixed in the beam of the ever-growing light rushing toward it as it sniffed along for food? He had seen many strange things along the tracks during his life, and this did not surprise him. One time he had come across a dead crow hanging upside down from a telephone wire.

It seemed that the tracks had been the principle conduit of his life thus far. The parallel relationship between the tracks and his life originated at Tweed's birth, when his family lived in the housing development clustered around the station down at Jamaica Center. Lore had it that the area was named after a popular drink called a "Jamaica" (hibiscus, ginger, rum and sugar) that General George Washington had ordered at an inn that once stood there.

Proximity to convenient public transportation had attracted his parents to the projects. It would be some years before they could afford a car, so Mrs. Kelley did the shopping, laundry and other chores by bus and train, frequently escorted by her cordon of squirrelly kids.

The next stop up the tracks for Tweed was when he started attending school in the White City district. His oldest brothers Buck and Mack had both gone to Longfellow Academy, which was a good neighborhood school, but it was closed by the time Tweed was of age because it was found to be loaded with asbestos and lead paint contamination. His next older brother Keiran went to Sacred Name School. This was an experiment on his parent's behalf, for while they were sacrament-abiding Catholics, they had never believed in placing all their eggs in one basket, as it were. And yet the results spoke for themselves, as Keiran was now in seminary. Despite its name, White City boasted racially integrated schools, and in that environment Tweed was just another ethnic kid.

The movement up the tracks continued when Tweed's family relocated to 'The Projects' near Rossie Square. This was the springboard to respectability for it wasn't long before Des and Christine had acquired a meager nest egg with which to finance the purchase of a house just outside the square.

There the tracks passed directly behind the Kelley's back door, and they also led to Tweed's new school, which he reached by way of a dusty rutted path that ran beside them.

It was at the Lucretia Mott School where he met the DEO (Drug Education Officer) who was to so profoundly influence his life, although he could now no longer remember the officer's name. The DEO carried a suitcase full of exotic goodies and when he arrived in the classroom he propped it open on a table like a sidewalk watch salesman.

"This here's your Black Beauty. Keep you up for days. This one here's your Red; a down-ah," he'd say, frowning.

There was something about the DEO's delivery, the hint of personal experience, of inner challenges sought and overcome, as well as the sheer ludicrousness of introducing narcotics to children that appealed to Tweed. He wanted to take the magic suitcase ride.

Furthermore, to top off his presentation the DEO always lit a joint of marijuana and passed it around the room so that everyone could smell and become familiar with the odor of the wicked drug. To Tweed it was like walking a pubescent boy through a harem and saying, "Smell that pussy, boy-you don't want any of that nasty stuff!"

Tweed's life continued up the tracks independently, heading away from the square. It wasn't long before he discovered Highpoint, where the McManuses lived, and ultimately Westbury Circle, near where LaGloria and Tweed currently shared an apartment.

From the Center to the Square to the Circle, Tweed had followed the tracks all his life, and in the meantime he used them when needed, whether as an escape route, a hideout, a dumping grounds, or a recreation area. The obvious significance of the rails in his life had never occurred to him before. Yet now that he thought about it, almost every important event that he could recall had happened here, from fistfights to camping out, to getting laid. If he had to be left without a ride on a rainy night, to limp home alone without being seen, he'd rather be here on the tracks than anywhere else.

CHAPTER 5

There weren't many nights when Des Kelley could be found at home, but as he was concerned with establishing his whereabouts, he thought it best to lay low and wait for developments. It was a wonder- he had been set up for execution and here he was worrying about his own alibi! *Oh, and where was I when they tried to kill me? In their gun sights, I believe.* He shook his head as he sat down to take a shit.

Chris was pleasantly surprised to see him home early from the club. He didn't want to tell her what happened until he settled in, although he kept reliving the experience in his mind.

He hadn't known what to expect when he learned that the message about Bricky was a fake, but he was wise enough to bring Harris and Simon as back-up, just in case. To think that when the boys originally discussed it, the plan was to go unarmed. There was a chance it could have been an FBI sting, an immigration ploy, or at worst, a ruse from Makepeace or one of the other Para operatives for God knows what reason. Saner heads prevailed, however, and Harris brought his twin cool-60s to the showdown.

The loop of that scene threaded slowly through his memory: the kid sitting in a slick black puddle with a look of disbelief and horror on his face; and the final flinch as if his expression might somehow deflect the bullet from Des' gun. That motherfucker had tried to kill him. He deserved it.

As he washed his hands Des realized that his shoulders were knotted and his arms were rigid with dynamic tension. He had been unconsciously clenching his teeth, and a headache was developing in his right temple. He might not have expected to be executed, and he certainly never expected to become an executioner.

One of Christine's fabulous neck rubs would work wonders right now, but Des wanted to talk, to tell her what happened, and he suspected that it was no longer safe to do so in the house.

They walked arm in arm through the neighborhood, staying fairly dry underneath the maple trees that lined the street, casually ambling toward their usual circuit around the ballpark.

"Chris, I have to tell you, someone tried to take me out tonight."

"Take you out? What do you mean?" She could tell by the strain in her husband's voice that he was upset.

"Take me out, you know, kill me."

"What?" Chris gripped his arm and looked in his face as if the details of the story would be there to see.

"It happened over at the Arbs. I was supposed to meet Bricky there. Or so I thought, anyway."

"Don't tell me Bricky tried to kill you?"

"No, no, let me start from the beginning. I got a message at the club that Bricky was in town and needed a place to crash. He was supposed to be waiting at the South St gate and I was going to bring him to the Mission Hill apartment, maybe get him some work. Later I happened to call Tom Morris, really just to say hi; but he wasn't home. I found out that he was away…away on a hunting trip up north with, of all people, Bricky."

"Tom, hunting? I wouldn't think that he'd go in for that sort of thing," said Chris, now bating her breath, confident in the knowledge that Des was whole and healthy and with her now, but also aware that he had faced danger that she found terrifying to contemplate.

"I don't think Tom went for the hunting...He'd probably call it a retreat. And Bricky was only going after red squirrels, anyway. But the point was that if Bricky was up north he couldn't be waiting for a ride to a safe-house, now could he?"

Both were silent for a moment as Des helped his wife over some roots that had broken through the sidewalk.

"Whoever sent the message clearly didn't anticipate that I'd realize it was a set-up. I could have ignored it, since I knew that it was bogus, but it bothered me to think that not only was I being targeted, but somebody had that kind of inside information to get to me. I mean, they knew the code words to use, and the story was perfectly believable. Bricky is wanted in Britain and Northern Ireland, that's common fact, but I didn't think anyone knew that he was hiding in the US. That alone has major implications, let alone the execution attempt."

"Oh, Des!" Chris was feeling the impact of the words in the pit of her stomach.

"I talked it over with Harris and Simon. We decided to go and see if we could learn more, like who was behind all this."

"But it was so dangerous!"

"We planned it right. Turned out I was supposed to walk into an ambush." He tried to say it cheerfully. "Two guys, waiting in the dark. But I had two guys and the element of surprise, as they say."

"What happened?" Chris had tears in her eyes, and she was holding her husband's arm rather tightly.

"See, at first I couldn't be sure if it was FBI, or ATF, you know, so I just drove up like I was supposed to, but Harris and Simon went in all stealthy to check out the scene."

"And?"

"They found a couple of shitbum kids, the McManus boys."

"McManus? Like LaGloria McManus?" Chris' head was churning with plots and suppositions, trying to guess ahead of the story that Des told so haltingly.

"Exactly- her brothers, I'm sure of it. They're dead now."

Oh, my Lord!"

"It was them or me, Chris."

Des stopped walking and turned to face his wife. They embraced.

"I know, I'm just thinking about LaGloria, and Tweed."

"Yeah, I've been thinking about Tweed myself."

"You don't think..."

"I just hope that he doesn't know anything that might get him into trouble."

"Have you talked to Storer?"

"No, I'll wait for him to mention it. Don't want to seem too inquisitive.

"Listen, Chris, right now I have no idea why those boys would want me dead. But I can figure that somebody put them up to it, and whoever did it is still out there. I've got to be real careful now.

"Storer's not going to be the only one looking into this, either. I mean, we'll use whatever sources we have, not only to understand it but to cover our asses. And then there's Makepeace."

"He'll help, won't he?"

Chris knew that by necessity AD Makepeace had connections in law enforcement and in the arms-smuggling world in which he thrived. Surely his assistance would be a great asset.

"Well, he'll perform an inquiry, and of course I'll cooperate, but I have to make sure that he had nothing to do with it himself."

"Why would Makepeace want to kill you?"

"Why would anyone?"

CHAPTER 6

"Love your car, Sharlae, it's wicked."

Sharlae knew that LaGloria didn't drive and didn't know shit about cars, but she thanked her for the compliment. Spending so much time in her car as she did, it had to be an extension of her apartment, and thus her personality. This modified Fairlane coupe was loaded with custom accessories, and it sported a stylish interior highlighted by the pink shag rug, velour seat covers and padded naugehide dash.

Working for Tweed, Sharlae put a ton of miles on her car, almost all city driving, and mostly at night. As one of the route drivers, or franchisees, Sharlae had a pretty regular clientèle, and she intended to keep it that way by being the model of consistency and punctuality. As long as Tweed could deliver the product, Sharlae would get it out there to her clients for rapid turnover. Her only problems were dickheads and double-dealers.

The dickheads always had a comment like, "You got anything else in that bag for me baby?" Or, "Do you come with the dope?" Yuk, yuk, it was to laugh.

The double-dealers figured that they were too smart for this operation so they were always looking for a way over. Where would we be without such clever individuals, whose idea of evil genius was to market the product as something other than what it truly was? Like the ones who made up outrageous names: "This is high-altitude Ztetloactatl- rarest fucking bud in the country." Or the ones who took perfectly good weed and cooked it up into hash oil in their High-Times easy-bake ovens.

The truth was that the operation ran smoothly without the added bullshit. Weed took care of Sharlae and the other distributors, who hustled to the middle men, or agents, and the agents peddled to the small-time dealers and users. She was the only distributor who had been given a franchise instead of working her way up or buying in. It had been a gesture from Weed, a way to help keep her on her feet after her boyfriend Carmine Gunther died of an overdose. Weed could be generous that way, although it wasn't his drugs that killed him or anything. Actually he really just wanted to make sure that the route got covered in Carmine's absence. Sharlae had been covering it ever since, but in three and a half years, this was the first time she ever had to give the boss's girlfriend a ride anywhere.

"So, where to?" She tried to smile, hiding the fact that it struck her as odd that LaGloria would go out looking for Weed this way.

"Let's go through the square, and then toward the Arbs. I hear there's a fire over there."

This wasn't as odd a request as it sounded. At one time Weed himself had been responsible for all of the fires reported in Arbs Park. They say he used to light bonfires to draw the fire department out so that after a few dozen calls, when they got sick of responding, he could bring hotboxes in for late-night demolition derbies. In fact, Sharlae had heard that the reason that those great big pillars were erected in front of all the gates was to stop him from driving in. Of course that made it more difficult to get the fire engines in, too, and thus Weed could work relatively undisturbed. Supposedly he had created a vast burial ground of stolen cars in there somewhere- a cemetery that represented millions in book-value insurance claims for the satisfied former owners who had paid him to make their cars disappear.

"To the square..."

She slipped from the apartment complex parking lot into the flow of traffic with the ease of a cab driver.

"Yeah, Sharlae, let's check the Cedars, and the 'Rock, and Fores. I get the feeling he might be partying with my brothers."

Cedars of Lebanon was a restaurant with a menu featuring authentic middle-eastern food, but since most of the floor space in the place was given over to the bar, it had a reputation more for boisterous customers than for fine cuisine. Weed occasionally stopped in there to meet with Jabbour, one of his sources for fine imported pot and hashish.

The 'Rock was actually the Silver Shamrock, kind of a work-in-progress, a cross between the reggae club it had been for a mere nine months, and the working-class neighborhood pub its owners envisioned. One of the investors in this little line-of-credit siphon was Wayne Kenney, another of Weed's sources, primarily for Afghan and Vietnamese specialty dope.

The Fores was a sports bar where Weed sometimes had dinner and a beer. He liked it not only because of the four strategically placed large-screen televisions that were tuned to games and scores for the convenience of the patrons, but also for the full glass storefront that permitted an open view of the street from his seat.

Sharlae had been in the Fores once or twice, when Weed brought her to have lunch with Eban, another distributor. At first she thought that he was trying to fix her up but then realized that with Weed it's always business. He had arranged the meetings because their areas overlapped, and he wanted to avoid any friction between his franchisees.

She didn't go to these places very often. Not that she didn't drink, she was as red-blooded as the next girl, but it was a matter of how she felt about partying. When she partied she wanted to have fun, something she could do anywhere, for instance, at home, or in the Arbs or at the beach. On the other hand, people who partied at bars always wanted something else, and not necessarily the same thing. Maybe it was drugs, or sex, or money.

She'd prefer to wait in the car, but looking at LaGloria, with her black hair and red lipstick, her gorgeous body and foxy clothes, she could imagine how long it would take for her to make her way through three crowded bars full of suddenly horny men.

"Weed? Partying with Nilvan?" she asked, then regretted opening her mouth. It was no secret that those guys hated each other, but it was obvious that something weird was going on, and it was none of her business.

LaGloria looked like she was thinking before she answered.

"Nil was giving him a ride home tonight. That's why I'm looking for him. They never showed up. I thought that maybe they stopped somewhere for a drink, and just forgot to call, you know?"

It was clear that she was worried, and sensing her concern Sharlae resolved to check those bars by herself, and quickly. She'd be at the Cedars in a minute or so.

CHAPTER 7

An old water pipe, long forgotten by everybody but a few old-timers, was the landmark that Tweed had been looking for. The pipe stood almost fifteen feet tall, with a perpendicular swing arm high off the ground and a spigot for filling the tanks on top of the municipal water trucks. Years ago they traveled what were then the dirt roads of the town in order to spray them and keep the dust down. When he was a little kid the pipe thing used to spook him out, as it looked somewhat like the gallows in a hangman diagram. Funny though, it never looked as spooky as it did now, standing alone at the side of the railway, rooted to the ground in an overcoat of creepers. Years ago one of the old railroad bums, a guy the kids called Buzzy because he spoke through a raw tracheotomy hole, saw him staring at the pipe one day after school and demystified it with the simple explanation about the dust and the water trucks.

From then on the pipe never bothered him so much, and the cool thing was that it marked the place where there was a hidden path from the tracks down to an industrial park. He just had to duck under the bushes and trust his feet to find it. If his memory served, there would be a retaining wall on the other side of the bushes, and then a short drop to a parking lot. On the far side of the lot there was a pay phone.

He suddenly remembered an adventure he had when his family first moved to the square. Somehow he had eluded his mother, who was also watching his brothers and a couple of nieces that day, and slipped away down the tracks. For such a little guy it was remarkable that he walked so far so quickly, but he emerged at the stop on Main, and blithely crossed the street in front of a disconcerted traffic cop. She promptly left her post to take the little boy by the hand and bring him to the soda fountain at a nearby drugstore where she attempted to ascertain his name and address.

In the meantime, a half a mile away the troop had been marked as AWOL, and all of the residents of the neighborhood were out searching for him and calling his name. They mobilized parties of volunteers to crawl into catch basins, under bushes, porches and basements.

When someone finally had the sense to call the police to report him missing, chubby Tumbleweed Kelley made it home, delivered by patrol car. The sirens were blaring and the lights flashing, as if he had been recognized for heroism and was to lead a parade. He arrived with his pockets full of candy, beaming a chocolate-smeared grin of triumph, and blissfully unaware of the trouble he had caused.

…The bushes were dense and impenetrable, but after surviving his jaunt down the hillside and rough treatment among the trees, he was not going to be deterred by mere foliage.

Whipped in the face, scratched in the ass, tangled, sweaty, and cursing, he fought his way through the thicket. He found himself standing at the top of a slope that was covered with broken glass, and to his annoyance he saw that the old path was still visible a few feet to his left; he had simply misjudged the entrance.

Well, the slope was new; and he hadn't been looking forward to climbing down a wall anyway, due to his sprained ankle. This would be easier to negotiate, but he was disappointed to see that the parking lot was no longer well-illuminated.

The only visible light was reflected from a myriad of glistening shards of broken glass that appeared to pave the entire surface of the old factory lot. The abandoned buildings were jammed up close to the tracks because at one time these factories had done all of their business by rail, off a spur that ran right through the facilities. When trucking became the preferred method of shipping and receiving, the rails were paved over and this area became a parking lot, with floodlights and a security detail.

It was here when, as a teenager, he had refined his patented vanishing act, which was especially useful when he was being pursued by the neighborhood beat cop. The overweight thirty-something cop would chase him down the street, and he would bolt around the corner, aiming for the block-long straightaway between the factories. There he could sprint for the wall, and then disappear into the bush, knowing that once he reached the tracks he could go wherever he wanted. Having lost his quarry, the gasping officer he left behind probably consoled himself that at least he'd surely put the fear into the kid.

There would be no sprinting now. The gloom and drizzle seemed to increase in the open and the way across the lot looked more daunting than he'd imagined. On the verge of turning back, he inwardly belittled his own timidity and walked ahead.

An odor of burning rubber perked up his wariness and he thought he could see embers glowing on the ground in the distance. As he approached, peering in a squint at the glowing red glinting in the crushed glass, he suddenly saw that there were bodies squatting around in a circle and blocking his view of a small trash fire.

He instantly felt dread and incipient panic- it was the second time in one night that he had walked into a situation unawares. But they were so low to the ground, huddled in the rain! What the fuck! Plus, they hadn't said anything, or he would have heard them.

Walking slowly now, he considered two basic options, 1) to acknowledge them and hope for the best, and 2) to ignore them, in which case returning by the same route would likely be awkward, to say the least. It occurred to him that one of the reasons that they were so quiet was because they were paranoid about seeing a stranger appear out of nowhere. Maybe he could use that to his advantage, indicating that he should take option 1. Then again, the reason he was worried in the first place was because he could imagine how he and his buddies would handle any stranger who came upon them in the dark.

"Yo-" he called, "-you gents just out digging the rain?"

No answer; this was actually a good sign.

There were four of them. One was smoking a tiny stub of a cigarette, another held an empty beer bottle, and the other two sat on their haunches hugging their knees.

"Nice talking to you guys. I'll be back in a few."

It was important to talk while he walked so that the semblance of conversation would permit him to face them until he was well away from the group. He would think that if they wanted to start anything they would have challenged him by now, but he angled for the darkest shadows to resolve the chill that was running up his spine.

"Hey! I know you!" shouted one of them, and Tweed stopped.

"Yeah?"

"You're, ah, you're that guy, ahm, Carl. You sold us that gold that time."

Hmm. Interesting. A good part of him did not want to stay and fuck around. But he turned and said,"The gold, huh? You got some of that?"

Just testing. He didn't know what the hell this guy was talking about.

They all suddenly joined in: "Yeah, that excellent gold bud. You sold us fat bags when nobody else had anything. Man, it was great."

"No shit." He smiled. See? Friendly.

"You got anything now, man?"

"No," he lied, weighing the possibility that they'd make him turn his pockets. "I'm out looking, myself."

"Aw, man, why didn't you say so? Look what we got!"

One of the dudes pulled a plastic bag from the center pocket of his hooded sweatshirt. Inside he found a foil packet that he carefully unfolded, occasionally holding it against the light of the dying trash embers, until he revealed neat rows of pink tabs of paper.

"T, man, tabs of T. You want any?"

Tweed thought it over. Buying some would probably put him on friendly terms with these bums and ease his departure.

"You got T? Shit, man, how much are they?"

The guy was gray-faced, with a split lower lip. He looked up into the rain. "Hate to say it, but I gotta get four bucks a hit for these suckers." Now the dude sounded mournful. "Just the way it is."

"I know what you mean, everything is too fucking high these days. Except me, that is. Listen, I'm going to head up the street for a few minutes and get some cash, then I'll take five of them."

The mere act of hobbling across the acre that separated him from the pay phone was excruciating, and he kicked himself mentally for saying that he was going to get money.

Finally he found the pay phone, right where he remembered it, kind of a half-shell hemi-booth bolted to a pole. But the cord was ripped and the receiver was gone. Now he was pissed. The vandals were probably the same morons who sat out in the rain selling hits of T on paper. Looking around briefly he knew that injured as he was his only option was to return to the tracks for the beeline to the next phone, or home, whichever came first.

The T peddler was waiting with a separated strip of five already ensconced in a tiny foil envelope. Tweed's anger, humiliation, frustration, and pain clashed in a flash of bad judgment. Secretly using his cash handling skills, he flipped a ten and two fives from the wad in his pocket and deftly made the transaction.

Now everyone was happy, slapping him on the back and encouraging him to consume the hits right away. Undoubtedly they had taken some earlier and were quite a few steps up the ladder of stonedom.

T, huh? In Tweed's experience, folks had used that name for a variety of chemicals that shared some of the psychotropic properties of common hallucinogens such as LSD. Sometimes "T" tested out as laboratory mescaline. Sometimes what was sold as T was the chemical equivalent of cannabis-supposedly pure THC. However, this time he was afraid that the paper might have been dipped in PCP, another high entirely, one that might account for the stupor in which he found the crew who sold him the stuff.

He stared at the envelope in his palm and pretended to pick at it, when one of the guys said, "Shit! The cops!"

A couple of things were conspicuous about that moment to Tweed. One was that the four peripatetic peddlers had vanished, yet none of them went for the slope to the tracks. Instead, they ran for the warehouses. The other thing was that as the police car sped across the lot in his direction, Tweed ate the strip of drugs in his hand instead of throwing it away, or stuffing it in his pants, or doing anything that would have made sense. Then he ran. To make matters worse, he cut his left hand severely on broken glass as he scrambled up to the path in what was undeniably full-fledged panic.

The tracks seemed welcoming upon his return: quiet, neat and simple. He stood there binding his wrist with a shred of his shirt, and shaking his head at his stupidity. His pulse throbbed in his hand, delivering a jolt of pain with every beat. Blood seeped around the ragged t-shirt bandage, and he knew that his bloodstream would soon be flooded with some kind of mind-altering drug. That would definitely put a crimp in any plans to visit a doctor for treatment. ("I don't understand it doctor, that patient needs several stitches and yet he sits there grinning like an idiot! Must be the blood loss!")

CHAPTER 8

Word came that the Makepeace delegation would arrive at 6AM. This was an indication of how Makepeace maintained his relative anonymity. His theory was that a dawn meeting in a public place was less likely to be observed, tailed, or bugged than a nighttime meeting held in seclusion. Whether his methods were effectively low-tech or just plain wacky, they seemed to work because like Des Kelley, he kept a low profile, and he was somewhat of an enigma.

Des had known him since the old days, since before he came over. He didn't know where he was from exactly, but his urban accent stood out in Kelley's County Roscommon pub.

AD Makepeace was an arms specialist, or more precisely, a procurement specialist who usually dealt in arms. In the center of military conflicts there are partisans and combatants, and then slightly removed there are those like Makepeace: nominally non-aligned parties who supply morale, provisions, and materiel for profit. While they may not make their political persuasions public, their claim of commercial neutrality was not altogether defensible. People like Makepeace have influenced the outcomes of wars.

Des Kelley's first real interaction with Makepeace occurred at a time when he and other members of the local militant cadre were going to ground and curtailing their activities. He arrived on the scene one day, offering to supply small arms at a nominal price. Folks speculated that he might be Gardai, Special Branch, or perhaps even IRA. Des Kelley tried not to think about it.

Years after Des emigrated and established his fund-raising activities in the US, he wasn't all that surprised to see AD Makepeace stroll into the biz club one day, looking for an order, per usual. Dollars were now by far his preferred currency, and since the Irish-American community was affluent and generous the deals increased substantially.

It was a time when the Troubles in Northern Ireland had been responsible for mass refugee evacuations over the border to the 26 counties. There was talk of civil war and the potential slaughter of thousands in the North.

Des had formed CAFÉ, the Citizens Arms Fund for Erin. Donations came in steadily and the fund was ready to take on contractors. Des knew that the money itself would cause problems unless it was managed properly, so he initiated an ongoing, long-term stockpile program. The idea was to create a network of bunkers in the Republic that would be systematically stocked, sealed and locked so they would be ready in the event of an all-out crisis.

His fund-raising acumen combined with Makepeace's initiative and expertise to result in some historic transatlantic arms hauls. Makepeace stepped in and made a series of significant deliveries in the early days, when the program was just getting underway. The benefit to CAFÉ was that he didn't force them to commit to purchase enormous quantities of weapons up front and accept delivery later; and he would do those one or two bunker runs.

There were some costly blunders among the successes. For example, on one occasion a cargo ship loaded with containers full of brand-new machine guns, grenade launchers, TOW and Redeye missiles and armor-piercing rounds had become disabled some fifty miles off of Long Island. The only boat that Makepeace could find in a pinch to offload, and thus save his shipment, was a barge- a flat-bottomed inland waterway type scow. The lame-brained compromise might have worked, too, if the goods could have been transferred at sea and if the barge could have miraculously made it back to a safe pier. However there was never really an opportunity to put it to the test, because of the vigilance of the US Coast Guard. They had been watching the barge move up the coastline, but when it started heading out to sea they thought the captain had either lost his mind or his navigational array and they promptly swooped in and interdicted it. An application of DEA tactics led to the serendipitous discovery of the 'mother ship' and the subsequent seizure of tons of valuable weaponry.

Des felt deference and obligation toward the arms merchant and in turn Makepeace protected him with what he referred to as liability coverage. He designed the policy to insulate his client, guaranteeing that in the event of apprehension, arrest or confiscation during transport, only he or his own people would take the rap. There would be no evidentiary, personal or other links pointing to Des.

Although seizures and other setbacks represented the loss of much-needed equipment and supplies as well as constituent's investments, it troubled Des that people who had no stake in the conflict might be arrested and imprisoned on his behalf. Yet he rationalized that their sacrifices would protect others, like him, who might then persist and continue the struggle.

CHAPTER 9

So he'd meet Makepeace in the morning. He wished that Tom Morris were in town. It would be a load off his mind if he could tell all of the facts to Brother Tom and have him handle the inquiries, and let his calm professorial demeanor offset Makepeace's deliberately provocative manner.

He reminded himself that there was no need to be adversarial. Yet he felt troubled because he had not accounted for his time. There was still no answer at Tweed's place; he was probably out with LaGloria.

For the heck of it Des called Harris and Simon again and had them try to reach any of their sons. He wanted them to keep a lookout for Tweed. Between Denis, Daniel, Jean, Jules, and Leo, one of the Fecteaus might run into his son tonight and pass him a message. And even though to Des' knowledge Tweed had never stepped foot in the biz club where Harris or Joe would see him, he might cross paths with one of the younger Tooles, Danny or Tommy.

The desire to establish an alibi was generating anxiety in Des but he also wanted to ask Tweed about these McManus guys. For heaven's sake, he was porking their sister, he must know something about them. But would he cooperate? It had been such a disappointment when Tweed failed to join the cause, and to exhibit any of the natural fervor that his parents would have expected. Would he have noticed if the McManus boys were suddenly flush with cash? Might he have seen them talking with anyone out of the ordinary? He would have to make Tweed understand the importance of these questions.

Tweed was always such an independent kid, and thinking back to some of his boyhood antics and his quirky behavior, Des smiled. For instance, Tweed rarely played with the other boys on the street, but he had a regular clubhouse full of girls keeping him company. And he had a habit of slipping away from time to time. Once they found him sleeping in a chestnut tree. He had climbed up with a pillow and a sack of snacks, then roped himself into the crotch of the tree to see if he could endure a night up there. He was also famous for his hideouts. One was in an abandoned caretaker's house at the local cemetery; another was in an empty garage that belonged to an elderly neighbor. Problem was that when he went missing his little gang was so tight-lipped about revealing his whereabouts. Seemed to be a born leader. His schoolwork had always been spectacular, really far better than any of his other boys, and that included Keiran.

But a change seemed to occur when Tweed was ten. Mack, Des' oldest, died in military service that year. It had supposedly been an accident, something that happened while he was on R&R. Of course he and Christine were heartbroken, but little Tweed never seemed to get over the loss of his brother. When Mack's uniforms were returned to the family, Tweed claimed them and wore them himself until they became threadbare.

Then it was later that year when the Kelleys took in a border, a young Jesuit named Brendan Tighe. The family had often invited Jesuits to dine at their home, and Tom Morris was a frequent guest. But Brother Morris was a strict conservative Christian Brother with traditional values and more often than not he was at odds with Brendan, while Tweed favored the young freelance missionary and the two became close friends.

Brendan became somewhat of a mentor to Tweed especially during his teen years. He had a way of showing up whenever Tweed got into minor scrapes, or committed misdemeanors that were typical of teenage boys. It sometimes annoyed Des how he would counsel Tweed when he got into trouble, even seeming to take sides with him against his father and mother. But Brendan also had a knack for making people laugh, for telling the right joke at the right time, and diffusing tension with a bon mot. With Brendan around, no one could stay mad at Tweed for long. There could be little doubt in the end that Brendan's influence had been positive, for Tweed turned out so well. He was always top in his class at school; he had moved into his own place at age eighteen, and he had been financially independent ever since.

It was just that they needed him. Buck was running the pub in Ireland, Mack was gone, and Keiran was in seminary. He and Chris had been counting on Tweed to take up the cause, to work as they had for Irish freedom, nationalism and unity. Sometimes he regretted not indoctrinating the boy when he was younger, but they had agreed that their children would have the freedom to decide for themselves. It just so happened that when they needed help the most, their son had gone his own way.

CHAPTER 10

The square looked rinsed-out and dripping dry, like linen whose colors had run and faded in the wash, pinned to the laundry lines of streets. Vehicle traffic was steady. A couple of greasers waiting at the light on chopper hogs stared hungrily at a group of pizza-soft teenage girls who were trolling the sidewalk. A bus sat idling at the curb next to the main intersection, pumping inky squirts of diesel smoke into the air. An ambulance raced by in the opposite direction, keening off-key into the distance.

"You like living here?" asked LaGloria, breaking the silence of the stoplight. Sharlae had just been thinking that she didn't belong to this town the way those girls on the sidewalk did. She lived on the edge of town, had not gone to school here, and didn't even have a library card. Work was her primary connection to the place.

"Yeah, it's home."

"To me, it's a market, a resource to be exploited."

Uh, oh. Here comes the LaGloria McManus School of Business talk. Sharlae had heard it before. Removing freedom from the free market, manipulating the dynamics of supply and demand, conning the consumer. She didn't know where LaGloria got this stuff, but she understood where she was going with it. She expected Weed to have a monopoly on dope. The laid-back style of business that had worked so well for him was simply not aggressive enough for her.

"I mean, look at this street! I bet that there are dealers in every other house. The people have to get their shit somewhere, right? You know what we gotta do is find out where the other dealers are and put them out of business, one by one."

"Yeah, no shit," agreed Sharlae, smiling, thinking, *this girl's crazy!* "We're here."

The Cedars was set back from the road as if a building in front of it had been removed for the courtesy of the small patron parking lot. At first glance it looked like a strip club; but the shake shingle roof and neon palm-tree logo gave it charisma. The place conveyed a sense of establishment, though not so much legitimacy; like a pawnshop that had been around forever.

Sharlae swung her car in and parked with figurative grace.

"Wait here, honey, I'll be right back."

As she climbed out she noticed that LaGloria had hunched down until her eyes were level with the window sash. *Is she searching or is she hiding?* Sharlae clicked her tongue and cocked her head in a quizzical pose. *Forget it.* She combed her hair with her fingers and tucked her shirt in, and then like a reporter assigned to cover a mall opening, she strode across the lot to the large glass front door of the restaurant.

She quickly scanned the lobby and the dining area and then entered the bar. Who should be leaving at that moment? None other than Og, another of the five local distributors who worked for Weed. She was nonplussed until she realized that this was his territory, after all.

"Hey, Sharlae!"

"Hey, Og!" she smiled. He was a scumbag. *Don't let him get too close.* They were standing in the doorway, and she surveyed the bar over his shoulder as they talked.

"What are you doing in this neck of the woods?" He asked, stroking his neck as if checking for a shave.

"Looking for my girlfriend. I think she's lost. I was supposed to meet her at the 'Rock but she didn't show. Figured she came in here by mistake." *Likely story.*

"Girlfriend, eh? Who is it? Should I get a buddy to join us?" He leered.

Weed was not here. The bar was crowded with a mixture of heavy-set kinky-haired Arabic looking men with black mustaches and beak noses, and a younger group of average after-work beer drinkers, mostly males. She took a pen and pad out of her pocket and started to write something. Og looked curious.

"What's that you got there?"

"Oh this? Just my appointment book, you know, how I keep organized." She closed it and slid it back into her pocket.

There was a look in Og's face as if he had seen someone he knew. Brushing past her he said, "See you around Sharlae. Look me up if you find your friend. We can party."

Gee, thanks. Now the next time she fantasized she'd see his warty puss.

Weed wasn't here but Jabbour was in the corner, holding a bull session around a table with smiling friends hanging on his every word. She had never met him but knew him by sight. Such knowledge could be dangerous, but she was fairly certain that he was one of the big dealers who supplied Weed. It troubled her that Og had been in the same bar. *What was he doing? Having a drink or doing some business on the side?*

Walking out she grabbed another of the free appointment books that an insurance company had left in the lobby. Sure enough, the one she had taken on the way in was gone from her pocket. At least she had the foresight to leave the jerk a note. Knowing Og's reputation as a pick-pocket, she had written: "Keep your filthy hands to yourself, you ugly fuck!" Right in front of him, as they spoke.

"They hadn't seen him in there," she told LaGloria upon her return. Then in an upbeat tone of voice she said, "At the 'Rock I'll try to call the house, too, you know, if he's not in there. You never know, while we're out looking he could be home."

Maybe she was talking too much. The way LaGloria hunched down in her seat made her wonder if they'd had a fight or something. Maybe there was another boyfriend involved, someone she didn't want to see. Maybe she was thinking too much.

"Yeah, right. Thanks, Sharlae, I really appreciate this."

They were passing the town common, the fire station, and the two-dollar movies. The square was illuminated in the amber radiance of halide street lamps like an alien force field that repelled the night.

All the characters were out now. There was Eddie Griffin, leaning against a bakery wall, legs crossed at the ankles, staring intently up the street. An elderly couple sat at a park bench, eating out of a shopping bag that was between them. A trio of boys on bicycles sped in and out of traffic, over curbs and loading ramps, hooting and calling dares to each other.

The 'Rock was next basically because Sharlae planned every trip like a delivery run, sorting the stops into a loop that pointed back home. Assuming for her own sake that they would have to visit each place LaGloria mentioned, then it made sense to visit the Fores last, since it was tucked on the corner of a side street that ran into South. From there they could check the park if LaGloria insisted.

CHAPTER 11

Detective Storer played with the change in his pocket as he pondered the facts of the apparent double homicide that occurred on his beat earlier in the evening.

How bad can it get? Take a town with 80 thousand or so residents living fairly close together, and tensions are bound to erupt into violence from time to time. But how bad can it get, when only a small percentage of those citizens actually own weapons, or have served time in jail for violent offenses? How bad can it get when the people have cars and bars and nightclubs and movies, a triple-A ball team, and an auto racing speedway to keep them out of trouble? When unemployment is only about 12 percent among males between 17 and 34?

Fucking people. Storer hocked, spat, then scratched his balls.

This was how bad it could get. Two local boys found dead in the town park. One of the boys was shot with a high-caliber weapon that clipped his side; but clearly the wound that killed him, the one in the forehead, came from a different, smaller bore gun at point blank range. The other had multiple gunshot wounds, but according to the grisly trail of evidence, what killed him was the blood loss he sustained while crawling some thirty yards from the point in the woods where he was shot to the road where he died near his brother. The kid must have had guts; well he did until he left them in the grass behind him, anyway.

Storer's partner, Jimmy Rima, was busy assembling the vital information that the paramedics, firemen and the first cops on the scene had collected. This would be easier in daylight, when they stood less of a chance of stumbling over clues and inadvertently trampling the crime scene. Det. Rima approached, following his flashlight to where Storer stood.

"I can hear it now- Gangland Style Slayings at the Park."

"Any press here now?" replied Storer.

"Not that I'm aware of, but it won't be long."

Storer pointed his flashlight at the gate, and swept the beam in a circle around the bodies.

"So who found 'em?"

"The fire department. They were responding to a call about a burning car- it's on the road around the corner-" he waved his flashlight, "and they needed to hitch up to the hydrant inside the gate here. The guy on the spotlight saw this one first," he pointed at Frankie, "then they found the other one when they got in here. Rude surprise, huh?"

"And the car?"

"Yeah, it belonged to them."

"Who are the victims? Any clue?"

"Oh, yeah, IDs on the bodies." He read from a notebook, but struggled with the pronunciation. "Francisco and Nilvan McManus, brothers. From Highpoint."

"Name sounds familiar. So what do we have? Theft? Drug deal gone bad?"

"I don't know, kind of looks like the OK Corral. This fellow had a rifle, and the other one left a shotgun over in the woods."

"Self-defense? A showdown?"

"They didn't shoot each other, that's for sure."

It was quiet except for the sound of the coins in his pocket falling through his fingers.

The preliminary work was taken care of, and the crime-scene folks were already at work. The back-up signal of an ambulance prompted him like an offstage cue.

"OK, have them take the car in and go over it for clues. I don't think we'll get a read on this until tomorrow, after we comb these grounds for bullet casings, footprints, the usual. Meantime, check up on the McManus boys, see if we got any history on 'em; find out about next of kin. I'll get this area sealed off- I want a quarter mile radius. Medical examiner's report will shed some light, too. We're going to need every shred of evidence."

CHAPTER 12

Someone once said that in the square there is a package store on every corner and in between there is at least one bar. That may have been an exaggeration, but it was true in the case of The Silver Shamrock. The block upon which it was situated was indeed bound like book-ends by Hilltop Liquors on one side, and then Sunnyside Wine and Beer on the other. However the 'Rock was not the only other business, there was also a teen center that was housed in a former real estate office.

The pub was being shoehorned into premises that had changed hands numerous times over the last ten years, defying the predictions regarding return on investment that the previous owner had made. When it was The Five Spot, a cheesy dive without air conditioning or pool tables or any other amenities that might normally be considered an added attraction for a local joint, it had lasted for decades. Since it closed and the original owner retired to Boca Raton, a number of hopefuls had attempted to duplicate his success. No maintenance had been done to the place in thirty years, and a layer of cigarette tar coated every surface within.

Successive renovations resulted in the addition of color television, live music, a grill, air conditioning, comfortable booths, pinball machines, pool tables, and theme decor. The most recent owners, with their dream of an authentic Irish pub, were undaunted by the prior failures of the Jamaican theme, the Polynesian phase, the disco phase, or the psychedelic coffeehouse era. But each generation had imagined that they would add the secret element, the gimmick that would pull in the boozers by the hundreds; and in this latest manifestation the draw was intended to be buxom red-haired waitresses. The reasoning was sound, for who could resist a wholesome, sexy red-haired Irish lass? The problem was that such women were not easily found, even in the Irish enclave of Jamaica Center.

In fact, when Sharlae walked in, with her hands in her back pockets and a determined expression on her face full of hope and purpose, she was about the closest thing to a real red-haired Irish woman as had been seen in the pub. And she was neither Irish, nor red. That didn't stop the barman, Myles Brennan, from offering her a job.

"Me? No, thanks, I'm just looking for a phone."

"Ah. It's over there," he pointed, dangling a washrag, "but if you change your mind, just ask for Wayne, or me, I'm Myles, by the way."

Sharlae looked around as if appraising the place. She winked.

"Right, will do."

Dan Toole had the stool on the far end of the bar where he could keep an eye on the traffic, and he liked what he saw, too. He nudged his buddy to point her out, but with nary a glance the dope said that she was too butch.

Nice ass for a butch chick.

No answer at LaGloria's place. OK, so he wasn't home yet. It wasn't the end of the world. She checked her own messages next, and heard that she had a delivery to make. Now she wished that he was home, so she could get this over with.

She thought for a minute, and looked around, noting the improvements that the new owners were proudly losing their shirts on. Dark paneling, smoked mirrors, quaint European style lighting.

The centerpiece of the bar was the new tap station. It bristled with over sized pull handles all bearing the names of the authentic stouts and ales that would soon become an acquired taste in the neighborhood, replacing the watery near-swill that passed for beer around here. Guinness, Newcastle, Murphy's, Bass. A Guinness sign over the bar proclaimed, "Ní féidir an dub a cur ina geal air." (Don't mix the black and the white.)

Feeling the eyes of Dan upon her but not quite able to see him and not quite willing to play peek-a-boo with some ogling shithead, Sharlae half waved to Myles the barman and walked out. He was just answering the phone at that moment and returned her wave with a flip of the washrag over his shoulder. The call was for Dan Toole, and it was his father, Joe. Dan had arisen from his seat to watch Sharlae walk to her car; and when he spoke to Joe he said, "Tweed? No shit? No, it's just that I thought I saw his girlfriend in a car with some chick that came in here a minute ago to use the pay phone. But I haven't seen him. I'll let you know if I do."

Noticing that the ogler was looking out through the blinds, Sharlae bucked it into gear and chirped out of there.

"No luck, kid. I tried your house, too, and there was no answer there either, sorry to say. Phew. Glad to get out of there."

She tossed her head and settled into her seat for the drive to the Fores.

"I know what you mean," said LaGloria, "I hate fucking Shamrocks."

"Oh, you been in there? Place isn't even finished yet. They're doing a lot of work to the place though."

"No, I don't mean The Shamrock, I mean Shamrocks, you know, phony Irish. The kind that turn green on St. Patrick's Day, and celebrate their heritage by drinking pints of Harp. My old man hated 'em, and I got no fucking use for 'em either."

"So, you're…Irish?" asked Sharlae, puzzled. LaGloria wasn't a name one would normally associate with the land of saints and scholars.

"100 fucking percent!" snarled LaGloria. "Well, my mother wasn't Irish, but when she married the old man he made her honorary Irish. My brothers and I were raised in the tradition. See, when other kids were hearing bedtime stories about Cinderella and Jack in the Beanstalk, we heard about Cuchulain, and the Heroes of the Red Branch, and Queen Maeve and the battles of Ulster."

Wow. This girl sure was a strange one.

"You ever been over there?"

"Every year since I was six. Spent my summers there, at our home in Connemara."

"You're shitting me!"

LaGloria turned and stared.

"No, I think that's pissa!"

The black-haired beauty shrugged and returned to scanning the streets and sidewalks for the men in her life.

CHAPTER 13

If his destination were anywhere else he didn't think he could make it, not in this much pain. But Tweed bolstered his resolve and determination by recalling that on each occasion in the past when he had to find his way home, even in the most adverse conditions, he had always made it.

Once he had driven into a flash flood on the Smoots Parkway, and his car had literally floated into a pileup of debris and vehicles at the base of a bridge abutment. After freeing himself of the wreck he had managed to wade in rushing chest-deep ice water and mud until he reached higher ground. Then because most of the adjacent roads were washed out, he was forced to walk miles in the rain and sleet. He remembered flagging down the first car he saw, and it turned out to be a police cruiser. The cops had the nerve to scold him for standing in the street and waving his arms as if there was an emergency. He said that hypothermia was an emergency and they, with their heated car, steaming mugs of coffee and warm mittens sitting on the dash, told him to call a cab.

…He wasted time looking for a stick to serve as a makeshift crutch. It occurred to him that the reason the guys at the industrial park had mistaken him for someone else was his appearance. Ragged clothing, torn boots, spattered with mud, and bleeding from cuts and contusions. With a crutch he'd look like a right bloody drifter. Not even LaGloria would recognize him.

The thought of LaGloria, waiting at home with care and solace and tenderness lit a warm spark in his chest. She would take care of him. She might bust his balls, but she loved him and he loved her deeply. Then he remembered the news he had to tell, and the grief that would stab her like a knife.

Why did she do it? What an insane idea, to send your brothers out to commit murder like sending them out to pick up a gallon of milk. He had gone along with it, too, even to the point of watching the whole thing go down. How had she convinced him? There were a number of points, he recalled. His father was in with Dapper Ferguson, a leading anti-drug councilman who was pressuring the police and the community to crack down on the drug trade. He was also friendly with the local hard-ass detectives who made life miserable for dealers like himself, by demanding payoffs and commissions as if they were selling the shit too. She had said that Des was the head of a vigilante group that emulated the IRA's neighborhood clean-up campaigns, and she warned that soon Tweed's people would turn up in alleys with their kneecaps blown out. And while she hated Des on the one hand for being what she called a "Shamrock", she also rejected his support of the IRA through his gunrunning, fund-raising and other activities.

When it came down to it, he didn't think she could pull it off. It was one thing to talk about it, to imagine the potential costs and benefits. It was quite another thing to imagine cutting his father down in cold blood; and he never really let himself think that far ahead. The idea hadn't struck him so viscerally before. Perhaps he was incapable of feeling compassion for the old guy, or else the whole thing had seemed a fantasy.

He was approaching the station now, and after the miles of dark solitude the bright signs of civilization smote his eyes like house lights coming up in a darkened theater. Avoiding the streets had been his intention and yet here he was walking through a major intersection. However, in his limping battered disguise he was no longer concerned about being seen. And he was halfway home.

CHAPTER 14

As was the nature of troubles, Des' seemed to be multiplying. Both Harris and Simon had reported back with news from the street. Harris said that he heard from his nephew Dan that he had seen LaGloria McManus out with a friend of Tweed's. On any other night they might have been bar hopping. Denis Fecteau had heard from a guy named Griffin who also saw them driving through the square this evening. Nothing terribly exciting there, except this was after she had spoken with him on the phone, asking if he had seen Tweed. If she was out looking for her boyfriend, then maybe there was more to the attack than he imagined. Maybe someone had gone after Tweed, too.

In the back of his mind he had already sketched out a plan to talk to LaGloria, but only after a respectful period of mourning had elapsed and only with the consent and/or presence of his son, of course. But now he felt an added urgency to see her face to face and find out what she knew. When was the last time she saw Tweed? What about her brothers?

He could see himself coming on too strong, possibly blowing it. Such things were better left to professionals, like Storer, or Makepeace.

His hands trembled. In the old days he would never have hesitated. He'd have hauled her in, fuck the consequences. If he didn't like what she had to say, then she might not be around to talk to the likes of Detective Storer. Let his boy find another punch, he'd get over her. The community would know that guilty or not, she had been made to pay part of the price for the crimes of her brothers. And others would pay and bleed until the truth came out.

He calmed himself. This was not the old country, and he was no longer a hard man. The poor girl was probably suffering, too. How would she have known that her brothers would accept money for murder? And if he was a target, and Tweed was a target, than who was to say if LaGloria wasn't one as well? If that's the case, then maybe he should have her picked up, just for her own good. Nobody has to be rough on her, he'll instruct his boys to tell her that she is to be brought to a safe place because of unspecified threats. He picked up the phone.

CHAPTER 15

"What do you do, anyway, LaGloria? For a living, I mean." Sharlae was just trying to be friendly; she could really give a fuck.

"I'm a photo consultant," she replied, disinterestedly.

"Oh? You sell pictures or something?" She imagined a mall kiosk or a studio.

"I didn't say salesperson, I said consultant. I tell people how to take pictures."

Sharlae looked at her quizzically.

"All right. You want to know? I'm a gay porn consultant. When a gay stud wants to do a photo shoot, I tell him what clothes to wear, how to pose, wear to put his dick, that sort of thing."

Sharlae practically guffawed. "You're kidding!"

"No, I'm serious. I make good fucking money, too."

"Gay guys? Why gay guys?"

"Well, for one thing I seem to have a knack for knowing what gay guys want to see. For another, they pay whatever I ask. For another, there is an unlimited supply of gay models out there doing photo shoots, and my skills can enhance their exposure, so to speak, their sales."

She never heard of such a thing. Nor could she imagine doing it herself, let alone imagine this obviously beautiful young woman doing it. Yuck. Gay porn?

"So, uh, how did you get started?" For some reason, Sharlae's heart was pounding.

"Look, do you really want to talk about what I do for work?"

In response, Sharlae just looked at her.

"OK, I just happened to see some gay porn one day, and I thought, these guys don't know what they're doing. I figured that anyone who walked in and told them a thing or two about dressing up, posing, makeup, you know, could make some money on the deal. And I did."

"Are there other, uh, photo consultants doing this?"

"Fucked if I know, and I don't care as long as I make money, but I imagine there must be, I mean, nothing new under the sun, you know?"

Holy shit. You learn something new every day. But really. First she had to run into butt-ugly Og, and now she had to get full-color visuals of naked queer boys playing dress up. What a night.

Fortunately forestalling any further conversation, they had reached the sports bar everyone called the Fores, although its name was really just Fores. It was down near the tracks in the stretch of town midway between the square and the railroad depot at Jamaica Center.

Sharlae had until midnight to make her delivery but a memo seemed to make a circuit of her mind every five minutes, making her feel like time was running short. If she could only skip this place and drive right to the park.

Now they were at the most distant point on the loop and she no longer held any illusion that driving around would be much use in finding Weed. Nevertheless she ran into the bar and looked around without incident or success. This time she simply shook her head when she got back into the car, and drove off in the direction of South Street.

The road curved a broad right before joining the short extension that ran under the railroad bridge. The streetlights in this section looked like they dated back to the days of the lamplighters, and they cast a feeble glow upon the surrounding mist and clouds of moths. Sharlae had driven through here a thousand times, using it as a shortcut to the wealthy 'burbs in the west. She drove quickly around the last stretch toward the stop sign, and came up short before a wall of flashing lights.

"Whoa! Check it out"

The police had South St blocked off with a fire truck, a patrol car and some saw horses emblazoned with neon lettering. At first it looked like traffic was still coming from the opposite direction, but then the girls saw that the police were only permitting a single tow truck to pass. LaGloria gasped when she saw the load the truck was carrying. Chained down to the flatbed, like a tortured wretch on a rack, was her brother Nilvan's car, burned almost beyond recognition.

"Oh, my God!"

Sharlae pulled over to the side of the road and both girls quivered as the truck drove off and the smell of scorched vinyl seemed to carry the hint of dire implications.

"An accident! What do we do?" asked Sharlae, trying to stay calm, and reassuring.

"We…get…the fuck…out of here!"

"What? Don't you want to talk to that cop?"

LaGloria seemed to be stunned, incapable of speech.

"Do you want me to talk to that cop? Listen, LaGloria, I'm gonna talk to that cop, OK? Tell you what, you stay here, and I'll walk over. Be right back, OK?"

LaGloria didn't look well.

Couldn't blame her. This was rough stuff. But it was better to know something than to imagine things. She kept looking back at the car as she walked toward the police officer.

"Um, excuse me? I'm sorry, can you tell me if there's been an accident?"

The cop looked her over in a split second and said, "Go home, miss."

"No, I need to know. My friend, see, she might know the owner of that, um, she might know one of the guys in that car."

"What's your friend's name?" asked the officer, not interested factually as much as implying that there was no friend.

"I'm sorry, man, I just wanted to help somebody who is really, really worried right now. I mean, what do I have to do? Call somebody?" She was talking too much again. "We've been worried half to death all night out looking for this guy. Now we come by here and there's his car, being towed away. Now what would you do? There's a nice officer, probably knows what's going on, but will he answer a simple question? No! Has to give me a hard time!" She stomped off in the direction of her car.

He followed, calmly noting the plate number as well as the model, make and year. When she had gotten back inside, he leaned in and looked at both girls for a moment.

"Yes, ma'am, a vehicle was recovered up this way tonight. It was burned, gutted. But there was also a shooting incident up here tonight, and I can't say any more about it."

"So the car was…"

"Can't say," he interrupted and looked carefully at LaGloria, who was shaking. "You alright, Miss- ?"

"LaGloria. Yes, I have to get home."

"L,A,G,L,O," he wrote as he spoke. "You'll want to talk to Detective Storer if you have any more questions. Now, turn around and get out of here."

After a minute Sharlae said, "Storer! Oh my God! What an asshole."

Somehow it sounded inappropriate.

They didn't talk much for the remainder of the ride. Her mind was full of questions, wondering what happened to Weed. *A shooting? Burned car? Were there any bodies? He didn't mention bodies. What do they do with the bodies? Should LaGloria call the hospitals? The cops?* She was glad that she didn't have to deal with it, but eventually this would affect everybody.

What would happen if Weed died? *Man, it's going to be rough making that run later. It'll be like delivering fresh rolls to a restaurant but not telling them that the baker was dead.*

CHAPTER 16

With every step Tweed took as he advanced down the length of the platform he became more acutely aware of the contrast between the evening bustle of the village and the bleak potent emptiness of the tracks behind him.

The platform passed over a small pedestrian walkway consisting of a tile-lined tunnel that was ideal for capturing echoes. Tweed could hear children entertaining themselves down there, whistling and screeching for the special effects.

For goodness sakes, it's dark out! Where are their parents?

Then he realized that the vacant lot to the right of the platform once contained a street-hockey rink where, when he was little, he spent many evenings like this engaged in earnest inter-neighborhood battles. Somehow it seemed safer for kids to be out at night in those days; but then he wondered how the welfare of someone else's children had become his concern all of a sudden. His maturity must be showing, or something.

By rights he should have been more concerned that there were no street dealers around. Was this not the profit center of his entire operation? Where was everyone? Here he was, the Ray Kroc of local dope merchants, walking through the McDonald land of the lucrative local drug market. Kind of a secret white-glove tour, except without the gloves. It would be gratifying to see the apparatus at work. He briefly imagined drive-by carhop service, with roller-skating hoodsies in cute uniform outfits wheeling up to waiting vehicles for orders.

"A lid? Yes, sir. Would you like some Thai-sticks with that?"

Tweed himself had started selling joints at a similar location years ago, when the pungent odor of marijuana had wafted about the streets almost as commonly as cigarette smoke. Back then the war was pumping users by the hundreds into the local economy as they returned from duty overseas.

However this hemisphere's variety of the herbal heart's-ease was less potent, less sweet, and less refined than what they had first encountered and become accustomed to in 'Nam. Over time however, entrepreneurial importers and domestic growers developed strains to suit even the most exotic tastes.

The sight of a row of pay phones interrupted his train of thought. The way things were going he expected them to be out of order. He hurried over and fumbled with his change. *Oh, baby. Pick up, LaGloria!*

There was no answer at his place. *Now what? She was supposed to be waiting. Where the hell could she be?*

Oh, no. Maybe Des got to her already. After all, he knows who went after him and he'll want answers.

But then, the cops were surely at the scene by now; maybe she had been notified, or picked up. Maybe she went to identify the bodies.

He cringed inwardly. No, wait, she may have simply gone out to look for them. But what if she did, and what if she ended up down at the park? She might see the wreck, and then despair. Who knows, perhaps she might do something rash. Tweed's heart sank as he pictured his girlfriend tearing her hair and sobbing. But then again, she might go right out and celebrate. She'll have a few drinks, and start planning her consolidation of the business.

Hardly consoled, he immediately thought to call Sharlae for a ride. Maybe she's got a run coming up and she can swing by and pick him up on the way. He started dialing and as the phone rang on the other end of the line he felt a thrilling sensation rising from his feet and then running throughout his entire body. It was a train, roaring into the station behind twin locomotives. Four sleek commuter cars and another engine in the rear all followed by a rush of gritty wind. He could barely make out the message on Sharlae's answering machine. By the time the noise subsided his time had run out, but then so had his change, and since Sharlae wasn't home, so had most of his options.

The last of the passengers disembarked from the evening commute, and as the train strained to pull out of the station, Tweed felt himself drawn along. He plodded unevenly, trying to clear his mind so that perhaps a spark might illuminate within and provide some inspiration.

A car kept pace with his walking, and he heard a polite beep. Looking up, he noticed a taxi near the platform, and the driver was beckoning to him.

"Hey! You look like you could use a ride!"

Tweed hesitated and checked his pockets, purely out of habit.

"Don't worry! Get in!"

The driver was a small bony fellow wearing jeans, a t-shirt and vest, and a leather cap. When Tweed made as if to get into the back as usual, the driver told him to sit up front, instead. As he switched places, Tweed noticed that the guy was missing his right arm.

"Tough night?" the cabby asked with a wry grin.

"Yeah, long walk," sighed Tweed. I'm headed to the Circle, if that's OK with you."

"Sure, no problem. Say, you want to smoke a joint?"

He could have cried. *Man, you see people do mean, fucked-up shit, and in the next instance you see folks like this guy, acting kind to a stranger, sharing out of the goodness of his heart. Kind of restores one's faith, makes you think that it can't be all that bad if people can be decent once in a while.*

"Love to," he said, grinning gratefully.

"Would you mind?" asked the cabby, handing over a bag of weed and a pack of papers, "I suck at rolling."

CHAPTER 17

Safe delivery. LaGloria was walking up to her apartment where she could take care of herself, and after wishing her well Sharlae was finally free to start her night. With one run already lined up she'd like to get home and check her messages, then kick back, pig out, and make plans.

For her part, LaGloria felt a deep obligation to Sharlae, especially in light of the fact that she had helped her through a critical moment, although LaGloria could not divulge the true nature of what that moment meant to her. She wished that she could do something in return to make up for her time and trouble. Perhaps give her some money? A hug? It was awkward. There were more important things to attend to, and any gesture to allay Sharlae's feelings would have to wait. Maybe she'd get a kick out of a signed glossy 8 by 10 from a gay porn star.

Sharlae's departure left her feeling suddenly significantly alone. Her thoughts kept her occupied.

The cop said there had been a shooting. In the worst case, that could mean that someone she loved might be dead. The torched car almost said as much. Three had left, none had returned. She tried with all her might to sense tragedy, to determine if she could feel the deaths of her brothers or Tweed. She felt nothing, other than the gnawing anxiety that had been working on her stomach ever since she witnessed the scene at South Street.

Where had her cockiness fled to, her self-assuredness? She'd need them along with a good deal of innocent poise, for regardless of the possible outcomes of the mission, she would soon have to deal with the police. They had her brother's car, and she'd like to know what else they had found.

And what about that bastard Des Kelley? How she'd love to call him to see if he's all right. "Oh hi, Des! Feeling any holier than usual? By the way, have you seen my brothers anywhere?"

In the best case, he was the one who got shot.

Events were moving of their own accord now that she had set them in motion, so it was vital that she maintain her grasp on the situation, in order to more fluidly manipulate it to her advantage.

Perhaps it would be advisable to call Des; call and plead for help, say that Tweed was missing and that she was at her wit's end with worry. That would throw the old fucker for a loop. Force him to offer her protection. Maybe that way she could pick up info by way of his connections to the local cops.

Man, Sharlae was right about Det. Storer. That guy should be arrested for impersonating an officer. And his roving shadow Reamer wasn't much better. Always shaking Tweed down. Shit, with the bribes he was paying, they could open up their own donut shop. Already the cost of bags on the street had risen due to the vicious cycle of handling fees. You pay a cop to look the other way when you truck the shit in, and another when you start divvying it up. The double dipping starts when you pay for local cooperation, and then you see the motherfuckers hitting up your customers. The con line these cop-shucksters used was usually something like, "You can pay me now, or spend the night in jail and pay the judge and maybe even a lawyer later, it's your choice." Few people would hazard the cell, the caprices of the court system, the missed days of work, and the possible criminal record instead of relinquishing their stash and a summary fine, paid on demand.

For the cops it was an easy scam, one that from their point of view appeared to achieve the same ends the law intended, but without the paperwork. But it turned them into predators who cruised the streets looking for the easy prey, while the crimes and safety issues of the town went unheeded.

LaGloria remembered seeing the efficacy of the constabulary vividly demonstrated during riots that had occurred at the basketball courts at the nearby playground some summers ago.

Rival gangs had arrived by the carloads to seize or challenge turf ownership. They were armed with clubs, bats, chains, nunchaku, bottles and knives. Yet the police, who had ample warning of the disturbance, sat in their patrol cars at the perimeter, watching from a safe distance until one group had emerged victorious. Then they went in and arrested the bleeding losers who were lying wounded on the ground.

That was also one of the reasons why she hated Kelley and his cronies. To her they represented the morbid lazy watchers who perverted the system they were charged to uphold. She understood that there was apparent hypocrisy in her position. She and Tweed were drug dealers, so they were in no position to question the morals of the police. But they couldn't help it if dealing was illegal. If they could get a permit and do it legally they would. Basically what it amounted to was her belief that it's better to be an honest drug dealer than it is to be a crooked cop.

There was a noise at the door. Someone was shuffling on the mat and fumbling with the lock. LaGloria froze, still standing in the spot by the phone where she had started to consider her next move. She drew a deep breath, preparing to scream if someone should attempt to enter. Suddenly the door was kicked open and her voice caught in her throat as she saw that it was Tweed. He was ragged, muddy and clearly in pain.

"Oh, hi, babe, I thought you weren't home, sorry I burst in like that, I..." he trailed off incoherently. The relief of having made it home was overwhelming him and he felt like dropping.

She rushed to embrace him and sensing his tenderness she helped guide him to the couch. She started to babble about where she had been while she eased his shirt off and then his boots. But she shut up instantly when, as she attempted to remove the boot from his swollen ankle, he went rigid and then passed out. With care she arranged his body full-length on the sofa and continued tending to his wounds.

It was fortunate that he was out, because it was going to hurt like hell when she cut this boot off. As she snipped away the straining laces, leather and sock she saw that his ankle and surrounding leg and foot were grossly swollen and purple; and when she elevated it, he awoke, promptly leaned over and vomited on the rug.

After removing that mess, she made the error of trying to help him to the bathroom. As soon as he arose from the couch he swayed, then toppled, again unconscious, only this time she had to catch him before he did more damage to himself. He was six inches taller and at least fifty pounds heavier than she was, and the best she could do was to cushion his fall with her own body. Winded, she decided to keep him on the couch for a while. But before she resumed cleaning his cuts and bruises she sat on the floor at his side and cried heaving sobs of accumulated fear and remorse.

CHAPTER 18

After rush hour the parkways fell slack and peaceful as the weight of the traffic was lifted, and the spaces between the streetlights were filled with pools of darkness.

Sharlae unkinked her neck muscles and sank into her seat as she anticipated her favorite part of the ride home. Once she had left the frenetic town streets it was a smooth languid cruise; onto Turtlepond Parkway, laid out as if it had been based upon the design of an animal burrow, then Stonybrook Parkway, that ran like rope bridges through the trees.

It was at the turn onto Stonybrook that she noticed the car behind her. Whoever it was had been following for miles, but now they were edging uncomfortably closer. She sped up slightly and moved as if to allow room for passing. They pulled alongside and she got a glimpse of three or four guys in a big sedan. But the car fell behind again and started high-beaming her. So they wanted to play games. Man, that sucked. Her neck started to tense up again and she gunned her little 6 to get some room. If they wanted some fun, she could oblige. Few people knew the streets around here as well as Sharlae did. Boundary Road was coming up on the right. From there she could duck into a veritable warren of side streets.

She took the corner without warning, coming as close to squaring a right angle as she could in a car that was never designed for high-speed maneuvers. Her aged aunt had owned the car before her and in 60 thousand miles had barely broken it in. Now as Sharlae careened over the crown of the road she opened it up on the straightaway that ran perpendicular to the parkway. Let's see them try that!

Well, what do you know? Not only had they made it around the corner but their advantage in engine size quickly overcame the gap between them as the sedan stretched out like a puma closing on a scampering hare.

She dashed down the first available side street, trying to simultaneously call up the mental map she had formed of this area back when she was delivering pizzas for a living. Settling on a tentative plan she convinced herself that since her car was quick and nimble and since she more or less had home court advantage, then losing these turkeys should not be much of a challenge. Afterwards she could try to figure out why they were after her in the first place.

This neighborhood had been established in the 1950s as cheap housing for ex-military personnel who were raising families and educating themselves on the GI Bill. Nowadays a lot of cops lived around here and Sharlae wasn't sure why that was, unless it was the natural order that cops move in when the military moved out.

Unfortunately these were town streets again so the quality deteriorated rapidly. There were potholes and fissures in the roadway and major depressions around the sewer covers. On the positive side, there was really only one route through this development, the rest of the streets were loops, cul-de-sacs and dead-ends.

The idea Sharlae had in mind was to lead her pursuers through the maze so that she might get them to zig when she zagged, and thus bog them down. Removing the element of speed from this game might detract from their enjoyment of it and perhaps they'll give up and find their way back to the parkway to pick on someone else.

It took a few tries, but after threading a ragged route through the roads of the complex and lurching from corner to corner at insanely dangerous speeds, she finally managed to outfox them. The big sedan was stuck on a blind alley one street over, and in order to catch up with her they would have to double back. By then she would be back on Boundary Road and out of there. But whoever was driving that thing was as crazy as she was, because instead of turning around, they simply drove through the intervening backyards, blasted over a picket fence, and bounded onto the road directly behind her.

Now she was becoming concerned, but only to the extent that she started to imagine that a confrontation, such as a shouting match, or worse, might ensue between her and the jerk behind the wheel of the other car.

Boundary rolled out along the town line, as the name implied, and also rode the perimeter of the old town reservoir. The town had long since hooked up to the city water supply so the reservoir had reverted to a lover's lane of sorts. During the day joggers pounded rings around the circumference, but at night couples parked along the water's edge. It was especially dark and private there, and generally no one bothered them, except the police.

As Sharlae tore around the bend in the road preparing to scream past the reservoir in the flutter of an eyelash, she saw that the police were in fact making the rounds of the parking area. In a flash of inspiration she cut the wheel rapidly to the left and skidded screeching into the parking lane. She parked as if it were the last available spot in a parking-lot musical cars death match. This had to get the cops' attention, and when they came over to hassle her the idiots in the other car would have to just drive on by.

The cops noticed her all right. She watched them turn on their bubblegum machine; just as the dark sedan stopped, and three guys leaped out of it, bolted to her car, and pulled her out. She felt disoriented in her amazement. She was yelling as loud as she could, kicking and fighting, and it made no difference. Incredible. Fucking cops sat there while she gets freaking carnapped! Two of the guys manhandled her into the back seat of their car and the other one ran to her car to drive it and follow them.

What a fucked up night this was turning out to be.

CHAPTER 19

Although still slightly ashamed of the manner in which he had fallen apart, Tweed had recovered from his trauma sufficiently to take a cup of tea. He commenced telling his tale while LaGloria wrapped his ankle in an ace bandage. Neither of them could remember if a sprain required heat first then ice or vice versa, but under the circumstances wrapping it seemed the sensible thing to do. If the police showed up at their door as they were soon likely to, then it would be advisable to have the injury appear dressed and treated and avoid any inquiries about it. If they did ask, Tweed could say that he twisted it while playing softball, or running for a bus.

His ankle was aching, his body was sore, his head hurt, and he felt the first flashes of the drugs in his system, but it was time to give his girlfriend the news.

"Babe, I'm sorry." He spoke softly and calmly and looked into her eyes when he said, "Nilvan and Frankie are dead."

It felt disrespectfully ironic to regard them with such solemnity.

LaGloria's eyes filled with tears but she didn't break down. She dabbed at them with the edge of the bandage and asked, "How?"

"We got there on time and they took off through the woods. I waited in the car, but after a couple of minutes I saw some other guys show up with guns, too. So I headed up the hill to get a view of the whole scene and," he paused, ever so slightly, "maybe warn them. I got up to a ledge on the cliff there in time to see that Frankie and Nil were ready. But then the car showed up at the gate, the other guys rushed them and..." He didn't want to describe his father's part in the killing.

"So he knew!" said LaGloria, bitterly.

"I guess so." Tweed hesitated. "The ambush got turned around on them. They put up a pretty good fight, too, but they were out gunned."

"I wonder if that prick ratted me out," she muttered to herself, apparently no longer concerned with the details. "So old D.K. got away, huh?"

"Yeah; not a scratch on him."

"What did you do then?"

"I tried to get back to the car."

"No shit, there were guns and ammunition in there. Took me and Nil weeks to get that stuff together. Did you get any of it? I saw the car."

"You did? No, by the time I got back down there one of the guys was torching it. I couldn't get near the thing."

"Fuck! That's evidence in there!" Her fury was a manifestation of her grief.

"Whatever was in there is gone now. The thing practically blew up, there's nothing left to find."

"There better not be."

"It's gonna look like a pretty sensational crime scene. I mean, when they find, uh, the bodies, and the car, they're going to wonder what the hell happened. But I don't think that any of it ties back to us. If anybody has to worry, it's my old man. And even then, I doubt that his guys left anything more than shells and footprints."

LaGloria spent some minutes in concentration while she gnawed on her cuticles. Finally she said,"You're right. If you look at it one way, then when the whole thing is over we'll be in the clear. Even if he suspects us Des can't pursue it without implicating himself. If he does, all I have to do is imply to the cops or the press that my brothers may have been selling or buying drugs from him."

Mindful of the fear he had while walking home, that Des would go after LaGloria for information about her brothers, Tweed considered using the only leverage they had at their disposal.

"There's another thing. Des was one of the shooters. He came in when it was over and finished Frankie personally."

The words sounded unbelievable coming from his mouth. Had all this really happened? Who were they, Bonny and freaking Clyde? He noticed that his voice was shaking as he spoke. "We can use that against him, and we don't even have to tell him how we know."

"What, can you prove it?"

It bothered him that she could be so calculating in the face of such stress.

"Leave that to the police. I'll just say that we have a witness."

It seemed to satisfy LaGloria to consider the possible advantages she had over Des, even though he had survived the attack.

Tweed looked at her while the implications of the affair sank in and attempted to suffocate him. Psychology was a factor here, he figured. LaGloria had sent her brothers to their deaths and now she wanted to put the best possible spin on things before they flew out of control.

The bandaging job was completed and Tweed changed his clothes before the discussion about alibis resumed. First she talked about her ride with Sharlae, and then he filled her in on his walk and the cab ride home.

"The driver was cool. We spent the whole trip talking about crazy places we had gotten high. I mentioned church, he mentioned the courthouse steps, but wouldn't you know it? We both got high, at different times, of course, in lock-up at the municipal jail. They had this basement cell block where everybody toked up."

LaGloria interrupted, "You got high with the cabby?"

"Yeah, why?"

"Where does he get his weed? Did you ask him that?"

"Babe, the dude gave me a ride and smoked a joint out of generosity. I wasn't going to question the man."

"That's the problem." She was pissed.

"What problem?"

"The problem with you, Tweed. For Pete's sake, you got stoned with this shitbum, you could at least have set him up with one of our agents and turned him into a customer."

It was always like this when they were together. He followed her around and tried to hold and kiss her, and she nagged the shit out of him.

"Alright, listen. We have to account for our time. You expected me home for dinner. You were worried because I was late. I twisted my ankle while running to catch the bus at Jamaica Center, so then I had to wait for the next one. Meanwhile you called a friend for a ride and went out looking for me. I hopped the next bus to Rossie Square and took a cab from there. By then you were home, too."

"OK, why were you taking a bus? Where's your car?" She was the cop, now.

"My car's in the shop," he said truthfully. In fact his car had been at Gary's Rod and Custom for over a month, receiving the equivalent of a peel, face-lift and makeover. "And what about you? Why did you go to South St? Did you expect your husband to be there?"

"Hey," she replied, scowling, "they might not even have seen me. But if they do ask, I'll just say that we were taking the back way to the station."

"Nobody is going to suggest that you killed your brothers, Love. We just have to make sure that our stories add up. Your only role in this is as grieving survivor. We have to make sure that it stays that way."

"Oh, shit!" she said as if in reply.

"What is it?"

"Nothing. I just remembered that Dad is going to have to be notified. He'll want to come up." Her father, John McManus, was living in solitary retirement in Sarasota Springs, Florida. Mrs. McManus had passed away when LaGloria was eighteen. The three children, who had proved so adept at taking care of themselves, were completely inadequate at caring for the elder McManus. He had opted to entrust his continued preservation along with his diabetes, glaucoma, angina and arthritis to an elder care community that had in return taken his life's financial worth in trade. When Nilvan realized that all he would ever inherit from his father was his name and a disease-prone genome it was a bitter parting. Neither he nor his brother spoke with their father after he sold the family home and moved to Florida. LaGloria maintained the required minimum communications with the old man and periodically updated them on his condition.

"Can he handle a trip like that at his age?"

"He will, and we better be prepared to put him up when he comes."

CHAPTER 20

The stream of insults threats and expletives coming from Sharlae's mouth seemed to be ineffectual at wearing down her abductors. If she had asked herself why they were allowing her to speak after taking away her freedom, then she might have permitted them to get a word in edgewise. She changed tactics.

"So you miserable sons of bitches have to kidnap chicks for kicks? Is that it?"

She glared, finally silent.

The driver responded patiently. "This isn't a kidnapping. A mutual friend of ours has asked that you be provided with some extra protection."

"Mutual friend? Who? You call this protection? What the hell is going on? I have work to do, and I'm telling you, my boss is not going to appreciate this. You guys are going to shit when you find out who you're fucking with."

"OK, whatever you say. Look, all I have to do is get you to a safe place. I can't help it if your plans are changed. You'd think a girl like you would be grateful when somebody comes to lend a hand. For what it's worth, ain't it better to miss work and be alive?"

"You're serious? What? You think someone is trying to hurt me? Who the fuck are you?"

The driver, a young brown-haired man in his early twenties who was wearing a rock band t-shirt under an insulated vest, sighed wearily.

"I'm nobody, OK? Jeez. I get this call, saying, 'Go get the girl and bring her in. She's in trouble and might be in danger.' Who knew that it'd be such a pain in the ass."

This was too much. Who would have ordered protection for Sharlae? Was it Tweed? No freaking way. If he did then he would have called her and told her. Besides, this wasn't his style.

"So you came to take care of me, huh? Why the heck didn't you just tell me what you wanted?"

The guy was becoming irate. "You're the one who wouldn't pull over. First you make me chase you through every street between here and Main, then you go and pull that stunt at the reservoir. There were probably a half-dozen calls to the cops about speeding cars in the neighborhood. What, did you think we were going to wait around and discuss it? Get into a little three-way chat? I can see it now, 'No, honestly, officer, we only wanted to help. The young lady must be confused as well as in danger.'" He spoke as if emphasis would make his point.

"Well, too freaking bad! Listen, shithead, you must have the wrong girl. Nobody gives a shit about me!"

He smiled. "You just said that your boss did."

"Yeah, he cares if I don't make it to work. And I'm telling you again that when he finds out what happened…Let me put it this way. He's connected, if you know what I mean."

Tiring of the bullshit, he replied, "I don't know who your boss is, or if you even have a job. But I do know that the guy I'm doing this for *is* connected, as you say. That's why he can offer this, ah, service."

Sharlae looked out the rear window and saw her car being driven by some half-assed goon. *He better not change my freaking radio stations! He better not even adjust my freaking mirror.*

She wished that she had a gun. Heaven knows that she had thought about it, especially in this line of work. You never know when some asshole is going to try something. Obviously. She entertained herself with the thought of blowing the driver's brains out the window. *Just signaling for a left! That's really using your head! Hah, hah.*

Escape looked to be impossible. Each of the dudes in the back seat with her had kept a hand on her arm ever since she started thrashing about. They stared out the window, apparently bored. Although they didn't seem to be paying attention, there was no room to crawl over their fat laps and throw herself out the door. Even if she did get out, they had her car, and could inadvertently run her over with it.

Where were they, anyhow? As far as she knew, this road led out to the highway ramp, and from there they could either go to the city or to the suburbs. *Fuck that!*

"Hey, asshole! I have to go to the bathroom."

"Then wait, you impolite, foul-mouthed bitch," he said with satisfaction.

"No! Pull over or I'll pee in this guy's lap!" she shrieked.

There was a moment of indecision. "He'd probably like that, but I'll pull over. What, do you want to squat behind a bush or something?" He seemed embarrassed.

"Right there." She pointed to a low wall at the edge of the woods.

"I'll go there. Just park so that nobody can see me."

They made a big deal out of leading her to the wall, and then standing around the car and trying to look large. Sharlae hopped over the fieldstone wall and dropped to her knees. She took a moment to brace herself, and to convince herself that she had to abandon her car to the creeps. Then she ran.

Whenin doubt, make it stout. The tall glass in Des' hand had a sensual appeal, smooth and curved, cool and solid. The bittersweet liquid within the glass imparted an effervescent aroma that bypassed the olfactory and stimulated the memory and imagination directly. When he raised the glass to his lips, images teased at the edges of his consciousness like glimpses in the corner of his eye of shadows dashing by. Crushed pine needles and salt-water spray, filtered sunlight on a fairway, rumpled sheets and soft skin glowing in the moonlight coming through a bedroom window, darts nailing a corkboard through a tobacco smoke cloud. Christine had delivered the drink to his study, and after half of the glass he was ready to try Tweed again.

He picked up on the third ring and sounded either surprised or annoyed, Des wasn't sure.

"Is everything alright T'weed?" he asked, reminding himself not to say too much.

"Well, yeah, I'm fine, uh, why?"

"Atta boy; good man you. No, I was just asking after your health, you see. I had a notion that you might be in trouble. I'll have to tell you all about it later. The reason for the call is that I need a favor."

"Sure, Dad, what is it?"

"The thing is this, son. If anybody asks, I'd like you to say that I was at your house tonight, you know, visiting."

"If anybody asks?" Tweed sounded reluctant.

"Yes, you know what I mean, boy. I'm just saying, if it comes up, then I was there between 6 and 8 or so for dinner, is that alright?"

It sounded like Tweed had placed his hand over the phone for a moment. When he returned to the line, he said, "But, Dad, I wasn't home myself, tonight."

"That's all right, you can simply say you were."

"Yes, but people saw me, I mean, how could I be in two places at once?"

"Oh, I see. Now I understand why I couldn't reach you earlier. Then how about this: I came over to have dinner with your lovely fiancée?"

The receiver was muffled again.

"You want LaGloria to be your alibi?" Tweed sounded unreasonably incredulous.

"Son, I just have to account for some time, alright? You know that normally I wouldn't ask, but it might come up, and I just thought that you'd help, that's all. I didn't think that it would be such a big deal. I'm also worried about you. How is LaGloria, by the way? Is she home now by any chance?"

"That's just it, Dad, LaGloria had some upsetting news tonight."

Suddenly the stout felt sour in his stomach. He hadn't intended to mention the incident. Could Storer have gotten to them already?

"Oh, and what would that be?"

"Well, earlier she went with a friend down to Jamaica Station, and on the way back she saw the police towing her brother's car. Looked like it was torched down by the park. Now she's all worried about her brothers."

"I understand." He paused and changed his tone. "Now, don't you do anything until you hear from me. I'll call some friends at the district substation to see if they know anything, and I'll get back to you. Why was she going to the train station?"

"To look for me because I was late for dinner. I missed my bus, but by the time she got there, I had already grabbed another one."

"Mmm, yes, alright. Just forget that other thing. Forget it, I'm sorry. LaGloria is more important."

"Yeah, she's worried that the cops are going to come calling with bad news any minute now."

"I'll tell you how to handle the cops, Tweed, I deal with them all the time. Some of my best friends are cops. Listen, I'll call you back as soon as I know anything. Maybe we can put her mind to rest; you know, it might have been stolen. I hear they recover a lot of stolen cars down there."

"Thanks; that's what I told her."

The last thing Des intended to do was to start asking questions about the incident at the park. But it wouldn't be too much trouble to pretend that he had discovered important information. Wasn't he one of only three people who knew what had really happened to the McManus boys? He decided to wait at least an hour before calling Tweed again. As he drained the last of the stout in his glass the phone rang and startled him. It was Simon.

"Des, I thought I should fill you in. Denis said the boys finally caught up with that girl LaGloria. They had her in the car and were bringing her to the farm when they lost her again, the idiots."

"LaGloria? Are you sure?"

"Well, yeah. Denis said that he saw her driving the Fairlane that his source described to him earlier. They stopped her over at the reservoir, but she told them that she had to pee, and bolted when they stopped the car."

"I don't blame her, whoever it was."

"What do you mean?"

"LaGloria McManus doesn't drive. She doesn't even have a fucking license. I think your boys grabbed one of her girlfriends by mistake. Blazes! It always comes down to communication!"

"Well, what should we do then?"

"Oh, don't worry about it. She's gone, right? I doubt that this chick will press charges. She probably had no idea who these guys were."

"There's one problem. We still have her car. See, one of the boys was driving it. He was supposed to follow them to the farm."

"Jesus, Mary and Joseph! One fucking thing after another."

It felt good to rage a bit, and he knew that Simon could take it. Before letting him off the hook he roared out more instructions for the boys, then slammed the receiver vehemently. The only way to see this thing through was to keep tight control over it, and that was impossible with shit-for-brains like Denis and his crew of numbfucks out there creating more trouble.

Another stout would do very well right now.

CHAPTER 22

Getting away from the weirdo protection squad had been the easy part of Sharlae's escape. The fat dude guarding her had probably stood there playing pocket pool for five minutes before he realized that she had bolted. The difficult part would be maintaining a pace that would keep her far ahead of any pursuers.

As she ran through a vast field that was overgrown with tall grass and scrub brush she vowed to lose some weight as soon as possible. 130 pounds was too much to lug around, especially when you have to dash for your life. She had intended to go on a diet anyway; it was one of those perpetual desires, but she was always deterred by the fact that nobody but her would notice any improvement. Her chubbiness was compact; her body was a small sort of slightly overweight package that guys called "cute".

This was no time to be thinking about guys. Some "guys" had just kidnapped her and stolen her car. Them and their stupid fucking stories. Who knows where that would have ended? Well, one thing was certain: they'd have to find some other girl to screw around with. As for her car, it was her home away from home and she missed it, but at least they couldn't try anything with it, the perverts. It wasn't exactly on the top of the list of most-stolen cars, either. Stripping it for parts would be a waste of time.

She reassured herself that there was little chance of getting lost in this vacant undeveloped parcel of land. They had pulled over just before the highway ramp, so as long as she continued in a straight line away from that road she was homeward bound. Not that the thought of home was much comfort right now. The goons could be waiting there for her. Before she went into the house, she'd have to make sure that she had either a large male friend to escort her, or a vicious dog, or a weapon of some kind. On second thought, she had better take all three just to be safe. A ride would help a great deal, too.

Who could she call for a ride? Fuck it, if she was going to call anyone, it should be Weed, to tell him what the heck had happened and why she wasn't out on her usual runs. Let him arrange a ride, maybe send a cab out. But that would require a phone, and they don't nail them to trees. She'd have to risk deviating from her course to try and find the old post road that ran into town from this backwoods vicinity. All she needed was a phone. And maybe some shoes. Her white sneakers were soaked and muddy and definitely not made for cross-country trekking. In addition her blue jeans with the fancy red stitching were stained with dirt and covered with sticker burrs and with flecks of the cat-o-nine-tail fluff that floated over the fields.

Hiking through the countryside like this was neat, considering that she couldn't remember the last time she had seen a dead rat, or a live toad, or a clutch of speckled eggs in a tiny nest, or any of the other fascinating bits of nature she witnessed along her way. It was like she was the proverbial city mouse seeing how the country mice lived. And yet she was relieved, no, downright thankful to come across the first sign of human habitation she had seen in almost an hour.

It was a low ranch-style building with a sloping roof, a stained brown exterior, and very few windows. The building sat off the road at the rear of an empty parking lot. No signs, no business; what was this place? Maybe a biker bar, or a so-called gentlemen's club? A cable ran from a corner of the building to a lonely phone booth that stood under a large rectangular floodlight at the edge of the lot. Excitement boosted a reserve of energy into her veins, igniting a sprint, and Sharlae was safe inside the booth moments after she saw it.

This was the first time in her life that it felt comforting to enclose herself in the aluminum and Plexiglas squeeze box.

Thank God, Weed was home.

He seemed preoccupied, but he calmed her down and told her that he had nothing to do with the carnapping. He was upset that she had been subjected to the abuse she described, and offered to send someone out to pick her up and drive her home. He promised that in the meantime he would make some calls to find out who had arranged her capture. He agreed that it didn't make sense that anyone would grab Sharlae and offer her protection, but alternative explanations were even more disturbing.

Just then a van pulled up and an obviously inebriated young woman asked Sharlae for directions.

"Hey, Weed, forget the ride. I'll be home in fifteen. I'm going to be paranoid about going into the house, but I'll call you when I get there."

The van was carrying not one, but two inebriated young women. Both of them were drunk, almost naked, and heavily painted up and perfumed. Apparently they were "dancers" on their way to a party, where they would be expected to dance, strip, and suck dick for cash.

The driver, named Chugga, said that they were getting 400 bucks an hour, to which her friend Honey whooped and giggled and slurped Southern Comfort from a half-pint bottle. Sharlae liked them right off the bat, but she became uncomfortable when they asked if she would like to join them for a gig someday. Looking at their long legs and tiny butts and boobs jiggling through their lingerie, she said, "Thanks, but I got a job already."

Honey snorted in laughter and replied, "This isn't a job, it's a party! You do it in your spare time!"

"That's OK; I guess I don't have the boobs for it."

They encouraged her not to sell herself short, and told wild tales of their adventures in party-girl life right up to the minute when they arrived at her street.

The contact buzz from being with these delirious babes wore off almost instantly, as Sharlae remembered that there were four psychopaths out on the streets tonight- and they had her car, IDs, and keys. She asked to be let out at the corner, then thanked her new friends and wished them good luck.

Chugga scrawled a number on a matchbook and handed it to her before she drove off. "Think about it, Sharlae baby!"

Tucking the book of matches into her pocket, Sharlae noticed that they had come with a long strand of blonde hair.

She had loved this street from the day when the real estate agent had first brought her here to show the house at the far end. There were only three other houses, spaced irregularly, each with a yard and driveway, and the street was situated away from the main roads and traffic noise. Buying the house had been a big step, one that required courage and persistence. Not unlike the bravery she would need right now to walk the length of the street and scope out her place.

It seemed normal. Other than a single fire pole with a lighted red globe on top there were no streetlights. It was quiet as always, except now she could hear her own footsteps as if amplified and echoing. A raccoon had taken the lid off of a trash barrel and was perched on the edge of the can, chewing on a take-out box. It regarded her serenely as she passed, like they were old friends who saw each other every night in passing.

She made it by Mrs. Albequerque's house and peeped at her own place from the shadows of a maple tree that grew out of the sidewalk. It was dark and still. Everything appeared normal. Except-her car was parked in the driveway!

What was this? Some kind of joke? Were people going to jump out of her darkened living room and yell "Surprise!" when she entered the house? She didn't know any people. She knew things. Some things about people, including a whole lot more about Weed's girl LaGloria than she wanted to know. And things in general, about the scene, and the trade, and the customers. But there sure as hell weren't going to be any people in that house, were there? No freaking scary fat dudes waiting to start a private horror show. Right?

By now she had made it as far as the front porch and was reaching for the screen door as if it were a live wire covered with nasty spiders. There was a note tucked in the bar.

"Sorry about tonight- my mistake. Car's in the drive-

Keys in the mailbox. It'll never happen again- promise!"

The night seemed to come crashing down all around her, like a pane of shattered glass. She took a deep breath and felt her pulse returning to normal. So it was all a mistake. She felt calm as she entered her home and turned on the lights in the hall. It'll never happen again. Radio- on. TV- on. Into the kitchen, and the fridge.

Now her anger was competing for dominance. Mistake all right! They never made such a freakin' mistake in their lives. They better believe it will never happen again! I'll see to it! Weed will see to it!

Wait a second- Weed must have seen to it! She called him and the next thing she knew, everything was back to normal. What a fucking guy. He was a regular, everyday, hot shit kind of guy and she loved him. Thank you again, Weed. She grabbed some ice cream and closed the door.

CHAPTER 23

"My old man called again. Still calls me Taweed, like it's two syllables."

LaGloria was coming out of the bathroom where she had been preening and preparing for a visit with the cops.

"What do you expect? He's a dumb mick!"

Tweed had half a mind to say, "So's your old man!" because he was, in fact, also a 'dumb mick'.

"He says that you don't have to worry about the cops. I got the feeling that he was letting on that he knew something about what happened. He said not to tell you because you might get upset, but in the case of deaths such as homicides the coroner's office makes the identification. In other words, there isn't going to be any scene at the morgue drawer like you see on TV. If the cops come, they're not going to take you anywhere."

"Stop it!" she shouted, "I don't want to hear what your ole Da said about his buddies, the fucking cops."

The door buzzer made them both jump. It was the police.

Tweed and LaGloria were speechless while waiting for them to climb the three flights of stairs to the apartment.

There were two of them. The first cop was a woman, and she looked unnervingly familiar to LaGloria. Her light brown hair was tied in a ponytail that draped from her dark blue 8-point cap, altering the crisp profile of her uniform. The other was an older man who had a look of apathy on his face. He was clearly less concerned with his uniform than he was with his sharp buzz-cut hair and grease pencil mustache. The woman did all the talking, and though the other cop displayed a distinct lack of enthusiasm he constantly scanned the apartment as if he expected criminals to come out of the woodwork.

They had come to tell LaGloria that firemen had discovered the bodies of her brothers Nilvan and Francis McManus while responding to a report of a burning car at Arbs Park. She listened over the nervous hum of her heartstrings. She felt unable to breathe. It appeared that they had been murdered, as both had apparently died of gunshot wounds. Police later discovered that the car in question belonged to Frankie.

The officer stressed that the investigation was in the preliminary stages, that they were still collecting important pieces of evidence, and as of yet had not established the time of deaths. The bodies had been removed and the coroner's office would contact her regarding paperwork, funeral arrangements, and death certificates.

They were also working on a motive for the killings, although there were no suspects in the case. In that regard, the officer asked if she might pose a few questions to LaGloria.

LaGloria was clearly distraught, and her composure had crumbled as the officer delivered the details of her report. She sniffed and asked what kind of questions they had in mind.

"It would help us a great deal, and you don't have to answer now, just think about this and call us, if you could tell us when the last time was that you saw your brothers. Did you know of any conflicts that they might have been involved in, or could you think of anyone who might want to kill them? And about the guns,"

"They had guns?" LaGloria's heart pounded heavy in her breast, beneath her tongue and in her ears.

"Yes, they each had one. Did they usually carry guns? Did your brothers own any guns?"

"You mean, like a handgun...ah...?"

"No actually, although we would like to know if they had any of those as well. No, we're looking at a military issue Colt M16 and a Remington 20 gauge pump-action shotgun."

LaGloria was horrified. She suddenly felt as if she could not speak. "No, no guns, not that I know of. I, I, uh..."

"It's alright, please, don't trouble yourself. We know this is a difficult time, and we don't want to make it any harder for you. But we believe that it will help if we can wrap this up quickly and find whoever was responsible for this terrible crime.

"As I'm sure you're aware, violent crime is not a regular occurrence in our community."

Both officers handed out business cards, and also indicated that Detective Storer would be leading the investigation, and that he could be reached at the same number. They then lingered in the living room as if they had to be told to leave. LaGloria understood that they were waiting for a response.

"Thank you, officer. I'll call Detective Storer in the morning and tell him everything that I know."

They started to move. "Yes, please, do that," said the female cop, "he'll probably want to meet you as well. It'll be an opportunity to go over the facts of the case and learn what we've discovered. He'll probably also want to know for the record where you were and what you were doing earlier tonight. Good night, Miss McManus."

As Tweed walked them to the door, the officer took LaGloria aside and said, "LaGloria, it's me, Bernie, Bernadette Diprizio. I don't know if you remember, but we went to school together."

"Bernie! Yes, I'm sorry, I was so wound up I didn't recognize you."

"It's OK, I understand. Take care, LaGloria, I'll keep you posted."

CHAPTER 24

The Bean and the Cod Restaurant was a convenient ten-minute stroll from the slip that AD Makepeace kept seasonally at the Cove Point Marina in Quincy Bay, and the walk along the docks was a pleasant prelude to the late meal he intended to have there. The stench of the inner harbor was abating as the tide came in and the wind changed direction. Seagulls perched on piers and mast poles, and Makepeace saw a lone cormorant standing on the bow of a dinghy, spreading its black oily-looking wings in a muscle-duck pose.

Earlier in the day he had overheard a sandy-haired boy who was fishing off the dock saying to a companion that he wished he could have the interest that was owed on the boats that were tied up at the marina. It amused Makepeace that such a sum seemed astronomical to such a wharf rat. But he knew that the value of his boat alone exceeded all of that combined interest along with the total cash value of all of the other boats at the marina.

His 126' super yacht was the current queen of the harbor, yet though it was a supreme symbol of opulence and extravagant wealth, Makepeace preferred to think of it as his livelihood. He worked and lived on board his yacht and when he went ashore he dressed casually to blend in with the crowd. This evening he wore jeans with a navy blue sweatshirt and rubber-soled blue canvas boat shoes. Tufts of white hair like hook and loop held a twill cap fast in place on his head and a day's growth of white stubble on his chin and neck completed the two-tone ensemble. The sleeves of his sweatshirt were pushed up to his elbows and his 5'8" stature seemed to be inflated by his vigorous sea-leg swagger.

The news from Des Kelley had come out of left field, so unexpected that it came across as a put-on or a mistake. Who would want to kill Kelley, other than, he considered jokingly, Makepeace himself? Perhaps he had enemies back in the days when he was in active service, but that was years ago. Since retiring from his pub to start a new life with his wife and family in the States he had given up fighting, both the B-Specials and his comrades, either due to strategy or fatigue. And yet he supported the struggle in his own way from abroad, and in so doing had helped to keep Makepeace busy for many years now. The steady business that dependable Des had brought his way, paid for by the donated dollars of the Diaspora, had helped him afford the long gradual transition from living in a hammock in a leaky trawler in wind-swept Bantry Bay to the sumptuous stateroom in his luxury yacht in fair Quincy Harbor.

As Makepeace walked he scanned the boats moored along the pier hoping to spot an evening reception still in progress or at least to spot a friendly neighbor or two who might accept an invitation to join him later for an onboard midnight nightcap. It was off season here and many of the regulars were still away on southern voyages. Of the vessels in the marina, few were occupied, and although a couple of them were gaily strung with running lights and brightly illuminated from within, the evening drizzle had discouraged folks from socializing. On the contrary he was raring to go, refreshed from the nap he took when he docked at the marina this afternoon after cruising down from Newport.

He could always drink with the crew, but fraternization was best done in moderation, lest it lead to lax discipline. And not only had he heard all of their jokes already, but getting laid was fairly high on his agenda, especially since he had to leave Newport prematurely, and not one of them could suck cock worth a damn.

When it came to dealing with Kelley he would have to tread lightly, not only to preserve his friendship with his old partner, but also to avoid risking personal exposure. He had a responsibility to look into the matter and to report his findings both to Kelley and to his IRA handlers as well. He knew that Kelley wouldn't talk to them directly, for ever since the organization's split in '70 he had reverted to a radical kind of republican fundamentalism. The 1916 Proclamation was his Bill of Rights and the IRA Green Book was his bible, but in his view the modern preachers and interpreters of these documents were blasphemers and idolaters, and the path to Irish independence had been lost when the Irish Free Staters, and ultimately deValera, accepted partition.

Des was in a curious position politically for although he could not align himself with any IRA faction, he shared their overall goals and aspirations, as one might eschew membership in a Christian sect and yet have faith in Jesus. He claimed that his civic defense initiatives were ultimately non-political, as they were intended to serve and protect Irish people despite their politics.

Yet his claim of relative neutrality was clearly disingenuous when one considered that by stockpiling arms throughout the countryside, Kelley's group had actually facilitated the IRA's weapons procurement program. Local farmers, ex-servicemen and other gun owners were more willing to donate their old shotguns, revolvers and single-shot Lee-Enfield rifles to the IRA when they knew that there were adequate stocks of modern armaments laid away nearby.

Perhaps the best way to initiate an investigation into the Kelley incident would be to rule out any potential conflicts in which the comhairle, ("committee") might have an interest. For example, if another paramilitary group had been behind the attack, then an investigation would certainly be warranted and pertinent. On the other hand, if it could be reasonably proven that the incident was not "relevant", that is, if say, a jilted lover had targeted him, then Des would be left to handle it on his own.

In any event, the first step was to gather information. He'd have to get his feet on the ground and get in touch with some of the characters in Des' greater circle of acquaintances, someone with a more or less independent perspective.

He also had a regular list of other resources and assets to call into play, but the process had just gotten underway. First he'd relax, have his dinner and a couple of drinks and mull his next move and then perhaps he'd make a phone call or two.

PART TWO

CHAPTER 1

If any reference to time and place could serve as the proper origin for the story of Tweed's life as it related to the murder of the McManus brothers, then one might consider a particular balmy June evening in 1974. For on that occasion, the actual date long forgotten, Brother Brendan Tighe had just completed his dinner and had taken himself and his bowl of strawberry shortcake dessert out onto the porch of the Kelley house. There he encountered young Tweed, who at 14 was half the age of the visiting Jesuit-in-training. Tweed had preceded his guest to the porch moments earlier, for the house was stuffy after one of Mrs. Kelley's famous dinners, and he longed for fresh air and the commencement of cookout season.

The two rested upon a pair of battered wicker chairs that sat like aged courtiers who had waited beside the door for many weary nights in weather both fair and foul. Tweed was careful to choose the one with the weak seat, for he was afraid that Brendan, who had been taking his dinner at the Kelley's rather frequently of late, might just plop right through.

The outdoors greeted them with a barely audible susurration from the trees surrounding the house. The chestnut, oak, magnolia, maple and pear trees all shivered as if in anticipation of eavesdropping on a juicy conversation. The one with the long drooping string-bean type pods swayed patiently.

"You were quiet at supper, Tweed."

"I guess I was thinking,"

"What about?"

"Nothing. I was just wondering how I'm going to make money this summer."

"You'll get a job, then?"

He had plenty of work; what he wanted was money. Between his chores, and the random tasks assigned to him by his father "to keep him out of trouble", and the odd jobs he performed for the neighbors, he was already putting in longer days than he had before school let out for the summer recess.

Just this morning after making his bed and folding his clothes, he'd worked his arms into gumby rubber beating the rugs out on the clothesline behind the house, then he'd helped his father disassemble and repair the gas stove, and hiked to the store for an elderly neighbor, all before lunch.

"Thinking about it."

"Like a paper route or something?"

A paper route was a given. He and each of his brothers before him had had a paper route for as long as he could remember, and unless he could think of an alternative, he'd soon be caddying at the golf course as well.

Tweed shrugged. He knew that there were ways to make money without working too hard, and suggested as much to his friend, who was licking his bowl for the last crumbs of shortcake and syrup.

"Ah, I see," said Brendan, thoughtfully. "Tell you what, then. Have you considered starting a prostitution ring? You know, with your little girl friends?"

"What? Hoodsie hookers?" said Tweed, aporetically.

Brendan's face was straight.

"Sure. And why not? Imagine the cash you'd be making!"

Well aware of Brother Tighe's penchant for humor, Tweed paused before responding to allow time for the punch line, if there was one, but also considered that this might be a lame attempt to elicit a conversation about ethics. Either way, Tweed was stumped.

He had only learned about prostitutes within the last year, and he still had difficulty with the concept. He remembered the time when, having first heard the word, he asked his friend Carmine to define it. Carmine had frowned slightly and shrugged his shoulders.

"A prostitute? It's a woman who sells her body."

Embarrassed to pursue the matter he had mulled it over privately, wondering what Carmine meant by that. How does one sell one's body? In pieces? All at once? What's left if you sell your body? Mary Magdalene was a prostitute, and Jesus had blessed her. Did this have something to do with lepers?

Some time later when the boys were shooting hoops at the end of the street the subject had come up again. On this occasion he gleaned a bit more. Apparently it had to do with sex. However, sex is pretty fuzzy to adolescents until they encounter it personally, and he was again embarrassed by his ignorance. One of the older kids had taunted him, saying, "You don't even know what suck means!"

Tweed has angrily retorted, "I do too; it means bad," thinking of various derogatory expressions he had heard.

"No, it means GOOD!" snorted the big kid, and he shoved him to emphasize the overall advantage he had over little punks like Tweed.

At any rate, prostitution was not what he had in mind, although as the months went by, he often wondered if he should have taken Brendan's suggestion more seriously and launched a career as a pimp. Instead he was planning to find out how the pot trade worked.

One would have to wear blinders not to see the dealers pushing joints from their regular locations on the wall at the end of the street and on the train tracks, especially if one walked along the path that Tweed took to and from school everyday.

At first their surreptitious movements and gestures had merely puzzled him, but he gradually became aware that they were transacting business of a sort, for as secretive as they were, he saw that money was surely changing hands. Again Tweed had directed his initial inquiries to Carmine, who was a year older and seemingly infinitely wiser.

Carmine's explanation had kindled the entrepreneurial spark in Tweed's breast, and after that he had been scheming and dreaming up ways to break into the business.

It was not like picking up a bundle of daily papers and delivering them for subscriptions and tips. If he wanted to start selling dope then he had to find a middle man to set him up with the smallest possible quantity he could turn over for a profit, and he imagined that he would have to fight for sales against an entrenched competitor. After all, even paperboys were fiercely protective of their territorial routes and customers.

Meanwhile on the breezy porch Brendan sensed the ambivalence in his young protégé and decided to let him off the hook.

"Too much overhead, eh? I can see your point. Where are you going to find a flop for the tricks? Although I imagine a sheltered spot in the woods or one of your clubhouses would do well enough. I remember Ruthie O'Connor used to do a little strip tease for the guys in the neighborhood where I grew up, and she used her father's garage. And how are you going to protect your girls and see to their needs? Next thing you know you'd be getting into hiring bodyguards and taxi drivers. Still though, I've seen some of the girls you hang around with, and I doubt that they'd take much convincing."

Oh, Tweed supposed, unlike me, right? He answered quickly.

"You're right. I can't see having them charge for what they're willing to give away for free."

Finally, Brendan smiled.

CHAPTER 2

Carmine Gunther had put forth his economics lesson in two parts. First he delved into supply and demand.

"What you see is a simple demand driven marketplace. There are those who want the product, in this case weed, and there are those who can supply it. It is the goal of the marketplace to ensure that there is a relative balance between the buyers and suppliers. When there is enough weed, the buyers can get it whenever and in whatever quantity they want, usually for a modest price.

"Suppliers set the price, usually based upon the recovery of the cost of growing, harvesting, curing, packaging and transportation, along with a reasonable profit and an additional mark-up for risk.

"In times of high demand, the suppliers may not be able to get enough weed, so they are inclined to raise the price in order to lower demand," he held his hands up like the two cups on a balance beam. "And in times of low demand the supplier may have too much weed, so they are forced to lower prices in order to stimulate sales.

"Like most agricultural products, weed is perishable. It has a certain shelf life, if you know what I mean. The supplier must turn over his stock of dope within a given time period so the shit doesn't go bad on him…"

"Go bad?" Tweed had asked.

"Yeah, it can get moldy, or stale, or dry and tasteless. The necessity for quick turnover affects the market also. Sometimes suppliers might have to dump everything they have just to break even; they'll even take a loss on a batch if they have to, so they can start again with fresh stock."

He then referred to specific marketing issues, first focusing on prices.

"Remember, if the price is too high you lose sales, so the idea is to know the difference between making a high profit on a limited number of sales, or a low profit on a large number of sales. For example, when cigarettes went up to fifty cents a pack, I had to quit. I just couldn't afford them anymore."

"No shit?" Tweed had a lot to think about.

"Other factors are important, too. To increase sales you have to offer a number of considerations to your customers."

"Considerations?"

"Yes, like allowing an occasional cuff, or offering small quantities for their convenience. Some dealers are afraid of getting stuck with an uneven bag, like when a shopper grabs a half-dozen eggs at the grocery store. The grocer has to hope that someone else wants a half-dozen, too." He gestured as if he were holding an invisible egg carton in one hand.

"Cuffs, eh?"

"Well, how else are you going to build loyalty?"

"If I cuff then won't they screw on me, and there goes loyalty?"

"No, usually customers want to deal with someone steady. They want a long-term relationship. It makes them feel secure about getting the next lid. Dealers don't mind deferring cash as long as the collection cycle jives with the restock cycle. They treat cuffs like money in the bank, but they need that money to re-up. You might get burned occasionally, but that's the cost of doing business."

Carmine smoked dope, and it intrigued Tweed that he could be so articulate and informative and yet be a stoner.

"I want to try selling weed."

"You ever smoked dope before?"

Carmine knew that he hadn't.

"I thought not. Shouldn't you try it before you sell it? How do you know what you're getting into?"

Tweed replied defiantly, "Smoke the shit and you lose profit, right? Plus you might get fucked up and forget your cuffs. I won't smoke it."

Carmine smiled indulgently. "Right."

CHAPTER 3

It was about a week before he tried it. Carmine and Jules Fecteau were getting stoned up in Carmine's attic, and Tweed was along to hang out and converse.

A small dark vial glistened in Jules' hand.

"Check it out!" he gloated.

"Oh, man!" cried Carmine, almost in a squeal.

"What is it?" asked Tweed.

"This, my boy, is hash oil."

Couldn't have said anything more incongruous than that. Hash oil? You cook hash with it? In the frying pan with the potatoes and onions?

Carmine took the vial and unscrewed the cap. A thick resinous odor filled the room. Jules pulled a pack of cigarette papers out of his pocket and prepared a leaf between his fingers.

It wasn't for cooking.

"What are you doing?"

"Don't worry, Tweed. Just watch."

Jules carefully rolled a pinch of marijuana into the paper, creating a lopsided pregnant snake of a smoke. After he had wet it between his lips and twisted it tightly to seal the ends, Carmine poured out a tiny drop of the thick black liquid, and Jules began working it down the length of the joint. Soon it was black and gooey, limp and disgusting looking.

"You guys are going to smoke that?"

"So are you, Tweed." Both of his friends started to laugh uproariously.

A rapid rationalization sequence occurred in Tweed's mind, nudging him ever closer to attempt breaking free of the surly bonds of rational thought. He had foreseen this moment a hundred times, and in every instance he had leapt at the opportunity to expand his consciousness, and finally taste of the apple that his old friend the DEO had often dangled in front of him. And yet there was a voice within him that warned of consequences, of lost memory and cognitive skills, of the irrevocability of this action. Proceed, and he would forever follow the beat of a different drummer. Probably a whacked out drummer, like Keith Moon, or Bonzo Bonham.

His primary objection was to smoking itself. He would undoubtedly not have hesitated if the hash-oil/reefer combo had come in a pill form. But having been raised in a household that included at least three smokers at any given time, and being long accustomed to the choking stench of cigarette smoke, he was exceedingly reluctant to follow their example. Ever since he could remember he had suffered through smoky meals, tar-stained kisses from his mother, as well as grossly overflowing ashtrays on every table and in every room. Unable to understand the allure of tobacco, he considered smoking to be an unnatural exercise, one that induced the veritable vapors of brimstone into the pure and sacred vessels of the human lungs.

The reefer had been re-lit twice already and was now clenched between the tiny teeth of an electrician's alligator clamp. Carmine had taken a gimp bracelet, adorned it with wooden beads and a feather, and crimped it to the end of the clamp, thus transforming the prosaic item into a custom "roach clip". Tweed accepted it and self-consciously drew on the end of the slimy snipe. Fearful of ridicule, he desperately held the expansive, esophagus-scorching drag of smoke as long as he could, to the chanting encouragement of Jules and Carmine. Releasing the blast from his mouth, Tweed hung his head between his knees and waited for the spots in front of his eyes to fade.

The joint circulated a couple of times while Tweed convinced himself that he was unaffected by the substance, concluding with a mixed sense of relief and disappointment that he was immune to pot's influence. Months later, when Tweed had acquired more experience and acumen regarding drugs, he would realize that it had been a miracle that the joint had burned at all. By then he had learned that the external application of the hash-oil had been an inefficient waste, since it was intended for consumption in a pipe, and if they had wished to use it on a reefer, they should have rolled it inside with the weed.

Nevertheless, after this first trial and exposure to dope, Tweed found himself in the back yard of Carmine's house, playing a curiously modified game of tether ball with his fucked-up friends. The radically altered game consisted of striking the ball with one's fist, and then collapsing in a giggling fit while the ball completed a few random oscillations and came to rest against the pole.

Tweed had never laughed so hard in his life. Laughter to the point of pain, to the point of exhaustion, to the point when he began to wonder if one could laugh to death. Carmine began to rag him.

"Oh, no, you're not high, Mr. I.M.Immune."

This, of course, was the funniest thing Tweed had ever heard. Jules and Carmine in turn began gagging in laughter over the bright red color of Tweed's face.

A shred of reason, likely born of paranoia, suggested that it would be wise of them to find a place where they could come down in private, or at least ride out the high without bothering anyone or becoming a spectacle. The afternoon movie seemed to be the obvious choice, so they left Carmine's yard and hiked off in the direction of the theater.

Two and a half miles and Tweed didn't remember any of it. They might have flown for all he knew, even though the route involved crossing fields, woods, and major roads and intersections. One thing had fascinated him, however, and as the movie started he still marveled at the transcendent glory he had witnessed in a traffic signal light. His friends had to tear him away from staring at what he perceived as a red, green and yellow beacon of beauty.

The color groove persisted as he watched the feature, *Song of The South*, unfolding with cartoon and live-action characters. He had never seen anything like it, a state-of-the-art multimedia extravaganza. It was overwhelming.

They were sitting too close to the screen anyway, and before Tweed could determine if the movie was a racist propaganda indoctrination film for children or a psychedelic class-conscious musical classic he had to leave his seat. Uncle Remus had seen right through him and the atmosphere in the theater had become as oppressive as a parlor full of fawning relatives.

A homing signal kicked in and he followed it although he had no recollection of making his way out to the sidewalk and rudely accosting an innocent bystander (his amazed buddies later swore that it was true), or of navigating through the unfamiliar streets. As he walked he sought in vain for the wits that he had surely left in little bits along the way, so he could collect them as a trail back to sanity. Or was that something Brer Rabbit had done?

The evening had reached his house just ahead of him and when he arrived he went straight to bed and shut down for sixteen hours.

He awoke refreshed and joyful to be in full possession of his faculties. It would be some hours before his friends shared their impressions of the previous day's events, and informed him about what an ass he had been. But neither the haunting feeling of blind humiliation nor the ache of regret at having forever lost some essential aspect of his self deterred him from wanting to try it again.

Another milestone, in fact one that would have a vital impact on Tweed's weed career, occurred within a month of catching his first buzz. Up to this point he had relied upon either Carmine or Jules to get him high by sharing their stash. It came as quite a surprise when Carmine told him that he was guilty of persistent mooching, an offense frowned upon in high society almost as severely as smoking alone. It had not occurred to him that he would have to buy his own dope and share it with others, since he more or less considered himself to be in a probationary period. So Carmine arranged an introduction for Tweed with his dope dealer, Wayne Kenney.

On one hand it hardly seemed necessary to observe formalities since Tweed had known the Kenney family for years. They lived in a two-family home three doors down from the Kelleys, where the elder Mrs. Kenney, Wayne's grandmother, lived alone on the first floor, and her son's family lived upstairs. In that crowded second-floor apartment, Mr. and Mrs. Kenney raised their children, Steven, Wayne, Gary and Edna.

When Wayne's service in Viet Nam had ended in '72 he was happy to return to his old room in his parent's home as opposed to striking off on his own or moving into an apartment with friends. He made a living by dealing dope and repairing and customizing motorcycles out of his grandmother's garage. For a recent veteran who had seen a brutal variety of front-line action, he had an upbeat, positive disposition; a demeanor that served as a foil to some of the surly and intimidating characters that made up his clientèle.

On the other hand Tweed had known Wayne only as one of the big kids in his neighborhood, almost as old as his brother Buck, and he barely recognized him since he had been overseas for so long. Wayne had never participated in the street-hockey or b-ball games and unlike many of the local boys he had no use for block parties or other social events. Furthermore, Wayne would not have acknowledged Tweed, let alone deal to him without an introduction, so Carmine's help was essential in this regard.

Walking up the driveway to Wayne's garage for the first meeting, Tweed looked over Carmine's shoulder and saw a figure seated Buddha-like at the top of the steep grade, obscured by the bright sunlight of the summer afternoon. Closer now, he recognized Gary, Wayne's little brother. At 16 he weighed approximately 250 pounds and was strong as a longshoreman. He tipped a sweating can of Pabst in greeting and smiled goofily. Carmine patted him on the shoulder, but Tweed passed out of arm's reach. He recalled how Gary used to grab youngsters in the neighborhood and grip them in a bear hug below the ribcage to knock them out for fun. Gary also had a reputation for his phenomenal throwing arm, and he was said to be able to reach low orbit with baseballs that kids were foolish enough to hand him.

The dark garage was cool and smelled of oil and gasoline. Wayne sat on a creeper beside a partially disassembled BSA. He held a box-end wrench in one hand and a drop light in the other.

"Good day, boys! Carmine, and Tumbleweed, I presume?"

Tweed nodded nervously in reply.

"So why do they call you Tumbleweed, anyway?" Wayne stood up and stretched, then placed the drop light upon the only vacant hook on a sheet of pegboard otherwise used for tool storage.

Tweed was embarrassed. He hated telling this story.

"My father had a thing for westerns, you know? He named my oldest brother Buck, and my other brother Mack, and I got stuck with Tumbleweed."

"Far out! Cool name if you ask me. I mean, how many Tumbleweeds are there?" He noticed the expression in Tweed's face. "Bet you'd rather be a Bob or a Johnny, huh?"

"No, Tweed's OK; I've gotten used to it."

"How about your brother Kerry? How does that figure?"

"I don't know, I guess my mother got dibs on that one."

Actually Tweed knew that Keiran had been considered special, having been the next to come along after his mother had lost a pair of twins in childbirth. Perhaps she had felt an obligation to tradition.

Carmine changed the subject. "Hey, Wayne, we wanted to grab a bag if we could." He looked around quickly as he spoke, as if worried about being overheard.

"Sure!" smiled Wayne. "Right this way!"

He led them to a small whitewashed room attached to the rear of the garage in which he kept an easy chair, a card table, an eight-track stereo and a refrigerator.

"What's it gonna be? A lid?"

Tweed fumbled with the cash in his pocket but remained silent.

"OK, a dime bag? A nickel? Speak up boys, don't be shy."

"Uh, Wayne, Tweed doesn't know what he wants. Could you show him what you have?"

Wayne placed his hands on his hips and cocked his head.

"All right. You have to understand that this is not how I usually do business. But I'll make an exception for a first-time buyer. Tumble-weed." He opened the freezer compartment of the fridge and removed a handful of plastic bags.

"Here's a lid. A dime. A nickel."

The crisp sandwich baggies were tightly rolled.

"Sealed with spit and frozen for freshness. Take your pick."

Tweed unrolled the lid and hefted it in his hand. This was more dope than he had seen thus far in his life and appeared to be far more than he would ever be capable of smoking, even with the help of his friends. Somehow the dime bag looked right and Tweed handed the nickel and the lid back with a sawbuck.

"Before you decide, I do have some gold in here...somewhere," Wayne fished around in his freezer. "Ah, yes; a nickel costs ten but it's worth it." He snapped a bag open and the aroma was like honey and roses, spices and citrus. "'Course I wouldn't have you buy it without a taste. Here, Carmine, twist one up for your buddy there."

So with the purchase of what turned out to be a dime bag of the gold stuff, Tweed became a user, and a buyer, but more importantly he gained continued personal access to Wayne. The benefit of the relationship was in the mentoring; the advice and counsel Tweed received regarding dealing as well as the ritual and culture of dope.

Among the important lessons that Wayne eventually imparted was the Happy Customers/ Happy Neighbors Rule:

-It is essential to have happy, smiling customers so that your neighbors do not become suspicious when they see visitors leaving your house or place of business

-In order to avoid the appearance of soliciting, all transactions, no matter how small, must be lengthy and irregular even if customers need to be detained to accomplish the goal.

Other lessons included:

-Breaking up quantity, and the use of scales from the hand-held gram weight clip balance to the precision triple-beam.

-Distributing chafe throughout the split, and maintaining volume with humidity control.

-Identifying quality, developing a nose for hybrid characteristics and an eye for all strains, classic, varietal, and evolving.

For examples of specimens, Wayne seemed to have abundant access to the best the world had to offer. Vietnamese longbud that came wrapped in waxed paper and tied with fine twine. Truly one-hit shit. The buds spoke of breeding and nobility, and one might only partake of them if one could genuinely, with full faith of spirit, honor the plants that would in turn reveal places, images, and dreams beyond the imagination. Hawaiian sticky-stick; short, fat buds practically dripping with resin and flashing highlights of yellow and green crystalline strands. Thai-stick, the inscrutable vegetation wrapped to stalks of green with thread like a bouquet garnee for the mind. Jamaican lamb's breath, sweet and dandy and coma-inducing.

But the regular smoke that Tweed bought and used and ultimately bought and sold was the Colombian red. In those days it still came into the country by airplane in loads of compressed fresh bricks about a kilo each. He planned to work his way up to kilo, but the $250 price was far out of reach yet, and he was also working out logistical issues. Even if he achieved his goal and purchased a brick, he would be crazy to bring it into his house and break it up. For one thing the smell would knock out the family and probably drive the cat insane, and for another, as the brick decompressed the risk of arrest seemed to increase exponentially. Tweed imagined the ratio between the unfolding surface area of the weed and the need for plastic bags, storage space, and security.

The incentive in the kilo level purchase was simply the price. A kilo yielded not merely the 2.2 pounds that a conversion table would suggest. Each pound represented 16 ounces, and in Tweed's realm of friends, contacts, and connections, very few people could afford an ounce that could go for as much as $40 for top-shelf grade. Besides, the lid was the standard bag, but the actual weight of a lid varied from dealer to dealer.

Dealing at this time involved a sort of happy consensual bartering, kind of like at a market where the butcher behind the scale says, "It's a little over, OK?" For daily users there was certain logic in buying only "three fingers" of weed at a time when the supply was steady.

Small-time dealers bought ounces because each ounce represented four quarters at 7 grams per. An average dealer could keep a quarter for himself and roll forty joints out of the remainder of an ounce, and sell them for a buck apiece; a "good" dealer could roll up to sixty out of the same quantity.

As an ambitious new salesman and dealer, Tweed wanted to encourage the trend toward many small quantity purchases. The greater the surface area, the greater the profit. For the remainder of the summer he concentrated on expanding the market, networking, meeting people, and getting out and advertising. He worked the concert venues, the ballparks, and the bar scene in addition to seedy alleyways and track side barker shadows.

This was all within the context of his connection with Wayne Kenny, and as Tweed's business grew, he risked alienating his friend, supplier and mentor. Wayne, however, was becoming increasingly occupied with his bike biz. The transformation from ex-GI to greasy biker was complete as he grew a 'fu-manchu', tied his long brown hair in a tie-dye kerchief, and adopted the colors of the local Devil's Disciples Motorcycle Club chapter.

At 6'2" tall, Wayne looked natural in cowboy boots and jeans, astride his custom chopper with the chrome trident sissy bar and the extra-long fork, throttling the sound of Satan's gargle out of an unmuffled bored-out motor. His newfound associates in the motorcycle club brought him as much repair business as he could handle and grandma's driveway was frequently blocked by a half-dozen hogs.

Whether they were picking up or dropping off, his friends and customers tended to whoop, holler, and peel out in eardrum blistering blasts of acceleration.

The increased noise provoked a reaction, and Des Kelley was one of many neighbors who gathered to demand that Wayne remove his business from the street, although it pained them to have to speak with an otherwise respected veteran in that manner.

By the time Wayne did pull his now burgeoning bike business out of his grandmother's garage, Tweed was back in school, where he encountered new connections and new market opportunities.

CHAPTER 4

The mechanism of tetrahydrocannabinol upon the adolescent brain was largely misunderstood at the time when Tweed began experimenting with it. Any psychoactive substance is likely to disrupt the normal cognitive functions, and possibly the reasoning, judgment and sense centers as well if it's worth its weight in gram baggies, and teenage users are highly susceptible to the euphoria and apathy inducing influence of the drug. Tweed recognized this intuitively, although he was less inclined to believe that it possessed addictive qualities. In his opinion, addiction was a phenomenon of the user, not of the substance, and among users he believed that it was universal.

A conflict was inevitable, for Tweed was a fine scholar for whom the annual return to the academic grindstone was as natural as the color-change of the trees in autumn. In order to manage his pot consumption he would have to put it on a schedule, along with his lessons and elective activities, his sports and after-school enrichment work. The dealing would continue whenever and wherever possible, but the smoking would receive low-priority on his agenda, ideally restricted to one evening per week, on a rotating basis.

By the end of September, settled in the school routine with his classes and track team practices, drama club rehearsals and student government meetings, homework and articles for the school newspaper, he was ready to take on his next goal. The school was full of dope heads, both in the student body and the faculty, and he knew that since the entire district was represented here, then there should be a wide variety of sources of weed for sale as well as eager customers to sell.

He mentioned the idea casually during lunch one day. He was one of a dozen boys and girls seated on seesaw-like benches at a long green table in the cafeteria. They inhaled their food, gurgled a steady flow of milk through carton straws and talked incessantly, all under the impassive gaze of the lunchroom monitors.

In a complete non sequitur like a ludicrous boast, Tweed said, "I bet I could get a pound of marijuana from someone in this school *today* if I had the money."

He waited for a reaction from his nerdish neighbors, Kevin Gormley and Kathy Dwyer.

They had been discussing chess or ballet or something and weren't sure if they wanted to respond to Tweed's challenge. Kevin had a pronounced lisp and an effeminate affect.

"Why would you want to? For heaven's sake!"

Kathy swallowed her bite of balogna, cheese and mayo.

"Not here. No way. There aren't any drugs here."

Tweed laughed derisively. "Any amount of pot before the day is out. I bet you anything."

Kevin felt the gaze of the monitor on his back. He lowered his voice.

"Who would you ask? You'd have to go to a burn-out senior. Or a jock."

"No, the kids out back," said Kathy excitedly. "Have you seen them out there? I think they sell mari- ahm, stuff before school."

"That's what I mean," said Tweed, with satisfaction. "There are plenty of kids selling dope here, and all you'd have to do is tell one of them that you have the money and you can get anything you want. Isn't that wild?"

"You're not saying that you're going to do something stupid, are you?" Kathy used what must have been her mother's tone of warning.

"No; I mean, it just occurred to me. I've seen them out back, just like you said, and I realized that in a school this size, there's bound to be somebody who has access to real quantities of pot. I bet those kids out there are selling hundreds of joints every day! It adds up."

Kevin frowned considerately. Kathy just shook her finger.

"Forget about it, Kelley."

The monitor looking over her shoulder seemed to reinforce that message, with an expression of suspicious curiosity on his face. Fixing Tweed with a stare he folded his arms, raised an eyebrow and beckoned with a crooked finger. "A word, mister?"

Tweed stood expectantly.

The lunch monitor leaned over Tweed and gassed him with garlic breath as he said, "I'd advise you to keep your voice down, Mr.-"

Tweed squirmed out, mumbling Kevin's name and homeroom number just as the end of period bell sounded, and he slipped into the stream of students shoving toward the exits. Now following the herd in the four-minute hustle to the next class, he looked at his fellow sheep differently, trying to pick out the ones who smoked dope, the black-sheep fringe.

And yet profiling was not going to provide the path to the most prolific pot purveyors. He lacked the specific talent required. For Tweed, who had always had difficulty remembering names and faces, clothes or shoes were of little importance. Furthermore, he had no fashion sense. If the stoners dressed distinctively he would be the last to identify the trend.

He needed to determine a more direct route to a source if he was going to make good on his assertion. However he had reservations about approaching the back-yard dealers directly. Discreet inquiries from an intermediary would be far more convenient. Perhaps he knew somebody who already had connections; somebody willing to trade their insights for a nickel bag.

Bone might be the guy to ask. He was a laid-back junior known for his ubiquitous artwork, the "turkey" graffiti series. Many of the buses, street signs, walls and billboards in the vicinity of the school were adorned with his characteristic magic-marker scrawls, humorous renderings of a turkey in various poses and attitudes. These included "turkey in a trench coat", "turkey on the run", "ninja turkey", "cool turkey", "psycho turkey", "turkey rock star" and a multitude of other peculiar pop-art turkey types.

Tweed had first met Bone at the start of the previous school year when he had overheard him lecturing to a small circle of friends in the back of a bus about the contrast between John Lennon's *Working Class Hero* and the Kinks' *Celluloid Hero*. Tweed had been trying to sleep, but he became intrigued by Bone's perceptions about the two archetypes in his dissertation. He explained:

"Lennon's working class hero is 'something to be', whereas for the Kinks, 'everybody's a star'.

"Let me put it in the context of free will and determinism.

"Lennon poses the hero as a worthy model, yet in a class-based society such as the one from which he emerges, how realistic is it to aspire to something that is beyond one's status? He acknowledges the prevalent caste structure by referring to his hero as 'working class'. The implied moral attributes of the society in which the hero struggles may transcend the bounds of class but they also form their own set of restrictions. For example, he says that society diminishes the value of the individual: 'As soon as you're born they make you feel small'; and it abuses the powerless: 'They hurt you at home and they hurt you at school'.

"Again, I believe that free will is an important consideration here, for Lennon seems to say that even those with ambition will never amount to anything, they will never exceed the pathetic roles into which they have been cast. The individual is impotent: 'You can't really function, you're so full of fear'; and blind: 'Keep you doped with religion and sex and TV'. Success in such a society may be attainable, but it comes at a cost: 'First you must learn how to smile as you kill'.

"For the Kinks, on the other hand, 'Everybody's a dreamer, everybody's a star'.

"Where is free will if everybody is a star? And if heroes are so common, then don't they lose something? Isn't their very heroism meaningless? 'There are stars in every city, in every house and on every street'.

"Throughout the song the Kinks juxtapose movie stars and the fans that worship them, trying to establish the relative merits of life on and off the screen: 'I wish my life was a non-stop Hollywood movie show'. However, they suggest that the star's life may be less ideal than many assume: 'People who worked and suffered and struggled for fame/Some who succeeded and some who suffered in vain'.

"Here too, there is frustration and impotence. Of course, it is worth noting that while the Kinks and Lennon are both products of Britain, the Kinks were treating society through the lens of Hollywood, the American icon, whereas Lennon described any contemporary, free and enlightened society."

Tweed was especially fond of the Lennon tune, with its bitter vocalizations and minor key strumming, and he found Bone's argument to be compelling and relevant.

When his brother Buck had moved to Ireland he said that he wanted to be a "working class hero". Having already lost his other brother in Viet Nam, Tweed came to identify the plaintive chant with hard choices, cynicism, and loss. The crackling 45 was one of the records in the collections his brothers had left behind, and he listened to it over and over through the headphones attached to his parent's hi-fi. However, he was not familiar with the Kinks, and when Bone finished talking, he introduced himself and admitted his ignorance of the band.

"If you've never heard of The Kinks, then it's not your fault, it's the fault of radio. It's just my opinion, man, but I think that these days commercial radio just repeats songs that people hate. See, radio execs figure that if they play a track enough times, then eventually folks will forget how they felt about it when it first came out, and maybe they'll even buy the shit.

"Anyway, The Kinks are an important band, musically, culturally, and historically.

"How so? Well, they sing about normal things, like life and people, without glorifying drugs or booze. And their repertoire, which has gotten huge over the years, has been a big influence on the rest of the rock scene. Just think of how many pop hits they had. Even if you don't know the band, you'd probably recognize *Set Me Free*, or *Waterloo Sunset*, or *You Really Got Me*.

"It all goes back to the Fender Stratocaster, man. The strat is the greatest musical innovation in the twentieth century, if you ask me. Most people think of the strat, they think of Jimi Hendrix, well, I tell you man, think of Dave Davies."

Bone was opinionated in a fiercely obstinate way. He would mention an opinion and wait for an opposing viewpoint, but most of his friends were accustomed to his lengthy diatribes on any of a dozen favorite subjects, and they were reluctant to rise to the bait and encourage him. When he failed to get a response he would simply issue a condensed version of his take on a topic, ticking off points on his fingers and thrusting his chin out for emphasis as he spoke.

Tweed hadn't anticipated such verbosity, and after names were exchanged he barely got in another word before the end of the bus ride twenty minutes later. As they parted at the station, he expressed his appreciation of Bone's analysis of the Hero songs.

"Oh, that?" asked Bone. "That's an essay I wrote, the same one I hand in every time I need one in school. Been using it since 9th grade. It's usually good for a B-plus. See you later, man."

…Now the school day was half over and without knowing Bone's schedule it could be difficult to find him. Then Tweed remembered that the upper classmen had lunch after the younger kids so he doubled back to the cafeteria. Sure enough, Bone was seated at a table in the back of the room in a section under the mezzanine overhang.

As he recognized his friend, Tweed noted that there were indeed similarities between him and the others at the table. They had a shaggy, unkempt look, and their apparel was individually accessorized by the addition of unique tokens such as leather pouches, roach clips with feathers, cannabis leaf patches, blown-glass beads, and rock band insignia.

"Hey, Bone, I was wondering if you knew where I might find some..." he hesitated, looking uncertainly at the other characters at the table.

"Peels?" asked Bone, smiling.

"Peels- oh, pills? No, man, weed," he said, in a whisper.

"Right, peels." He flipped his bangs up away from his eyes, which Tweed noticed were gray-blue. "No problem, dude. How many are you looking for?"

This was one of those idiomatic usages that made Tweed uncomfortable, like rhyme-speak, or pig-latin. Bone undoubtedly referred to joints as pills, which he pronounced as "peels".

"Bags. Whatever I can get, quarter, half, whatever."

"What? You're looking for an Oh-zee?"

Tweed felt embarrassed and exposed. "Not quarter ounces; quarter pound, half-pound; you know, quantity."

A couple of the other juniors at the table laughed.

"Yeah, well, alright, whatever you say, ah, it's Ted Keely, right?"

Tweed felt his cheeks burning. "No, Bone, Tweed Kelley."

"Just shitting with you, man. If you're serious, I can check around. Get back to me at the bus stop this afternoon before you go home."

Inventing an excuse for his tardiness to class was not as difficult as actually sitting through the remainder of the day. Boredom wasn't the only obstacle that prevented him from following the course work, for in the back of his mind Tweed was preoccupied. The comment that might have been no more than an idle proposition to his classmates at lunchtime had become a bit more probable by seventh period. He watched the minutes fall away from the institutional wall clock in his classroom as he wondered what he would do if Bone did find some quantity. He hadn't really saved enough money for a major score yet, and if he did obtain a stash he wasn't sure if he could move it.

CHAPTER 5

"He standa like a shitabum, like this."

For some reason the memory of his old neighbor Mrs. Falconetti comparing her son's posture to her bent little finger came to mind as Tweed picked Bone out of the crowd at the bus stop. He stood stooped or bowed as if in perpetual fear of being struck about the head and shoulders; which was completely in contrast to the benign expression on his face. When he wasn't talking, Bone tended to look as though he was enjoying a private joke, with a wry little half-smile on his lips.

"Terry Haar," he said, enigmatically.

"Who is she?" asked Tweed, his anticipation rising.

"He- is the guy you gotta see for the peels. I told him to hook up with you. You can catch him over at the Crystal Pond Park stop."

"What, I have to take the west bus?" Tweed took the southbound bus home from school, and although he could just as easily take the west bus in order to meet Haar, he had no idea how to get back from there.

"Yeah, he didn't come to school today, but he'll be waiting at the stop for his girlfriend. She's a freshman. Sam something or other. You can walk to his house from there."

"So how am I going to know this kid?" asked Tweed.

"You'll know him. Yellow-orange wild hair, wicked pale skin, crazy-ass look, and his girlfriend will be there. She's black- island black, from Trinidad, I think."

From the outside one bus was pretty much the same as the next. They were parked under a row of hickory and Norway maple trees, waiting as usual for the students to pile on for the end-of-day commute.

Just standing in the west line, and seeing a different uniformed fat guy in the driver's seat created an eerie sensation in Tweed. An adventure was about to begin.

There were no seats available and the standing room was sufficient as long as everybody breathed in unison. The bus had been full when Tweed boarded, and it would have been humane to prevent any more kids from squeezing in. At departure it was little consolation that the overcrowding would diminish with every stop. After witnessing how many people they crammed on the west bus, Tweed would never think of the southbound bus as crowded again. This should be called the black bus of Calcutta. The close proximity of this many kids at one time would normally instigate the conditions for chaos, but without freedom of movement mischief simply wasn't an option.

Perhaps he had misjudged the potential of collective will. All of a sudden the bus started to rock from side to side, out of sync with any external influence of the route or road conditions. At a traffic light the bus pulled alongside another student transport, a large yellow van for the handicapped and those with special needs. Like the propagation of a wave, it too started swaying before the light allowed the traffic to proceed, and a cheer went up from the occupants of the westbound bus.

The full body press was making Tweed sweat, and the lack of visibility made him nervous as he traveled into unfamiliar parts of town. Sidling toward the front of the bus so that he could watch the stops and possibly ask the driver where to get off, he found himself standing near a petite, stunningly beautiful girl. Mashed into the student body, he was in no position to see much of her, but he did notice that she was short, perhaps 5' tall, and that she had large breasts for such a small girl. He wished that there were fewer people between them so that he might be pressed against her, instead of being wedged in between a goon with halitosis and a faceless head of tightly gelled curls.

From that moment he lost track of the stops as he focused on her fine features and smooth ebony skin. Her hair was tied in a ponytail that hung far down her back, out of sight. She seemed to be concentrating on the passage of streets and stops, and when she turned to get off the bus, Tweed noticed that they had arrived at Crystal Pond Park.

The bookbag was holding him back, snagged among the locked limbs of a trio of straphangers. Yanking urgently, he threatened to uncork the bottleneck in the front of the bus as he hurried to the door, dragging a knot of bodies behind him. If he hadn't worked the bag loose he would have spilled a half-dozen kids out onto the sidewalk as he leapt free of the bus. The pneumatic doors contained them and the bus hissed an insult under its breath as it rolled away.

"Sam?"

She was walking quickly for a short girl, and carrying a load of books as well. She turned and almost saw him when she heard her name called from the other direction. Terry Haar had just arrived at a jog, up the stairs from the train tracks that ran beneath and perpendicular to the bus route. For a moment Tweed's attention was taken by the tracks, strange rails that did not pass through his neighborhood, but apparently ran off into the same city that his rails did.

"Yo, Terry!" He sprinted to catch up with the couple, before they turned down to the stairs. Terry stopped and raised a hand.

"Oh, yeah, Weed, right?"

Tweed's head snapped a quick rotation of insecurity. It wasn't cool to yell out drugs on the street.

"Sam, this is Weed, he goes to the same school we do. I forgot I was supposed to meet him here today."

Sam took in Tweed with a sweet smile, and nodded recognition. He had trouble looking away. But he wanted to clear up the confusion about his name.

"Yeah, good to meet you, Terry, Sam, I'm-"

"I know, I know, Bone told me all about it. Let's head to my place, it's right down the tracks." He quickly ran down the two flights to the lower level.

Tweed had never been in this part of town before, and he had no idea where he was in relation to his frame of reference, but he felt relaxed and happy. It was a crisp autumn afternoon, he was with cool people, and he and Terry had something in common.

During the walk Tweed listened as Sam filled Terry in on the events of her day, and about what was happening at school in general. She spoke with a practiced enunciation that would make a finishing school grad jealous. Precise English varnished with mellow Caribbean refinement, as much an improvement over the American slur as Trinity English is over standard Eaton.

As impressed as Tweed was with Sam's exotic beauty and obvious poise and intelligence, he was also bewildered as to how she had ended up with skinny, ugly Terry Haar. In Tweed's eyes he looked like an emaciated Mick Jagger junior with red hair. His arms were thin and bony, he was pale as a scurvy victim, and his hair looked as though he had tried cutting chunks of bubblegum out of it with rusty scissors, while looking in a broken mirror. He also kept up a rude by-play, interspersing his conversation with comments such as, "Hike up your panties, my dear, it's time for lunch," and,

"What do you say after we look at our homework we play bouncy-bouncy?" When he did so, Sam simply pursed her thick luscious lips and said nothing.

Terry led them through a gap in a rusty chain-link fence, down a rutted dusty path that spilled out on a delta of rain-water deposited rocks. They were now on a sidewalk at the junction of an intersection, where the street upon which Terry's house stood formed the leg of the T.

The house was a large blue Victorian with ornate white trim and multiple added dormers that appeared like tree houses through the optical obstruction of a massive beech tree in the lawn.

The kids walked up the driveway toward a white garage that had its mouth full of an orange Dodge Charger, and entered the house through the side door. Tweed couldn't help noticing that the garage needed a new roof, and that the car was on blocks.

Inside the house was dark and damp and cool, and it smelled of other-family funk. Terry explained that he lived there with his three brothers, but his oldest brother Dickie was in prison right now, so he and Scotty and Dave had the run of the place. Terry was the youngest. When Tweed asked if his brothers were in the house, Terry said that they were, but since Scotty was with his girlfriend and Dave was doing heroin, then they would be unlikely to see them.

Down a short hallway into a kitchen that was so messy and filthy that cleaning was less of an option than total gutting and remodeling; up a winding flight of servant's stairs to the second-floor hallway.

As the trio walked along the hall Tweed peeked into the bedrooms on either side and in one of them caught a glimpse of Terry's brother Scotty balling his skanky scag-bag girlfriend in a naked heap on the floor. Relieved that he seemed to be the only one who had noticed, he trailed as they ascended again, this time on the main stairs of the house, to the attic and Terry's room.

"So, Weed, man, what can I do you for?"

Tweed wasn't sure if Terry had a problem with his name or a problem with word order.

"Ah, as much as I can get. A pound?"

"A pound of dope you say? How about two?"

Since this must have been levity on Terry's part, Tweed simply laughed self-consciously.

"I can give you a pound of red, but I happen to have a pound of gold, too."

"Acapulco gold?"

"None other. Sticky, sweet, I'll tell you man, you can sell this shit for twice what you get for the red."

"How's the red?"

"Shit, man, it's Colombian; top shelf, tight bud, almost pure resin."

"Well," said Tweed, against his better judgment, "let me check it out."

Sam giggled from Terry's bed. "Man, Weed, you're so serious!"

"Hey, Sammy," said Terry, "Roll one up, will you? While I take care of my man here." He reached under his bed and dragged out a battered army-green footlocker, from which he produced a brick wrapped in a plastic bag.

Tweed kept one eye on Terry and the other on Sam, feeling somewhat disappointed to see her handling marijuana, although he did not know why. She sat lotus style with an album cover stash kit on her lap and concentrated on her task, while Terry tore open the bag and offered it to Tweed for inspection. The pound was packed in a dense brick that looked like it would be difficult to break up. The aroma was heavenly, and despite himself, Tweed began salivating. Highlights of nutmeg and cinnamon, citrus and rich loam, the condensed smell of an eastern breeze wafting across the spice trail.

"Shit!"

"Shit, man? No freaking way! That there is the best Colombian red you can get right now."

"What about this gold you were telling me about."

Terry smiled appreciatively. Oh, the man's got an appetite. Hang on a sec'."

He disappeared out into the hallway, and when he left, Sam beckoned Tweed over to the bed. He hesitated; his blood suddenly rushing hot and fast to his extremities.

"Don't you want this?"

"Ahm, spark it up!" he said, his mouth now dry.

"Oh, I don't smoke, honey. I only roll it because Terry doesn't know how."

Taking the symmetrically rolled reefer from Sam's hand, he looked into her eyes and melted.

He lit it, and drawing deeply thought with wonder that he would never have expected to be smitten by a black chick.

The smoke helped to clear his mind, and he started to scheme about how he was going to score some of this excellent weed.

Terry returned, looking over his shoulder and carrying a duffel bag. "Here we go, dude!"

The gold was even tastier than the red. This pound was fluffy and almost pure bud. The color was that of Vietnamese long bud, but the characteristics of this cannabis were unlike anything he had seen before. Flat oval buds bristling with glistening red hairs attached to sinewy stout branches that still displayed machete marks where they had been cut for curing. And whereas the red had been like a fine aperitif, the gold was a meal in itself, giving off a heady, hoppy bouquet. Tweed had thought that he lusted after Sam until he saw the pound of Mexican gold.

"OK, so how do we do this?"

"You want 'em both, 600. The red only, 250."

Shit. 250 was more than he expected to pay, and 350 was unheard of. But then again, it was gold, surely worth more on the street than regular commercial. An idea occurred to him: a unique product like this would do well with novel marketing, such as selling buds as opposed to bags. Charge 5 bucks for a gram rather than the standard 3.5 grams. Plus, if he took both pounds, he could sell the red primarily and thus subsidize the gold, while prolonging its shelf life, and in the long run keep more for himself.

"I'll take both pounds, but I hate to tell you that I have to go home and get the money first."

"Don't worry about it, Weed! I'm not worried about it, I know where you live."

"You do?"

"No, but I know where you go to school. Just give it to me there."

Holy shit, this was going better than he had thought possible.

"Now, let me pack it up for you...did you have gym today?"

"Yeah, why?"

"Perfect! Wrap them up in your jock, or your socks. That way if you get hassled by the cops, knock on wood," he knocked himself on the head, "they won't find it."

The weed safely stashed in his bookbag, Tweed sensed that Terry and Sam were anxious for him to leave.

"Will I be able to get more of this, do you think?" he asked.

"The red, for sure. The gold, I don't know. I stole that off of my brother. But don't worry, he stole it from someone else."

Now Tweed was feeling uneasy. He was holding enough pot for an army, and he was a long way from home with no clue as to how to get back there. He asked about the trains.

"Fuck, man, it'd take you forever to get home by train! First you'd have to go all the way inbound then switch lines outbound, and by the time you catch your bus, you'd be lucky to get home by midnight."

That was an exaggeration, but it was a daunting prospect nonetheless, especially as Tweed had never done it before. All of his travels by train had been along one trunk, one spoke from the hub of the city. He had followed it from end to end, but had never tried another spoke.

"Tell you what, I have an idea." He stood in a thoughtful pose for a moment then started pacing and waving his arms as he spoke. "You could pull it off; after all, you have your student transfer and it's just a matter of time, right? But you don't want to carry two pounds of pot around town all day. So instead, wait here while I make a call- I'm going to get you a ride home."

He turned back to Sam before he left the room and said, "What do you want on your pizza, babe?"

Terry's plan was devious but elegant in its simplicity. The first step was ordering a pizza for delivery to his house. Then when the courier arrived, Terry and Sam intended to detain him long enough for Tweed to steal the guy's car. Terry stressed the importance of the next part of the plan. After Tweed got home safely he was to leave the car parked so that it could be recovered intact and returned to the shop that owned it. Then perhaps they could avail themselves of the same scam again someday.

Terry was celebrating his cleverness and Sam was hungrily awaiting the arrival of the fresh, hot, hamburger, onion and jalapeño pepper rings pizza; but Tweed withdrew into a clammy shell of anxiety. Having bid his new friends goodbye, he was hiding on the far side of the garage, crouched in a squat, clutching his bookbag tightly in his sweaty hands. The plan was in effect and he was going along with it, but he would have liked to work it out in a bit more detail before proceeding.

He foresaw problems, and although he tried not to think about them, they formed the nucleus of a ball of nausea in his stomach. First of all, his experience was limited, as the only thing he had driven was a gravity motivated wooden go-kart, and he had been no closer to driving a real car than pretending while sitting on his father's lap as he drove. Secondly, he had no idea how to get home from here, in fact he did not really know where here was.

Crystal Pond was a once-pristine habitat west of town that had been set aside as a wildlife reservation; and The Park was a housing development that had been thrown up between the tracks and the reservation for low and moderate-income families. Tweed understood that most of the middle and high-school aged kids in this neighborhood commuted across town to the district school just as he had since matriculating from White City.

Fortunately he did not have much time for thinking. A sagging black Lincoln Continental with suicide doors pulled up to within a few yards of Tweed's hiding place. At first he could not believe that it was the pizza delivery because even with the recent lifting of the Arab oil embargo and the end of the gas-rationing regime it was insane to deliver pizzas in a Continental. But sure enough, a kinky-haired kid wearing white painter's pants climbed out of the car with a boxed pie in his hand and shuffled to the side door of the house to ring the bell.

It was becoming increasingly difficult to hear his cue over the beating of his own heart and the throbbing of the ill-tuned idling V-8, but Tweed made out Sam saying, "Could you come in for a minute? I have to find something smaller than a fifty."

At the moment the driver followed Sam into the house, Tweed crawled around the car and slid into the front seat. No time to adjust the mirrors, he had to blast off. The steering column shift handle was loose as a feeble handshake, and it took a moment to find reverse. When he did get it into gear, the car thunked loudly and coughed up a lung full of blue smoke before shuddering spasmodically down the driveway. He swung it in a wide arc that bisected the opposite curb, mashed it into drive, and floored it. The car died with a wheezy gasp.

Wrenching the keys in the ignition, Tweed heard himself praying fervently over the whinnying spin of the starter motor, and then he thanked all of Creation when the motor started and he was rolling again.

The steering wheel felt oversized and off-center, and it seemed to require a lot of effort and rotation to maneuver the car around corners. It was fine when he was on the long straight street that paralleled the railroad tracks, but when he started heading east he encountered lane drops, roundabouts, and one-way streets that not only challenged his skill with the wheel, but also appeared to impede his progress. It was tempting to pull over and ask a cop for directions.

There was a Ford Fairlane Coupe in the right lane ahead of him, and he could see from the profile that the driver was an elderly gent wearing a felt hat. Tweed's father said that drivers who wear hats always go too slowly, so he pulled in behind in order to calm down and assess his situation. It was then that he noticed the large sausage and mushroom sitting beside him. Lifting the lid he became engulfed in a steamy exhalation of cheesy vapor that reminded him how hungry he was. Within moments he was experiencing the great American pastime: cruising down the road and eating pizza. The caricature of the chef on the cover of the box seemed to wink approval.

So enraptured was he that he failed to notice the police cruiser that had pulled alongside him at a traffic light, until he saw that the officer behind the wheel was staring at him. Tweed just smiled and raised his slice of pie in salute. The cop smiled and waved in reply, and drove off when the light turned green. Making sure to stay well behind the patrol car from then on, he was presently rewarded as he realized that the cop had led him to the border of Jamaica Center.

From here it was a matter of staying low in his seat so that no one would recognize him. This was not a problem because even with his recent growth spurt he was barely large enough to reach the pedals and see over the dash. And yet the joy he had experienced on the thirty-minute drive from Crystal Pond rapidly gave way to profound fear. He was a fourteen-year-old driving a stolen car, and hiding two pounds of marijuana in the sweat pants in his bag. Furthermore, he had eaten someone else's pizza. It was time to come down to earth.

He could not know it then but this was only the first of countless adventures Tweed would have in stolen cars. And yet looking down the long years of his subsequent hot-box career, this would ever be the most memorable. For as a novice operator he was absorbed in familiarizing himself with the quaint knobs and switches on the dashboard, as well as with controlling the momentum of the abused, asthmatic Lincoln. It waddled and swayed when it was under way. The wheel behaved like the helm of a ship, and the chassis responded in kind, pitching from the right rear to the left front even on the smoothest roads, bouncing several times over every bump and squealing like a motel box spring.

The odor of stale pizza, dried coffee and cigarette tar, the broken down seat with faded fabric and no safety belts, and the drone of the radio that received only one station and apparently could not be shut off. Indelible impressions Tweed would later fondly recall whenever he drove a "borrowed" vehicle, whether it was a fine luxury sedan, a sporty foreign compact, or an RV.

CHAPTER 6

Sunday dinner was a big deal at the Kelley house, and this week it was a special event, with full courses and wine, fine linen, the best china and silver, rolled napkins and lighted candles. All on account of the guests, of course. Brendan Tighe had been away all summer studying at Lemoyne, and Brother Morris had just returned from a visit to the Holy Land.

Mrs. Kelley had been preparing food for the affair since Saturday night, and Mr. Kelley had spent the morning cleaning the house. But Tweed had dawdled on his return trip from the ten o'clock Mass and he had been trying to keep out of sight since then.

Sunday was a stolen day as far as he was concerned, a weekend day that he was not free to enjoy. Redundant chores and obligations in the morning, and then a stifling period of family time, and later either entertaining guests, or worse, visiting relatives. His parents gabbing interminably while he sat in front of a television beside cousins he barely knew, boredom eating his heart out.

Tonight Brother Morris would undoubtedly repay his hosts for their hospitality with a boring lecture and a slide show. Tweed would be assigned to operate the projector, and he would be expected to advance the carousel with enthusiasm as if he could not wait to see the next frame. Dreadful as that was, he had no desire to see Brendan either, because so much had changed since they last talked.

Just this past Friday in school he had paid his newest pot supplier Terry 500 dollars as an installment on a major 2 pound deal. The money represented all of his cash and the proceeds from his first significant sale. The day after he had bought and sorted the weed, Tweed sold a quarter pound to one customer. After paying Terry he had hoped to spend the weekend pushing bags to build up his money supply again, but now he was a hostage in his own home.

The sermon at Mass was called "Trust In The Lord", and although the gist of the homily was fading quickly from his memory he thought it had to do with the difference between trust and faith. The reference text was printed on the weekly sermonette, which he held close below his chin like a tray. This was to prevent telltale crumbs from falling on his Sunday suit and revealing that he had spent his collection basket coins on donuts again.

> Trust in the Lord with all thine heart; and lean not unto thine own understanding. In all thy ways acknowledge him, and he shall direct thy paths. Be not wise in thine own eyes: fear the Lord, and depart from evil. It shall be health to thy navel, and marrow to thy bones. Trust in the Lord, and do good; [so] shalt thou dwell in the land, and verily thou shalt be fed. Delight thyself also in the Lord; and he shall give thee the desires of thine heart. Commit thy way unto the Lord; trust also in him; and he shall bring [it] to pass.

Since early adolescence Tweed had experienced an insatiable curiosity about Christianity, and about the life of Jesus in particular. Having been raised in a Catholic family he was familiar with the simplified child's version of the bible story, from the Garden of Eden to the Garden of Gesthemene, and he had a childlike faith. But when he was ten years of age his faith was shaken by the death of his brother Mack, and further upset by the sudden onset of his brother Keiran's religious fervor.

As a young teenager wondering about the age gap between Mack and himself, Keiran had learned that his mother miscarried twins in the interim before successfully delivering him. He believed that God had conferred special status upon him, and as his parents had taught him that all babies were gifts from God, he also concluded that he was a divine gift to his parents.

Tweed was willing to humor his brother to a certain extent. But when he vowed to devote his life to religion, Tweed began to suspect egoism at work rather than selfless dedication. For Keiran fantasized about becoming a latter-day prophet and about possibly being the reincarnated Savior. Tweed's rationalization that other Christian children might share similar fantasies about themselves only served to make his brother seem slightly less weird and the other children slightly more so. Who knows how many other religious fantasies were woven in the minds of the faithful? Christians had been taught to venerate the translated visions of fanatics throughout the ages.

Yet Tweed also viewed religion selfishly, not seeing it as the relationship between his soul and the divine, but rather as a sequence of prayers that he uttered by rote with all the hope and innocence of *Twinkle, Twinkle, Little Star.*

In an attempt to encourage thought and reflection, Brendan Tighe had suggested that religion could be the path to self-discovery. But recently that path was becoming overgrown with a certain weed. Tweed began toying with the notion that the weed itself could aid in the process of self-discovery, for perception-altering drugs and techniques had been used traditionally throughout the world as a means of achieving enlightenment. He had recently acquired *The Teachings of Don Juan* by Carlos Castaneda and from it had learned that the Yacqui Indians used the hallucinogenic properties of peyote as a means of enhancing religious visions and prophecy. Hadn't Jesus gone into the desert and fasted for forty days? For that matter don't all spiritual teachers and mystics speak of self-abnegation, of ritual consciousness expansion and cleansing of perception? And in Health class he had learned that marijuana had been cultivated and used as a recreational drug for millennia, but in ritual use it had often been controlled and prescribed by priests and shamans. It seemed that pot and religion were compatible, and Tweed decided that insofar as the weed could aid in his voyage of self-discovery he could use it more frequently.

It was fitting that he would end the week on a theme of Trust and Faith. Hadn't faith led him to his first big score? And wasn't trust a major component of dealing reefer, if not the major component?

After driving home from the dope deal, abandoning the pizza parlor's stolen delivery car at the Rossie Depot parking lot and hurrying to his clandestine clubhouse for a quick bagging session, Tweed had spent the night and much of the following days inculcating a strong sense of self-preservation. He decided that paranoia was the key to longevity as a dealer. In order to thrive on the streets as a dope peddler he would have to have an unerring nose for snitches, cops and thieves. At first he conceived of it as a kind of "Spidey-sense", a magical tingle that would run up his spine when trouble was nigh. But he didn't have any radioactive reefer to smoke, and anyway he didn't need super powers to sell pot. He simply had to avoid getting ripped off or busted. Without too much analysis it was plain to see that what he really needed was a highly refined sense of paranoia- a codified, professional paranoia.

Common sense told him that the first rule designed to reduce risk should refer to talking. As harmless as pot seemed to him and millions of other users, there were some people who honestly believed that marijuana was "evil weed", or "wacky tabaccy". It had been demonized in popular culture since the 1930s as the cause of a wide range of ills, from moral decay to madness. Furthermore it was a controlled substance, placed on the federal narcotics list alongside Cocaine, Heroin, Morphine, and Barbiturates; therefore it was illegal to buy, sell, cultivate or possess. Accordingly Tweed resolved never to speak of the drug by name whether in person, on paper or on the phone, and to devise a system of designating quantities for his contacts and customers. In this manner he could reduce normally incriminating transactions to bland chat that would hardly arouse suspicion:

"Hey, Tweed! Did you see the game last night?" (Got any weed?)

"Yeah, it was great." (Sure thing, how much are you looking for?)

"I saw the first quarter..." (I'll take a quarter) "did you catch the score? (How much?)

"We were up by five." (5 bucks)

There was no code, he simply told everyone to improvise and thus references to weed gradually took the guise of references to homework, quarts of milk, weather predictions, etc.

It was much easier to get through dinner than Tweed had imagined, not because of the tales Brother Morris told of his barefoot pilgrimage on the Via Dolorosa, but because of the perfectly roasted beef, the mashed potatoes, brown gravy, fresh green beans, pearl onions in cream sauce, sweet rolls, and garden salad. Everyone praised Mrs. Kelley, somewhat more passionately than they had thanked the Lord for the blessing of his bounty before the meal. She would have none of it, in fact she did not eat with the family. Instead she bustled about from the kitchen to the dining room, bearing steaming pots in her mittened hands from stove top to trivet. She hummed happily, making sure that plates were full and glasses were brimming, and that the food kept coming until the guests pushed away from the table.

The boys took up the job of clearing the table and starting the dishes while the adults pursued a lively after-dinner conversation. Each time Tweed came into the room for another armload of plates he heard a different topic being discussed. The economy, the war, the President's resignation. He preferred the sink full of greasy pots and pans instead of wading through the political bullshit in the other room. The impeachment hearings had been great drama throughout the summer, and Tweed's personal Watergate scandal scrapbook dated back to the first headline, but his interest was fading. As far as he was concerned, the image of Nixon's last helicopter ride had seemed to put an end to the spectacle of the failed administration.

On most occasions Tweed would join in debate, usually to bolster the liberal position of his mother against the strangely conservative views of his father. Tonight however he was hoping to remain unnoticed until he got an opportunity to slip out of the house. And the kitchen was conveniently close to the back door.

He imagined that there must be others in the area who longed to get out of their stuffy houses and away from their boring families as much as he did. What was on television right now? Lawrence Welk? Mutual of Omaha's Wild Kingdom? Wouldn't folks rather go out and buy a bag of fresh sticky red? Perhaps he could meet them for a walk. Marlin Perkins was a heck of a lot funnier if you watched him when you were stoned.

As Tweed finished the first batch of dinnerware there was a transition in the dining room. The dessert china was laid out, issued from the wall hutch like a pretty promise of good things to come. Then in another skillful display of synchronized entertainment, Mrs. Kelley served the pies, lemon meringue and blueberry, just as the coffee finished percolating.

The twinkle in his eye should have given him away, but the usually staid Brother Morris actually caught Des Kelley unawares with an unexpected story. He said, "Des, did you hear that Pat went into the pub recently and sat down at the bar? Mick the barman asked him,

"'Pat, you look dejected, what's the trouble, my good man?'

"Pat looked up wearily and replied, 'Ah, Mick, I just came back from the doctor's. He told me that I haven't long to live.'

"Mick shook his head and said, 'I'm sorry to hear that, Pat. Tell me, is there anything I can do for you?'

"'There is, now that you mention it. After I'm dead and buried, would you take a bottle of your best Jameson's, and pour it on my grave?'

"Mick thought for a moment and answered, 'That I will, Pat, but, could I run it through me kidneys first?'"

Christine Kelley laughed hysterically and Tweed thought it was funny, too, but Des kept a straight face, and Keiran just smirked. Tweed could tell that his father was searching his memory for a suitable response, but he was probably stuck looking for a clean joke.

Brendan probably had one at the tip of his tongue but unlike Des he wouldn't want to upstage his elder friend and colleague. He left his seat and entered the kitchen in order to have a quick chat with Tweed before dessert began in earnest.

"Run it through me kidneys! Oh that's a good one," he chuckled.

"Yeah, you know, it reminds me of something my history teacher said a couple of weeks ago," said Tweed, as he crouched to place a colander under the counter. "That almost all of the great figures in history were drunk during all of the important events that ever took place."

The Jesuit did an intentional double take. "He did, did he? Is that what they teach in public school? I told your parents to send you to St. Thomas' Academy."

"Well, it's true, isn't it?" asked Tweed, trying to keep his mentor on the defensive. "The Declaration of Independence? The Magna Carta? Treaties and surrenders, scientific breakthroughs?"

"Well," began Brendan, as if he were singing the introduction to a solo vocal part, "You have to understand that alcohol played a different role in society, I mean, there were times when people drank alcohol basically because they couldn't drink the water."

"That doesn't mean that they didn't get off on it," said Tweed.

"No; well, think about it, when somebody drinks all the time, do they really get drunk? For one thing you have to understand is that in many cases the alcohol consumed was not hard liquor, but rather near-beer or weak wine, what they called spring wine. It had hardly any kick at all."

"OK, sure. I'm talking about soldiers and statesmen, historical figures, people who mattered. I think they got shattered. During the Revolutionary War, the Civil War, heck, any war, everybody got as wrecked as they could."

Brendan tried another tack. "Do you blame them? You're talking about times when the overall life expectancy was low, and they had no antibiotics, no anesthesia, and only primitive surgical techniques."

"I'm just saying that I agree with what my teacher said, and that it's amazing to think that these people we honor in our history books were really soused during their greatest moments. Just think of how many times wine is mentioned in the Bible."

This was something that Brendan felt more comfortable discussing.

"Yes, again a reflection of society. Wine was an important part of culture in Biblical times. It was important to trade, to religion, to daily life."

"That reinforces what I'm saying. The religious folk drank wine while they worshiped, and the pagans worshiped the god of wine."

"Tweed, I must disagree. You say the Bible is full of references to wine, and that's true, but it also admonishes those who partake in it. Listen to this selection from Proverbs:

"'Who hath woe? Who hath sorrow? Who hath contentions? Who hath babbling? Who hath wounds without cause? Who hath redness of eyes? They that tarry long at the wine; they that go to seek mixed wine. Look not thou upon the wine when it is red, when it giveth his colour in the cup, when it moveth itself aright. At the last it biteth like a serpent, and stingeth like an adder. Thine eyes shall behold strange women, and thine heart shall utter perverse things. Yea, thou shalt be as he that lieth down in the midst of the sea, or as he that lieth upon the top of a mast. They have stricken me, shalt thou say, and I was not sick; they have beaten me, and I felt it not: when shall I awake? I will seek it yet again.'"

"It seems to me," said Tweed, tentatively drawing upon his earlier conclusions, "that the spiritual experience and the high experience are a natural combination, one that's been practiced by people in many cultures, not only the Judeo-Christian."

Brendan shook his head. "Again, Tweed, let me quote scripture, from Romans:

"'For I say, through the grace given unto me, to every man that is among you, not to think more highly than he ought to think; but to think soberly, according as God hath dealt to every man the measure of faith.'"

For the sake of appearance Tweed did not go directly to his family Bible to check up Brendan's citation. However, as he finished dessert and then helped out during the slide show, the notion bugged him that the Bible actually contained a reference to being high. It seemed more likely that his friend the Jesuit had taken liberties with his own interpretation. On the other hand it was reasonable to assume that nowhere in the scriptures was there an endorsement of catching a buzz, by any means.

The slide show accompanying Tom Morris's lecture about his visit to Jerusalem was lengthy and as hard to follow as the homework instructions from the last teacher on a Friday afternoon. The images looked overexposed and under composed. White rock, white sand, vast expanses of white buildings. Many shots of Tom in his khaki pants and straw hat, placed in the pictures as if to provide scale.

His lecture did keep Tweed's attention for a while as he brought together the latest information from discoveries on the Dead Sea Scrolls, excavations of archaeological sites, and comparative studies by leading cross-cultural scholars. As he proceeded to the gospel descriptions of the fateful conflict in Jerusalem, Tweed's mind started wandering. Boredom had pulled out its whittling knife and was carving years from Tweed's life. Hadn't he been to church once already today?

This was too much, although the mystery of Christ's death and resurrection had formed the foundation of Tweed's faith in the risen Lord...

A couple of years ago a number of local Catholic churches had started offering "folk" Masses that featured a casual atmosphere, contemporary live music, and a new pervasively joyous approach to the liturgy that brought parishioners in by the droves. However after only a couple of months the church that the Kelleys attended abruptly stopped the folk Masses, returning instead to the traditional Mass, with the High Mass offered in Latin. When the archbishop at Sacred Name announced his decision, the congregation accepted it meekly and without complaint, and in fact if he had left it at that there would have been no further controversy. However, the archbishop used the occasion of the announcement to lambaste folk Masses altogether. He condemned them for contributing to a trend toward loosening of moral and traditional strictures that bound the community together. In response a number of parishioners, some of them longtime pillars of the community, stood in unprecedented protest and walked out, and Tweed followed them. From that day forth he attended church separately from his family.

It was at his new church, the Church of the Annunciation, that he had a profoundly touching experience of faith. It occurred during his first visit there the following Sunday at the point in the Mass when the Priest was leading the Liturgy of the Eucharist. Thus far there had been slight variations in the ritual from what Tweed had seen countless times before. They did it a little differently here. Unlike the Priest at Sacred Name who mumbled over a chalice with a tiny wafer in his hands, this Priest held a large segment of flat bread aloft before the congregation, and in a loud voice proclaimed the mystery of the body and blood of Christ, the Consecration and transubstantiation.

As the congregation stood and clasped hands, the meaning of the Sacrifice suddenly became clear to Tweed. All at once he understood that Christ had died for him, a sinner who could gain heaven only through Jesus. Alone in the pew, with only strangers beside him, Tweed wept. Although humbled and joyful, he was not converted by this revelation, this vision of redemption. It had created a baseline in his awareness, from which he hoped to grow and develop. God had tracked him down and caught him and placed his foot on his throat. Getting up and accepting his role as a Christian was something he would have to do on his own. Until then he would recommend the church for the folk Mass but he would not proselytize for the faith.

...Finally Tweed seized the opportunity to break away from the gathering. It was 9PM; the adults had retired to the den for party games, liqueur, cigarettes and chat. He caught Brendan's eye with a wink as if to say, "Cover for me!" then rolled into his sweatshirt and out the back door.

How could his parents afford this extravagance? As a child he had taken his family's economic situation for granted, but now that he was a young man making his own money he wondered about it for the first time. His father didn't work and never had as far as Tweed could tell. The Kelleys still owned a pub in Ireland, and Des called himself a businessman, but Tweed wasn't sure how he qualified that claim. Was it the two annual trips to Ireland, or his "membership" in the Rossie Biz Club?

Mum worked for as long as he could remember, and as hard as she could without detracting from the tender loving care she lavished upon the house and family. She earned most of her money as a private word processor for a professor; a published author named Alton O'Hegarty. She had met him onboard ship on the passage from Ireland, and they had stayed in touch ever since. For the past couple of years she worked in the mini-office she had converted from her sewing room. There she would don headphones and sit for hours, transcribing the professor's tape-recorded dictation into neatly typed stacks of paper.

It was hard to believe that the pub could generate enough profit to pay for the airfare, the middle-class lifestyle, and a home in the city. But these things existed, and were further ratified by the family's friends and associates, the churchmen and cops and politicians.

His father was well connected; especially for a guy who never felt at home in the US. Here was a guy who, since he emigrated in 1960, had worked for dual citizenship, had lost a son in the service of the US military, had been a stalwart tax-paying member of the community, and yet still saw himself as Irish. No matter how compelling a local referendum might be, or how exciting the hometown sports teams, or how close his American friends were. He followed the Irish press by mail, and the BBC by short wave. With all of the relations he had back in Roscommon, including his son Buck, who had lived there since '71, he had a living link to his roots and Irish community, and he never let his family forget it. Of course to anyone who met him in America, the accent was a dead give away.

After glancing back at the house to make sure that nobody was watching, Tweed slung his body under the back porch, sliding on his heels in order to keep his butt off the dirt. There was a crawl-space under there suitable for stowing rakes, push-brooms and snow-shovels, all of which he had moved aside earlier when he had gone in there to hide his dope. It was wedged up against the floorboards where he had left it, snug and secure, but this was no way to operate. Soon he would have to solve the storage problem. For now he would head to his clubhouse where he would inspect his weed and taste and compare the high grade Mexican gold marijuana with the Colombian red. All thoughts of family or religion were forgotten.

His sweatshirt was just compensating for the chill, as long as Tweed moved briskly and worked up some heat. The path to the local hangout wall was deserted and dark. The air smelled of piled oak leaves and dry grass, and the breeze kept low to the ground in brief gusts.

As he walked Tweed dug the toe of his sneaker into the piles of debris along the edge of the path, hoping to dislodge an object suitable for kicking. Here the ground was uneven and full of obstacles, but soon he would reach a stretch of asphalt where he could run across the road and pass a rock from foot to foot with sharp kicks.

There, peeping out of the grass on his left, was a shiny black rock striated with thin parallel red and white layers. Tweed cocked his leg and skipped toward it like a football player lining up an onside kick. Just as he reached his foot out, another foot appeared from the shadows and swept his rock aside. He heard a self-satisfied cackle and saw the neighborhood boor, Og, dusting his hands and grinning.

"Tumbleweed tumbles!" he roared.

Tweed recovered, and keeping his eye on the rock, tripped over and back-kicked it through Og's legs.

"And he scores!" countered Tweed.

"Hey, man, that could've hit me!" Og complained.

"I know, I tried, but I just missed..."

"You dumb mick-"

"Ugly camel jockey-"

"Fuckin' potato eater-"

"Goat fucker-"

"Fuckin' green, boozin', fuckin', leprechaun-"

"Queer Arab raghead-"

"Heh, heh, how's it going, eh, Kelley?"

"Not bad, yourself, Og?"

"Heard you got something good."

"Indeed I do, sweet and tight as Susan Gosling's cherry."

"What? Man, did you ever do Susan Gosling?"

"No, but I can dream, can't I?"

"I don't know..."

"What?" asked Tweed.

"Smoke a cherry? Doesn't sound right."

"That's OK, she can smoke me."

Og smiled. "Oh, I get it! She can smoke me! Oh, man!"

"Hey, you want to check it out? Got some with me right now."

"I thought you'd never ask."

CHAPTER 7

The attraction of the clubhouse lay in its orientation. Cocked akimbo, seemingly at a whim, it stared off into space indifferently. Functionally it was a garage but there were at least two reasons why it probably never served as such, at least not since the days of horse drawn carriages.

First, it was not attached to the house to which it belonged; in fact, at first glance it was hard to tell whether it was part of any property at all. Its odd position suggested that it might have predated the surrounding structures, as well as the street itself, like an obstinate boulder that defied civilization to build around it.

Secondly, in order to approach the garage in a car one had to cut diagonally across a moderately busy blind intersection and then carefully creep over a steep curb and up the driveway.

The elderly owner of the property, Mr. Wolff, parked his car on the street in front of his house. His garage faced in the other direction onto a different street like a difficult child with its back to the house. For many years he had cleaned and maintained it by himself, usually sweeping it out in the spring and late fall. Lately even those rare visits had ceased as he delegated the chore to neighborhood kids who did odd jobs for pocket money.

The garage was safe, cozy and comfortable for Tweed and his buddies, the current occupants since they evicted a family of gray squirrels. More than merely dry and convenient, it imparted a homey sense of responsibility. Perhaps out of respect to old man Wolff they did little to customize the interior, other than applying token brands of territorial possession. Even these were little more than hash-marks as there were no graffiti artists within the clique.

An old workbench in the rear of the bay served as the communal gathering point, for when the door was open those seated at the table had a tactical view of the street, an element that made them feel secure in the cave-like environs. Favorable lines of sight also assured privacy by virtue of the prominent elevation.

In his clubhouse command post Tweed sat like a feudal lord at the head of his court.

Carmine arrived unexpectedly, provided the distraction that Tweed needed so that he could discreetly remove some pot from his pocket without revealing the total quantity he was holding. When Og had finished greeting/abusing Carmine, Tweed showed him a sample.

"Check it out. A lid of red."

Greedily fingering the baggie Og raised it to his beak-like nose and inhaled. "Smells good…"

He selected a bud and rolled it between his thumb and forefinger, "Dense…" and squeezed a seed like he was popping a zit, "Not too seedy…"

So all of a sudden Og was an expert? The sight of his friend running his fingers through the dope brought to mind the old Three Stooges routine: "I'm a corner sewer, nyuck, nyuck!"

"You gonna roll it or you gonna make love to it? C'mon!"

Tweed frisbeed a pack of papers across the table.

"Marfils? I got something better. Take a look." He tossed two packs back in return.

"Reefer Rollers? What the-?" Tweed puzzled over the unorthodox design.

"Yeah! 'Fine papers for over forty years', or some bullshit slogan like that. See, there's a roach clip in every paper."

"Roach clip? Looks like a piece of 18 gauge wire."

"Exactly. See, as you burn the reefer, the wire becomes exposed along one edge. You just bend it back, voila!"

"Don't you mean voici?"

"Who gives a fuck?"

"Looks like it'll canoe"

"Man, don't put them down until you try them."

"You're holding the bag, Og, and here are your papers. Twist one up!"

In moments, Tweed regretted handing the responsibility over to Og, who obsessed over every detail of the operation. First the choice of buds, because he would not settle for the loose chafe that had settled in the bottom of the bag. Then came the fastidious cleaning procedure to remove every seed, stem, and Mantis-turd from the dope. Next the preparation of the paper, for although Og apparently preferred Reefer Rollers, he had to crimp and pre-roll the leaf to encourage conformity to his preconceived notion of the ideal reefer. Then, with a pile of pure cannabis on the one hand and a properly prepped paper on the other, he commenced the assembly and rolling phase. This was critical in Og's opinion. "If you overlap, that's what makes it canoe. The wire is just a holder, but the paper will canoe if you don't roll it right."

Canoeing was the undesirable tendency of joints to burn along one side, forming a paper "canoe" full of unlit weed. One way to deal with a canoe was to simply burn it like some kind of aboriginal rite of sacrifice. Get it smoldering and cup the hands around it so that taking hits was like peeking into a little shrine and sucking all of the incense out of the air.

Another way to deal with canoes was to prevent them by rolling correctly.

This notion of proper technique, of 'reefer etiquette' was something that struck Tweed as pretentious. It was one thing to observe idiosyncrasies; in fact weed smokers had some fascinating quirks and traits. It was another to impose some kind of standard.

"Hey Og, are we going to get to smoke that tonight? You're not fashioning a monument to Colombia over there, you're rolling a joint. How long is this going to take? Do you have to be such a freaking perfectionist?"

Og used his standard reply: "Fuck you, man."

"I'm serious. Does it matter if there are seeds in there? For Pete's sake!"

"Look, you want a friggin' 4th of July special?"

Carmine joined in. "Snap, crackle, pop?"

"I'm just getting old waiting over here. It's like you're building a watch or something. I can see you putting on rubber gloves, 'Scalpel, forceps, hemostat...'"

"Fuck you, man, alright? Now I'm going to Bogart it. You don't deserve to smoke this joint. That's right. Fuck you, man, I'm going to smoke this all by myself."

"Go ahead, man, Bogart."

"I will! This joint's too good for you. Fucking watchmaker, rubber gloves!"

"That's right, Og. You go ahead and do that one to your head, because I have a bag of Acapulco Gold here and me and Carmine are going to do a doobie of that while you smoke your god-damned icon."

"Gold? Fuck, man, I'm just trying to roll this so it burns better."

"He's right," said Carmine, "a clean joint is a tasty joint."

"Well then, why don't you ask Bogart if you can get a couple of hits off his clean bone, while I twist up a fat joint of this gold. Because I'll tell you, when you got gold, it's all good: the stems, the seeds, the chafe."

"He's got a point there," said Carmine. "I mean, if I had, say, Thai stick, I wouldn't throw away anything."

"Seeds are worthless, no matter how good the dope is."

Og had spoken.

"Not so," said Tweed, "There is a thin coating on each seed that contains a substantial amount of THC. If you know what you're doing you can remove those coatings and smoke them separately. Takes time, though."

"How the fuck do you know?" asked Og.

In response Tweed rolled his forefinger and thumb together in the universal gesture for cash, and smiled, implying that he had rubbed off the seeds himself. Actually, he was just repeating some of the lore that Wayne Kenney had imparted to him during marathon bong-sessions earlier in the year. He had no idea if it was true or not. But he wanted to knock Og down a peg before he became unbearable.

Carmine held out a book of matches.

"Don't you start now!" growled Og.

"Doesn't do any good unless you smoke it, dude."

"I don't want to smoke it, now."

"Why not? You know Tweed's gonna smoke both kinds with you."

"That's just it. I don't want to smoke the red if there's really gold to be had. That's like having a Twinkie before having a parfait."

Tweed shook his head. "Man, you better buy some of this fuckin' dope, for all the bullshit I have to put up with."

He did not, however, wish to expose the full bag of gold buds. Fortunately he still had a primo number in his pocket that he had spun up earlier. "Alright. Here." He made a show of handing the joint to Og but when he reached out for it, smoothly faked and tossed it to Carmine. "Light this, will ya?"

Two tokes later Og was begging him to sell some of his stash.

"Can't do it, man; at least not until I find out if I can get some more. Hey, I'm turning you on aren't I?"

It was a mistake to mention the gold when he wanted to sell the commercial red.

"That's all you have, man? C'mon, break some out, I know you have it."

"All I have to sell is the red. Try it. You'll like it."

The joint had been stationary in front of Og's nose for five minutes now. The train had broken down in Ogsville.

"Hey, Og!" said Carmine, "Pass the thing, will you?"

This was an historic toke, an inhalation of epic proportions. He had already filled his lungs, his bronchs, his esophagus; now he was cramming smoke into his cheeks, his sinuses, his brain cavity. Short whuffing tokes like an air compressor.

"Hey, Og!" cried Tweed, "You're gonna pop there, man. Take it easy!"

Og started rocking back and forth with each huff, probably so that the water that was pooling in his eyes would roll off his face. Either that or he was about to keel over.

"Pass it!" demanded Carmine. But the joint was gone, and it had taken Og with it.

Normally Og looked somewhat primitive, hence the name. Black bowl-cut hair, dark complexion and baggy eyes, a neckless hunch and a brooding stare.

Now he was caught in the ineffable moment, the blissful Purgatory of oxygen-starvation, the kaleidoscope head rush. Crumbs of glowing paper flared out on the tip of the wire between his fingertips, and still he sat, contemplating the heroic ascent of his star within the cosmos.

"Tweed, do you want to step outside?" asked Carmine, gesturing around Og's inert form.

They walked out to the side of the garage, where there was a concrete concavity somewhere in shape and size between a rain gutter and an alleyway.

"Just wanted to tell you, man, that Og palmed a couple of your buds when he was checking out your bag."

"Yeah, I know. I figured that I'd sell him that bag when he asked for one."

"But if he has some buds he might not buy a bag."

"True, but let me put it this way: whenever he asks for a bag he'll get this one. He's just robbing himself. Thanks, anyway."

Syrupy smoke trickled from Carmine's nose.

"Well, I'll take a bag...but I don't want that one."

"No shit. Let's go inside, I'll cut one up for you."

CHAPTER 8

In relating the story of Tumbleweed Kelley's career, it was appropriate to pinpoint its origin; the evening when he first seriously contemplated dealing drugs and when his path in life diverged from all others that he might have taken. His father's story on the contrary, broader, deeper and more complex by comparison, can just as easily be picked up at the end of the same dinner party that had bored Tweed and driven him out of the house.

For Des the price for skipping out after dinner had been a minimum of cleaning chores with a measure of butter-up bribes to the wife. He walked to the biz club with a full belly, a light heart and an active mind. Exercise quickened the flow of coffee and alcohol through his system, resulting in a throbbing ache in his temple and a flush of exertion on his face. The trademark cardigan Aran sweater he wore on his evening strolls felt a bit too warm as he left the close tree-lined streets of his neighborhood and approached the broader avenues of the town. He undid the hand-woven leather buttons and shrugged the heavy wool off his shoulders so that he wouldn't sweat in the cool evening air.

Delightful company always stimulated him but tonight the combination of his old friend Tom's insightful pedantry and Brendan's hilariously barbed banter had left him eager for more colloquy. He felt as though his betters had intellectually invigorated him and now he in turn must be more articulate and argumentative, glib and apropos. With any luck he would encounter the usual cast of wooden bar brooms, dull-witted stool jockeys, hammered has-beens and bleary-eyed blow hards at the watering hole, and he would let his newly primed verbal pump run freely for a while.

It was a shame that his guests had declined the offer to come along, even though they mockingly chastised him because it was late on a Sunday night. Indeed only certain civic organizations, charitable groups and clubs were exempted from the state's blue laws that restricted the sale of alcohol on Sundays; thus one advantage of membership was that the biz club intentionally exploited that gracious loophole. Des understood neither the archaic, regressive law nor the moral indignation with which society enforced it. His own pub in Ireland stayed open well past midnight on Sundays, and "last orders" wasn't until 11PM. "Holy hour", when all pubs closed, was still observed from 2-4PM; but that was no more unreasonable than the current demand by American Catholic bishops that sporting events not be scheduled on Sunday mornings, so as not to detract from attendance at Mass.

Thinking of his pub brought a pang of homesickness, as well as a care for his son Buck, who had run the pub since '71. In fact the damp chill in the air this evening reminded him of his hometown Boyle. He would be there soon enough for his annual Samhain visit, but until then he would have to quell his obsession with matters relating to his homeland, for they remained tantalizingly distant.

An old IRA partisan himself, Des remained keenly aware of developments in the armed and political struggle for a united and sovereign Ireland. When he visited earlier in the year, in May, the Northern Ireland Executive had just voted in favor of the Sunningdale Agreement. This action, designed to provide for a cooperative consultative assembly in the north in the form of a Council of Ireland, seemed to incite the anti-power-sharing Ulster Worker's Council to strike, thus bringing the northern province to a virtual standstill.

The strike elicited frustration and violence among the populace, and before it ended 22 people in Dublin and five in Monaghan had been killed from bombs placed in cars that had been hijacked in the Loyalist areas of Belfast. The failure of the military to restore order had further reinforced Des' conviction that civil war was inevitable.

In addition, the seizure in '73 of the Claudia off the coast of Waterford with five tons of armaments destined for the IRA had created additional urgency to his personal efforts to protect his homeland and people.

However the IRA of 1974 was not the organization to which Des Kelley had pledged his loyalty back in 1940. That was two years after the Dail Eireann, the separatist parliament that had laid claim to the newly proclaimed Republic after the revolution of 1916, had formally handed the reins of government to the Army Council of the IRA.

Although they were few and politically insignificant, republican fanatics like the Kelleys held on to the illusion of the legitimacy of that government, even as they witnessed the partition of Ireland by the Government of Ireland Act, the internecine futility of Michael Collins' civil war, the Machiavellian heresy of deValera's constitution, and the formation of the 26 county republic.

The town of Boyle was near enough to the border to be convenient for troop billets and arms caches, and young Des Kelley was a member of one of the small squads that performed border raids during the 1950s. The spirit of "the rising" reared in every generation, and these actions came under the heading of "The Campaign of Resistance to British Occupation". In response the Irish Taoiseach deValera imposed internment, a perennial tool of repression since the inception of the Special Powers Act of 1922, to great effect against the insurgents in 1957. Pressures such as these and internal upheavals in the movement itself led to the abandonment of the campaign in 1962.

By then Des Kelley had taken the advice of his friends, comrades and relations, and removed himself and his young family to the US. It was understood that the work was not finished, and that in his new life not only would he enjoy the benefit of connections to the bedrock Irish community abroad but he would also exploit the vastness and relative wealth of the Diaspora as well.

As a businessman with legitimate interests in Ireland, Des could travel regularly and freely in and out of the country. This was initially useful for smuggling cash and information, and later for transferring small shipments of arms and explosives. One of his more successful schemes involved rounding up donations of armaments that Irish-American servicemen had collected during their military careers. In the years leading up to the Troubles he shipped everything from small arms, souvenir rifles, hand-grenades and anti-personnel mines, to canteens, weapons clips, field glasses and camouflage.

During the latter half of the 1960s Des was still dealing with the same regime, a seemingly quiescent organization that was laying in wait. However in 1969 the situation become considerably more complicated; first, in August when the "Battle of Bogside" revealed the vulnerability of republican, nationalist and Catholic families living in the north. Clashes between the Unionist Apprentice Boys and their supporters, and mostly Catholic civil rights activists, led to days of brutal rioting and destruction in Derry. Then in December the IRA leadership split into factions over issues of strategy and ideology.

Thus in early 1970 Des found himself to be politically isolated with the old guard, venerated republicans who had suddenly become irrelevant.

Despite his personal values, his feelings of betrayal and anger, he believed that it was his duty to continue working to arm those whom he saw as the victims of the aggression, the underdogs who could not legally obtain arms for self-defense. Des watched from afar as battle lines were drawn in Belfast with the formation of the Ulster Defense Regiment and a host of splinter unionist paramilitary groups.

As the death toll started to rise, as homes were burned and families were displaced, the call for arms went out across the south in the Republic and to the associations of Irish brethren in the US.

Already established by then, Des was in a unique position to respond, immediately ramping up his activities as much as possible within the constraints imposed by secrecy and safety. Ironically, the Arms Trial affair (surrounding the attempt by several important Dublin political figures to procure and supply guns to the north) provided a key distraction in that regard during 1970. Des was able to analyze and exploit the Garda's cordoning tactics as effectively as he had already defeated customs.

CHAPTER 9

"You're going to have to do better than that, you know."

Tweed had tossed together a couple of dime bags and was holding the remains of the lid up to the light.

"What? They're fine! You saw me weigh them!"

"That's what I mean. You're weighing dope on a mail scale. That won't do."

"I have another scale here too-" he indicated the kitchen calorie counter.

"Look, man, it's embarrassing enough that *we* can see you using this shit to weigh weed, but think of all the customers who don't know what you use, who assume that you're really weighing it out?"

This was really something. Until recently accuracy in weight had been the least of a dope smoker's concerns. You'd be happy just to get a bag, and then if you did you judged it by eye, or by finger. A one-finger bag, or a three finger bag, for example. It was a true sign of excess when people start quibbling over grams.

Tweed suspected that there was another message here, or an ulterior motive that he couldn't quite justify. Then again, now that he was moving quantity it did make sense to have a reliably consistent scale.

"What's your point?"

"Just let me pick from these bags."

Tweed groaned.

"What?" said Carmine, "Man, you better get used to it. Offering pick of the bag is one of the ways you keep customers."

"Right. I let them paw through my weed so they can pick a bag, and then they turn around and cuff it, right?"

"I'm just saying. It's good customer relations to always offer a choice of bags. Lets the customer feel like he's in control of the sale, when really, you both know they're going to buy."

"I'll think about it."

"Well, you should think about consistency, too. Say you do hand someone a couple of bags. They should be pretty much identical. And the only way you can guarantee that is by having a good scale. You need an Ohaus, no two ways about it."

"Ohaus? What is that, an Irish house or something?"

"You should know. No, man, an Ohaus is a balance beam, a wicked accurate scale that can weigh everything from a hundredth of a gram to a pound. They use them in laboratories."

Og was coming around, picking his nose and rocking in place on his seat. "I know where I can get one for you."

CHAPTER 10

1 74 lives were lost in Northern Ireland during 1971 as a result of the military conflict, and in an attempt to exert more control over the rapidly devolving situation the British executive again imposed internment without trial.

But the galvanizing event not only for Des Kelley, but for all Irishmen everywhere, was the massacre by British troops of 13 civilians in Derry on January 30, 1972, henceforth to be remembered as Bloody Sunday. The year had started tragically, and by its conclusion 467 in all had perished, including partisans, soldiers, and non-combatants.

From where Des Kelley stood this was not a crisis of the north alone, not merely the echo of a distant cry or a troubling news item. He saw it as the culmination of centuries of British repression and occupation, and the beginning of a human tragedy involving the mass movement of refugees, the slaughter of innocents, and the taking of political prisoners.

His fears were born out when the subsequent cross-border flight of the displaced became the largest refugee movement in Europe since World War II.

250 more died as a result of the conflict during 1973, and as '74 progressed there appeared to be no let up in the hostilities.

Meanwhile, significant advances by British Special Branch operatives in Belfast created difficulties for the IRA leadership. Vital strategy documents were uncovered during a raid on a Myrtlefield Park safe house and ammo dump, prison-block organizations were infiltrated, and on the streets black-ops and dirty tactics kept the guerrillas off-balance.

Record numbers of young men and women were volunteering to fight for the IRA, but arms and supplies were scarce. The serviceable weapons and ammunition went to the front for offensive and defensive operations, while volunteers shared well-worn weapons at rural farmhouse training facilities.

Gradually, as Des' ambition evolved, he began to justify his participation by rationalizing that his arms shipments were purely for defensive purposes, and that in the event that a sufficient deterrent could be created, then the blood-thirsty enemy would cease hostilities.

It was easy for him to distinguish the enemy, because he had a fundamental belief that all Irish people shared a desire to see the island united and free, and therefore the enemy consisted of non-Irish interests such as Unionists, the British military, and multi-national corporations. Irish people shared a universal green-ness that was evident in a love for Irish language, literature and myths, as well as Irish folk music and dance. In his opinion, any love that Irish folk might have for the Crown was secondary to their love of Ireland herself. And Ireland, the long-suffering mother, was worthy of the love, and care, and the passion expressed as her children rose to protect her.

It was the innate response to threats against sovereign Erin that Des sought in his sons as they matured. He had felt it growing up, but his father had been a dyed-in-the-wool republican and various uncles and cousins had been involved in the struggle back to the days of the Irish Republican Brotherhood. Some had been imprisoned, some had clashed with the RUC. With these examples and others, Des found heroes to emulate throughout the movement.

Except Tweed all of the boys were born in Ireland but they remembered little if anything of their early years, as their experience was eclipsed by the move to the US and the novelty of adjusting to their new environment. Kids have the chameleon-like ability to blend in, but Des stubbornly clung to his ways, and anchored his routine around the Mass and the bar, both of which he attended with equal devotion.

In his attempts to inspire his boys he avoided what he considered to be dogma or propaganda, and instead focused on his view of the truth. His persistent and heartfelt assertion was that the British were ruthless warmongers who looted and pillaged the world over to satisfy their own need for resources. They would cling to the six counties in defiance of decency, human rights and international law to the detriment and endangerment of the inhabitants therein, only a slim majority of whom were loyal subjects. Having watched their empire dwindle from its peak days of glory to the current meager commonwealth, the proud British would never willingly cede this remaining acquisition of conquest. Spoken like a true Anglophobe.

CHAPTER 11

Even in a consumer-driven marketplace there were considerable limits to packaging and product presentation when it came to pot. Marijuana growers had not advertised since offering hand-painted crates and farm-stand signage in the 1920s, and they had never wasted much money on cellophane shrink-wrap or other common devices designed for bringing produce to market in a fresh, presentable fashion. Instead marijuana came wrapped in burlap sacks, oilskin duffel bags or heavy-duty polywrap and duct tape. Due to the illicit nature of the product all signs pointing to the grower vanished by the time the weed reached the buyer.

A savvy user might trace his dope back to a certain country of origin, or possibly even a region within a country, simply by examining the weed closely and noting certain identifying characteristics. But the grower, no matter how sophisticated, no matter how successful at breeding hybrid show-ribbon dope, remained hidden, secret, and incognito.

Like any other perishable goods marijuana is best when it reaches the market in the proper phase of the product cycle. Each step in the process, from cultivation, to harvesting, seasoning, curing, and bundling, must occur in due time so that the pot is fresh, tasty and potent for market. In order to achieve this, both the plant and the grower need a stress-free environment. The plants need an adequate supply of well-drained sandy loam and abundant filtered sunlight. Though the plant is a weed it improves with grooming and fertilization.

In order to accommodate a product that requires so much time and care, the grower ideally needs freedom to go about his business, without the threat of prosecution or working at gunpoint. The grower manages the crops over the long-term, and studies plot rotation, and seed propagation. Interruptions in this cycle are detrimental to the finished product and account for a substantial portion of the substandard weed that is available for sale in the US. For example, prematurely harvested weed can be bitter, or cause headaches.

Improperly cured weed can develop mold and mildew. And these are only some of the hazards to which marijuana is subjected as it makes it way to market.

In the early '70s dope was still being smuggled into the US by airplane, which made for some tasty fresh weed, indeed. Weed that had sat beside a dusty airstrip in South America, Mexico or the Caribbean yesterday could sit in a New York warehouse today. However in the '80s a new phase commenced in the war on drugs with the intervention of the US military and improvements in detection and interdiction technology. As a result air smuggling became too risky. Soon it was relegated to the foolhardy few running small private hauls.

The bulk of the weed, the commercial tonnage, started to come into the US by boat. In the freight holds of cargo vessels marijuana was subjected to new threats and contaminations. Diesel fumes permeated the packaging, bilge water soaked through the bales, and worst of all, time itself destabilized the product. A shipment of primo Jamaican bud might leave Kingston in Grade-A condition, only to arrive at its destination as a crumbling mealy mass.

Mexican growers combated this trend toward old and moldy by trucking dope into the US by the ton, and if it weren't for the fact that Mexican weed generally sucked, then the ravenous American consumers would have welcomed the solution. In the end, Mexican pot basically tided the market over until Yankee ingenuity solved the problem of dope supply and demand.

By the mid '80s American growers were cultivating plants indoors on the large scale. They established vast indoor gardens that featured automated controls over feeding, watering, light and humidity. They sped up the maturation cycle and crossbred strains for potency. And most importantly, they communicated with each other and traded seeds to invigorate the stock. This trend toward hybridization paid off when outdoor farms made a resurgence in the latter part of the decade.

Regular rural American subsistence farmers, tired of being screwed by the government over price supports and subsidies, turned to Cannabis as their new crop of choice, and they formed an alliance with the seed wizards. Soon regional dope from the US was surpassing weed from Afghanistan and Viet Nam for flavor and potency. States from Kentucky to California saw the emergence of a new agricultural, economic and political powerhouse: the pot farmer.

Tweed witnessed all of these changes in quality, packaging and distribution during the years of his acquaintance with pot, but starting with the first bags he purchased from his friend Wayne, he noticed that some strange things turned up in weed from time to time. A random assortment of items fell out of the bricks and bales as he broke them up. The idea of keeping these curios and starting a collection came from his serendipitous discovery of a box of empty preserve jars in the clubhouse garage. Old man Wolff may have intended them for sorting hardware or for cleaning paintbrushes; but now Tweed was putting them to use. One jar was for the snags of strings and ribbon he removed from the weed, another for the many insect bodies and bits of beehives he had found, and a third was for storing any particularly robust-looking seeds.

In the years to come his collection would grow to fill a dozen jars. He would also augment his collection with a series of unique labels he had removed from bricks of hashish imported from Lebanon and Syria; as well as the wax-paper wrappings for opium that retained the sticky sweet aroma of the lumps they had contained; various bottles and vials that had held hash-oils and liquid LSD; and an assortment of wild and wonderful cocaine envelopes.

The bonus bric-a-brac added an element of surprise to the chore of cleaning the weed and weighing out smaller quantities. If he were a wealthy, massive dope smoker he would leave the pounds intact because the pot looked so attractive when the buds were on the branch. But in order to serve his customers with consistent bags of uniform quality he had to strip the branches bare and reduce the buds to their smallest constituent size. The process resulted in a virtual rain of seeds and chafe that quickly altered the value and appearance of the smaller bags. A few seeds and stems in a lid didn't look too bad, but the same ratio made a nickel bag downright seedy.

The issue of what to do with shake was one that each dealer handled in his or her own way. Some separated all of the shake and sold it wholesale. Some distributed it in evenly to all of the bags. Tweed removed the bulk of the shake and discarded it, as a cost of doing business. He had decided on this remedy only because he was willing to do something else that few other dealers would contemplate, and that was raise the price.

CHAPTER 12

The stories Dad told his boys when they were sitting around the parlor were of the *Tain Bo Cualaigne*, of the Heroes of the Red Branch of Ulster, and of Pearse and Connolly. The tunes he favored were the songs of rebellion about '98, '47 and '16, and the bittersweet ballads of loss and privation that only the Irish could sing.

As a further incentive to spur interest in their heritage, Des brought his oldest son Buck with him on a visit to the old country in '65, and he brought Mack along in '67. He used these occasions to demonstrate his abiding personal connection to his country, and by introducing the boys to all of their relatives, to help them understand their vital connections as well.

Yet however focused his intent, and however parochial Des' concerns may have been, his sons were subject to the influences of greater world events. Like millions of other young American men they became eligible for military service at the time when the US became entrenched in its own international conflict in Viet Nam. The new draft was in effect under the Selective Service Act of '67 and although the boys were of age, they both somehow "dodged the bullet".

Counting himself as a conscientious objector Buck was relieved to have avoided service, but Mack went ahead and enlisted. As soon as he did so it seemed to both Mack and his family as if a whirlwind had taken him away from home to boot camp and then on to field action. Before he knew it he was "in country", in combat.

Then in late November, 1970, Des and Christine were notified that their son had died in the war, supposedly after having drowned while on R&R. Many families were losing sons in the war then and the noble sacrifice was supposed to be borne stoically; but the small, close Kelley family was devastated, and Des was inconsolable.

For his part Buck, now the oldest, decided to opt out. He, for one, would have no more to do with American politics or the war machine. Rather than embrace what might appear to be the alternative, he also rejected the burgeoning counter-cultural scene associated with his generation, along with its icons, including hippies, free love, and rock music. After eleven years away in the US, he returned to Ireland permanently, to become the new manager of the family pub in Boyle. There he learned that the harder the physical work, the blunter the emotional pain.

This year it was supposed to be Keiran's turn to visit Ireland with the old man. He was only 4 when the family moved to America, and until now Des hadn't been able to afford or justify taking him back for a visit. But his instinct told him that it might be a good idea to pass Keiran over this time and to take Tweed along instead. As he arrived at the biz club he pondered his ambivalence. Perhaps it was because Keiran, a normal well-adjusted American kid, had never demonstrated any interest in his heritage. Or was it that Des and his wife were afraid of traumatizing the boy by exposing him to the conflict first-hand? Maybe emphasizing the significance of his dual citizenship would result in undue confusion. But what made him think Tweed could handle it? Was he any different?

Des needed help and he naturally expected his sons to throw themselves into the cause just as he had when he was their age. Yet for all of his talk he could not force their awareness or concern, and to ask for help would mean openly revealing to them just what it was that he had been doing all of these years.

It seemed unlikely at his age that Keiran would understand the lesson he was trying to get across, that prevailing injustices in the world sometimes cruelly forced people to reject authority and to break laws in order to defend themselves. He seemed to possess a strong moral sense, a naive expression of his idealism. Des would never forget the time when the boys were 9 and 5, and they were brawling over some trivial spat when Keiran sneered at his little brother, "Tumbleweed, you don't even know the altitude of God!" The offbeat insult initially struck everyone (but Tweed) as funny. Des on the other hand proudly wondered where his precocious boy had come up with such a profundity.

CHAPTER 13

Manipulating the market was an essential part of Tweed's business strategy and retail price control was one of the tools he believed he needed in order to implement it. However prices had been fixed and static for a relatively long time compared to other similar goods and services. A nickel bag was 5 bucks, a dime was 10. For quantities beyond that it was often a matter of haggling and negotiation between the buyer and the seller.

Various reasons accounted for pot's stable selling price. One was that the product itself was considered to be like dirt. As a weed it was the lowest form of agriculture, and only rare super mind-blowing potency would alter that perception, literally or figuratively.

Furthermore, on the user level, transactions were carried out between friends, on a cooperative basis.

Unlike other illegal drugs, such as amphetamines, or hard drugs such as cocaine and heroin, pot lacked the pusher figure. Instead weed proliferated through a vast organic structure in which users were the furthest outlying peripheral cells. Mid-level dealers such as Wayne and Terry were like branch managers of the network, representing storage and distribution nodes that condensed and intersected. And yet the nature of the business and the product was such that competing dealers might obtain their inventory from the same source and not even know it.

Tweed aimed to change all of that. He would control the supply chain, he would control the prices and he would control the distribution. But first he had to dominate the market, something he planned to accomplish by strategically releasing the gold for sale after he had created an artificial drought.

The holiday season was coming, the perfect time at which to offer golden baubles for sale.

CHAPTER 14

The door to the club was heavy, ill fitting and pinched into the jamb. A casual customer might conclude after a tug that it was locked, and give up and go away, but a biz club regular such as Des approaches with determination. Without thinking he sets his feet, braces his shoulders and hauls away as if clearing debris from a mineshaft.

A gust of air smelling of stale urine soaked tobacco fled the premises as he entered. Harris Toole's voice penetrated the redolent haze.

"Des! Wondering when you'd get here. Are you going to announce a special collection?"

His eyes hadn't even adjusted to the tar-tinted light within. The club occupied a converted storefront in a space originally designed for a dry cleaning business. Cheap remodeling such as dark paneling, indoor-outdoor carpeting and a dozen scattered tables effected the less than magical transformation. The bar that Des approached was in fact the dry cleaner's old customer counter, which had merely been pushed back to make room for the seating.

"Special collection? What for?"

"Haven't you heard? Bombing in Guildford. Yesterday. 5 dead, 54 wounded."

Des' mood suddenly faltered as if it would turn, escape the bar and slink off to seek comfort elsewhere. He rubbed the bridge of his nose and closed his eyes for a moment.

"JC Byrne called from the Mission looking for you. Wants to get together and coordinate, like the last time."

The last time had been the occasion of the horrific so-called "M62" bombing of a motor coach near Leeds in Britain, earlier in the year, in February. The IRA had designated the bus as a legitimate target because it was used to ferry soldiers; however, some of the servicemen had families aboard, and 2 women and a child died in the blast as well.

Cynically capitalizing on the carnage and the resulting outpouring of grief and empathy, Des and his comrades had established a survivor's fund for the victims. From this experience he learned that donations for the cause of relief amassed much more quickly than donations in the name of defense, ballot, or civil rights initiatives.

The Guildford massacre sickened him, as did the entire IRA bombing campaign in Britain during the '70s. But Des was a hard man who knew that bombs were being used on both sides of the conflict, and he'd also heard that on occasion British SAS operatives had even planted bombs in loyalist strongholds in order to implicate the IRA.

The more he thought about it, the more he appreciated the advantage another special collection would give him as he prepared for his return trip at the end of the month. Perhaps the funds would enable him to afford an infusion of conventional arms so that he could make a case for returning to a defensive posture.

"OK, Harris, we'll set up a CAFÉ committee meeting…Is it alright with you if I hold it here? I hate that fucking dive over in Francestown."

"Of course, Des, whatever you need. But if you call the Geese a dive, I can imagine what you think of this place."

"What, do you got pub envy? Let me put it this way; at the Geese the door to the Gents leads to an alley."

"No shit?"

"I wouldn't, not there, anyway. But tell me, what do you know about this bombing? After Mass this morning I spent the day getting the house ready for guests."

"Thanks for inviting me. Not much, just what I heard on the news. Place they hit was called the Horse and Groom, and it was full of soldiers who were out for a drink on Saturday night. Apparently they were just back from duty in Northern Ireland. Made a bloody mess of it, bodies everywhere. On TV they interviewed a Brit bigwig who raved about hunting down 'the maniacs and animals' who were responsible."

Des listened, sipped from his stout, and muttered "Good Lord", and "Jesus, Mary and Joseph" and "Fuck no" while Harris spoke.

"Is this what it's come down to, Des? Bombing the fuck out of pubs and buses?" Harris leaned with his arms rigid from his wrists to his shoulders as if he was defending that spot on the bar.

Mentally awash in images from his last trip to the North, Des replied, "They walk around the streets with machine guns...they park armored personnel carriers at every intersection- you don't know what it's like over there." He hesitated, gulping back emotion. "It's Brits out and they'll do whatever it takes. I'm not saying I agree with their methods. You know me better than that."

"Yes, but instead of Brits out, they're taking regular people out; women, kids, little old ladies. It ain't going to help in the long run."

Des placed his hand over the bartender's.

"Murder never helps anything. It's a sin and a shame, a sin and a shame what's happening over there." He shook his head slowly.

"Slán agus beannacht." Harris removed his hand and placed two tumblers upon the bar between them, then complemented them with equal portions of whiskey. The bottle from which he poured the tribute would remain at hand, to be offered as a libation sacrifice while the two men solemnly contemplated the suffering that folks like them were enduring in England and Northern Ireland.

"Amen, and may God have mercy on the souls of the murdering bastards who blew the place up."

"Blew it to kingdom come, you might say."

"Well, I suppose dynamite will get your soul to heaven quicker than say, dying in your sleep."

"I never thought of it that way, but I think you've got it all wrong. I mean, who's to say but that the soul don't move at the speed of light, now?"

"And if it does?"

"Well, if at the time of death the soul departs your mortal coil at the speed of light than all souls leaving at a given time would reach heaven at the same time."

"You mean to tell me that if two fellows die at the same time, then the soul of the poor fellow who's been blasted to pieces doesn't have a head start for heaven over the soul of the poor fellow who dies in bed? Wouldn't he get a boost from the blast?"

"I don't know, Des, Einstein said that if you shined a flashlight from the front of a spaceship that was moving at the speed of light then the light from the flashlight wouldn't go any faster than the spaceship."

"Toole, we were talking about the poor people who were murdered in England, not nuclear physics."

"You started it, *a run mo chroi*."

"Hey, only my wife calls me that."

"That's not what she tells me."

"You know, that does it; I've decided. I'm not going to bring Tweed over next trip."

"Tweed? I thought you were going to bring Kerry?"

"Neither of them. This changes everything. It's too hot right now. Besides, if the fund-raiser goes well I'll be too busy to show them around. Next time."

The tweetling trill of worn hinges and the thud of the firmly closed door signaled the entrance of another patron, catching the bartender's attention. As he looked up, the light from a fixture over the bar illuminated his features. He looked pale and tired, like a resigned prisoner apprehended in a searchlight.

Des heard footsteps approach and stop directly behind him, and he saw Harris nod recognition to the new arrival. Another man might have started when a hand suddenly clamped upon his shoulder, but Des had either anticipated it or he had thick skin.

Ignoring the bartender's protest the stranger said, "I knew that I'd find you here, Kelley. Now how about a welcome for one who traveled 3300 miles to see you?"

Des casually slurped the remainder of his drink as if it were lukewarm soup and then set the empty glass aside. He glanced at Harris, whose eyes were still fixed upon the face of the newcomer. Deliberately he slipped off the stool, ducking so as to turn from under his assailant's grasp. Like a display of animal dominance before competing males, Des stood tall, flexed his muscles and swelled his chest. Just as quickly he deflated with a gasp.

"Makepeace? Is it you?"

"None other, Des, my man. Sure and it's good to see you after so long."

"So said the coffin maker to the stiff, am I right? What in God's name brings you here?"

"To give you the short answer, you do, and I'm hoping that you'll give me reasons to return regularly."

"I see; but is *túisce deoch na scéal*, a story requires a drink, so let's have you sit and wet your whistle. My good friend Harris Toole and I were just sharing a bottle of his best bottom shelf stock."

Makepeace and Toole shook hands and exchanged nods of greeting as if to say, "Any friend of Kelley's..."

Having been promised a drink, Makepeace sat squarely in front of the bottle and examining the label said, "Bottom shelf, you say?"

"That's right; a clever publican, Toole is, to keep his best below the bar."

"Well then; from below the bar to below the belt..."

Harris produced another glass and served the precious uisce beatha.

"Slainte, fad saol agat is gob fliucht!" ("Health, long life and a wet mouth!")

"Maith go leor!" ("Very good!") rejoined Toole merrily, and the heart-felt toast made the drink all the more heart-warming.

"Might I ask what occasion you're celebrating? I mean, it's rare friendship indeed that rates 'bottom shelf' liquor on a Sunday night."

"Ah, old man, if I'd known you were coming I could have said that it was to celebrate your arrival. But the truth, sadly, is that we were taking a drink in respect to the dead and injured from yesterday's blast in Guildford, England. Another 'success' for the IRA, Lord have mercy."

"Mmm, I heard about that; although knowing you, I would have thought that you'd be cheering them on, not mourning the victims."

Des looked at him silently for a moment before answering.

"Perhaps you don't know me as well as you think, then."

Striving to dispel the awkward tension that had settled between the old friends, Harris asked, "Tell me, Mr. Makepeace, what is your business here? What do you do?"

Before he could respond, Des interrupted, "He's a brewery rep. Used to visit me at the pub and try to get me to bump my order. You know these salesmen."

With years of experience sizing up his customers, Harris looked Makepeace over in a glance and noticed his beefy callused hands, weather worn face and wiry white hair. Oxford shirt, fleece jersey, coarse brown denim worker's jacket.

"Oh, yes, I know salesmen." He was no salesman, but no matter. "Are you staying in town, Mr. Makepeace?"

Again Des put in before his friend had a chance to speak. "I'm sure you know that you can stay at the house with my family; Chris will be only too happy to put up a room for you."

"That I do, Des, because she told me so herself. You see, I came here from your place just now. That's how I learned where to find you. Fine woman, Christine. You're a lucky man."

"Don't I know it."

"So it's a vacation then is it?" asked Harris, "Will you be here long?"

Des shifted uncomfortably on his barstool, apparently stifling the urge to answer again.

Makepeace smiled. "No, it's business, Mr. Toole. I'll be here as long as it takes. You see, I'm expanding my territory, looking for new opportunities, as it were." He turned and winked at Des.

Flustered, Des stood and pulled his sweater on.

"It's past time, now. I've got to get home early tonight to start on the phone calls. We'll see you tomorrow, Harris."

"Sure thing, Des. Good to meet you, Makepeace."

"Likewise, and thanks for the drink."

Rim-rolling the bottle like a teetering bowling pin, Harris appraised the remains of the contents and then corked it. It struck him as odd that Des had lit up with genuine joyful recognition when he first saw Mr. Makepeace, (if that unlikely name was real) and yet during the subsequent conversation he treated him more like a bill collector than a friendly "brewery rep".

Harris would keep his doubts and observations to himself. He was Des' right hand man because he could be trusted. The less he knew the better, like the smattering of Irish phrases he swapped with Des. Still, he wondered what the A.D. stood for.

CHAPTER 15

"Pleased with yourself, now, 80?" Blind-siding me like that? In a bar?"

"Now don't be mad, Des, I wanted to surprise you!"

"Thought it would be funny, didn't you, you blasted-"

"Come now, no need to overreact. What is it, Kelley? Aren't you glad to see me?"

Shoving his hands into his pants pockets Des resumed walking home and stumbled, bumping into Makepeace.

"You're a sly motherfucker, you, and although I am happy to see you, I would have liked a little notice, some advance warning."

"Well, I'm here and we'll have to make the most of it. Say, mate, what's wrong with your friend Toole? You don't trust him?"

"Harris? I trust him with my life!"

"Now, Des, when Chris told me that you were at the Rossie Businessmen's Club," this he stressed as if he were referring to a swank establishment. "I thought I had it figured. This was your new base of operations." His voice echoed along the empty street. "Now I see that you can't even talk in front of your bartender."

"The way I see it," grumbled Des, sourly, "with some people the less they know, the more trustworthy they are. And you know damn well that any precautions I take are for your protection as well as my own."

"Of course, of course."

"So did you fly?"

"No, no, took the boat. And my boat is following, to meet me here."

Des looked at him suspiciously. "What for?"

"Well, my friend, as much I hated to I came over empty, so I plan to return loaded, understand? I'm sure that you can help with that. In fact, I'm sure that we can help each other."

Not another living soul had crossed their path during the walk home, but Des still looked around in all directions before answering.

"You want to do a run from the US? Are you crazy?"

"You tell me. You've been here for a few years now. Don't tell me that you've been sitting on your hands all this time. I know what you've been up to. And if Guildford is any indication, things are heating up over there. Wouldn't you like to start some real shipments, with significant quantities?"

"You have a plan, a proposal, connections?"

"Carpe Diem, Des, the time is right. You raise the money and I'll load the boat. People are counting on us."

"We haven't got much time before I leave, myself."

"That's right, Des, I understand. If we play it right, you'll be there with plenty of time to arrange the offload. We spend the next three weeks lining up the deal, you fly on ahead, and after following a leisurely fishing route back I should arrive some three weeks behind you."

"Isn't that cutting it close? I'll only be there the month."

"Which is to our advantage, don't you agree? As soon as you see to the receipt of the order, you fly on home and nobody's the wiser. I think it works out rather well."

On his way out this evening Des' mind had been buzzing with ideas, but now he had more to think about by an order of magnitude. This plan was ambitious but logical, simple but elegant. He might have dismissed it out of hand, considering that even with the funds he had collected to date he would have been hard pressed raising enough for a shipment large enough to make the trip worthwhile. But the bombing tipped the scales, and he would tap the outrage of the aftermath by soliciting donations from militants as a representative of the Citizen's Arms Fund for Erin, and from non-militants, to whom he claimed to represent the Citizen's Fund for Erin.

By either name, the organization had grown by virtue of persistent and strenuous grass roots efforts that he and Chris had undertaken over the years. Working with other local groups and individuals through a widely scattered network of sympathetic neighborhood bars, restaurants and taverns they secured a steady source of financial support for CAFÉ. They also siphoned off some of the flow for other needy organizations. These included legal aid, employment counseling and women's services, as well as free-press entities and prisoner's families relief.

Des considered that there was another incentive motivating this scheme, for he knew that Makepeace would not have come all this way in the off chance that Des could help him put together an arms deal.

More likely this was an IRA operation from the start and he was either working for them directly or looking for a piece of the action.

Personally Des' sympathies were with average citizens, the workers, the families, and the voters. Thus his fundamental philosophy was more in line with providing for a militia, or arming citizen-soldiers to fight and defend themselves against domestic tyranny. Although he agreed with Sinn Fein's basic strategy of keeping an armalite in one hand and a ballot in the other, he would rather avoid contact with any of the radicalized paramilitary splinter groups that would advance their causes by means of terrorism. It was becoming increasingly difficult to maintain that distance.

CHAPTER 16

On the way home from school Tweed cranked up his powers of observation as he tried to account for a feeling that something had changed. He saw that the trees were in the full blaze of autumn color. The air was cool and carried a tantalizing scent of burning leaves. Days were getting shorter. Seasonal transitions such as these were expected, and although change was apparent in the process, it was predictable. The difference affecting him was more immediate, but noticing a change didn't mean that he understood its cause or significance. He felt the same, looked the same, and he was eating and shitting as usual. Personal pot consumption was up slightly, but he tracked it closely and from a subjective viewpoint there were no appreciable side effects thus far.

The difference could be external, like the gravitational influence exerted between bodies of mass when their orbits draw them into proximity. That must be it. Sam was definitely one heavenly body whose influence was having an effect upon Tweed. He was still reeling from the one-two punch of learning first of all that she was not Terry's girlfriend, and secondly, that Terry had dropped out of school.

For two days he had carried Haar's money around school as he fruitlessly searched for him, and then he finally sought out Sam, hoping that she would help to relay the cash in order to pay off his cuff debt. But Sam told him that she would not be going to Terry's house anymore because he no longer needed a tutor, since he was quitting school.

Barely able to contain his glee, he asked, "A tutor? You were his tutor?"

"Yeah, it was his last chance to catch up on his work. What did you think I was doing over there? Watching TV?"

"I thought that you were going out with him."

"With Terry Haar? Oh, c'mon! That scrawny, disgusting...You've got to be kidding!"

"No, well, it's just the way he talked to you, I thought..."

"It was the way he talked to me that was so gross! Man!"

"I know! I'm sorry! I wish I'd known."

"Known what? That I was his tutor? That I didn't like him talking to me that way?"

"I wish I'd known that you weren't going out with him. I'd have asked you out myself."

"Well, what's stopping you?" She'd said, less irritated and with a shy stammer in her voice.

Seeing his own reflection in her eyes, Tweed realized that if anything stopped him from dating this beautiful buxom black babe, it would be a "who", not a "what". The prospect of introducing her to his old man induced a chill that his hot blood quickly dispelled.

"Sam, my name is Tumbleweed Kelley. Pleased to meet you."

"Likewise, Weed." She took his hand and lowered her eyes.

"Would you like to go out with me tomorrow night? Get something to eat and then catch a movie?" He felt faint.

"What do you want to see?"

He was about to suggest *Herbie Rides Again* until he caught on to the suggestive lilt in her voice.

Having survived the interview, he simply had to handle the wait until the date.

In the meantime, there was another star in his firmament: the new lodger in the house, AD Makepeace. It was tough to figure the old dude out, let alone to understand why he was staying with the family all of a sudden.

This guy was a character. He could be coarse and hilarious, but then kind and philosophical. Showed up that night after the dinner party and moved right in. It had been a few days now, and Tweed still wasn't accustomed to having a stranger living in the attic. Of course, Mum said that he was no stranger, just another friend from the old country who hadn't been around for a few years. She suggested that the boys treat him with all of the fondness and respect due to a beloved uncle.

Well, he was the hard-drinkingest, swearingest, letch of an uncle he ever knew, and Tweed was pretty sure that the old salt was hitting on his mother. His behavior seemed harmless and in good fun, but whenever Mr. Kelley left the house, old uncle Makepeace started hovering around the old lady, reminiscing, cracking wise and touching her a lot. Keiran said that he saw Makepeace pat her on the butt, but it was hard to believe she'd put up with that.

Anyway, he only went out at night, and during the day he stayed in the house. For entertainment he hassled the family or listened to corny music on his portable stereo phonograph. Had a real thing for Orff's *Carmina Burana* and Beethoven's *Battle of Vittoria*. Made it out to be a real honor when he let Tweed flip through his record albums, but seeing the collection made Tweed wonder why he bothered to bring them all the way across the ocean. Swingle Singers, The Village Stompers, Tom Jones, a handful of classical LPs, and a stack of worthless 45s. Who the heck were the Clovers, Larry Verne, or The Royal Guardsmen?

The cool thing about him was that he had a knack for telling stories. They were outrageous when they didn't contain any hint of truth whatsoever, and even more so when they did. Most compelling were the ones that included a Des Kelley, who was certainly no relation, especially if he was as bold, crazy and colorful as described. Tweed noticed that his mother frowned disapprovingly when Makepeace made free with tales of the past, and that only encouraged him to resurrect stories that involved a beautiful young hell-raiser. It took a moment for Tweed to link the unlikely heroine with his mother because Makepeace referred to her by her maiden name.

Yet the wonder that he felt at hearing his parents enlarged and enlivened by either truth or fiction was offset by his suspicion that they were in some way being conned or taken advantage of. The bullshit bluster struck Tweed as another form of inappropriate flirtation.

Still, it bothered him that whatever change he thought was taking place in himself might be noticeable to others. One way to find out if that was the case was to hang out with his best friend, Jimmy Col. Not to mention anything, but just to see if he said anything. He and Jimmy knew each other well; better in fact than if they were brothers. They had shared adventures, hopes, dreams and secrets, and they had even had their first crushes on the same girl, Rita Hotchkiss. Funny to think that just a year ago they were fantasizing about that gorgeous little blonde, when now he was planning to date a beautiful black chick.

Better not mention that to Jimmy, either.

Down the trail from the Arbs Park bus stop was the ballpark where some of the neighborhood kids were making the transition from baseball to football while others were lazily tossing a frisbee. The park formed the point at the base of the exclamation mark that was Jimmy Col's street, a cul-de-sac he passed before he reached his own street. The houses here backed up against the park like a retaining wall, separated from each other by quarter-acre yards and private gardens.

Mrs. Col worked tireless miracles on her property to maintain it to the standard acceptable to her demographic. Yet for all of her efforts and the slave labor of her children, the yard usually looked like a Nouveau American salad, all dandelions and alfalfa sprouts. Neatly positioned objects of questionable origin decorated the grounds, including a tin plate windmill, a set of toddler-sized Adirondack chairs, a cedar vendor's wagon with a furled red and green striped umbrella, a silver ball on a pedestal, and a swollen garden hose that hissed like a snake as Tweed stepped over it.

As he hooked the corner into the house he caught a flash from the window of the house next door. It was creepy old lady Bemans looking through her blinds for a sign of trouble from the Columkille kids. The shiver that ran up his spine goosed him to step lively into the house, and he called for Jimmy with a falsetto pitch in his voice.

He'd sat in this kitchen a thousand times but it always seemed odd; he lived only a few streets away yet this home was so different from his own. The whole house was weird in a unique, charming way. For instance, Col's family put milk in their tomato soup, and mayo on their hot dogs. He had learned to politely refuse food after having seen how they ate. Ketchup with mac and cheese, and cheese with french fries. If something didn't taste right to them, they usually flavored with sugar, as opposed to salt. Mrs. Col tended to overcook vegetables to a uniform mushiness that Tweed would have expected to run right through the strainer and down the drain with the water in which they were boiled.

He yelled again, intent upon avoiding the necessity of actually looking for his friend in this maze of chaos. Maybe the Cols liked living this way, but he never got used to it. First of all, they coexisted with a flock of live finches that had air dominance over the first floor. Jimmy claimed that they were never sure how many birds they had, and it must have been hard to tell since they were always flitting from room to room, from armoire to hutch to chandelier. His own mother had a fondness for birds, but you wouldn't see her inviting a single one into her house, even if it was mad Sweeney himself, and him in a cage.

Mrs. Columkille's penchant for sharing her home with finches seemed incompatible with her appreciation for antiques, and her knack for acquiring them. The house was a veritable museum of mismatched antique furnishings, décor and objects d'art. He had trouble with the contradiction that birds were permitted to shit upon furniture that he wouldn't feel comfortable sitting upon. He figured that the stuff must be valuable, if only to compensate for its intrinsic ugliness. There were African totems of ebony in the living room sitting opposite a vast obsidian Buddha. The pagan icons were subconsciously disconcerting to Tweed on their own merits so that he felt that the room practically cried out for a proper crucifix. A tapestry on the wall appeared to have suffered critical attack from an army of moths, leaving it with the approximate ragged profile of Stuart's portrait of Washington. Cast-iron toy trucks and tired raggedy-Anne dolls sat on tables at either end of a leather couch, and the coffee table in front of the couch held a stuffed 3-foot-long crocodile. The couch and the crocodile appeared to be similarly upholstered.

Comfort was not a major concern here. In fact, Mrs. Col appeared to have arranged it so that visitors who might naturally wish to take a seat would instead end up looking at obscure curiosities while trying to duck away from swooping finches.

Another thing that bothered him was the lack of privacy in Col's house. Despite the overall size of the place and the number of rooms there were seven kids living here along with occasional boarders and a menagerie of pets. The Kelley home was small but his family had respect for personal space to the extent that one could always find a place in which to be alone. If Jimmy came over, the boys could go to Tweed's room to play cards or a board game, and be totally undisturbed if they wished.

Jimmy's room on the other hand had a barracks-like atmosphere because of the two bunk beds that he shared with any of his 3 older brothers or 3 younger sisters. And if the first floor was a reflection of Mrs. Col's creativity, then upstairs belonged to the kids. Their clothes, toys, musical instruments, books, projects, posters and stuff-in-general was strewn all over the rooms, bathrooms and hallways.

Tweed often wished that his mother would lighten up on her fanatical obsession with neatness, but seeing the total opposite end of the tidiness spectrum made him appreciate the order and decency she demanded. On the other hand, he still felt betrayed by the memory of daily threats she had made to him when he was younger. "Make up your bed, army style. The police will be here after you go to school to check your work. And do a good job so they don't have to come back and arrest you." He had lived with the fear of that conviction for years, much to his subsequent humiliation.

Suddenly little Missy Columkille thumped her way through the swinging door that led to the dining room. Framed in the doorway like a gunslinger entering a saloon, she paused, swinging a floppy stuffed dog by one ear.

"Hi Tumble-dee-bum-bum."

"Hi, Missy!"

"My name's M'rissa!"

"I know, Melissa. Would you do me a favor and go get Jimmy?"

Melissa clearly had other plans, but was torn by her innate desire to please. Tweed fished in his pocket for a suitable bribe. He had been working in the school library earlier and must have something that would entice a three-year old.

"I'll give you these stickers."

She went up on tippy toes and looked closely at them with expectation.

"What's that say?"

"Ex libris. It's for books. You stick 'em on books and that says they're yours."

"Kay!" she said.

"You going to go get him?"

She nodded big, emphatic nods.

"OK, here."

She took the stickers and ran off. Melissa was the youngest, then came Susannah, then Megan, a 13-year-old going on 20. Next oldest was Jimmy, then his brother Peter, and the two oldest, Eric, who was 20 and Todd, who was 21. The birth of Melissa had caused considerable speculation around the neighborhood because Mrs. Col had been divorced for a few years and did not claim to have a boyfriend. Tweed knew, but only because Jimmy told him, that ever since Jimmy was born Mrs. Col had raised the kids herself. She had been involved with different men during the years when she had the girls. He was also aware of the scandal that she had originally been married to a guy who was later put away in prison for life, and that she after she divorced him she married the cop who put him away.

The only thing that mattered to Tweed was that she was a cool old lady who was always nice to him and interested in what he had to say, and that Jimmy was his best friend.

Just then Missy returned with a large book, *Tales Told Under the Green Umbrella*. She had placed one of her new stickers on the cover.

"Where's Jimmy?"

"I don't know."

"You were supposed to find your brother, not a book!" Exasperated, he considered dispatching her again, this time with a swat on the butt. But then he heard his friend's voice behind him.

"Hey, man!" Jimmy had just entered the house from outside. "I was just looking for you! We gotta talk!"

"All right, let's hit the Arbs." He turned to Missy, "I'll get you next time!"

"Tweedle-bum-bum!" She replied, and razzed him with her drooly pink tongue.

CHAPTER 17

"OK, so what's happening?"

"Man, you have to check this out- I found a room in school that nobody knows about."

"A room? So what? Where?"

"You are going to fucking love this place, man! We can get stoned in there and everything!"

"In school? What are you talking about?"

"I've been looking around lately, checking the whole building out and shit, wondering where certain doors lead to. Well, sure enough, I found a secret passageway."

"Where does it go? Where is it?" asked Tweed.

"I have to bring you down there, man, and you are absolutely going to love it, but we have to be careful and keep it quiet. I don't want to get busted and I don't want a whole mess of kids showing up. Nobody was in there for years before I found it and I want to keep it private."

By now they had crossed over the boundary into Arbs Park. Tweed produced a rumpled bone from his secret stash but held off from lighting it until they were well within the park and away from the perimeter.

"Where is the damned room, dude?"

"I'll tell you, Tweed, but first I want you to hear an idea that I have; something serious."

"What? Are you going to ask Rosalind Matchett out for a date?"

"Huh? No, you crazy son of a gun, I'm not talking about chicks. You know the Hilltop Liquor store? I think I know a way that we can rip it off, man!"

"Rob a liquor store? What, have you fucking lost your mind?"

"Well, shit man, I wasn't going to rob it, of course. I said rip it off, not rob it. Look, the store has a little driveway where the trucks unload, see? Well there's two ways we can do it. One- when the guy is unloading he sets a few stacks of cases on the ground and then wheels them into the store a stack at a time with his two-wheeler. Brings in a stack of fulls, brings back a stack of empties. OK..." He braced himself for emphasis. "We do a grab and dash- while he's inside- and whip a case or two. Easy!"

Tweed tried to keep an open mind. Maybe this was something that Jimmy had seen on television.

"So we run off with a couple of cases of bar bottles, huh?" He spoke slowly, "You ever carry a case of beer? It's heavy, man, I'm telling you. Imagine running with one, while some dude is chasing you."

Col looked grim. "So, you're saying...?"

"I'm saying that it might be better to get a two-wheeler someplace ourselves and whip a whole stack instead. For one thing, it'd be easier. For another, the guy might not notice a missing stack right away."

"Alright, Tweed! I was just wondering if you'd be interested. Because what I really have in mind is the other way. Have you ever looked at the back door to Hilltop? There's nothing to it. I bet we could pop that door and take our time cleaning the place out. Remember, the driveway is right next to the tracks, near the Hope Street bridge. Perfect cover. We just haul everything down below the bridge and then clear out from there."

What had come over Col? What a delinquent! So Tweed wasn't the only one going through changes.

Then again he had to admit that it fit a pattern. Ever since they were little kids, Jimmy was always ripping shit off. It was no use denying what was so apparent. Now that he thought about it, Jimmy was a thief. He remembered how Col would always end up with extra milks in school, and sometimes snacks, too. He'd get up and make the rounds in the lunchroom, snagging a couple of freebies while the lunch ladies weren't looking, then scamming the tables like a casino chip hound. Hoovering up raisin boxes, and bags of cookies, and then returning to exult over his plunder.

And later, when they were ten, little Jimmy Col showed Tweed the five-fingered discount. What scores he pulled! The little felon and his accomplice would sit on the hill behind the five-and dime stores, munching on chocolate and poring over purloined comic books. One day Tweed's older brother Mack found them there and since it was clear that there was a slew of rules, laws and commandments being flaunted in front of him, he grabbed Tweed by the ear and dragged him all the way home. By the time they arrived he had extracted a story of confession from his sobbing little brother and strongly reiterated the Christian precepts he was supposed to obey. His ear felt like boiled shoe leather, but he was relieved to hear Mack let him off with a warning, instead of turning him over to his parents for additional punishment. He took up the issue of personal atonement and correction in his prayers, and after that it was quite a while before Tweed ever enjoyed Jimmy's ill-gotten gains again.

Well, that is if you don't count all the times Jimmy made crank telephone calls and the boys laughed it up when folks on the other end of the line got furious. Looking out over the neighborhood from his bedroom window with gleeful malice, he'd call taxicabs out for non-existent fares, and had everything from flowers to pizza delivered to bogus addresses. He was a master at pissing people off, and his phone abuse made great entertainment. Tweed would never have personally dared any of the shit Jimmy pulled, but he loved being there to watch it unfold.

Harmless pranks were one thing, but this liquor store nonsense was a bit ambitious. Tweed had too much at stake now to risk getting in trouble over a couple of cases of beer. Best thing would be to discourage action on the theft at least until the weather deteriorated. Not that he was seriously considering it, but a job like that would definitely be safer on some shitty evening during a sleet storm. On the other hand, the secret passage bullshit sounded interesting, and maybe if he made a big deal about it then Jimmy would forget about the liquor store.

"When I think of some the places you've 'discovered'..."

"What? You mean the maze?" Col was referring to a hedgerow maze that he had stumbled upon when trespassing upon the grounds of the National Society of Arts and Sciences near Westbury Circle. Their subsequent adventure there was unforgettable. Hiking through the woods for an hour to reach the place by sundown; seeing it from the brow of an adjacent hill, and then instead of entering the maze, walking right into the arms of a private police detail that had been assigned to patrol the grounds after dark. The cops accused them of knocking over the oversized vases that decorated the surrounding garden. Col had insisted that not only were the vases in that condition before the boys arrived, but that the cops were showing their ignorance by not knowing that the vases were supposed to be knocked over. In response to interrogation he had gave a false name, but he swore that his mother was an antiques dealer, and that these vases were objects of antiquity that were designed to convey an image of age and decay. It wasn't until the cops tried to push them into their car that the boys made their break and bolted through the bushes and down the hillside into the darkness.

"The maze, the sewer..."

"Hey, that wasn't really a sewer, Tweed, it was more of, ah, an aqueduct."

"It ran under the street; there were rats in it; I call it a sewer." Col's aqueduct was supposed to be a magical tunnel to secret places. Secret places like the swamp and the river.

"Well what about you? You've brought us to some pretty crazy places, too."

"Like where?"

"You're always bringing me tree climbing and cliff climbing and stuff."

"Yeah, well that's the difference; I like to get high."

With that Tweed sucked the fiery remainder of the roach into the back of his throat and began to choke on it. Jimmy couldn't help himself from laughing.

Tweed staggered, hacking and gasping and performing charades as if to say, "I'm going to beat you for laughing while I'm dying."

But Col was saved by his older brother whose hollered summons echoed off the trees and houses. He ran off for his supper yelling back to Tweed, "Remember what we talked about!"

Tweed had other things on his mind. Last night he had been tallying his cash and projecting earnings from the dope sales and was thrilled to see how much money he stood to make. Starting with the pound he had gotten from Wayne, he realized that he had sold it over 46 transactions. 1 quarter pound sold at $90.00; 6 ounces sold as lids over twelve deals for $300.00; 12 dime bags for $120.00; and 21 nickels for $105.00. All told he had generated $615.00 in sales, for a profit of $365.00. Not bad, but now he was working on the second pound, and at the rate he was selling, he would make an additional $375.00 before Thanksgiving. A quarter pound of gold would stay in personal reserve, thus limiting the potential earnings from the third pound, but his intention was to raise the price after withholding the supply for a couple of weeks, and thus offset the loss of revenue by increasing his margin. If all went as planned, he could earn $970.00 for himself by Christmas and have a quarter pound of gold for his head.

Thanksgiving was a month off yet, and there was still a shitload of pot to deal before then. Moving the stuff was no problem, as long as he had the time to spare. The demand was so strong that it seemed like all he had to do was stand on a hilltop and whisper "Weed!" and folks would come running in droves to buy it from him.

But it didn't help that his father wanted him to come along on the rounds to help pick up donations for his new Irish charity work. If he had the time for volunteering, he'd do it at the local hospital where all the cute candy stripers worked.

"Now, Taweed, I don't ask much now, do I?" his father had asked in his gruff, self-deprecating tone, "You know I'm going over at the end of October and I want to have the money together by then. There are people waiting for assistance over there, people who have worse problems than having their father ask them for a couple of afternoons."

There wasn't much Tweed could say to that. It wasn't like he had a job or anything. As far as the old man was concerned, Tweed would only waste his time reading anyway. He had cultivated the image of a bookworm over the past couple of years, partially to serve as a foil for his adventurous side. It was helpful to be known as a straight-laced goody-good honor student, especially when grown-ups were looking for a culprit. Who had picked all of the grapes off Mr. Tucci's arbor? Not Tweed. Who shaved racing stripes on Tusic, the O'Connor's old dog? Couldn't have been Tweed, he's such a good boy!

The only problem with having a reputation as a responsible young man was that some parents expected him to be more steady and sensible than their own children. They were always sending Tweed someplace or other with their bad-apple kids, hoping that his shine would wear off on them somehow. More often than not he would lead the troublemakers toward worse trouble than they had ever contemplated being in before; but if he taught them anything, it was how to get out of it so no one got hurt, or punished.

For example, there was the time when Mrs. Handy sent her son Jackie along with Tweed to the ball game, thinking that at the least, her son would be off the street, and at best Tweed would be a good influence on him. But in the event, Tweed showed his new friend how to sneak into the park so they could save their money for snacks, and after they got into the game he led him down to the locker rooms where they stole caps from each team to keep for souvenirs.

Much of the inspiration for his mischief came from the very books behind which he hid most of them time when he was in view of his elders. He preferred books about clever boys who managed to solve mysteries, who could contrive simple machines out of everyday objects, or who made adults appear simple and foolish.

Recently however, his intellect demanded writing that was challenging, and most of the bulk young-adult pulp fell far short of the mark. He read because he craved stimulation, and as a consequence his literary appetite began to encompass works by authors such as Herman Hesse, Thomas Merton, Charles Dickens and Ernest Hemingway.

As books were the conduits to ideas beyond his imagination, then the library was the supermarket of the soul. There he discovered how much there was that he didn't know. The local library was a satellite on the municipal branch system, and its modest holdings were a mere token collection, yet it represented a sample of the vast wealth of ideas available in print. To Tweed it was like a fountain from which he could draw off knowledge books at a time like pitchers of refreshing water. As soon as he was old enough to go alone, he would walk the half-mile to the library on Saturday mornings and spend the entire day there curled up around a select pile of books in a study carrel. The librarians all knew him by name.

Reading imparted a sense of security and connection to the world at large. He easily imagined being part of a community of intellectuals who shared ideas, and he dreamed of discussing thoughts with the writers he admired. And yet these fantasies did not encourage wanderlust, for he believed that books would always bring the world to him, hence there was no need to go out and seek it.

Recently he had read the biography of Ireland's former president, Eamon DeValera, both to satisfy the requirements of a book report pending at school, and to get an objective assessment of the man his parents revered as a leader and statesman. The biographer also had placed DeValera upon a pedestal, and gave a glowing account of his career from his days as a young revolutionary to his role as leader of a modern republic.

Tweed would have liked to identify with his subject; to feel some personal affinity for him although from Tweed's perspective he was a man from a country that was as distantly removed as the era in which he lived. One of the items of interest about DeValera that Tweed had chosen to elaborate upon for his report was the fact that in 1916 DeValera was an American citizen fighting with the IRA. He was an immigrant from New York who took up Irish studies in Dublin and later joined the Gaelic League where he could immerse himself in the Irish culture. Recruited into the IRA he soon found himself participating in the Easter Rising as part of the Dublin Brigade under Thomas MacDonough. The Pyrrhic Revolt resulted in the arrest and execution of many of DeValera's friends, comrades and contemporaries, including MacDonough. DeValera himself had been spared only due to the reluctance of the British to execute an American.

But as a comfortably complacent American citizen himself, Tweed did not find inspiration in the story of DeValera's life. This was partially because it seemed to have little relevance common to Tweed's life, personally, historically or politically; and partially because of the ambivalence that his parents had shown toward Dev, whom they sometimes praised and sometimes cursed.

The only political event that had any impact upon Tweed, an adolescent with a minimal awareness of current events, was the impeachment of President Nixon. But that had more to do with the packaging of the affair as a made-for-TV mini-series, with a colorful cast of characters, a full schedule of original episodes, and a mostly family-friendly format of programming and content. The impeachment had coincided with the arrival in the Kelley house of a new second-hand color console television with a 19" screen and a wooden chassis large enough to get buried in. Almost as soon as that set was turned on, Tweed's favorite TV friends became Kimba the White Lion and Leon Jaworski.

CHAPTER 18

Chris Kelley watched her husband prepare for the committee meeting while she folded laundry from a wicker hamper. He was moodily quiet and preoccupied. Not surprising since the planning for these meetings was always needlessly complicated. JC Byrne had insisted upon holding this hastily called conference at Cu's Pub. Although Des was busy and preferred to stay local, he had agreed to travel to the Mission district for the meeting. He'd hitch a ride with Ed Cleary, who commuted home to the Mission from his job over here at the Municipal Water Works; and return with Charlie Cotton, who worked at the Mission Waste Transfer Station and commuted to his home in Westbury Circle.

The clothes were still chilly from hanging out on the line and they seemed to draw the warmth out of the room. A stipple texture of goose bumps plastered the backs of her arms. Des stopped puttering, stood behind her and wrapped his arms around her waist. He smelled freshly showered and the heat from his body warmed her back. She wished that she could slip inside his t-shirt with him.

"Your hands are cold."

"I've been out gathering the clothes in."

He turned her around to face him, cupped her hands in his, then warmed them with his breath.

"80 going with you?" she asked.

"No, he's got his own thing."

"Yes…" she hesitated, thinking, "he certainly does. You know, I saw his baggage being dropped off."

Des knew his wife well enough to know that she had probably been watching for the arrival of Makepeace's things.

"Oh? And? Something about his bags?"

"Well, it wasn't his bags, so much, it was the driver."

"What about the driver?" He sounded slightly impatient.

"It was just that, well, I know all of the drivers."

Security was the foremost concern for the Kelleys and their associates, so they used only known and trusted drivers, whether for deliveries of people or things.

"And you didn't know this fellow?"

"No, I never saw him, or his car before."

"Maybe 80 didn't know him either. Maybe he just caught the most convenient lift."

"He knew him. They talked for some time. No money was exchanged…though it did look as though they agreed to meet later. I'm just saying…"

"I know." He guessed her concern. "It was strange enough that he showed up out of the clear blue, but…"

What if Makepeace was being run, that is, directed by unknown agents to get intelligence on Des' activities, or worse, what if he was setting them up, for a scam or a bust? It could be a significant problem.

"Maith thú!" ("Good for you.")

"I'm not saying that we have anything to worry about, but be careful."

Des nodded, well aware of his situation. For all the years they had been in the US, the Kelleys had lived almost exclusively on illegal and unreported income. If any of his activities were to come under official scrutiny he could encounter severe difficulties from both the Revenue and Immigration services. Operating as a non-profit without permit, incorporation or taxpayer-ID was bad enough, but Des had also invested donated funds as a management stake into a number of small local contractor's outfits in order to generate personal income. He would set up crews of fresh-off-the-boat Micks and Paddies with painting, masonry or carpentry work, and he collected a percentage of their earnings for his trouble. In order to ensure the success of these companies, he also lined up their contracts and provided basic advertising and transportation, yet he neglected to license or insure them and he kept all financial transactions under the table.

He had always thought that by maintaining genial relationships with local law enforcement authorities he would ever avoid any legal entanglements; that well placed friends would serve as a buffer and deterrent. Now the thought crossed his mind that 80's presence might somehow threaten or compromise that assumption.

80 had proved to be a valuable ally on a number of critical occasions. The association between the two men went back over 15 years. During that time Des had never pressed Makepeace for information, for the less he knew about the man, the better for both of them. Expedience was the master of necessity, and standard operating procedure aside, he believed that as long as he obtained the maximum amount of arms with a minimum of exposure to risk, then he was justified in his approach with respect to Makepeace's privacy.

This time it was 80's approach that was questionable. It would be vitally necessary to follow up on Chris' observations and to determine whom he was working with, where he was going and what his intentions were.

The problem was that 80 was not an idealist like Des, he was a practical businessman, generally self-motivated. His position as a middleman supplier placed him in close proximity to the militants whom Des wished to avoid. Furthermore, as a weapons man he had acquired a pragmatic understanding of modern armaments. He would spout stats from Jane's like a tout quoting handicaps from a Racing Form. The functionality and cold certainty of weapons was as enjoyable to him as the smell of Hoppe's nitro and gun grease.

There was no time for this. 80 had laid down a challenge that Des was naturally inclined to accept, and yet the impending deadline had him so busy that he lacked the time to perform due diligence.

"Can you keep an eye on him?"

He expected a sarcastic reply from Christine, like, "Sure, I'll just fit it in with the cooking, the cleaning and chasing after the kids." But instead she said, "I think we had better."

"Do you have any ideas?"

"I'll get the girls on it."

She was referring to Mna In Eannacht, a kind of women's auxiliary, a network of wives, girlfriends and volunteers.

"That's my girl." He smiled, and kissed her quickly on the lips.

There was one more thing to do before leaving.

Keiran complained incessantly and Tweed grumbled ungratefully but Des pulled them out of their rooms, got them up and into sneakers and coats, and pushed them out the door ahead of him.

CHAPTER 19

Anchors have already been dropped into the biographical time streams of both Tweed Kelley and Des Kelley so it may seem superfluous to highlight yet another essential milestone in the story.

Nevertheless, their individual stories were merging and their choices were beginning to have relevance to one another, so at this point the overall narrative may proceed like a fishing vessel trailing lines in order to trawl the past.

The trip to Mission was memorable, for while Cleary was making up bullshit stories about the old man, Keiran was moaning into the door panel on his side of the car, Tweed was complaining, and Des, who was in the front passenger seat, was periodically snapping back at the boys to behave themselves. Tweed thought that "Uncle Ed" Cleary bore a striking resemblance to the cartoon character Fred Flinstone both in voice and appearance.

Cleary: "Did you know that your old man served on a coal tender during the war? Took a torpedo in the North Atlantic and had to be rescued at sea with his shipmates? No? He was a bloody hero, he was!"

Keiran: "I want to go home...*Star Trek* is on!"

Des: "Cut the baloney, Ed. They know that I was never in the war."

Cleary: "Don't let him fool you, boys! He still can't talk about it but someday he'll tell you the truth about how he stared down the barrels of a Jap zero."

Tweed: "I thought you said the Atlantic?"

Keiran: "How long will this take?"

Des: "What did I tell you? That's my son you're talking to! He knows when you're pulling his leg."

Cleary: "Sure! Didn't you learn anything in school? The Japs were all the way up to Maine! They were running recon up and down the East Coast!"

Keiran: "I'm not feeling well, Da."

Des: "Cut the crap, Cleary! You're going to miss the turn..."

Tweed: "Dad, did you know that there is an abandoned Nike site up in the woods between Roosevelt and the Reservoir?"

Des: "Don't you start now."

Cleary: "That's right! Listen to your Dad, Tumbles, because you can get in trouble for talking about things like that."

Keiran: "When are we going to get there?"

Des: "Oh, here we go now!"

Tweed: "Things like what?"

Cleary: "Exactly. Good boy. We never had this conversation."

Des: "I wish that we hadn't."

Cleary drove a dark blue 1969 Chevrolet Impala sedan that looked like it had tinted windows from the accumulation of tar from countless unfiltered Camel cigarettes he had consumed in the car. The smoke and ultra-violet rays had interacted chemically with the vinyl interior to leave it feeling as spongy and sticky as a "Nerf" football taken from a dog's mouth.

Tweed was perched on the edge of the rear bench seat with saucer-sized steel springs cupping his butt cheeks through the threadbare polyester seat cover. His feet rested upon a carpeted hump that bisected the floor of the car longitudinally like a keel box. From here he surveyed the road ahead and kept track of the route.

Of course he was too young to drive, and if he knew his parents, they'd be in no hurry to help him acquire his driver's permit even after he turned 17. But as recent experience had taught him, he wouldn't be a passenger for the rest of his life; and if by some chance he did end up driving again he would like to know how to get around.

Then again, a sense of direction was almost as good as a road map, as long as one was familiar with the natural geophysical features and landmarks in an area. In this instance, heading from Rossie to Mission, Tweed remembered that they would have to cross the commuter rail, pass by the municipal skating pond, and drive over Moss Hill and the river before they merged with the parkway that led out of Jamaica toward the Mission. Cu's Pub was in a neighborhood located near an off-ramp on the last section of the parkway before it reached the junction with several major highways that flowed on into the city, about 9 miles from the square, deduced reckoning.

Tweed shifted over next to the door opposite his brother. This street was in poor repair and he enjoyed placing his forehead against the glass whenever he was in a car on a bumpy road. The vibration soothed him and called to mind the euphoria from a hit off a joint. So perhaps this was part of a life-long trend, this compulsion to buzz off.

As Tweed zoned out, he realized that for as long as he could remember he had gotten off on one mind-altering experience or another. As a toddler rocking in his bed to get to sleep. Or later, walking around the house with a mirror under his nose, trying to get his vision to flip. Doorways had looked like hurdles, and ceiling lamps had defied gravity like alien artifacts.

Then he recalled that every summer as a child he'd spent frequent afternoons at a grassy slope at the edge of Arbs Park, where he would climb to the summit, lie full out on the ground and then roll himself all the way down the hill. The object was to go real fast and get dizzy. Pull your arms in tight for speed and end up flailing like a discarded rag-doll. The fun part was trying to stand once you came to a stop at the bottom. Some kids puked.

Then there was another popular buzz that kids tried by squeezing each other from behind, knotting their fists under the solar plexus in order to induce blackouts. Usually the bigger kids did it to the little ones, and the trick was to stop squeezing just short of asphyxiation. If there was nobody available to squeeze, you just held your breath as long as you could, trying to see spots in front of your eyes.

And everyone knew that fevers or fasting could make one go hoopy.

So maybe getting high was a normal life function, like sneezing, or orgasm. It was a natural tendency that gave way to a conscious desire for repetition; probably with the onset of puberty, he rationalized.

If there was a natural predisposition to getting buzzed then it followed that it must be universal, that everyone shared it to some degree. But how did that explain people who never got high? His father for example had said many times that not only did he not drink for the buzz but that he had never been intoxicated. And he was a barman- he knew all about getting drunk.

Even as he considered the question he was losing track of the street signs in the flaring and fading glows of passing traffic and street lamps. He was almost asleep when Cleary abruptly announced their arrival at the pub.

CHAPTER 20

A cold breeze frisked the boys cursorily as they walked from the car to the bar, and they yawned in tandem, at once sticking their fists out wide and hunching down into their coats for warmth.

Inside the door a drafty hallway followed an S-shaped path and emerged in the pub proper at a stainless steel counter at the end of the bar. The wretched cloying odor of cheap tobacco filtered inadequately through boozer's lungs gave way to a fresher, gaggingly rich admixture of fumes from a variety of smoking devices, from pipes to snipes.

A sign in a small frame stand read "Please Wait To Be Seated". Ignoring the request, Des walked directly toward a group of men who were talking among themselves and seized one of them by the elbow.

"JC, how are you?"

Byrne, a small wiry gent was wearing gold-rimmed glasses and a navy peacoat over a faded striped shirt. His polished shoes and crisply creased brown trousers made him look like a factory floor foreman.

"Holding my own, Des, and yourself?"

After greetings and introductions all around they spoke privately.

"If you're ready, Des, here you go."

He withdrew a parcel from his coat, and removing green velvet wrappings, revealed a ceremonial shillelagh. Des received it and pounded his open palm as if to signify the seriousness of his intent.

"Afterwards, Des, I'd like to run something by you if I may."

"What is it, JC? I have my boys with me tonight," he pointed to Keiran and Tweed, who were ambling over to a pinball machine, "-and I may not be able to stay long. Can we talk about it now?"

"I suppose..." he mumbled and raised his hand to his chin. "You see, I was going to ask if you would consider letting me go, you know, take the trip in your place this time."

"Take my place?"

"Yes, well, just this once. I may not have a chance otherwise, not before, uh..."

"What is it, JC? What's happening?"

"I've got to tell you Des, and I apologize for putting you on the spot, for being blunt like this. I've been meaning to tell you, but I only really found out recently. I have cancer. What's worse, I don't have long to live."

In that moment Byrne's face seemed to come into focus, suddenly shrunken and gray. The pathos and clarity of the image startled Des.

"Jesus, Mary and Joseph! Is there nothing the doctors can do for you?"

"You know how it is. Blasted doctors. It started in my leg, and now its spreading; they want to take the leg but I'll be fucked if I let them. At least not until I have a chance to go home."

"You want to go over alone? I only have the one seat reserved. What about Mary? Your seven kids for heaven's sake?"

JC looked miserable. "It's just that I wanted to see the old home before..."

"Well, listen JC, let me work on this. I don't know why we shouldn't be able to get you and Mary both over there. I mean, there are emergency funds available, I'm sure. We can work something out. Let me think about it. I don't know if taking this trip is the best way about it; but if it is, then so be it, you'll go. I'll study on it and let you know." He kept talking to avoid becoming unnerved by his friend's tragic news. "I'm sorry to hear this, old friend. It's hard, indeed. But you go over for me and you'll be having my work to do, and how would that be on top of everything else? You'll want a rest, a vacation, not a bloody working trip with border crossings and bullshit to deal with."

"Ach, you're right, Des. I'm sorry I asked, I was just…well, I was feeling homesick, you know?"

"I understand, of course, JC; and believe me when I say that I'll do whatever I can to get you over there soon. Let me think about it."

"Well then, first things first," he replied jauntily. "Let's get down to business."

He took his seat slowly, maintaining a placid visage and steadying himself with a trembling hand.

Gaveling the assembly to order, Des saw the usual representative delegates seated in front of him and also other new volunteers who had come along to assist in the effort. Pat Devaney brought a couple of friends from The Brew and Bard in Marshfield; Tom Connolly was with some associates from The Tavern in Crystal Pond Park. Woody from the Wild Geese represented Francestown and his group hailed from Dawestown. JC Byrne of Cu's Pub covered the local Uptown and Mission districts, and of course Des Kelley of the RBC stood for Rossie, Roosevelt, Jamaica and Westbury in addition to his administrative responsibility.

When Kelley was at the dais with gavel in hand the meetings were marked by decorum, moderately deliberate pacing and adherence to Robert's Rules. There were no flowery phrases, undue formalities or personal anecdotes. He addressed the state of affairs, presented an operating budget suitable for public consumption, and ticked off the roles, goals and duties of various sub-committees.

The boys paid little attention as their father reviewed some of the various revenue sources represented by his organization. Irish music promoters, language school coordinators, radio personalities, gallery owners, skilled and unskilled laborers, cops and pols.

In the pinball alcove they held a desultory competition, trying to rack up a substantial number of games on the machine. Both boys had learned how to sweet-touch a tilt table from big brother Buck back when they were little and he was still living at home. They practiced on a lame old machine located at the drug store in the square. It had dead bumpers and erratic flippers but the kids fed it quarters like it was a familiar old panhandler. This machine was Aces High, by comparison a modern, straightforward unit with standard ramps, toggles and targets. It pivoted slightly at a nudge because the adjusting bolt on the left rear leg of the machine was wedged in a crack between adjoining checkerboard linoleum floor tiles. Whenever it matched a free game it startled the bar patrons with a resounding wooden knock that sounded like a rap by the bony hand of fate upon the hollow coffin of destiny.

Peering over occasionally, the boys saw that their father and JC Byrne looked ghoulish in the flickering fluorescent light accentuating their pale skin, hollow eyes and cheeks. They appeared like members of a convocation of lesser demons, breathing smoke and alcohol vapors, with red eyes and sallow complexions.

Mr. Kelley spoke again. "I'll thank you for coming out tonight by keeping my remarks brief. You all know what is at stake. There is no need for me to tell you what you already hear in every letter and phone call from your folks back in Ireland. But I will mention a few facts to remind you of why we work hard to collect money to provide and protect resources.

"When the Troubles broke out again in earnest nobody knew how long the violence would persist. For centuries each generation has had to deal with the conflict, whether they were trying to get through a difficult period or laying plans and provisions for extended hardship. Each generation must have thought that their time presented particular challenges. Likewise, I say as we observe the current crisis developing in Ireland that it seems as though the peril, the potential for escalation has increased due to factors presented by the modern era.

"In addition to encountering the classic weapons of repression such as intimidation, suspension of civil liberties and the imposition of emergency laws, our people are also facing modern military tactics and hardware. Nationalists and Irish Catholics living in Northern Ireland endure unprecedented harassment. In 1971 the British Army conducted over 17,000 house searches in Ulster. By last year that number had risen to over 75,000. Indeed members of Crown forces in Northern Ireland outnumber nationalist males by more than 2 to 1.

"Now we hear there is a rift developing within the IRA leadership. I believe that bodes ill for the future of Ireland no matter how it is resolved. There is no doubt in my mind that the split is being exacerbated by British intelligence operations, and that as a result, the organization is generally being discredited. A recent article in the Sunday Times baldly asserted that members of the leadership are guilty of embezzling funds from the cause. And recent raids by the SAS revealed the IRA's emergency contingency plans. All such plans have thus been rendered ineffectual.

"We must do what little we can to provide a reliable, decent alternative for assisting the helpless victims of the conflict. Aid and relief organizations play an important part in any war, and though our numbers are few and our contribution limited, we will continue to raise money and raise awareness of the plight of our Irish brethren.

"When you ask people to give for Irish relief, this latest bombing in Guildford will be fresh and raw in their minds. So with all respect to the poor departed, who were so cruelly taken from God's green earth, we must now go forth and solicit donations in their names."

He paused to confer with JC Byrne and seeming to gain his assent, went on to say, "I'd also like to ask that everyone kick in a little something extra for our good friend and host JC Byrne here, who I am sorry to say has been stricken with a life-threatening illness. He can certainly use whatever help we can give him now in the hour of his need."

His comments swallowed up in a concerted murmur from the crowd, Des stepped away from the podium. He realized now that his concern about the change in venue had been unwarranted. It seemed petty to have worried about JC's motivation, thinking that he wanted to avoid the biz club because he thought it was a dive. He couldn't blame him in his condition for not wanting to travel across town. On the other hand he was desperate to travel overseas with a salmon-like will to reach Ireland, the place of his birth, before he died.

Would he care, Des wondered, if he should be buried in the US or at home in Ireland? It had never occurred to him before, but the threat to his friend's mortality made the question suddenly relevant. He had considered that he might prefer cremation to burial, but was reluctant to pursue the matter for he feared that it might conflict with Catholic doctrine.

In order to dispel such uncomfortable thoughts he decided that if in the event of his death Extreme Unction were performed then he could face his Maker with a full slate of sacraments. He'd be judged for his sins long before his loved ones fulfilled his wishes and cremated his remains, and they'd "take the heat" for it if need be.

"Poor bugger," he thought as his business in the bar concluded.

JC had come over in the '60s and had spent a tough couple of years struggling to get on his feet. Then with God's blessing he met and married a girl who, though born locally, looked with her red hair, freckles and fine figure as if she could have sprung from the Clare countryside. She spent the next ten years bearing their children in rapid succession. The children, seven in all from toddlers to pre-teens, were uniformly fair and freckled too.

What a tragedy if JC should die; then she would be left to handle all of that on her own.

Des permitted his imagination to show him a glimpse of how events might occur. First, a funeral and a gathering of friends- he'd be sure to milk that crowd; then, the grieving widow Byrne receiving a solicitous visitor -of course it's Des himself, doing the right thing by her and delivering a hat full of checks from community well-wishers. Then, "Please allow me to express my gratitude, Mr. Kelley..." Ah, yes.

The real-time sight of the still quick JC Byrne chatting with Keiran and Tumbleweed at the pinball machine interrupted his reverie. He appeared to be conducting a lesson in Latin.

"Certe, Toto," he said, smiling, "Sentio nos in Kansate non iam adesse."

Keiran enjoyed a linguistic challenge, especially without the pressure from an audience of classroom peers; and although Mr. Byrne was a bona fide Latin teacher he gladly wrestled with the translation.

"For sure, in all...ah, I feel, ah..."

"Good work, boy! Indeed, what I said was, 'You know, Toto, I have the feeling that we're not in Kansas anymore.'" He winked.

The boys laughed, pleased to converse with this friend of their father's. His erudition was as evident as his inebriation yet he was hardly condescending. But it was hard to avoid staring at the tufts that sprouted from his ears and nostrils as if his head was stuffed full of hair, the same steel-wool color as his eyebrows and carpet-stubble.

"How about this, then? 'Illiud Latihe dici non potest'."

"It is not possible to speak latin?" guessed Tweed, hesitantly and self-consciously.

"Close, son, but the real translation is, "You can't say that in Latin'."

Des spoke up, "When I was a boy the sisters pronounced it 'deechy', not 'deeky' like you do."

"An indication of the influence of church vulgar, no doubt," said Byrne, nodding.

"Semper ubi, sub ubi!" said Keiran, with a giggle.

"Speaking of the vulgar, eh?"

Des collared his sons and made for the door. "Sic transit gloria mundi," he said in a lilting growl. He was grinning, but noticed the slight double-take in the weary eyes of his colleague, and understood that those words would have a different significance for one so afflicted with a terminal illness.

A few minutes of stamping about in the cold outside the pub helped to shake off the tobacco stench and to clear their heads. Des stood at the curb with his arms folded and stared down the street.

Speaking in a low voice to Tweed, Keiran wondered aloud why his father had thought it necessary to bring them along.

"What's the point?"

Tweed thought for a moment, and seeing Charlie Cotton arriving in his big Buick to pick them up for the ride back to Rossie, was content merely to have completed his duty. But he replied, "Moral support, I guess."

CHAPTER 21

Rising out of his dreams or rising out of his waking desires, like a well-irrigated corn stalk reaching toward a new sun, a bulbous hard-on tented Tweed's pajamas as he awoke to beat down his alarm clock. His swollen penis led him out of bed and toward the bathroom, practically glowing with heat and achingly sensitive to the movement of every fiber against which it strained. He hesitated to touch it; his reluctance originating as much in Catholic shame as in fear of further upsetting it. He had boners before, but this was a beaut- almost worth admiring in the mirror. Urinating helped to take the edge off, but even as he washed up he was obliged to stand away from the sink.

Sam must be getting up now too, he thought. *She could be admiring herself in a mirror, maybe in her underwear.* Maybe thinking about him. To tweak his fantasy Tweed imagined Sam living right next door in the room across from his. What if she could see him now? He looked down at his pecker, now throbbing in a renewed tempo. Maybe she'd be horny too. He imagined the two of them each looking at themselves and proceeding through the morning mirroring each other's thoughts and actions. He was tempted to grab himself and choke out a load of relief, and would like to think that she was doing the same, but that was going too far. He had only recently learned how to get off and had only vague notions of how girls did it. And lusting after another and expecting that she shared his compulsion to sin would surely compound any guilt he would feel for sinning with his body.

But what if she got dressed at the same time that he did? What a hot thought, Sam standing in front of her bureau, picking out a set of clothes and hopping into them. He'd love to see that. *Man, how do you tuck those jugs in, anyway?* And what if she did dream of him, stepping into his civvies, trying to calm his rod to fit in there with his balls, flexing his muscles as he stretched a shirt over his back. And the both of them whipping through breakfast and hurrying out the door, and in his fantasy arrangement, seeing each other on the sidewalk outside. They would embrace and after a passionate kiss set off for school arm in arm. Whoa.

The sidewalk was deserted as usual when he emerged from his house and the day looked to be overcast and dismal. Fantasies forgotten, he hustled toward the bus stop shouldering a brown canvas sack of books and homework.

He hoped to have enough time to pick up a cup of coffee before he had to waste another day at Munie. There was a decent diner across the street from the rear of the school.

Tweed's stride was inspired by the Grateful Dead song, *Truckin*. His loosely-tied basketball shoes appeared to plod ahead of their own accord and pull him along behind them in an even straight-leg gait as if he was putting his foot in it with every step. He affected an aggressive demeanor by lowering and fixing his gaze to a spot on the ground ahead. One arm swung in parade-style sync while the other crossed his chest and held his book bag.

Bearing the weight of their respective disciplines, the assorted tomes within the bag were bound in a conspiracy to upset his walking rhythm. He preferred slinging the bag over his shoulder like the jocks and the stoners as opposed to swinging it at arm's length like the sissies and the geeks. Another sub-set of the student class carried their books in camper's back-packs, and an even smaller minority employed briefcases. With peer-group instilled confidence he accepted the notion that you could judge a kid by his or her book bag, but deemed it to be less a matter of convention than individuality. It was style versus cool. Regardless of the burden, he was still trucking on and it was a new morning with the potential for adventure and experience.

Halfway to the bus stop he noticed that the neighborhood was utterly quiet and he was apparently alone. It was rare for the area to be so devoid of activity. Where was everybody? Walking slowly, he looked around for signs of life. No cars, no dogs, no birds, no people. He stared at the twigs on the branches of a nearby tree to see if the air itself was moving. Curious now, he walked on wondering if he hadn't forgotten a holiday or something.

Thus preoccupied he was almost disappointed to see Col's sister Megan approaching the path from the direction of the cul-de-sac with two of her friends. The spell was broken with a lingering regret like the recollection of a bittersweet dream. Before hustling to overtake the girls, he reflected that he could really appreciate occasional moments of peace in his life.

"Morning, ladies!"

Megan Columkille hesitated long enough to make Tweed think that she was going to ignore him, but then she answered, "Long time no see, Tweed".

Her friends, girls from the neighborhood whom Tweed didn't recognize and Megan didn't bother to introduce, smiled and seemed to dash off quick messages in code with their eyelashes. Sisters, probably. Shoulder-length brown hair, prominent overbites, the kind of figures that come from drinking Pepsi with cereal for breakfast. One wore a blue corduroy coat with a nappy fake fur hood, and the other had on an unbuttoned, unlined black leatherette jacket. Tweed's attention was on Megan, who looked petite in jeans and a heavy sweater.

"Yeah, well, you look great!" he blurted.

The girls giggled in unison and he felt embarrassed and out-numbered, yet somehow emboldened.

"But I'll tell you," he said, "you should walk more often, because then you'd have a nicer butt."

Her chorus twittered and cooed but Megan was unruffled.

"You could use some exercise yourself- you still have your baby fat."

Congratulatory squeals from the gallery.

"Baby fat? I walk all the time- miles a day. I'm in shape!" He pouted as a lure for sympathy.

"Hey Tweed," said Megan coolly, "Is it true what they say about you and the Stapleton sisters?"

A flush of unease spread from the pit of his stomach to his chest.

"What do you mean? The Stapletons...that moved away a couple of years ago? What do they say?"

"Well, I heard that the three of you put on sex shows for the boys in the neighborhood." She said the word 'sex' like it was the name of a venomous spider. Her friends looked away without comment.

"What? Who said that? I did what? Are you kidding?"

"Hey, I didn't believe it either until I heard it from, uh, two different people. They both said that you and the twins got naked in the back seat of a car while people watched."

Discomfort had spread throughout his system and his glands responded with copious amounts of sweat that ran cold down his sides and back. He squirmed inside his coat. He was starting to recall his participation in episodes that he had put out of mind for years.

The Stapletons, Jennie and Tamara, were cute, blonde-haired twins who had once lived in the house across the street from the Kelleys.

"Who...who told you all this bullshit?" he demanded haltingly.

"Listen, I'm sorry I brought it up, OK?" Her freckles had been obscured by a bright blush.

"Come on, Megan, please tell me where you heard this."

"OK, it was my brother, alright? Now are you happy? Jeesh!"

He felt like he had been hit below the belt, and lagged behind to take a breath and to put some distance between him and his accuser.

The goddamned truth was that Tweed had in fact done all sorts of crazy things with Tammie and Jennie; not only in a parked car but also in a garage and under the porch behind their house. They'd tie him up and smother him with kisses, then stick their hands down his pants. Then they'd untie him and let him stick his hands down their pants.

The sex shows must have been organized by older kids who exploited the opportunity to watch two little girls strip down and mime sex acts with their little boyfriend. Disturbed to realize that he had been blocking these memories, he was also profoundly ashamed. To hear this from Megan Columkille, of all people. Why, just last summer he had gotten to second base with Megan during a sleep-over hosted by her brother Jimmy at their house. He vividly remembered her sweet eager face and the wetness of her experimental kisses.

A few years later when she was 18 he would meet her on the street one day and notice that she had the words 'Crew Slut' tattooed in gothic lettering above her breasts. But now she was the not-so-innocent kid sister of his best friend. No relationship had developed from fooling around together and he was content to know her as a friend, but he certainly did not want to offend her.

Anger added to the mudpie mix of emotions stirring within him. So Col was telling stories about him behind his back. Saying things that Tweed could not recall ever discussing with him. Shit that hadn't crossed his mind in ages.

The girls were well ahead now, their heads still bent in a huddle as they went.

"Yo- dude! Wait up!"

Man, how do you like that? Think of the devil and up he pops. It was Jimmy Col, chugging up the sidewalk, his sneakers untied, his barracuda unzipped, and with half a Pop-tart in his mouth.

Tweed waited just long enough for Col to match his pace then turned and greeted him vehemently.

"So, what are you, my freaking conscience, now?"

"What? What are you talking about?"

"I just talked to your sister man, and she told me what you said about me. Thanks a lot."

"Is that why your face is so red? You're welcome. I have no idea what the fuck you're talking about. What did I supposedly say?"

"The story about me and the Stapleton twins, the thing in the car, you know." Tweed placed his hand to his face and then looked at it, as if to verify his coloring.

"Well, yeah, I know the story, but I never said anything. She musta heard it from the same place I did- my brother Eric. He was telling stories with his buddy O'Toole a couple of weeks ago and that one kinda slipped in there. He was talking about all kinds of people- I don't think he had it in for you or anything like that. But I know he's an asshole."

"Asshole? Holy shit, man! Now Megan thinks I'm a pervert!"

Col hocked a lungie about 7 feet off into the grass.

"Look, Tweed, for one thing, that shit probably turned her on more than anything else; and for another, you are a pervert."

"Fuck that, man! I wonder where he heard about it."

"He was there supposedly...he was one of the kids who got to watch, I guess. So, is it true? Did you and them really do it?"

"Fuck that, man!"

Tweed drew the line at saying "Fuck you" and in turn expected the same consideration from his friends. Jimmy simply changed the subject.

"Listen, Tweed, I know you're pissed, but I was going to remind you about that room at school. You have to check it out."

He calmed himself and replied through clenched teeth, "I intend to. When?"

"Tell you what- hitch up with me at gym, 3rd period. We'll talk about it then."

They could just as easily have discussed the matter during the long bus ride to school, but Col sensed Tweed's need for space, and at any rate, Tweed had decided against taking the school bus. It took a little longer and he had to pay for the privilege, but he enjoyed riding with the regular working commuters on mass transit. Turning into a strap hanger and memorizing the passing street signs.

Fifty minutes later he was simultaneously taking the last sip of his coffee and the last hit of a roach as he approached the entrance to the school. He had fashioned a convenient joint holder by poking a pen through the upper side of the cup. With the plastic lid securely fastened, the morning java became a disposable bong and the mixture of sweetened coffee and honey resin dope within was lip-smacking delicious. The smoke was disguised in his vapor exhalations in the morning chill, the odor of his breath was masked by the coffee, and the oversized trash barrels stationed at the rear stairs to the building provided means of disposing of the remaining evidence. Now to get by Mr. Deodato, the brooding history teacher standing watch at the next landing.

"Morning, Mr. Kelley. I see you came in the back way this morning." Deodato, a short, squat man, spoke in a sing-song manner like a sycophantic maitre'd.

"Very observant, sir! Good morning!"

The teacher caught Tweed's smirk with a lifeless stare. "Do you see those students out there, Mr. Kelley?" He indicated the groups of dealers and jokers and smokers who were standing at the perimeter of the school yard.

"Yeah?"

"Do you know what they represent?"

Tweed frowned considerately.

"I'll tell you, Mr. Kelley. They represent failure, sloth, indigence. I don't know why they bother coming into the school at all after wasting time out there."

There was only a minute to spare before the first bell rang, but Tweed felt it necessary to say something in defense of the kids who, although he didn't know them, did not deserve to be slandered by someone he considered to be an uninspired staff hack at Munie high.

"I wouldn't judge them so harshly, sir," said Tweed, warming up. "I think they represent commerce and capitalism at its best.

"Everyday they stand out there selling their wares to a client base who in turn are benefiting from the level of competition in the market. Sellers and buyers alike are learning lessons of free-market economy that simply can't be taught in a classroom, and amassing valuable experience as they prepare to enter the expanded world of business and industry."

Mr. Deodato had a curious expression of fascination and disbelief on his face, and his glasses appeared to be fogging just a little. He passed a hand over his bald head without speaking.

"Think about it. The dealers buy in quantity to take advantage of volume discounts, but in order to make a profit they must be aware of the going price on the street, as well as the cost of doing business, and establish an acceptable margin while encouraging new business and trying to squeeze out competitors. Sounds like quite an education to me, a real-world application of standard principles."

"Well, Mr. Kelley, what a pleasant surprise! Now I assume that the next time I ask about the principle cash crops in Colonial America you'll have a ready answer. Alright, scram before you're marked as tardy."

Across the threshold school was not merely another place in which to spend time, it was also a state of mind. He handled such transitions easily, whether in the fervor of religion, the tranquility of nature, or the adrenal rush of athleticism. It was like swinging on a vine from tree to tree. Now he had swung from drug induced euphoria to the tree house of academia, an environment in which he was especially comfortable. In this regard he had two advantages over most of the students who had matriculated from district schools. First, he enjoyed blending in with the crowd and the anonymity of being lost in the shuffle, and Munie was certainly overcrowded; and second, thanks to his above average intelligence he had yet to be challenged by anything he encountered in the curriculum.

When he was at school he tried to exemplify the model student that he personally emulated. Attentive in class, ready and willing to volunteer, motivated to learn, personable, articulate, and intellectually proud but open to criticism. Believing that school offered a valuable return on any investment of effort, he threw himself into all of his scholastic endeavors. He avoided social conflicts as much as possible, mainly by avoiding cliques, gangs, groups and persuasions.

At 5'8", medium build, with his curly brown hair and frank, open face, plain pocket tees and seat-beat blue jeans he was no threat to anyone. Except perhaps some of his teachers.

And thus far two months into the term he had managed to separate school and pot. The morsel he did on the way in this morning was an exception, a lapse from his usual behavior, justified, he rationalized, by the unexpected need to deal with the confusion and anxiety arising from his encounter with Megan Columkille. As for the disturbing issue itself, it would remain quarantined in the back of his mind like a neglected textbook in the depths of his locker.

His schedule called for Spanish and History before Gym class when he would meet Col, followed by English and then lunch when he would find Sam. The classes were typically uneventful except for the fact that at one point during her lecture on irregular verbs, the Spanish teacher had sat on Tweed's desk and absent-mindedly ran her fingers through his hair. She had whispered that she would die for hair like his and asked him to save some for her the next time he visited the barber. He told Col about it while they warmed up for a run.

"It was weird, Col, I mean, she was twirling my hair around her finger while she was teaching."

"Miss Kendall's fine," said Col, dreamily. "Hey- maybe she wants you. What did you do?"

Fine in a mousy demure way, thought Tweed inappreciatively.

"I didn't do anything. She was practically sitting in my lap. I was just hoping that she'd go away. Everybody was looking. It sucked."

"Well, don't let it bother you, man. But if I were you, I'd go for it. She has nice legs."

They had completed some token calisthenics and had split off from the rest of the gym class to jog around the basement perimeter. On the way down the hall Col suggested a detour. "There's a janitor's closet at the other end of the building at the point where we come around for the back leg of the lap. How about we stop in there and do a quick bowl?"

He was freaking crazy. Smoke during school? In the building? They could be caught, censured, busted, expelled.

On the other hand Tweed had tucked a small stash into the waistband of his shorts so that it wouldn't become a gratuity for locker room pick-pockets.

What the hell?

"That's cool. But duck in and close the door fast- and we had better leave quick too!"

Suddenly their footsteps sounded like the flapping of clown shoes, echoing the length of the barren basement corridor. Blood rushed in Tweed's ears like a freshet over rapids.

They reached the anonymous wooden door and Col swept it open silently. Both boys vanished into the closet and were swallowed in senseless blackness. Tweed fumbled for his measly half-gram stash and Col crouched to pull a jiffy one-hitter from his sock. "I keep it on me for good luck- and it worked! I brought the bowl and you're…"

He stopped talking at the instant the door knob rattled behind Tweed's back. Tweed concealed the dope with deft sleight of hand, and his buddy stayed down on one knee, in a pose that both saved and condemned them. The unexpected visitor was not the janitor as they might have feared, but the gym teacher, a brick shithouse of a football coach sporting a crew cut and a whistle dangling from a rope around his neck.

"Kelley- Columkille- what the hell are you doing in here? Oh, my God! Don't answer that. I can't believe it; not from you boys. This is a disappointment, a terrible disappointment. Of all the things- I never expected to find you guys making out in a closet!" He walked away sadly shaking his head while also physically projecting all of the machismo at his disposal.

Relieved but shaken, Tweed wondered how he would ever live it down. On the positive side, at least he hadn't been the one on his knees.

"What do you say?" asked Col nervously. "Want to go see the room I found? Coach is probably planning to humiliate us when we get back to the gym."

"So you want to hide out, eh? I think it'll be worse if we don't show up right away. Besides, if he's going to say anything, I want to be there to hear it."

"Yeah, no shit. OK, we meet at lunch at the stairwell by the nurse's office."

It was a better idea, but it put Tweed in a bind. He had intended to meet Sam in the cafeteria at lunch. Well, maybe he'd have time for both.

"I'll be there…"

They jogged back to class separately.

Fourth period, English Comp, room 217, second floor rear, overlooking the soccer field and the alumni parking lot. About as far from the nurse's office as you could get within the building.

The three minute allowance for travel between classes usually resulted in a time deficit going into the 20 minute lunch period. The remainder of the break was chewed up pretty quickly just pushing through crowds and standing in line. If he was going to get back to the caf before Sam left he would have time for only the briefest glance at Col's discovery. No lav, no locker stops.

He skipped rapidly along the hallway, kicked a pair of safety doors back on their hinges and raced through them toward the far stairway. But upon reaching the stairwell doors he saw through the wire-reinforced glass panels on either side that a dense throng choked the stairs. The students were running, yelling, pushing and falling. He worked his way into the swirling counter-clockwise drain of humanity and heard a teacher's voice from the landing at the top floor: "Proceed calmly! Don't panic!" Tweed asked no one in particular what was going on. The answer emerged from a couple of different voices, muffled and smushed in the press. "Explosion in chem lab!"

This was no time for drilling outside in the cold with a horde of frightened underclassmen. When the handle of the door came around in the shuffle like the gold ring on a merry-go-round, he seized it at the bottom of the next landing, and pulling it open a crack, squeezed out to a deserted hall. Sprinting, he reached Col in moments.

"Almost didn't make it!" he panted. "Explosion in chem lab- they're clearing out the whole third floor!"

Just as Col opened his mouth to reply, the emergency signal rang on bells throughout the school, one of which was directly overhead. He clapped his hands to his ears and pointed downstairs with his elbows instead, and Tweed followed him to the basement. Once they arrived at the bottom of the stairs, Col suddenly turned and ducked below the lower steps and beckoned Tweed to join him.

"See!"

There, out of sight in the shadow of the stairwell, was a small wooden door, about 3 feet square, finished with maple lacquer and gilt block lettering that read "Dedley Room".

Col turned the knob with a ceremonial flourish and waved Tweed ahead. Entering on his hands and knees, Tweed was amazed to see that the "room" was in fact a tunnel that followed the outer wall of the school.

The boys scuttled ahead in a crab-walk and examined the tunnel with wonder. It was remarkably quiet, and they got an impression of forced perspective looking at the distant vanishing point through dust filtered light.

"What do you suppose it's for? Drainage? Inspection?" asked Tweed.

"Beats me. I mean, they got a boiler room and an electrical room, right? So what do they need this for and why is it called 'Dedley'?"

Tweed was baffled.

"Hey! Check this out!"

They had come to a window that was partially submerged below grade. The lower half opened upon a blank concrete window-well, and the upper half permitted a view of the outside where there were legs and feet milling about at random.

"The fire drill!" said Tweed, delighted.

"Ho! Yeah! We can check out some of the babes from here!"

Tweed thought of Sam. "Did it occur to you that the building might be burning down? We could be the only ones still in the school."

"If we are, we're probably safe in here," said Col, uncertainly.

"Well, we either have to head back or find out how far this thing goes." He instantly regretted mentioning a second option.

"I know how far it goes- all the way around in a giant horse shoe to the other stairwell on the opposite side of the building- to another door that says 'Dedley Room'; only that one's locked and the lettering is faded."

"No shit?" said Tweed, his eyebrows drawn and mouth agape, "What a funky place."

"Like I told you. I'm hoping that we can come here and hang out, do a little graffiti...party, you know."

"The Dedley Room Clubhouse?"

"Something like that. What do you say?"

"I say let's head out of here. I gotta go do something, and I want to find out what happened in the lab." Tweed realized that in the event of a general alarm, the kids in the caf would have filed out to the athletic fields for muster. He would have to find Sam out there among the legs.

The emergency alert and evacuation actually bought him some time, as the bell schedule had been interrupted, and fortunately Sam was not hard to find. Even at Municipal High there was a relatively low minority population, and besides, most of the girls in the yard were like cold farts in dixie cups. Sam was like hot shit in a champagne glass.

By now the students had organized themselves into groups formed up by class for roll. As he approached her he became intensely nervous.

"So, how was lunch?"

"We're not missing much," said Sam, "unless you like fish sticks."

"Like, if the explosion didn't kill you the tartar sauce will?"

That sounded stupid, he thought, but she encouraged him with a smile.

"When I saw you standing here I realized that I don't know your last name. I guess it's between L and P anyway." He gestured up and down the line.

"Mickle," she said, "Samantha Mickle."

Coming from her the name sounded like an exotic Caribbean vacation destination. "I didn't tell you before because I wasn't sure..."

"Sure of what? Of me?"

"I wasn't sure that you were serious when you said that you wanted to go out with me."

"I'm serious. We're still going out tonight, right? Actually I was hoping that we could do something after school, too."

She thought about it. "I'm going to a meeting of the school newspaper in the auditorium at 3. If you can wait around, I'll see you after that."

Satisfied, Tweed beamed off into the crowd, hearing a riff from the song, *Getting Better All The Time...*" running through his head.

Whenever he passed through the student activities quad, a hallway and adjacent rooms at the rear of the school auditorium, Tweed sensed a crowd of ghosts whose traces could be detected in the softly worn amber bricks in the floor, in the eggshell-thin brass doorknobs, and over next to the steam pipes, in the sensuous wooden benches, the seats of which had been rubbed to an almost liquid contour by the friction of countless restless torsos.

Waning sunlight descended a tenement-style air shaft and penetrated the hall through pinholes in a pair of spring-loaded shades that might once have been pale yellow, if they hadn't been tinted with a gradient of grime that grew darker closer to the roll. A persistent squall of dust and ash had settled over a decade of Sundays upon windows whose flawed glaze might have illuminated days of the roaring past, when boys in spats and argyle socks, linen shirts and suspenders passed to and from their classes along this corridor. Those heavily lidded eyes, occluded with motes and cataracts, offered no such insights; yet opposite the windows, crisp inverted images of the sooty exterior could be seen slowly drifting across the wall like bubbles in a rising tide. Each pinhole projection depicted identical walls cross-hatched with identical institutional windows.

Tweed had come here after finding the auditorium locked and empty and surmising that due to lower than expected turnout the newspaper had taken its meeting elsewhere.

One room looked pretty much like another, and as a result of his unexpected intrusion the ham radio operators association took the opportunity to solicit him to join their ever-dwindling fraternity. Tweed politely declined, mumbling something about a conflict with his chess club schedule, and promptly barged into the next room. Here a small gathering of perhaps six or seven students were seated in a semi-circle. They looked at him as if he knew the answer to a riddle and then as if to prove it, one of them asked, "SciFiWriCri?"

After a brief round of answer the question with a question he learned that this was the Science-Fiction Writer's Critical workshop. Two rooms down and three or four to go.

Meanwhile in the hallway members of the school newspaper staff were splitting toward the exits, their meeting adjourned. Tweed followed the trail of stragglers back to a room that also served as storage for props and stage equipment. There he finally found Sam, waiting alone.

The relationship that started that afternoon between Sam and Tweed was one of passionate intensity proportional to the overall brevity of its duration, and it seemed to pick up on the theme of discovery that Tweed had been following all day. Whatever fascination the process of self-discovery held for him, he preferred the excitement of experiencing adventure in the Dedley Room spider hole with his best friend Col; and now, thanks to Sam, his introduction to the catwalk that was located high above the auditorium stage.

The catwalk was accessible from a ladder in the rear of the prop room, stage left. He looked up the ladder with trepidation and placed a hand upon one of the lower steel rungs.

"Is it safe?"

"If you want, I'll go first," replied Sam, Tweed's presence having given her the boldness to act upon something she had only dreamed of daring.

"No, I mean, they still use this, right? The stage crew?"

"Every time there's an event in the hall, yeah."

"OK, then…" He pulled himself up, reconsidering that he should have let Sam go first. Then he'd have an excuse to look up at her butt.

Never having been up this particular ladder, and not being too fond of ladders in general, Tweed proceeded deliberately, peering upwards into murky shadows that seemed to magnify the terror of his ordeal, and wondering how he would know when he had arrived at the top. He figured that the climb had to be at least as high as the curtain rise, but he never anticipated arriving at and standing upon a scaffold-like platform of dusty wooden planks that was illuminated only by the light from below, nor could he have imagined the perilous thrill of the transit.

Approximately 18" wide, the catwalk was an exposed gangplank that spanned the breadth of the stage at a height of ten meters or so. It was equipped with no more of a hand rail than a length of loose wire strung through steel eyelets along the I-beam supporting the lighting rigs.

Without talking Sam and Tweed crossed together clinging to the guide wires and shuffling in a heel-toe step as if their feet were magnetized. If there were a show in progress down below they would have had a unique perspective on it, but under the circumstances they were not inclined to stop and admire the view.

In addition to the lights and bundles of cabling Tweed could make out huge suspended speaker horns and memorial banners strung between the rafters.

Having survived the crossing they let out hushed sighs of relief, feeling as if they had shared a life affirming experience. Now they stood at the end of the platform over the room at stage right.

"What do you suppose is up here?" whispered Tweed, thinking that he couldn't wait to tell Col about this place.

"You mean like bats and bugs?" Sam moved closer.

"No, I meant like whatever. I wish I had a flashlight."

He stretched out his hands and swept them around, unseen in a circle.

"Hey! I just felt another ladder!"

"Don't you go off without me!" cried Sam, betraying her anxiety.

He reached for her hand and placed it on the ladder.

"I wonder where it goes. I'll go first."

"Catwalk over the catwalk? Maybe to an attic?"

"Stairway to heaven…"

Tweed's pulse throbbed under his tongue as he climbed and he tried hard not to think of how far he might fall if he should lose his grip.

He imagined the headmaster shaking his head and saying, "And to think there was a light switch right over there…if he had only known."

Suddenly he bumped his head and struck wood with a hollow thud.

"What was that?"

"Just using my head. Wait a second."

A trap door on hinges- he pushed it open and was rewarded with daylight and a gush of cold fresh air. The ladder continued upwards for a few more rungs.

The third major discovery of the day was Tweed's to make as he climbed up to the roof of the school building into the cupola, a crow's nest over the city neighborhood, a balloon basket above the world. When Sam climbed up to join him he turned and relinquished his gaze on the panoramic vista so that he could catch the expression on her face.

"The cupola!" said Sam, and Tweed, not familiar with the word, looked around to see what she meant.

It amazed him that this architectural embellishment could actually serve a functional purpose and accommodate two people for sight-seeing. It was roughly hexagonal in shape, about 6 feet across the interior with painted horizontal slats on the exterior that made up a cylindrical louver affair. From where Tweed was standing, the dome looked as if it had been constructed by a colonial carpenter, with stout elaborate cross-braces supporting the massive weather vane apparatus, which as he recalled, included a copper-colored ant figure.

Together in the tower they were alone, superior, and aloof, like royal heirs who had ascended to a lofty turret in their castle in order to survey their domain. The boy, the son of an immigrant, and the girl, a naturalized citizen, had superseded the stratified society from which they came. Sharing the view, the physical closeness and the soaring thrill created a romantic experience beyond the significance of words for them to express, and beyond the intimacy of a caress for them to have touched. For those moments the light conspired with a gold expanse of burnished hills and the breeze wove treetops and bird flight, and sounds came from all around in varying halos of distance and delay.

Due to the fixed angle of the louvers they couldn't see anything in the immediate vicinity but they had a rapturous command over the landscape at a distance of 2-5 miles. By manipulating loose and weathered slats at various points around the compass they expanded the viewing range even further. On one side the city lay before them denoted by converging vectors of commercial and industrial progress and sectors of civic blight and renewal; in all other directions feudal towns and suburbs formed a slouching skirt tethered on stays of highways, rivers and rail lines.

Most impressive however were the trees, which from this vantage appeared to form a canopy over the entire Municipal district as far as the eye could see. At ground level it was somewhat noticeable that the city had retained an abundant variety of trees to line its side streets and thoroughfares, but from the roof of the school the myriad nodding crowns of oaks and maple, chestnut, poplar and sycamore, ash, birch, spruce and cedar created the impression of a protective shield, an organic version of the domed city fantasies of science fiction.

In these exalted circumstances the young idealists let their fancies take flight and they spoke to each other about their most sincere desires and secret fears and they pledged mutual vows of heart, mind and soul. Tweed would never remember specific words, or what they were wearing, or even what they did exactly, but later he often experienced a feeling that he had known Sam all his life and that he would know how she would react in any given situation. That confidence, that familiarity came about as a result of their conversation in the cupola. And yet the fact that they broke up less than a month later could be taken as a caution against putting too much faith in the magic of one special afternoon.

As he descended the ladder from the cupola to the catwalk Tweed had an impression that a number of things had been decided, but he wasn't sure what they were. Then when they were leaving the school he realized that his arm had been around Sam's waist for some time and although he didn't recall placing it there, it felt natural, despite the bumping of their hips.

CHAPTER 22

It was a routine Friday morning for Christine Kelley: starting her day at five o'clock, getting the men out of bed and starting the chores. Breakfast for four at six so the boys get out of the house by six-thirty, then she dressed for the walk to church with Des at half-seven.

The Mass was an ordinary weekday service during the lull in the Catholic calendar between the Celebration Of The Cross and All Saint's Day when there are no feasts or holy days.

It was disappointing to see so few parishioners scattered throughout the pews. Not long ago Mass had served as a roll-call for the faithful in the community as well as a means of keeping informed about their mutual health and welfare, and Chris was sure that the faces she saw here every day were the same ones she would see in heaven by and by. Today, in addition to the Kelleys, there were perhaps a dozen supplicants, all of them considerably older and infirm. Their presence was a testament to the constancy of their faith, but their numbers also pointed to the disparity between generations in the congregation as to duty, charity, humility and obligation. Daily Mass might seem like a burden and an anachronism to Catholics of her age, but it was clear that fewer young people were attending Sunday Mass altogether. Was there no room for the Word of God in the lives of today's working folk? Was it no longer comforting, instructive or relevant? How could people survive without moral guidance, the loving Hand of God upon their shoulders and the Light of Truth to mark their paths? Lord knows, those tempted to ignore the teachings of Christ would likely include anyone caught in the conflict between right and wrong, especially the ones who have to discern fine shades of morality and legality in an age of ambiguity.

It was largely Chris' influence that convinced Des to donate some of the money they collected to causes other than arming the "citizen soldiers of Ireland", and her conscience was clear and strong as long as her relationship to Christ and the church was sound. The foundation of that relationship was established in confession, and her experience of God in daily life came directly from the cycle of sin, atonement, penance and redemption.

Sacred Name Church boasted fine Italian masonry, cathedral vaulted ceilings supported by rows of stately columns adorned with ornate scroll work, a vast balcony for the choir with a glorious pipe organ, golden crucifixes, marble saints, stained glass stations of the cross, and hand carved woodwork from nave to narthex. Yet of all of the places in the church, Chris preferred the confessional booth because it was plush and private and personal. She realized that she had enjoyed the one-to-one setting with the priest since she was a child attending Sunday school.

Practicing with her class for the upcoming rite of First Communion she had participated in exercises that included marching in file from the school to the parish church where the students lined up to take turns at confession. They had already been coached in form and etiquette and then at the last moment they were sweating the fine points of sin. If the penitents couldn't think of any specific sins they had committed, they were told to speak in general terms and claim one or two of the big seven.

The confessional had looked tall then, and forbidding, like a miniature child-sized church with barbed spires on the corners, dark oak panels and crimson velvet curtains covering the windows. Blind sputtering nervous when she entered the booth, Chris was instantly put at ease in the cool dark quiet of the interior by the rose-soapy smell coming from the priest and by the gentle sound of his voice. She exhaled the rote portion of her confession all in a rush and then breezed through her sins, making up some details on the spot and forgetting to mention others that had troubled her conscience for weeks. She received her penance like it was a homework assignment on her favorite subject, then skipped light-hearted out of the church to join her friends and compare notes.

She had a strong desire to talk right now as well because she wanted to tell her husband everything she had learned about Makepeace before he went to work at the club for the day.

When Des and the boys went out to the meeting at the Mission on the previous evening, Chris found herself home alone with Makepeace. Although she had known him for years his presence made her uncomfortable for there were some things about him that she didn't like. She had to admit that he was damned handsome, funny and sociable too, so how come he never had a girlfriend about? It also bothered her that he was so hard to place. Most people, you hear them talk, you know where they come from. Not so Makepeace, not by a long shot. He could be from Cornwall, or Wales, or he could be a tin-eared Irishman for that matter, with little inflection and a flat understated urban dialect.

Furthermore, it irked her that he had showed up unexpectedly, acting as calm as if he just walked into the pub back home, and talking as if he had just picked up a conversation they left off years before.

While she didn't want to spend any more time with him than necessary, she would fulfill her promise to Des, and at least keep track of his whereabouts.

"It was a good thing," she said to her husband as they walked home from church, "that he happened to mention that he'd be going out later in the evening.

"I told him that I was going out to visit a friend myself. I thought if I got to Paula early enough she might let me borrow her car for the evening and I could follow him.

"Well you know how I hate going up the tracks after dark, but I walked to the Dolan's and knocked on the door. I couldn't call because Emmett has the one phone and he keeps it in the attic for business. Paula met me at the back door and apparently Emmett was doing more than numbers up there because she was mad to get out herself and said that I could use the car only if I brought her along.

"Not that I said anything about Makepeace mind you, just that I had to keep an eye on somebody. Paula loved to play at eye-spy and so off we went, first for coffee, then to wait for 80's ride to show up.

"Yes, it was the same fellow as before and they went straight to the highway and headed north. Before we knew it we had followed them well out of the city and I was wondering what kind of adventure I'd let us in for and whether we shouldn't turn back.

"Paula was driving after all and just as I mentioned the idea, the other car took the ramp to the north shore road. We were careful to avoid appearing to follow them, so for the next few miles we hung back and almost lost them. Then they pulled in at a strip club and parked in the lot. I thought it was odd because it seemed like along way to drive to get to a tittie bar.

"Well, wouldn't you know it? In a few minutes another car pulled in and parked right beside them. 80 and the other driver got out, shook hands, and the two of them walked into the club together, carrying on like grand old pals.

"80's driver waited in the car, and so did we, for a time, but it looked like they were going to be awhile, and we weren't about to wait around outside that place. So I made a note of the make and number of the car and came home so I could be here before you got back."

She handed the inscribed napkin to Des for analysis.

"You do good work, girl," said Des. "I'll get to work on this and you let me know if anything else comes up."

A tough woman, Chris had become accustomed to the formal distance that Des kept between them when they were working, but before she let him go she had one more item to add.

"We got pulled over on the way back, up in Bedford."

"Speeding?"

"Yes, Paula was a little excited, pushing 80 on the freeway. The blasted trooper had no sense of humor."

"I'll see what I can do about that as well."

They embraced briefly and went their separate ways.

CHAPTER 23

The girls in Hansen's Swedish Bakery were always ready for Des' arrival after church on Friday morning. Two large black coffees, a danish for Harris and a bran muffin with margarine for himself. In turn he charmed them with his smile and his ribald language. He leaned over the counter, the smell of fresh air and incense clinging to the wool of his sweater.

"Diane, darling! I have something for you my dear!"

The older woman was stuffed into a starched white uniform like footballs and basketballs in a pillowcase. She wore a stiff blond Pat Nixon hairdo, hospital white hose over legs that would have suited Liberace's piano, and white orthopedic work shoes. She giggled coquettishly, hunched over conspiratorially and said, "Oh, Des, I hope it's a big pile of money, yeah? Is that it? I don't see any bag or anything."

He raised his knee to rest his foot on the rung of a stool and took her hand and boldly placed it on a bulge filling the inseam on his upper leg next to his crotch.

"Here it is, dear."

She squealed in shock and yanked her hand away as if she had touched a live wire, almost striking Ingrid, her associate who had leaned over for a peek after waiting on another customer.

"Dear Lord, Des, what is that?"

"Just happy to see you, love..."

"Oh my God! You naughty, naughty man!"

At this Des laughed loudly, holding onto the counter to steady himself, while tears of hysterics streamed from his eyes. Lowering his leg and carefully reaching into his waistband, Des retrieved the copy of the weekly church missalette that he had rolled lengthwise and strategically stashed in his shorts prior to entering the shop.

"Oh, I got you good this time, darling!"

Diane laughed so hard she couldn't respond, and combined with Ingrid's howls, the effect was like a pair of randomly whooping burglar alarm sirens. Her face flamed red through her cakey makeup and the resulting contrast with her dyed hair made her look like one of her raspberry-lemon pastries.

He carried on this foolishness as much for the satisfaction he derived from amusing his Swedish sweethearts as for the free coffee and goodies with which they rewarded his antics.

A few minutes later he arrived at the biz club, and when he transferred both cups to one hand in order to pull the door open, he spilled some coffee. As he entered the bar he shook his wet hand and searched his pockets for a handkerchief, finding the napkin upon which his wife Chris had jotted her notes.

"Take these off my hands will you Harris?" he shouted, and as the bartender rushed over to assist him, Des noticed that Makepeace was seated alone at the bar.

"Oh, sorry 80, I didn't know you'd be out so early; I only got the two coffees; here, take mine." He swiftly palmed the napkin and shoved it back into his pocket.

"No trouble, Des, I prefer tea myself," replied Makepeace. "But I'll take that muffin off your hands, my love."

"There's no tea in this bar, and since I see that you've already got a drink, and since bran muffins go better with coffee than with whiskey, I'll eat this myself, thank you."

"Fuck your muffin! I don't need it…it won't help this hangover, anyway."

"Tied one on last night, did you? So that's what you've been doing with yourself. How are you getting around, anyway? Not taking cabs everywhere, I hope."

"No, no, I've got a chauffeur and my own personal limousine service."

"No shit? And I've a bleeding jet pack…"

"Yes, I noticed the exhaust gases to be sure…but seriously, it's Reggie, a fellow from my crew. He's over for the holidays, staying with his girlfriend and her roommate, and using her car. He'll be heading back with me on the boat. In the meantime he's been a big help, like yourself Des."

"Oh! By the way, I'll be spending the weekend with him so you'll have your house back to normal for a while."

"What? I expected you for Sunday dinner! I wanted to introduce you to a couple of good friends who are coming by, men of the cloth."

"In that case, I'll return before Sunday dinner, and again, I thank you for your hospitality."

Harris, who had been absorbed in studying a crossword puzzle, swallowed a sip of coffee, cleared his throat and said, "That's OK, Des, I probably have something to do on Sunday anyway, so don't feel embarrassed about neglecting to invite me to dinner." He left the table and busied himself in the back room while his patrons talked.

"Toole, I know you too well," shouted Des after him, "to expect you to sit through a religious lecture and discussion for the sake of a plate of food. Makepeace here, on the other hand could use a little more religion and less, ah, spiritual persuasion."

"It's only hair of the dog, Pater, no need for sermons."

"You're right, I've had enough of sermons myself today."

"How about your collections? How are they coming along?"

"I think I can guarantee that the baskets will come back full. But what about your end? Do you have everything lined up?"

"Not yet. We haven't discussed your needs. So tell me, what kind of miracle are you praying for?"

"Collections are for good works, not for miracles, and I believe that our needs are modest. Body armor, automatic weapons, hand grenades, anti-personnel mines, rocket propelled grenades, field glasses, radios, ammo. Will you get it?"

"Sure, but I expected you'd be going for armor-piercing rounds, mortars, stingers, demolition gear…"

"Well it is then that you consulted with me instead of following your own lights."

"My lights? I've seen what they're up against over there. You can't win a guerrilla revolution with body armor and hand grenades."

"Revolution? These aren't the old days, 80, and we're not talking border raids or skirmishes. Our concern is solely defensive. We're thinking of the isolated rural nationalists as well as the urban Catholics facing harassment from sectarian paramilitaries…

"I wish it were a revolution, I wish it were all-out war, with Dublin getting into the fray. But it's a bloody puppet Republic in the South and they turn their heads when the North is on fire."

"I won't argue with you, my friend, after all, money is money as far as I'm concerned and I really don't care what you buy. But I've talked with others who might care."

"They can fuck themselves, old friend, because I think that sometimes the provocative actions they undertake are responsible for the backlash that results in suffering for our people. It's violence begetting violence."

"Come now, you're no pacifist, Kelley. What do you expect people to do with the guns you put in their hands?"

"I'm surprised that you'd ask about consequences; I thought that it was none of your business what happened to the weapons you sold. You start thinking about cause and effect and pretty soon you'll find you're taking sides. You can't afford to let that happen."

Makepeace stood and cast his gaze around the empty bar as if he were surveying a crowd for a familiar face.

"I'm just saying, Des. You know, making sure that I got the order right, trying to please the customer, what? Anyway, you're right…I could give a fuck about how my guns are used once they've been sold and delivered. But I'm sure that you can appreciate that I do have an abiding interest in the nature of the conflict and the relative strength and, shall we say, viability of the combatants. One does not always have the luxury of picking one's customers, but one should strive to stay on top of the market and be aware of who the best potential customers may be."

"Oh? Frankly, Makepeace, I thought you were saying that if the IRA had arranged this run they would have made a substantially different selection of items to fill the hold. But I'll tell you, I wasn't really counting on them to help with the offload, anyway."

"No? You know that you can't do it without them, Des."

"Not without their awareness, certainly; but it is rather short notice and as it is I'll be counting the days until your arrival, and I'll have no time to waste lobbying for their support.

"Like the tailor said, we have our work cut out for us. But while you were out getting plastered last night I was rallying the local troops. We've less than 20 days left before I leave."

"You'll have to be ready sooner than that. I don't want to put the deal off to the last minute if I can help it. I'm no tailor. Let's say you have 14 days."

Des was disappointed that Makepeace hadn't taken the cue to defend himself by referring to his trip to the strip club.

"Alright, 14 days then, two weeks. And now that I've had my coffee I'll get back to work. What about yourself? When are you leaving today?"

"At noon time, but I have errands first so I'll be off. See you Sunday. "Harris!" He shouted toward the back of the bar and the bartender emerged with a dust pan and brush in hand. "Slán, Harris!"

"Agat, Mr. Makepeace, slán abhaile!"

CHAPTER 24

If anything could be said to suck about dealing pot, it was the way it took so much of Tweed's free time. He considered how his liberty had recently been diminished on Saturdays as an example. Sleeping late did not seem to be a choice but a requirement of his 14 year old body and he figured that many of the physical changes he observed in himself had probably occurred during the weekend puberty hibernations. Then ablutions, chores and other household obligations kept him occupied almost until mid day when he was finally ready to go to the library.

The two most intense periods for dealing pot were Friday evenings and Saturdays from 2 to 7PM, but since he had been out on a date with his new girlfriend Sam on Friday he had inadvertently left a number of regular customers in the lurch. As a result, demand and anxiety among his clientèles would factor in as well, making for a particularly busy afternoon.

With only a couple of hours to spend at the library it hardly seemed worthwhile going there at all. Nonetheless, when he arrived at the clubhouse at 2:30, he was carrying a stack of newly borrowed books. He had chosen them as an alternative and supplement to the tedious reading required at school.

After checking to make sure that no one else was approaching the garage he quickly removed a parcel he had stashed in a compartment hidden beneath the butcher block work bench surface. Relieved at finding the dozen or so bags just as he had left them he decided that it was worth the risk and henceforth he would keep a couple of ounces here at all times. Not only was it convenient, but he liked the idea of hiding it in plain sight as it were.

Tweed took a book from his pile and spread it open before him. As he idly perused the first few pages he cleaned and rolled a thick joint of sweet choice gold, using the cover of another book as the cleaning device. *Someday I'll have kids of my own*, he thought, *and I'll recognize the sound of weed seeds rolling down a smooth surface, and the sound of a half gram being scooped into a sheaf of rice paper. Then I'll either bust them, or ask if they wouldn't mind turning the old man on.*

After toasting the joint to his head it seemed as if he had thrown a switch, so suddenly was he stoned. He wondered if a person could get stoned so often that being straight becomes in effect their alternate reality. Does Bob Marley get really fucked up if he doesn't smoke ganja?

Looking up from his book, Tweed viewed the street framed by the garage bay door and obscured slightly by the bright light dazzling his field of vision. Just as the image appeared two-dimensional it suddenly gained depth like one of those jiffy line-drawn optical illusions, and he saw the street as a shoe box, bound by houses, the street, and the sky. Artificial gray cardboard props standing in for the real thing. Or was it an illusion? The leaves on the maple tree across the street formed up into patterns of letters seeming to spell out a jumble of meaningless poetry.

He wondered how long he had been staring into space and attempted to focus for a moment on something close by instead. He had never realized that the cracks in the concrete floor beneath his feet were so deep. Paint and grease stains took on the appearance of recognizable celebrities. There was Henry Kissinger, and there Chairman Mao.

"Hey, Tweed, you feelin OK?"

It was Og, flanked by Bone and a couple of dudes Tweed didn't recognize. "Sorry; didn't mean to startle you."

"No, it's just...I looked out that door a second ago and didn't see you coming."

"Came down the side, from the back."

"'Course! That's cool. What's up, Fugly?" He was annoyed that Og had broken the first rule of the clubhouse by inviting strangers. Now no matter how cool they were, no business could commence until they had left. On the other hand he was pleased to see Bone, an infrequent visitor, and he acknowledged him with a nod.

"You know man, I wanted to take care of some business, you know; talk things over."

Tweed stood and walked toward the door.

"Business? Let's go for a walk."

"I think we better do it here, man."

"I can't, Og, and you should know that." He looked pointedly at the guys he didn't know.

"Oh, they're alright, they're with me. This here's..."

"Og, I'm glad it's cool, and since it's cool you won't mind talking while we walk." He brushed past Bone and the others and let the slope of the driveway pull him down to the sidewalk where he commenced walking briskly in the direction of Arbs Park.

"Wait up!" Og hustled to catch up and whispered, "Man, I got your scale here!" He pointed at a gym bag he had folded under his arm.

"It's the Ohaus we talked about, the real deal, with calibration weights and everything! Don't you want it?"

"The scale? What the fuck? Who said I wanted...Oh! The Ohaus! No shit? Where did you get it?"

"From the chem lab, man! Remember that false alarm yesterday in school? I pulled that to clear out the science labs so I could score this baby."

"You blew up the lab?"

"Just a little. Enough to get everyone out of there. So here you go, man; it's all yours." He shoved the bag into Tweed's hands.

"Well, OK, thanks! What do I owe you?"

"That's why we came down here, Tweed, to make the swap, to get paid."

"Who's 'we'?"

"Ah, me, and ah, Bone, and Pete and TJ there..."

"Four people? I have to pay four people? How much do expect to get for this scale, anyway?"

"Six people, actually. I don't want much, just a bag apiece, you know, that's fair isn't it?"

"Six! Six bags? Why did it take six people to rip off a fucking scale? What kind of bags? You better be talking nickel bags!"

"Hey, man, don't get all bent out of shape! It took six people because that was how many it took. I needed help with the explosion, look-outs at the stairs on both ends of the hall, and help getting the thing out of the school. This took careful planning and it'll be weeks before they realize that the thing is missing. Look at it this way- you get a professional lab scale at no risk to yourself, and all it cost you is a couple of bags. I was thinking dime bags."

"60 bucks? You want 60 bucks for it? You know how many bags I have to sell to make 60 bucks?"

"I don't know, uh, six?"

"No, man! A hell of a lot more than that! If I had known that the scale was going to cost 60 bucks I never would have agreed to it. In fact I never did agree to it!"

"I don't want cash, man, I want weed; the gold, hopefully."

"I should give you cash and make you buy your weed elsewhere! You're lucky if I buy the thing at all!"

"Hey- you want to be like that, and I'll just keep it. You'll see that you really need this thing if you're gonna keep dealing and then when you come asking about it the price will be double."

"Fuck that! I'll give you a lid, you split it up between you guys, and it'll be the red, not the gold. I told you, I have no gold for sale."

"A lid? How the fuck am I gonna split a lid between 6 people?"

"You should have thought of that before you recruited so many to help you!"

"C'mon, dude! Make it an oh-zee at least. And we'll use the new scale to split it up."

"Alright. Tell you what. You meet me back at the clubhouse later, say five o'clock. Alone. Then I'll bring your oh-zee and we'll see about splitting it up for you. Fucking thing feels like bad news already, and I'm going to be paranoid using it."

"No you're not, man you're gonna love it! Every big dealer has one of these things. Do you know how much they go for? Believe me, 60 bucks is cheap."

"Og, I'll tell you. Shit that's hot only sells for a third of its regular value. A third, that's all. And that's when the hot item is in mint, brandy-new condition. This thing is clearly used."

"Look, all the pieces are there, it works, and it only cost you a bag. You should be happy."

"I'd be a lot happier if you remembered that part of what makes the clubhouse special is that we don't have kids from all over town using it. So don't bring people around, showing them our place, alright?"

"Touchy, touchy! I can see I caught you in a bad mood. Never fear. These guys aren't from around here anyway. I doubt that they'd be able to find the place if I wasn't leading them. But OK. I'll see you at 5 then." He ambled off in his loping, dejected way.

CHAPTER 25

It was remarkable how much Des could accomplish from his "executive suite", the small table to the right of the bar in the Rossie Businessman's Club. The tools of his trade included a telephone, a newspaper, a pocket notebook and a pint of stout. All of the critical information needed for maintaining control of his various enterprises was stored in his head: contact and financial data, influence capital reserves, as well as the whereabouts of and relative threat posed by personal and political foes. He considered himself to be disciplined and organized, although if you asked his wife Christine, her opinion might differ somewhat. But she knew the gentle father and loving husband as well as she knew the tireless champion of the causes of Irish "freedom, welfare and exaltation among nations", and the former was a far sight more easy-going, casual and garrulous than the latter.

As he had explained to his wife, his sons and his comrades, the priority business occupying the last few weeks before his departure for Ireland was the fund-raising effort his people were running for the supposed relief for the victims of the Guildford bombing. This day however his primary objective was to exploit the information relating to Makepeace that Chris had scrawled upon a napkin outside a strip club on the north shore last night.

His best opportunity for completing that objective would occur just after the shift change at the local precinct house, when his friend Officer Storer usually visited the Club after going on duty. Storer had been trying to cut back on the number of his visits to the Club ever since he was caught there by his supervisor playing in a darts tournament. This when he was supposed to have been interviewing witnesses in the Larchdale Projects after the apparent homicide of an elderly school teacher. It would have gone worse for him if his supervisor hadn't also been a regular at the Club, but since he wanted to make detective he rededicated his efforts toward being more conscientious, punctual and professional.

He couldn't stop visiting the Club altogether because Des Kelley was a valuable connection in the community who occasionally helped to sort out intractable cases, and who also provided a steady source of additional revenue to make life a little easier for a poor beat cop. And the money was only one of the benefits of his relationship with Kelley. Whenever he needed work done on his Roosevelt section split-level ranch, he relied upon Kelley to send a crew of skilled laborers; polite deferential Irishmen who were content to perform the work for tips and beer. And they were grateful too, because once their undocumented status had been exposed to Storer, he had something over them that not only guaranteed good work, but a continued relationship based upon fear and trust.

Des on the other hand always managed to have something over Storer, just a bit of insurance should the payoffs and the back-scratching not prove to be enough of an incentive to continue cooperating. He never really considered this to be a disadvantage however because he genuinely liked Kelley and because his ego generally would not permit him to see the true nature of his bargain with the local 'Ceann Mor', the harp term by which the workmen referred to Kelley.

When he arrived at the biz club he was only too happy to run the plate numbers that Des provided, especially when he found out that the owners weren't locals who might have connections of their own, but merely seemingly random names attached to vehicles registered in towns far north of the city. For his five minutes on the radio Des rewarded him with a double sawbuck and his choice of dates in a sky box at the ballpark if or when the home team clinched a berth in the playoffs.

The speeding ticket Des wanted quashed was another matter, especially as it was issued to the car belonging to a notorious local bookie. But seeing how his wife was driving at the time, and how Des seemed to have a personal interest, (probably banging the broad, he figured), then he'd see about calling in a favor from a friend on the State Police who was stationed at the turnpike barracks.

As soon as he got the information Des virtually forgot that Storer was still in the bar. One of the cars Chris had seen last night was registered to a Faith Bunting, probably the girlfriend of Makepeace's crewman; and the other belonged to a Stephen Darrager. Could this be Makepeace's arms contact? Or was he an IRA cell, a member of Cumann na Gael, or some Noraid-type subsidiary?

CHAPTER 26

By the time five o'clock rolled around Tweed was obliged to return to his house to reup his dope supply. 12 bags in two hours had to be a personal sales record and the day was young yet. The question was how much to get? An ounce for Og, then an additional quantity for the evening rush. At least splitting it up would be interesting as he became acquainted with his new toy. On the way back to the clubhouse he hitched up with Col, who met him with disturbing news.

"Hey Tweed, there's something I'd like to talk to you about. First off, did you hear about Jimmy Black?"

Jimmy was a friend of Col's. He was a skinny, red-haired, freckle-faced kid with glasses who looked a couple of years younger than his age. One of those kids that Mrs. Kelley had always identified as a suitable playmate for Tweed also. Tweed, on the other hand, liked to stay away from the obvious bookworm weakling types because he liked to think that he had an image to maintain- that of the 'regular guy'.

"What about him?" he asked disinterestedly.

"He killed himself. Today. Hung himself in his room."

"What? Jimmy Black? Your Jimmy Black, the little…"

"Yeah, you know him, lives over on Scott Street. Lived."

Tweed had been taking hits from courtesy joints all afternoon. He used them to entertain his customers, to give them a treat and to slow the pace of the transactions so the neighbors would be less likely to notice the flow of traffic. The cumulative buzz had created a haze of cognitive disassociation. He was slow to respond.

"Well, what the…what happened?"

"It's a long story, Tweed, and that's what I want to talk about."

Og was lurking in the shadows near the clubhouse.

"Hey, you guys, did you hear about Black? The kid killed himself! Can you believe it? How bad can it get, I mean, jeesh! I wonder why he did it."

Now Tweed felt downright nauseated as the facts took hold.

Col had his hands in his pockets and stared at the ground as he replied, "Over a girl, I guess."

"You heard about it? It was over a girl? Who?" Og demanded.

"Look, I don't know the details, you know, the kid was my friend, OK? Yeah, it was about a girl, and I don't know who. I just…heard that his parents found a note and it mentioned a girl."

"Man! You'll never hear about me killing myself over a girl! I mean, how old was he, 12? How serious could it be, for Pete's sake?"

"Og, shut up will you? He was 14 and I guess it was pretty serious or he wouldn't have killed himself, right? Anyway, think about it…he's one person you knew who is gone forever now. And I'll tell you, you only know so many people in your life, know what I mean? It's a small world, you know?"

The three kids walked into the clubhouse without any further discussion. Tweed hit the lights over the work bench.

"All right, let's see this scale."

It was a beauty. Triple beam, 610 gram capacity readable down to a tenth of a gram, with the balance indicator on one end and a large shiny specimen pan on the other, all in a sturdy desk-top configuration. It included the optional tray of calibration weights.

"I'm bound to lose these suckers," said Tweed, examining a gram weight. "Alright, here's your bag. I threw in a couple of extra fat buds to make up for your trouble." Setting a business tone helped to reorient Tweed and to calm himself.

"Pissa!" said Og, his smile lighting up like the Cheshire Cat.

"I'll take those!" He sifted the bag for the largest buds and deposited them in a separate baggie which he hid in his shirt pocket.

"So, you're not going to share the bonus, eh?" asked Tweed, trying to determine if Og had any conscience whatsoever.

"I look at it this way. The plan was my idea, so I get the bonus, and besides, I already told everybody how much they're going to get, so there's no use changing the deal now. So, can we split this up, or what?"

Tweed knew that Col was waiting for Og to leave so he could talk about whatever it was that was bothering him, but he also knew that the best way to get rid of Og would be to patronize him.

"Yeah, sure, let's test this puppy. First let me try a gram weight."

The scale had obviously been calibrated to spec because the gram came out spot on. Og insisted upon splitting the bag himself, and it was clearly his intention to keep all of the larger pieces aside in one bag and to split the remainder as chafe and shake. When he had finished, there were 5 oversized but seedy nickel bags and 1 chunky bag that disappeared into Og's shirt pocket along with his "bonus" bag. After he concluded his business, Og strutted out of the garage with a look of cool satisfaction on his face that was accentuated by the lit spliff between his teeth.

Col observed, "Did you notice how he thumbed the scale? Shit, I'm glad he's not selling dope. I mean, your bags are like the baker's dozen, and he's like the friggin crooked butcher. Man!"

"Thumbed the scale? What do you mean?"

"Each time he weighed a bag for one of his 'friends', he kept his thumb on the edge of the plate for extra weight. Like when they try to cheat you at the deli."

"Shit, I didn't even notice."

"Yeah, well that's because you're too freaking honest. Just because a guy has a scale doesn't mean that his bags are always right. There are all sorts of tricks you can play with a scale to make it look like you're careful and precise."

"Like what? Man, Carmine told me that I had to have one of these things. Now I'm beginning to wonder."

"No, he's right. If you're going to deal you need one, at least to make sure that the bags you're buying, I mean the quantity, is right. But the scale does lend an illusion that you're all scientific, when an unscrupulous dealer could just as well calibrate it to shave a gram off of every quarter; or you could add extra grains in the pan instead of keeping your thumb on the plate."

He showed Tweed how the plate unscrewed to reveal a storage bin for ballast lead. He pointed to the beads. "Don't lose this shit, man. In fact, you should probably keep this thing on from now on, because you know that the scale is correct, and if you fuck with the ballast you might screw it up. Some scales are sealed with a tag after they've been calibrated to show that they can't be altered. The electronic ones are self-calibrating, but they cost a shitload of money, too."

"How do you know so much about scales?" asked Tweed, as he dumped another quantity of pot on the pan.

"You take languages, I take science courses. I took Chemistry last semester; and besides, I used to have a little toy version from a science kit I got for Christmas one year."

"Now the problem is, where am I going to keep this thing? If I put it in my room, my mother will find it for sure."

"Yeah, that's rough. Listen, I have a problem too, man. It's about Jimmy Black."

Tweed's stomach felt nervous, as if he anticipated trouble.

"What is it? I thought you said that he was depressed about some chick."

Col sighed and folded his arms. "I lied. And there's more to it than that. Jimmy was my friend, and I'll never say anything bad about him, especially now. I still can't believe that he's dead, and there's going to be a funeral and all that. Man, I can imagine how my parents are going to take this."

"So...what's the truth? What's bugging you, is it because he killed himself?"

"Yeah, I mean, I guess it bothers you too, but the thing is, you see, he came to me recently, and...it's not going to be easy to hear this man, but I trust you and I want to hear what you have to say about it. Anyway, he came to me and told me that he had a crush on me."

"Jimmy Black? What do you mean, like he loved you or something?"

Col hid his face in his hands. "Yes, I'm telling you that he was a fag, and he thought that if he told me that he had a crush on me, then I might be a fag too or something, I don't know. Hey, don't look at me that way. I'm not queer. And I told him so. I mean, I tried to be nice about it, you know, I didn't say 'get away from me you fucking gaybo', or anything like that. I just said that I couldn't believe he was a fag and I told him to think about it and make sure he knew what he was doing, because if people knew he was queer, it was going to get rough."

"He didn't touch you or anything..." Tweed felt uncomfortable now, and his heart was throbbing in his chest.

"Well, man I can't believe I'm telling you all this, the thing is that a couple of days after he told me, his mother took the both of us to her work because they have a swimming pool there. She works at night and there's usually no one using the pool then. So anyway, I'm still trying to be his friend and all, and I went to the pool with him. But when we were in the showers, there were a couple of dudes there, too. Big guys, maybe even college age, I don't know, and they were horsing around, slapping each other and yelling shit, you know."

"Were they naked?" Tweed felt foolish and embarrassed.

"Well, yeah, of course they were naked, it was a shower, you know, like at the pool? So this guy comes over to me; and I'm standing at the next shower over from Jimmy, and he says, 'Hey, boy, do you know how to play with yourself?'"

"What? I hope you socked him."

"Listen, man, I wasn't sure what was going on. I mean, these guys were obviously older and they were fooling around, you know? I couldn't be sure if they were serious at first. And like I said, they were naked. I mean, I was wearing a bathing suit but I wasn't about to get any closer than I had to."

"So what happened?"

"I ignored the dude; but he goes, 'C'mon, kid, I asked you if you like to get a boner.' And he starts flopping his dick around."

"So you stood there and watched while this fucking fag stranger starts waving his dick in your face?" The story reminded Tweed of the time an upperclassmen had streaked through the gym at school. Later, one of the girls who had witnessed the event commented vividly, "All I saw was this big hairy thing coming toward me!"

"He wasn't waving...anyway, I wanted to get the hell out of there, so I bolted for the pool, and Jimmy's mother was in there, and the guys didn't follow me or anything."

"That was the end of it?"

"Not exactly. I was scared shitless that the weirdos would be waiting for us when we got out. They weren't, but when we went to get dressed, Jimmy admitted that these guys were his friends, and it had all been a set-up to get me to go queer or something. I guess they thought that if they stood around and played with themselves I might join in or something."

Tweed noticed that Col was trembling.

"You didn't, right?"

"Tweed, I'm telling you that I am not queer. What the fuck would you have done? So anyway, I had to tell him again that I wasn't interested, that I was sorry, but he'd have to find another boyfriend. He told me that he already had a boyfriend but they broke up last summer. I don't know who, so don't ask. But what's bothering me is that yesterday he apologized at first, then he tried one more time to convince me and I got pissed off and shut him down hard this time. I...I told him that I hated queers and I thought it was a sin, and I'd be damned if I was going to fuck around with another boy when I haven't even fucked around with any girls yet."

"You haven't?"

"Look, that's beside the point, OK? See, he went and killed himself after I told him off."

The story had ended so abruptly that Tweed's emotions felt like lemmings that had been swept over the edge of a cliff.

"So? I mean, I'm sorry he went and died, but that's not your fault."

Col just stared at him.

"What? You think that because you told him the truth and because he couldn't take it, then it's your fault he committed suicide? Come on!"

Col thought for a moment, clearly uncomfortable with the notion of laying any blame on his dead friend.

"All right. So maybe it's not my fault. Do you think I should tell his parents about what happened?"

"NO! No fucking way! What, do you want them to blame you or something? The less they know, the better. How would you like it if you found out that your son killed himself because he was a fag? Don't you think it's better if they remember him they way they want to, you know, like, ignorance is bliss?"

"I think it's my responsibility to tell them that I knew why he was despondent."

"So that bit about the note he left was bullshit, too?"

"Not exactly. He did leave a note, and I don't know what it said, but I think it was just that he was unhappy and he couldn't handle it. One more thing. He didn't hang himself, either."

"So how did he die?"

"He shot himself with his father's gun. The folks were sitting in the kitchen right next to his room when they heard the gun go off. The bullet almost came through the wall. They ran in and found he'd blown his head off."

"Holy shit!"

"Right. There isn't going to be any funeral, or if there is, it'll be closed-casket. Now what do you think?"

Tweed looked at his friend and felt a great sense of empathy. Col was suffering, no doubt.

"I'm telling you, man, forget about it. If I had a kid that killed himself when he was just 14 it wouldn't matter to me if he thought he was queer or not. I'd figure that he was a confused kid who needed help. In Jimmy's case his parents never got the chance to help him, so the best thing to do is let them think of him as going to heaven, innocent, you know?"

Col was crying. "What you say makes sense, Tweed," he sniffed, "and I guess I should thank you, but it also convinces me that I should say something. You're right. They never got the chance to know their own kid, and now they'll let him go wondering what could have made him do it, and whether there was anything they could have done to prevent it.

"I won't say anything, but I should. I should have back when he first came to me. I should have told my parents, and his parents, and then maybe this whole thing would never have happened."

Somehow under the circumstances it didn't seem right to comfort Col by touching him in any way. But not touching him made Tweed feel miserable. His best friend had told him a story so painful that he doubted he would have had the honesty and courage to confide.

"Hang in there, bud. It's going to be alright. All I can say is to remember when you feel sad, and I will too, that there is nothing worth killing yourself over. And if you ever feel that way, I mean, like killing yourself, do me a favor, OK? Talk to me first."

"As long as you promise to do the same."

"Sure thing, man. What are friends for?"

CHAPTER 27

We're looking back, it's important to remember. The year was 1974, the month October. A dozen eggs cost 78 cents, gas was 53 cents a gallon, and the average income was $11k. The distinction we're highlighting here is not evident in specifics however, but in generalities. From a 1986 point of view, '74 was a simpler time; gullible but not carefree, naive but not innocent.

In the neighborhood where the Kelleys lived, people locked their cars only when they parked in the city, and they locked their homes only when they went on vacation. And yet if they were to look back a dozen years as we have they might observe that their sense of pride and security in a community that had existed homogeneously since the 1950's had been gradually eroded by the inexorable trickle-down influence of international events such as the war in Indochina, conflict in the Middle East, and the Arab oil embargo; and domestic issues such as the Watergate scandal, forced busing of school children, and the counter-cultural revolution in general.

Resisting these external pressures, folks struggled to maintain their local identities by practicing civility and hospitality and by observing communal rites of tradition.

To the Kelley's recollection their old neighborhood in Jamaica Center was far more civic and neighborly than Rossie was now, but back then the families were practically living on top of each other, circumstances that encouraged a forced conviviality. And yet in the single-family-home environment of Rossie there were block parties and neighborhood cookouts and fireworks displays, and everyone pitched in without the need for asking.

Families were more prolific then, and frequently had to sort their kids from the neighbors' because the uninhibited children moved freely from house to house. And the kids had their own subculture, a separate society less concerned with boundaries or proprieties than its adult counterpart. They taught and entertained each other, and played and prayed and fought together.

But the strife that had torn at the composure of the community had also frayed the fabric of the family. Intolerance and cynicism, selfishness and insecurity teased at the threads that bound the family together; while society, dazzled by the glamour of vanity and conceit, slowly lost interest in the common good. Cults of personality supplanted the essential personal element in culture.

The Sunday dinner Des planned could be construed as an attempt to reinforce a stereotype, a comforting ideal that he relied upon as if to say, "as long as this is right, then my life at least is still right". Besides, when you can gather with friends and family in the comfort of your own home to enjoy good abundant food, can there be much in the world that is wrong? Is that not why we humbly ask the Lord's blessing and express our deepest gratitude for the meal? For the feast ignored the hunger of neighbors, it denied the deprivation of the multitude, and with aloof smugness it thumbed its nose to the plate glass window of the world and said, "We're quite comfortable in here, thank you! Sorry for speaking with our mouths full, but the food is so delicious!".

In reality Des looked forward to the dinner as if he were a politician anticipating a donation-per-plate fund raiser. Christine looked at it as a lot of work and would just as soon have everyone sit down early so that she could get the house cleaned early.

Tweed basically resigned himself to another wasted afternoon stuck in the boring house with the old folks again. But this time he had no desire to slip out because recent events had left him feeling a bit shaken and vulnerable. It seemed like the whole town was buzzing with the news about Jimmy Black's suicide, and Tweed thought that if people had paid half as much attention to the poor kid when he was alive then it never would have come to this.

Keiran was floating around quietly, keeping out of his mother's way and acting as if he too were grappling with some awful secret.

Makepeace arrived just in time to help set the table but not until he had stowed away another couple of large travel bags up in his attic room. Chris Kelley shook her head and said that Makepeace had a queer habit of leaving the house empty-handed then returning with his arms full of bundles as if his kit had magically multiplied.

Brother Morris came to the door like an itinerant line preacher, holding his hat in hand and issuing soft polite greetings while patting his belly as if to hint at its emptiness.

As if drawn to the address by the aromas of baking potatoes, roasting beef, fresh bread and boiling onions, Brendan Tighe was last to arrive. He swept into the house like a performer visiting the children's ward in the local hospital, as he pulled a Kennedy half-dollar out of Keiran's ear, elicited a smile from the dour moody Tweed, and lifted the pace of Mrs. Kelley's steps. Immediately after the introductions were performed by the host, he sensed a personality clash between Makepeace and Morris that he hoped to offset with his own presence.

The weather was ideal for October in New England, for touch football on a leafy quad of grass, for apple picking at a hillside orchard, or for an annual foliage survey expedition. Balmy, breezy and a blue sky for any late season Columbus Day weekend barbecues.

The guests gathered in the dining room and everyone at the table commented about the weather. For once it was not idle ice-breaking chat as much as a polite way of saying that although it was a shame to spend such a glorious day indoors, the sacrifice would be endured in the name of friendship. Conceding the point, Mrs. Kelley attempted to draw in some of the outdoors by opening the front and back doors and letting the autumn air sweep the kitchen cool.

The doors were situated opposite each other so that if you were standing on the front stoop you could see clear through the front hall, the kitchen and the back hall to the back porch. Then from front to back on the right side of the house the living room, dining room and den made up the remaining rooms on the first floor. The house faced sunny side south with its back to the tracks, and Mrs. Kelley had recently removed the lacy summer curtains from all of the windows and replaced them with heavy winter drapes so the air inside was still warm enough to raise bread.

An early dinner differs significantly from an evening affair. The appetites of the guests, their respective energy levels, volubility and sociability are affected to varying degrees by the hour and the absence of alcohol. Furthermore everyone except Makepeace had attended the low Mass together at Sacred Name and they were chastened, somewhat contrite and reflective.

Since arriving at the house Brother Morris and Brendan Tighe had been busy discussing the subject of the sermon. The priest, who was relatively new to the parish, had over the last few weeks been attempting to draw parallels between the scriptures and modern culture. This week his theme had dealt with the popular song, *A Bridge Over Troubled Water.*

"I'm not so sure that Simon and Garfunkel were trying to sound Christ-like in the first place," said Brother Morris as he removed his jacket and placed it on the back of his chair. The jacket had concealed a paunch he carried like a medicine-ball under his sweater, and when he sat down it looked as though he were trying to balance it upon his knees.

"Well, was that really his intention, I wonder?" asked Brendan, with a curious inflection that dipped instead of rising in the interrogative.

"Whose? The songwriter's or the priest's?"

"The priest, Father Boylan; I mean, was he really saying that the words could have been spoken by Christ, or was he saying that they reflected a Christ-like sentiment?"

"What's the difference?" asked Morris with a sniff. Formerly a teacher, he was now an administrator at a Christian Brothers school not unlike the one in which he had been educated. "If you ask me, the best source for Christ-like sayings is the Bible and no mistake."

"Last week he talked about Disney," said Des, as if complaining.

"What? Snow White as a modern-day parable? Or was it that Mickey Mouse was Christ-like, with Minnie, Pluto, Donald Duck and the rest as latter-day apostles?"

"Now you're being silly," said Brendan. "Reverend Boylan was clearly trying to make a point relevant to his congregation. I don't blame him for illustrating his sermon with contemporary cultural icons."

"No, I don't imagine you would," replied Brother Morris as if he were addressing a student accused of cheating on an exam. "But again I say that the Word of God is the only valid reference for theological instruction. In fact I find it rather disturbing that he expected his congregation to be familiar with a hippie folk song in the first place."

"It won a Grammy award a couple of years ago; I'm sure that folks knew what he was talking about. And you must admit that when he took the song line by line the words were undeniably relevant. 'When you're weary'...'When you're feeling small'...'When friends just can't be found'... 'Like a bridge over troubled water I will lay me down.' I think it's valid to say that these sentiments echoed Christ's message."

"I'd go along with that," said Tweed, though he was intimidated by Brother Morris. He privately referred to the loud, pedantic, elder gentleman as 'BroMo'. "But I wonder how Father Patrick would have handled the second verse of the song."

"Eh? What do you mean?" asked Des.

"It goes, 'Sail on silver girl, sail on by, your time has come to shine, all your dreams are on their way.'"

BroMo folded his arms on top of his stomach and as he looked down his face receded into folds and creases.

"I'm wondering how he handled Disney. What did he say, anyway, Des?"

"Well, um, as I recall he said that Walt Disney was like Jesus because he looked after the little children, and he got his message across through cartoons, er, like Jesus spoke in parables, you might say."

"Well, I wouldn't say. You might as well compare the Lord our Savior to Carl Yaztremski, for all of that, or Captain bloody Kangaroo."

"Oh, come now!" interjected Brendan quickly. "Don't we look for examples in our daily lives? If our fellow man is moral and honest and decent, doesn't he deserve our love, respect and attention? Should we not strive to be like those whom we admire for their goodness? Jesus taught us all to follow his example, and to set up the house of God within our hearts, so that we might one day come to the Kingdom of Heaven."

"If you're leaving aside the Holy Trinity, the angels and the saints, and keeping strictly down to earth, but Jesus, Mary and Joseph are too old fashioned for you, then why not look to the Church, the Pope, the Cardinals, Bishops and Priests, God's anointed representatives on earth? I say they are better examples than clowns or folk singers."

"But my dear Brother Morris, didn't you start by questioning the sermon as given by the priest at today's Mass?"

"Alright. He's young and inexperienced. I criticized him for his choice of words and for the examples he selected. Walt Disney and Paul Simon, indeed!"

"And are we not all sinners? You're right. The Word of God should be our one true guide, but we elaborate, we broaden our understanding of the Word by comparing it to concepts relevant to our daily lives. You know, Einstein helped us to understand the theory of relativity by placing it in the context of word problems, like a math teacher does."

"So Jesus' message was too complicated to understand? He needed somebody to dumb it down for Him, or for us?"

"No, I didn't say that, but you must admit that some of His parables are difficult for us poor mortals."

"His contemporaries understood them!"

"Perhaps they did. I would agree that some did. But in addition to spreading the good news, part of the function of the church was to promulgate and edify the Word.

"If I might make an analogy, the framers of the constitution expressed the ideals of democracy but the process of interpreting and fully understanding the document has been going on for two hundred years now and it takes all three branches of government to do it."

Morris turned to Makepeace, who had been silent thus far, and asked, "What say you, Mr. Makepeace? Jesus as Walt Disney?"

"Don't ask me, Brother Morris, I'm only a simple fisherman. When I try to picture Jesus in my mind I see him with the bread and the fishes you know, things we can all understand, and I see Him making miracles with them, something no one can fathom. I always confuse Jesus with God Almighty, anyway."

"But they are one and the same, aren't they?" asked Morris, solicitously.

"Please," his face colored; "I think this is more your area than mine. God sent His only begotten Son, so says the Bible. We're talking two, mind you. God, one, sent His only Son, two, and I don't think it makes any sense if you say that God sent Himself as His Son. But if you want to say that God is working through Walt Disney, then I'll go along with that. I mean, we teach little children that God is in everyone and every thing, am I right?"

"As long as you're not confusing monotheism with pantheism," muttered Morris.

"That was a militant group in this country, wasn't it, the Black Pantheists?"

Brother Morris looked up, startled.

"Just kidding, sir. Like I said, religion is above me, and anyway, like politics, it's just not good dinner conversation, to my mind."

After an awkward pause, Brendan amiably pursued a neutral topic of conversation.

"So you're a fisherman, Mr. Makepeace?"

"Yes, for lo, these many years."

"Then you've traveled a bit off course, to end up here, haven't you?"

"Sure," said Makepeace, taking a sip from a tall glass of beer, "...but the world is getting smaller, and nowadays trawlers from Dingle to Killybegs will fish down to Lisbon and Setubal, and on after the catch wherever it is. Even off the coast of Newfoundland or George's Bank."

"You're from Dingle yourself then?" asked BroMo, now on a fishing expedition of his own.

"Oh, well, I've been out of Dingle, CastleGregory, Belmullet."

"And how did you become acquainted with Chris and Des?"

"Maybe I should leave that story to Des. What do you say, Des, remember Vallapuentes?"

"Vallapuentes? Is that where you met?"

Des gave his friend a hard look and then answered Brendan's question.

"You might say that; yes, I believe that it was Vallapuentes. But really, 80 is an old customer of mine from the pub. He's here on holiday, spending a couple of weeks visiting friends in the area. We haven't seen each other in what? Years!"

"Too long, Des, and that's why I had to visit while I was here. It's been grand and I am glad to have met you as well, Mr. Morris."

He raised his glass in salute.

"Likewise I'm sure," said BroMo.

"I apologize for all of the questions," said Brendan, "But I'm simply fascinated."

"Oh, I love to talk. And any friend of Des, as they say. Anyway, until you get to know him, a man is only as good as his story. I mean, you can only judge a man by his story."

"I guess I'd agree if by story you mean word..."

"Yes," said BroMo, "Story can mean many things. For example, it can mean lie, or alibi, or..."

"Or joke," added Brendan, with half a wink.

"Gentlemen, I'm not playing at word games with you. Tom, I believe that Des said that you were a teacher? And Brendan, a scholar if I am not mistaken, so I will defer to you on matters of semantics. I merely meant that beyond taking someone at face value as it were, you listen to how they describe themselves, what they do, where they come from, like we did when we met. We form our opinions from that. So there is no need to apologize."

"Deep thinkers, these two," said Des, shaking his head. "Sometimes Tom, you think too much."

"You'll never accuse me of that," cried 80.

"No, that's true."

"There are times when matters come before us that we must consider, like or not," said BroMo.

"I've been considering some serious matters myself lately," replied Des, as if to himself.

"Well, I was referring to the suicide of that little boy in your neighborhood. My sympathies go out to his poor parents."

Makepeace restrained himself during the obligatory moment of silence, then asked with sincere concern, "Suicide? When? Someone you knew?"

As Christine related the news, Makepeace realized that under the circumstances tact would tie her tongue and euphemism prevent from her explaining the details of the tragedy. He tried another approach.

"Have you ever had to deal with a case of, ah, one of these before, in your line of work, Tom?"

"Not among my students, thank Heavens...but there was an incident," Morris became dewy eyed as he recalled, "...when I was in college. A classmate of mine...defenestrated." By way of demonstration, his hand ran a little race to the edge of the dinner table on two fingers and leapt off into his lap. "They put out that it was an accident, but those of us who were close to him knew the truth. He had been despondent and took his own life. I could never understand adding the sin of self-destruction to whatever failing or loss he had suffered."

At this Keiran blurted, "I have been thinking too, and I want to announce a decision. I am not going to play pinball anymore."

Tweed turned to his brother in disbelief. Kerry was sitting rigidly with his hands on his knees, leaning forward with an intense expression on his face to meet the identically quizzical stares of his parents.

"I am not going to play cards anymore, either. And after I graduate from high school I intend to enter the seminary."

"Keiran?" asked Des as if he had heard it from a third party.

"The seminary, boy, are you sure?"

"Yes, I am, Uncle Tom, and I would like to go to Bible camp next summer if I can save up the money between now and then.

"I think you're right about Father Boylan. I think he is reaching out but I'm not sure if it's doing any good. But I do know that he needs help. The church needs help, and in whatever way that I can, I would like to serve."

Brendan felt it necessary to intercede.

"I think that we had better talk this over, Keiran. I mean, I commend you but don't you think that you should talk to someone who has actually been in the seminary? Find out what you're getting into?"

"I wouldn't care if it was gruel and sack cloth; if it was straw pallets and vows of silence; penance and prayer and work and fasting."

"That's a pretty good picture you've drawn there, but I think I can fill in the blanks for you. Not to convince you one way or the other, mind you, but just so that you are better informed."

Des managed a smile and said, "I don't remember there being any priests in the family so this will be a first; but Brendan is right, boy. If you're serious about this you should talk it over with him first. Then we'll talk. I know this thing about Jimmy Black got you pretty shook up. We'll see how you feel in a couple of weeks, say, after I come back from my trip."

Mrs. Kelley removed and wadded her apron, then dabbed her cheeks and chin with it before tossing it into the kitchen hamper.

"Dinner's ready!"

Somehow it sounded anti-climactic.

During the blessing Tweed looked around to gather impressions that he could later relate to Sam.

With the extensions out and the extra leaf in, the mahogany dinner table was almost too large for the gathering. None of her tablecloths suited the augmented board so Mrs. Kelley had draped cloths of lace and linen across the length and breadth, leaving the corners bare like the shoulders of a woman in elegant evening dress. A pair of brass candlesticks served as a centerpiece with tall unlit yellow candles crookedly pointing at the candelabra light fixture that hung on a chain from the ceiling over the table.

BroMo remained in his seat to Des' right, his face florid and heavy, gray eyes twinkling behind gold wire-frame bifocals. His thin brown hair resolved from finely trimmed silver sideburns to a patina of razor stubble covering his saggy jowls, and these formed an even roll over his crisp striped collar. When the food arrived he squared his chair to the table and drew himself up straight.

Opposite Brother Morris sat Brendan Tighe: tall, lanky, with brown eyes and long brown hair combed over to conceal a receding hairline. A long friendly face with deep laugh lines next to narrow eyes, a mouth that seemed ever full of quips and puns like a squirrel has acorns in his cheeks. He wore a white v-neck sweater over a dress shirt & dickie combination with a wide mod belt and brown corduroy pants.

AD Makepeace took the odd seat on the corner furthest from Des. He had a stocky build of average height but imposing. Light hair, blue eyes, an insincere smile. Physically fit but ham-handed, with fingers like sausages. Jeans, sneakers, and a sweatshirt Tweed recognized as belonging to his father.

At the head of the table sat Des Kelley himself: heavy build, thick neck, Irish mug, brown hair, brown eyes. He kept his shirt sleeves rolled up over the cuffs of his navy blue suit coat, and his collar was unbuttoned as well, with the lapels riding over the jacket like some typecast tacky tourist.

His wife on the other hand was dressed neatly in a plum skirt with a matching floral, almost wallpaper-pattern blouse. At 5'4" she was the smallest person in the room but having raised four boys she had the strength and stamina of any one of them. She kept her dark hair in a loose aerosol mold but a couple of fingers occasionally fell in front of her blue eyes; and brushing at her bangs was her trademark gesture of annoyance.

Every dish of the meal was produced in excess so that even if each of the large hungry men at the table ate several pounds of food apiece there would still be ample leftovers.

A long train of clinking earthenware and china vessels snaked across the table, vigorously shaken as Des carved the roast beef on the tray at its head. A basket of warm bread made the rounds to provide a sop for the incipient saliva and for the luscious gravy that was waiting in boats fore and aft. There was a profusion of glassware, some tall and fluted, some cylindrical and lead-bottomed, others with mellow bowls on short stems. The silverware sat tucked in tidy blankets done up like hotel beds, and the plates were the ones from the top shelf in the hutch that Keiran and Tweed were forbidden to reach although they had long since had the height.

Des served up the crisp roasted onions that had caramelized on top of the round alongside the meat as an appetizer and garnish on the first tray of sliced beef. There were pearl onions in white sauce, baked potatoes, gravy, steaming heaps of cauliflower and fresh boiled green beans. For a matter of minutes all conversation except polite conventions ceased as platters passed and plates were filled, forks chattered and glasses splashed to the brims with milk, water and wine.

The boys knew that they always got plenty to eat so at formal dinners like this one they didn't fuss about portions. Usually the lion's share went to the young Jesuit, Brendan, simply because he was quick and voracious and he seemed to have no compunction about leaving all of the serving bowls empty. Today however he was competing with seasoned chow hounds, not so much Tom Morris as AD Makepeace, who ate like a man who had once lost a staring contest with starvation.

Even as he recorded the vivid sensations of delicious food, wonderful smells, the warm bright room, and the vibrant charismatic people, Tweed felt alienated and he had difficulty following the conversation. He kept thinking about his stupid brother and his stupid dramatic announcement that he wanted to be a priest. And Brendan was acting like an eager coach presented with a hot prospect for next season. First Col, now this.

So Keiran wanted to help the priest? Well maybe he could bring him up to date on the music scene. Bridge Over Trouble Water was practically an oldie. You want relevant, take the album Before the Flood. Tweed had purchased the record during the summer right after it was released and he had played it so many times that every song, skip and pop was ingrained in his memory. You want material for a sermon? How about: *I Shall Be Released, The Weight*, or *Blowin' In The Wind*? The homilies practically write themselves! Personally Tweed preferred *Stage Fright* and *The Shape I'm In*, although *It's Alright, Ma* reminded him of his dead brother Mack and *Cripple Creek* reminded him of Sam.

And that was another thing that pissed him off about Kerry's flash in the pan. This would have been the perfect opportunity to make an announcement of his own, using the buffer that the presence of guests provided, to tell everybody about Sam. Not that it should be a big deal. He was kind of relieved actually that moment had passed now and he no longer had to build up his courage. In fact he wasn't sure what made him most nervous; telling them that he had a girlfriend, or telling them that she was black. "Mum, Da, I've been meaning to tell you. I have a new girl. Her name is Sam, she's from Trinidad, and she's black as the Ace of Spades. Um…Da, your jaw is in your gravy there." There had never been any overt bigotry in his family, but he imagined that his parents would get pretty creative with seemingly non-biased and pragmatic reasons not to pursue a relationship with a colored girl. Sitting here thinking about it he wasn't able to understand that fundamental intolerance. Was it that Sam was black, or was it that almost everyone else he knew was white?

How did she see him? He was as far from black as you could get, from skin to soul. But he had an advantage, if you could call it that, of having been exposed almost daily to ethnic diversity. His family were immigrants, and his neighborhood and his schools were all examples of classic American salad-bowl diversity.

For Sam's part, she didn't live in a black ghetto and never had. In fact she was from a well-to-do family that lived in a townhouse with an attached garage and security at the gates. On the contrary, back in Trinidad her neighbors and classmates had been more racially uniform, but then, almost everybody was black.

His mother was blabbing on about something and suddenly Tweed looked at her in a new light. What the heck did she have to do with Makepeace? Last night, when Carmine had called to shoot the shit, he said that he had seen Tweed's mother out on the night that he went to Cu's Pub with the old man. Carmine was walking home from the square that night and had decided to stop by and see if Tweed was home. On the way up the street he saw Mrs. Kelley sitting in a car parked on the corner, seemingly waiting and looking at her own house. He said that he kept walking, wondering what was going on. Then a car pulled up in front of Tweed's house and blew the horn a couple of times until a guy came out of the house and got into the car. As Carmine was about to climb the front steps, he thought to look back at Mrs. Kelley, having the odd feeling that she might be watching him; but at that moment she was driving by, and it was obvious that she was following Makepeace, the dude who just left.

"...And Chris would pick up bits of sceal as she traveled with her father from town to town. It's a keen talent that, being a good listener." Now Des was finishing some story about the old days.

"But nowadays the news isn't very good at all I'm afraid. I wonder if they talk about the Troubles in the market towns."

There he goes again, hoping that someone will give him an opening to spout some rebel Republican rubbish. Up the 'RA and all that. Tweed had heard it all a thousand times.

CHAPTER 28

"**O**f course, Des, the people in the South have always been sympathetic, and I'm sure that it is a great source of frustration to the British that the so-called terrorists melt away over the border."

"Well, we all know the role of the British in the current difficulties," said Des, with disgust.

"And do you think that a terror campaign will change that? Bombing pubs and buses?"

"You know I'm not in favor of bombing or terror but I do believe that one man's terrorist is another man's freedom fighter, and that the British are a bellicose people who have brought war and tyranny to every inhabited continent on earth. All they understand is conflict, and only when push comes to shove do they move to the bargaining table."

"So might makes right, is that what you're saying, my friend?" asked Morris, dryly.

"I'm asking you, Tom. I thought that there was a kind of post-colonial realism that had taken hold in the world. Nations had more or less agreed that sovereignty was to be respected, international borders were to be redrawn only by mutual consent, and acquisition of territory by force would not generally be tolerated. Am I right? I mean, I thought that it all went along with a 20th century morality, although some of the principles were hard fought and reinforced in global wars and regional ones too. It seems that it took a while for some nations to get the message that it wasn't alright to invade one's neighbor for land or resources and commit genocide or rape and pillage. And yes, I'm lumping what Britain did in Ireland in with what some other rough customers on the world stage did and I think that they deserve it! I call the partition of Ireland an act of aggression and a continued wrong that should be redressed in front of the world community. Ireland has pressed England to relinquish its claim to Ulster over many years and in many ways. In the meantime the non-loyalist citizens of Northern Ireland suffer oppression similar in ways to that experienced by blacks in the American South of the 1950s."

"Come on, now, Des…"

"No, I'm asking you, isn't it right to use force in certain circumstances? For example, self-defense? How about declared war? I'll tell you something, Tom, my boy Mack told me when he was in Viet Nam that the camp chaplain used to line the boys up every day for Communion and he'd send them off with a little blessing that went something like this: 'Father, Son, Holy Ghost, now go and kill them commie sons of bitches.'"

Brother Morris rubbed his forehead thoughtfully before responding.

"So you are saying might for right, Des. You see an apparent contradiction. On the one hand Jesus said to turn the other cheek and on the other hand Christians wage war. I might remind you of a passage in Matthew, I believe, in which the Lord Himself speaks in war-like terms:

"'*Think not that I came to send peace on earth: I came not to send peace but a sword. For I am come to set a man at variance against his father, and the daughter against her mother, and the daughter-in-law against her mother-in-law. And a man's foes shall be they of his own household.*'

"Also in Luke: '*But now, let him who has a purse take it along, likewise also a bag, and let him who has no sword sell his robe and buy one.*'"

"And there are many more instances in the old testament.

"In the Book of Numbers, God issued a command to destroy the Midianites that Moses and his army took quite literally. They killed every Midianite warrior, wiped out every Midianite village, rounded up the remaining Midianites and killed all of them except the virgin women (who were kept for the Israelite men) and burned all of their possessions.

"The Bible is chock full of references to war and violence. If another example is necessary, then in Psalms there is the famous line that says: *'Happy shall be he that taketh and dasheth thy children against the stones.'*

"But make no mistake, my friend, there can be no moral justification for war, nor can violence promote good."

"Islam permits war in self-defense," said Brendan, earnestly.

"In the Koran it says *'Fight in the cause of God against those who fight you but do not transgress limits. For God does not love transgressors.'*"

"Surely there is a moral right to self-defense at the very least," said Des, "A man must have the basic right not to be killed. We naturally seek self-preservation, and in so doing we protect our loved ones and our communities. There is by extension a moral imperative to self-defense."

"Right, but on the other hand there is never a moral justification for killing, because the Lord said Thou Shalt not Kill."

"Then shalt thou be killed?" asked Des with a frown.

"Laws have dealt with these issues for millennia, and in the Book of Exodus when Moses delivered the ten commandments he also delivered the judgments of the Lord that outlined specific crimes including murder and lesser infractions, and applicable punishments all along the 'eye for an eye' 'tooth for a tooth' model."

"OK, then short of killing, how about the morality of rising against unfair rents, religious intolerance, disenfranchisement, starvation? Is there not a moral basis for stopping hooligans from burning your home? Or from looting stores, or smashing cars?"

"Well," said Morris wearily, "Paul, in Romans, ties the commandments to civil obedience in general. He says that it is essential to obey authority, as rulers do good in God's name, and furthermore the authorities execute God's wrath upon evildoers. But it is important to remember that Paul ends that passage by saying that Love is the fulfilling of the law."

"I can understand cautioning against vigilantism, especially in times of peace. But in times of conflict, when emergency conditions exist, then I believe that it is the duty of motivated citizens to respond to the needs of their communities. A society in crisis needs civil defense, engineering, public works and construction as well as communications and transportation expertise."

Des was shifting the gist of his argument. He had sought to frame his politics and activities within a moral context. Now he wanted to focus on the moral implications of the actions of individuals such as the militant defenders of Catholic Northern Ireland insofar as they affect a given community in crisis.

Although he would not openly discuss the matter in frank terms he would like his friends to condone his arms smuggling activities in principle at least; but it was clear that he was not going to get even tacit agreement on a hypothetical discussion. It was beyond his reckoning that this was not, on the face of it, a moral issue for them, and he felt disappointed. But although he could not claim the high ground on this matter his personal feeling of righteousness was undiminished.

Meeting the gaze of his wife, Des seemed to take a silent cue and he turned his attention to his plate.

The tenor of the discussion might have amused Makepeace if he were paying attention and he undoubtedly would have thought that his host was taking himself far too seriously. He did not know why Des had thought it necessary to try to impress him with a fancy dinner, highbrow guests and esoteric conversation.

While Des and the gent whom he treated as his father-confessor blathered on about politics and religion, Makepeace dwelled upon memories that had been illuminated upon the flickering projection screen of his mind by the mention of Vallapuentes, and the story of Christine Kelley's intelligence gathering work for the IRA back in Ireland, although it hadn't been described as such.

Ah, Vallapuentes! A tidy profit, that. Community of ex pat Irishmen with no-hassle connections to cut-rate European arms. Makepeace had assumed the risk of running the freight in his boat and Des Kelley had handled the logistics, offload and security.

In the early stage of the transaction, deposits of cash and faith were being made good as all of the principles gathered at the picturesque villa belonging to a gregarious Galwayman named McElheny. Food, women, and drink provided by McElheny, and the exotic Mediterranean location combined to intoxicating effect for an unforgettable weekend of booze, bullshit and debauchery. For people who needed to know as little about each other as possible Makepeace and Kelley got to know each other pretty well.

As for Christine, Makepeace knew that there were women among the partisan activists working in the pro-IRA community, but of course their role was clandestine, especially in the Republic. Stories such as the one Des had told helped to fill in the gaps on the exciting biography of a woman he had long admired.

But this domestic scene was hard to accept, and after a week of exposure, it was becoming rather tiresome. What was Des trying to prove? That he and Christine had managed to lead a respectable life? That his family was socially adept and integrated?

He'd look at the lovely Christine anytime, but why parade these poncy pals in front of him? Des was a radical Republican arms smuggler. Did he really think that it would appear that he'd had a religious conversion? If so, he was more of a hypocrite than Makepeace gave him credit for. He felt like shaking the man and saying, "You're an outlaw, you cheat on your wife, you're a lousy father, and you drink too much. Who are you trying to kid? Me? Or yourself?"

And Chris herself was a poser; pretending to be a doting wife, but all the while well aware of her husband's occupations and diversions and deceptions. For all Makepeace knew, she could be the brains behind Des; the real schemer and tactician. Who knows what kind of shit she got into? After all, you can never really trust a spy.

Then look at the boys: Tweedle-dum and Tweedle-dee. The older one looks like a bleeding bookworm and wants to be another lousy priest for God's sake! Well, he didn't get it from the old man, that's for sure.

And the younger one was into something peculiar, although Makepeace wasn't certain what, probably nothing worse than wanking. He had an independent air like he was accustomed to sneaking out of the house, or making his own decisions and fending for himself. He was perfunctorily considerate in a way that reflected well upon his upbringing, yet inattentive in a way that suggested that inwardly he wanted nothing more than to avoid the family that had reared him. But then, he was at a tough age. Telltale rat hair on his upper lip, acne on his cheeks, and the sheen of body oil on his forehead spoke to that. When he emerged from his struggle with adolescence, this growing boy was clearly going to be the largest of the Kelley offspring. Though come to look at him, he could just as well be the offspring of Christine and the local milkman.

Well they were a fine family and no denying it. If this is what they wanted, then so be it. Given the circumstances however, it would have been easier if he despised Des, because then he would feel less uncomfortable about concealing the true reason for the trans-Atlantic voyage of the Cor Mor. For despite the 50-ton capacity of its hold, the boat had been chartered for a very small cargo indeed: one man, his luggage and effects.

He resisted the urge to reexamine the sequence of events that had resulted in his position of obligation and hence his arrival here. Needless to say if the mission objectives hadn't somehow coincided with his ulterior motives then he would still be plying the waters off of Spain and Portugal. It was only after he'd been pressured by his contacts in the IRA to do the job, to make the crossing and return to Ireland with the American that Makepeace had thought of Des. And it wasn't until he started asking if anyone knew his whereabouts that he realized how irrelevant Des had become, especially in the minds of his former comrades. The information was freely available because nobody cared any longer.

By persuading Des to load a cache of arms into his empty fishing trawler, Makepeace guaranteed a greater return on the trip than the expenses and per diem promised by his Irish employers. All they were concerned with was the safe return of the American fellow; and all he'd been able to gather about him was that he was an engineer or an avionics expert.

There in a nutshell was the contrast between the young turks and old Des Kelley: in order to pursue their strategic goals they were hiring advanced electronics specialists; and he on the other hand was still seeking conventional small arms and defensive weaponry.

Yet, having intentionally complicated matters, it was essential for Makepeace to maintain the integrity of his missions.

The IRA had charged him with the safe pick-up and delivery of one individual and they would not tolerate any significant deviation from the deliberate execution of that mission. He had considered it a blessing when a shortage of manpower had prevented them from placing a watchdog operative on his boat. Having the specialist aboard would constitute enough of a hindrance. Not that he wasn't sensitive to their urgent attention to matters of security. He understood that they would not look kindly upon having Des learn about their plans, no matter how loyal a nationalist he was or had been.

In order to pull off this phase of the operation successfully, Makepeace would need to arrange a transfer at sea. He'd have his guest take a small charter fishing boat well off the coast to rendezvous with the Cor Mor soon after it had been loaded with Des' merchandise, and just prior to its departure for the open sea.

The integrity of the mission he was to perform for Des lay in the commitment he had made to deliver, a la Vallapuentes. Maintaining the illusion that this was strictly an arms run might be increasingly trickier at the point of delivery. Des did not wish to have the IRA breathing down his neck when he attempted to offload his cherished cache of hard-earned weapons, but they did have a legitimate interest in meeting the boat when it arrived at its destination.

Makepeace deemed that it would be to his advantage if he could arrange for the American to simply walk off the boat with the rest of the crew upon docking. He still had some time to think of a way to convince his business associates that it was in their best interest as well.

He'd already met his passenger, told him about the boat and its seaworthiness, characteristics and comforts, or lack thereof. They reviewed the schedule that he had outlined to the best of his ability, anticipating the arrival of the Cor Mor, and a brief two to three day layover for maintenance, refitting, inventory and refueling. Then with a full crew complement assembled and refreshed after a chance to stretch their legs, he'd order them to sail his boat out with the local fishing fleet to await further instructions. The American, a quiet, likable chap, was to make his final preparations for the journey and sit tight until he received word that it was time to go.

CHAPTER 29

Indicating that his stomach was as full as his plate was empty, Keiran politely begged permission to leave the table and was promptly excused. To Tweed's surprise, no one challenged him when he excused himself moments later in order to follow his brother.

He wasn't in the bathroom, the first place in which Tweed had thought to look for him. He was sitting on his bed facing the door apparently expecting a visitor in his room. Tweed briefly considered wrestling his brother into a full nelson hold, then dismissed the idea and laid into him verbally instead.

"So! You're giving up pinball! What the heck is that supposed to prove? Huh? Priests don't play pinball?"

"I was trying to show that I'm serious."

"Serious? Sounded pretty funny to me. I almost cracked up. Man, I bet priests play poker in the parish rectory, (the card game, that is) and they probably have their own pinball machines."

"Listen, Tweed, priests take a vow of poverty. They don't have pinball machines…they give all of that up for their vocation. Self-denial, like during Lent, you know? That's what I'm doing- giving up gambling for my vocation."

"You really want to be a priest? Or a monk? 'Brother Keiran', is that what you want? Take the vows, join the orders? For what? To please Mum? I think the plan will backfire on you, because her dream is for you to make a lot of money someday, not to make none."

"You are so…typical. A typical teenager. Man! How can I explain it to you?"

"Typical teenager! I am not! I'm not like other kids!"

"Yes you are, Tweed. In more ways than you know. You're just a self-centered, confused, insecure adolescent. You don't know who you are, or what you want. But hey, don't sweat it, happens to everybody."

"Fuck that, Keiran! I don't follow the crowd. They follow me! I set the trend. I'm the influence. Typical teenager? Shows how much you know." He wasn't ready to be on the defensive.

"Look at you! Drinking coffee all the time and reading, reading, reading. Soon as you think you're a big man you're ready to chuck your life and start doing the Lord's work instead? Who's confused?"

"Oh, I see. No room for the spiritual in your life, I suppose, eh, Tweed? You go to church all these years, you went to catechism; you even quit the parish to join an unorthodox sect. There's something going on there. You have a relationship with God but you don't want to talk about it. Well, don't knock it when I say that I'm going to explore my relationship with God."

"Yeah, I don't have to join the seminary, though. Are you sure that you do?"

"Mack went into the army, Buck went into business. How many choices do you think I have? Dad wants me to work with him. He's not interested in seeing me go to college. Remember- you went to public schools. I went to Holy Mary and Sacred Name. Seminary is a natural progression for me, and I really do want to serve. See, you blend in, you're good at that. I never would have made it in White City or Munie."

"But think of all the things you'll have to give up."

"Like what? I mean, there's bound to be sacrifices, but name something I'd miss."

"Shit, man, practically everything, right? Sex, drugs, rock 'n roll for starters."

"Yeah, right. Well, you can't give up what you don't have to begin with. Anyway I can do without all that."

"Well I couldn't. You should see the babe I'm going out with now. Her name is Sam and she's freaking gorgeous."

"I believe you. Chicks always seem to dig you; though I don't know why."

Tweed shrugged his shoulders then pretended to look out the window.

"If I were you I'd party my ass off while I still had the chance. I can get you a couple of sweet gold reefers if you're interested."

"As if you'd have a clue where to find stuff like that!"

"I'm only saying. You want to get fucked up so you can really think things over, let me know."

Keiran stared at his brother critically for an instant.

"Sure, sure. Why don't you tell me more about this girlfriend of yours? When are you going to bring her around?"

"Um, well, there's a problem. She's from Trinidad."

"So? She doesn't speak English or something?"

"Of course she does, man; but Sam's..."

"She's not pregnant?"

"No. She's black."

Keiran laughed. "Big deal. Are you afraid that your family will embarrass you? You bring your black girlfriend over for dinner and Mum keeps telling her to wash her hands before we eat? Or Dad tells her that she's getting too much sun?"

"I don't know. I guess I'm worried that he'll come off like Archie Bunker."

"No, Tweed, Archie was a WASP. There's a difference. He'd be uncomfortable having either Dad or Sam as a guest for dinner."

"I don't know. Can you picture me walking down the street here with her on my arm? I can imagine the comments from Og and them."

"That's your problem, Tweed, that you'd worry like that. You don't know how people will act and it shouldn't matter to you anyway. Besides, you were just old enough to have missed busing, but most of the kids in this neighborhood go to schools in black neighborhoods. I wouldn't be surprised if there were other kids around here with black girlfriends, or girls with black boyfriends."

There was no sense in arguing with an idealist. "Carmine says that someday there will be a Mulatto majority in America. He says you drive around now and you see mostly white folk, but over time, what with intermarriage and different growth rates in different populations, skin tones will darken overall."

"Yeah, he might be right. Just think, you marry a chick from Trinidad and you'll be helping that happen."

"That's good, Kerry. And everybody thinks that you're so serious. Hey, speaking of funny- after you left the table Brendan tried one of his so-called 'stories'."

Keiran groaned. "Alright, go ahead." Tweed sucked at telling jokes, and he wasn't in the mood to hear one.

"There was this novice at a monastery where the monks maintained a vow of silence all the time except one day a year, when they hold a special banquet. This novice found it hard to keep his mouth shut for so long and looked forward to the big day when he might finally speak. On the day of the banquet the Abbott stood at the head of the table and signaled the temporary suspension of the vow.

One of the monks raised his hand, the Abbott acknowledged him and he arose to speak. 'The gruel is too thin!' said the monk in a rusty croak; and after permitting a brief murmur from the brethren, the Abbott signaled the resumption of the vow.

"Another year passed, and finally the day of the feast arrived. On this occasion, a different monk arose when prompted, and said, 'The gruel is too thick!' That was the extent of the conversation for the year.

"When a third year had elapsed, the monks were again assembled at the dinner table awaiting the freedom to speak. The young monk was anxious to have a turn at speaking after so long, and was fortunate to find himself selected by the Abbott when the time came. Nervously he arose and said, 'When are we going to stop this bickering?'...Get it? When are we going to stop bickering?"

"Yeah, that sounds like one of Brendan's stories alright."

"Lame; I know," said Tweed, thankful that he had remembered enough details for the story to at least make sense. "But Makepeace came back with a story of his own, and it went like this: A teacher was leading her elementary school class in a vocabulary lesson when little Timmy raised his hand. 'Yes, Timmy?' asked the teacher. 'I gotta take a mean piss!' said Timmy urgently.

"'That is not the proper way to ask for lavatory privileges, young man! Now you may leave the classroom, but when you return, I expect you to use the word 'urinate' in a sentence.

"So Timmy marched off to the boy's room and when he came back to the classroom the teacher was waiting. 'Have you come up with a sentence, Timmy?'

"'Yes, teacher, here goes. You're an eight, but if your boobs were bigger, you'd be a ten!'"

Tweed's was glad to see Keiran laughing and he joined him with an arpeggiated giggle of his own, his annoyance with his older brother having passed. Soon they were chatting as amiably as brothers can, Tweed as always feeling slightly inferior, as if he were a couple of steps down the staircase of wisdom and experience. He was surprised to learn that Keiran had been worried about their father's upcoming trip to Ireland.

"I guess it was supposed to be a surprise, but Mum told me a couple of weeks ago that I'd be going with him, you know, over to visit Buck. They were taking me out of school for the month and everything."

"Why didn't you want to go? I'd be psyched!" he lied.

" A month alone with Dad? The airplane trip alone would be murder. Imagine twelve hours of lectures about the menace of the military industrial complex and the merit of the free socialist state." Now mimicking his father, *"the heroes and martyrs of the revolution- dreams deferred and denied."*

"And then...being dragged around to visit aunts and uncles and cousins and who knows who else. I don't want to have to make up a month of school just so I can get in with Dad and his bunch.

"When I go to Ireland I want to do it on my own terms, touring the sights and hiking the countryside, not wasting hours in smoky taverns waiting for Dad to do his deals with the men in the black hooded anoraks."

"What do you mean?"

"I just mean that this trip is supposed to be for business not leisure and I don't want to have to be there to see the kinds of deals 'Des Kelley' makes."

"What are you talking about? What deals?"

Keiran's face twisted into a skew of disbelief. "Tweed, did you ever wonder about what happens to the money that we raise supposedly for Irish relief?"

"No, why, do you? I mean, they're always talking about this bullshit but that's their business. What do I know? What do you know? What happens to the money?"

"Forget it, Tweed." He set his lips firmly and shook his head, but then said, "But sometime you might want to consider how Dad runs his business.

"Anyway, he went and changed his mind and now I'm not going. I only found out Friday. Mum said that he won't bring me when there's bombs going off left and right over there. Come to find out that he wasn't going to bring me anyway. Get this- he had already decided to take you instead!"

"What? To Ireland?"

"Yeah, no kidding! When he planned the trip he originally intended for me to go like Buck did when he was 16. But then just recently, after Mum told me that I was going, he decided to take you instead. She only told me because she knew that I didn't want to go in the first place. So now neither of us are going."

"Well, that's good, because I've been looking forward to this next month when he's away; not that I won't miss him."

"No, I know what you mean; me too. I think we're all going to get by just fine when Da's gone. Gonna be mellow around here." Keiran gestured evenly with his hand, signifying calm waters.

CHAPTER 30

Events were piling up and burdening Tweed with complications and consequences. He preferred to follow a repetitive schedule like the block grid pasted in his notebook that depicted his 35 weekly classes. The grid told him where he had been, where he had to go when, and when he had to go where. With advance notice he could comfortably integrate virtually any item into his school or personal calendar, but unexpected events disrupted and annoyed him.

Yet his desire wasn't so much for order as it was for control. Tweed enjoyed having a full academic course load and he allotted the remainder of his time to extra-curricular pursuits as well as partying and dealing pot. Perhaps someone who didn't have so much on their plate wouldn't mind the addition of an unexpected item or two. But on top of everything else, having a lodger at his house, going out with Sam, dealing with Col and Jimmy Black's suicide, and coping with the ramifications of his brother's decision to become a priest had left him feeling troubled and disoriented. He had an acute sense that all of a sudden his words and actions had a heightened importance, as if he could no longer speak casually about any subject to anyone lest he regret his words later. But why? Who was paying attention? Who would call him to task over some offhand utterance? He wished that he had the opportunity to talk with Brendan after dinner on Sunday night. Maybe he could have explained this abashed feeling. But Brendan had come up and knocked on Keiran's door, interrupting the boys' conversation. Tweed had been obliged to leave so that for once Brendan could counsel Keiran privately.

Now that he thought about it, Tweed realized that he had always been aware of people watching him. Some watched closely, with critical interest; others, who watched from afar tended to check up on him periodically. There were parents and close relatives in authority such as aunts and uncles and grandparents, then there were 'honorary relatives' who maintained an abiding interest, such as godparents and close friends of his parents who were regarded as aunts and uncles. Then there were teachers and community contacts such as priests, policemen and librarians. In addition there were friends and neighbors, and peers. All keeping an eye on him to see how he well he performed, how he turned out.

One example of the way in which folks kept tabs on him occurred on Halloween, the next big holiday on the calendar as far as Tweed was concerned, although he was getting too old for trick-or-treat. In years past when he was making the rounds on Halloween, it was not uncommon that certain neighbors would invite him into their homes where he would be expected to give an account of himself. The pleasant neighbors, who were usually the parents, aunts or uncles of his friends, would sit in their living rooms eagerly listening as he hastily reported as to the health of his family, his recent grades and accomplishments, as well as any anecdotes he could recall about his brothers. Sometimes he would even recite a short poem.

And yet all of these people watching him only represented the active observers. He was also aware that there was a 'record' being compiled, for it was frequently mentioned in school. A teacher might say, "Do a good job as the audio-visual equipment monitor, and it will go on your record." Or conversely, "You don't want to get too many demerits; it looks bad on your record." Records were kept by bureaucracies and he had been taught that bureaucracies were inherently corrupt so he felt that there was more than a hint of conspiracy in record-keeping. Birth record, student record, police record, financial, academic and community records all conflated over a lifetime into a flawed biography. This reinforced Tweed's belief that it was best not to be noteworthy, and that one of the advantages of not being outstanding was that it reduced the probability of setting any records.

Keiran had said that Tweed was good at blending in, but he had no idea how difficult it was to achieve that level of anonymity. Especially as an illegal dealer of a controlled substance he strove for the kind of average appearance and unassuming air that resulted in friends saying, "Oh! I didn't notice you standing there, Tweed!"

The week following the dinner party had a considerable impact upon Tweed's faith in relying upon routine to provide structure in his life. In fact the reason that the events of this week merit inclusion in this retrospective narrative is due to the manner in which they affected his outlook regarding initiative and adaptability. Forced to deal with incidents as they arose, he began to relish the creative potential of decision making, and on the flip side he appreciated the gambler's thrill of random chance. You made the call as long as you were prepared to accept the beat. But if poker was to be the metaphor, then Tweed wanted to be holding all of the cards and last to act on the hand.

On Tuesday Bone caught up with him at the bus stop and told him that Terry Haar was looking for him. Said that Dave Haar was pissed when he discovered that his gold was gone and he told Terry to get it back. Bone, who usually seemed to be under the influence of cerebral inertia, appeared to be awaiting a response as if he could be trusted to become a liaison between principals. Partly out of panic and partly out of dumb stupidity Tweed said nothing one way or the other. He merely expressed mild surprise and shrugged off the news.

But he began to plan how he was going to get away with satisfying the Haars and keeping the gold for himself. For a while he studied over the idea of appeasement, trying for some kind of negotiated settlement involving the surrender of quantities of inferior weed and perhaps a cash adjustment. After all he did not want bad blood with the Haars, who were known convicts and scag addicts, any more than he wanted to contract a case of venereal disease; nor did he want to precipitate a crosstown conflict. However for each rational scenario to which he envisioned a successful conclusion, he also fantasized a matching spectacle of humiliating failure or personal injury.

Wednesday Bone met him in school again and told him that on the following afternoon Terry would definitely be coming to find Tweed to talk to him about the gold.

In the meantime Tweed was trying to see Sam as often as possible. On Mondays, Wednesdays and Fridays she had choir practice after school and he gladly escorted her to rehearsal.

Although it was a school organization the choir met at the local YMCA because the building contained an auditorium that was noted for clean lively acoustics. Choir members were permitted to walk the two and a half miles to the Y if they wished but a bus was provided to ensure that they arrived punctually and prepared to sing.

Sam believed that the walk was doing her some good; surely there were benefits from deep breathing and from developing increased stamina. She wasn't so sure however about the frequent stops for kisses. It was nice to get all romantic and horny but it messed up her appearance and she risked being late for practice. Wednesday afternoon the dowdy choir director met her at the entrance to the hall and sneered disapprovingly as Sam kissed Tweed goodbye, then warned her that tardiness would be sufficient cause for dismissal from the choir. This was no idle threat. The rigorous practices were intended to prepare the chorus for an annual conference and competition that would be held in Washington DC in early November. If Sam or any other member of the team were to be cut now they would miss out on the trip as well.

Finding himself a couple of miles out of his way and in a part of town with which he was not familiar, Tweed decided to make the best of his situation. He scouted the area around the Y and merely by being observant and inquisitive on the street he was fortunate to encounter a new customer upon whom he could unload any stash he had leftover from his school-day dealing. He sold the bags at a discount, but the extra cash compensated for the hassle of dealing with late afternoon trains; and his customer, a one-armed pool-hall broom named Rod, was happy to get quality hooch for a change.

From Rod's apartment, a third-floor walk-up situated over the pool hall/pinball arcade, Tweed was able to get his bearings and orient himself. He heard the comforting squeal of steel on steel from the wheels of the commuter trains rolling along on banked rails between parallel roadways in the nearby ground-level transit corridor. Yonder, perhaps another mile or so distant, was the boundary of the Mission district. He could just make out the profile of the hilltop church around which that neighborhood had been built.

The streets in this section of town were lined with rows of dilapidated townhouses like the one in which Rod lived. At one time a generation of wealthy gentry had lived here, close to the business center and the swinging nightlife of jazz clubs and restaurants. Nowadays the clubs and the commerce were gone as were the upscale urbanites, and these uptown blocks looked more like skid row. Prostitutes stalked the corners; cops and hoods and winos played a tireless game of hide and seek. Trash and the detritus of modern society, such as shopping carts and wooden pallets, abandoned vehicles and household appliances accumulated in the vacant lots between buildings.

For a fourteen year-old boy whose only frame of reference was his own small neighborhood, it was liberating to be out on the town; and he realized that a map composed of bits and pieces he had learned separately was coming together as a whole inside his head. His world was growing larger, expanding beyond Jamaica Center, Rossie Square and Westbury Circle. Recent exploits had enabled him to encompass Crystal Pond Park, the Mission and points between into his realm of awareness, and he could envision someday knowing the entire Metro region and all of the related boroughs. But by then he would have to have a better way to get around than public transportation.

Before he left Rod's place he rolled himself a solid joint to smoke on the platform while he waited for the train.

Rod amused himself critiquing Tweed's technique.

"You always crumple up the paper first?"

"Yep." People frequently asked him about the crumple.

"Gives you better traction, huh?"

That was the first time anyone figured out why he did it.

"Sure does." He was licking the seal.

"I think you get a better roll from a pre-rolled paper, myself."

Here we go. Everybody had their own method and for most of them, their's was the right way, the proper way, the only way. Someday, Tweed thought, he'd have to write a book about all the regional, ethnic, generational and downright peculiar variations that existed in the world of reefer.

"Yeah, some folks put a little crease in it first, some roll it between their fingers like you do. I crumple it up, then stuff it and twist it up like a tamale. The way I see it, it's just a joint."

That wound Rod up. "Just a joint, you say?" Rod was an older dude, well over six feet tall though he listed to one side, likely to favor his good arm, and he walked kind of pigeon-toed, with a limp. His hair was long, dirty and uncombed and he lashed it about for emphasis as he spoke. He reeked of alcohol and Tweed suspected that he worked at the arcade primarily because of its proximity to the bar across the street.

Speaking through his sinuses he continued, "What if you were to die today? Huh? Think about it. That would be your last joint. Your last reefer. The last number on the day your number comes up. The last spike before they nail you into your coffin. The last high before you soar up to the sky. Now wouldn't you want that to be a fine, fucking joint? I mean, man, I would want my last joint on earth, the last thing I smoke before I die, to be the best, I mean the best fucking reefer I ever smoked. Rolled clean and even and oh-so fat. I don't want no canoes, no popcorn reefer, no ducktail pinner for my last joint."

"Well, that's different, isn't it?" answered Tweed. "You didn't say I was on death row. Warden comes in and says, well Mr. Kelley, you got yourself a choice, a nice juicy chicken, a nice grilled steak, or a nice fat reefer, and hell yes, I'm taking the weed, fuck the meal, thank you. If they let me do up the last number to my head before I'm dead, then damn right it's going to be a slow-smoking stogie, sweet and neat, no seeds or stems; a joint to remind me of all the other joints I've ever smoked; the paradise lost of reefers."

"Paradise lost, right. You've lost your mind, my friend."

"Well if you find it, hold onto it for me until the next time I visit, will you?"

"Sure, and the then I'll tell you about how you pass the roach funny."

"Oh, go to hell, Rod!"

Despite the effort and good will that went into preparing the joint, Tweed was forced to put it out as soon as he had lit it because the train arrived. He noticed that there were no other riders and chose a seat for himself near the front of the car across from the conductor's station. As he sat down he inadvertently lost his grip on the bone that he had just pinched out between his fingers, and he watched with dismay as it quickly rolled down between the seat cushion and the backrest.

Tweed immediately tried to force his hand down into the crack between the cushions but there was little room and since the sections were ten feet long it seemed impossible to remove the bench in order to look under it. However at that moment the conductor entered the car and as he approached he noticed Tweed searching and asked if he could be of assistance.

"Drop something down there? Happens all the time! Just take me a moment to get it out." The conductor, a short man whose excessive girth was barely contained within his uniform, tugged on Tweed's arm to budge him off the seat. Then in a swift brute motion he wrenched the bench forward on hinges that were located out of sight below the cushions.

He and the teenager peered down into the box below.

"A joint? You were looking for a joint? My word! I pulled up the seat so you could get a joint! Well, tell you what- since I have this thing open, you take a look down in there and pull up anything else that you find."

The gentleman had been good enough to help him recover and return his lost weed, so Tweed fished down among the heating ducts and wiring conduits in the dusty aluminum seat box and did indeed find some items that had clearly fallen from pockets or purses; but nothing of value or interest.

"So what do you do with all this stuff?" he asked.

"Key chains and pens and such we throw away. Wallets, purses, books, umbrellas, they all go into lost and found at the end of the line."

The conductor smiled as if he had shared a secret and then took his position in a cabin at the head of the car. Tweed settled into the restored seat with his back to the window as the train rolled on towards home.

He wasn't alone in the car for long. At the next stop a group of young black men entered the car looking, for all Tweed knew, like a gang. They carried golf clubs, bats and tire irons and while it was obvious that they were not sportsmen out looking to assist stranded motorists, it was also clearly no coincidence that they chose the bench opposite Tweed. They were all larger and older than Tweed and the smallest of them outweighed him considerably. Staring at him intensely, they began thumping the floor rhythmically with their weapons.

He had no dope, some money, but they might not even be interested in money. What were they after? Just out to beat somebody? He sat passively, alert and excited but not particularly scared, wondering what would happen next. The thumping persisted, louder and faster, and suddenly the conductor took notice. He leaned into the car and caught Tweed's attention, glancing over as if to indicate that he was aware of what was happening. Tweed did not feel reassured, for he doubted that the conductor would wish to face seven or eight armed and hostile teenage boys. He took a deep breath and prepared to do the only thing he could think of in the circumstance: bullshit his way out the predicament. As Tweed began uttering the first words of a feeble greeting to the gang, the conductor suddenly burst out of his cubicle like a horizontal jack-in-the-box, wielding a small caliber revolver that looked as though it would fit in his sock.

"All right then boys, take it easy! Everyone is going to get off the train at the next station, even if it's not your stop. Get it?"

No response; all eyes were fixed on the barrel of the gun.

"Good, I see that I have your attention. Now sit quietly until we pull in at the platform. Don't get up to leave until I say so."

He stroked his whiskers and winked at Tweed surreptitiously as if to say 'That's twice I bailed you out.' Tweed looked down and shook his head, concealing a grin.

In minutes the train stopped at the next station and all of the angry young men departed. But not until they had contributed sundry items to add to the conductor's lost and found collection.

"That was pretty ballsy!" said Tweed admiringly.

"Nah, I let this baby do the talking for me," replied the conductor, patting his pistol.

That gave Tweed an idea, inspiring a plan for dealing with the Haars.

CHAPTER 31

He was so pleased with himself at having arrived at a solution to his problem that it wasn't until he was in his last class on Thursday that he realized he had forgotten to implement it. This was the first time that Tweed wondered if a potential side-effect of pot consumption was the erroneous impression in a smoker's mind that an idea, once considered, became in fact accomplished. It would become a problem, for him at least, for the remainder of his life. For example: did he complete that homework assignment? He must have, because he had thought about it. The bills must certainly have been paid, for he had previously considered doing so.

It wasn't a matter of intentions unfulfilled, it was a matter of a defective mental link between the goal and the assumed completion of that goal. It was almost as if by imagining it, it must be so. Would that it were. On every occasion he would be surprised to learn that he had never completed a given task he had set out for himself, and by the time he had realized it, it was usually too late.

He compensated for this synapse-lapse, or whatever it was, by becoming strictly organized, as if precise record-keeping would serve to check his other perceived shortcomings. In addition, he assumed an overbearing personality so that he could achieve his ends by having others, hopefully more competent people, complete his tasks for him. Ironically, he facilitated the control of others by providing them with dope, the same substance that had impaired his own abilities in the first place.

After school Tweed was kicking through a pile of leaves at the base of a tree, waiting for the throng of students in the departure area to surge aboard the buses, when he noticed Bone leading Terry Haar through the crowd and heading in his direction. What luck. How had Bone known that he would be here? He was only taking the bus twice a week now that Sam was attending choir rehearsals, and given the odds, he might not have found him in the crowd. Perhaps Bone intended to get on the school bus with Terry, figuring that if they didn't find him on the bus they would probably find him in the neighborhood or at home.

Flinging his sack over his shoulder so as to obscure the view of his face, Tweed wheeled about and scurried toward the queue forming outside another of the outbound buses. As he pushed in among the kids boarding the unfamiliar bus he kept an eye over his shoulder and noticed that Bone and Terry were last in line at his regular bus, and they too were scanning the milling crowd, surely looking for him. Finally the buses got under way, and Tweed was oddly relieved to find himself heading off toward Francestown on a route he had never before taken.

CHAPTER 32

The ensuing journey was quite unlike his prior adventure on the bus to Crystal Pond Park. For one thing the bus was surprisingly empty. There were fewer students living on the route so Tweed had no trouble finding a seat. And on this occasion instead of heading to a specific destination with the intention of meeting Terry Haar, he had no idea where he was going and his immediate concern was evading Terry Haar.

The course of the bus route was almost leisurely and wound along extensive tree lined parkways. The other kids on the bus all seemed to be settling in for a ride, opening books and nodding off. There was none of the bustle, pranks and shoving so typical of the bus he usually took home. As he tried to enjoy the ride without getting too anxious he reasoned that the logical course of action was to take the bus all the way to the last stop and see if the driver would permit him to remain onboard for the return trip. Then at least he would get back to the area near school where he could pick up the train.

However the next thing he knew the driver was shaking him gently by the shoulder.

"Last stop, kid, c'mon, get off. I gotta clean up."

"Huh? Aren't you turning around, you know, heading back?"

"Not me. End of the line. I get another route here that heads out to the industrial park. You want to head back you're going to have to wait awhile. See, this is a school bus, and you're going to have to get on the city route. The stop's just down the street there. Should be another one along in about an hour."

Tweed stumbled out of the bus in a groggy fog and as he walked away he heard the bus bleeding off air pressure with a blasting hiss. He was standing in front of a small red brick building alongside which were parked several idle buses. The door to the building was open and Tweed could see a couple of bus drivers within smoking cigarettes and drinking coffee at a small table.

There was a tingling sensation in his abdomen that he recognized as the onset of adventure. It should have triggered an instinct to call home to tell his mother that he was going to be late, or ask if there was anybody who could come out and pick him up. He walked past the building and down the street following the direction the driver had indicated but he continued on past the bus stop also and kept walking, trying to clear his head and to get a sense of what kind of place Francestown was.

After about a half-mile he came to a small shopping mall preceded by a parking lot. In the center of the lot was a large sign mounted on a concrete pillar that was rooted in the center of a raised island with grass around the base. A Lincoln Continental was parked at the curb next to the island, idling with the headlights and radio on. The door was open and there was nobody in the car. Tweed approached cautiously, looking around for the owner. He was there for perhaps a minute, at first puzzled and concerned as to why someone would leave a luxury car parked in the middle of an empty parking lot; and then feeling a sudden thrill, a spasm of desire and wickedness. He walked boldly to the driver's side and got in, confidently closing the door behind him. The handle was made of mahogany and felt heavy and valuable in his hand. The seats were soft black leather and the stereo was a quadraphonic rig that made the music come at him from everywhere. It was power everything from the seats to the mirrors. He shifted it into gear and drove away as if he were the guy who had paid off the note on this gleaming hunk of machinery and was proud of it. The thing flew so smoothly that he didn't realize how fast he was traveling until he hit fifty, and the road had only two lanes. He eased back and cruised, keeping one eye on the little compass atop the dash so he could make a wild stab at heading southwest toward his neck of the woods.

What a car! Not that he would ever buy one, even if he had the money. It was too fat, too long, too rich. For the cake it took to buy this monster a person could get a sports car. But you could hold eight people in it and have yourself a party. Tool around in the Conty, pick up some hoodsies, then pack the trunk with beer and head to the Arbs to crank the tunes and get laid. Awesome. Too bad he didn't have a joint right now. He had sold the usual day stash at school but hadn't brought out anything for himself. Then again it was just as well, for if he happened to get pulled over, any slim chance he might have of conning his way out of trouble would go up in smoke. And he was plenty nervous and paranoid without the added chemical enhancement.

On either side of the road there were cemeteries, and on the right beyond the headstones and the trees he could see a river flowing broad and peaceful in the same direction he was headed. Then he encountered a series of roundabouts that brought him swinging closer to home as if he were taking advantage of some orbital accelerative effect. He began to relax, knowing that he would be home soon. The glowing blue digital clock on the dash indicated that he shouldn't be too late that a lame excuse wouldn't cover. It was a stroke of genius to grab this baby and motor on home. But where to park it? He remembered Terry Haar's admonition about the pizza delivery boy's car, to leave it so that it could be recovered intact, so the kid would get it back, no harm done. Tweed had no malice against the owners of the Lincoln, he merely thought they were stupid. He'd love to repay their stupidity with a spectacular stunt, like driving their car off the Jamaica Center trestle so that it ended up nose down in the middle of the intersection below; or bringing it to the top of Pippin Hill and rigging it up with a rock on the accelerator to see what kind of swath of destruction a two-ton car could make through the woods. But in order to do that he'd have to arrange an audience, and so that would require first finding a parking place.

As he thought he unconsciously reached for the keys, and to his horror, there were none. In fact there was no ignition at all. He shrank into his seat as if the steering wheel had become electrified. There was a gaping hole in the steering column that he hadn't noticed before. What an idiot! He broke out in a cold sweat. The car was stolen! Stolen before he stole it. Holy shit! Who knows how long this thing had been on the hot car list? He had to get out of it immediately. There could be cops looking for it, owners looking for it, insurance men, guys with baseball bats...

He was entering Westbury Circle from an oblique angle and it occurred to him that he could leave it at the cinema. It was convenient and the place wouldn't open for another couple of hours so the lot would be vacant.

He pulled in trying desperately to drive casually, and parked in the second row, away from the building. He immediately regretted the choice, feeling exposed, but not wanting to sit and think it over he grasped at the hole in the ignition and realized that he could not shut the car off! He opened the door, leaped out and hustled away, but a couple appeared seemingly out of nowhere and called to him.

"Hey! You-hoo! Yoo-hoo! Mister! Could you help us?"

In terror he turned back to look at them.

"Have you got a jack? We have a flat and our jack is no good."

He was a college kid; clean-cut, blue-eyed, fair-haired, standing with a lovely auburn haired cutie. They implored him once more.

He stammered a response, "Uh, I'll be right back, uh, I have to get something."

"Hey, mister, you left your car running!"

He started to run, and bolted to the back of the theater where he knew the alleys that lead to the streets he needed to follow. His heart was pounding and his vision was obscured by black spots in front of his eyes. Gasping, he stopped to bend over and pull himself together. He almost vomited.

It was a close one but he was OK. Nothing to get upset about.

So it was stolen car. Big deal. What if the guy who had it before him went through the same thing he did? What if some other kid jumped into it now? It was sitting there idling like a big fat invitation: steal me. Could be the most stolen car in town. Could be a chain of thieves all picking it up and dropping it off like a loaner. First some rich bastard in the suburbs went out in the frosty morning and started the car, leaving it running so that it would be toasty warm for him when he was ready to leave for work. However, while he was sitting in his breakfast nook drinking coffee and reading the Wall Street Journal, he noticed a young man enter his vehicle and brazenly drive away. Outraged, he called the police immediately, but he was disappointed to learn that stolen car cases were not given high priority by the police because so few of them resulted in a recovery or a conviction. Meanwhile the erstwhile joyrider, who only wanted a warm ride to school, had left the car outside a corner store, and had taken the keys with him. In fact he decided to leave the car there, intending to return for it after school.

Some time later a genuine street hood, fancying the wheels, hopped into the unlocked limo and with a dent puller and the skill of experience, yanked the ignition assembly from the dash with aplomb. In moments he had taken possession of the car and was casually taking it for a spin with a couple of friends as passengers.

That scene went bad, however, when one of the boys said that he wanted to take the car for a quick ride by himself before they stripped it, and then he ditched the others. Tables were turned for him when he went to pick up his girlfriend, because she in turn ditched him. And it was when she was cruising with her girlfriends that she got spooked by a police car, thought she was being followed, and abandoned the car at the Francestown Mall.

He started to laugh and started jogging again.

CHAPTER 33

On most Fridays, teachers will try their hardest to dampen any growing enthusiasm among the students about the coming weekend. Quell the daydreaming and nip the high spirits in the bud. But pop quizzes and open ended essays didn't bother Tweed. He said 'bring 'em on'. Most of the stuff they threw at him was geared for the lowest common denominator in the class anyway, so it wasn't much of a challenge. And he handled his writing assignments by turning in what were, in effect, long rambling letters to his teacher in which he took the tone of an avuncular colleague, at once tritely philosophical and meanderingly meaningless. They usually came back to him graded B minus, with the added comment, "Too Pompous".

Today he was looking forward to his walk with Sam because he wanted to ask her to go to the movies with him on Sunday. He had noticed that *Thunderbolt and Lightfoot* was up at the Westbury Cinema again and he had missed it the first time it came around. If Sam was any fan of Clint Eastwood then this could be a date.

But when the time came she was non-committal. The day was raw and cold and she kept her hands buried in her pockets and her collar turned up around her face. Maybe she didn't like the idea of going to a movie in the white middle-class enclave of Westbury Circle, or maybe she had other things to do, but she wasn't saying. She walked quickly and talked little and didn't look at him much. Tweed was beginning to feel unappreciated and that he should have packed her on the bus and been done with her.

They were nearing the YMCA and he wanted to make sure that he got a kiss before he left. If he wasn't going to see her until Monday then it was going to seem like a long weekend. A sudden gust of wind forced them to seek shelter in the doorway of the Y and as they huddled out of the gale, Tweed pulled Sam against him and kissed her passionately. That was just about the time when things started to go wrong. At that moment the chorus director stepped out of the door and seized Sam by the arm.

"That's enough, young lady!" she snapped. "I've had it with your attitude! We can't have young ladies such as yourself representing this organization. You may as well turn around and go home. I am removing you from the roster. I'll have to bring in another soprano to take your place on the trip to Washington DC. You can thank your boyfriend for this unfortunate outcome."

Sam broke down in tears instantly and didn't bother to protest.

Tweed on the other hand shouted at the woman who was walking away as stiffly as if she had a baton up her butt. In a fury he vowed that he would file a grievance and have her fired. However when he turned to Sam to console her she refused to talk to him. Even though they were both heading to the train station she refused to walk with him, and he ended up following her until the point where they took separate stairs to opposite platforms.

She looked sweet and sexy standing across the tracks from him with tears in her eyes, her nose stuffed up and her lips all puffy, but despite his pleading she would have none of him. It was that image of her that he would carry in his mind for months after they broke up.

He traveled home in a funk, not really believing that he was responsible for what had occurred, and wondering how he could convince Sam of that when he called her later. Then as he got closer to Jamaica Center he remembered that Bone and Terry Haar could well be waiting back in Rossie for him to return to the neighborhood, and he turned his thoughts to handling the next anticipated crisis. Fortunately, he was better prepared for this one.

CHAPTER 34

One of the advantages of the clubhouse was that to the casual observer it usually appeared like a vacant garage sitting on the crest of an embankment surrounded by bushes. Only a regular visitor or someone with a trained eye could tell whether or not the garage was occupied at any given time. The building itself was easily overlooked beneath its shabby overcoat of ivy tendrils, and otherwise it blended into the row of houses like a smeared detail in a pointillist landscape.

For Tweed, detecting strangers in the clubhouse was like feeling the twitch of a dowsing rod in his hands- he could sense them without actually seeing or contacting them. Klaxons went off in his head, and his heart rate and respiration increased perceptibly. The feeling of outrage and violation was only tempered by the almost certain knowledge that the people in the clubhouse were none other than Bone and Terry Haar. It would have been extraordinary if true strangers had suddenly appeared in his personal little hangout, and if any ever did then he would have to think about moving to another one.

It was more than just pride and jealous greed, it was a matter of security. Tweed was stashing his quantity in there.

And what the fuck did Bone have to do with this anyway? Was he simply caught in the middle because he was the one who introduced Tweed to Terry? Or was Terry offering Bone a commission, a percentage of the recovered dope in exchange for leading him to Tweed? Either way he wished that Bone had kept his mouth shut and stayed out of it.

At any rate now that they were here he had to deal with them. From where he was sitting the situation looked satisfactory, especially since his adversaries were bottled up and out of sight in the garage.

He trotted around the block to the Kenney's house and called on Gary, Wayne's younger brother to come out and accompany him back to the clubhouse. Gary had agreed to provide back-up should the need arise and now was the time when, like the train conductor's handgun, his bulk would make the most favorable impression.

As they walked Tweed briefly entertained himself with the notion of physically challenging the pair waiting in the garage for them. He imagined saying, "You want the weed? You're going to have to take it from me. And if you want to get to me, you're going to have to go through him first."

Gary was a big mutha, built like a V8, with arms like tree roots. No speed, not much brains, but strong as Adam's off ox. Ideal in enclosed spaces like the clubhouse. Shit, all he had to do was catch Terry in a bear hug and crush the living shit out of him. And as for Bone, Tweed didn't think that he'd put up much of a fight if it came down to it. Not unless he brought the Kinks into it.

He could picture Bone holding him in a head lock, saying,"*Nobody puts down Ray Davies! Aaaaargh!*" and furiously scribbling his trademark 'Turkey in a trench coat' on his face. "*Take that!*"

Gary interrupted his daydream.

"So…you sure about this, man?" he asked, in a childish voice that belied his massive size.

Tweed looked up at him.

"It should go like I said. You stick to your guns and act tough. Think about how mad you'd be if it happened to you. Do it like you were going to be on TV or something."

"No prob; I've been thinking about that, like you said. I'm just wondering what I'm supposed to say if none of this shit gets talked about the way you think it will."

"Well, Gary, if that's the case, then I have nothing to worry about, do I?"

They were approaching from the rear, from the house side. He preferred to walk up the drive, but this time he wanted the advantage of surprise. It always troubled Tweed whenever he had to sneak past old man Wolff's house like this. It was one thing to use his garage, but it was another to creep along under his windows when the friendly old dude could be inside and spooked by the noise.

He could hear Bone's voice coming from inside the garage. Droning on about something in the sing-song conversational tone he used, and periodically coming up short with the word "man," like a record catching up on a scratch. The other voice however was not familiar.

It didn't sound like Terry Haar.

Turning the corner now and stepping through the convenience entrance that was cut out of the bay door, Tweed came face to face not with Terry, but Dave Haar.

"Here he is now," said Bone.

"This is Weed?" Haar's eyes narrowed and he pursed his lips.

Thin as a runway fashion model, standing as if his back pained him, eyes dark like a raccoon, raw track marks visible on his arms like a hideous rash, he was menacing like a ghostly apparition.

"Ahm, Tumbleweed, Tweed Kelley," said Tweed, nervously offering a hand. "Who are you, and what are you doing in my garage?"

Dave stepped back like he had been slapped. "In your garage?" He turned to Bone. "I thought you said this was a community place?"

Bone started to speak but Tweed interrupted him. "You know, Bone, I've had to speak with you before about bringing people in here! What if every Tom, Dick, and...what did you say your name was?"

"Tweed," replied Bone, almost pleading, "This is Dave Haar, Terry's older brother. You know, Dave, looking for the gold."

"The gold! The gold? Did you hear that, Gary? He said he wants the gold." His stomach ached as he pushed ahead with his plan.

"Yeah, I heard," said Gary, sullenly. "I guess everybody wants the gold, huh?"

"What do you mean? It's mine!" said Dave Haar, with an edge of hostility in his voice.

"Oh? You mean like finder's keepers?" asked Tweed.

"What the fuck are you talking about? My brother Terry sold you my Acapulco gold and I want it back. I never said that he could sell that stuff, and since neither of you asked me, I'm here to take it back."

"What about the money? I paid for that weed and I'll tell you, from my point of view, it was more than fair, what I paid."

"Hey, I'm taking a loss on that shit, and I want it back. I don't give a rat's ass about the money. You can take that up with Terry. That is, after he recovers from the ass-kicking I gave him yesterday for not catching you after school."

"Yeah, he kicked the shit out of Terry," added Bone.

Tweed ignored him. "So you say the weed is rightfully yours? Terry said that you stole it," he said pointedly.

"That's right!" shouted Gary, startling everyone.

"Look, it's none of your business where I got the weed..."

"Oh, I think it is. You see, my friend Gary is here to represent the guy you ripped off. Him and Gary are best friends." For a visual, Tweed twined his forefingers together like a liquorice stick and then jabbed at Dave for emphasis. "Gary here doesn't think it would be right for you to steal the weed twice, so to speak."

"That's right!" said Gary again, vehemently.

Dave paused, and gave Gary the once-over. He was a big kid, and ornery-looking, too. Dave could be a wild man in a fight, and might not do too badly in a two-on-one mix up, but he knew that this other freaking kid Bone would be practically useless. He only had avarice on his side, whereas Tweed had Gary and the payback motive.

Tweed noted Dave's indecision and spoke up, "You want to jam over this, that'll be fine, because there's nothing I love more than a good brawl. But either way you're not walking away from here with any dope."

But Dave wasn't ready to give up yet. "So you and Rick Rose are tight, eh?"

Tweed prayed silently that Gary wouldn't fall for a lame old trick. He didn't.

"I don't know any Rick Rose, but I do know Jim Kuhn, the guy you ripped off." Now Tweed silently thanked Sam for having provided the vital information, the name of the dealer whom Dave had robbed.

Gary went on, "He's a decent shit who unlike you wouldn't stoop to hitting another guy's stash. But I tell you, he's pissed off about this and so am I."

"On the other hand," said Tweed, in a conciliatory tone, "He'll be pleased that you came forth like this...that's real stand-up. I imagine he'll enjoy following up on it personally."

At this moment Dave knew that he could piss and moan; he could take a swing and take a beating; or he could get out while the getting was good. Either way the trip was a failure and he was coming away with nothing. That pisser Weed had managed to sleaze one over on him.

"Fuck this shit. I'm out of here. Better keep in mind, Weed, that I know where you live. And you better stay the fuck out of my town, if you know what's good for you."

Haar looked at Bone as if to say, "Are you coming?" and then stalked out of the garage, venting rage by kicking the flimsy plywood door out of his way.

Tweed walked Bone to the door and stepped outside with him. Sunset had repainted the landscape while they were inside, and their faces and everything around them was illuminated in radiant gold and flashes of greens and reds. As the glow from the horizon intensified, a light breeze picked up and carried with it aromatic hints of acorns and oak leaves, chimney smoke, and cooking food. The mood of tension and aggression among the boys suddenly lifted and Tweed felt like playing touch football, or riding his bike and following the sun with the cool breeze at his back.

Without a word, Bone smirked as if to say, "I know it, I'm a shitbum," and he ran down the drive to catch up with Dave Haar.

"Well, shit!" said Gary, smiling widely. "And you better stay out of this neighborhood, if you know what's good for you. Hah!"

"Be cool for a minute," said Tweed quietly, watching until the pair had disappeared down the street. "They'll hit the tracks and Bone will bring him to the square. Maybe he has a ride."

"What difference does it make? He's gone. We did it! You were right, man! So tell me; who the heck is Jim Kuhn?"

"Fucks knows. I just hope that he doesn't come looking for the stuff now."

"Speaking of which, you got that bag for me?"

"Yeah, yeah, here you go..." Tweed gladly handed Gary a sack of select gold buds as a reward for his fine performance.

"24 carats."

Just then Carmine's voice rang out.

"Looks like I'm just in time."

He was coming from the same spot from which Tweed had observed the clubhouse earlier.

"Did you catch that sunset? Freaking awe inspiring. I said to myself, 'I hope somebody's in the clubhouse getting spliffed right now, because a good buzz would go perfectly with those colors.'"

"But we got ourselves a quandary," said Tweed, facetiously. "Can't stand out here and smoke; if we go inside we can't see the sunset, and if we hike up to the hill the sun'll be down by the time we get there."

"Fuck the sunset, let's get stoned!"

"No, man, you're right," said Tweed, "Let's just stand here and enjoy it while it lasts, then go inside."

"Man, I can't tell if you're busting my balls or what."

"Believe me, Carmine; you'd know if I was busting your balls."

"No shit," laughed Gary, "we just got through busting some guy's balls, and "I think he's gonna be sore for a while."

Tweed let Gary tell the story while he rolled up a celebratory number. He knew that Carmine would be content to listen to Gary crow for a moment, but that as soon as the joint started to circulate he'd have stories of his own to tell.

CHAPTER 35

Regardless of whether they were elective or imposed Makepeace did not normally enjoy vacations, so he kept himself relentlessly busy during the weeks prior to the arrival of his boat, the Cor Mor. Each day he was actively engaged in advance work for the upcoming voyage, and in his spare time he reviewed nautical charts, surveyed the weather and tides and toured the waterfront.

His crewman Reggie accompanied him on most expeditions and he also displayed an uncanny penchant for finding genial pubs, and then 'crawling' from one to the next.

Reggie's girlfriend had a similar knack for shopping and she introduced Makepeace to all of the bargain discount warehouses, flea markets and factory outlets in the area. She had fun watching the men browse and spend but she was less thrilled about hauling all of their purchases back to her place for storage. At the end of the month when Reggie finally left her to rejoin his crew mates onboard the boat, the void in her life would be all the greater.

By Saturday, October 19, the pressure brought on by an impending deadline was as palpable to Makepeace as an approaching weather front. The tension strangely enabled him to relax for the first time since he had arrived in the US, as if it reminded him of who he really was and what he had to do. It felt familiar, like an object from home stowed away in his luggage.

Tonight he would rendezvous with an important contact, one vital to the success of his mission. He had found her on a short list prepared for him by a colleague in a British Special Branch counter-terrorism unit, of advantageously placed resources, corporate agents who were well-established in these parts. The fact that she was the only woman on the list had encouraged him that she might also be the most likely to be able to show him a good time.

He was to coordinate with her on a kind of joint task force on American arms suppliers. It was becoming clear that American arms were finding their way onto the streets of Northern Ireland and ending up in the hands of militants on both sides of the conflict and the British wanted to know how that was being achieved.

As a freelance operative Makepeace had not been entrusted with any cash for a potential buy. If he did manage to line up a transaction in a bid to demonstrate how the paramilitaries were doing it, then his contact would have the authority to advance a modest sum for the purchase.

As soon as she had arranged for him to meet with the arms dealer, he would turn to Des and tell him to pull his cash together. Setting the transaction tentatively for October 24 should permit time to arrange the deal, with allowances for anticipated blown meets, fuck-ups, and miscommunications.

His new colleague was wealthy, young and attractive. She was a member of the horse-set and polo scene in Hamilton, and the current guardian of a slip in Swampscott harbor that had been owned by her family for generations. By virtue of her pedigree and position she was well prepared to assist Makepeace in procuring a bulk order of arms and supplies, just what Des Kelley required, and all through legitimate wholesalers.

Working to build her prestige over the course of a year by splashing money around with a dowager's largesse, she had gained the trust of local merchants who were suspected by the British government of funneling hardware to loyalist paramilitary organizations in Northern Ireland. The dealers had unknowingly become the focus of discreet official inquiry because of their remarkable ability to circumvent the red tape, tariffs and customs restrictions that would normally make such freight transactions if not impossible then at least increasingly unprofitable.

As the British attempted to deal with problems associated with the violence and discord in Northern Ireland they were already spending vast sums of money, applying the bulk of their available resources directly to the source of the conflict. However in order to tackle illicit activity of this sort, which was far removed and incidentally a low priority in the scheme of things, they would have to dedicate money, manpower and political capital to the effort. The expenditure seemed unreasonably high given the projected return on investment. Furthermore, the operation would ostensibly require the cooperation of American CIA, FBI, and who knows how many other state and federal agencies, without even considering extradition issues.

In lieu of launching a substantial cooperative covert effort with the Americans, existing agents in place had developed the intelligence on exporters, manufacturers, shipping agents, et al. In the end, the most cost effective method of advancing the operation was to exploit the opportunity Makepeace had presented. He was going to the States anyway, building his cover in the face of increasing scrutiny by the IRA. The British were very keen to know who it was that the IRA considered so special as to send a personal transport for him.

Combining the missions was pure expedience. While in America he could look into the arms market, and determine whether it was indeed as easy to smuggle arms as they feared. And if he returned with a sample cache of arms then army intelligence could set about gathering information from the weapons themselves.

Expediency had placed Makepeace in an awkward position because he was representing himself as pro-republican to the Irish and pro-loyalist to the arms dealers. Even though those factions were at odds there was a slim chance that if the right people compared notes he could wind up painfully having to explain himself.

Makepeace had his own priorities, however, and wanted to one-up the whole arrangement. He would use Kelley's cash to demonstrate his good faith with the arms dealer and make the initial purchase. At the same time he'd promise additional orders and encourage an ongoing relationship with the dealers.

He'd persuade his new associate to split the advance money that was originally intended for the buy and then they would go their separate ways. Having made the introductions his colleague would resume and maintain her cover in Hamilton and the investigation would proceed with deliberate speed.

This was how Makepeace ran a freelance operation, and he would take advantage of his friends in British intelligence, and any of the other parties involved if he could get away with it.

If all went according to plan, then his suppliers would never know that the arms he purchased were not going to loyalist street brigades in Ulster but to nationalist storage depots in the Republic. And of course Des would never know that the arms he had purchased were supplied by British-American ideologues who intended them to be used by Protestant death squads in the indiscriminate murders of Catholics.

But then it was essential both to his continued effectiveness as well as to his very survival that not the slightest hint of any link between him and the British Special Branch should ever become apparent to either Des Kelley or to any of his other clients.

The entire mission was shaping up to be a complicated series of misdirections and compromises. The challenge was to serve many masters while keeping his own best interests above all else. Fortunately his British handlers had facilitated matters by giving him a great deal of latitude in order to complete his assignment. Their overall mission objective was to track down American sources supplying arms to loyalist factions in Northern Ireland. Makepeace, on the other hand, was merely paid to provide information. He was not expected to initiate action or to attempt to influence the outcome of events.

Likewise, his IRA clients, believing that they had him at a disadvantage, had permitted him so much freedom in planning and managing their operation that he had copped a side-deal with Des Kelley in the bargain.

Yet despite the duplicity and machinations he saw himself not as a double agent but solely as a pragmatist. He had long since hammered out his priorities and copper-fastened his loyalties, and had neither doubts nor misgivings.

The truth was that he couldn't have fabricated a scenario like the one in which he was now involved. Something this fucked up could only occur spontaneously, and he could only laugh as the pieces of the plot fell into place.

The only thing that bothered him was having to intimate a necessarily tough bargaining and acquisition phase where none existed. The deal was practically prearranged so he was spared the usual back and forth haggling over money and logistics, yet in the meantime he would have to let on that this deal was no different than any other so as not to arouse suspicions.

It would help if he could spend less time around the Kelleys, but he had accepted their hospitality for the duration of his visit and he was already staying away as much as possible.

CHAPTER 36

"So what can you tell me?" Des asked his wife Christine as he entered their bedroom at midnight. He had just come home from the biz club after a long evening of extending the glad hand to his constituents and then adding up all of the combined receipts from the latest fund-raiser. "What is our man up to?" He looked at her over his new pair of bifocals.

Chris was accustomed to the stench of cigarette smoke that clung to her husband like a geis, as well as his beery breath, his poorly hidden inebriation, and his utterly consistent lack of consideration. She hugged him nonetheless and wearily reported her findings.

"How the fuck should I know?" she sighed, exasperated. "I followed him, north again, to what amounted to a dinner date with a young lady. They met at a posh polo grounds of all places- out where the homes all look like country clubs, and from there they went to a restaurant. I thought for sure that I'd be following him to a motel afterwards, but instead they went out for a sail off Marblehead. Almost six bloody hours wasted tailing the lovebirds, when I should have been home."

"Ah, well, you tried. He's having his fun anyway. I wonder when he's going to get around to that little list I gave him. Less than a fortnight and I'll be winging away. Doesn't allow much time, I'd imagine, for the type of diabhlaíocht he gets up to."

"And tomorrow?" she yawned.

"Leave him be. We want to be careful but not foolish. No sense wasting time or money trying to prove a negative."

"So be it. 'Níor dhún Dia doras riamh nár oscail Sé ceann eile.'" (God never closed one door without opening another.) "I'd like to be home anyway, to keep an eye on the boys. Tumbleweed has been down ever since his girl dumped him, and Kerry's awful quiet, don't you think?"

"Ah, too bad I can't take Ta'weed with me this time. It would have done him good, no doubt."

"He'll take care of himself, I'm sure. He's as independent as he is stubborn."

"Like myself, I know. As for Keiran, well...you know, still waters run deep, they say."

CHAPTER 37

Sailor, smuggler, fisherman, spy. Considering his lot, Makepeace felt a mixture of arrogant pride and scornful self-loathing. He was an independent operator, free to seek his fortune in the world. And he was self-made to a degree certainly greater than any of his peers in his graduating class at Harrowdon, where as a callow youngster he had been recruited by Special Branch.

In those days Makepeace had been a natural athlete in competitive intra-mural sports, and he also excelled at outdoor activities such as boating and fishing; skills that were valued and encouraged by his handlers.

They trained him as an informant and confidant, so that he could serve as an unobtrusive conduit for intelligence. However during his brief indoctrination by the SAS he had been most intrigued by his introduction to weapons, in the armory, the firing range and the ballistics laboratory.

The same factors in his upbringing that had been a disadvantage for him at Harrowdon were ultimately to determine how he might best be employed to serve the crown. For his parents, who were loyal British subjects, had raised him in Ireland; and in accordance with his mother's wishes he had become a devout practicing Catholic. Furthermore his uncle had died while serving in the RUC, and while the cause of his death had been ruled accidental, his parents perpetually blamed the IRA.

Thus Makepeace fit the profile for the ideal covert operative in the struggle to counter the threat posed by the IRA. Working "under cover" on fishing boats, he soon met and befriended Irish nationalists including Des Kelley, and he found it easy to fraternize with local Republican leaders and to insinuate himself into a position of trust and acceptance.

At that time, before the SAS had officially deployed at the Royal Engineer's base at Castledillon, Armagh, covert operations were conducted under the auspices of the Northern Ireland Training Team, or NITAT. Internment had for the most part failed to suppress the IRA, and British military commanders wanted to combine intelligence gathering with more aggressive patrolling of Republican areas. These early counter-insurgency efforts led to the creation of the army's secret Military Reconnaissance Force, or MRF, which was dispatched to Northern Ireland in 1972 in order to launch covert ops intended to disrupt and discredit the IRA.

The onset of the civil rights movement in Northern Ireland and an increase in violence and unrest associated with what was perennially referred to as the Troubles presented new opportunities and gave prominence to operatives such as Makepeace. His assigned objective was to infiltrate the Republican ranks, yet he strove to avoid full-fledged induction to the IRA, instead offering his services as an ardent sympathizer and supporter.

He loved his work, but not the hierarchical structure under which he imagined he suffered. The combined influence of his ego and his desire for independence convinced him that he would enjoy an advantage working freelance. When he separated from the service he believed in his naivete that he could continue to be effective while maintaining a reasonable distance from people and situations that might place him in moral or professional conflict.

In total contrast to Makepeace, a world away and yet sitting directly across the table from him at the polo club bar, was Mrs. Heather Harrad-Farquhar. She was thirty-ish, blonde, lithe, svelte and beautiful. He didn't like blondes as a rule, but she was so disdainfully icy, so temptingly beyond him that he wanted her.

Frustrated, he felt angry at her and himself. The emotion rose in his blood like a convenient excuse for almost any behavior.

Here in her element she was safe and secure, haughty and irreproachable. But when he got the chance he would turn the tables and show her his qualities.

She had things that he needed, and he intended to get them from her. First of all he wanted to get out on the water to feel the sun, the air, the spray and the buoyant irregular swell of the sea. Perhaps she could take him fishing in the area where he would soon launch his mission to rescue the American defector. Then perhaps he could experience her swells and her buoyancy.

However when they boarded her smart spanking ketch for a sail she refused to travel beyond the outer harbor marker. The water in the inner harbor was choppy but out past the buoy the ocean was gray, grim and forbidding.

Like him she seemed to relax during the sail and she let down her guard enough for him to learn that she was a divorcee. He asked her why she hadn't reverted to her maiden name and she said with a laugh that she had. She also seemed to enjoy his pleasure at taking the helm, and impressed with his proficiency she wrapped herself in her sweatshirt and quietly took in the scenery. The wind was brisk and the current strong but the boat felt like a toy under his control as he manipulated the sails and the rudder and began tacking a zig zag course back to shore.

She had already given him the details about his meeting with the arms rep, stressing the fact that she had vouched for his skills as a weapons expert. His expertise in appraising weapons and his overall knowledge of the commodity could be valuable and increase his appeal as a trading partner over the long term, although it could also put the dealers at a disadvantage when the time came to agree on a price.

He risked mentioning his plan to charter a boat for the offshore passenger pick-up. He asked if she might know someone prudent enough to take such a job.

"Someone you have to trust? Forget it! That's no good. What, were you planning to pay for discretion? No way."

Undaunted, he figured that he could find a suitable boat for hire, and he regretted bringing the matter to her attention.

She did not let it drop. Becoming excited, she said, "You know, this could be a god-send, a golden opportunity. Yes, it's perfect! I know just the outfit to do the job."

Makepeace no longer wished to divulge any additional information about his plan. But she didn't need to know any details; in fact, to suit her purposes, the less she knew the better. She smiled and smote him with the full impact of her charm.

"I have a certain, uh, competitor who works out of Nahant. Get him to make the drop for you. When the job is done, you can kill two birds with one stone."

"What do you mean?" he asked, fully captivated.

"You don't want the captain to talk, right? So when your passenger is safely aboard your vessel, you sink him."

"Oh! I sink him! Simple as that, is it?"

"Yes." She moved closer to him. "Simple as that. Knock him out, shoot him, doesn't matter; then flood the boat to the scuppers and watch it sink." Her breath was in his face now.

It made sense. Her idea was brutally elegant. It would succeed in delivering the passenger and furthermore it would impress upon him the seriousness of his endeavor, likely scaring the shit out of him.

And it would be the means by which he secured a new permanent status, as deceased. The accident, if it could be arranged as such, would be reported as the cause of the American's disappearance. He couldn't buy a cleaner getaway.

They had reached a suitable mooring point and weighed anchor.

She was running her fingers lightly over the hair on his chest when he agreed to her proposal. In moments he was following her below deck where, on a cramped u-shaped love seat, he had the most satisfying sex in the most uncomfortable positions he had ever attempted.

CHAPTER 38

The mark that branded Tweed as a dope smoker was less conspicuous for its appearance than it was noticeable for its odor. It consisted of a delta of discolored skin on his right thumb-tip, with a corresponding resin smudge on his forefinger. These he rubbed together in the manner of an impecunious miser.

Some smokers prized their "built-in roach-clips" to the extent that they didn't even flinch when the last of a budhead flamed out of existence between their fingers. Either they had developed heavy callouses on their oft-charred fingertips or their nerve-endings had been burned to insensitivity.

But Tweed felt conflicting impulses regarding the signs that were evident on his hands. Self-consciously aware of the sweet herbal aroma, he feared that others might take notice of it as well. It was like waving a flag and shouting, "Hey, I'm a pothead!"

He didn't need that kind of attention.

Then again it was like a subtle badge, a tattoo that signified his membership in an elite club. A lot of people might have tar stains on their fingertips but how many could boast that theirs were caused by Acapulco gold resin?

In his case it couldn't be helped; when he smoked the gold, resin came bubbling out of the end of the joint like honey dripping from a straw. It was delicious.

He had acquired the habit of sniffing his fingers like a man whose hands were anointed with fresh pussy juice. Yet he used every means to eliminate the traces. He rubbed his fingers over coarse surfaces to abrade them raw, and rolled fresh mint leaves between them. He took to stripping evergreen branches and placing the handfuls of needles in his pockets. In this way he deodorized his jacket and had a ready supply of pine needles to manually pulverize in order to mask his digital funk.

Simply handling the gold and rolling a joint left a sticky coating on his fingers, and when he peered at it closely he noticed fine feathery red hairs and minuscule crystalline granules embedded in the oil.

The second hit of the reefer was always the best, for the first was not inhaled, but only used to burn off the twisted tip of rice paper; and subsequent hits started to taste of accumulated resin. The smoke became harsher as the joint diminished in length until it became a roach that had filtered and distilled the essence of all of the previous hits.

Usually he smoked each joint down to nothing, but occasionally he saved the roaches in a matchbox and then tore them open to fill a new joint consisting solely of roach weed.

Carmine Gunther was a pipe and bong man, and he claimed that a purist like himself appreciated the flavor by placing only a pinch of weed in the bowl at a time. Each toke was savored and appraised and the high was also evaluated gradually, the better to avoid over-indulgence. But Tweed had a fundamental objection to pipes- they smelled worse than his fingertips and they were difficult to conceal.

Carmine himself had recently experienced the awkwardness of carrying a bowl. He was entering his house after partaking in an afternoon head session at Arbs Park with Tweed and a couple of other friends. By chance he encountered a lazy yellow-jacket bee that was living out the last days of its life in autumn-induced slow motion. Somehow it flew into the collar of his heavy woolen sweater, where, becoming trapped and disoriented, it began to frantically buzz about. At that moment Carmine, who was walking in through the back door and hallway, noticed that his parents and a neighborhood couple were seated around the kitchen table, playing cards.

Everyone looked up from their hands to greet him just as the bee stung him on the back of the neck. The searing injection at his hairline caused Carmine to yelp loudly, and to the amazement of everyone in the room, he suddenly tore his sweater off over his head and began beating it upon the floor.

His compact Meerschaum had until then been safely hidden in his shirt pocket, but suddenly it fell to the floor and skittered to the center of the room, where it spun like a top on the linoleum.

Conversation had ceased and all eyes were upon Carmine as he retrieved his pipe, recovered his sweater and his composure and simply said, "Bee sting! Gonna need some baking soda!" before dashing off to his room.

When he heard the story, Tweed said that the incident proved that bowls were a nuisance. Carmine replied that it proved nothing about pipes, but rather he took it as a punishment from God. Tweed replied that it was more likely that if the Lord had acted through the bee, then He had stung Carmine only in order to force his parents to become aware of his dope habit. It might have been painful, but it was constructive.

Now, sitting on the brow of the hill in Arbs Park at his favorite bogarting site, Tweed started to chuckle as he imagined a fable originating: *The Story of The Boy and the Bee*. But as he tried to work it out he became stuck on the ending. "And the moral of the story is"…something appropriately pertinent or pertinently appropriate.

After smoking a chubby number to his head, the resulting high was like what he imagined an out of body experience might be. Gazing up at the clouds that were illuminated by the setting sun, he felt that it was like the moment in *The Wizard of Oz*, when Dorothy's farmhouse had come to rest in Munchkinland, and her visual world suddenly shifted into full sensual color. That was the effect of weed upon Tweed, a subtle shift into another reality, where everything was more vivid, as if his senses had become fine-tuned.

There on the hillside he began his listening game, trying to isolate sounds that were very near to him, and then expanding his awareness until he was simultaneously listening to all of the noises within his range of hearing. From crickets at his boot heels to jet engines passing overhead at fifty thousand feet.

The game took him away from himself, and he imagined soaring down the hill a few feet over the grass like a low-flying Superman, led by the rich cacophony arising from the vicinity, a mixture of highway and traffic, factory and hospital, school and church and neighborhood noises.

He began to see cops and children, trucks, geese and insects, houses, trees and cars, fields and rivers and highways. The thrum of humanity and nature took precedence over his own heartbeat and breathing; and as if in counterpoint, he heard a tuneless electromagnetic whine ringing off the grid of high tension wires, telephone poles and radio transmitters.

Overwhelmed, he lay upon his back physically and stared at the darkening sky; but mentally he was soaring far and away from the planet's surface, toward a distant group of stars that were visible through a patchwork of high clouds. He panicked, and began to look for signposts, tree tops, anything he might seize to slow his ascent into the heavens. But he had already risen above the trees and he was rapidly reaching the altitude of hawk flight.

With a gasp he tore at the grass on the ground by his sides and pulled his awareness down to earth, feeling the tingle of circulation restoring his limbs, and the congested rale in his lungs. Safe, whole, sane but still significantly wasted, he sighed and relaxed.

The pot was almost too good, but well worth the high if one could handle it.

When he wasn't stoned, Tweed experienced everything straight-line, one-to-one, on its own merits. There was seemingly a linear sensual connection between him and his environment. Whereas when he was stoned, his experience was sensually fuller, more rounded. The connection between him and any external stimulus was enhanced, augmented, inflamed. It was as if when looking at a given object, his vision encompassed a greater peripheral awareness.

And despite this somewhat frightening episode, he was becoming increasingly adept at functioning while under the influence. It seemed that when he was stoned, schooldays were less of a bore and homework less of a chore. His enjoyment in listening to music was also greatly enhanced, but television, which had never held much appeal for him, seemed confusing and prone to inciting headaches.

He wondered if either of his parents had ever tried smoking pot. Knowing them, they wouldn't want to be caught dead near the stuff. Still he imagined his father explaining the possession of a bag to a police officer. He'd cast the matter in terms the cop could understand.

"Well, officer, you see, it's like this…when cops work a security detail at a gate for a concert or a sporting event they frisk people as they pass into the arena, and sometimes they discover and confiscate a certain amount of contraband. Now, say another cop comes along and sees one of these fellows standing there with all of this contraband. What is he going to think? Was he doing his duty, holding all of this stuff, or might he be holding personal stash, for his own consumption, as it were?

"You see, it's like that for me, being a parent, because sometimes parents and cops have similar obligations. I came across this stuff going through my kid's pockets, for the laundry don't you know, and tried to do the responsible thing, taking an illegal substance away from the boy. Now, you can't blame me for holding it until I got a chance to destroy it, can you?"

No, it was hardly likely that the old man would recognize pot, let alone know what to do with it. Beer or liquor, on the contrary, he would recognize instantly, and if he were to find Tweed with any imbibable spirits he would confiscate them immediately. And he would suck them down not long afterwards.

Having realized that his father was a big drinker, Tweed had resolved some time ago in a pact with his brother Keiran never to abuse alcohol. He couldn't say that he would abstain completely, but that he would never permit himself to get to the point where his father was now, and where his mother and older brothers had been as well.

It was plain to see that the trouble Buck and Mack had experienced on account of alcohol was at least partially caused by the example that Des had set for them. Yet he failed to consider himself a problem drinker; not Des Kelley, businessman and pub owner, even as he pointed to problems that others had with booze.

Tweed would never forget the time when the police had arrived at the door looking for Des. It was about a year after the family had moved from Jamaica Center, and Mack, the oldest, was almost 16. He was rather large for his age, and the cops had him in the back seat of the cruiser, parked in front of the house with the emergency lights flashing to ensure the complete attention of curious neighbors.

It seemed that a group of boys had taken up a collection and persuaded Mack to try to buy beer at the package store in the square. The store owner had no problem selling a case of Pabst to the friendly curly-haired teenager, in fact he hadn't even thought to ask for ID. But when the cops saw the same boy carrying the beer down the street on his shoulder, they detained and interrogated him. Officer Rima figured Mack for 16 because of his baby face, and he might have gone easy on him if he had told the truth when asked his age. But Mack lied, opting to try to pull one over on the greasy-looking rookie officer, by spouting out an improbable birth date for himself that would have had him clearing 18 years.

Rima offered to hand Mack over to Des to punish as he saw fit. From his point of view it was a waste of time to bring the boy into the station, fill out a ream of paperwork, process him into a cell and an arraignment only to have the parents come down and bail him out anyway. But Des was humiliated to see the patrol car in front of his house with the lights blazing and his son cuffed and hang-dog in the back seat. He refused to accept the officer's kind offer. He said, "Take him...he's all yours...I don't want him here." At the time Tweed was shocked, but not half as much as Officer Rima was, and not nearly as much as Mack.

Later in the evening his father did indeed retrieve Mack from the station, whereupon he brought him home and whipped him with a belt mercilessly from one end of the house to the other. And Mack hadn't even had a beer.

It wasn't without a smack of irony that the memory of the event led Tweed to consider adding another modern fable to his growing anthology, this one entitled: *The Tale of the Boy and the Beer.* And the moral for this one was- "Quit while you're a head!"

CHAPTER 39

Like pugilists tapping gloves at the commencement of a match and then warily circling away from each other to a respectful distance, 80 Makepeace and Des Kelley met at the biz club on Wednesday night to watch the Bruins game and to discuss matters of mutual importance.

"You've been scarce, 80."

"Out and about, around and about."

"So, you're 'on the go', eh?"

"Well, you know what they say about idle hands, Des."

"I do indeed, for you'll never see me sitting on mine." Des took a long swig from his glass of stout.

"That's for sure, Des, because you're always sitting on your arse."

"Alright, now," he replied quickly, wiping his mouth on the back of his sleeve, "Tell me, what have you been up to?"

"No good, to tell the truth, my friend. But I have been up to Marblehead and up to Cape Ann and up to Lynn Shore Drive as well."

"Have you now?" Des would patiently endure.

"Yes, and I've also been talking with some brokers about last minute freight and supplies I'll be wanting to load aboard the Cor before I ship out."

Des was not prone to emotional responses. Although he had been quite anxious to receive an update from Makepeace he would be satisfied with a minimal report. His face showed neither relief nor pleasure and rather than look at Makepeace he gazed at the television.

Harris Toole had brought his own black and white set from home so he and his patrons could watch the game. A television set was not normally part of the decor in the bar, but then, only rarely were any of the furnishings improved or brought up to date. For example, the clock was still set on daylight savings time, and the only calendar in the place was inexplicably pinned open to April 1969. Perhaps that was the month when time stood still in the biz club. Or maybe Harris fancied the featured picture of a New England pasture blanketed with wildflowers so much that he had forgone the promise of other months, like a man infatuated with a centerfold girl.

"It'll be a costly load, this last one."

Makepeace waited for a response and Des nodded.

"So, I'll be needing the cash, Des." Again he waited.

Des also waited for a moment before saying, "You didn't say how much, 80."

"Right, well, I was working off of your order."

"And? Did you manage to get everything?" He might as well have been discussing the groceries.

"No trouble there, none at all. Now, I'd like to arrange to make the actual buy for Friday."

"Fine, yes that sounds good. But I do have some concerns. I mean, am I going to see a sample of the merchandise?"

"Well, Des, this isn't a bloody flea market; and besides, it's my job to look out for your interests in this deal."

"Uh huh. I'll tell you right now that I want to see that freight before it goes aboard. I'm not going to pay for a boatload of cargo sight unseen and merely hope for the best."

"See the cargo, Des? You want to touch it, handle it, do you? Would you like to load the crates, too? I'm sure we can use an extra pair of hands."

"That's well and good because if it were up to me, I'd turn each and every box out on the pier and account for every bolt, clip and cotter pin."

Makepeace snorted behind his glass.

"You think that's funny, now?"

"I'm just trying to picture you there with all of your crates open, up to your elbows in it, when the harbor patrol comes along and asks you what you're doing. . . . 'Inventory' says you!"

"So what about it, 80? Am I going to see what I'm paying for or not?"

"I'd prefer it if you would limit your contact with the consignment, and it's only for your own good. But if you insist, I'll see about getting you in there somehow. It's short notice, understand. I mean, we've only got a limited window of opportunity."

Hearing Makepeace acquiesce, Des almost regretted pushing him, as he instinctively wanted to keep the relationship between them positive and amiable. But he reminded himself that it would be better to smuggle the cash itself into Ireland than to hand it over for a boatload of empty promises. This affair had seemed odd enough all along to warrant taking extra precautions and when it came down to cash on the barrel, he wanted to see the goods.

The rabbit-ear reception was poor in the bar but Des could see that the Boston Bruins had concluded their game with the Pittsburgh Penguins with a tie score, 5-5.

CHAPTER 40

A miserable series of indistinct days shuffled past, but Tweed hardly noticed as he was hopelessly disturbed, out of it, fucked up, and he had smoked hardly any dope. It had been almost a week and the idea was finally taking hold that Sam had dumped him and she was not coming back. At first he had told himself that the trouble would blow over, that she would settle down and forgive him, and that their relationship would resume where it had left off. But when he had finally confronted her after days of searching her out in school, she had been cold and succinct, saying, "Forget it, Weed! You're no good for me. I mean, it's not just because I got kicked off the chorus. It's because you will always care more for your friends and your pot than you would for me."

He sensed the finality of her words but failed to appreciate their meaning or their sincerity. Wasn't the fact that he was no good for her one of the reasons that had made him so appealing to her in the first place? He was a white Irish kid from the wrong side of town. Of course he was no good for her, but that's what made it so sexy. When she said that she hadn't broken up with him because of the chorus thing, he figured that she meant that it was because of the chorus incident, otherwise, why mention it? And as for his friends, the weed, and her, well, they comprised a set that he would not normally lump together. There were his friends, there was the dope, and there was Sam, and he refused to weigh out his love for each of them like bags on a scale.

Yet despite his inability to understand it, her refusal to see him was breaking his heart. He had thought that they made a good couple; that they could learn a lot from each other, and that she would enjoy sharing experiences with him. He desperately wanted another chance to explain to her how he felt and to encourage her to reconsider. She could be making a big mistake.

***

He no longer needed to escort Sam to the YMCA, but he proceeded to the same neighborhood on Friday afternoon because he had made a commitment to deliver a couple of bags to Rod at the arcade.

Rod was obviously playing middle-man now, scrounging a head stash out of a couple of dimes that he then split up into indeterminate amounts in miniature manila envelopes that he sold for five dollars apiece.

Since Tweed was accustomed to selling his weed in plastic sandwich bags so his customers could plainly see and feel the product before buying it, he was dismayed at the prospect of folks buying the same stuff sight unseen in mean, grubby little envelopes. Then it occurred to him that someone who had forked over a fin for a palm-full of dope could in turn divide that quantity again, and sell it in joints, perhaps even adding a few grains of tobacco to fatten them up. However the law of diminishing returns states that there are only so many ways one can split a bag.

He arrived at the arcade early and decided to wait outside until Rod's shift ended. The day was raw and bitter cold and the sun was lost behind the glaring screen of an overcast sky. The streets and traffic and buildings were only distinct in shades of gray, and pedestrians hustled by, faceless behind turned up collars and scarves. Sparse flurries of snow flakes hung swirling in the air as if they needed directions to the ground, and passing vehicles drew them along like trains of fairy dust.

Sitting alone on a bus-stop bench, Tweed wondered where his willful independence had gone, the feeling that usually fortified him in moments like these.

A boy about Tweed's age sat on the bench beside him and struck up a conversation. He outweighed Tweed by a good hundred pounds, had a bushy Afro, and despite the cold, wore only a tan barracuda, blue jeans and pristine white basketball shoes.

"Hey, man," said the stranger, "I bet you're looking for some good hash, huh?"

"Hash?" asked Tweed, surprised.

"Yeah, like this." He was holding a gummy ball of some dark substance between his thumb and forefinger.

"You holding?" asked Tweed.

"I can get some, if you want. What do you need? A couple of grams? An ounce?"

"Let me check it out..."

"Man, all's I got is this little bit. You want some I can get it for you."

"Where?" He sniffed, trying to get a whiff of the hash if that was what it was.

"Right over there." He indicated the arcade.

"No shit? How much for what you got?"

"Five bucks. Tell you what. You give me a five spot and I'll go in there and get you one. Then afterwards we can do a couple of hits out here on the bench."

"I'll go with you."

"No man, that's not cool. This dude don't like meeting people, you know what I mean?"

"I don't have a bowl," said Tweed.

"No prob. I'll borrow one from a friend who's playing pinball in there, and I'll even fill it first if you do, too."

"Yeah, all right." He fished in his pocket for a five and handed it to his new acquaintance, saying, "Get me a good one."

Suddenly Tweed's senses came up to full alert as he watched the kid waddle across the street and into the arcade. He couldn't believe that he had ignored the advice of his friends and mentors, and broken a cardinal rule of street transactions by trusting a stranger to make a buy for him. His nervous paranoia had him standing and staring at the door to the arcade like an anxious bettor watching for his horse to round the last bend at the track.

Within five minutes he suspected that he had been scammed. He walked over to the arcade and entered, not really expecting to find the con-artist within.

Rod was just preparing to leave, thrusting his good arm into the sleeve of a greasy, dandruff-powdered jacket, and struggling to drape his other shoulder as if with a cloak. The empty sleeve was fastened to his pocket with a safety-pin.

"Hey, Rod, you see a chubby black kid come in here a few minutes ago?"

"Who, Rollo? Yes, I saw him. He ducked out the back. Don't tell me he got you, too!" Rod chuckled and leered at Tweed's reddening face.

"Got me for five bucks." Tweed was indignant. "Where can I find him?"

"Aw, forget it, man. Live and learn, live and learn. What'd he try to sell you? It wasn't oregano, you'd know better than that."

"Hash, or shoe polish, I don't know." He was becoming increasingly irate.

"Fuck it, Tweed, my boy. Five bucks you can lose. You're lucky that's all he got."

"Fuck that, man! Where can I find him?"

"You don't want to know. I can promise you that if you did find him, he'd be surrounded by a dozen of his buddies, and besides, he probably already spent your cash."

Tweed recalled a day in gym class when he had been paired with a similar chubby black kid for a wrestling match. When it looked as though Tweed was getting the upper hand, a number of other kids had piled on to bring him down to the mat. But Tweed stood his own, throwing them off one by one until he was victorious.

It didn't matter how much money was at stake; he'd fight to get it back even if it had only been bus fare. It was the principle of the thing. He came down here to sell dope honestly and he wasn't about to be taken for a chump.

"I just want to talk to him, Rod. Do you know where I can find him or not? If you want me to keep coming here you had better fess up."

"Alright, you crazy motherfucker, follow me."

Rod led him out through a back door that Tweed had never seen before, to a street that was darker and dirtier than the one from which he had come. It was as if the townhouses on the main drag were erected solely as a front to hide the squalor behind them.

A couple of elderly winos lay like piles of rags on a sidewalk grate that issued billowing plumes of steam. Litter and broken glass was strewn everywhere like some kind of perverse urban landscaping decor, and graffiti adorned the store fronts, billboards, bus stops and parked cars.

"How much further, Rod?"

Limping ahead in an off-kilter shuffle, Rod mumbled in reply.

"What'd you say?"

"I said we're here. Now you wait while I go in and find Rollo, the fat fuck. Let me see if I can get your five bucks back before you go and make things worse."

Throbbing disco music shook the windows of an old Chinese laundry that had been converted to a smoke shop. No one had ever bothered to remove the original signage, an incongruous display of Chinese characters that obscured the glossy ads for Salem, Winston, and Kool cigarettes that had been placed in the shop windows.

Tweed waited outside while Rod swung the door open with an awkward bodily motion and lurched inside to confront the group of teenagers who were gathered around a rack of Playboy and Jet magazines.

A moment of panic flash-froze Tweed's organs as he imagined Rod slipping out another back door and abandoning him to the ghetto gutters. But through the frosted glass he saw him addressing the kids sternly, and gesturing widely with his one arm. Rollo stepped forth and it appeared as though money changed hands. Soon there were grins on all of the faces and a couple of kids clapped Rod on the back as he exited the store waving a crumpled bill in his hand. Rollo and the others followed Rod out to the street and Rod said, "Don't say a word!" below his breath as he passed Tweed.

Sure enough a round of catcalls and insults ensued as Tweed gritted his teeth and pursued his elder friend back toward the pool hall. "Yo, homeboy! Go on back to where you come from! You don't belong 'round here!"

"Hey, whitey! Your mama's calling!"

"Next time we git you for everything you got!"

"Shit, man!" said Tweed, talking to Rod's back, "Is this the way it's got to be? I'm not prejudiced, for Pete's sake!"

"No? But they are, my boy. Look around. Imagine living here and ask yourself if it would affect your attitude. Your white-ass Sunday school niceties have no place here."

Rod was right. The Kelleys had always been poor, and had started in the public housing projects when they came to America, but the projects in Jamaica Center and the streets in Rossie were clean and well-kept. This neighborhood looked like it was at war with itself and the city. The graffiti could have been the inspiration for a Jackson Pollock painting. It was difficult to imagine walking to school along trash covered sidewalks, stepping over homeless individuals and drunks, and not having the Arbs Park to explore and play in. He began to question whether he even wanted to return here to deal bags to Rod and his cronies. Why expose himself to this blight, this despair and decay?

On second thought, Rod was a twisted, crippled and wasted reflection of his environment, yet he had become a friend whom Tweed valued for his street-wisdom and his slurred sagacities. Was he that far removed from the biz club clientèle whom his father regarded as esteemed comrades?

When they arrived at the arcade, Tweed was anxious to finish his business with Rod and to get out of there as soon as possible.

Suddenly he did not feel comfortable in the dim noisy pool hall where the air smelled of stale cigarettes and the floor was sticky with spilled soda pop. He felt the stares of the pool players and avoided physical contact with the pinballers as he retraced his steps to the front door, where freedom and fresh air awaited.

But just as he passed the front counter, he noticed a familiar face on one of the kids who was changing a bill for quarters.

It was one of the Byrne boys, a son of JC Byrne, Des Kelley's business associate from Cu's Pub in the Mission district. His father had told him that JC was dying of cancer, and he could not in good conscience walk past one of his sons without greeting him.

"Hey, ahm, Mike, is it? Remember me? Tweed Kelley from Rossie?"

Startled, the young man turned, and after a moment his expression turned to one of recognition. "Sure! It's Mickey, not Mike. I do remember you! From one of those lame meetings your old man held at the bar. At Cu's, right? Sure! How are you, Tweed? What are you doing here?"

"Just hanging, man, but I'd ask the same of you! Aren't you a long way from home?"

"From home, yes, but the old man's bar is just a few blocks from here, and the place where I work is even closer."

"Oh? You work around here?" With his curly red hair, freckled face and innocent smirk, Mickey didn't appear to be much older than Tweed.

"Yeah, up at the Esso under the El. You should come and check it out sometime."

Esso gas stations had been officially renamed as Exxon in 1972, and yet many of the local stations still retained their original signage; but even at stations where the signs had been changed, customers were generally slow in adopting the new brand identity.

"What do you do there?"

"Pump gas, what else?" Mickey smirked again. "Tell you what. I'm heading back to finish my shift in about fifteen minutes. Why don't you come with me? I'm only on until five and we can hang out and goof off."

Tweed agreed, and by the time he returned from Rod's apartment, Mickey was ready to leave the arcade.

Mickey had allowed himself only ten minutes for the walk back to work so he had to hustle. Tweed was hard-pressed to keep up with him.

"I thought you said it was only a few blocks!" he panted.

"Not far from here, now. You see that billboard? It's only a few blocks after that!"

All told it must have been two miles, anyway. When they arrived Tweed realized that he was now on the border of the Mission district, a good two or three stops down the inbound commuter line from the YMCA.

Situated on a busy street corner directly below the elevated rails, the gas station primarily served a local cab stand and a number of other commercial accounts. Only a small percentage of the business came from commuters or residents in the local community because relatively few of them owned private cars. Inner-city folk depended upon municipal buses and trains for transportation.

Mickey showed Tweed how he spent his time between customers: shooting paper darts across the intersection with compressed air, whistling at any young ladies who happened to walk by, reading newspapers and comic books. Tweed told himself that if he weren't dealing pot he would like to have a job like Mickey's; carefree, independent, and within walking distance of a pinball arcade.

Yet the icing on the cake, as far as he was concerned, became apparent after Mickey had waited upon a particular customer who had pulled in for a fill-up.

Tweed noticed instantly that the driver of the car was none other than his former girl-friend's former chorus director, the woman who had summarily kicked Sam off the squad, thus dashing her hopes for attending the competition in Washington DC with her teammates, and ruining his hopes for making it with Sam.

After the woman had driven away and Mickey had returned to his usual seat on a stack of tires with his feet up on the cash register stand, Tweed told him Sam's sad story. He concluded saying, "I wish I could have waited on that bitch...I'd have filled her tank with washer fluid."

Mickey folded his arms and thought for a minute.

"You can do better than that!" he said, retrieving a charge slip from a Rolodex stored beneath the register. The slip represented the chorus director's account with the gas station, and on it Tweed saw a series of charges for fill-ups, all consistent as to gallons dispensed and dates of service.

"So what?" he asked, wondering what advantage the slip might give to him.

"So, you charge more gas to her account!"

"Big deal! So she owes more money! What good is that?"

"Well, for some guys, doing her out of some cash would be a form of revenge. But for guys like us, spending her money is even better, wouldn't you say so? What we do is add a few charges to her account, careful not to make it look too weird, you know? Then, since the station is theoretically collecting money for gas that was never sold, we can pocket the difference!"

There was a certain malevolent logic to the scheme that Tweed appreciated. Together the boys worked out and entered into the unsuspecting customer's record a reasonable schedule of additional fraudulent charges; and to show his faith and certainty in the success of the scheme, Mickey took thirty dollars from the register and handed it to Tweed, free and clear. He stuck an additional thirty in his own back pocket for good measure.

"OK, we can't do this again for another few weeks, or at least until the bills go out at the end of the month."

Shit, Tweed could take a cab home if he wanted, and when the time came, he did. He liked Mickey's cleverness and self-confidence and agreed to meet him again at the arcade on the following Friday. He also resolved to bring a couple of fine joints, because Mickey, who was probably stressed out over his father's illness, could stand to get fucked up, and Tweed owed it to him.

CHAPTER 41

Carmine and Tweed took a stroll through the Arbs Park on Saturday morning to have a talk and a smoke. The woods were glistening after a relatively benign autumn rain storm that had raged throughout the previous night. It was the kind of weather that might have been far more inclement a couple of months later, when the same blustery winds and gusting precipitation would have resulted in drifting snow.

To keep himself from moaning about his romantic troubles, Tweed was ragging about the clubhouse. On numerous occasions he had insisted that it was essential for the perpetuation of the clubhouse that the regulars respect the place, keep it clean, and avoid telling others about it. He had been especially firm in his conviction about the latter, and he had tried to convince his friends that bringing outsiders to the garage was a sure way to ruin it for everybody.

But over the past month or so the clubhouse had gained an elevated degree of notoriety and had become a Mecca for seekers of weed. Since they were drawn by the fame of his good deals and abundant supply, then perhaps Tweed was partially responsible. However it had never been his intention to have his patrons lining up at the door to the place where he liked to kick back and party. He had taken care to personally deliver bags to his best customers, and to make regular rounds so that people would know where to find him without infringing upon his privacy.

The situation was getting out of hand, Tweed insisted, and he admitted that he had already started to contemplate abandoning the garage all together.

He and Carmine thought that they were walking aimlessly, yet before long they arrived at the top of the hill near Tweed's favorite spot for watching occasional sunsets. There they came upon a tree that had fallen out of a proud grove of hemlocks that arose from the top of the ridge like the spines on a hedgehog's back.

The peculiar thing about the tree was not so much that it had succumbed to a storm of no particular violence, but that it had landed with its top resting on the lowest branch of an adjacent tree. The dead tree had snapped at about 8 feet above the root line, and the now horizontal trunk formed a beam that was over 60 feet in length. Its branches, having been firmly embedded in the soil by the weight of the fall, had formed an even row of supports like wall studs on 24 inch centers.

In short, nature had provided a wonderful new lodging in the woods, featuring a room that was 40 feet long, 8 feet high and 12 feet across. Tweed saw it as a naturally superior alternative to the now defunct clubhouse in Mr. Wolff's garage.

With a mighty tree-trunk ridge beam and rafters, the whole structure looked like the inverted frame of a wooden ship that had been thatched with fresh pine boughs.

The enclosure was remarkably cozy, inspiring the boys to hurry home to gather whatever items they could find to make it more comfortable. They returned later in the afternoon with a couple of chairs, a telephone cable spool table, and an assortment of produce crates. They arranged the "furniture" at the base of the living tree, under the narrow end of the trunk beam, and then gathered a pile of rocks with which they created a fire pit. The fireplace added a degree of comfort for the chilly late October days and also served as a focal point and a source of entertainment.

Tweed and Carmine claimed possession of the new hangout by virtue of having discovered and decorated it, and they dubbed it "the fort". The feeling of sole proprietorship was further reinforced by the isolation of the site in a section of the park that rarely saw visitors. Having decided to move into the new ready-made hangout, Tweed simply had to find a safe place to store his stash.

CHAPTER 42

The rain storm that had toppled an ancient tree in Arbs Park had also blown the Cor Mor into harbor. Fishing boats working off the coast of New England typically encountered such weather in mid-autumn, with sustained winds of 22 MPH, an average temperature of 40 degrees, limited visibility and steady rain. For an Irish crew it was like coming home.

AD Makepeace heard the news about his boat in a phone call early on Saturday morning from his crew mate Reggie, who also reminded him to pack his duffel bags. Reggie's girlfriend was clearing the crap out of her car so that she could drive the two men and all of their gear to the dock. She wanted to dump them there unceremoniously and avoid a tearful separation.

Makepeace planned to first greet the crew and stow his gear. Then after he inspected the boat he would give his men a couple of days of R&R, restricting them to the general vicinity and requiring them to check in regularly. Reggie was to stay on board and watch the boat, alone at first, since Makepeace would be going to meet his arms contact and then to a final tryst with Heather Harrad-Farquhar in the evening.

The time had come to get the money from Des, and to explain to him that he needed it now even though the transaction might not occur for a couple of days, because he could not afford to return to Rossie in the meantime. Furthermore, Des was packing for his own voyage, collecting his bags and his travel documents, passport, and tickets, and making last-minute preparations. Makepeace would have to convince Des that despite his desire to attend the purchase and to inspect the merchandise, it would be counter-productive to get involved when he had such pressing demands upon his time. He'd vow to keep Des updated as to his progress and to notify him the moment his freight was secure in the vessel's hold.

He located his man by following the sound of shouting from his quarters in the attic of the Kelley home down to its source below. It sounded like the bellowing of a bullfrog who rolled his R's. There wasn't much time left until his own arse would have to be rolling so he trotted downstairs and found Des in the sewing room on the second floor flipping through a rack of clothing on hangers.

"Jesus, Mary and Joseph!" he roared, "Am I blind or are you hiding my striped shirt, Christine?"

He turned abruptly, expecting to see his wife, and met Makepeace face to face.

"It's probably in your bleedin' bag," he said, helpfully. Just then Chris yelled from the kitchen, "It's already packed!"

"Well, I'm off then, old man," said Makepeace. "I've got Keiran hauling my bags down to the stoop." He had never bothered to unpack, having bought clothes and borrowed them when needed instead of pulling them out of his luggage.

"So that's it, is it? And when will I hear from you?"

"Hear me now, Des. I'll need the money before I go." He held out his hand as if Des would have it in his pocket.

"The money?" Des bluffed, "I thought that you might have forgotten."

"Hardly. And if I did, then my associates would remind me rather strenuously."

"Right…" he smiled. "So I give you my money now, and then what? I see the shipment tonight?"

"Honestly, Des, I can't say when the deal will happen, it's just…"

"So when you find out, you'll call me right away, then. No sense carrying all of that cash around." He lowered his voice. "I mean, we're living in a world of danger, and uncertainty."

Makepeace didn't know whether to bully or bluster.

"I'm afraid I can't come back here to pick it up later. I'll be either on the boat or seeing to business. I must be ready at a moment's notice."

Des seemed to speak through his stare. "I understand, 80. It's not the way we did things in the past, but then, this is a unique circumstance. We're not in the old country."

"That's for sure, Des. It's a new world."

It took another fifteen minutes of gentle persuasion and cajoling before Des relinquished his cash. By the time he stopped talking, Makepeace felt low and shameful. He had wheedled like a Liverpool street hustler until he convinced Des to act against his better judgment, as if he would have done the same thing if he were in his shoes. The shame wasn't so much getting the money out of Des, it was the whole arrangement. Caught between working for the British and working for the Irish, and trying to get over on everybody, including Des.

If he had simply pursued the mission to trace Loyalist arms sources in America, and to report his findings, then the additional deal with Des might not have been such a bad idea, even if he had ultimately been forced to admit to the British that he had facilitated an arms sale for the Irish to boot.

The situation became rife with intrigue when he added American emigre Darrager to the equation. And yet if Makepeace hadn't originally reported about the IRA's plan to recruit the American weapons expert, then the mission would never have taken place.

He had offered the use of his own boat in order to provide a secure ferry service so the American wouldn't be traced at the usual points of departure. The only other option had been for Darrager to travel in disguise, incognito; but that method required some subtlety on his part, and inevitably left a paper trail.

Makepeace had been doing odd jobs for the Republicans for some time, but until now he had never been in such a position of trust. The successful completion of this deal would enhance his reputation immeasurably. The irony was that what would look like a success to the Irish would also be a victory for the British, because they would soon know all about Darrager, his whereabouts and his prospects as well.

If Makepeace owed Des anything for his faith and hospitality, it would be repaid when he completed this job and delivered the freight to the proper destination. The ends would justify the means.

He paused on his way out to thank Christine again, to complement her on her beauty and cooking and the loveliness of her home. She acted cool and polite, while Des was practically shooing him out the door.

He also wanted to shake hands with the boys, and Keiran was willing but the younger one was nowhere to be found.

It amused him that Christine checked the street through the curtains before she opened the door, and he noted the surreptitious manner in which she scanned the perimeter as he climbed into the car beside Reggie.

Taking a last look back at his gracious hosts, he saw Des standing primly with his arm around Christine's waist, and he noticed the tight look of tension draining from her face. No waving or smiling, rather, it was if they were watching the tax man leave after performing a lengthy audit.

Well practiced in packing for overseas trips, Des worked methodically, placing items of clothing one by one into the deep wells of the luggage lying open on his bed. The heavy antique alligator-hide bags smelled of storage, like moth balls and attic dust. In their time they had traveled tens of thousands of miles to places diverse and exotic, stowed in the cargo holds of ocean liners, airplanes, trains, cabs, coaches and cars. Yet they were none the worse for wear, although the satin linings were frayed and the heavy grips were stiff and brittle. The exteriors of the bags were mottled with layers of shipping labels, some intact, some partially peeled, randomly featuring the names of various countries, ports and cities. Des had received the luggage as a gift from a friend in Lisbon who told him that he had found them in a Beirut hotel.

Although he was packing for a month-long visit, Des was no tourist; on the contrary, he was, in effect returning home. In fact he had an advantage because for him packing was mostly a matter of remembering what he did not have to bring, whereas the average tourist worries about forgetting what he did have to bring. He did not bother with common travel necessities, nor did he carry any of the comforts of home, for they would all be waiting for him at his destination.

Aside from his clothing, which he rolled carefully into neat cylinders and stacked like scrolls, the bulk of the space in his luggage would be reserved for gifts and parcels that he would deliver to and for friends.

He was however obsessed with one detail, a part of the process that had become successively ritualized over the years- the selection from his extensive collection of religious memorabilia of items he deemed appropriate for the trip at hand. He kept a sample assortment on display at all times, proudly integrated with the decor in his bedroom. As if waiting for inspiration to guide his selection he stood in front of the dresser, perusing an array of scapulars, medals, cinctures, relics and rosary beads.

Although these were holy objects and Des was a pious Catholic, there were a number of factors affecting his decision that were not entirely spiritual in nature. There were aesthetic considerations; especially considering the size, textures, shapes and colors of the items, and concerns for taste, pragmatism and superstition.

Most of the items were designed to be attached to clothing and for the most part served to identify the wearer as a Catholic or more specifically as a member of a particular group or lay community among the faithful.

Scapulars in their modern form were derived from an article of clothing, a part of the monk's habit, usually a broad piece of cloth worn over the robes with an opening for the head and hanging to the feet in front and back. Members of religious orders wore the scapular every day and most considered it a privilege to be buried in it when they died.

Gradually brethren were permitted to confer the scapular upon members of the lay community, men and women who regularly interacted with the order and held positions of service and responsibility. This smaller version of the scapular was essentially a manner of conferring recognition, like a badge displaying the colors or sign of the order. Conferees were expected to keep their scapulars close to their persons at all times lest the blessings, privileges and indulgences granted to them diminish.

Over time the exclusive use of scapulars by various orders and their attendant confraternities and consororities gave way to a broader use of religious badges among the faithful. And as the scapulars and medals were disseminated so was the lore and mystery surrounding each one.

It is the nature of the pious to make personal and referential associations with their icons. Catholics frequently pray to saints who possess specialized virtues, personalities or histories that make them uniquely qualified to provide divine intercession into their affairs when difficulties arise. Indeed the saints frequently take responsibility for multiple issues of concern. Saint Columba of Ireland for example is the patron saint of bookbinders, floods, Ireland, poets, and Scotland; while Saint Anthony of Padua is the patron saint of American Indians, amputees, animals, Brazil, elderly people, faith in the Blessed Sacrament, Ferrazzano, Italy, fishermen, harvests, Lisbon, lost articles, mail, oppressed people, Padua, Italy, paupers, Portugal, pregnant women, sailors, seekers of lost articles, shipwrecks, starvation, starving people, sterility, swineherds, Tigua Indians, travel hostesses and travelers. With 4867 saints from which to choose, the Catholics have a vast resource of patronage and intercession on their behalf.

Scapulars and religious medals are also personal and referential, and they represent another line of defense for the faithful in need, since all of the icons are blessed, and many of them have miraculous origins and virtues.

According to pious tradition, the Blessed Virgin appeared with a scapular in her hand to Saint Simon Stock at Cambridge England on Sunday, July 16, in the year of our Lord 1251, and said, "Take, beloved son this scapular of thy order as a badge of my confraternity and for thee and all Carmelites a special sign of grace; whoever dies in this garment will not suffer everlasting fire. It is the sign of salvation, a safeguard in dangers, a pledge of peace and of the covenant."

Thus began the custom of extending the special grace of the scapular, a tradition which quickly spread to other orders throughout Europe.

Des remembered that bishops in Ireland had attempted to distribute the Brown Scapular of Our Lady of Mount Carmel to all members of the local militia, not only for the personal safety of the soldiers but also to provide them with freedom from Purgatory.

Other scapulars had their origins in the visions of saints as well, including the Blue Scapular of the Immaculate Conception.

Jesus Christ came in an apparition to the Venerable Ursula Benicasa, foundress of the Theatine Nuns, and promised favors for all faithful who would wear a sky-blue scapular. Later Clement XI and successive popes granted certain indulgences for the wearing of the scapular. By Des Kelley's time the number of plenary indulgences attached to this scapular had risen to 433. (Plenary indulgences allow for the removal of some or all of the temporal punishment due for sins already forgiven.)

Jesus also blessed a sister of Saint Vincent de Paul in 1846 with a vision in which He showed her a scapular to be worn on Fridays for an increase of faith hope and charity. This came to be known as the Red Scapular of the Passion.

In order to obtain the grace of the scapular the wearer must repeat a specified number of prayers in honor of The Holy Trinity and Mary Immaculate. In some cases the scapular must be kissed repeatedly.

One must also ask for the plenary indulgences to receive them, keeping one personally, and giving the rest of them to the Holy Souls in Purgatory. One plenary indulgence gets a soul out of Purgatory.

Des was less concerned about plenary indulgences or Purgatory than he was with covering his own mortal ass as it were. He was an Irishman, influenced by Catholic reverence but also imbued with profound respect for the supernatural. He was also aware that there was a sacred corollary for every heathen prayer or ritual. In his experience he had found little difference between religious icons and pagan talismans, for both could be potent in their own way. Indeed there were places in the countryside where Des grew up where even a breastplate of holy medals would be of little consequence in the face of heathen powers at play, for the subtle charm of the wee folk was great and perilous.

Throughout his life he had always balanced his ill-defined and misinformed respect for the potency and authority of tokens by carrying clover and rabbit's feet in addition to his saint's medals and scapulars. He gave no consideration as to the relative merits of one over the other, for after all, a warrior may carry many weapons, both offensive and defensive.

Keiran had entered the room bearing an armload of laundry and a message from his mother that dinner would be ready in half an hour.

"If you're picking those out for your trip, they won't do you any good, you know," he said.

"Why do you say that, Kerry?"

"Well, Da, let me put it this way. A couple of weeks ago you brought me over to Cu's for a fund raiser to benefit the victims of the Guildford bombing right?"

"Yes, that's right, so?"

"So how many of the victims, how many of the people in that pub do you think were wearing their saint's medals when the bomb went off?

"And didn't you give Mack one of your medals to wear before he went off to Viet Nam?

"And one day last summer when old Mrs. Donovan saw me riding my bike in front of her house, she stopped me and pinned one of these things on my shirt for good luck; and wouldn't you know-" he reached out toward the frame of the mirror where the scapulars were hanging and flipped one of the small rectangles of cloth irreverently, "-that was the day I fell off the bike and broke my arm!"

CHAPTER 44

The dorm room standard extra-long single bed in which Makepeace had slept during his stay at the Kelleys had been fine and suitable and he was grateful for it. But tonight would be the last time, for some weeks anyway, when he would sleep in a comfortable bed with soft pillows, clean sheets and a sexy naked woman beside him. Heather had gone out of her way to make their association professional, mutually profitable and pleasurable.

"For queen and for country, love," she said with a smile, her face just visible over the sheets. The bed was a four-poster, seemingly too large for the room which Heather had reserved for the weekend in a cozy seaside inn.

He'd only known her briefly and had only fucked her three times so far, but thought he knew her well enough by now to know that her true motivation was more likely 'for green and for cunt!'

But what a stroke of luck to find some proper British ass here in America of all places, and while he was dealing with micks no less. A genuine Darbeyshire heifer, she was; beef to the heels, but without a spare ounce of fat on the whole stunning package. He placed his hand open flat on her hip and felt the solid cool mass of her, relaxed and torpid beneath his palm. The draping bedclothes followed the curvature of her figure and suggested a delightful caricature of her body.

Heat seemed to radiate from his chest, making him feel smothered. He swept off the top sheet with the flourish of a stage magician and the air smelled like his sweat molecules and hers were mingling and fornicating. Then he thought with some amusement that each man on the crew would undoubtedly carry some essence of pussy back to the boat. A well-laid crew is a happy crew.

"So, love, I want to make sure that there is no misunderstanding about Captain Jack."

"No," Makepeace returned to reality with a deflating prick, "Not unless you're going to tell me that it had all been a lark, and that you weren't really serious about sinking him."

"Oh, I'm serious. For reasons that really needn't concern you, Jack and his boat must be destroyed. But if it helps, the world will be a better place with one fewer asshole around; the claims adjusters and insurance companies will enjoy picking over his estate; and my business associates and I will be sincerely grateful to you."

He had already considered the potential benefits of complying with her request. By using and then eliminating Capt. Jack, he ensured a clean getaway for Mr. Darrager, and helped to avoid the risk of returning to dock with a cargo-hold full of illegal weapons. With any luck, after the harbor master logged the Cor Mor's departure, the boat would be only one of a million plying the North Atlantic.

But now he weighed the worth of her gratitude. There was no need to try to convince her to split the money and look the other way when he could just as well keep it all for himself and proceed with his plan with her none the wiser.

"So you'll make out alright on the deal? Then I want something in return."

"What do you mean?" asked Heather, suddenly sitting upright in bed, her breasts coming to rest in an accusatory pout.

"Well, it's all over but the report now; I mean, you establish the contacts, I make the buy, we prove the existence of at least one American source of arms for the Irish loyalists. That was supposed to be the extent of the mission, and I imagine that after we file our report, someone else will be along to clean up, to take action, whatever."

"Yes, and...? What do you have in mind?"

"The report, Heather. I want you to say that it was Capt. Jack who was to deliver the freight, but when his boat was destroyed the cargo went up, or down, with it."

"So...you want me to..."

"That's right. You say that Jack was the contact, the middle man handling the actual physical transfer. Everything was going smoothly, you say; the arms were bought and paid for; but then during the transfer things got a bit dicey, shots were exchanged, and unfortunately his boat was sunk, with the loss of cargo and all hands."

"But if they do ultimately get around to shutting down this supplier, and they make arrests, what if they discover that the stories don't jive?"

"By then it won't hardly matter. We'll claim that it was my idea to hire Jack for transport. I subsequently discovered that I couldn't trust him and was forced to eliminate him. On the other hand I don't want to imply that he was one of the primary targets of the investigation because I wouldn't want to make it look like I destroyed a boat belonging to the dealers, and killed the golden goose, as it were.

"Anyway I intend to have a couple of crates to hand over, as if to say, 'See, I managed to salvage some evidence despite the difficulties.' And if pressed, I'll say, 'Bloody hell, I went over there, dealt with the assholes, stuck my neck out and got in a firefight, what more do they want?'"

"Very convincing."

She did not sound convinced. But she was going to get what she wanted out of the deal, including the removal of a competitor. There had been other perquisites as well.

"The only thing I don't get is why? After all this work...Why would you want to report that the arms were lost after you bought them? What do you intend to do with the weapons?"

In response he said, "Would ten grand be enough to make you forget that you asked that question?"

"What question?"

Heather's complicity in removing her competitor had already assured Makepeace of her cooperation, but with her acceptance of the bribe Makepeace was certain that he could deliver Des' shipment without official inquiry or suspicion from the British side. His business with Kelley had little impact on their investigation and would remain secret as long as he could make a profit from the relationship.

Des was no terrorist, he was not the enemy. He did what he did out of fear or paranoia. Try as he might Makepeace could not see Des as one of the "murdering Taigs" his colleagues in Special Branch wanted to exterminate.

His friends in the IRA, the murdering Taigs themselves, were more likely than MI5 to discover that he was smuggling arms for Kelley again, but he would have plenty of time in the next few weeks to come up with a story to justify his actions.

That was one thing about the Irish that had always fascinated him. They liked a good story, whether it was true or not. If he said that the pope shit gold potatoes, the offense would be forgiven if the story were entertaining and well-told.

While his Irish contacts had always been fairly receptive to his stories, there was one occasion when he had been acutely worried about his credibility. It was during the job that had gotten him into this mess, the botched mission that had resulted in the death of his friend and colleague Cormack Green.

Makepeace stood naked at the window and gazed out at a private beach and cove across the two lane road in front of the inn. The window was open slightly and the crisp night air licked the sweat from his neck, chest and shoulders. Heather's reflection was caught between the panes of glass, and she appeared to be floating on a cloud of blankets ten feet outside the room.

"Did I tell you how I got this assignment?" he asked, knowing that he hadn't, and surprised at himself for bringing it up.

"No, why? Is there a story behind it?" She reached behind her head and doubled up her pillow.

"A story…indeed.

"Over the period of a year or so I had developed a reliable source, information that wasn't sensational, but valuable nonetheless. It was peripheral stuff, you know, the kind of data that intelligence types use to deduce what is happening elsewhere. About six months ago one of those blokes from Joint Services, a guy named Green, joined me on the job to observe first hand. He was a regular guy, friendly and outgoing. Married, two little kids back home. Anyway he blended right in and everyone seemed to like him.

"We worked hard to build confidence with the locals, especially with a fellow I'll call Cork," this Makepeace mockingly pronounced 'Carrig', "and after some months I thought I was finally in position for a breakthrough…" He was trying to avoid being specific in any way.

"I was going to meet some people who were being sought by the RUC, outlaw republican nationalists wanted in connection with attacks in Northern Ireland.

"Well, they were going to arrive at-, at the dock where I had a regular commercial berth, and I was going to bring them over to…a private residence. It was to be a pleasant, routine two-hour crossing during which we could get to know each other. Green was working with me that night, hoping for a glimpse of some infamous characters, and ready to report to his RUC and SAS commanders.

"But when the group arrived, Cork pulled me aside. He said he had news for me, that he was sorry to tell me, but he had learned that Green was a spy, and he was using his position on my boat as an observation post, to gather intelligence on the local command.

"I don't know how, but they had everything on him; his unit, his hometown, everything. I realized that I was under suspicion now too, that in fact the whole thing had been a set-up. I was being introduced to the hard men so that they could kill me."

"Oh, my word!" cried Heather, "What did you do?"

"It was a test. I knew that in order to prove myself, to save myself, I had to watch Green die; I had to let him die."

He almost said kill Green because that was what he really had to do. It had to be clear whose side he was on. "You're sure about this, now?" he'd asked Cork. "I mean, anybody can be anybody for all I know, but the man's been working on my boat for six months at least. He knows his work, never seemed suspicious…" He regretted that last bit instantly, so he blundered on, "But if you're sure, then I say kill the bastard. I'll do it myself if I have to."

Cork was mollified. Makepeace had bought some time.

Next he had to alert Green, to get him off the boat.

The trip went ahead as planned and from the moment they cast off the vessel seemed to be crowded with passengers. It was impossible to speak privately with his crew-mate. Cork remained in the wheelhouse while Makepeace took the helm, Green ran chores all over the boat, and the guests went below for coffee and whiskey.

Heather lit a cigarette and Makepeace kept talking.

"The mission was too important to hinge on the life of one man. If it were me, I would have given my life so the operation could go on."

That was easy to say, but bland rationalizations usually are.

"I was lucky that I didn't have to kill him myself," he lied. "But I did have to turn on him, to call for his execution, and, God help me, to stand by when they carried it out.

"Dumped his body at sea and for that I don't deserve forgiveness. His family wouldn't even get the decency of a proper burial."

Heather was pale and she unconsciously gathered her clothing. This man had betrayed a comrade, someone like herself, a British agent. She considered how he might be dangerous. They had compromised each other so how could he threaten her? She did not want to hear any more of the story but found it difficult to ignore. He was standing in front of her, attractively sexy, aggressively masculine, nakedly hairy; and she felt compelled to pay attention, especially after he had set her to rights with a pounding as pure as the driven pile. This was something in the manner of a post-coital confession. He had to unburden his soul as he had his body. She started to dress but otherwise encouraged him to finish his tale. How had he witnessed Green's execution? Did they kill him right there on the bridge of the boat?

Makepeace welcomed her questions. He wanted her to make it difficult, to put him to the test. After all she had trusted him.

Green had trusted him too. Trusted him when he called him out on deck, where the eager killers waited, smoking and grinning and chatting in obscure street slang.

Initially Makepeace had intended to quietly warn him. The scene replayed in his mind with a new heroic slant: "Green, my man, you've been made. They know you and they'll kill you. You'll have to swim to save your life. I'll keep them busy in the cabin while you slip off into the water. God be with you, mate."

But on the night in question he'd had other overriding concerns. It had occurred to him that Green might have been part of the plot as well, that he could be working with the IRA to expose him. His only option was to play it out as Cork had indicated, and see what developed.

"There was no warning," he continued. "He was on deck, standing by the rail. When they shot him he went overboard."

"Did you report his location? So they'd know where to search for his body?"

"I couldn't call in until the next day, and by then the body would have traveled a considerable distance.

"And that wasn't all there was to it. Cork didn't want to hear about search parties or what not because that would have meant that I had tipped off the authorities about Green's disappearance and about where to look. Though if anyone came looking for him, I was to say that he hadn't showed up for work recently and that's all I knew."

"You did report it, right? You told them how he died?" A touch of cold horror had crept into her voice.

"Yes, of course. I gave them the whole story."

A story not substantially unlike the one he had fabricated for her. True enough to account for Green's disappearance, as this version had been true enough to relieve some of his own guilt.

Cormack was gone, ashes and dust to a bloated mass, a lifeless hulk, pulverized by gnashing rocks and torn asunder by myriad creatures of the sea. Another victim of war, one who had fulfilled the highest demand of duty. But what of purpose? Had Green achieved anything in life or death? Did his sacrifice advance the cause of peace, the certainty of victory? Did it balance the accounts of injury and vengeance, blood and treasure? His sentence had been avoidable. Perhaps his enemies had imagined that he had already done them damage, or misjudged his potential to hurt them. But they did not have to kill him. They could have interrogated him or simply monitored his activities or demanded that he be removed from Makepeace's employ. It pleased them to kill him, at that time, for whatever gain could be had. Perhaps they were sending a message to the SAS and maybe to Makepeace as well: Don't fuck with us!

Makepeace would live with his guilt, and worse, with an awareness of his own capacity for deceit, betrayal and treachery. At the conclusion of the nightmare episode he had been wracked with fatigue, anxiety, depression, and felt a strong desire to abandon his career.

But the British had been unfathomably complacent about the incident. His debriefing had been carried out in an almost congratulatory fashion. Pats on the back, platitudes, and a disconcerting shift from a condescending to a more conciliatory tone.

It took some time for him to understand that the way they looked at it, the incident had demonstrated that Makepeace was in the right place, doing the right thing, and that Green's death had locked him into an unassailable position with the Irish.

For Cork it was business as usual, and he behaved as if nothing had happened. The IRA were in the process of exploring legitimate business concerns as a revenue source to fund their armed resistance to British rule in Northern Ireland, and had already had some success in pubs, bookmaking and taxicabs. Makepeace was of some assistance in this regard as he and his boat provided an example of the potential of exploiting a share of the fish market. Sales of the catch were but one means of making money. In addition there was the wholesale tier, and distribution and restaurants. One obvious advantage was that the boat permitted relative freedom of travel between the various ports and fishing villages north and south. There were no road blocks, land mines, Gardai cordons, or border crossings to deal with. Not that they could afford to be careless, for the Irish fishing grounds were scrupulously patrolled, but primarily to restrict foreign access to that rich national resource.

Yet despite Makepeace's newfound wariness and caution in dealing with the Irish, it wasn't long before he was involved in another IRA operation. When Cork mentioned the plan to bring an American specialist over to Ireland, Makepeace initially thought that he was being fed bogus info that could be tracked back through sources. He was still feeling exposed and vulnerable because it was conceivable that someone in British intelligence had sold out Green. But after he offered suggestions to help refine the plan, he ultimately found himself in full charge of the mission, like a back-seat driver who had been handed the keys. He had insisted that he was not acting as a member of Cork's unit, that he was not volunteering for active service. But Cork said that by serving as a contractor as it were, Makepeace actually added a layer of separation, a bonus element of deniability. Yet for all he knew this mission was another test of his loyalty and viability, and he was being closely watched.

CHAPTER 45

Christine and Des Kelley never discussed child rearing, and if they did stop to think about it they would likely conclude that their children wouldn't have turned out much differently even if they had. They missed out on the Dr. Spock phenomenon entirely and since neither of them were particularly well-read they had never been exposed to any of the contemporary literature. Even if Christine were to come across an article on parenting while browsing Ladies Home Journal or Better Homes and Gardens, she would probably skip it in favor of another containing tips about spot removal or items about window treatments. She did however find it helpful at times to pick and choose from the profusion of advice that was offered by well-wishing friends and relatives, although they hadn't had much luck with their own kids.

If they had employed any method in raising Mack, Buck, Keiran and Tumbleweed, it was the same one that their parents and generations before them had used: practicing on the first-born and applying the lessons learned from the experience to the next progeny and so forth.

Objectively speaking there were principles by which they evidently abided. These included discipline administered by caring parents; the guidance, instruction and comfort of religion; a nurturing home where none wanted for shelter, clothing or food; and an education based upon fundamental skills, classics and humanities. Essential elements for a happy family and well-rounded kids.

The Kelleys furthermore relied upon the family dinner as the tried and reliable means of uniting and reinforcing the family unit. Earlier in this narrative there were allusions to the importance of family gatherings in the Kelley home, particularly Sunday dinners to which extra guests were invited. Now in the final days before his departure for Ireland, Des especially wanted to enjoy the company of his family.

On days other than Sunday there were occasions when for one reason or another one of the four family members might not attend the evening meal. This Saturday night Des guaranteed that everyone would participate whole-heartedly because he had announced that he was treating them to dinner at their favorite restaurant, a Rossie landmark for over 40 years, the Pleasant.

"That's fine," said Christine upon hearing the news.

"I had only thawed the links anyway for bangers and mash. I'd rather have veal parma-gee-ann any day, myself."

"Mmmm," moaned Keiran, clutching his stomach as if he was famished, "A big plate of spaghetti and meatballs for me."

"Spaghetti!" exclaimed Des, "You can have that at home! When you go to the Pleasant you have to order veal or pizza."

"I'm going to have minestrone and anti-pasto," said Tweed, speaking like a cartoon wop.

"Oh? And some wine to go with your meal, sir?" kidded his mother.

"No, mum, beer will be fine," he winked in reply.

Within half an hour everyone had washed up, changed into neat clothes and assembled in the parlor, raring to go.

The restaurant was full when the Kelleys arrived, but when John, the head waiter recognized Des, he raised a finger in the air as if he had a notion to bid at auction, then hurried off into the dining room. While he was gone the family waited in the vestibule, delighting in the warm, inviting, appetizing aromas wafting from the kitchen.

The waiter reappeared presently and beckoned them to follow him. Indeed there were no vacant booths or tables but John had been clever and resourceful and also a bit presumptuous in order to achieve the miracle of seating the Kelleys promptly. Knowing that their good friends the Fecteaus were already seated in the dining room, John had produced a utility table and butted it up against their table in order to accommodate the larger group. It was a tight fit, elbow to elbow all the way around the table, yet the Fecteaus graciously denied any imposition and welcomed the Kelleys as if they were family.

Many of the folk in the restaurant were friends or acquaintances. Simon Fecteau, of course, and his wife Janine. Joe Toole was there also with his wife Kathy. And city council member Dapper Ferguson was making the rounds while he waited for his extra-cheese, pepperoni and olive pizza.

Chris sighed, knowing that once Des started talking to Dapper, a change would come over him that she likened in her mind to the transformation Lon Chaney underwent in becoming the Wolfman, except instead of lupine he became loopy. Dapper was a politician and Des was a fabulous bullshit artist, so when the two of them got together they were knee-deep in no time. Des considered it a challenge to outshit a shitter and he was ready to take Dapper head to head on any topic.

Chris laid a hand on her husband's arm as Dapper worked the tables, heading in their direction. Des wasn't rising from his seat or anything, it was simply a signal telling him to calm himself.

"Remember, Des, you invited us to dinner yourself!"

"And dinner we shall have by Gor!" he chuckled, but his eyes were on Dapper.

"How are things at work, Simon?" she asked, trying to force the conversation upon the man at whose table she was a guest.

"Oh, fine, fine, you know, it's the start of the busy season for us, for us."

Simon Fecteau worked in appliance repair for the gas utility. He was a big round bear of a man about 40 years old, with thinning brown hair. A sweet generous disposition was flawed somewhat by his unfortunate echolalia. The condition caused him to repeat the last words of every sentence and sometimes to repeat the words of those to whom he was speaking, or others who were nearby. His friends hardly noticed, but others found it annoying, or ignored it or otherwise compensated. The problem was that it was kind of contagious.

"Oh, with the cold weather, you mean?" asked Christine.

"You mean? Yeah, yeah, the cold weather really keeps us hopping, hopping. Lots of pilot lights, furnace work, furnace work."

"I can imagine, imagine." Chris was keeping an eye on Dapper's progress, fully intent upon creating the semblance of a lively conversation at the table so that, if he was any gentleman at all, he might feel averse to interrupting their talk and their dinner.

Keiran giggled into his napkin and then he stuffed it into his shirt collar like a bib. Tweed was hiding behind his menu card; and Des was drumming his fingers on the tabletop. What a bunch of louts.

Not that Tweed gave her any trouble, and a good thing too because she had her hands full, figuratively speaking, with Des and Keiran. She knew that her husband would never admit it but he'd be lost without her. Sure he talked a good story. In fact almost all of the money he made came from talk in one form or another. Requests, demands, persuasion, threats, negotiation, intimidation- he always had a winning way with words. But she kept the books, ran the accounts, and knew what he was good for at any given time. And she ran the house, a job that he surely did not make any easier, for by nature he was chauvinistically untidy. He was her love, a cushla mo chroi, but also the cause of her grief. She wanted to believe that as a God-fearing Christian he was an honest father and a loyal husband. But in reality he only paid lip-service to the church, he slept with other women and he wasn't much of a father. She bore him four sons and she nurtured, cared for and raised them. However, just when she had finished raising her eldest, when he had become a man, the Lord had called for him all too early, and she was left with three sons. Then when Buck left home to move back to Ireland she was down to two boys. Now Keiran was going to give his life to the Lord as he pursued a vocation that left her wondering why God kept taking her sons away. She realized that Keiran must be suffering, for the choice of a life of pious chastity was not one that any son of Des Kelley would make lightly. She looked at him as he sat quietly picking at his food and worried that the serenity visible on the surface was only a mask that covered a deeper disturbance. Tweed on the other hand held nothing back. He expressed every wish and whim vocally or verbally. That was why she felt that she never had to worry about her youngest, because she could read him like a book.

At this rate she might as well resign herself to awaiting the pleasure of Dapper's company. But as fate would have it, when Dapper finally approached to greet them, John also arrived to take their orders, thus heading him off. Rather than stand behind the waiter waiting for an opening, the gregarious pol ambled toward another unsuspecting couple of potential voters in an adjacent booth.

But Chris' satisfaction was short-lived, because Dapper hailed John before he could hustle back to the kitchen, and requested that his table be moved so that he could sit between the Kelleys and the Tooles. In this way he would approximate his usual seating arrangement at the Rossie Biz Club, where the three gentlemen frequently met and drank together. John could either acquiesce and make his work more difficult by placing the table in an aisle, thus leaving little room for maneuvering, or he could refuse Dapper Ferguson and redirect all of that hot air in his direction. He chose the former course of action and soon Dapper was seated cheek by jowls with the rest of them, wedged in between the tables with a magnificent 16-inch pizza practically in his lap.

"I'm off for home this Wednesday next," said Des, with his mouth full of bread.

"Are you now?" replied Dapper, strings of cheese and gobs of tomato hanging from his lower lip. "I don't blame you for taking a vacation when things are so bad here. I'd get away myself if I had half a chance but I can't be leaving when the town is in crisis, now."

"What are you talking about?" asked Des as if the man was crazy.

"Crime on the streets, the drug problem, the schools…"

"Going on vacation? Who said I was going on vacation?"

"Vacation," said Simon, as if playing Simon says.

"The kids, the kids these days, with their drugs, their beanies, and their poppers and their hypers. It's a menace, I tell you."

"You ain't on the blasted school committee, Dapper; and what would you do about crime?" Now he was playing into the campaign act, too.

"I'll tell you what I'll do," said Dapper, but he glanced at Tweed and Keiran and seemed to think better of revealing his strategy. "I'll ask you to pass the Parmesan- I want to shake a bit of it on my pie here. If you're not going on vacation, then why are you going?"

"Business, of course. Have to conclude some transactions, visit my estate, view my holdings. Expect to meet with some highly influential individuals regarding projects of mutual interest. And I will of course be delivering aid to the needy victims of the tragic circumstances in Guildford. Plan to make a personal presentation to the mayor on behalf of the good people of this city. I'll try to remember you to him if I can, Dapper."

"I always said that Ireland is the land of saints and scholars, and you are either one or the other, I'm sure," said Dapper.

"I'm sure," said Fecteau.

"It wasn't you who said that," said Toole, "it was Brian Boru."

"Boru, Boru."

"Boru? No, it was Pearse, before they executed him."

John had swung in with the food like a high wire unicycle act.

"So, you going to Ireland, eh, Des-ah? Good-ah for you! I was there you know!" Rapidly and precisely he dealt the plates off his tray.

"No, you weren't." Des received his entree with a nod.

"Yes! Yes, sir! Back before the war!" He tucked his tray under one arm and brushed his hands outwards as if pushing an imaginary pile of poker chips into a pot.

"Really, John? What were you doing there?"

The tall Italian straightened, frowned and passed a hand through his hair, "Well, that was the old days-ah, you know, maybe we talk some time, eh? Yes!" He smiled again, collected some plates and silver from the table and departed hurriedly.

Now Des frowned. The waiter's comments had created a distraction in his mind. Could John really be old enough to remember visiting Ireland before the war? The old guinea sure looked good for his age. He had probably spent two thirds of his life hurrying between the steam-greased kitchen and the cigarette-stuffy dining room but he looked fit and his complexion was fresh off the fairway. Des marveled that he looked as young for his age as Dapper looked old for his.

Comparing the two men Des saw that Dapper was indeed the polar opposite of his Italian host. Paunchy, white-haired, haggard and slouching, Dapper apparently bore the burden of his ambitions. But it wasn't his looks that got him where he was, it was his voice, and that was still stentorian. He used it effectively to promote himself and the causes, concerns and constituents he represented. In addition to the voice, he had balls, and a flair for bullshit; that was the real Dapper Ferguson, the person Des admired. In fact he secretly wished he too could run for office, if not for a council seat like Dapper's, then for the mayor's seat itself. With the legitimacy of elected office in his favor he could address some of the inadequacies and injustices inherent in the current bureaucracy. Politics as such mattered little, rather it was the power that appealed to him. Friends were plentiful and his influence was renowned but legitimacy would ensure his place in history and the esteem of his peers. His experience as an immigrant who had always worked outside the system led him to fantasize about manipulating it to his advantage. But Des could not become a public figure. At least not to any degree or any respect more so than he was already. He knew that he couldn't survive the test of official scrutiny without incurring indictments for successfully maintaining an illusion of propriety, or plaudits for eluding prosecution. Taking a sip of the house Italian Rosé, he decided that in the event that he should ever become a fully legal and law-abiding citizen, he would rather be a politician than a restaurateur. No disrespect for John; the man's marinara was a masterpiece.

Like everyone else at the table Des had fallen to, and fallen silent as well, chewing his food steadily while clutching a fork in his left hand and a bread roll in his right. There was nothing like this in Ireland, not even in the so-called Italian restaurants, where the sauce resembled ketchup and the pasta was water-logged and mushy. On the contrary the pasta accompanying the veal fillet on his plate was tender and delicious, although he was irked that it had been poorly drained and sat in a puddle of water. Somehow the memory of soggy Irish spaghetti made him think of his money and Makepeace. Now he risked spoiling his dinner. Suddenly his esophageal sphincter felt like the loose lid on a pot of boiling coffee.

He thought it over. It was Saturday night, so Makepeace was probably making his connection right now and arranging to pick up the weapons. Rather than roil himself further with fret and worry, Des decided that whether or not Makepeace called with news he would take the initiative and visit the boat at its current mooring on Sunday night in order to perform a little due diligence.

Tweed winced as he bit into a rolled slice of Prosciutto- he had added too much dressing to his antipasto, and the meat was dripping with oil and vinegar. However he still intended to eat everything on his plate, from the first slice of hard-boiled egg to the last olive. He had already finished the starter course of bread and minestrone soup, a sentimental favorite of his ever since he had attended elementary school. His parents had always taken him to the Pleasant in order to celebrate special occasions such as recitals or report cards, and in time he had developed the custom of starting his meals with minestrone and ending them with spumoni ice cream.

He had heard that Col's sister Megan was working at the take-out pizza counter. He made a mental note to return later in the week so he could see how she looked in her uniform. Ever since he broke up with Sam, Megan had become the default target of his fantasies, and he wouldn't mind getting to know her better. On second thought, that would mean that he'd have to speak to Col, something he hadn't done since the memorial service for Jimmy Black. Actually, on that occasion he had only mumbled a few words; the last time they had really talked was when Col had confided in him about Jimmy's death.

OK, so Jimmy was gay whatever that meant, and Jimmy was gone; nothing could be done for him now. But it troubled him to think that his friendship with Col had been laid away like Jimmy's remains. Something could be done about that, and he resolved to call his friend as soon as he got home.

Invariably, the less he hung out with Col, the more time he spent hanging out with Carmine, and he could appreciate the difference. When Tweed was with Col, he was in charge, he was the authority, the brains, the idea man. But when he was with Carmine he was like Carmine's little brother or something. Carmine was the mentor, the wizard, the cool head. As much as he admired and respected Carmine, he resented the fact that he had somehow become locked into a position of deference toward him. Not that he minded so much, it was just that sometimes he got tired of behaving obsequiously. After all, it was Tweed who ran his own business, Tweed who supplied the dope, and Tweed who had expanded his boundaries to encompass practically the whole city. Carmine would probably be happy to stay in Rossie his whole life, but Tweed had his sights set on an ever-receding horizon.

He and Jimmy Col had often discussed the idea of traveling the world together. First they planned to hitch hike across the continent to Alaska, America's final frontier. Then after bumming around the tundra for a while, they'd head south, procure a 44' yacht, and continue their voyage westward on the open seas. They had chosen the vessel for the journey of their dreams from a yachting magazine that Col had stolen from the waiting room at his family dentist. For all of the hours they had spent poring over the glossy pages of the obsolete periodical, they had dedicated no thought at all to practical considerations such as how they would make their living, where the money would come from, or where they would obtain the skill and knowledge to operate such an ocean-going boat. Their goal was simply a given, so real to them that they had even contemplated looking back on their carefree days of shared experiences and travel when they were older still and more settled.

All of that seemed so immature now. Everything had changed in their lives with the late introduction of puberty, reefer, girls, suicide, and to some extent, rock and roll. A trip around the world wasn't out of the question, but instead of Col he would now be more likely to want Megan for his companion.

Tweed's musings were suddenly interrupted. A family of five had finished their dinner and gotten up from their table to leave the restaurant. He had scarcely noticed as the parents and then their daughter, a girl about his age walked past carrying their coats. The daughter, who hadn't seen Tweed, was LaGloria McManus. She wouldn't actually meet him until sometime the following year.

But the two sons, who looked a bit older than Tweed, dawdled near his table, apparently waiting for their parents to exit the dining room. One of them cleared his throat, a-hemming for Tweed's attention. As far as he knew he had never seen either of them before and was surprised to hear the kid call him by name.

"Hey, man, hey Kelley, uh, Tweed! It's about that, uh, sawbuck, right? OK?"

Confused, Tweed replied, "What are you talking about? What sawbuck?"

"The one I owe you, remember?" he nodded knowingly in the direction of Tweed's father as if it were a hint to do so.

"Yeah, sure, I remember now." No, he didn't, but neither did he want to be embarrassed in front of his family.

"Alright, then! We'll catch you later, right?"

"Sure thing!"

The stranger gave him the thumbs up. Then the kid and his brother finally departed, walking as if they had springs in the heels of their sneakers.

Who the heck did they think he was? They seemed to have the name right, like they really knew him. Could it be that Tweed had forgotten not only uncollected debts but the faces of guys who owed him money? Impossible. Not a couple of jokers like them. Now it was going to bug the shit out of him until he figured out who they were and what it was that they were after.

Furtively he glanced out of the corners of his eyes at his parents. Fortunately his father was talking to his cronies and his mother was scolding Kerry for slurping his spaghetti. The pasta whip-lash had left a brand of sauce on his cheek like a fresh wound. Come Halloween a couple of tomato-sauce scars like that could pass for hideous disfigurement.

At his age Tweed was feeling ambivalent about trick-or-treat this year. He had no desire to go out in costume like the little kids but neither did he want to miss what might be his last legitimate opportunity. Maybe there would be a party in the neighborhood, some place where he could drink and dance and celebrate his old man's departure. Maybe he could even bake some pot brownies-something he had wanted to try since he first heard about it- or better yet, why not weed-sketti? Wayne Kenny had introduced to him the concept of altering the potency of dope. He said that in order to prepare weed for consumption as food it was necessary to break down the fiber membrane of the plant either by freezing it or by cooking it. Other would-be pot alchemists had described folk remedies for treating weed as well. For example, one procedure allegedly produced the Black Death, a substance so powerful as to be considered hazardous to health. In order to create BD, one had to bury an ounce of marijuana and wait until it decomposed and putrefied to a black viscous liquid. Supposedly you dried the slime then smoked it, but Tweed had never tried it. Not that he doubted the soundness of the theory, just that he couldn't imagine parting with an ounce of pot for an experiment. As it was the quality of his dope had been pretty high, high enough to exploit its psychoactive properties simply by smoking it. Eating it could be an efficient way to get off, too, as long as he prepared it correctly.

A plan was shaping up in his mind. He would talk Col into hosting a party at his house on Halloween by promising to cook dinner. Tweed would sauté the weed in a pan with a little garlic and butter to mask the odor. The weed-sketti would get everyone nicely wasted and then he'd see what fun would develop with Megan later. If Col went along with the idea then he'd have to come up with a list of people to invite. Maybe he could get that kid Mickey to come over.

"Hey, Da- guess what?"

"Now, Taweed, how in God's name am I supposed to know? You just tell me, sweetheart."

"I was going to say- I ran into Mickey Byrne after school the other day. He's working at a gas station."

"Mickey Byrne? Good for him, now. Who's Mickey Byrne?" At this Des laughed uproariously, as if he had been witty indeed.

Now Tweed was discouraged from pursuing the matter. Already the old man's attention had wandered to some comment he overheard from another table.

"Mickey is JC's son, Da- he's my age. I met him at Cu's once."

He wasn't sure if he got through. For a moment Des stared vacantly as he seemed to recall some matter of importance.

"Mickey Byrne! Oh, Mickey Byrne!" he repeated as if his son had failed to include this vital bit of information. "He must be about your age now, am I right, Taweed?"

CHAPTER 46

Sunday, October 27, 1974

After chores, after church and after brunch- another feast his mother had laid out for the neighbors as a sort of going away party for his father- Tweed finally tore away from his family. There was a prevalent mood of tension in the Kelley house, probably precipitated by Des or by the disruption caused by his departure. Normally Tweed wasn't affected by his parent's vicissitudes but he was feeling smothered and had to bolt for the relative freedom and expanse of Arbs Park. Once he was within the park he would look for Carmine, whistling out their familiar call pattern and waiting for a response.

Ask anyone in the neighborhood for directions to Arbs Park and they'll refer to the wooded area opposite the ball park just down the railroad tracks heading toward Jamaica Center. That was where Tweed entered; at roughly the tail end of the rugged 600 acre tract.

The boundaries of the park were poorly marked but he knew when he had passed within because even at the perimeter the air seemed to improve…becoming sweeter, lighter, more rarified. And once he was within the park proper he became enchanted with the magic of the place.

The park was periodically groomed and maintained by crews of grounds keepers with mowers and tractors but was otherwise inaccessible to vehicles. That in itself restricted the number of visitors somewhat. Furthermore, very few visitors would enter the park on a chilly Sunday afternoon like this one, when the sun gave cold cheer through a flying checkerboard of clouds. Any who did were unlikely to plan an extended stay as Tweed had. He intended to meet up with Carmine at the fort, build a fire and then kick back for the remainder of the afternoon.

The plan depended in part upon the park being deserted. It would be a major bummer to have their peaceful toke fest interrupted by some well-meaning civic first-responder who was checking a report of smoke coming from the woods. Anticipating this they had already worked out that they would build the fire at the base of the tree. They figured that ideally the heat would rise along the trunk, drawing the smoke like a chimney to the upper branches where they hoped it would feather off into the breeze.

Tweed had been whistling on and off since entering the park and had as of yet heard no response from Carmine. Approaching the base of the final hill of the hike his pace quickened. Carmine was probably up there comfortably enjoying the fort all by himself. That was enough incentive to march up the slope double time but he stopped suddenly when he noticed a magazine lying discarded at the side of the trail. Bending to pick it up he saw that it was copy of *Playboy*, July '74. It was heavy and glossy in his hand and he stared at it, numbly transfixed as if he had seized hold of a live wire. Then just as suddenly he folded the magazine into his back pocket and resumed his climb to the fort, pumping his arms and breathing heavily.

How to broach the subject to Carmine? Now he wished that Carmine had not preceded him to the fort, or better yet that he had left the magazine right where it was. He didn't want his friend to think that he had come to the hide-out simply to read girlie mags. This was ridiculous- he was unaccountably nervous and his hopes for a happy high had turned into clammy cold sweat and a gnawing in his nuts.

At the brow of the hill he scanned the approach to the fort, looking for some sign of Carmine's presence. The grass lay flat in wax-bean colored clumps that all leaned generally in one direction, slicked down against the surface of the hill by seasonal rainwater. The trees in the grove resisted the steady breeze with an occasional shrug of their heavily drooping boughs. No bird calls, no squirrels or chipmunks. It was hard to say whether Carmine had been here; but then, a deer or moose for that matter could have passed through here and Tweed wouldn't know the difference. Looking up he saw a hawk chasing its tail high over the trees. He interpreted his momentary impression of the lane outside the fort as proof of his solitude, and advanced, feeling a bit disappointed that he would be the one waiting for his friend to show up.

At first glance the fort looked unimposing- more like a brush pile than a wig-wam. But then he saw that the view had been foreshortened by the angle of approach. Seen at full length from the side, the fallen timber looked like a shaggy green leviathan beached at the base of a tree.

Taking advantage of a gap in the hoop skirt of evergreen boughs that wrapped modestly around the lower trunk, Tweed ducked inside his new home away from home.

It was surprisingly dark, causing temporary blindness until his eyes adjusted. The first thing he saw when the dazzle of sunlight had passed was the inert body of Carmine, passed out on the ground like a college freshman after a kegger. Tweed kicked him in the sneakers and Carmine started, saying, "Now?"

"Now what?" Tweed asked with a laugh. "Get up, you bum."

"No, what now?" replied Carmine groggily. "I was just…I can't remember."

"Hey, man, how long you been waiting?"

"I was asleep. How the fuck should I know? What time is it?"

"I don't know…2:30? Let's build a fire."

"Yeah, alright," he stood and stretched and scratched his balls.

"I'm stiff from lying on the ground."

"Well help me find some kindling and shit will you?"

"Oh, so you can build the fire? Do you know how? Did you ever build a camp fire before?"

"I can build a fucking camp fire. What, are you a boy scout or something?"

"I was, and I know how to build a fire so that you can start it even if all you have left is one match."

"One match? Big deal. I thought you boy scouts could start a fire without any matches. But I'll accept your challenge. I'll build a fire and get it going with just one match."

Soon they were crashing through the underbrush like a couple of retrievers flushing grouse, arguing all the while about what constituted kindling and what was suitable for fire wood. The exchange became particularly heated after Tweed caught Carmine trying to tear a limb from a live tree.

"Green wood? Some boy scout. You only use green wood as a last resort. There's plenty of windfall and dead branches about; you just have to pick them up."

"Fuck that, man! This green branch will burn hot and help get the rest of the wood going. You don't know what you're talking about."

"I know that you shouldn't be removing branches from good trees for the fuck of it! I was talking to one of the guys who work here and he said that's how trees get infected with diseases and parasites."

"You're a friggin' parasite. Wait'il you see how it works."

On his hands and knees with his face not six inches from the base of the wood pile, Tweed steadied his breath, preparing to serve as a human bellows.

"That sure is a freaking gorgeous pile of wood, don't you think?" joked Carmine. He was trying to unsettle Tweed because by now the chore of lighting the fire had become the primary focus of their attention and energies. It had assumed mythic significance, as if large wagers and personal reputations were at stake. Tweed held the match as he awaited a propitious moment at which to strike it, sensing the air currents with the very hairs on his cheeks. Perhaps the stack of wood was a trifle over-engineered. But with Carmine hassling him over each stick and every twig, it had been like two architects using Lincoln Logs to collaborate on a scale model of the Notre Dame cathedral without either of them having seen the original.

He lit the match, cupped it in his hand and applied it to the underside of a cluster of dried oak leaves. For a time they seemed fire-proof, brown and leathery and merely reflecting the heat. Carmine spluttered a guffaw over his shoulder. Tweed continued holding his breath and steadily rotated the match as it was consumed by the shrinking flame. Suddenly the leaves caught just as the match went out. The flame spread to a shred of birch bark that flared up as if it had been soaked in kerosene and in turn torched a spray of pine needles. The fresh needles went up in a crackling blaze.

"See! What did I tell you?" gloated Carmine over his contribution of green branches.

Tweed couldn't answer. He was turning his head back and forth like a swimmer doing the Australian crawl while he sucked in air away from the fire and blew it out upon the base of the fire. Yellow spots swam in front of his watering eyes and his head was spinning.

"What's this?" cried Carmine, noticing the magazine protruding from Tweed's back pocket. "Whoa-ho!"

"Give it to me," wheezed Tweed. He snatched it back and began fanning the fire, force-feeding it oxygen. "More fuel for the fire," he said finally as he sat back away from the heat of the growing blaze.

"No way! I want to read it first!"

"You didn't read it already?" asked Tweed suspiciously.

"No...what do you mean?"

"It's just that I found this thing lying on the ground outside the fort there, not fifty yards from here. I figured it was yours."

"Not mine," said Carmine, "...must have been some kid up here beating off. Check to see if any of the pages are stuck together."

Tweed actually flipped a couple of pages before tossing it back to Carmine- "You check!"

Carmine immediately opened it up to the centerfold.

"Oh, my God!"

"What is it? Let me see..."

When Carmine turned the book to show the centerfold to Tweed, it was as if something profound was being revealed to him. There on the pages of Playboy magazine was surely perfection in human form. The most beautiful, sexy woman Tweed had ever seen, dreamed of or imagined. The little half top she wore came down just to her nipples and her perfect breasts jutted out over a slender creamy waist, a flat golden-haired abdomen, and a v-shaped bikini bottom that damply defined her peachy pussy.

"Bet you'd like to do her, huh?"

Tweed wanted to look away but he could not. How could something of such beauty grace the pages of a men's magazine? Were there really women as sexy as her in the world, or was this some photographer's effect? How do you contact a girl like her? Could he write to her, plead the insanity of his love for her? It was suddenly very warm in the fort.

"You like that, huh? You ever seen anything like that before?"

No, he hadn't. Closest was a photo he once saw of a nudist colony. His brother had pointed it out in a magazine at the library, having been told the issue and page number by a classmate of his. So Tweed joined a long line of adolescent boys who had ogled over the periodical Just like he was ogling now. He had to snap out of it. He licked his lips and tried to sound casual.

"Izzat your sister, dude?"

"Fuck you, Tweed. My sister's not nearly as nice as her, although this one's too, uh, white for me, you know? Me and you have to go to a strip club someday and see real naked chicks in person."

Tweed had to allow a wave of rage to pass over him. How dare he say anything to denigrate the goddess? Then jealousy overruled. Let Carmine look at other girls- Miss June would be for Tweed alone.

"You should jerk off, man before you blow a load in your drawers."

"Fuck that, Carmine."

"What? Don't you jack off?"

"None of your business, asshole!"

"Oh, so you do jack off. But not now, not here, is that it?"

"Fuck, no!"

"Why not, man? We're friends. I ain't gonna molest you or nothing. You think I care about your dick? I wouldn't touch your dick with a ten foot pole. I just thought that you might want to relieve yourself. That's all it is, you know, like taking a piss."

"Yeah? Well, I wouldn't even take a piss."

"What? Man you've pissed in front of me plenty of times. I can't remember all of the times we've pissed together. We're like a couple of mutt hounds, man, we piss together so much."

"You make it sound like all we ever do is stand around and pee. Alright, so we piss together. That's not the same."

"Oh, so you're embarrassed to shake your dick one way but not the other. I don't get it...you have hang-ups."

"Look, just because I don't want to whack off in front of you doesn't mean that I have hang ups. I think it's normal."

"And I think it's normal to get off when you need to. Shit, me and a friend of mine got busted jerking off together. No big deal."

"What do you mean 'busted'?" he asked, although he wasn't sure he wanted to know. Carmine Gunther had just told him that he had been masturbating with some other kid. Was this another homosexual confession? How many homos were there in the neighborhood, anyway? Jimmy Black, that guy Tommy Toole, and now maybe Carmine, plus whoever his friend was. Holy Shit. On the one hand it was like, more chicks for him, and on the other it was like, what the fuck was going on? The idea of men touching other men sickened him and he dare not consider any other form of male intimate contact.

"Well, me and this kid were up at flat rock looking at a Playboy together and the fucking babes in it were so awesome we both started beating our meat, you know, just kind of flopping our dicks around, when all of a sudden this old dude come up and starts giving us a hard time. He was like, 'You boys like-a-you preeks, eh? You like-a play with your preeks and maybe get in trouble. Maybe go to hell, eh?' We told him to go to hell."

"What? Are you kidding? You were just laying there with your dicks out, trying to get your rocks off in broad daylight and in public? Are you insane?" The mental images were killing him. A moment ago he had seen surpassing splendor, a figure of womanhood that would forever serve as his model of ideal femininity; and now he saw nothing but ugly worm-white adolescent penises. He wanted to throw up.

"Shit, it's not like we were sitting on the steps of the library or something. We were just jerking off, you know. Innocent boyish behavior."

Mentioning the library just about did it for Tweed. No spunk stains on the library steps, thank you. He dropped Miss July gently onto the pine needle floor and stumbled outside for fresh air.

Carmine followed, doggedly pushing his perverted agenda, and laughing at his friend's discomfort. "Heh, heh, I'm really getting to you. I tell you Tweed you have to broaden your horizons." He attempted to pat his friend on the back but Tweed shied away.

"Broaden my horizons? I don't go for boys, you know?"

"Neither do I, but I wouldn't turn down a circle jerk. I mean, some things are a biological necessity."

"Circle jerk? I don't even want to know." He turned away, avoiding Carmine's eyes.

"You don't know what a circle jerk is? It's when a bunch of guys sit around and stroke..."

"I said I don't want to know." But it was too late. Goofy teenage kids with their thumbs hooked in their underpants, earnestly straining to...

Our Father, Who art in heaven
Hallowed be Thy name...
...Hail Mary, full of grace,
Blessed art Thou among women...

Prayer took him down the hill toward a small frog pond that in another month or so would ice over for skating. He scanned the sky for the hawk he had seen earlier and witnessed a v-line of geese soaring rapidly and high, high.

He too had wanted to get high, not to wander in the woods praying for escape from the dreadful revelation of his friend's kinky proclivities. Could he party under these circumstances?

It would be a shame to abandon the cozy little fire that he had triumphed in building. He couldn't leave it unattended.

Besides, he rationalized, he also had to rescue Miss July from getting her pages stuck together.

Carmine was still standing outside the fort, glumly picking the seeds out of a pine cone. After Tweed returned neither of them said anything for some time. Carmine puttered around doing housework and Tweed squatted near the fire, taking his turn at picking seeds- from a small pile of weed he had crumbled into his palm. Satisfied of its cleanliness, Tweed twisted the dope into a single leaf of rice paper and gummed the assembly tight with a silver strand of saliva.

"Got a light?"

There. He could have lit the joint himself since he always carried papers and a lighter for good luck, but now the ice was re-broken. It was funny...Rod always asked for a light too, even though he kept a book of matches in his shirt sleeve.

"Did I tell you about Rod?"

"The guy with one arm? What about him?"

"Well," Tweed inhaled deeply and spoke through the smoke, "I was with him the other day, down at the arcade. He wanted to buy a couple of bags. Anyway, before he got off work I was waiting for him outside and got to talking with one of the locals. Turns out the kid was a street hustler. Sucked me in for five bucks."

"No shit! You kick his ass?"

"No. You might say I got what I deserved since I was dumb enough to get taken that way, but I did get my money back..." Tweed then told Carmine how he insisted that Rod lead him to Rollo's hideout and confront him for the money.

"So, all's well that ends well, huh?"

"I guess so, but Rollo never gave the money back."

"He didn't? You just said that when Rod came out of the laundry he had your fin."

"Yeah, I said he had a fin. Thing is, it wasn't mine. He didn't get it from Rollo, he just pretended to. He went in there and most likely told those black kids to play along while he acted out a scene for my benefit. After a minute or so he pulled a five dollar bill out of his pocket, waved it over his head then walked out and handed it to me. I was supposed to think that he had intervened on my behalf to settle a dispute, right an injustice, you know."

"And you're saying that he didn't do that?"

"No, he didn't. He couldn't afford to make waves with the locals. They rip off people all the time. What's he gonna do? Play one-armed bandit? No fucking way. He gets on their wrong side and next thing he knows they're hassling him every day on the street, then his apartment gets torched. Old cripple dude can't get involved."

"But you knew this? You knew what he did? You took his money?"

"Ahm, not right away. I figured it out later, when I was heading home. Yeah, I got his five bucks. Serves him right, the ugly old fuck. I guess I'll make it up to him on his next bag."

"Don't say nothing, though. I mean, dude's probably got pride."

"I won't unless he does, man, not that is, unless he decides to lord it over me."

"Would he do that? Do you know him well enough?"

"Heh, well let me put it this way. One other time when I was there dropping off a bag, Rod asked me to go to the store with him, to help carry bags. So I go to the store and I was following him around while he picked shit out; and pretty soon it looks like he has some things to buy so I scoop them up. Wouldn't you know, he starts hollering to everyone in the store, going, 'This guy took my stuff! This guy is taking my groceries!' I mean, he's pointing at me and yelling, 'I'm crippled and this creep is taking advantage of me!' I tell you, I was mortified."

"Were you really taking his stuff?"

"No, man! Like I said, I was picking the stuff up so he didn't have to carry it. That's what I was there for."

"So what'd you do?"

"Well, the people in the place looked like they were going to gang up and kill me, and I was saying shit like,'Hey I really don't want his stuff, I was only...' But freaking demented Rod kept spouting nonsense about me ripping him off. So I left. Walked off and left him cold."

Tweed paused to tend to the reefer, touching it up with a moistened fingertip.

"When he came out of the store- struggling with all of his shit, I might add- I reminded him why I was there in the first place. And you know, he thought it was funny? I mean, he realized that he had fucked up, that the booze had made him so paranoid that he forgot that I was going to carry his bags. But looking back at it, he thought that it was the funniest thing that happened to him in ages. Laughed all the way home."

"Was kind of funny."

"Yeah, in a third-person perspective kind of way, but look at it from my point of view. I could have been arrested for harassing the handicapped!"

"You would've got off."

"That's beside the point!"

"Hey, well, speaking of ripping shit off, I have this plan that you have to hear."

"A plan to rip shit off?"

"Yeah!" replied Carmine enthusiastically.

"Then I don't want to hear it."

"Decide that after you hear it. It's a good plan. You know the new convenience mart that opened up next to the field?"

"Near the courts?"

"Yeah that's the one. I knew someone who works there."

"So?"

"So, she can be our inside person when we rip it off. We go in there at night, acting like we're going to rob the place, see, and she acts like she's all scared and everything and opens up the register for us."

"All that for register cash? Do you know how many things can go wrong with a plan like that?"

"No, not for the register cash- that's the diversion. What can go wrong? It's not like we're really robbing the joint."

"Speaking of joints, toke up, dude. If it's not for the cash why do it? And I'll tell you what can go wrong. While we're pretending to hold up this market, a cop could wander in, or some concerned citizen. Does the place have cameras?"

"For the booze, man, the booze! We just go through the register so they think we got away with fifty bucks or something. What we're really there for is the cooler out back. See, while I have my friend occupied at the counter, you go and tape the back door so we can get in later. Then when the place closes, we sneak in and clean it out."

"Why go through the motions of robbing the place? Why not just go back and tape the door?"

"Two reasons. 1) To cover up the theft. See, if they discover that booze is missing, they'll chalk it up to the theft. And, B) To cover up the theft. No one will expect the store to get robbed twice in the same night, will they? Shit, the register's already empty, right? Besides, I want my friend to keep her job. Could come in handy again some time." Carmine grinned like he had just worked out the variables in a quadratic equation.

"Too complicated, man. But I have to give you credit for all of the effort you put into this. Shit, you must have been scheming."

"Complicated? It's the essence of simplicity. We'd probably go in there to pick up some munchies anyway. All's I'm going to do is go up to the counter and say,'This is a hold up; open the register!' and act like I could rough up the clerk. Meanwhile, you slip into the walk-in chest, go over to the loading door and tape the lock. We leave, she calls the cops. At the end of the night we wait for the lights to go out, then we duck in the back door and hustle all the full cases out.

"Maybe an hour's work, tops. Believe me, it'll be well worth your time."

"Yeah, you went over it twice now, and I still say forget it. You don't want to have a record for larceny. I don't want to have a record at all. I have to keep my nose clean."

"You and your nose! C'mon, Tweed, take a chance! Live a little! We're not going in blind, we have an in!"

Tweed's resolve would not be shaken. His father knew practically every business owner in the square, and there was no way that he would risk getting busted for ripping off some friend of his father's. At least not while his father was in town. It wasn't inconceivable that he'd have a change of heart after the old man had gone to Ireland. In fact, one thing that bothered Tweed was that the plan was so downright appealing. He knew that the new market was perched on a berm of sod that had been bulldozed up from the ball park. That berm would provide essential cover so they could work undisturbed hauling cases of liquor out the back of the place in the dark. Transportation was another matter. Once they had all of the contraband they'd have to stash it somewhere until they could sell it.

Thinking this far ahead was useless. Tweed could not permit himself to get wrapped up in Carmine's devious schemes. After all, when Carmine was locked away in Juvie or Munie detention, he'd want Tweed to be free on the outside to visit him and smuggle in snipes and what-not.

He did know how to live, and he did take risks, but he also believed that there was a distinction between sociopathic crime and victimless crime. He'd sell all the dope he could get his hands on, but he'd have to have a damn good reason to bust in and steal someone's livelihood.

It was time to change the subject, to throw Carmine off his train of thought. "Hey, I almost forgot…a strange thing happened to me last night."

"Strange things are always happening to you, man." His inflection was somewhere between jealous and disgusted.

"Well, shit, what do you expect, I was born on Friday the 13th."

"No kidding? Isn't that supposed to be unlucky?"

"Unlucky, strange, it's all the same. Anyway last night my old man took the whole family out to dinner at The Pleasant. So when I was eating, in the middle of dinner, these two kids come up to me and tell me that they owe me ten bucks, and that they'll see me later to clear it up."

"Doesn't sound strange to me. Or unlucky."

"No, except that I never seen them before and they sure as hell didn't owe me any money. I mean, I pretty much had it figured that were just trying to get my attention."

"Probably wanted some weed."

"Bingo. Later I saw them hanging outside the clubhouse. Just happened to notice as we were coming home. They were lucky I saw them; I don't even go there anymore. After a while I went out and headed over to see if they were still there. Sure enough…standing there waiting for me to bring them a bag. If I didn't have one on me I would have told them to screw. Buggin' me in front of my parents! While I'm eating!"

"Low life motherfuckers. I would have told them to beat it."

"You know what makes me mad, though? It's the lack of privacy. Goes to show what I was saying about the clubhouse."

"The garage?"

"Yeah, man, like I said it was getting out of hand. We can't have people from all over town-strangers- dropping in at the clubhouse because they happen to be looking for weed. Next thing you know we'll have plain clothes cops in there and who knows what else."

"Yeah, I suppose, but it sure is a good location. It's easy to find. That's why it gets so much traffic."

"That's traffic I can do without. There's plenty of business without opening a friggin' street bazaar. That's the reason I'm here. It's peaceful. You have to have a place where you can get away from people, you know? Present company excluded, of course."

Who was excluded? Carmine wondered, mistaking the phrase.

"Well, you got your privacy here, anyway."

"I'm not so sure. If what you said earlier about the magazine is true, and assuming that it didn't fall from heaven," his own view of the divinity of the centerfold aside, "…then at least one kid was up here recently. And I'd have to guess that the grounds crew knows about this place, or at least about the tree, anyway, because they always trim out the deadwood. They're bound to come across it sooner or later. It's peaceful but I wouldn't call it private."

"Doesn't look like anyone's been here," observed Carmine, somewhat taken aback, and speaking almost defensively.

"Well, nobody should bother us here. We're alone now, right?"

"We should be. As far as I'm concerned, we found this place, and it's ours."

"They do cut up diseased trees and the ones hit by lightning, but maybe when they see this one, you know, appreciate the cool way it landed. Anyway, I don't think they'll bother with it until the spring."

"They don't appreciate shit. I saw a poplar once that got hit by lightning and the scar ran all the way down the tree from the top to the roots. The bark was blasted right off, all over the place. They cut that one down."

"Lots of trees like that in the park."

"True, but on this one the scar was a perfect spiral around the tree; and some of the bark was embedded, like friggin' spears, in other trees. Can you imagine the force of that explosion? I can see cutting down a dead, blasted tree, but this one looked like a unicorn's horn carved by lightning."

"I remember that tree- over by little hill, right? It had a deep spiral groove, all of the grass on the hillside was burned, too."

"Yep, that's the one. They should have left it up."

CHAPTER 47

Plot a line from Des' house to 80's boat and it's what, 13 miles or so? By car the trip is of course longer than that, but if you were going to drive then you would have to decide which route to take. You could head west out of town until you reach one of the circumferential highways. They link the outer suburbs to the city and loop back toward the ocean whether you go north or south. Then simply follow a coastal route to the harbor. Or you might try a more direct route, traveling east. However the city jealously holds the harbor around which it was built in a choking half-nelson. To get to the harbor you'd have to drive straight through the interposed city, which, while not practically impossible is possibly impractical.

Fortunately Des did not own a car, so when he decided on Sunday night to pay a visit to Makepeace, he chose public transportation, easily the most direct and efficient route in any event. By taking the bus and then the train into the city Des didn't exactly achieve the directness of a bee line to his destination, nor the rapidity of a crow's flight. But he knew that the last inbound stop on the commuter rail placed him within walking distance of the commercial wharf where Makepeace had obtained a temporary berth at a private dock. Makepeace must have paid dearly for the convenience both in terms of the fees he had paid for the berth as well as the grease he had been obliged to apply in order to stop the squealing of various authorities and officials. For as he had told Des during his stay, if he couldn't keep his boat out of sight he could at least make people look the other way.

The motivation for Des to sacrifice an evening he normally would have spent in pleasant company at the bar, was his desire to take a look at the boat himself. Makepeace had failed to keep him informed so in order to preserve his peace of mind he wanted to see if the boat was still tied up or if it had been moved. If the boat was idle then it was likely that the arms deal had not yet occurred, for as far as Des knew, it was 80's intention to disembark as soon as the cargo was secure. If, on the other hand, the boat was gone, then any number of things could be happening and Des would have to restrain his imagination. Either way he was not looking forward to confronting his friend, the captain of the vessel, because he did not wish to appear too anxious. He'd walk to the dock, take a peek, and then return home regardless of what he discovered.

The affair was frustratingly beyond his control now, and trust, the only thing that might have checked his frustration, was not something he bestowed with much confidence. Des had been certain that he could trust his own judgment although the ease with which he had been persuaded to part with his money had perhaps signified a lapse in that regard; and he could trust his principles. Furthermore he could trust his wife, but that was the extent of it, because he was not sure when it came down to it that he himself could be trusted.

People entrusted their money to him because he encouraged the perception that he was responsible, an honest steward of just causes. Despite the conventional wisdom that trust must be earned, Des had gained their trust almost effortlessly and then casually betrayed it. In other words the fact that others placed their trust in him did not mean that he was trustworthy. He applied that lesson to Makepeace accordingly.

And yet he also believed that in a business relationship trust was not as essential a component as it was in a personal relationship. The dynamics of business eliminated the need for trust. Parties entered into a business relationship for mutual gain; and unless both parties are satisfied contractually, materially, financially, etc., then the relationship falls apart. In his opinion he did not have to trust a business associate like Makepeace as long as he got what he paid for. This ethical compensation permitted him to deceive his "customers" as a function of doing business.

He smiled at the irony of contemplating trust as he neared the wharf, for he was sneaking up on Makepeace in an attempt to keep him "honest."

The air was warmer near the water and an eerie mist rolled into the streets as if a vast assembly of ghosts had turned out for a protest march. Visibility was reduced to the distance from one street lamp to the next so that he hardly noticed the transition from office buildings to warehouses on his left. Then he was strolling beside a seemingly endless chain link fence, which he knew must border the water, although he couldn't see it. He heard waves as clearly as if they were lapping at his feet and the coughing chortle of seagulls conversing with each other from perches atop pier pilings. The odor of decaying seaweed, dead fish and diesel fuel permeated the fog and seemed to be augmented in the same way that the dampness facilitated the transmission of sound. The breeze tasted distinctly salty.

Signs appeared on the fence at regular intervals warning that the pier beyond was unsafe and that trespassing was prohibited. But after a hundred yards these gave way to signs advertising boat repair, deep sea charters and fish markets.

Finally the chain link fence terminated at a large gate through which passed a cobblestone access road. Des had reached the entrance to the commercial wharf and fisherman's row. He emerged from the mist and gloom into an area illuminated by yellow floodlights that glared with the intensity of perpetual daylight.

He relaxed a little as he realized that he was again among people. For a cold Sunday evening there was a considerable amount of activity along the piers. Men were still working at this hour, some loading trucks. After a moment he realized that most of the individuals he saw were either coming from or going to a bar on the pier that appeared to be disguised as a fish and chips shack. The property was marked off with squat decorative peened-over pier heads linked together with stout ship's rope. The shack itself sported port-hole style windows framed with life preservers under a weather-beaten corrugated tin roof. The off-beat charm of the place appealed to Des and he felt a sudden urge to go in for some rest and refreshment. But as he gazed at the bar he happened to notice that next to it, behind another sagging rusty fence, sat a lobster boat grounded in the center of a parking lot. The old wooden tub had been painted and fixed up as a gimmick, advertising Bayshore Shellfish and Lobster. The pound, a large corrugated metal building standing on the edge of the pier with its toes hanging over the water, was his destination, the place where Makepeace had secured his boat.

The gate to the parking lot was locked and the place was dark, but Des was undeterred. He would have to find a good vantage point from which to determine if there was a boat back there and if so, to verify whether it was the Cor Mor. Bayshore may have had boats of their own but the building wasn't large enough to conceal more than one trawler.

Like any fifty year old male Des had long since ceased performing certain physical activities. To be honest he would have to say that he had left off doing more of them than he had carried on, and climbing fences was certainly among the first he had abandoned. Nevertheless he judged that it would be within the scope of his ability depending upon the level of necessity and, in terms of the particular fence, the level of difficulty.

After approaching Bayshore from every angle and finding himself stymied it was quickly becoming a matter of choosing the fence. For example to the right of the dockside bar there was an alley leading to a dumpster and the rear of the establishment. However there were no windows in the back of the bar and the dumpster was backed up against a ten foot stockade fence. Des could see that the bar had no need for access to the water and that furthermore it made sense to prevent tippling patrons, tipsy or otherwise, from toppling into the drink back there. The dumpster might provide a platform from which to climb either that fence or the one enclosing the parking lot next door, but it also gave off a stench worse than the harbor's foul breath. He might draw attention clattering up the wire so close to the bar anyway, so Des began to consider his other options. The gate was in full view of the road and lit up like a prison yard, so he'd have to make that a second option. The fence on the far side of the parking lot was practically leaning against a two-story cinder block garage, but the building came out further into the street so even if he went at it from that side it would still be a frontal assault. However he noticed that due to the placement of the streetlight the garage cast a shadow across the corner of the lot. The darkness would give him an advantage and in addition it was clear that an old sack of malt like himself would need the corner post if he was to have any hope at all of pulling his fat arse over the fence.

This was really no time for stealth. He had been walking around for ten minutes already and had probably been seen by a dozen people. Not that Des had much experience with this type of thing. When he was a youngster he'd had a lot of brass, and he'd been brazen throughout his subsequent career, but this was different. It was going to take a lot of nerve to vault that fence and he was going to sweat out every second of it.

Just as he was prepared to advance and make the attempt, a car suddenly pulled over to the side of the road and parked directly under the street lamp. Ignoring his own instincts, Des tried to get a glimpse of the driver, but his view was obscured by the light reflecting off the windscreen. He hesitated, breaking stride and feeling foolish. Why wouldn't the blasted fellow move on? There was nothing to see here, and Des was certainly not going to mount the fence before a witness as if he were a bloody street performer. Playing the roles of detective and prowler were enough for one night. Now he'd have to stroll down the pier again, as nonchalant as Harold Lloyd.

He had whistled all of *The Pigeon On The Gate* before coming around for another pass, and when he returned he was disappointed to see that the car was still parked in the worst possible spot.

Come off it, he thought, *I haven't got all night!* The guy was probably watching him in the rear view, practically compelling him to continue walking, as it would look odd for him to loiter about. *Or would it?* he wondered. Perhaps he could force the car away simply by standing there and staring at it. If Des were sitting in that car he'd find it pretty intimidating to see a stranger hanging around. He stopped and tried to adopt a menacing pose. It didn't work. Instead he was surprised to see the tail lights go out, the door open, and a man emerge from the car. Without paying any attention to Des, he proceeded across the street, took hold of the fence with both hands and stood there at the very place where Des had intended to climb, facing the dark, vacant parking lot.

This was too much. Curiosity got the better of Des and he decided that he had nothing to lose by asking the fellow what he was after. His footsteps resounded loudly on the cobblestones as he approached but still the fellow did not respond. Lost in thought perhaps. All the intimidation had gone out of Des now, and a bracing dose of adrenalin sped to his brain, triggering contradictory primal impulses.

"You work here, mate?"

The stranger turned, startled. He was a young man, about Des' height, wearing glasses and standard business attire. A professional, yes, but not in money, and therefore not in legal or medical. Some sort of civil servant then, or a teacher.

"Me? No, I, uh…Why, why do you ask?"

Soft pudgy features, pale. Clean-cut with medium-length brown hair. Clearly nervous.

"Oh, I didn't want to trouble you; I was just looking for a friend of mine here...at Bayshore Lobster." He hooked a thumb toward the fence but kept his eyes on the stranger.

"Well, I'm looking for a boat, actually, a fishing boat."

Des couldn't keep his eyebrows from shooting upwards. Who was this guy? "So you're going fishing, then? At this hour?"

"I didn't catch your name, Mr...?"

"Loughlin," said Des, supplying his wife's maiden name as a clue to Makepeace, should this ever get back to him. "I'm here about the Cor Mor myself." See how he responds to that.

"Ah, Mr. Loughlin, I'm Darrager, glad to meet you. Where is it? Back there? Are you going aboard?"

Where had he heard that name before? He wasn't a member of the crew, that was certain, and he was not here to go fishing. Police? FBI? Perhaps he had said too much.

"Likewise, I'm sure. I imagine so. It had better be, hadn't it?" Answering a question with a question was a basic defense mechanism.

"I haven't seen it yet; I was just stopping down here to see what it looked like."

What it looked like? What was he, an investor? An insurance man? A boat buff?

"To tell you the truth, I'm not even supposed to be here," he continued.

"No? Why not?" asked Des, with only a tenth of the interest he felt internally.

"Mr. Makepeace...you know Mr. Makepeace? He wanted me to stay away. Said he'd tell me when the time was right. Kind of like a surprise, I guess."

"Oh, yes, I know him well. He likes his little surprises, Makepeace. That's who I was looking for. Wanted to say hello before he cast off, you know? If you see him, tell him you saw me?"

"Sure, next time I talk to him. Maybe you'll have a chance to get together; I think he's going to be in town for a couple of days."

"Thanks, Darrager. Well, nice to meet you; I'll be off now. Have a train to catch."

"Where? At Central? Do you need a ride to the station?"

"Sure, I'd appreciate it...but didn't you want to see the boat?"

"Place is closed, and I can't very well break in now, can I? I'll just have to be patient."

Des couldn't break in now either, apparently.

It was hard to figure this fellow Darrager. He was direct in a naive, pudgy way, and kind enough to drive him to the train station. If he was a cop then he was putting on an elaborate act.

The next train boarded in twenty minutes. Des shared the platform with a pair of plump, stone-gray pigeons whose bobbing and pacing reminded him of a couple of white collar commuters annoyed that the train was not waiting for them instead of the other way around. As the sole passenger Des would at least be assured of his pick of seats once the train arrived.

In the meantime he reviewed his conversation with Darrager. The guy knew Makepeace, and Makepeace was going to notify him when the time was right, whatever that meant. Was it Makepeace who had mentioned the name Darrager? He didn't think so. Where then had he heard the name?

Just then a thought occurred to him and he checked the pockets of his sweater. Sure enough it was still there. A napkin, now greasy with palm sweat, that his wife had given him one night recently after tailing Makepeace by car. On it he saw the two license tag numbers she had noted, along with the information his contact in the police had provided- the names of the individuals to whom the tags were registered. There it was, Stephen Darrager, a resident of a town he recognized as a north shore bedroom community. He recalled the story Chris had related; Darrager was the guy Makepeace had met at a strip club. During the course of her surveillance she had also seen him meet with his lady friend from Marblehead, and with his man Reggie.

Were these people connected? Was there a thread that tied them all together? Could they have anything to do with the deal he had arranged with Makepeace? The more he thought about it, the more concerned, suspicious and angry he became. No matter how he looked at it, Darrager was bad news. The deal was between him and Makepeace alone. No one else should know about it. If Darrager was going to board the Cor Mor, then he could possibly learn about the cargo that was on board.

It was a matter of security. If Darrager wasn't a member of the crew, and he didn't appear to be, then he shouldn't have been there; unless, of course, he was an arms dealer himself. Somehow that didn't wash. Des had known arms dealers and smugglers of various stripes, and this guy didn't fit the profile. He lacked the ego, the drive and the marketing skill. You want to sell arms, or anything for that matter, you have to sell yourself too. Darrager was too timid.

And it was a matter of jeopardy. With every contact Makepeace had created another opportunity for risk, betrayal, arrest, or rip-off.

And, damn it, it was a matter of trust. If he was going to bring other people in on the deal, then at the very least he should have let Des know. Didn't Makepeace realize what was at stake? The money alone should have made the difference. It should have reminded him of the degree of obligation.

OK, so he was down at the wharf looking for his partner, 80 Makepeace, and instead he met Darrager. Was it a chance encounter, a set-up, or a flipping coincidence?

CHAPTER 48

As we roll into Halloween week, 1974, it may be helpful to review the events described thus far before proceeding to the conclusion of this retrospective.

Des Kelley, who had dual citizenship and lived in the US with his wife and family, was planning the latest of a series of bi-annual trips to Ireland, his ancestral homeland. He would remain for the month of November, staying for the most part in his old hometown of Boyle. There he still owned a pub that had been in his family for generations and was now run by his eldest son Buck.

Whether he professed to be traveling for business or pleasure, the true purpose of his trip was to smuggle in money and/or illegal weapons, purportedly to defend Catholic, nationalist and republican Irish against aggressive northern loyalist paramilitaries and the forces of the British Crown. A former member of the IRA and an ardent activist for the cause of Irish independence, Des was born with a genetic predisposition toward republican dissent and had been indoctrinated at an early age into the politics of Irish freedom.

Throughout his life Des adhered to a concept of a socialist republic that had been politically obsolete before he ever left Ireland in 1960. He had emigrated to the US with the specific intent of tapping the wealth of the diaspora, deliberately targeting established Irish-Americans such as cops, pols, tradesmen, entertainers and publicans. Having secured their patronage virtually by dint of his ambition and genuine entrepreneurial spirit, he used it to support those in Ireland whom he deemed to be the true heirs and standard-bearers of the revolution. In time he was able to create a quasi-legitimate and self-sustaining fund-raising entity called CAFÉ. The Citizens Alliance for Erin, ostensibly formed to collect funds for Irish relief, and alternatively known as the Citizens Arms Fund for Erin, became the ideal front for a modestly successful weapons smuggling operation during the latter part of the 1960s.

However, less than a month prior to his departure, when his plans were already in disarray due to the chaos and uncertainty engendered by the IRA's current bombing campaign, Des received an unexpected visitor from Ireland. AD Makepeace was an old friend and arms dealer who operated out of his own fishing boat back in the old country. Kelley had dealt with Makepeace on a number of occasions in the past and had even recommended him to his comrades in the IRA. Yet his arrival in the US was almost as startling as the proposal he delivered, for he suggested that Des hire him to make a daring and, as far as he knew, unprecedented trans-Atlantic arms run.

Violence had been escalating in Northern Ireland since the IRA began lashing back at the loyalist factions for the depredations they had committed in response to the civil rights movement in Derry and Belfast. The Troubles persisted, continuing in a bloody tit-for-tat fashion. On October 15th for example, the IRA planted a bomb in London, and six days later the Ulster Volunteer Force assassinated two Catholics on the Falls Road in Belfast. The distinction between provocation and retaliation became blurred again on Monday, the 28th when the IRA killed two British soldiers in a bomb attack outside Ballykinlar British Army base, County Down.

With Makepeace supplying American weapons, Des could make substantial progress in the effort to arm the border communities against what he feared would be an all-out assault by the

British. Thoroughly persuaded, he ultimately decided to take the risk for a major weapons haul, and he paid over to Makepeace the bulk of his receipts for the past six months.

For his part, Makepeace was also running a variety of scams. He was trying to make a profit from his deal with Des Kelley, to enhance his earnings for a voyage that he had already undertaken for the IRA. They wanted him to smuggle in a new recruit, an American electronics and avionics engineer whose skill and expertise could help them to offset the technological advantage currently held by the British. The British had also hired Makepeace (making the circle complete), to track the source of American weapons that were ending up in the hands of loyalist street gangs in Ulster.

Throughout all of this he was less concerned with failing to fulfill the promises he had made to his business partners than he was with being discovered by any of them as a two-timer. Unfortunately for Makepeace, Kelley had been especially assiduous regarding all aspects of his transaction. His normal professional suspicions were heightened by a chance meeting with Darrager, the American engineer. This encounter threatened to shatter the illusion of separation that Makepeace had woven about his missions, although Kelley had yet to understand how Darrager was involved.

In the meantime we have been observing events and activities in the life of Kelley's youngest son Tumbleweed. An independent lad of 14 years, 'Tweed' was the only of Kelley's four sons to be born and raised in America. And though he seemingly fell far from the tree he was the apple of his father's eye, for Des expected him to assume the outrage, guilt, fervor and passion befitting a true son of Erin as he matured, and to join him in his radical Irish agenda. The youngest child, in the throes of puberty, was dealing with a different set of priorities, and he had yet to exercise his powers of observation, judgment or perspicacity. The only significance he attached to his heritage was that it was responsible for what his friends called his "accent", which, despite his efforts to speak 'normally' was detectable in his distinct enunciation and syllabic emphasis. He was more interested in experiencing the sacramental rites in the new holy trinity of sex, drugs and rock 'n roll. To this end he had taken up dealing marijuana, and had gradually expanded his market base from friends in his neighborhood to customers in school and points beyond.

As for sex, he had yet to rationally accept the fact that in his brief life he already had more sexual experience than most boys, even those among his peers who had already achieved manhood. In his prepubescent days he had frequently been a somewhat passive and unwitting participant in raw sex play with a pair of girls his age, twins who lived across the street. The precocious trio had also displayed their naughty intimate games as the featured attraction in shows they staged for the benefit of the older kids. He had almost forgotten these incidents by the time he reached puberty but now he was driven by a relentless desire for female companionship. His frustration was particularly acute since his first relationship with a girl had flared and fizzled in a matter of weeks.

Yet his closest friends were boys, one of whom had recently experienced sexual trauma in his own life, and the other who expressed a view of sexuality that made Tweed uncomfortable. Furthermore both of his friends were petty criminals, prone to thievery and other sociopathic behavior that they exhibited by committing crimes of nuisance and vandalism.

Tweed felt that he was well on his way toward becoming his own man, self-made and self-reliant. His father's departure would do little to change that one way or the other. The old man went to Ireland on business twice a year. It had never mattered to Tweed before and he had little anticipation that it would matter now.

Nevertheless, it was clear that Tweed was receptive to influences. And one consequence of his father's absence could merely be that he was beyond his influence, and perhaps vulnerable to other influences. As an adolescent, Tweed was still shaping his character, molding his nature to suit the positive elements he recognized in other people. To watch him in conversation one would think that he was performing a running medley of impressions, as his face took on expressions he had gleaned from the friends he emulated. By turns, a thoughtful pursing of the lips, a la Carmine Gunther, and then the elevated left eyebrow, a la Brendan Tighe. Eventually his face would portray him instead of caricatures, but it was notable that nowhere in his repertoire did he employ any of the gestures, mannerisms, words or expressions of his father, Des Kelley.

But lest we forget, the reason for the extended examination of this period in the lives of the father and his son, this flash blast from the past; was to help determine how, twelve years later, Tweed was to become involved in a plot to kill his dear old Da. Not to paint too broad a picture, but the lingering image of the parochial Irishman winging away to smuggle guns into the land of his youth while his son holed up in a forest fortress scheming the expansion of his drug empire may resonate far more effectively than a prolonged dissertation on the subject.

CHAPTER 49

By Tuesday, October 29th extreme agitation had set in and Des felt a preternatural malaise of confinement and impotency, as if an inner beast in his breast demanded release and satisfaction. What good was it to go home with nothing to show for it? How could he have been so gullible as to give everything he had to a blasted ghost, a pookah who had conjured his way into Des' life and then conned him out of his money? What recourse did he have? Call the police, the Coast Guard? Track him down in Ireland? The fellow lives on a freaking boat, for God's sake. Get the IRA involved? Fat lot of good that would do, except to make Des look foolish and perhaps even to cause himself to be dragged in front of a court of inquiry. He could do without the hooded debriefing session, thank you. It was time to call a friend with a car and ask him to drive down to the dock where they would smash the gates if they had to; and find Makepeace, the sneaky bastard, before he lit out onto the open water. That is, if he really had brought his boat over. Could have all been a ruse. Never saw the boat, never saw the guns. Got nothing for his money except for wind sauce and air pudding. And not only did that taste like shit, but the portions were too small.

Des thought that he was easy to get along with. He had behaved as a friend and as a host, and had been repaid with deceit and treachery. Normally self-contained and placid for an Irishman, his blood was now boiling, and in his rage he vented abuse and vituperation upon Makepeace, who was not available to wither in the storm of vitriol. So he spent the better part of the last afternoon before his voyage in a spiral of anger and self-reproach. At last he decided that he could do worse than to go to the biz club, believing that ale and exercise would surely put him back to rights.

It was well that he did so for it was there that Makepeace finally called him. Joe Toole pulled the phone up from beneath the bar, handed the receiver to Des, and said, "Your man."

He heard Makepeace speaking before he even raised the phone to his ear. "Des? Des? We're on, mate!"

Des was momentarily speechless, like he had caught a sucker punch.

"80? How kind of you to call. Are you done, then? And still sticking around?"

"Nearly done, Des…"

"Then write your mother," muttered Des vehemently.

"What's that? I said good news, old man. Just calling to let you know that it's a go…"

"So you have nothing to show me?"

"Like I told you, this isn't a Tupperware party. And as you say, I want to move on as soon as possible. Let's take this a step at a time. If I can see you before I go I will; but either way, I'll call."

"Better than that, 80, I'll come see you- right now."

"What? Now, Des? I don't like talking to you on the phone like this, but…"

"That's why I'll come down there and see you in person."

"…but I'm busy, you know? I'm on the job, damn it. It'll take you at least an hour to get here, and I don't know where I'll be in an hour. It's a waste of time, I tell you, Des. Wait to hear from me, when I have more good news to tell. Then we'll see."

"I'm going to drive down there and we'll talk then. If I understand you correctly, then you are waiting anyway. I'll take my chances that you'll be there. As for how long it will take, well, I think

I'll wait out the afternoon traffic, then go along directly. Say, after dinner. Perhaps we'll have a drink together, to celebrate." With that he rang off resoundingly.

Passing the phone back to the bartender he said, "Joe, can you get Dan in here to cover for a couple of hours?"

Joe stood, flipped a washrag over his shoulder and placed his hands on his hips, assent in his eyes.

"And I think we'll see if Simon is up for a ride in town."

Des wasn't merely looking for someone with a car and some company for the ride. He was looking to deliver a message with impact, a message that he was no man to trifle with. He and Joe Toole and Simon Fecteau were an imposing trio but for extra muscle they also arranged to pick up Woody from the Wild Geese. The combined weight of the squad topped 900 pounds, a load Joe's Bonneville was well-equipped to carry. The weight of additional lard-asses only seemed to make it handle better.

By 7PM the group was leaving Francestown, following the curve of the greater harbor southward toward the center of town. By boat they could have cut the trip in half, even considering speed restrictions and convoluted buoy controlled traffic lanes in the inner harbor. But Des had announced his intentions and would gain nothing with the element of speed or surprise.

This wasn't the first time that Des had rallied his friends to back him on a mission of might and intimidation. He was their motivator-general in any event, and although he demanded discipline from his cadre he was always generous in gratitude. Nobody in the car asked why they were driving to the docks and Des declined to fill them in. Instead he chatted breezily about his upcoming trip, current events, and, knowing that Simon's brother-in-law was a publisher's sales rep, about the latest novels. Simon said that he had just finished *Tinker, Tailor, Soldier, Spy*, by LeCarre, and he'd loan it to Des. Less approachable, in his opinion but no less intriguing was *Gravity's Rainbow* by Pynchon. Simon called it a thumper, because every time he tried to read it before bed it periodically thumped down on his chest and woke him.

Des turned to Joe, "You taking the kids out for trick or treat?"

"They go out on their own; but I'll be helping with the block party, you know, the one we hold every year."

"Oh, yes, the block party. I usually miss that when I go away. What'll you be doing? Cooking hot dogs and such?"

"No, I call the dances. It's a shame that you can't come, Des, it's a lot of fun. I expect to see your boys, though, because every girl this side of the square will be there. "

"Call? Like a barn dance, a square dance?"

"More like the *Bunny Hop*, the *Hokey Pokey* and the *Chicken Dance*. Get all the youngsters wearing costumes into a big circle, and dance them to death. I do Simon Says and musical chairs, too."

"That's what it's all about..." sang Des, merrily.

Soon the *Hokey Pokey* tune had insinuated itself into his head, providing a musical accompaniment as he mused on what it was all about.

It was about his pride and his principles and it was about the money. It was about getting an advantage, and helping to provide an advantage to people back home who were eking out an existence threatened by fear and intimidation. People for whom a simple drive to the North to buy a television or a refrigerator was a harrowing experience, for it required crossing multiple military checkpoints manned either by callous Gardai, masked insurgent gunmen, or surly British thugs. Caught between the passively complacent government in Dublin and the terrorists in Ulster, the folks in the rural countryside of Leitrim, Fermanagh, Monaghan and Armagh were exposed and vulnerable. Des had been working to level the playing field, believing that with every cache of weapons he also delivered peace of mind. And yet, when they needed it the most, when the crisis was already upon them and things could only get worse, Des feared that he would fail, and arrive with empty pockets and hollow excuses.

At least he was no longer beholden to the IRA, but for all of that he couldn't help wondering if they had something to do with his current difficulties. Finding himself a day before departure with the deal yet to be consummated, it was no stretch at all to imagine that they were using Makepeace to get either his money or his guns. If that were the case, then it would do no good to contact his old comrades, for they'd then be obliged to deal with him directly, and that could only come out badly for all concerned. Not that he had any real qualms, for he had long-established self-preservation protocols and self-defense mechanisms in addition to a network of allies and safe houses.

The Kelley name was known and respected from Sligo to Cork, from Donegal to Down. If he had been ripped off, he wouldn't take it lying down, that was for sure. Whether it was Makepeace himself or the IRA, Des would find a way to settle the score, and to make up for any losses, real or perceived.

"It's up on your left now, Joe, at the end of the fence…"

The big car rolled slowly along the water's edge, and the men gazed out through the fence at the harbor. Spotlights in the distance reflected as shimmering spikes extending a quarter of a mile across the black water. A pair of container ships were briefly visible in silhouette, anchored for unloading at the massive Subaru receiving dock across the quay.

"The public lot up here?" asked Joe. A sandwich board sign on the right advertised hourly rates, but no attendant appeared to be present.

"No, keep going, take a left."

"Right onto the pier? Can we park down there?"

"We're not going far, and there'll be acres of parking, as they say. Now look for the dry dock lobster boat."

Bayshore Shellfish and Lobster was closed and dark and desolate as it had been the night before but Des was undaunted. The chain link and aluminum gate was locked with a stout chain and padlock. When Des told Joe to nose his car up to the gate and to gun it, he figured the chain would go before the padlock, but in fact, it was the hinges that popped. The gate folded and wrapped the front of Joe's car as if in a coat of mail. Joe proceeded to drag the entire assembly across the barren parking lot until the frame and cross members of the gate fell aside, clanging in showers of sparks.

The four men emerged from the car with alacrity like a clown posse arriving at a circus fire act. Instead of a rescue trampoline they picked up the Bonny's new hood ornament by the edges and promptly removed the fence to the ground.

After an anticlimactic moment as they stood around wondering why no one had paid attention to the gate crashing, Des led the way toward the pound, feeling uneasy because he hadn't yet been challenged.

The building was two-stories tall and spanned the width of the lot, with a colonial gable-style shake-shingle roof. Offices upstairs, a wholesale operation on the first floor left, and a retail counter on the right. A walkway leading to the pier ran between the shops on the first floor. The passageway was dark and seemed to be too long for the apparent distance it traversed.

As the men walked on, they were met with a fetid exhalation of warm sea air that gushed outward in their faces, rank with fresh fish and seaweed, sea-gull droppings and mildew. Yet they heard only their own footsteps and it occurred to Des that the place could well be deserted. Emerging from the other end he saw that there was another empty lot in the rear, and a loading area beyond, with a smaller building adjacent to the actual pier. Des breathed a bit easier now that he was in the open but remained wary that his only retreat was back through that passage. A moment's hesitation, then he signaled his men silently and advanced, encouraged by the sight of a fishing boat tied to the dock. Des' heart was pounding heavily now and he started to jog to dispel some adrenaline. Groans pursued him as the group picked up the pace for what became a fifty-yard trot across tar and cinders. But they came up short as if stunned by the beams of two searchlights that turned on them suddenly. Then as if to surround them, all of the lights in the area were illuminated. AD Makepeace approached from the opposite direction as if he had been standing on the dock and awaiting their arrival all along. He issued a greeting that fell flat in the damp evening air, and Des responded with a bellowed retort.

"You got my money, Makepeace?"

"Des, we had a deal. You're not backing out now, are you?" He stood with his hands raised in an exaggerated shrug.

"I gave you the money, 80. What have you got to show for it?"

"I told you that everything is set. You'll get what you paid for, as agreed. Patience, my friend."

"And you'll get what's coming to you as well," Des snarled, and stepped closer, now nose to nose with his business partner.

"No need for threats, now...We've known each other too long for that, haven't we?"

"You call this a threat?" asked Des, hauling back and punching Makepeace in the face with a walloping right that opened a small cut on his cheek. Before Makepeace had finished staggering back under the blow, three of his men had rushed forth from the boat, making for Des. But they were matched man for man by Joe, Simon and Woody on Des' side, and in a moment the scene erupted into a general melee, with elbow-throwing, shin-kicking, knuckle-busting, and knee-crashing.

The two sides were coincidentally well-matched. It was like orang-utans versus chimpanzees, block-bodied bar brawlers against sea-legged sailors with arms like braided steel. But experience gave the upper hand to Des' complement. Simon and Joe were both veterans; an ex-Marine, Simon had survived Korea, and Joe was ex-Navy, capable of singlehandedly clearing a barroom of inebriated troublemakers.

The scrap was all over in minutes, and though the sailors got the worst of it, it was the older men who would ache for days afterwards. Reggie the first mate, the only one still on board the Cor Mor, had blasted the boat's air horn as if to signal the end of round one. Makepeace, panting and red-faced, raised his hands to capitulate and he spat upon the dock.

"What do you want, Des? This wasn't necessary. Maybe it made you feel better to kick my ass, but for Christ's sake, it was dangerously stupid, don't you think?" He spat again.

"Ballsy, you mean?"

"No, stupid," he lowered his voice, "...for all you know I could be sitting on a load of weapons here. I guess it does take balls to walk up to a fucking battleship, especially when the crew is nervous and paranoid. We're keeping a low profile here, you know? No attention from Coast Guard or police harbor patrol. So, OK, you avoided a firefight, but it's almost as bad to be thrashing like street gangs."

He yelled toward the boat that was still hidden behind the glaring searchlights, "Reggie! Get these men some whiskey...and ice!"

Des waved weakly for Joe, Woody and Simon to go aboard. Joe shrugged, rubbed the back of his neck with his right hand, and pushed his buddies up the narrow gangplank ahead of him.

AD Makepeace remained outside with Des. A seagull descended in a graceless arc through the frosty air to alight near them upon the pier. It strutted about and cocked its head at the men, appraising them like a gym coach who had just broken up a fight between his students. Des made as if to say something to scare the bird off, but thought better of it and closed his mouth.

"He's looking for a hand-out," said Makepeace, thickly.

"Is that what you were looking for…like this filthy gull…a handout?"

"Now wait a minute. I told you that I could get the guns and I got the guns."

"Where are they? Show me."

"I haven't got them yet…"

"Did you pay for them?"

"Des, why are you doing this? Let me do what I have to do. You should be getting ready to leave."

"I know what I have to do. I have to take care of myself, and I'm not leaving until I have either my money or the guns."

"Is that it, then? You don't trust me to do it after you leave? I brought my boat and crew all the way from Dingle just to con you out of some cash? What am I going to do, head home with your money? It would cost me that much just to hide for a month. I'm telling you, it's under control. That is, if you haven't fucked it up by coming here. I told you not to expose yourself. Now you'll have me worried."

"I gave you that money on Saturday. I thought that you'd have left by now."

"Like I said, I couldn't come back to your place. I've been busy lining this thing up. Look; it happens tonight, alright? I'm just waiting for the all-clear. But you have to leave be, if you still want it to happen. Get out of the way."

Des started to respond but 80 continued, "I don't blame you for being careful. Since when can you trust your friends?"

"I'll go home when I have some answers, 80. You had me fairly flummoxed when you arrived unannounced like you did, and I've been trying to figure it out since then. Your idea for this scheme didn't explain much, but I was willing to go along with it."

"What do you mean, Des? I told you why I came."

"Well, you know, it seemed that you stayed with me but you were being put up by the IRA if you know what I mean."

Makepeace stared at him steadily for a moment. "I don't have to tell you that a man can tell the truth and yet avoid talking of things that would be harmful for others to know."

"Hey, like I said, I was willing, was I not? I didn't need to know how they are involved, but I do need to know how someone in particular is involved." He paused to gauge 80's reaction.

Only a flutter of doubt passed over his face as he replied, "Who? Reggie?"

"No; I don't need to know anything else about Reggie, or about your wealthy lady-friend for that matter. I want to know about Darrager."

A poker player's version of a double-take preceded his response. Concerned as much with learning what Kelley knew as he was with concealing his surprise, he said, "Stephen Darrager?"

Des simply pursed his lips as if to say, "Come off it!"

To which Makepeace asked, "You know Darrager? How?"

"I want *you* to tell *me* about him. You owe me a little honesty right now."

Gritting his teeth Makepeace cursed his luck. His mission could be in jeopardy. He performed a little round-robin exercise in his head, connecting the players across the board, Des to the IRA, the IRA to Darrager, Darrager to the British and the British to himself. In conclusion he reckoned that Kelley could do little to damage him with his intelligence.

"I know Stephen Darrager. He's an American, lives just outside the city. I had lunch with him once or twice. Why do you want to know about him?"

"You've asked me how and why. I might as well tell you where and when, too. Here and now I need to know because he doesn't, or I should say, shouldn't, have anything to do with our deal."

"You talked to him?" Makepeace almost sounded amazed.

"I'm asking you, 80. Tell me about Darrager. What the fuck is he doing on your boat?"

To Makepeace this line of questioning was disturbingly reassuring. Kelley had done his homework somehow and had put him in a spot. That was disturbing. But he didn't seem to have any idea how Darrager was involved.

"Nothing," he started.

"Fuck!" shouted Des, "Tell me the truth, damn it!"

"Nothing to do with our deal."

Laughter could be heard emanating from the open bulkhead on the Cor Mor. Apparently the boys had patched things up and were enjoying themselves. Des marveled that these men who didn't know each other were equally complacent about toasting each other as they were about fighting. On the contrary Des and his old friend were locked in mutual distrust and suspicion. He suddenly felt tired and wished that he were home.

"Fair enough, 80. Then why, pray tell, is he going aboard the Cor Mor? Because I'll tell you, knowing what he isn't isn't enough. You say he isn't a part of our deal; well, he isn't part of your crew, either. What else isn't Mr. Darrager? I hope your answer includes things like US federal agent."

"Alright, Des. I can tell you what he is, if you really want to know."

"I think the benefits outweigh any possible disadvantages right now, all things considered."

Makepeace shook his head gravely and spoke reluctantly, "Then I'll tell you- I'll tell you everything. That way you can decide if you have learned enough to be satisfied, if you need to know more, or if you know too damn much already.

"I'll tell you about the IRA and about Darrager, but don't say that I didn't warn you, because you might not like what you hear.

"Darrager is IRA- a recruit, a new recruit, a volunteer actually. Not particularly Irish; I mean, he was born and raised in the States...but he's motivated. You see, he's wanted to get involved ever since Bloody Sunday, when he became aware of the civil rights movement and he saw scenes on television of British soldiers beating down the peacenik demonstrators in the streets of Derry. He was a college student at the time. Stayed in school, avoided the draft and earned advanced degrees in electrical engineering and avionics. Started working at Northrop before he even finished school. On his way home from work he would often stop at an Irish bar near the plant, where he ultimately met the people who recruited him and got this whole thing started.

"Now he's going over, and I'm giving him a lift. Then my part will be done, and he'll be off to parts unknown. It has nothing to do with the guns."

"It does if he's aboard. I've always accepted your vouch for the crew, but he's not crew."

Makepeace had sold the trustworthiness of his crew as part of a pledge he made to Kelley that he called his liability clause. Basically it stated that in the event that the boat was detained, searched or seized, then only Makepeace and his crew would take the fall, thus protecting the buyer from apprehension or prosecution. In fact he made this pledge duplicitously, for his men were all protected by the mercenary arrangement he had with British Army intelligence.

"He knows nothing about the guns, and since I'm taking the freight aboard before I take him aboard he won't learn about them."

"I don't like it, 80."

"He'll disembark with the crew before you and I meet to unload. He'll never see the stuff. And even if he did, you already told me that you figured the IRA would know what you were doing."

"Frankly, I'm just as concerned with them ripping me off as I am with you ripping me off."

"This isn't a fucking rip-off. I told you I'd haul the freight and I shall."

"I might have felt better, I mean I might have been less suspicious if you had told me what you were up to. For all I know this Darrager fellow isn't the only fucking passenger. You could be hiring to haul illegal immigrants. And I'm not so damned casual about what I let the IRA know about my business. I only said that I wouldn't expect any help from them, that's all. I'm sure they'd like to know about this...they'd love to know what I'm up to, and to make a grab for themselves."

"No, Des," Makepeace looked down at his shoes, "They couldn't care less. They don't want to know. They only care about Darrager. You're ancient history."

"Ancient history, you say? I was just there this Beltaine past."

"Yes, but just as you have nothing to do with the new leadership, they have nothing to do with you. Lord knows I wouldn't tell them about our arrangement, but if they found out, it wouldn't make a difference. I mean, they haul guns in by the trawler-load."

"This load in nothing to sneeze at!"

"I agree. I'm just saying that whether you succeed or whether you are arrested they look at what you're doing as a matter of no consequence."

"The feeling is mutual. Communists and criminals, the lot of them. It's not like the old days."

"Precisely. It's not like the old days. You can see the proof of that when they start bringing in guys like Darrager. You're one of the old-timers, and the old-timers have become irrelevant. They no longer have any influence." He told himself to drop the subject. Des looked pale and withdrawn. "So, will you give me until tonight, anyway?"

"I suppose I can stick around for a while," mumbled Des.

"No. Go home, man. I don't need you hanging around; and you are too busy at any rate. Tell you what...I've got an idea..." He searched his pockets. "Yes, I've got it. Here, take this." He handed Des a stiff white invitation card.

"What is it?" Des squinted at it from arms length and then tromboned it a couple of times in front of his face.

"Look at it! It's an exclusive ticket to an invitation-only event- the Ali fight on closed-circuit TV. The match is in Africa so it'll be running late here, but you'll see it live- as it happens. Tonight. You can go any time after nine. Personally I think Foreman will take it, but still it'd be great to see The Greatest regain his heavyweight title."

Kelley stared at the card in wonder, apparently placated, at least for the time being. "This is tonight?"

"Where have you been? It's the fight of the century, the Rumble in the Jungle, Des. Yeah, it's tonight- history in the making."

"Alright. Alright then, fine." Des seemed satisfied as he carefully tucked the invitation into a coat pocket.

"Good man. You enjoy yourself. That ticket came from our connection, the one who set this up. So you might take that as a sign of good faith. And you know, after the fight, get yourself home and get some rest before your flight tomorrow. You won't hear from me unless there's a problem. Later in the month I'll call you as we discussed. Between now and then just put me out of your mind."

CHAPTER 50

"So is it cool with you, huh?"

"Shut up, will you? I'm trying to make a shot."

Col balanced a basketball on the fingertips of his right hand and lined it up with the end of his nose. When he went up with the ball a bolt of mucus ran like quicksilver out of his nostrils and he wiped it on the sleeve of his sateen windbreaker. The shot stunned the backboard as if he'd clobbered it with a brick, then on rebound it skidded off the rim and fell close to where Tweed was standing. The support posts vibrated like a tuning fork, and the ball rang off the pavement with a hollow rubber ping and dribbled away. Tweed made no effort to catch or retrieve it.

"Thanks, man!" said Col sarcastically as he shouldered his friend out of the way. His ball was rolling rapidly toward the far end of the court, and if he didn't hustle it would continue out past the fence and pick up speed on the slope down toward the street.

As he sprinted after the ball he saw Carmine jogging into the park, headed in his direction. "Yo! Gun-tha! Grab the…"

Carmine had seen the runaway basketball and without breaking stride he scooped it up casually and carried it back to the court.

"Too cold for b-ball, man!"

"Thanks! Nah, I'll play 'til there's snow on the ground."

"Yeah, but the ball doesn't bounce for shit!" Carmine fired a gut-shot cannonball and one-hopped it over to Col to make his point.

"Hey, Tweed, we got a problem. I came to tell you as soon as I could. I was just coming up from the Center and since I had to cut through the park I thought I'd stop in and check out the fort, you know, see how it's doing?"

"And? What's wrong? Did they cut it down?"

"No, man, worse. Somebody found it. When I went in there I found all sorts of shit lying around. I mean somebody's been using the place! They built a fire in there and everything, like the place belonged to them."

"No shit!"

"No man, I'm serious. This sucks. Couldn't believe it. Fuckin' soon as you get something fuckin' good somebody comes along and fuckin' spoils it."

Jimmy Col was a bit confused, trying to piece the story together from what he'd heard. "The fort? What fort?"

Tweed answered, "Yeah, I meant to tell you about it. We, ah, Carmine and me found it the other day after the storm; remember that storm last week? Well, we were up on hemlock ridge, where you cut over to get to the stream, and there was this tree that was blown over. The cool thing about it was how it landed against another tree just the right way so that it made this huge fort- it looks like an Indian lodge, like a big wigwam, you know? Fucking incredible. I mean, you'd have to work all day to build a fort that good. Freakin' roof's like ten feet high! We built a fire pit in there and brought up some chairs."

"Yeah," said Carmine, still excited and breathless, "Except now somebody else is using them. Moved right in and made themselves at home. You want to go check it out?"

"Let me think about it." Tweed looked pensive.

"What? You have to think?"

"No, I got shit to do. Gotta make a couple of deliveries. Anyway, the fort isn't going anywhere. At least not yet."

"What do you mean?"

"I mean we should head up there tonight, when hopefully we'll find whoever it is that's using our place. I say we drag them out and teach 'em a lesson."

"OK...alright! Sounds like a plan, sounds like a plan." Carmine smacked his right fist into his left palm for emphasis. Col also nodded approval.

"Usual time, usual place, then. Catch you later."

The boys split off in separate directions. Tweed walked to the square to sell almost an ounce of pot (including another dime bag for his new customers, the McManus brothers); Carmine headed to his girlfriend's house to see if he could mooch some food; and Col hurried back to his house to put away the ball, grab a cup of hot chocolate, and blow his nose.

The evening was considerably colder and windy when the boys returned to the park, whistling to each other like bombs falling in the dark. Having found each other at the path inside the tree line they followed the perimeter of the neighborhood for some distance, and the lights from the houses on their left pierced the gloom like signal fires from watch pickets.

Ahead and to the right the expanse of the park loomed larger in their imaginations than in reality. Despite the fact that for years they had explored every square foot and knew the place as if it were an extension of their own back yards, at night the park seemed to swallow them up. This was partly because of the absence of visual cues, and partly because there was less noise coming from the surrounding streets to hem them in with audible boundaries.

Rationally they had no reason to fear the park, having lived next to it for most of their lives, and for the most part they would happily spend any time of night or day in any area within the park. Indeed their parents trusted them to "play safely" on the hills, fields, trees, ponds and streams that made up the property.

Yet there were parts of the place that the boys avoided for a variety of reasons. For instance there was "The Witch's Kitchen", actually the bleached remains of an old caretaker's cabin. The exposed foundation of marble and brick, which would have held little interest to an undergraduate archeology student, resisted the overgrowth of creepers and weeds and the encroachment of the brush, and maintained an eerie presence in the grove of willow and chestnut trees it inhabited. Somehow each successive generation of children who roamed the park inherited the fables and lore regarding such places in the park. They learned to give the "kitchen" a wide berth lest they fall prey to enchantment by the mysterious witch's hex, and become imprisoned in the dungeon that surely lay hidden below the forest floor.

Another such area was the "Indian Steps", a primitive stairway cut into a steep grade ascending to a scenic overlook, one of the highest points in the park. Many locals swore that the stairs "felt funny", describing an aura that some considered spooky, others considered sacred. Either way the steps were haunted and therefore to be avoided, even though the process of going around them was toilsome, a difficulty that pointed to the need for the steps in the first place.

Another dreaded spot was "Deadman's Curve", a bend in the access road that led to the top of Motley Hill. It was said that over the last hundred years a dozen people had died there while attempting to descend the hill at high speed on toboggans, go-karts, bicycles or skate-boards. A stalwart Paul Bunyan of an oak tree stood guard at the critical spot on the curve where control of acceleration was either won or lost by foolhardy daredevils as they attempted to earn renown and notoriety at the cost of limb or life. If the grounds-crews who maintained the park had any conscience they would have removed the oak long ago, for in the absence of any obstacle, those who had failed to negotiate the curve would have simply wiped out, suffering bumps, sprains, or humiliation.

In addition there was a storm drain called the "Mob's Oubliette". Located near a culvert on the first base side of a baseball diamond that the neighborhood kids had carved out of a field in the hollow of a natural amphitheater with a backdrop of majestic spruce trees, the sewer had been stuffed with the bodies of two alleged informants. Prior to their tandem interment, the ill-fated pair had been preparing to testify in the high-profile trial of a crime boss. Tweed remembered well the hoopla and drama of the incident that had occurred the same month he turned twelve. The frustration of the search and rescue units was almost comical as they tried to gain entry to the park with their vehicles and equipment, and Tweed took it as a lesson that he filed away for future reference. Apparently even Mafia hit men were aware of the impenetrability of Arbs Park, a feature that Tweed would come to value in later years when he used it as a hiding place for stolen cars.

Superstition kept the boys away from the Witch's Kitchen and the Indian Steps, places where any threat was imagined, the fear having been engendered by legends. However in the case of the Oubliette, the story was no urban myth, no legend. A neighborhood couple had discovered the bodies in the "manhole" during the course of their early morning jog, and many people had subsequently witnessed the police removing the evidence. And the danger of Deadman's Curve was real. Tweed himself had witnessed a fatal accident there in February of '71, when a Westbury Circle teenager had flown off his sled and struck the tree, apparently trying to ditch. His back was broken and he died instantly. Paramedics on ski-mobiles arrived promptly. Failing to resuscitate him they towed his body away on a toboggan. Like a morbid consolation to the other sledders, the word went around the hill that if he had survived the accident he certainly would have been paralyzed.

For Tweed and his buddies danger was not always a deterrent or else they would never have enjoyed such perilous pursuits as swinging over the abandoned quarry, plummeting down the rock slide at the back of the cliff on shreds of cardboard, or running a pulley tram on a cable strung between two telephone poles a tenth of a mile apart alongside the tracks.

Yet common sense dictated that they stay out of areas such as Skunk Cabbage Swamp, a half-mile long crescent-shaped stretch of low-lying bogs that were said to contain treacherous camouflaged pitfalls of quicksand and sucking mire. Tweed had explored the bogs and determined that they were well worth avoiding, if only because of the stench of muck and methane that hung about the place, but also because of the abundance in that area of bloodsucking insects and hostile vegetation including sticker burrs, cat-o-nine tails and exploding milkweed pods.

Also off-limits were any trails or attractions that were designed for or frequented by tourists. No more than ignorant interlopers, the tourists never saw the park as it truly was, but were instead satisfied following a rodent's maze of trail markers and information placards. The boys saw themselves as elusive and silent as prototypical Indians, invisible and undetectable as mountain rangers; one with their environment among the trees. They observed the tourists but were not observed; and they moved freely and directly through the park, while other visitors rarely strayed from the color-coded trails and paved pathways. And yet if Tweed looked closely he would notice that he and his friends, brothers and neighbors had over the years created trails of their own, as well-worn and established as any that were built by the municipal Parks and Rec. Dept.

"So you never answered me, Col…is it OK to have the party at your place?"

"I guess so. I don't know what my mother expects, but for some reason because you're involved she thinks it's a great idea. She's taking Melissa to the block party."

"Oh, shit, the block party!"

"It's alright, my mother is going to be busy for a while working a table selling hot chocolate and donuts."

"No, I mean I just hope people will come to our party. I forgot about the block party. All the babes go to the block party."

"So invite them. My sister has some friends who might want to come."

"Yeah, well, as long as Megan's there."

"Don't tell me you're after my sister now."

"Why not?"

"Look; she's my sister. Believe me, you don't want to have anything to do with her."

"I just want to party with her." Tweed kept his voice as level as his gaze.

"Yeah, sure. She likes Timmy What's-His-Name, anyway."

"Timmy who?" Now he was suddenly animated. "Not the cross-eyed kid?" He skipped ahead and walked backwards in front of his friends.

"I don't know...I don't keep track of..."

"No shit...Timmy whats-his-name, huh? Goofy sucker...used to go to White City?"

"A lot of goofy suckers used to go to White City," he said conspicuously. "Forget it man, you're wasting your time. I can't believe that you're getting all worked up about this."

Tweed turned to Carmine, who had been following along quietly.

"Don't look at me," he said. "But Jimmy, you can't blame Tweed for going after Megan. He's frustrated, you know." And he made the universal air jack-off sign.

"Cut the shit!" said Tweed, as if disgusted.

Suddenly Col held his hand up to bring them to a stop.

"Hey, what the-? Look!"

They had been walking along a ridge with cliffs on either side. The left side dropped off to the park dump, so close that they could spit in it, and on the right lay a giant slab of weatherbeaten pudding stone known locally as "Pancake Rock". The site was a favorite of wall-climbing enthusiasts, for the ridge pitched upward at a fifty degree angle and Pancake Rock was a sheer face about twenty meters from the base to the top. Jimmy pointed down toward the base, calling his friend's attention to a group of kids who were huddled around a small fire. The kids were plainly visible in the fire light, talking and horsing around.

"I bet they can't see us from there!" said Tweed. "People standing next to a fire at night are pretty much blind to their surroundings unless they step away and allow their eyes to adjust to the darkness." Seeing an opportunity that was too good to pass up, Tweed decided to play a small prank on the unsuspecting night visitors. He positioned a grapefruit-sized boulder at the edge of the rock face.

"Check this out!" he hissed under his breath.

He kicked the boulder and sent it hurtling down the face of Pancake Rock. Unimpeded on the smooth inclined plane, the boulder careened downward, skipping off the rock face like it was in a desperate race to the earth.

"What, are you gonna bowl them over?" giggled Carmine.

At the last moment before reaching the bottom, the ball of granite suddenly took a freak hop and pitched- smash! into the middle of the fire, sending up a plume of sparks and scattering burning sticks and embers in every direction.

"He scores!" Tweed exulted quietly.

Down below, his victims were in various stages of shock and terror. Their cries seemed out of sync with their frantic movements. It was as if a meteor had dropped out of the heavens directly into their midst. Some of them had fallen on their butts, some had gone scrambling for the hills. After a few moments, the rattled group reassembled at the base of the Rock and were peering upwards in a vain attempt to see the origin of the assault. Tweed, Carmine and Col were fit to burst, trying to restrain their laughter. The possibility that Tweed might have crushed someone's skull with the boulder did not occur to any of them.

"Hey! You! I know you!" shouted one of the unfortunate ones from below.

"I thought they couldn't see us!" whispered Col.

"They can't!" replied Tweed, "They're just guessing. Rock didn't come from nowhere." He drew himself up to inflate his apparent size, swelling his chest and spreading his shoulders like his mother always asked him to, and then stood at the lip of the cliff.

"Oh, yeah! Who am I?" he shouted in a false voice, booming like the Wizard of Oz.

The kids below seemed to confer among themselves, then the speaker responded. "You're that guy, that guy that had the beef with Mr. Eddie, right?"

"Oh, jeesh!" said Tweed, sotto voce.

"Who's Mr. Eddie?" asked Col, puzzled.

"Mr. Eddie lives at the projects; he's a lot of things. Pimp, dealer, fence, you name it. I wouldn't want to have a beef with him."

"Nah," said Carmine dismissively, "Eddie's alright. You just got to get to know him. Did you know he hunts squirrels out of his apartment window? He pops 'em and yells down to the little kids- 'Hey- bring me up dat dere squirrel and I'll gib you a nickel.'"

"Yeah!" laughed Tweed, "That's just the way he talks. Like Satchmo or something."

"So how you going to play this?" asked Carmine, indicating the waiting group below.

"Like this!" said Tweed, and filling his lungs with air he yelled, "Yeah! I had a beef with Eddie, and if you don't watch out, I'm going to have a beef with YOU!" And at that, he ran straight down the face of Pancake Rock, faster than his legs could carry him, his body almost horizontal, an incoherent rale of shouts, howls and obscenities streaming from his mouth. Col and Carmine followed instantly, yelling like the Mongol hordes, and simultaneously praying that they wouldn't end up smashing their faces or breaking their legs in the attack.

It was a rout. If the poor kids had been scared by the fire-smashing boulder from hell, they were panic-stricken by the sudden onslaught of dark forms from atop the cliff. The pursuing trio was hard-pressed to keep up with their prey, for they fled as if demons were close on their heels. As he ran, Tweed thought to herd everyone toward the closest exit gate, but the group split up and he found himself chasing only five or six of them. Looking to his flank he saw that Col and Carmine had also each taken a smaller group, and now they all ran on independent vectors, racing toward the perimeter.

Five minutes after they launched their attack the friends met up at the base of the ridge again, laughing and high-fiving, and each recounting the experience as if the other two hadn't been there.

"So do you think they were the ones who were in the fort?" asked Col.

"No way," answered Carmine, "or else they would have been warming up inside the fort. No, that was another bunch of shitbums who won't be around for a while. Man, we're gonna be cleaning up tonight!"

CHAPTER 51

The fact that there was no name tag on the back of Woody's favorite stool didn't mean that it wasn't his, and that was a dictum he was all too happy to enforce. On this occasion a hapless innocent beer swiller received correction for his indiscretion when he was suddenly hoisted by the scruff of the neck and unceremoniously dumped from the end of the boom crane that was Woody's mighty right arm. For added flourish, Woody cleared three additional adjacent stools at the bar for his pals Des, Joe and Simon. The indignation that flared in the eyes of the displaced patrons flickered and faded ever so quickly when those same eyes beheld Woody. His piano-mover's frame, pumped to the pink by his recent calisthenics down at the docks, seemed to negotiate for him, preempting needless arguments.

Des removed his sweater, folded it over the back of his stool and took a look around at the interior of the Wild Geese before sitting. Overall the place was reminiscent of a regrettable romantic liaison, in that he wasn't sure if it would seem more depressing before or after drinking. But he was still feeling fairly unsettled, in fact too upset to get loaded, though he knew he could come around in time to go to the fight. He checked his pocket, and finding the ticket felt better by degrees.

Closed circuit television, my goodness! Will wonders never cease!

Last night in America and he was going to witness an event that, although it was international in almost every respect, was still essentially an American spectacle. The raw brutality of a fight between heavyweights Muhammad Ali and George Foreman was a symbol, emblematic of US power and aggression. Des wondered why the venue was in Zaire of all places.

The beers were up, but Des did not receive his in good humor because the bartender had winked at him as he placed the glass down in front of him. That was something he could not abide, even if he hadn't already been feeling snide and vinegary. He grew up in a pub, had worked all of his life in a pub and had spent most of his time either in front of or behind a bar. He enjoyed people, whether they were boisterous or moody, reserved or garrulous, crude or considerate, broke or flush. Like many publicans he thought he had seen it all: acts of humanity and depravity, gestures of touching decency and incorrigible contempt. But personally he loathed the knowing wink, flashed on the sly; a secret dared as a secret shared; the 'I got you, you're alright with me, mate!' signal. He didn't even know the man, but he was damned well sure that if the situation were reversed, and he walked into Des' place and ordered a pint, there was no way in hell that Des would wink at the fucker. It would be different of course, if it had been Des who had done the winking. It'd still have been ambiguous, however, for what in fuck's name does a wink mean, anyway? And taking the other scenario, where, say the weirdo walks into Des' pub and orders a pint, well then, he can wink all he wants. He's paying, isn't he?

But didn't the Geese make Des feel homesick for the biz club. A hazy reference came to mind, something along the lines of you can't ever picture the face of the one you love. Des was trying to picture his place in the Club, the seat where he did all of his business, where he got most of his drinking done, and he drew a blank. Now that too was depressing. Soon he would be in Ireland… what if he were unable, in a Roscommon daydream, to recall his watering hole away from home? Substitute Christine, and see what happens. He couldn't really focus her face in mind either, but then, that might not be a good test because recently every time he thought of his wife, he imagined another woman he'd rather be balling.

None of this was important at the moment, compared to the queasy grind in his stomach, originating in a question that had been simmering like a pot of cabbage on the back burner. Was it true that Des was 'ancient history'? Was his work really irrelevant? And did his friends hear any of that, and if so, how did they take it? Would they take him seriously, and could he hold their respect? He had to put a good face on the situation, make a story out of it. As he drained his first beer he composed his thoughts and formulated the rough outline of a speech.

CHAPTER 52

"Wow! So that's the fort? It's huge!"

Tweed didn't answer as he had paused to pee. The broad arc of urine sounded like a sheet of muslin being torn as it pattered down upon frozen leaves and twigs, and a cloud of vapor arose as if Tweed were standing next to a hot spring. Carmine had hurried ahead and entered the fort, and his muffled exclamations could be heard from without.

"Damn!…What the?…Holy shit!…"

Jimmy Col approached the fort looking for the entrance but he stopped when he heard Tweed yelp behind him.

"What is it? You OK?"

"Yeah, man, I just got stuck in my zipper, that's all. Shit! I'm bleeding!"

"Don't expect either of us to kiss your boo boo," laughed Carmine.

Looking up from his injury at Carmine, Tweed snorted back a giggle. Not as a response to his friend's quip, but because Carmine, whose upper body was now visible leaning out from the door to the fort, himself looked like a big dick hanging out of the zipper of the tree.

"Stop fooling around. We got a situation here. They've been here since this after. Take a look."

Limping because of his wounded dick, Tweed hurried ahead and ducked into the enclosure. Col followed close behind, thankful that he had found a reason for carrying a flashlight for the entire expedition.

There was no doubt that someone had recently been there. The air inside was warm and smelled of doused fire and fresh spilled beer. A steel milk carrier sat next to the fire, apparently to be used as a grate. Carmine was kneeling in the dirt examining a sample of the graffiti that covered all of the items he and Tweed had left in the fort.

"Recognize it?" asked Tweed.

"Maybe. I'd say project rats. This is their style. Marking shit like dogs; fuckin' moving in like vermin."

Tweed grunted then removed a cigarette-sized spliff from a belt stash and a disposable lighter from his jacket pocket. Rotating the joint he carefully burned away the tip, then took a heavy hit and got the pilot lit. Now it would burn evenly through clean leaf, fresh bud or seeds and stems. Retaining the smoke in his lungs, he passed the bone to Carmine, then crouched down to pick up an empty beer bottle.

When Col handed him the joint he released what was left of his first hit and took a deep breath before toking again. "Hey Col, light the fire, will ya?" he said on the intake. He posed, perusing the beer bottle, hefting it and wrapping his fingers around it.

Carmine was bent over dusting off his pants, and Col was preoccupied with lighting a handful of twigs he had torn from the tangle of vertical branches that made up the walls of the fort. Without warning Tweed wheeled about in a mighty head-down knee-up wind-up and with a full-force delivery slammed the bottle against the base of the tree, smashing it to splinters. The sound of the crash was rather like the popping sound of a light bulb, but Col and Carmine reacted violently, shouting at Tweed while cowering behind raised arms, hands and feet.

"What the fuck! What did you do that for? What are you, some kind of maniac? What an asshole! I can't believe you did such an asshole thing!…"

Rah, rah, rah, they went on like that at length, while Tweed said, "What's the big deal? I broke a bottle! Do you know how hard it is to break a bottle in the woods? I mean, on pavement, it's nothing. But unless you're near a boulder or something, good luck!"

"What the fuck? Why would anyone, why would *you* want to break a bottle in the woods? What a stupid thing to say! Man, that's *litter*. I can't believe you'd litter in the park. Arbs is our park, man, we don't shit on it like assholes." He indicated the graffiti. "Man, what an asshole thing to do!"

But Tweed would not defend himself or his actions. He had broken the bottle deliberately, with the intention of provoking a specific response from Col and Carmine. He wanted to put them in the right frame of mind so they would be more receptive to what it was that he planned to say.

CHAPTER 53

Des wasn't one of those blokes who sat in the pubs night after night with their pipes and their pints and their debates, bantering theory and philosophy, and arguing every item of political or social relevance. It seemed to him that there were thinkers and there were doers and he placed himself in the latter category. He was a man of deeds who acted according to his own conception of the greater good. As a son of the sod, an Irishman born and bred, he felt a sense of obligation, a duty not only to respect and defend his native country, but to help to fulfill a shared vision of a united Ireland, a proud and free member of the community of sovereign and independent nations. But even a simple pragmatist such as himself had not come upon his convictions merely by absorbing the prevailing doctrine. Loyalty was a part of his very fiber, like any other characteristic he had inherited from his forebears; but his beliefs were further reinforced by personal experience and a sense of his place in history; and his attitudes had been hardened in the heat of conflict. He often reviewed the events and circumstances that had affected his path in life, like a trauma victim asks "Why me?", or "What could I have done differently?" But while any member of the proletariat might acknowledge the futility of questioning his or her role and/or fate, for Des futility itself was a sign of oppression, and questions were symbolic of the grievances of successive generations.

For some the struggle to defend Ireland had been ongoing for 800 years, and they did not care to differentiate between the faces and races of various foreign invaders and occupiers. And even though Des himself had received his education in the modern Irish republic with the benefit of a civilized, northern hemispherical twentieth century perspective, his personal pantheon of heroes and idols contained personages from previous centuries. For example, 18th century revolutionary leader Theobold Wolfe Tone, the father of Irish republicanism, who had wished "…to substitute the common name of Irishman in place of the denominations of Protestant, Catholic and Dissenter"; and Robert Emmett, who had said upon being condemned for treason in 1803, "When my country takes her place among the nations of the earth, then, and not till then, let my epitaph be written."

Another of his heroes, Daniel O'Connell, had fought for and won Catholic Emancipation in 1829. From the black years of famine in the mid-1800s came more martyrs of Irish rebellion and the formation of the Irish Republican Brotherhood. Such was the tradition of dissent in Ireland that such names, including Fenians Philip Larkin, Michael O'Brien, and William Allen still deserved and received reverence from common folk like the Kelleys by the time Des was serving in the IRA in the 1950s. But his generation gave special prominence to the leaders of the rebellion of 1916: Pearse and Plunkett, MacDiarmada, MacDonough, and Connolly. For they had immortalized, in their Revolutionary Proclamation, the demand of the republican movement and the Provisional Government on behalf of the Irish people: "…the right of the people of Ireland to the ownership of Ireland, and to the unfettered control of Irish destinies, to be sovereign and indefeasible."

In the view of Des and others like him, the rebellion of 1916 was a logical outcome of the failure of Home Rule petitions that had been brought before the British Parliament on three occasions starting in the 1880s. Home Rule was a controversial measure to both the Irish and the British, but the attempt to pass it in 1912, though failed, had elicited an inordinate degree of concern from loyalists in the north of Ireland.

At that time there had been a rebirth of interest in Irish culture among nationalists in Ireland. Irish myths and legends were reintroduced by a new generation of writers and storytellers. Douglas Hyde and Eoin Macneill, representatives of a new generation of classicists, founded The Gaelic League in order to assist in the restoration of the Irish language. In addition the Gaelic Athletic Association promoted ancient and traditional Irish sports.

The loyalists responded by forming the Ulster Volunteer Force, initially a paramilitary organization some 100,000 strong; and by creating the Ulster Covenant, a document designed to reinforce the pledge of loyalists, "to stand by one another in defending for ourselves and our children our cherished position of equal citizenship in the United Kingdom…" The fact that 470,000 loyalists had signed the pledge, and that they further promised, "to defeat the present conspiracy to set up a home rule parliament in Ireland and…to refuse to recognize its authority" only exacerbated the fears and concerns of republicans, who were increasingly threatened by discrimination and brutality.

But when Sinn Fein became a political force to be reckoned with, and the IRA under Michael Collins forced the British to the negotiating table, a crucial opportunity was at once won and lost. For in the event, after Sinn Fein leader deValera had finally hammered out consideration of an Irish Free State during meetings in London, he ultimately sent Collins to sign a treaty with the British. The achievement of the treaty, and as a consequence, the partitioning of Ireland, became a source of dispute between deValera and Collins that led to a foolish and disastrous civil war. Collins referred to the agreement as a 'stepping stone', a base from which to launch further military actions against the north in order to force the complete and utter withdrawal of Britain, and the ultimate severing of the link with the Crown. deValera focused on the lingering dominion status of Ireland and the requisite Oath of Allegiance to the Crown as the source of his discontent. Collins became a casualty of the war, and it would seem that the dispute died with him.

So partition was in fact the end-result of the failure of the doomed Home Rule petitions, and the failure of the revolution, and the failure of deValera. For he had taken the bitter pill of partition as the cost of creating the Republic of Ireland, a pill that many republican partisans were not willing to swallow. And it is there that Des Kelley pegged the core claim of his argument. He and others of his generation believed that the death of Michael Collins was the pivotal event in the modern history of Ireland, and they accorded the "Big Fella' a greater degree of honor and significance in the wishfully revisionist view of history than he had received at the time of the actual events.

With the current re-emergence of the Troubles, the IRA had been reinvigorated, only to see its leadership and constituency split along factional lines. Diverse influences such as Marxism, the American Civil Rights movement, the free-speech and counter-cultural movements all had a hand in altering the political landscape as well as altering the military and economic objectives of the revolution.

Now almost fifteen years after he had taken himself out of Ireland, trusting God's grace, his own free will and the golden promise of America on the toss of a coin that had self-preservation on one side and his potential to help his country on the other, Des stood accused of irrelevancy. Like a laborer whose skill had been toggled into the operation of a machine that represented technological innovation and efficiency, he was, if he was to believe Makepeace, thus rendered redundant and obsolete.

Was it vanity that was behind his refusal to accept this notion, was it pride, or did the facts themselves fly in the face of the assertion? How could he doubt his own importance to the cause in which he believed? It wasn't simply a matter of saying that you're only as irrelevant as you feel, like a crusty old pensioner; or that relevancy is only skin deep, like a plain woman. He could do better than to rationalize his value, the significance of his contribution, or his leadership. He could point to the success of his various business enterprises, to the size of his organization and to the consistent flow of arms and supplies that he had smuggled into Ireland over the years. When Ireland is free and united, and the British are no more than trading partners; when the history books have been written and the dust of objectivity has settled upon them, then Des' name will be found among the principals in the rolls of Irish distinction.

Of course he was relevant, that was certain. He had raised thousands of dollars since the Guildford bombing, and he had purchased a boatload of arms for the defense of his homeland. Within a month's time he would celebrate an unprecedented transatlantic arms run, and success in this admittedly hazardous endeavor would pave the way for additional operations. And as he personally had made a difference, so the weapons and materiel he smuggled in would make a crucial difference. For when the people have the option of self-defense, when they no longer see themselves as helpless victims, their foes the British and their loyalist henchmen will be forced to reconsider their actions, and they will realize that there is a high price to pay for the violence they perpetrate.

"It's a damned good thing we're doing, you know," he said, raising his glass as if for a toast.

"What's that, Des?" asked Joe, cocking his head to hear better.

"I say, here's to the Wild Geese!"

"Here, here!" rejoined Woody with a hearty grin.

"And here's to Cu's Pub, and The Brew and The Bard, and the Tavern, and of course, here's to our own Club. And let's have a toast for all of the work that you men have done, getting the word out about the collections, and helping me to prepare for the Samhain trip."

"Sow-en?" asked Woody, around a mouthful of suds.

"Sahmain, the Irish Halloween," said Simon, knowingly.

"Yes, summer's end, All Saint's Day, you know."

"Well then you're leaving soon!" cried Woody.

"Tomorrow," affirmed Des. "And in a couple of days I'll be making a delivery on behalf of you men and myself, and all of the other folks who contributed to the relief effort."

"Then, here's to Des!" said Joe, a little too loudly, so that a number of the melancholy drunkards in the bar joined in, glad for a reason to celebrate, and hopeful of a free round.

"Ach, I do my part," said Des humbly, "We make but small gains in the face of great odds. Blessed are the peacemakers, and I am truly blessed indeed, especially having such good friends. Here's to you, Joe, and Simon and Woody, and thanks for helping out tonight."

"So, did you straighten out your friend the fisherman?" asked Joe, not so much curious as conversational.

"Oh, to be sure; he knows which side of the bread gets the butter."

"Heh, heh, well, I think he'll be wanting a nice slab of London Broil instead of butter, to take the swelling out of that shiner you gave him."

"He can slap a mackerel on it for all I care," replied Des, "but are you boys alright?"

"I think we have the cure for all of our ills right here!" So saying, Joe drained the remainder of his beer.

"Let me just say, again if I might, that what we've done is important, and I can tell you before I even get there, that in addition to raising money, we've generated a great deal of good will, and that the folks back home will not forget it. You can be sure that should you ever go over, the debt of gratitude will be repaid with hospitality, and you'll never want for drink, neither will you have to pay for meals or lodgings."

"…lodgings. That's grand, Des," echoed Simon, "I'll tell you, I wasn't expecting a reward, and certainly no key to the city or ticker-tape parade. As for drinks, I'll get the next round, round."

CHAPTER 54

"I saw this thing on the TV the other day about science, about the planet earth. They were talking about how smooth the world is. Of course it's mostly water, so it looks pretty smooth when you look at it from space. You ever seen one of those pictures from space? The whole planet is like a marble, a big blue cat's eye, spinning away with barely a wobble. I'm not talking about the shape, I'm talking about how smooth it is, you know? On this show they said that if you could hold the world in your hands, 'He's got the whole world in his hands,'…you wouldn't be able to feel the tallest mountain- Mt.Everest would be smaller than a pimple on the ass of the earth. Same goes for the Grand Canyon, the Great Wall of China, the biggest freakin' thing you can think of- no more than a blemish, like the little bumps on the hide of a b-ball."

Tweed paused to make sure that he still had an audience. His friends were still pissed off but at least they were listening. He smiled as he imagined how crazy he must sound. Probably seemed as if he was capable of anything.

"So, say the biggest mountain on earth is no bigger than a c-hair on the pussy of the world, then can you dig how infinitesimally small a person is? Take all of the people on the planet and put 'em in one place and from space they'd look like an ant colony. If you could make them out. Three billion people and if you could hold the world in your hands you'd probably squish them without even knowing it. Oops! sorry God! You'd better take this back, I think I squished your worshipers." Tweed gestured as if he were handing a beach ball over to an imaginary friend.

"Yeah, one person is pretty darn insignificant compared to the whole world, you know what I mean? So just think how small, how insignificant one person's trash is. There's no doubt that as a race people have been fucking things up. I mean, garbage is no joke. Freaking cities bribe each other to take it off their hands. You got New York shipping most of their garbage to New Jersey, and hauling the rest to sea. But right there it kind of makes my point. Like, all of the people on the eastern seaboard flush their toilets every couple of hours and where does all the shit go? Out to sea! And they've been doing it for two hundred years! Other folks pump it into the ground or truck it to treatment facilities. Millions of tons of shit and garbage every day; and do you see it, do I? No, it practically disappears. We've gotten pretty good at eliminating our waste, forgive the pun. It's not like the freakin' middle ages when they just threw it all into the streets. People dying of dysentery left and right.

"How do we live this way? I mean we make more garbage than anything else. More than clothes and cars and books and furniture and everything! Because, think about it, almost everything we make that isn't garbage will be garbage some day. It's like they say, one man's treasure is another man's trash. How do we do it? I'll tell you. We live in an environment that's constantly self-regulating, self-sustaining. The garbage is part of the whole scheme of things. The Earth is just like one big waste disposal and recycling plant. Look at road kill, you know, like *'Dead skunk in the middle of the road, stinking to high heaven'*. Well, that song's talking about a skunk; one skunk. What about armadillos, possums, dogs, deer, horses, elephants, whales? They drop dead all over the place. Does anybody bury 'em? Do they scrape 'em up and cremate 'em? Nope, they just sit there and rot, or scavengers take care of them and you know what that means- more shit. OK, so sometimes the bones remain, and fossilize and what not, but see, what I'm saying is that nature takes care of these things. They talk about contamination of the environment, oil slicks, industrial pollution. I'd say there's probably been worse natural contaminations of the environment than man-made ones. There's places where oil seeps from the ground, there's tar pits and acid lakes. A volcano blows up and a zillion tons of ash and crap spews into the air.

"But you have to care about these things. I'm not saying that everybody should just throw their shit everywhere. I mean, if every asshole walking down the street just decided to smash bottles whenever they felt like it, then it wouldn't be long before you couldn't, you wouldn't stand for it. We all have to live together so we can't allow that kind of behavior- despite all the examples I've given to the contrary. You're right to get upset when you see someone trash the place; one of the oldest rules of society is that you don't shit where you live...or is it where you sleep? Anyway, you get the idea. I'm trying to make a point here, to draw your attention to something. But sometimes actions speak louder. You've got to admit, if I just started spouting off about pollution and stuff, you'd probably yawn and tell me to shut the fuck up. I mean, sometimes you have to take bold action, you know? You gotta do something that grabs people's attention. Sometimes you even have to use reverse psychology."

"OK," interrupted Carmine, "So you smashed a bottle in order to make a point about how wrong it is to break a bottle?"

"No, man, I'm saying that sometimes you have to do something big, something unexpected to make people think, to make them realize that what they've been doing is wrong."

"So you smashed the bottle because we didn't expect you to?" asked Col incredulously. "I sure as hell didn't expect it. Shit, I guess it worked."

"No, man, I smashed the bottle because I felt like it. I smashed the bottle because I was mad. I was mad because someone came into our new clubhouse, I mean our fort and they shit all over it. Smashing the bottle had nothing to do with this. I'm not talking about the bottle; that was just a way of focusing attention, and energy.

"No, the reason I brought all of this up is not because of what I did, but what I plan to do. I'm going to teach them a lesson."

"What lesson? Horn in on our fort and we'll break one of your empty beer bottles?"

"Carmine, you still don't get it, but that's OK. See, they wreck it for us, we'll wreck it for them. If we can't enjoy the fort then nobody can."

With that Tweed kicked the steel milk case so that it flew the length of the fort. He then proceeded to pull on the overhead branches as if to tear them down.

"You're going to wreck it? You can't wreck a freaking tree, dude. Fucking storm couldn't wreck it, I don't think you can."

But Tweed was in a destructive mood now. He turned all of his attention and energy toward tearing down the fort- swinging from branches, kicking the improvised seats, scattering the stones that made up the fire pit.

"Wreck it?" he said, "I'm going to burn it down."

CHAPTER 55

"So, what about that horse's ass?" Dan Toole fixed Simon in an accusatory stare with both eyebrows raised like the lid of a jack-in-the-box.

"Who? Your father?" Simon Fecteau had just come in out of the cold.

"And where is that other blasted clown?"

"Clown. Dan, listen now, Joe wanted me to tell you that he'll be late coming back tonight. You were to just go ahead and you know, finish his shift and close up for him."

"Oh? That's all! Why not? What else would I be doing tonight? I'm always waiting to go down to the shit hole on a moment's notice and serve panther piss for a few hours. The old fart's going to owe me for this!"

"Owe me...Hey, now don't call the club a shit hole, Dan. There are better words to describe it. I mean, it's a sleazy dive, but it's our sleazy dive."

"Excuse me, Simon, you're right, shit hole is a crude term for this moldy God-forsaken armpit of the square."

"Armpit? An improvement, but how about, say, belly-button? Isn't that more like it? Come to the Businessman's Club, the navel of greater Rossie."

"I don't know; armpit works to describe the stench, and navel works for the image of accumulated lint and crud, I guess. Alright, I'll go with navel because it's halfway between armpit and butt-crack. So what did they do, ditch you?"

"Ditch you? No, no they didn't ditch me, they left me at the station and I blasted home on the late commuter train. I didn't want to go with them, anyway. See, Des come up with tickets to the Ali fight they're showing tonight on closed-circuit TV at Curley Hall in Dawestown."

"No shit?"

Simon stumbled a little because of the interruption. "Shit? No; for real, for real. Well we had Woody with us you know, and had to drop him back at the Geese, and that's in Francestown; and to give me a ride they would have had to come all the way back here only to turn around and go back again."

Dan stopped him again. "Because Curley Hall is in Dawestown...I get ya. And Joe went with him, the lucky stiff. Man, that burns me! I have to stay here tending the mushrooms and he scores a ticket to see the Ali fight, the Rumble in the Jungle- Live from Kinshasa! I'd say that one will run late, alright. Zaire is like, ten hours ahead of here, right?"

"I don't know, Dan, eight at least. I'll tell you though, I can't wait to hear about it. Neither of them knows where the hall is. And I know that they're not familiar with Dawestown. Especially at night."

"Where is Dawestown, Simon?" asked Dan, from the short end of the proverbial stick.

"Dawestown? It's where they fight like this!" Taking up a defensive crouch Simon started wind-milling his fists and backing away.

Dan laughed, "I get it, I get it...but seriously."

"North and West, north and west..." He took a seat. "Up past Francestown on the way to the north shore. I worked up there a couple of years ago. The place they're going to is like a large Elks hall, you know, about the size of a shriner's auditorium. Has a bar, maybe a couple of bars. Should be a nice place to see the fight."

"Why didn't you go?"

Simon massaged his right elbow. "Got to work in the morning. Fight's too late and work's too early to be staying up on a Tuesday night. You should have seen the two of them, though. Des was yelling directions and grabbing at the wheel. Joe was going nuts...he hates back seat drivers. And Holy Mary, Mother of God, I swear, when Des wasn't giving Joe a hard time he was yelling at the other drivers on the road. If I was driving, I'd have to stuff him in the trunk."

"Like to see that, Simon." Dan was losing interest. After Simon left it would be a long boring night. The place had shit for entertainment. "This place doesn't even have a radio, does it?"

"I don't remember seeing one, but if you'd like, I can get you one from my car. It's a pretty good short-wave. I take it with me to work sometimes."

"What, your car's out here? Why, I'd really appreciate that, Simon. You're all right, no matter what they say about you."

"Say about you," he repeated, then looked keenly at Dan, "What do they say?"

"Beg your pardon, just kidding."

"Kidding, oh! Hah, hah! I'll be right back! Hey- if the reception's any good, maybe you can tune in the fight..."

Initially Dan had about as much luck picking up the boxing match on the shortwave as his father had driving around Dawestown and searching for the hall. Dan finally located the broadcast on the dial but in order to tune it in he had to place his hand on top of the receiver and act as a human antenna. This was tolerable until he had to answer the phone or get something for one of the slugs in the bar.

***

In fact Joe in his frustration had almost called looking for directions. He was tired of driving around without a clue as to the direction of his destination, and he was hoping at the very least to shut up Des, who had been hammering him incessantly since they left Francestown. When he realized that he had been driving in circles and that he had passed the hall at least twice, he finally pulled in. To his dismay he found the parking lot full, and so was forced to seek parking elsewhere.

Dan did take another phone call during the remainder of his shift, but that one was from AD Makepeace, looking for Des Kelley.

Anticipating that Des may have passed up the chance to see the fight, he had intended to tell him that the deal had gone through as promised, that his boat was loaded with Des' merchandise and that he was ready to leave. In a sense it was a shame that Des wasn't there, because he had also prepared an elaborate story hinting at the personal risk, hardship and physical labor he had undergone to accomplish his task. Of course, in reality the deal had gone off smoothly and efficiently; it was cash and carry and come again, thanks.

He'd save his tale for another time, perhaps when he met Des in late November, and by then the story would be refined and colorized.

Now other than taking a piss, his last task to perform while on American soil was to make another couple of calls before disembarking. First he contacted Capt. Jack, giving him minimal notice as agreed to prepare to launch the chartered tour boat. He also reviewed the tentative route and confirmed the coordinates to which Jack would deliver his passenger. Then Makepeace called the passenger, Stephen Darrager, to give him the go. Calmly he issued orders, telling him to grab his duffel, make a quiet exit and to hurry to the pier to board Jack's boat for the ride to the rendezvous.

It was convenient to leave Darrager with the impression that the Cor Mor would be waiting for him out beyond Gloucester Harbor. Having further to travel in a larger boat, Makepeace would have to make haste so as not to end up pursuing Capt. Jack northward to the meet.

As he plotted his course he knew that his charts were up-to-date and reliable, and despite navigating in unfamiliar waters he had confidence in his own skill and in his boat and crew. Likewise he was confident that Capt. Jack would follow through and carry out his part of the bargain; confidence inspired not by Jack's reputation or because he had a gut feeling about his integrity, but rather because Makepeace had provided his own insurance. He had dispatched his right-hand-man Reggie to meet Darrager and to accompany him on Jack's boat. Reggie would hold Darrager's hand if need be, but he'd also keep an eye on Jack, and see to it that they reached the rendezvous.

Meanwhile, Des Kelley and Joe Toole were among the last ticket holders to show up at the big event at Curley Hall in Dawestown.

The stylish contemporary building lacked the modesty that typified the decor of most of the civic and community halls Des had seen before. This was not a Knights of Columbus meeting room, or a bingo hall, but an opulent auditorium.

High inside the showy atrium a massive crystal chandelier was suspended like the sword of Dionysius, and Des briefly imagined seeing it fall and crush the crowd into the crimson pile carpeting below.

Safely within the comfortable main auditorium the assembled guests had already stifled the atmosphere with hot vapors of body heat and nicotine, through which Des and Joe could make out large television screens mounted in pairs at the corners of the room as well as at several key vantage points near the bars and rest-rooms.

Des did not regularly enjoy watching television. He had been aware of the miraculous innovation prior to leaving Ireland but didn't see it as an improvement over radio, which he had loved since childhood. Neither he nor Christine had ever owned a television until they moved up from Jamaica Center and their youngest boys had practically demanded that they acquire a set to go along with the new house. But other than experiencing the undeniable delight of seeing the Ed Sullivan Show in color, Des had little use for it. Now he found that it was quite disconcerting to see multiple sets all flickering the same grainy picture through the haze of cigarette smoke, and wondered what kind of damage his eyes and mind were sustaining in the cross-fire of electron beams. The only remedy was alcohol and plenty of it. It was time to relax, time to enjoy himself, along with the spectacle and the company of his good friend Joe. And yet his head ached and as he became increasingly inebriated he also became restless and belligerent.

He began to realize that it had been an error on his part to accept the tickets to the fight. Since when had he been a boxing enthusiast? Here he was at a showing of the world heavyweight championship and yet, if asked his opinion about it, he would say that the best fighters in the world were Irish, make no mistake. Knowing little about the careers of the contenders, he had no favorite between the two, and in any event, he was having difficulty following the action. Two large Negroes were slugging it out on the screen; that was about all Des got from it. The next thing he knew, Joe was nudging him awake.

"You alright there, Des?"

He felt mean and irritable. With anger tasting bitter in his mouth he cursed himself and Makepeace and Darrager and Muhammad Ali.

He would be spending the bulk of the following day, Wednesday, cooped up in an airplane, and by the time he arrived in Ireland it would be Thursday, the 31st, due to the time zone difference.

Why hadn't he stayed in his seat at the club where he could be cozy and complacent? He might even have stayed at home with Christine for a change. After all, he wouldn't be seeing her for almost a month.

He grumbled loudly and incoherently, not speaking to anyone in particular, and one of the fans nearby told him to shush. Des instantly looked to Joe, as if to say, "Can you believe that asshole told me to shush?" But Joe was swept up in the action in the ring, and he swung his fists and 'oofed' and 'aahed' in sympathy and admiration.

In hindsight, standing at that moment was probably not the wisest thing for Des to do, especially considering his actions subsequent to rising. For he failed to stand erect, feeling as if the floor had suddenly rolled or pitched under him, and he lost his balance. Thrusting a hand out to steady himself, he inadvertently knocked a cup of beer off the table and onto a stranger's lap. As Des lurched toward the gentleman who had insulted him, the gentleman with the beer soaked trousers leaped up and accosted him. The ensuing melee was worse by far than the one in which he had been involved earlier, and instead of sore knuckles and a feeling of abashment, this time Des came away with a black eye and a swollen lip; in addition, his clothes were dirty and torn and a chunk of hair had been yanked from his already thinning scalp. Joe had tried to act the peacemaker, and although he was drawn reluctantly into Des' latest scrap, before long he found himself being dragged out of the hall at the hands of three burly Dawestown policemen. It had taken four of them to remove Des Kelley, who, when Joe found him, was puking at the space between his shoes as he leaned spread-eagled against the hood of a black and white cruiser.

Fortunately the local cops did not see much percentage in charging or booking the two out-of-towners. Instead they escorted them to the town line, sirens blaring and lights flashing as if they were accompanying a foreign dignitary with pomp and honor. For Joe at least there was a bit of a silver lining in the whole dark affair, because the fight had ended in the eighth round, just as the police had arrived to break up the fracas. Des had given up caring about the boxing, and he reinforced his disdain by repeatedly asking, "So it was Sambo that won, was it now?"

CHAPTER 56

On hemlock ridge, in the section of the Arbs Park that pointed like a craggy finger toward Westbury Circle and beyond, Jimmy Columkille and Carmine Gunther were both working earnestly and single-mindedly. With no thought for common sense they were following the gleeful evil commands issued by Tumbleweed Kelley to burn and destroy the tree fort. They moved swiftly with branches flaming like torches in their hands, touching them to the exposed leaves, twigs and pine needles along the inner walls of the structure. After a minute or two, dense hot smoke threatened to choke the living daylights out of them, so the boys were forced outside to complete the destruction of their former playhouse in the woods.

"Holy frijole! Look at it go!" shouted Tweed over the growing roar of the conflagration. Almost immediately the heat was so intense that the boys were forced to retreat into the open field. Sweat evaporated off their faces, and their clothing gave off faint wisps of steam. The branches lining the inside of the fort had been fairly well dried out by the camp fires the boys had lit at the base of the tree. The fire spread rapidly outward from these branches, consuming green and dry wood alike. The dead tree that made up the fort lay like a pile of kindling at the base of a pyre, and as it became engulfed in flame it threatened the mighty hemlock against which it had fallen.

Thus the still-living tree was to become a sacrifice in the purification ritual Tweed had initiated. An updraft swept the flames higher and higher, catching the lower limbs of the tree.

"Look!" cried Col, pointing at the tree.

Vapor seemed to be issuing from cracks in the bark at places along the trunk.

"It's cooking from inside!"

The tree was popping and groaning and the wind seemed to rush in toward the tree from all directions, feeding the flames and sending them higher into the old evergreen. Shielding their faces from the heat, the boys stood cowering at the base of the tree, transfixed by the tremendous spectacle, yet rapidly becoming overwhelmed by the heat and smoke.

"What's that? Is it raining? Shit!" said Carmine.

Tweed held out his hands to feel the rain and instead felt a stinging prickle on his exposed skin. "It's raining alright..." shouted Tweed, "it's raining pine needles!"

Like a massive road flare the tree stood blazing on the hillside, and as it burned it sent thousands of scorched pine needles soaring skyward in an updraft, like a swarm of fireflies. Now they were falling back to earth as a rain of incandescent sparks. Some of them were still hot enough to burn tiny holes in the boy's clothes.

"Let's back off!" suggested Tweed, and he started looking for a new vantage point from which to watch the remainder of the fire. But as the boys retreated they found that the rain of needles fell over a widespread area, and their view of the giant torch was obscured as they descended from the ridge.

"Quick! Up to the top of Mots!"

They would have to jog a quarter of a mile in order to get away from the hazards of the fire they had set. From the elevation of Mots Hill they'd have an open view across the park and they could watch the fire while sitting comfortably on park benches. Furthermore up there they would be undisturbed. Anyone else who might have been in the park would surely head toward the fire that now looked like a towering chemical explosion. As the boys ran they could hear the sound of fire engines approaching from station houses in White City, Westbury Circle, Jamaica Center and from as far away as Roosevelt. There was no cause for the boys to be alarmed for they knew that even when the fire engines arrived at the gates of the park it would be some time yet before they would be able to gain entrance and make any progress toward the ridge. Any concern they felt come not from fear of apprehension or blame but rather fear that the tree would be saved. Undoubtedly the firemen would eventually manage to bring their equipment close enough to the fire to determine that it was beyond their abilities to manage this emergency. The tree would burn to the ground like an abandoned triple-decker in Mission Hill.

CHAPTER 57

Keeping the focus on Makepeace at this point might make for good storytelling, but it is important to remember that we are not primarily concerned with him, or with Darrager, but with Des and Tweed Kelley.

From what we have learned so far it is clear that Makepeace was a principle character in the life of Des Kelley, and furthermore we know that he will survive at least until 1986, and that he will be involved in the events that we are waiting to see unfold. And yet, though it would be ideal to wrap up this retro episode with a proper denouement, and though it would be fitting to tie up any literary loose ends while wringing a moral and historical perspective from the twisted rags of our tale, there is also a certain danger of distraction in following this side-plot to its conclusion. A newspaper journalist might condense a handful of facts from what is publicly known about the voyage of the Cor Mor and using color, spice, unsubstantiated rumors and unofficial speculation, hash out a column of limited interest, possibly worthy of a page-three insertion below the fold. Our purpose here is best served by simply acknowledging that elements of his story not only balanced but also enhanced some aspects of the larger story of the Kelleys, especially insofar as they helped to demonstrate the consequences of Des' actions in particular.

Settling into the command of his boat for the trip across the harbor and then 'across the pond', AD Makepeace felt like a farmer planting his arse in the well-worn and comfortable seat of his tractor. He plowed the greasy seawater at a controlled steady pace, and feeling the familiar pulse of the powerful engines he was eager to open them up and finally reach cruising speed. Now that he was underway at last, it galled him to have to pull back and idle in the open water for the rendezvous. Arriving at the coordinates he let his boat drift in the 2-3 foot swells and as he awaited the arrival of Capt. Jack, he thought over the events of the day with some satisfaction.

First he had settled up with HHF, his erstwhile liaison, and was only slightly peeved that she felt it necessary to remind him to take care of Capt. Jack. There he was, being uncharacteristically suave and romantic, promising to look her up back home come the holidays, and she was nagging him to murder the wretched bugger.

Then he had swung his boat up to the north bank of one of the many local rivers whose foul effluents have fed the fetid harbor with toxic contamination for centuries. The horrid outflow had always been proportional to the trade and commerce flowing in and out with the tides, although at ever greater orders of magnitude.

The traffic and bustle of the modern seaport provided a screen of activity behind which Makepeace felt secure as he docked at the arms warehouse and transacted for tons of illegal weapons. The consignment was stowed in the hold of his vessel, all as if he were merely taking on ice or supplies, except that his men hardly had to lift a finger. But he wouldn't have had it any other way because he believed that furtive movements were the most suspicious and clandestine arrangements most susceptible to discovery.

Despite feeling complacent, he still had a dozen stories planned in mind should the need arise to bluff his way past a local harbor patrol or coast guard unit. Only under close scrutiny would it seem irregular for an Irish fishing boat to be sailing off the north shore past the light at Gloucester point, which was why he had picked this particular meeting place. It was unlikely that anyone would see the boats this far out from land, and the area was regularly socked in with heavy fog, hence the light.

At the moment he spotted Capt. Jack, Makepeace was thinking about the tussle he had with Des earlier on the dock, and how it was seemingly over Darrager. Perhaps it was reasonable for Des to be anxious about his money after the few days it had taken to pull the deal together for the buy. But he really seemed to be steamed about Mr. Darrager as if the guy were an American spy or something. Now here was the controversial Stephen Darrager himself, coming to join the Cor Mor for a nasty, cold, and bumpy ride to the North Sea. For added excitement Darrager would be treated to an unusual docking transfer at sea, so that should he survive he may remember that he started his new life with an act of courage and daring.

(Not that it would do him any good. Less than a year later Darrager was apprehended by special units of the Gardai in a flat outside of Dublin where he was working on electronic counter-measures for the IRA.)

CHAPTER 58

For a view of the city there's no place like the top of Mot's. Tweed knew this because he had spent countless hours there. He had seen the shrubs and bushes that dotted the hillside spring into blossom, then bloom in the summer and fruit and fade under the chill of autumn winds and winter snows. By observing over a lengthy period of time the iterations of traffic from the distant municipal airport he had learned to anticipate overflights and to predict the arrival and departure of the jumbo jets. And it was here on the top of Mot's where Tweed learned to appreciate his place in the cosmos; witnessing the procession of planets and stars and all of the dear natural phenomena a sighted person might behold, from rainbows to aurorae, from eclipses to halos. But in all the years that he had been coming up here he had never seen anything so spectacular, so beyond fuck all as the tree-fort fire on hemlock ridge. The flames from the fire were so bright that they illuminated the entire hillside in an eerie brilliance. All of the objects caught in the light seemed to glow fiercely in the dark, and they also cast deep and sharply defined shadows. The fire roared skyward in a stationary jet like a torched petroleum well-head, yet it gave off little heat. On the contrary, it sucked in the night air, causing an odd inverted breeze. There was very little smoke coming from the blaze, and Tweed knew that the black jet emerging from the top of the flame consisted mostly of hot ash like a volcanic plume.

He had done this. Tweed himself had lit the great Arbs Park fire of '74, the fire that would be talked about for months and remembered for years to come. With smug self-satisfaction he noticed the forms of people in the distance hurrying toward the fire, caught in high relief like figures frozen in a night-club strobe. What could they do, converging on the scene like that? There was no way that they were going to put it out, and that was the beauty of it. They might as well accept the fact that Tweed had started the unstoppable fire. He tore his gaze away from the welder's torch glare long enough to look at the faces of his friends, to see the awe and admiration reflected in their faces as brightly as the fire light.

"Fuck ass fire huh?" said Carmine, in his peculiar way.

"You said it," replied Tweed.

"I bet every able-bodied person in the neighborhood is rushing over there right now to help save the forest," added Col.

"Psssh!" scoffed Tweed, "The forest isn't in danger! When that tree burns out the show will be over. It ain't gonna spread."

"Imagine if it did, though," said Carmine, "Can you imagine seeing that whole row go up one by one? Man, they'd drain ponds to put it out; they'd call in helicopters to fight that sucker."

"My old man took me for a ride on a fire-boat down at the harbor once, but I've never heard of a fire-copter," said Tweed.

"I bet they have 'em. So is your old man a sparky or something? Will he be heading up here now, do you think?"

"No, he has a friend in the department. I doubt that he even knows about the fire. Dudes down at the biz club wouldn't know if the whole square burned down around them."

"What's a sparky?" asked Col.

"It's like a fire groupy, someone who enjoys listening to the scanner and following fire trucks around and watching the firemen; like Arthur Fiedler…he's a sparky."

"Yeah, well, Arthur Fiedler will come up here before my old man ever does," said Tweed, realizing that he couldn't recall the last occasion when his father had entered the park.

"You get along with your father, Tweed?"

"My dad? I don't know; I guess so. He's not what you'd call a dominant figure in my life. My mother's the one we watch out for, the real 'authority' in the family. Take now for example…the old man is heading off to Ireland for the month of November. He goes there twice a year to stay with my brother. The rest of the time I hardly see him, but then I wouldn't, unless I want to go into the friggin' dive and look for him. Actually, I'll tell you, Moe the fruit man is more of a father figure to me."

"Moe? That old weirdo? The guy with the blue truck?"

"Hey, Moe's a cool dude. Used to give me rides to school when I went to White City. If you ask me, I'd say that he's probably a 'father figure' to a lot of the kids around here."

"What do you mean?" asked Col.

"I mean, look, the guy's been driving around the neighborhood for years selling vegetables to all of the old ladies, and all the housewives, you know? I bet he stops at some houses for longer than others, if you know what I mean."

"Delivering the zucchini, you mean?" laughed Carmine.

"Yeah, something like that. You gotta figure, he's probably got a half-dozen little Moes running around."

"Shit, man, did you ever notice that Og kind of looks like Moe?"

"And Bobby Dukas, and others; come to think of it, Col, you kind of bear a resemblance to Moe yourself."

"Aw, fuck you, man! My old lady didn't screw no freakin' fruit man!"

"Why not? She…" started Carmine, but Tweed interrupted.

"Hold it, Gunther, you're talking about his old lady, here; don't say something you have to take back."

A spark not reflected from the tree fire briefly flared and died in Carmine's eyes. "Yeah, OK, I was just making fun."

"My mother doesn't even like zucchini!"

"Yeah, alright Col; -and don't knock Moe, man. You ever heard him play the piano?"

"The piano?" asked Col as if he were setting up another punch line.

"Yep. I was at the Porgio's house one time when Moe was bringing in the string beans or something and he went ahead and sat down at Mrs. Porgio's piano and played some Chopin for her. Had fingers like Vienna sausages, but still he played pretty damned well. My old man sure as heck never played anything."

"Not even the skin flute, eh, Tweed?"

"I'll remind you, Carmine, when I hear you talk that way," started Tweed in an exaggerated deep lilt, "That your immortal soul is hanging in the balance. At the rate you're going you might just skip Purgatory altogether."

"Don't give me any of that Catholic bullshit, Kelley."

"Bless him, Lord, he knows not whereof he speaks."

"Spare me."

CHAPTER 59

The mid-ocean docking maneuver was one of those things that was easier said, as in, "I'll just pull alongside there and you hop off that boat and onto this one..." And someone like Capt. Jack might nod and say, "Sounds good!" But it didn't exactly come off like some scene from an action movie sequence. The Cor Mor displaced a lot more water than the Capt. Jack and the difference in size between the two vessels was only one problem. The seas were at 2-3 feet with winds gusting at 15-20mph, and the two boats, which were relatively small by ocean-going standards, bobbed about like water-logged corks.

After the exacting work of securing lines, making fast, seeing to potential hazards and to the safety of the crew, it was a breathless moment as Darrager slung himself aboard. Yet what followed was surreal by comparison, as Makepeace watched Reggie carefully and calmly place a .44 to the base of Jack's skull and murder him as efficiently as possible under the circumstances. Reggie then paused only long enough to glance at Makepeace as if to say, "That's done!" before he set about sinking the Capt. Jack. Of course Darrager was suitably horrified and distraught, and he blubbered on and on. But it had taken longer to line the boats up and secure them than it had to kill and sink Capt. Jack, and the Cor Mor was underway before Darrager settled into the wretched nausea that was to mark the remainder of his voyage.

AD Makepeace spent some days under the silent oppression of remorse, guilt and self-hatred. However, unlike his unfortunate passenger, Makepeace thrived on the plunging, pounding sea, the raw bracing air and the conspiratorial freedom of adventure with his crew. No matter how or when the facts regarding the demise of Capt. Jack should ever come to light and call the circumstances of the tragedy into question, he would have nothing to fear. Who had pulled the trigger? Who was the executioner, was it Reggie, the IRA, Heather Shockley, Des Kelley, Makepeace himself or all of the above? In the end he had to justify the episode as an example of the cost of doing business.

CHAPTER 60

The firemen did ultimately manage to position their engines close enough to the fire to use their hoses, however they sprayed the water not on the burning tree but on the surrounding ones. Any fool could see that the mighty hemlock was a loss and nothing could be done to save it, but with vain optimism the crew struggled to defend the rest of the grove, and whether or not their work was successful or even necessary, they did deliver a good soaking to the hillside.

Invigorated, emboldened, enlightened…Tweed had been radically affected by recent events, though perhaps not on a conscious level. After his father left for Ireland and the hubbub about the fire had died down, Tweed found himself willing to contemplate ideas and deeds that he would certainly have considered too risky or downright foolhardy in the past. For example, he looked forward to popping the back door at Hilltop Liquors with Col, and to exploiting the devious imagination of his buddy Carmine.

The Halloween party wasn't quite the groovy gig that he had imagined. Megan showed up only briefly, and seeing her was like seeing a commercial in color when you've been watching a black-and-white movie on TV. But he was pretty fucked up in the first place, having downed the better portion of a bottle of home-made apple-jack and having smoked a couple of stiff spliffs. He spent most of the evening taunting the other chicks at the party and arguing with his friends about cars and tunes. Some awful music could be heard echoing from the neighborhood block party. It sounded like they were playing the top 40 on AM radio, stuff like *The Way We Were*, and *Sunshine on My Shoulders*. Meanwhile at Col's party, his speakers were pumping out volume-distorted hits including *I Shot the Sheriff*, *Bennie and the Jets*, *Band On The Run*, and *Angie*.

Tweed was never sure if it was justified to blame the weed with which he had laced the chili and the pizza, but it wasn't long before the guests at the party started sagging toward couches and onto the floor, as a general mood of somnolence came over the affair. Blitzed by any personal, legal or medical standard but not incapacitated, Tweed himself slipped out of the house and headed toward the park, looking for Megan.

Now it was too late for trick-or-treaters to be about, but many porch lights were still on and the piercing whine of television sets resounded from every living-room on the block. Fragments of shattered pumpkin spattered the street, eggshells littered the gutters and toilet paper shrouds adorned some of the trees.

He spotted Megan coming out of the park with three older boys, one of whom appeared to be holding her arm. Upon seeing Tweed she disengaged herself; and yet when they drew near, she intentionally brushed past him without speaking. He had never seen the guys before. The smallest of the three was dressed in a varsity jacket with the sleeves pushed up to his elbows, a black t-shirt, jeans and basketball shoes. His buddies were dressed alike in barracuda windbreakers and workout gear. Tweed looked them over quickly, but feeling concerned and confused about what Megan was doing with them he called after her.

"She don't want to talk to you," said the short one. "She's with us now."

"Yeah?" asked Tweed, "Who the fuck are you?"

"I'm Billy Gibbons, lead singer of ZZ-Top, and this is my band," he said, hooking a thumb toward his comrades.

"And I'm James Joyce," replied Tweed with a hint of sarcasm.

"Hey, James, do you live around here?"

It didn't take a fan of ZZ Top to point out that these guys were not them. Tweed turned and looked after Megan, who continued walking toward the sidewalk.

"Go ahead and get in the car, babe, I'll be right there," yelled the mouth. "I say Jimmy boy, I asked you a question."

The big ones crowded near now, as if to muscle an answer out of Tweed.

"Oh, yeah, I live around here," said Tweed, puffing himself up.

"This is my street, this is my neighborhood, and that's my park. You want to go through here you got to talk to me first." He had no idea what he was doing.

"Oh, so you're the head honcho around here, eh? The big cheese. Shit, I never heard of James Joyce before."

"Apparently," commented Tweed.

"What do you mean by that?"

"I mean if you heard of me you wouldn't be walking through here, and you wouldn't be giving me a hard time." Tweed stepped closer to Gibbons and leaned over him to emphasize his height advantage. In response his friends formed a wall of goon between them. Tweed was not impressed.

"Listen, kid, me and my pals here can take care of you ourselves, but in case you're interested, we have two other friends in the car. Why don't you be a good boy and run along now."

"Yeah," added the other one, "Go home and look through your candy."

"I don't have any candy for you boys, but it's kind of late now for trick-or-treat, so why don't you take off the freakin' masks?"

"Oh, shit, he thinks he funny. I'll tell you what's funny. Hey Billy, look,"

The two kids who had been waiting in the car had decided to come out and join the fun. They carried open long-neck beer bottles and sauntered slowly toward Tweed from behind, backlit by the streetlight.

"Well, I'll leave 'Joyce' here with you guys. I'm going to go catch up with Megan."

Billy trotted off toward the street, and Tweed found himself surrounded by four guys, any one of whom had a distinct size advantage over him. Figuring that discretion was the better part of valor, and being truly worried about Megan, Tweed made as if to leave and pursue her. The strangers had other ideas. One of them tomahawked a full beer at Tweed, striking him on the shoulder. The bottle bounced off, dropped to the pavement and smashed, filling the air with the sweet smell of lager. Tweed was unhurt and unfazed, but he was also furious. Reason, logic and self-interest were superseded by blind thoughtless rage. Summoning up whatever hereditary courage or innate strength he might have at his disposal, Tweed basically went berserk.

Seeing that he had withstood the beer bottle, one of the other attackers came at him with a cast-iron crow-bar. He swung and missed and Tweed dodged and grinned. He swung again and Tweed simply raised his hand and stopped the blow in mid-swing with his fist. It wasn't until later that he found that his hand had been broken. Craziness like that was not what the guys had expected from a single unarmed kid, and Tweed could see hesitation and doubt pass over their faces. Seizing the opportunity, he turned the tables and attacked, running at full speed toward the one who had thrown the bottle. Without waiting, his target turned and ran as if Tweed were a rabid dog.

"Oh, so you got some balls, huh?" shouted another one.

Tweed wheeled about and ran at him now, hollering at the top of his lungs something that sounded like the orchestral crescendo in *A Day in the Life*. As soon as he was within range he unleashed a rocket right that threatened to take the kid's head off. The spurting blood had an unreal quality to it in the artificial light of the street lamps, as if Tweed had smushed a tomato in his face.

"You fuckid broag my dose!" Whined his second victim, as he doubled over with dry heaves.

"Crazy motherfucker!" said one of the remaining assailants. "Fuck this, I'm getting into the car!" The joker fled and leaped into a navy blue Chrysler Newport, and the last of the four thugs took his wounded comrade by the arm and started to escort him toward the car. Seeing that his attackers were going to get away, Tweed sprinted after them, pumping his fists and grimacing like a demented warrior. The driver floored the Newport in reverse and inadvertently smashed into a parked car. Now his car was bumper-locked to an AMC Gremlin, but when he saw Tweed running at him at full speed he clearly thought 'fuck the bumper'. The car tore down the street in a horrendous smoke-show, dragging, or rather pushing the Gremlin ahead of it. When he cut the wheel to come about, he lost the Gremlin, which in turn smashed into two other parked cars. There was no retreat in that direction, but the delay allowed Billy and his friends a chance to pile into the car as if they were pulling a college fraternity stunt.

Terrified but safe all together, the group charged at Tweed in the car as if to run him down. Tweed stood his ground like a blind matador, impassive and irrationally assured of his own invincibility. Sure enough the driver of the Newport swerved to avoid him at the last moment and clipped another parked car before screeching off into the night. The last Tweed saw of them was the frightened face of Megan Columkille, staring out the rear window at him as if he were an apparition.

After all the excitement, the normal quiet of an October night seemed strained and artificial, and Tweed was amazed at what had transpired. It was as if he had stood by and witnessed the whole thing as a spectator. After a couple of minutes dogs started barking and folks started coming out of their houses to inspect the damage to their cars, and the renewed activity made him realize that it was time to head for home.

As he rounded the corner past Col's street he encountered Mrs. Col coming back from her volunteer shift at the block party.

"Hey Tumbleweed, I want you to go right home now. I hear there's been trouble down at the end of the street leading to the park. The police are looking for some kids who vandalized a couple of cars down there."

"Yes, ma'am, sure thing," he said and stopped short of asking after Megan. No use getting her into more trouble than she was likely to be already. It wasn't the image of a parental dressing-down that caused him to be worried for Megan's sake as much as it was his imagination's rampant depiction of her being undressed by a gang of chicken-shit idiots in the back seat of a banged-up Chrysler.

Incidents such as these effectively molded his character for better or worse as part of an annealing process that would continue throughout adolescence, eventually to establish his individual temper.

A healthy, well nourished lad placing in the 95th percentile for height and weight and in the 99th percentile for intelligence, Tweed was, in other words, a strapping precocious boy; but still only fourteen years old. In addition to dealing with the physical and emotional dynamics brought on by puberty, he was also experiencing a psychological growth spurt while various traits of his personality waged a dogfight within him for dominance.

He was naturally curious and intellectually insatiable, yet he had no concept of equating his blessings and endowments with any advantage. Neither did he see education as a means to an end, though he enjoyed learning and derived satisfaction from all of his academic pursuits. Why, he wondered, was it necessary to continue attending school until he acquired enough knowledge to secure a position in a lucrative profession? He already had a lucrative position, the job requirements for which were ambition and common sense; and neither of those could be taught or certified with a diploma.

Though it was really no more than a chip on his shoulder, he was acutely aware of the hurdles and boundaries facing the underprivileged in a class-conscious society, and yet he knew that he personally had profited from the free-market. He might acknowledge that he was a budding entrepreneur, but he refused to salute the flag of competition and he utterly decried elitism. Admittedly the breadth of his experience was limited, but in his opinion competition only punished non-conformity and promoted mediocrity rather than rewarding excellence. Elitism on the other hand served to codify the misappropriation of resources in society according to a skewed scale of perceived merit.

He had heard about individuals who had supposedly given up their identities including name, rank and social-security number in order to live "off the radar". The idea held a romantic appeal for him and he almost wished that he too could "go underground". But Tweed was a realist and he accepted the fact that if he couldn't live within the system, then he could at least find ways to beat it without hurting anyone.

The standard model of success in America was portrayed in terms of the coequal potentials of either the prince or the pauper to someday become the President of the United States. For his part Tweed held no such illusion about his destiny, and he reckoned that an impoverished immigrant's odds of attaining the presidency were no better than his odds of winning the lottery. In fact, given a choice between a chance at becoming the leader of the free world and a free lottery ticket, he'd take the scratch card.

Not that Tweed spent much time considering such matters, or pondering his fate in general. He was far too busy to waste time on idle reflection. There was dope to sell and an image to project. Selling a bit of himself with every bag as he put it required constant refinement and reinvention of his legend and persona. To this end Tweed adopted a new look and a new attitude, and he even tried changing his gait. Truckin' was still in as far as he was concerned and he adopted a modified version of the loping limbo strut, with the result that he appeared to be suffering from either a sports injury or a congenital defect.

For the creation of an after-hours alter-ego he purchased a couple of worn, baggy three-piece suits from the goodwill store at church, and retro-accessorized them with a vest watch-chain and a feathered fedora that he borrowed from Carmine's senile grandfather. Fine glad rags such as these were not designed to impress his peers, and he wouldn't be caught wearing them in the neighborhood (because in order to beat him they'd have to catch him first.) However his outfit provided stunning proof of the adage that the clothes make the man. He had to carry them with him and change at Rod's apartment, but once he was thus accoutered he was admitted without hassle into a nearby uptown jazz club, "The Chamber". There he developed an appreciation for cool combo jazz, and sultry older women. For a peach-fuzz faced kid like himself, the women initially seemed unattainable but the goal of dating them was consistent with his friend Col's advice that he avoid the local girls.

The Chamber was the ideal half-way point for meeting his new friend Mickey Byrne, and together the two underage boys spent many an evening at the jazz club, grooving on the music, sipping tequila and ogling the college chicks. Mickey's companionship was a refreshing change, and Tweed soon began to emulate his friend's wry, world-weary outlook on life. Mickey latched onto Tweed as well, finding a kindred spirit in the Rossie dope dealer. The boys were both the youngest children of large Irish families, and also the only American-born among their siblings. Their shared experience gave them common ground, and they found fast friendship that was completely independent of money, dope, work or girls.

Tweed had also provided solid comfort as well as some much-needed distraction for Mickey during a difficult time in his life. Shortly after Tweed's father had left for Ireland, Mickey's father JC died, having refused the treatment that might have extended his life. Despite his obstinacy he had done his best to prepare himself and his family, settling his affairs and living out his final days with admirable gusto. So JC Byrne had gone to the embrace of his maker with composure and dignity, and he was honored with the respectful tributes of countless friends, loved-ones and survivors. Yet his death made a powerful impact on his son Mickey. Stressed by the ordeal, worried about his family and cynical about his own future, Mickey might not have rebounded without Tweed's help. But JC's death had made an impact on Tweed as well, for he was obliged to represent his father, and to serve as a kind of intermediary during the wake.

There was no shortage of hard-feelings toward the Kelleys, for JC's widow had let it be known that Des had denied her dying husband's last request. To add insult to injury, Des did not attend the funeral because he was in Ireland traveling on the ticket he had refused to give up for poor JC.

Of course when Des learned about the passing of his close friend and indispensable colleague JC Byrne, he fell into mortal anguish. On top of his grief and sorrow he piled shame and embarrassment for having to excuse himself from returning for the funeral. He was in fact entrenched in advance work and negotiations to handle the receipt and distribution of the coming shipment; but he could no more admit to that fact than he would admit to refusing JC's dying wish. During the phone conversation with his youngest son Tweed, who, as the bearer of the news, had demanded an explanation on behalf of his friend, he hastily improvised that there was a misunderstanding about the nature of JC's request. He asserted that rather than asking for a ticket to Ireland, JC had actually asked for advice, and that Des had, in good faith, offered him sound advice at that. Besides, he said, if JC had wanted to travel to Ireland he had both the means and the opportunity.

In his heart Des felt that he had in truth given the bum's rush to a loyal friend, and by so ill-treating a fellow Irishman he had also betrayed himself and his ideals; but worse still, he had besmirched his reputation. He fancied himself to be a champion of the working Irish poor, a man who would give you a hand to pull you out of the gutter, not one who would be the first to throw dirt on your grave. Unable to manage effective damage-control from afar, Des could only authorize Christine to help organize the mourners. He told her to work the wakes as fund raisers, to see if they could help to defray the costs for the funeral, flowers, and burial, while also leaving a decent sum as a gift for the widow Byrne.

Having made basic arrangements, Des had to leave the matter in his wife's hands and hope for the best because he was still reeling from the realization that he had celebrated the simplification of his job too soon. For indeed his task had suddenly become vastly more complicated.

Arriving in Ireland he had marveled at the difference in the whole experience, in the fact that he could almost enjoy traveling when he wasn't smuggling anything. However, his heart felt as light as his bags only until it dawned on him that, a) he had never before handled a shipment of this magnitude, b) he had very little time in which to work, and c) he didn't know whom he could ask for help. There were a number of organizations with the manpower, skill, and brass to offload and distribute a haul of arms like the one he was bringing in; but most of them were the same governmental and paramilitary groups he was trying to avoid.

On previous smuggling runs he had worked with a network of trusted and old local cronies, men from his generation who despite some differences, shared his basic philosophy. But as he settled in to live with his son Buck, he knew that few if any of those friends and connections would be willing to help him with something so grand, and so risky. The greater the size of the haul, the greater the possible hazard, as bribes were paid, lorries were hired, and greater numbers of men were brought in to work.

In the end a crisis was averted when a highly diplomatic delegation from the IRA convened a meeting with Des to convince him that he had nothing to lose by welcoming their participation. First they argued that Des and the leadership shared a vision with similar goals, and therefore their commonalities outweighed their differences; secondly they pointed to the fact that there are only so many people one can trust in an endeavor such as the one he was undertaking, and that sometimes it's better to deal with the devil you know. Furthermore they claimed that Des' plan fit in exactly with their long-term plans as well, for they said that strategic stockpiles of arms provided a couple of important advantages. One advantage was security, for one controlled dump was easier to manage than myriad small stashes; and the other advantage was as a negotiating card. The IRA envisioned using their arms dumps as leverage in talks with British and loyalist factions, although admittedly, at this stage in the game it was difficult to see how that scenario might come about. Another persuasive element in the talks was his own son Buck, who had up to that point been stodgily independent. When Buck started advocating the position of the IRA, Des knew that he would have to give in.

So the local leadership was able to co opt Des and to get him to hand over his first major shipment, all the while assuring him that his arms depots would be secured according to his plan. There can be no glossing over the fact that the IRA looked at Des as an old crank, and furthermore that they looked at him as an American, someone who was only around for two months out of every twelve. If he was willing to raise money in the States, and to go out of his way to smuggle in weapons, then who were they to stop him? It would've been better if he'd smuggled in the items they wanted, but he was by no means their exclusive supplier, and over the years the hauls Des shipped in allowed for the steady rotation and upgrade of arms in the field. The depots were gradually emptied and restocked with older, obsolete guns as the newer American guns went out onto the streets.

A separate volume of literature could be dedicated to the story of the first CAFÉ arms shipment, starting with the agreement between Des Kelley and AD Makepeace, progressing to the deal between Des Kelley and the IRA, and including comprehensive details about the arrival and offload of the Cor Mor, and subsequent hauls. However the task we are now in the process of concluding does not encompass such as vast topic, but is instead primarily focused on introducing Des the man, and on providing insight into his character and his motivation.

For a gentleman who had been relatively self-secure as an individual, a well-established and mature man of 50, Des was surprisingly unsettled by the events surrounding the Samhain trip of '74. He learned that he could take on even greater challenges than he had thought possible. In fact he was so impressed with his own ability to manage people, money and projects that he came to think of himself as a CEO of an international organization. And yet on the eve of his first great triumph he had learned that he could be a callous heel for whom the lessons of Scripture and the daily sermon seemed to have no meaning. He had forgotten a friend in need; he had ignored the plea of a suffering man, possibly hastening his untimely death. This had precipitated a crisis of conscience in Des to which he responded in strange and contradictory ways.

As soon as he heard from Makepeace that he was thought to be irrelevant and inconsequential to the Irish republican cause, Des had set out to prove otherwise. Thenceforth all of his work was motivated by the desire to earn his place in history. He had a personal pantheon of Irish heroes, consisting of both real and legendary men and women whom he admired for their various words and deeds; and he hoped to someday occupy a similar place in a pantheon of heroes honored by some future generation, perhaps his own sons and grandchildren. In order to accomplish that goal he worked hard to build his organization both at home, with his employment and protection rackets, and in Ireland, where he continued smuggling arms and providing safe passage to America for people in need.

Events in the world persisted beyond and despite the efforts of Des Kelley to influence or abate them. In 1974, 216 people would die in Northern Ireland as a result of the political, social, religious and economic conflicts, with British regulars, pro-British loyalists, and a largely Protestant constabulary on one side, and the civil-rights, Christian democratic, socialist, nationalist and republican factions on the other. And yet not all of the news was bad, for a cease-fire between the IRA and British forces started in December of '74 and would last at least until April of '75. In 1975 however, 247 would die, and in July of that year the infamous Miami Showband killings occurred, the investigation of which would reveal startling implications about the extent of dirty tactics being deployed by both sides in the conflict.

The pattern of death, deceit and destruction continued unabated throughout the 70's, with 297 perishing in '76, the year in which Sinn Fein VP Maire Drumm was assassinated while convalescing in her hospital bed; 112 dying in '77, the year the British implemented their 'Ulsterization policy' in an attempt to place events under local control; 81 dying in '78, the year of the 'dirty protests' by republican prisoners; and 113 dying in '79, a year of spectacularly bloody successes for the IRA, including the killing of 18 British soldiers on one day in County Down, and the murder of Lord Mountbatten and three of the guests onboard his boat in County Sligo.

In the early 1980's the spirit of the Provisional government reared in glorious prominence once more. Controversial hunger strikes by republican prisoners in the H-blocks in Long Kesh prison brought international pressure to bear on the British regarding the plight of political prisoners and also revealed the appalling conditions of their imprisonment. Capitalizing on the outrage, Bobby Sands stood for and captured the seat as Independent Republican MP for Fermanagh/Tyrone while on hunger strike in his cell in Long Kesh. Bobby Sands died on day 66 of his hunger strike, and nine of his blanket-protest comrades soon died on hunger strike as well, but their sacrifices would galvanize the nation, and provide impetus and inspiration to the republican movement at large, while demonstrating the moral inadequacy of the British position.

Needless to say Des revered the 'ten men down' as highly as he did the martyrs of '16. During the early '80s he marveled at the advances made by Sinn Fein, and celebrated the emergence of the new northern leadership under Gerry Adams and Martin McGuiness. The number of casualties seemed to be decreasing, and political rather than military activity appeared to be foremost.

As Des got older he reexamined his religious faith and increased his dependence upon the church for salvation; yet he seemingly failed to see the contradiction between his faith and his actions. A place in history might be attainable in any number of ways, as evidenced for example by any given saint, serial-killer or boy with his finger in the dike; but he certainly could not take a place in heaven as granted. Since the death of JC Byrne he had gone out of his way to prove his common decency and worthiness with countless acts of charity and redirected philanthropy. And yet even as he prayed more and attended services more frequently, he also flouted civil laws and lied to his constituents. It was as if he felt a need to balance the scales, so that for every act of contrition there had to be an offsetting act of sinful volition. By the latter half of the decade he had embarked upon a pattern of behavior that was as irreconcilable with his religious beliefs as it was detrimental to his well-being and prestige. He started cheating on his wife, having a series of embarrassingly public affairs with local women, some of whom were also acquaintances of Christine Kelley.

Mrs. Kelley could be patient as the day was long but she was tolerant only to the extent of her ignorance. That is, she would abide misbehavior if she wasn't aware of it, and she preferred it that way. At any rate she was too busy working and raising her boys to pay much attention to her husband, and of the two boys, she tended to worry most about the one who wanted to become a priest. Keiran was an intense, complicated boy who needed supervision and direction while her youngest seemed to be more than self-sufficient. For instance she couldn't remember a time since he was ten years old when Tumbleweed ever needed any money for school, work or play; whereas the other two mooches in the family practically lived out of her pocketbook.

It had never occurred to Tweed that it was unusual for a teenage boy to be so self-reliant. On the contrary, the trouble Tweed had was that he didn't know what to do with all of his money. He was clever enough to realize that he could not be conspicuous about his wealth, so he refrained from purchasing a stereo for his room and from splashing his money around. Even taking into account his weekly nightclub expenses and his personal pot consumption he was still far enough ahead that he would have difficulty explaining any deposits he might consider placing into a savings account.

The logical solution to the problem of excess cash was clearly to reinvest it. Of course, without looking too far ahead he could see that there would be a limit to the extent that reinvesting would work to ease the surplus. He didn't have to go so far as working out a formula to understand that the more money he made, the more he would have to reinvest. Besides, it was one thing to re-up and continue doing business at a consistent rate, it was quite another thing to sell exponentially more pot over time. Tweed was ambitious when it came to selling weed, but his ambition and his imagination weren't accustomed to working together.

He thought that he'd never forget selling the gold, or smoking it for that matter. He'd licked and sealed a lot of baggies before he started selling the gold, and he'd lick many more for years to come, but those bags of Mexican gold, the ounces, lids, quarters, eighths, and grams were the tastiest, funkiest, all-around ass-kickingest grass he'd encountered thus far.

After Christmas of '74, when he'd run out of all but his private stash, his immediate concern was finding a new supplier. Looking back he realized that he had been fortunate to have scored the quantities with which he started his business. Now that he was established as a dealer, there were a number of reasons why it wasn't practical to look for new sources on the street. First off, it was bad for business, because even without any stock to sell he couldn't afford to create the perception that he lacked a consistent source. Whether or not his customers acknowledged the addictive qualities of the stuff, they felt a great deal of comfort in knowing that their next bag of it was readily available. This of course was the fundamental element of his success, because every business thrives on repeat customers, and dope consumers were loyal indeed. Another problem with asking around was that it was like issuing an open invitation to all of the assholes, low-lives and con-squads in town to approach him with their rip-off proposals. If he wanted that kind of participation from the general public he'd start a marijuana cooperative and have the community pool their resources to procure allotments for their own consumption. And furthermore he wanted to avoid pot-buying by committee, a situation he imagined resulting when his well-meaning friends and other interested parties gathered to give him advice on the matter and stress their particular concerns.

Yet his quandary was temporary, and by the end of the winter school break he fell into another connection. Luck and propitious timing might have had something to do with it, or it might have been the case that he was the only person in a position to take advantage of the opportunity, but either way he managed to pick up a kilo of Colombian red that became the new standard by which all other weed was judged. For the remainder of the new year and for some years to come, red became the commercial grade product. It was as much an improvement over, say, Mexican green as bottle rockets were over firecrackers; affordable for the regular smoker but significantly less potent than exotic strains such as Vietnamese or Hawaiian.

Tweed could thank the McManus brothers for setting him up with his new supplier. Ever since he first met them, the McManuses had been troublesome clients. They seemed to approach him at the least opportune moments, they were demanding and obnoxious, they teamed up on him, and in what would become a running gag between them, always pestered him to cuff. Yet for all of that, they had unwittingly introduced him to Donal Harding, a local recluse who not only consistently secured adequate supplies of the best dope, but who was also to become a lifelong friend and mentor to Tweed.

Like Tweed's friend Wayne, Harding was another survivor of the US involvement in Viet Nam. His combat stint was framed like a chunk of time line between two major events of the war, as he had arrived in theater just before the Tet offensive and shipped out just before President Nixon fulfilled his campaign pledge by ordering the withdrawal of US troops. Donal's exit from the war had already been guaranteed by a shrapnel wound he had received one February night in '69 that had started out bad and had suddenly become worse when the Vietcong launched one of their last major assaults against US troops. Donal was gravely wounded, but over 1100 of his comrades were killed that night in and around Saigon.

The lingering pain and disability from his wound had likely aided in Donal's withdrawal from society, and he did little to improve his hermit-like image. Perpetually clad in his left-over combat fatigues, he wore a beard and handle-bar mustache and grew his hair long. He lived on a dead-end street in one of a tract of houses that had been built specifically for ex-GIs in Rossie.

But the trappings of his lifestyle and his personal demeanor only served to conceal what he was really doing with his sharp mind and his military training. As Tweed was to discover, Donal was one of a group of vets who had aggressively pursued a career in dope smuggling after the war. They had gone to Colombia and purchased land and boats and airplanes, and they had made connections with growers and middle-men, in effect setting themselves up as drug lords. Once the dedicated dope smuggling operation was underway, they ensured the success of every run with military-like efficiency, using advanced radio telemetry and radar to avoid detection and observation. This small group remained intact until the 1980s, at which point they had invested and diversified to the extent that it was more profitable to look after their real-estate and other business concerns than to continue competing in the new era of cartels.

For Tweed his relationship with Donal Harding proved to be equally profitable, for he went on to build his organization on the model Donal provided. In addition, Donal introduced Tweed to some of the most rare strains of pot, hybrids that made the gold of '74 pale by comparison; as well as to other choice drugs that helped to expand his consciousness and his appreciation.

As the '70s turned the slow revolution down the drainpipe of history, Tweed sampled from a virtual dessert-cart of illicit substances. Cannabis was the aperitif, the palate cleanser to which he always returned, but in addition he enjoyed hashish, hash oil, cannibinol and opium. Also in the organic realm he tried peyote and mescaline and mushrooms. He sampled the powders cocaine and crystal meth, and the pills STP, and DMT, chloryl hydrate, Librium, Valium, Demerol, and Quaaludes. For inhalants he enjoyed nitrous oxide and chloroform, and in addition he had brief flings with the nitrate sisters butyl and amyl; but he lumped these together with PCP and angel dust as the drugs of last resort. And rarely, usually on a carefree summer's day, he would elope in the embrace of LSD, slipping a tab of windowpane or blotter under his tongue and throwing caution to the winds. By the early 1980s, an analysis of the chemical bouillabaisse he had ingested would reveal that even with the breadth of his experiences with hard drugs he was no more than a dilettante; and yet when it came to pot, he was a true connoisseur.

BOOK THREE

CHAPTER 1

The municipal police district encompassed a diverse amalgamation of boroughs and hamlets with varying population densities and crime rates. The Rossie Square police station, like many of the outlying precincts in the district, operated fairly autonomously. As the primary law enforcement entity in the area the Rossie police dealt with a range of issues and challenges, some common to the entire district, some unique to the community. Yet one thing it shared with all of the other precincts in the city was that it lagged about twenty years behind the times in terms of equipment, technology and communications.

Furthermore, due to a difficult history of labor relations and public relations, the department also suffered from a shortage of qualified personnel as well as a lack of trust and confidence on the part of the citizens.

There were relatively few homicides in the precinct, but when they occurred such crimes were turned over to precinct detectives who handled all investigations, not exclusively homicides per se. Of the killings that did occur, most were classified as crimes of passion, committed by people who knew, were related to, or were romantically involved with their victims. There were accidental killings, and unintended killings, but none of the incidents in precinct records were unsolved.

As the lead officers on the McManus murder case, Detectives William Storer and James Rima were keen to maintain the chain of responsibility and evidentiary control at the scene of the crime. Although they would have free rein to proceed with the investigation in the manner they deemed necessary, they would have to coordinate with the state medical examiner's office, the county coroner's office, and the central municipal task force that served as a clearinghouse for all violent crime investigations and control efforts.

By the time the detectives made their first thorough walk-through of the crime scene the site had already been combed, measured, examined, photographed and cordoned-off.

"Can't be easy for the guys from forensics," observed Storer as he gazed through a rectangle made up by his two hands, held in front of his face, thumb and forefinger to thumb and forefinger.

"At least it's still fresh," muttered Rima, crouching beside a patch of blood-stained grass.

Indeed there was an incongruous freshness to the air, as a drying breeze picked up with the dawn. The sound of irregularly random but steady splashing emanated from a stream that was hidden behind a shadowy bank of brooding rhododendrons. Rima had already been down to the stream, following the trail of blood across the dewy lawn as he attempted to reconstruct the movements made by Nilvan McManus before he died.

"I say this one was in the road over there first, then he bolted down toward that brook. I'm guessing he tried to take cover near those bushes when he got nailed."

"Bolted away from the road?" asked Storer, though he was facing in the opposite direction and pre-occupied with his own observations.

"Yeah, could have seen his killer coming and headed for cover, like I said. Then after he gets shot, he crawls back toward the road, toward his brother there." He indicated the area that his colleague was examining.

"Why did he start in the road? Why couldn't they have split up? One takes the road, the other hides in the bush?"

"Why be here in the first place? They weren't sight-seeing, that's for sure."

"No, they weren't casual visitors who happened to be shot while walking in the park. Clearly they were here because it's isolated and quiet."

"So they came here knowing that there was going to be trouble?"

"Why else bring a shotgun and a rifle to Arbs Park? It's not like they have a problem with bears or mountain lions here."

"So back to the meet, or showdown idea. They showed up for a meeting, ready for the worst, and the worst was what they got. Whoever did them in was apparently more prepared, or more paranoid."

"Boy scout motto- be prepared. Only I doubt these guys were boy scouts. So you're thinking drug deal?"

"Maybe. Could be anything. Private beef, bad business, whatever."

"Alright, so who goes to the park after dark…what's today, Friday? Who goes to the park after dark on a Thursday night?"

"Well, none of these actors were regular park patrons…"

"No, I'm not thinking of them, I'm thinking of possible witnesses. Who else might have been here last night?"

"The park is of course public. It was donated to the town about a hundred years ago with the provision that it remain free and open and accessible. That's why you don't see no turnstiles. There's no admissions, not even suggested donations. I suppose you could make up a profile of average park visitors and then factor in the time of year, time of day, weather, etc. and eventually you might come up with an idea of who might have been in here last night. Best thing to do would be to ask for help from the locals. Put out an announcement, tell people that we want them to come forth if they were in the park between certain hours last night. Then when we get a response, if we get a response, we ask them if they heard or saw anything 'unusual'."

Storer grunted in agreement.

"Crappy weather last night," added Rima.

"Early on, yeah, but it cleared up later, thank God. Most of the action took place on the pavement. Don't know if we'll find any footprints from the shooters."

"What makes you say that?"

Storer looked toward the gate and pointed. "My guess is that the shooters came from out there. Stiff number one, what's his name, Francis? He was facing the gate when they found him. This guy, Nilvan?"

"Yeah, yeah, Nilvan," Rima reported helpfully.

"He was coming this way, too." Storer directed like a traffic cop, with his arms toward the gate. So I say they were facing guys coming in from the street."

"OK, but their car was way the fuck over there," Rima pointed over his shoulder at the bulk of the hillside.

"Yeah? And?" Storer prodded.

"And it looks like they came through the woods there. Now to me, that looks like stealth, you know? Like they were the ones planning to creep up and maybe take someone by surprise."

"So it was a setup? You think the killers were waiting here inside the gate, then the kids come sneaking up from the brush?"

"That's what it looks like to me," replied Rima, optimistically.

"So if they had the element of surprise, why were they the ones who got blown away?" Storer said this as if he were exposing an obvious flaw in Rima's reasoning. The younger cop hesitated a beat, then answered. "Good question."

CHAPTER 2

"I'm putting on water for tea. Do you want a cup? Might help settle your stomach. What's the matter? Are you going to be sick again?" LaGloria talked while she busied herself about the apartment, trying to provide an outlet for the adrenalin-spiked energy that was frazzling her nervous system.

Tweed looked uncertain. He gripped the handle to the freezer door on the refrigerator, staring at the manufacturer's emblem with the Nordfrost logo embossed on a stippled metal badge that appeared to glide and ooze like a chrome slug. As he turned to focus his gaze upon LaGloria's face, the room suddenly seemed to pitch in a cartwheel spin. Despite what the drugs were telling him, he knew that since his position relative to the refrigerator was fixed, then he would be alright as long as he stayed put.

"PCP for sure," he muttered, his suspicions confirmed by the tell-tale asynchronous hum of the buzz.

"PCP? What are you talking about? I said hot tea, not T."

There was a distracting flash from the checkerboard linoleum floor, as if it were made up of clashing colors. Tweed tried to find something bland and neutral to look at, something plain and reassuring. The surface of the counter top was decorated in a classic 1960's American motif, like confetti scattered over a rose-colored field, with a narrow textured aluminum rail around the perimeter. The dose of nasty street chemicals Tweed had consumed altered his vision so that the confetti shapes seemed to float apart from the substrate, the reddish tint of which was reminiscent of the interior of a mouth. Looking at it Tweed was at once becoming hypnotically drawn in and viscerally repulsed. The apartment he had shared with LaGloria since 1983 was suddenly an alien environment, scary and disturbing. But closing his eyes was no solution because the terrors of the dark lurked within and he was not up to facing them. Better to deal with so-called reality than to pit himself against what his imagination could throw at him. He attempted to speak.

"I have something to tell you, babe. On my way home I picked up a couple of hits of T."

His girlfriend seemed to leap into his face. "You ate PCP! Tonight of all nights! Why did you have to go and get fucked up now? Fucking shit, Tweed! You're no help to me now! Come on," she took his arm, "you should go to bed and sleep it off."

He wouldn't budge, reluctant to relinquish his dwindling grasp on reality, represented by the handle of the fridge, to which he clung with all of his strength.

"Damn it, Tweed, let go!" she shouted, trying to pry his fingers free from the cold metal bar.

"Leave me here, love, leave me here. It's safe here."

"Oh my God, you're hopeless! What? Do you want to stand there all night? You're just going to guard the fridge, is that it? Tweed, let me help you to the bedroom."

"No, babe, I can't let go. You go to bed. I'll be OK."

"I'm not going to bed, you are! You crazy, fucked up lump! I'm telling you right now, you can't stay out here in the kitchen all night hugging the freaking refrigerator!" LaGloria had a repertoire of different voices she used for different occasions. She was now warming up her shrill nagging voice, the type of chalkboard rending tones that any henpecked husband in the northern hemisphere would recognize as the signal for the onset of protracted difficulties, likely to include bickering, backbiting, insults and the frosty withholding of affection. He relented and relaxed his grip a little before changing his mind, but his hands felt like boxing mitts and LaGloria was too quick for him. She yanked his arm and pulled him bodily toward the bedroom.

"Oh, shit, I can't do this!" he said, pitifully. His ankle felt as though it had gotten caught in a bear trap. The walls of the room were closing in and the frame of the doorway leading to the hall looked trapezoidal. The hardwood floor in the hall was rolling toward him in waves. He would have to step high to avoid them.

"What are you doing? There's nothing there, god dammit! Just walk. I don't want to have to drag you all the way."

They had made it as far as the bathroom.

"Gotta stop here, babe. Hold on just a second."

LaGloria groaned in exasperation. "Are you going to be alright in there?"

"Yeah, no problem," he said, "I'm fine," and he stumbled within and closed the door behind him. *There- that would do.* Dropping to the floor as if collapsing, Tweed grabbed the side of the bath with one hand and rolled himself into the tub. *No safer place in the house.*

As soon as he had found a comfortable position he realized that there was an annoying noise coming from somewhere nearby. It was LaGloria, pounding on the door and yelling.

"Hey, Tweed! Did you die in there? What are you doing? I'm coming in!"

But by the time she entered he was gone, off on an adventure in the realm of his unconscious imagination.

"Fuck it," she cried, "you're sleeping there."

Her anger was quick and hard to control but it was useless to wrestle with that emotion when so many others were clamoring for outlet and expression. Her fists were clenched at her sides when she stomped out of the room, her head high and her spine erect, but she would just as soon curl up in a ball and sob. With Tweed incapacitated, there was no one to console her, no one to hold and comfort her. Frankie and Nilvan were gone. Tweed was gone. She was alone.

The teabag was still in her cup where she had left it moments ago, stewing bitterly like herself. Almost mechanically she traversed the kitchen, fetching milk, sugar and a spoon. Then as she sipped the strong hot tea she paced repeatedly to the broad bay window in the den, briefly parting the curtains and peering out at the street with each iteration.

Damn, she thought, she should have had a plan. She had considered the possibility that her brothers might screw up, that they might fail to follow her explicit directions, but she had discounted most of the scenarios she imagined developing as a result. It would have been counter-productive to permit worry, paranoia, fear or pessimism to embellish her more pragmatic concerns. She knew her brothers all too well; well enough to convince them to help her and well enough to be realistic about their proficiency. Frankie had managed to earn his diploma a year late after flunking out of the college-prep course at Munie and bouncing to the school of industrial arts to complete his education. Nilvan had never even finished high school, having had just enough intelligence to know that he couldn't cut it. But they both did OK for themselves, hustling day to day; and despite their differences, bickering and fist fights, they helped each other to survive. They also maintained the pretense of looking out for their little sister, caring for her with their peculiar blend of truculent tenderness and sociopathic solicitude. And yet she had long since dominated them with the authority of her gender, the cunning of her intellect and the force of her personality.

How could she have predicted that Des Kelley, the fat Irish bastard, would turn around and blow her brothers away? Now his debt to her was even greater, and she would have to double her resolve to even the score. There could be no doubt that she would truly be justified in taking his life.

After all, the worthless piece of shit had made her life miserable, starting years ago, when he had first seduced and then abandoned her mother. LaGloria was 18 at the time, still living at home, working part time, attending night school and dating Tweed. Her father had recently retired after working for 35 years in a boiler shop and he was finding it difficult to adjust to a life of leisure. To aid in the transition he spent the majority of his time in the local VFW post, ostensibly to stay connected with his peers and to gain a perspective on the remainder of his life. In fact he was drinking and avoiding his wife. He wasn't accustomed to spending free time with her, never having had so much of it before, and furthermore he felt increasingly uncomfortable and inadequate in her presence. There wasn't much to talk about; and he could not afford to travel, to redecorate the house, to improve his education, or anything that might help stimulate conversation and interest between them.

How her mother had met the smug, self-righteous prick Des Kelley, LaGloria did not know. But their affair lasted for a few months, most of it carried on right in the McManus home. Des would visit in the early afternoon. Rose, her mother, would be waiting in the parlor with a pitcher of Manhattans, and one thing would lead to another. LaGloria met him at the door once as she was going out. He scanned her with the eye of a sidewalk flirt, muttered an unlikely pretext, and entered the house as if he were a long-time friend of the family.

Frankie and Nilvan were on their own, having moved out of the house as soon as legally possible, and LaGloria was busy enough with her own life that although she resided at home, she really only slept and showered there.

Her mother was basically free to entertain her gentleman friend, knowing that her husband was occupied at the post, and that LaGloria was no deterrent even on the rare occasions when she was home in the afternoon. Apparently she believed that her daughter was old enough to understand, and if not, she was at least smart enough to keep her mouth shut. Not that Rose was really hiding anything, for if her husband had known about the affair, she would have enjoyed his humiliation. She used to say, "When I married you, you were like a Greek god. Now you're like a god-damned Greek!"

LaGloria did not understand her parents. Surely they loved each other, for they had always kissed and hugged and otherwise doted on one another. Or so it appeared in LaGloria's memory. Usually a couple's body language provided a clue as to the intensity of their love. Take her and Tweed for example. Even at a glance a casual observer could see that not only were they in love, but they couldn't keep their hands off each other. Then again 20 plus years of togetherness could conceivably have tempered that kind of ardor somewhat. Would the body-language test even apply in the case of people who in those days were rarely in the same room together? At least at that time they still slept together, didn't they? Sure, thought LaGloria, her father and mother did sleep in the same bed, only he had no idea who was warming the sheets.

At any rate the hanky-panky ended abruptly. Not, however, because of any discovery her father had made, but because of a discovery on the part of her mother. She was diagnosed with ovarian cancer in the fall of '78, and subsequently underwent a complete hysterectomy in December, only to be stricken with heart disease in the spring of '79, followed by lung cancer in '80. Rose McManus doggedly held on to her increasingly uncomfortable life despite the deterioration of her body, her dignity and her self-esteem. She died in 1982, far too young for her, far too early for those she left behind. Des Kelley was conspicuous for his absence at her funeral.

Essentially a broken man after losing Rose, Mr. McManus never regained his independence. Various age-related infirmities reduced his vigor and limited his mobility, and he resigned himself to loneliness and isolation, gradually permitting his world to grow smaller and smaller.

It was time to check on Tumbleweed. As she gently pushed the bathroom door open it groaned loudly on its hinges, making her cringe. Her boyfriend on the contrary was completely inanimate, his stillness causing her to catch her breath until she heard the reassuring whisper of his breathing. How vulnerable he looked, how sweet and trusting. He was at her mercy like this. She could turn the cold shower on him or she could just as easily leave him in peace. The idea of tormenting him caused a nipple-stiffening thrill to course through her body and in response she pulled her head out of the bathroom and reminded herself that she was mourning. She would have to watch her behavior.

How was one supposed to act when one's family members had been murdered?

Genuine emotion was a poor substitute for the bloody rage that had festered in her heart over the years, engendered by the crimes and depredations of Des Kelley. The destruction of her mother was just one of his cruelties, and even in her own family, her mother was not his only victim.

Des Kelley the humanitarian, Des Kelley the philanthropist, Des Kelley the pseudo-ward boss had allegedly planned and funded the creation of the Christian Youth Center of Rossie. When it opened in 1976 to community-wide acclaim, "Cycor" was promoted as a recreation center, a place where teenagers could come in off the streets and play pool, air-hockey, foosball and table-tennis. The center was staffed with "youth counselors" who organized activities and instructional seminars for the teens. The display in the store-front window was plastered with self-help pamphlets, fliers from local churches and charities and help-wanted postings for current job openings in town as well as opportunities for those who might wish to return to school or to earn their GED.

LaGloria had never personally been inside the youth center, but she had always suspected that it was a front for something criminal or nefarious. Maybe it was a numbers operation, or loan-sharking; perhaps they pushed drugs or ran a general fence and money-laundry. Whatever the facade of the place covered up, it didn't look like much. In fact, Cycor was an eyesore. Situated directly on Main St on the seedy side of town, it blended in nicely on the block it shared with a tattoo parlor and a check-cashing dive. The community action committee responsible for converting the place had of course awarded the work to contractors recommended by Des himself. Although renovations continued well after the grand opening, the center still resembled the shabby five-and-dime that had previously occupied the premises until it had failed during the recession.

Rumors, her personal suspicions and the doubts of other concerned citizens aside, there were real scandals associated with the youth center, scandals that ultimately forced the police and municipal authorities to close the community outreach facility. The problems started when a young man (who subsequently moved to another town with his family) reported that he had been sexually abused and assaulted by members of the staff at Cycor. Soon other teens joined in a swelling chorus of accusations against the very counselors who had been responsible for encouraging and helping the youngsters they had allegedly abused. If LaGloria had only heard such accusations in the press, or second or third hand, then the impact upon her and her family would have been minimal; but in the event her brothers Frankie and Nilvan were among the first to come forth with corroborating accounts of abuse.

As a naive younger sister, LaGloria could never be sure if the boys were telling the truth, having been a frequent victim of their pranks, fibs and outright lies. But Frankie and Nilvan stuck to their stories from the first time they related them and throughout the ensuing ordeal of interviews with cops and psychiatrists and lawyers and advocates; through a series of hearings "downtown", through the physical exams, the media scrutiny and a thorough review of their academic and criminal records.

LaGloria would never know if her brothers had been truthful regarding their accounts of abuse, but she was certain that they suffered, if not as a result of the assaults, then definitely as a result of coming forth. For their friends, classmates and sometimes even total strangers went out of their way to harass them and belittle them for supposedly being diddled against their will.

Perhaps they sought justice and lawful retribution, perhaps they were in it for the private settlement that the plaintiffs ultimately reached with their alleged abusers. But whatever peace they were able to achieve after the controversy had died down was never shared by LaGloria, for she took the episode to be further proof of the evil potential of Des Kelley. He had supposedly originated the idea of Cycor; he alone had profited from the opening of the center and he initially benefited from the positive publicity. She could only imagine how he must have gained otherwise, but she had an active imagination and could hardly conceive of any sin, crime, or pernicious deviation of which he could not be considered capable. He was not, however, ever charged in relation to the alleged crimes at Cycor, nor was he in any way connected to them, for once the place closed his name was scrupulously dropped from press accounts as if he had never been associated with it.

CHAPTER 3

None of the booths in the Salonika Restaurant were particularly accommodating and usually a large group that wished to sit together would take a table. But Eban, one of a party of five, had insisted upon a booth because the gorgeous Linda Mesthene waited the booths, whereas her mother, a dour archetypal middle-aged Hellenic matron waited the tables.

If the rose-tinted contact-lenses of love weren't obscuring his view, and if he would permit himself a bit of dispassionate deduction, Eban might see a portentous relevance in Mrs. Mesthene's appearance, that is, a resemblance of things to come. She was said to have been a great beauty in her time, and that should have been the tip-off right there. There were even women like her in his own extended family, but when he looked at her he couldn't see past the dark hair net, the shawl and black woolen stockings. Solid, severe, and partially androgenated, she looked as though she could have held the world record in squat-thrusts.

A lithe part-time karate instructor with almond skin, curly black hair, and classic Middle-Eastern features, Eban had for some weeks now been pursuing her daughter Linda, who was blond, bright, curvaceous and taller than him by four inches, all of them good. He of course had recommended the restaurant to his fellow franchisees as a suitable place to hold an impromptu meeting, and when everyone took their seats he made sure that his was on the aisle, facing the kitchen. Eban's market territory covered the broad, still surprisingly lucrative corridor running from White City out to Roosevelt.

Og, Bone and Kuhn respectively took the opposite bench, and Sharlae crammed into the wall seat beside Eban, with her feet folded up in her lap.

"Oh, crap!" she said, "I lost the pompom from my right ankle sock!" More unexpected consequences of her sudden flight through the fields. Sharlae's franchise, the one originally controlled by Carmine Gunther, encompassed a chunk of the pie roughly perpendicular to Eban's, heading all the way out to Crystal Pond Park.

Og blew air out of his mouth and rolled his eyes as if to say, "Big fucking deal". Og's wedge of the aforementioned pie was favorably situated in the congested heart of Rossie, between the Square and Westbury Circle.

"So rip the other one off," suggested Eban.

"Yeah, but then what do I do with it?" Sharlae knew from experience that if she tore off the pompom and saved it for a spare she would never need it, but she was equally certain that she would lose another pompom only if she threw this one away, as if it were a magic charm.

"Are you serious?" asked Bone, looking at her as if she had interrupted the final sequence of operations in a lengthy mental calculation. Bone's portion of the distribution network represented a stake in the Mission and uptown markets. He milked it for all it was worth. "You chuck it. Here, let me have it."

"What are you going to do with it?" she asked suspiciously.

"I'm going to chuck it!" He laughed abruptly, catching cola up his nose.

Sharlae looked from his face to Og's to Kuhn's and felt a twinge of protectiveness. She furtively reached in and secured the pompom to a safety-pin she kept in the pocket of her jacket. She'd keep it. It was either that or go through all of her socks and tear off all the freakin' pompoms and be done with it once and for all.

Later she would add the pompom, or was it a pom now that it was alone? -to the clutter of odd mis-matched items on her bureau-top at home. It should be a welcome addition to the motley buttons, tokens, coins, stickers, tampons, ticket-stubs, crayons, bottle-caps, pins, buckles, matchbooks, coasters, and unread religious pamphlets that were lying there as well.

"Let's get serious," said Kuhn, who was generally the quietest of the bunch. Kuhn had bought in on the ground floor as it were, taking Tweed's favorite sector of Jamaica Center and mopping up the abutting areas. He was frequently accused of zone violations by Og and Eban.

"What do we know, what do we have to do? Has anyone spoken with Weed?"

Og was picking his nose, Eban was staring dreamily, and Bone was idly stirring patterns into a pile of sugar on the table top with his finger. Sharlae answered.

"Last time I talked to him was before midnight last night. I was just checking in, and didn't know at the time what had happened."

The waitress arrived, interrupting an uncomfortable moment when each of Tweed's associates remembered hearing the news about the McManus brothers. She relayed their orders via hand signs and verbal cues directly to her father, whose visage appeared through the mist of the short order window like a mask out of Greek tragedy, with blazing blue eyes and tail-light red cheeks framed by tufts of black hair and eyebrows.

Mr. Mesthene owned Salonika Restaurant, a tiny joint coincidentally located on Corinth St in Rossie; he also prepared the food and when he found a willing listener, he extolled the virtues of the original Salonika, the Greek city from which he and his family had emigrated when Linda was still a toddler.

Here he was the master of his domain insofar as his wife permitted him to be, and he felt in no way threatened by the procession of eager young gentlemen who entered his store seeking to gain the attention of his beautiful daughter.

When he looked at Eban, for example, he didn't measure him against an ethnic or cultural standard, nor did he consider the criteria of tradition, heritage or religion. Instead he placed the young man on a demographic scale, and considered his family connections, his net worth and his prospects. Demetrius had learned very early upon arriving in America and settling in Rossie that being established counted for a great deal in this society. An immigrant might ambitiously join into the community, he might work hard and make friends, he might buy a home and start a family and send his children to school, but still not have half of the advantages enjoyed by established snobs who could not care less about any of those things.

Glancing quickly from Linda to her father, Eban felt a flush of anxiety radiate from his chest. In that instant he caught a premonition of a scene in the near future when he might have to present himself more formally to the Mesthenes for inspection and approval. He'd already met old man Mesthene, and had heard the Salonika rap. Seemed to be an alright dude. Reminded him of one of his uncles, particularly the one who used to growl at him in a deep accented voice:

"Eban! Remember the camel! You don't let the camel stick his nose in the tent! If the camel sticks his nose in the tent, the next thing you know, the camel is inside the tent and you are outside, sticking your nose in the tent!"

Eban had no intention of having anything to do with tents or camels.

Those old guys worked so hard, always trying to prove something, to prove that they're as good as everyone else, that they buy into the Ponzi-scheme of the American dream.

Linda touched his arm- light, dry fingertip contact that lit up his nerves like a whack on a funny bone, and brought his attention back to the present. "So you guys heard about the shootings over at the Arbs? Pretty scary shit, huh?

"I don't think it was a random killing or anything," said Eban, then he stretched, locking his fingers high over his head and cracking his knuckles. "But yeah, it sucks that violence like that should come to a place as peaceful as the Arbs. I still don't think the park is dangerous."

Bone added quickly, "Then again, I heard that they had a shotgun and an M16. Can you imagine jogging through the gate and getting pinned down by crossfire?"

"I can't imagine you jogging anywhere," said Sharlae.

"An M16, huh? I wonder where the McManuses got an M16."

"Did you know them?" asked Linda.

The members of the group looked at each other uncertainly. They had all known the McManus brothers, but their reluctance to share that information was no reflection on their regard for the waitress. It was a matter of training and discipline to avoid volunteering, especially when they were in each other's company. Og responded.

"Ahm, I went to school with the younger one, that was, uh, Nilvan. But I'm talking back in elementary."

"Well I'll tell you something- they were in here just the other day," said Linda, pointing at Og with a stubby pencil. "Came in here pretty often actually, for breakfast. They'd each get the special and the older one drank a lot of coffee. I seen 'em around the square sometimes, too."

"They're seeing them all over the Arbs, now," muttered Og.

"Og! I swear!" said Sharlae, her face reddening.

Linda imparted a special smile to Eban that seemed to say, "Good luck with this bunch!" and then resumed her duties.

"Like I said," said Kuhn, "What do we have to do? Is there any way we can help?"

"Things are going to be pretty fucked up for awhile," said Bone, as if he had pretty much summed up the situation.

"They're fucked up already," Sharlae replied, almost by way of rebuttal.

"I know what you mean," sighed Eban.

"Oh yeah? I don't think so. Last night I was kidnapped. How's that for fucked up? How much more fucked up can it get?"

She had their attention now, although Bone's face betrayed a trace of skepticism, Og looked as though he'd like to kidnap her himself, and Kuhn seemed to think her story was amusing.

Sharlae could tell a good story. She had developed most of her technique by imitation, as she had spent heaven knows how many hours listening either out of boredom or fascination to the bullshit that flew when her boyfriend and his buddies used to sit around and get wasted. Carmine had been the consummate verbal artist, even when stoned. In fact most of his interactions with other people, and most of his relationships with the other guys in Tweed's circle were precipitated upon scams, snow jobs and in at least one instance, upon an outright, unjustified and unresolved rip-off.

Carmine had noticed the latent talent in Sharlae; he had encouraged her to speak up and had pointed out that not all skills can be acquired through osmosis. From time to time he actively coached her in some of the more subtle devices and nuances of story telling, which, as he went to great pains to point out, was not the same as lying. But Carmine told his tales and spun his cons as part of an enduring match of one-upmanship, either against himself or his perceived opponents. His death by drug overdose was shamefully pointless, especially for a storyteller. For her part Sharlae had learned to always stick as closely as possible to the truth, to strike and establish the tone of the tale like the ringing of a tuning fork. For she knew that her listeners would follow that pitch no matter how outrageous the tale became in the telling.

"So I was up on Toilet Paper Parkway," she began, "cruising home and minding my own business when, I swear to God, just like in the movies, I picked up a tail. It's only two lanes running through there so unless you're alone on the road you're either leading or following somebody. This time it was obvious that, I mean these guys weren't following me, they were chasing me. I didn't think I'd done anything to piss anyone off, although you never know, these days it doesn't take much...Anyway you could spend half of your life trying to reconcile the perceived grievances of every shitbum you happened to pass on the street. And you know my route, I'm always running around out there." Sharlae waved her hand expansively, almost brushing the tip of Kuhn's nose at the peak of the sweep. "Oops, sorry!"

"So you were being followed. What did you do? You said you were kidnapped," Eban prodded in response.

"What would you do if you had guys on your tail?"

Eban quickly answered, interrupting Sharlae, "Ah, gee, I think Og would know the answer to that one. What do you do, Og, when you have guys on your tail?"

"What is this?" Og grumbled, "Shit on Og day?"

Sharlae answered her own question. "Right! You lose 'em...I tried that up in Geritol Estates, but my foxy Fairlane was no match for their big block Olds. I even pulled a stunt like the one I did that time up at the Community College when I thought the rent-a-cops were after me, you know, a quick power-slide into a parking spot. That time it worked and I lost them; but not this time...Next to the reservoir, that's where they grabbed me- in front of the cops- right in front of them, not 50 yards away! Stuffed me into their car and drove away like it was nothing."

"No shit? This was last night?" asked Bone.

"I'm telling you, man. It was bad enough they put me in the back seat with two freakin' goons with bad breath, but I could see that they got somebody driving my car! And you know, the whole time I was saying to myself, 'If they so much as put a scratch on that thing!'"

"OK, so what was this? An ex-boyfriend or something? I mean, you said you were kidnapped, but you're here now."

"Yeah well, Og, I'm getting to that, and no, I have no idea who those bozos were. The driver was saying that he grabbed me for my own protection, that they were taking me to a safe place. Not that I believed them, don't get me wrong. As far as I was concerned, I was dealing with a bunch of sick fucks who did it because they thought they could get away with it." Sharlae took a sip of coffee and wiped her mouth with the back of her hand. Despite herself, she was attractive when she was animated like this, glowing in the heat of the gaze of her peers.

As she went on to describe her escape she had to resist the urge to withhold the ending. By now, despite the fact that she had omitted the details about her new girlfriends Honey and Chugga, she had strained her credibility to the extent that her narrative sounded more like a romantic fantasy than an account of a criminal abduction.

"Here's the part I can't get over. When I called Weed from the road, he must have known already...about what happened at the Arbs, I mean. And he didn't say anything. You know how cool Weed is. Sounded like he was only concerned about what happened to me."

"Probably just being polite, you know?"

"Yeah, except he didn't say anything like, 'Listen, Sharlae, I'm in the middle of something right now', or, 'I've got problems of my own'. And here's the kicker- I got home and there was my car, parked in the driveway. And there was a note on my front door- an apology!"

"An apology?"

"Right. Figure that out. Not signed, but it said 'Sorry- won't happen again'."

"Now I know you're putting us on," groaned Kuhn.

"I'm serious, man, sometimes the truth is strange. I figure Weed straightened it out, made a few phone calls or something."

"So you're saying that you were practically forced off the road, then you were grabbed and your car was stolen."

"Uh huh."

"But you got away and made it home on your own, only to find out that whoever it was put your car back where it belonged? Ah, Sharlae, you didn't say how many joints you smoked before all of this happened."

"Very funny, Bone, but you know that I stay straight when I'm working."

"Hmm...wild!" said Kuhn, "I can't imagine how Weed could have helped you. I mean, the only way he'd know who those guys were would be if he sent them after you himself. But man, that sure was fucked up!"

Sharlae was troubled by a sudden realization. She had been with LaGloria at about the time the killings were supposed to have occurred, and she had said that Weed was out with her brothers! And she remembered talking to the cop! -Oh, oh. Could she have been stupid enough to tell that cop who they were looking for? She searched her memory, frantic.

"What is it?" asked Eban. "You look like you just got slugged or something."

"Oh I, ah, I was just thinking. You don't suppose that Weed could have had anything to do with..."

"What? Hold it right there, babe. This is Weed we're talking about. What the fuck? Five minutes ago he was your hero."

"I know, I know, it just occurred to me that when something like this happens everyone is a suspect, right? The cops will be talking to Weed for sure."

"Yeah, and anybody else who knew Frankie and Nilvan. They might even talk to us."

"That's alright," said Bone, with authority. "We don't know anything. But I say ixnay on the ocktay about eedWay, OK?"

"What did you say?"

"Never mind."

"No, man, what the heck is ick-snay?"

"Kuhn, it's pig-latin, you know? Ixnay, ixnay," Bone replied with impatience.

"I know it's pig-latin. What the fuck is ick-snay, is all I'm asking. Nick? Nicks? Nicks on the talk? What's that supposed to mean?"

"Jailhouse Rock, dig? You got it now?" said Bone, wearily.

"What? No, I don't." Now Kuhn was fed up.

Eban tried to dispel his aggravation. "Jailhouse Rock, it's an oldie. It goes, ah, let me see, 'Lefty said to,' ah,..."

"No, man," said Bone:

"'Bugsy turned to Shifty and he said, "nix nix"

I wanna stick around while I get my kicks'"

"I still don't get it," sighed Kuhn, "but that's alright. I should have known it was before my time."

"Oh, like I'm so much older than you." Bone's sarcasm was misplaced, since he was indeed a couple of years older than Kuhn. "I was trying to be inconspicuous, you know, cool, like? *Un-ob-tru-sive*? All I meant was that we should stop talking about Weed." He concluded his statement in a low hiss.

"Well, why didn't you just say so? Ick-snay on the ock-tay! From now on it's ick-snay on the ig-pay atin-lay, own-Bay!"

"Yeah, well uck-fay oo-yay oo-tay!"

"Boys! That's enough! Man! I'm glad we don't have these meetings very often."

"Hey, we don't have to have them at all as far as I'm concerned, but right now we have ourselves a situation."

"Damn right it's a situation; especially if we can't get any product." -Bone

"Who says we can't?" cried Sharlae, "You know something we don't?"

"All's I'm saying is that Weed is likely to be tied up for a while. He's gonna have to lay low. You mentioned talking to the cops, well that's not the half of it. Him and LaGloria are gunna-hafta deal with all sorts of bullshit, autopsies, funerals, the whole nine yards. All's I'm saying is be prepared to hunker down until the heat blows over."

CHAPTER 4

A man of habit, Des Kelley took pleasure from the regular, predictable trappings of an unvarying, prosaic routine. Every morning he walked the same route to the town square and was gratified to note that familiar landmarks such as homes and businesses, sign posts and trees, hedgerows, alleys, streets and ditches remained as he had left them on the previous day. And though all of these objects were fixed and stationary, he delighted in the daily variations in appearance, the differences caused by light, weather, season, decay and renewal.

The path he followed, the lanes upon which he walked had been in place long before his arrival, and would doubtless remain long after his passing, but for now they were his very own, the feeling of attachment enhanced by a sense of safety and privilege. The place he considered to be his true home was far away across the ocean, yet he belonged here.

However, this morning there was no joy to be found in any of his customary haunts, no respite from a gathering pall of doubt and anxiety that clouded his thoughts and perceptions.

When Father Patrick's seven thirty sermon had failed to lift him out of his funk he had actually considered going upstairs in the church to wait for a turn in the confessional. As he slowly walked up the broad stairs leading from the lower chapel to the narthex he felt the impulse to seek redemption and absolution diminish with each successive step, until his resolve was worn down like the marble steps themselves.

"Bless me Father, for I have sinned," he thought bitterly.

"It has been eleven years and six months since my last confession…" Let the padre swallow that. Perhaps not such a shocking statistic for some sinners in this godless world, but prior to October 1974, and the death of his dear comrade JC Byrne, Des had been a faithful and regular penitent, and he received communion at every mass. The change occurred when Des deemed himself to be partially responsible for his friend's premature death. It had seemed futile to seek absolution from any human agent of the Lord's mercy here on Earth. No heartfelt pledge of penitence would make up for his negligence; no sentence of penance, no claim of moral cleansing could remove the stain of fratricide from his hands. As a result Des waited in mortal dread for his own day of reckoning when, called before the Lord to account for his sins, he would surely be judged worthy only of damnation.

Des had selfishly ignored JC's request that he hand over the ticket he held for passage to Ireland. It had been a simple request, based not upon his scant faith in the restorative power of such a journey, but in a romantic desire to spend the remainder of his life in his homeland. Des might have easily granted the wish, for he traveled to Ireland twice a year, and had acquired the ticket at nominal cost through connections. Instead he slipped away, declining to respond to JC's needs and deferring consideration until his return a month later. He had turned his back on one of his oldest and closest allies, and it should have been no surprise when he learned while in Ireland that JC had died back in the States.

When he heard the news Des punished himself despite the fact that JC would have died even if he had gone back to that green and pleasant land. For the terminal cancer that originated in his leg had metastasized and spread rapidly, and furthermore, he had refused treatment. Unable to cut his trip short and return to the US for the funeral, Des did arrange for an ersatz wake and memorial service to be held at a pub in JC's hometown. Meanwhile the faithful departed's remains were laid out in his family plot at Forest Lawn Cemetery near Jamaica Center.

In addition to forsaking the sacrament of communion, Des had also abandoned his scapulars, holy medals and rosaries, no longer considering himself worthy of their marvelous protection. Yet despite the cynicism with which he regarded his own fate and his chances for salvation, he began a trend toward even more orthodox and parochial religious expression, participation and belief. In short, he became a hypocrite, a great holy name dropper, who liberally invoked the angels and saints, the Holy Trinity, and the Holy Family. He no longer saw himself as a common sinner with an average chance of salvation; he stopped trying to rationalize his behavior; and as if resigned to a sense of fatalism he proceeded over his subsequent career to flout every common, civic, and religious law.

Next on his morning agenda he would usually visit the bakery for the sake of the sweet treats to be found there, namely Diane and Ingrid, and maybe for a cup of coffee and something to eat as well. But today he was reluctant to enter the cozy establishment- its tantalizing aroma and titillating temptations were too rare and refined for a low-life murderer with blood under his fingernails. How could he face his girlfriends with any semblance of genteel behavior? He had proved himself to be utterly unworthy of any human respect and he deserved only contempt, if he weren't already beneath such regard.

For years as he had struggled with his remorse the knowledge of his failure had ironically become a motivation for him. Although the guilt he felt lay primarily in the admission that he had broken faith with a friend, until last night he had been haunted by a death for which he may have been only partially responsible. JC's illness after all was the ultimate cause of his death, and that illness was ordained by God.

But last night Des took a life- he had committed intentional, premeditated murder. Another human being, a young man, wounded and down no less, had looked him full in the face imploring mercy, and Des had shot him to death. Whatever potential that individual may have had was now irrevocably gone. He had been judged, with no opportunity to improve his chances for salvation, no chance to pray, no moment spared to ask the Lord for forgiveness. No pre-death conversion, no confession, and still the kid probably stood a better chance of getting into heaven than Des did. Because Des had done him in, and that changed everything.

He walked past Hansen's Bakery, his stomach hollow but heavy. The regular early risers were out: the paper-boys, bakers and florists, beat-cops and store-keepers and yet he felt isolated in the pre-rush stillness of the square.

Up to the right on Corinth he saw a group emerging from Salonika's, and they looked like Tweed's gang. Wasn't that Dogg, or Wogg, what's-his-name? They were out bright and early this morning, and all talking seriously, as if in a business meeting. Des strolled casually across the town green, basically a delta-shaped traffic divider dressed up with park benches and lilac bushes, and he dawdled near the war memorial. Sure enough, the kids had stopped and were huddling around the phone booth on the corner. Now what were they up to? That was the phone that Des had his bookies use so as to keep the traffic off the biz club line. They had to be spreading the news about the McManus kids. What might they know about those boys? Although it crossed his mind he would not approach Tweed's friends to ask them that question.

He'd get what he could out of his son, but somehow it bothered him that the dead boys weren't total unknowns. Not that he could recall ever having met them, but he had known their mother, for God's sake! His son was dating their sister. They were practically family. That was what stuck in his craw, what galled him.

It was virtually inconceivable that someone in the greater circle of Kelley acquaintances should try something like this. There were too many problems with the scenario. For example, what possible motivation could they have had? Did they really expect to succeed? They weren't wearing masks or disguises...weren't they concerned about being recognized? Did they see themselves as his enemy?

Either they had acted out of self interest or they were hired to do the job. If Des were to allow for the possibility that they had acted independently, then he couldn't imagine why they had chosen to act in the manner they did. Why try to assassinate your sister's father-in-law? What possible gain might they derive from such a move? Surely it would not help LaGloria in any way. After all, it wasn't as if Tweed stood to gain substantially from Des' passing. The bulk of any estate would go to his wife and eldest sons. No, there was no financial motive. Then again they might have been compelled by virtue of some unimaginable incentive or powerful persuasion...But why? Could it have been some twisted impulse of honor, some adolescent revenge fantasy arising from an inability to cope with their mother's infidelity? It was ludicrous! Such a theory presupposes that they had known about his affair with their mother, that it troubled them, and that years later they had suddenly decided to do something about it. No, they had to have been working in concert with someone else. And if so, then who? Where had they gotten the guns? Did he still have a dangerous enemy out there somewhere? A mysterious foe who now hated him not only for some unknown insult or injury, but also for dispatching his hit men? Hit men? More like human sacrifices.

He had better speak with Tweed as soon as possible. He needed to know whatever his son could tell him about the McManus boys and if his little blackbird could add anything then all the better. Were they close, LaGloria and her brothers? What about Bricky? Did he know them? Does he know Tweed or LaGloria? Granted that most murders are committed by and against people who know each other, this one was almost too coincidental. Perhaps it was a stroke of brilliance to employ the McManus boys. Perhaps by their very proximity to Tweed and LaGloria they had gleaned enough information about Des to enact the plan to lure him to the park. Furthermore Des imagined that if they had gotten away with the deed they would have been easily overlooked when the police rounded up likely suspects.

It was clear that his would-be assassins were not experienced; Harris' assessment had told him as much. Were they counting on beginner's luck? Or were they so confident of Des' ineptitude that they believed he would gullibly fall into their trap? Looking back, it was too bad that they had killed the boys. If they had merely wounded them, then they could have questioned them and avoided all of this doubt and anxiety.

You don't send boys to do a man's job. Someone had underestimated Des, and they would be wise to realize that he would try to maintain that advantage.

No matter who his enemies were, Des would out-think and out-smart them. His attackers hadn't survived the assault, but the loss of life in no way balanced the scales. If there was an unknown enemy then they would soon know the full extent of his taste for revenge.

CHAPTER 5

"Hey, man, got a full house here, just wanted to touch base, you know, see if every thing's alright. We heard about Nils and Frankie, and man, that's tough. Anything we can do to help out, man?" Bone felt confounded that he didn't know what to say. At least he knew what not to say, avoiding names whenever possible and never mentioning anything illegal.

"Thanks, dude, I appreciate that."

Weed sounded weary. It had been a long night. He clearly hadn't expected to receive a phone call from his crew at what must have felt like the crack of dawn. This was just payback for always insisting that they carry out their transactions in the early morning.

"The old lady's in rough shape, of course, and we have to see how it's all going to shake out. It's good of you guys to call, but I think we're OK right now."

Eban took the phone, "They were alright dudes, man, it's a shame, that's for sure." His voice was deeper than usual and uncharacteristically solemn. "I remember when Nilvan came up to the studio looking for lessons. Said that he wanted to be a kick boxer like Jean-Claude Van Damme. I took his deposit, told him to start running and to come back when he could run five miles a day."

"So Nilvan took kick boxing, huh? I never knew that," said Tweed.

"No, man, he never came back..."

Now Kuhn grabbed the receiver. "Hey, I just wanted to add my two cents, you know, I mean you guys are going to have some hard days ahead and I hope that you remember that we're here for you. Speaking of which; remember that time out at the state park- remember? When Nilvan and Frankie were there at the cookout?"

"You mean the Hopkinton car hop?"

"Right! We were all up there partying and the site was pretty packed by the time, ah, who was it? You know, ah..."

"Yep, I remember. Carmine and his girlfriend showed up." Tweed had heard the story many times, and had told it himself many more.

"Yeah; but there was no parking and it looked like they was gunna-hafta leave their car out on the road and hoof it the three miles back in to the site. But Frankie and Nilvan, man, they turned around and said, 'No friggin way are you walking in this heat!' And they picked up that AMC..."

"Right!" laughed Tweed, despite himself, "The Gremlin."

"Uh huh, by then we had all got a hold of that car and wouldn't you know, we carried it right out of the parking spot and left it in the middle of the lot! Carmine was like, 'Thanks for the spot, dudes!' And the owner of that Gremlin, he pro'lly freaked out."

"Yo, brother," Tweed switched to his strictly-business voice. "I gotta ask you something...You working today or tonight?"

"Uh, what's today, Friday? Yeah, I'm on at one o'clock, working 'til ten."

"Cool. That's what I wanted to hear. I may need to ask you for a favor; get you to do something for me."

"Shit, of course, Weed. Whatever you need."

"You're alright Kuhn. Call me before you go in today. I'll go over it with you then."

Sharlae was sniffling when she got on the line. "Hi, Boss, I'm really sorry to hear the news. It wasn't until this morning that it hit me..." She was crying openly now. "I was with El-Gee last night-maybe right when -it happened."

"It's alright, babe, be cool."

She welcomed the sound of his voice. Weed's voice always soothed her. This business could be nerve-wracking, even when killings and kidnappings weren't involved.

"She's alright; we're OK. You didn't know them, did you, Sharlae?"

"No, not really. Well, there was that time, a party up at your place, I mean your old place, when Frankie tried to hit on me, but I never really got to know him or his brother. But listen, if there's anything I can do..."

"I know. Thanks. There is something I wanted to tell you." Weed cleared his throat and coughed, "I asked someone, a friend, to call you. Now, he's gonna-wanna hear everything you can tell him about what went down last night."

The hairs on the back of Sharlae's neck suddenly stood on end. Everything about last night? Was Weed looking for an alibi?

"Descriptions of the dudes, the cars, the where, the when and how, you know?"

Oh, that. Phew.

"He's going to look into it for me and it'll be a big help if you can tell him whatever you know."

"Sure thing, of course, Weed. You know me, I have the next best thing to a photographic memory."

Tweed resisted replying, "What, you mean a hot bod?" And instead remained suitably mournful, waiting for the next of his suck-ass dope dealers to pay their respects. It was Og.

"'Sup, Weed? Listen, man, I was sorry to hear about Frankie and Nilvan, man. I mean that's gotta really suck."

Tweed couldn't be sure if he meant dying or surviving.

"I never really hung with them or nothing, but they were hot shits, both of 'em. Just thought I'd say it, not that it does 'em any good, now."

"Yeah, OK, Og, listen, give the phone back to Bone, will you? I got a little job I want you and him to do for me."

"No shit? What is it?"

"Uh, Og, give the phone to Bone now, will you?"

Tweed's patience was unlikely to outlast the dime Bone had paid for the call, and yet before the allotted time ran out he managed to outline a job that, due to present circumstances, he would be unwise to perform by himself. The details of the task were encoded in a shorthand that Tweed had developed over the years with the help of his associates. In essence, he said that he wanted Og to accompany Bone to one of the stash-houses he rented in order to retrieve a bail of pot for processing into pounds and smaller quantities.

When Bone filled him in as to what was expected of them, Og was thrilled. He had heard that Weed found his stash-houses by making deals with people in the porn business. Supposedly the same houses were used for discreet, nondescript film locations. Although he had already visited a couple of the places without having seen any evidence of activity; no sets, no props, no cameras, his enthusiasm was undimmed. He fantasized about stumbling into the filming of an orgy, or encountering naked starlets rehearsing their scenes. Although Og knew that the essential element of truth was sometimes missing from rumors and second-hand news, what he didn't know was that in this case the facts would not support the least of his wishes. Tweed had indeed leased the suburban split-level ranch and other homes like it from connections in the porn industry, thus enabling them to earn additional revenue from properties that were convenient both as tax write-offs and as innocuous sets. And the sets were indeed for porn shoots. But it was gay porn.

So even if Og had ever visited one of the sites when filming was in progress, he would have been in for the disappointment of his life. Yet, for all his friends knew, Og had never had a girlfriend, let alone sex. Who knows? Maybe exposure to male-on-male hardcore was just what he needed to prime the plumbing and to broaden his horizons.

Bone, on the contrary was relieved. He had wanted reassurance, and though he hadn't asked for it, he also wanted confirmation that the dope supply would continue unabated. There was a lot at stake, from business considerations to personal concerns.

At the same time he was excited. If Weed's participation in the management of his enterprise were compromised, if he was in effect hamstrung by private obligations or by police scrutiny, then Bone had an opportunity to step up to the plate and demonstrate his abilities. Maybe Weed would see that Bone could be of more service to him as a right-hand man, a partner in the local dope business. Then Bone would gain control over bales, tons,…shitloads of weed. And he would have first pick of the primo, choice, all-bud stash that the high-level dealers like Tweed kept for themselves.

After his associates rang off Tweed sat on the edge of his futon, holding the phone in one hand and rubbing his eyes with the other. The two telephone components were molded from plastic into the shape of a pair of hands, and when cradled they approximated a friendly clasp, the base half palms-up and the "hand set" palms-down. Damned awkward new-age piece of shit that served more suitably as a conversation piece than as a means of conversation. LaGloria had picked it up in New York during one of her business trips down there. In fact the whole apartment was decorated with items reflecting LaGloria's taste, and LaGloria's style. Perhaps it was her way of ensuring that he could never bring another woman up there without revealing that he was firmly wrapped or whipped or whatever.

And there she was, still sleeping but hardly distinguishable from the pillows and other lumps and rolls of bedclothes strewn across the mattress.

Traces of PCP were yet distorting Tweed's cognitive faculties so it took a few moments to recall how he had ended up in bed, when he was fairly certain that he had started his night's rest in the bathtub. Slowly the details of yesterday's strange journey home floated to the surface of his awareness like the cryptic messages in a toy magic eight ball. Ah, yes, LaGloria had been sweet and kind when he arrived. He was suffering from the pain of an untreated sprained ankle and then after she had tended to him and comforted him, he bore witness to a tale of horror and tragedy. Later an injudiciously ingested dose of drugs had wrestled him to the floor of the bathroom, and there he remained for most of the night, sleeping in the dry tub. But in the middle of the night, still some time before dawn, he had emerged from his sarcophagus and had hobbled into the kitchen, only to find LaGloria still awake. She was drinking coffee and pondering her part in the deaths of her brothers, in turns feeling guilt, then rage, then despair. At the time Tweed was hardly in the best state of mind for comforting her, yet he sat up with her until daybreak, consoling her, reviewing and discussing the event, and planning their next course of action.

Now he started to chafe under the burden of the necessity to act. And he was unnerved by LaGloria's penchant for scheming, of which she was seemingly capable even when she was under stress.

How many times had she insisted that he repeat the story of the attempt on his father's life? She had focused on details such as the number and timing of the shots, and the number and description of her brother's killers. However, her principle obsession was with the guns, and at length, from her point of view at any rate, she had been fully justified in harping on that subject.

"Damn it Tweed, I spent a lot of money on those guns," she had said both vehemently and repeatedly in his recollection.

"It's not like you were expecting to get that money back," Tweed had objected.

"I'm not worried about the money. I know that I wasn't going to get my money back, that's not the point. You don't buy an M16, shoot someone with it, and then return it like some expensive tool from Sears. But of all the possible outcomes, the worst would be to go out and not merely miss your target, but also to lose the guns to the police afterwards. Fuck! It's like stealing a car to use in a bank robbery only to have it towed away for leaving it in a no-parking zone."

"OK, so what are you worried about? That the cops will trace those guns back to you?"

"Well, yeah, maybe…" LaGloria's faith in the Rossie police placed them as slightly more competent than department store clerks in her estimation.

"But you said that the reason you bought that gun was because it was practically untraceable. I admit that it sucked to lose such a nice piece and all, but if they can't trace it, then what difference does it make?"

"That's just the M16, Tweed- what about the sawed-off? I mean, the numbers were missing but who knows if the police already have a forensic match on record for that one."

She could have a point there, Tweed had realized. The sawed-off had been a gift to Tweed and his girlfriend, given to them by Col's uncle Bryan Dyer at their first apartment-warming party. Bryan was a clear sociopath, with a record of violent confrontations with law-enforcement authorities. Who else would give a shotgun to a young couple starting a new life together? There was a better than even chance that he had in fact used the gun during one of his standoffs or assaults.

With this in mind Tweed had had a fateful recollection.

"Love, I was just thinking…didn't the officer, you know your friend Bernie there…didn't she specify a Remington 20-gauge?"

"Yeah…so?"

Here LaGloria's ignorance of guns was revealed somewhat problematically.

"So for one thing, our shotgun was a sawed-off, which she never mentioned, and for another, it was a 12-gauge. In fact, it wasn't even a Remington."

"What are you saying?"

"Well, either she was describing another gun that they found at the scene, or your brothers had a gun that you didn't know about."

"So…" LaGloria seemed to be cogitating. "What about the sawed-off?"

"Let me see. I kept the sawed-off in an oil-skin bag, wrapped in a heavy chain…"

"A chain? Wasn't that overkill?"

"The chain was used for hanging the bag. See, I used to hide the thing in the chimney."

"The chimney? Where? Here?"

"Yeah; I wasn't about to keep a freaking sawed-off shotgun in the house, so I went up to roof of the apartment complex and dropped the sucker down the chimney. Just propped a rod in there to hold it in place, then left it."

"Is it still there? I thought Frankie…"

"No, I took it out when the landlord had that work done on the furnace. That chimney hadn't been used in years, but I yanked it out anyway just in case they needed to look in there or fire it up or something."

"I thought that Frankie had it," LaGloria said again.

"He did, in a way. After I pulled it out of the chimney I still needed a place to hide it, and so I stashed it down in the trunk of Frankie's car."

"Did he know that?"

"Well, it was still my car then, as you may recall; you know, right before I signed it over to him. But uh, yes, when you were planning all this we talked about it from time to time. Even so; as I said before, it was no Remington 20-gauge, so he must have found another one. I don't blame him; I wouldn't want to rely on an old shit-kicker like that in a fire-fight."

"So where is it? What happened to the sawed-off?"

"If I had to guess, I'd say that it was still in the trunk of the car."

Suddenly LaGloria had become animated. "Tweed! You have got to go and look! You have to get that gun back!"

At that moment Tweed had felt what little remained of his spirits vanish with a whimper.

"Uh, LaGloria, I saw that car burn…burn and explode! I can imagine what's left of the shotgun, if it's still in there in the first place."

"That's just it, Tweed. If it's in there we don't want the police to find it. You have to check first, see if it's in there, and if it is, then take it out for God's sake!"

"OK, so I'm supposed to sneak into the police lab, crawl through a burned wreck and remove evidence from a murder investigation?"

"The way I see it, it's either you find it or the cops do. And if they do, then they find us, see? Whose fingerprints do you think they'd find on that gun?"

Not that he could deny any of her requests in the best of circumstances, Tweed was beginning to be swayed by her reasoning. Claim as he might that the gun in question had nothing to do with the crime in question, he would still have to answer a lot of questions about it, should the police actually recover the gun. But who was he kidding? If the gun was still in the car, and if they found it, they may well end up with the crucial evidence with which to solve a number of old cases, and hence charge him in connection with them.

He remembered how he was taken aback when Bryan had presented him with the gun. Yet he had accepted it gratefully. You don't insult a psychopath when he's trying to be nice. As Tweed recalled with a lingering twinge of discomfort, Bryan had taken LaGloria for a spin on the dance floor at the party, leaving Tweed holding the bag, as it were. And considering some of the things that Bryan was alleged to have done, Tweed had kept the parcel at arm's length, at once afraid to touch it, and at the same time afraid to put it down. Bryan's nephew Jimmy Col had said that the gun may have been the murder weapon used in the infamous Crystal Pond Bowladrome murders. If so it was a clue, long sought-for by the police, to the unsolved crime in which three employees at an isolated bowling alley were robbed at gun point, made to lie face down on the floor and then shot in the back of the head.

"Alright", he sighed. "Let me think a minute. If they towed the car," he began slowly,

"They towed it! I saw it on the flatbed!" interjected LaGloria.

"OK, if, as you say, they towed it, then it must have gone to a municipal tow yard first. You know babe, we could be in luck. I'm pretty sure that all of the municipal tow jobs around here go to…"

"Rossie Towing!"

"Right!"

Rossie Towing, located incongruously in Jamaica Center was a well-established operation that handled private tow work, emergency road service calls, contracts for local repair and body shop facilities, as well as wrecker service and scrap and junk removal.

However, few people in Rossie knew that the company was actually owned by two local cops, none other than detectives Storer and Rima. Tweed and LaGloria knew it because of their connection with Kuhn, who worked there as a driver and lot hand. Kuhn had also told them another little known fact: that it was the ultimate goal of the two detectives to sell the towing company when they retired from the force, and to purchase a gourmet bakery out in the suburbs. With wry amusement Tweed had occasionally conjured the image of old Storer squeezing a pastry bag instead of squeezing his customers and colleagues for pay-offs.

"And if it's Rossie Towing, then maybe I can get in and check it out."

"Kuhn can get you in there, can't he?"

"Well, I don't know if I'd want to have him let me in as much as I'd like him to look the other way when I 'sneak' in."

"Well shit, Tweed, do it! We don't have much time!"

"Hold on, I'm still thinking." Tweed said this as if it were something he rarely did with much success.

"I'll make a couple of calls- maybe I can get a friend in the department to slow things up. The order telling Rossie to release the car for transport has to come from down town."

"If that's the case, then maybe Kuhn can move a wreck in the way or something, you know, make it hard to get it out of there," LaGloria added helpfully.

"And it is Friday; you know how hard it is to get things done on a Friday afternoon. It's reasonable that the tow down town might have to wait until first thing Monday."

"Alright! If it does go that way then you'll have all weekend to get in there and strip it if you have to."

"Hey! I still have a sprained ankle, you know? I may have to scale fences, crawl through brush and shit. Don't expect me to strap a friggin' toolbox to my back too."

After that LaGloria had calmed down, apparently satisfied. She had even permitted him to enter the bed. His own bed. Although she had pulled a cruel trick on him, tipping him onto the floor once for good measure before he fell asleep.

Now here he was, what, minutes, or was it hours later? Awakened by a gang of dope mules who still called him "Weed". When did that get started, he thought. The first time he smoked a joint? It seemed that Bone had always called him Weed, and the other numbskulls simply followed suit. Despite the codes and the caution, the euphemisms and double-entendres, his own people still called him Weed as if it were no more or less of a nickname than 'Joe' or 'Timmy'.

At his age Tweed was long accustomed to the consequences of having an unusual name. His name elicited comments and questions, caused double-takes and raised eyebrows, and underwent verbal mangling. As a youngster there was no need to be outlandish in behavior or appearance because his name alone ensured that he would receive attention.

He would like to think that a name was simply a means of identifying an individual, that it was simply a verbal cue to which an individual responded when hailed. But in fact in most cases it seemed that one's name became an intrinsic part of one's identity. Indeed some names suited their owners more aptly than others. Accordingly Tweed believed that when people engaged in the process of creating and assigning nicknames they were really attempting to ascribe names that were more suitable to their friends and loved ones. Furthermore some names became indelibly associated with the personalities they represented: John, Paul, George and Ringo. Jimi and Janis. Honest Abe and Tricky Dick.

And while the mental image most commonly associated with the word tumbleweed was that of a desolate, one-hitching post ghost-town, the shorter nick-name Weed was eminently more suitable as a verbal reference between the man and his product. For a pot seller even the name Herb wasn't as good as the name Weed.

Anyone who didn't know better might think that he had chosen the name deliberately. And in fact he had been given the opportunity at age 18 to do just that- legally select his own name. And yet on that occasion- an opportunity which was rarely granted to most citizens- he chose to retain Tumbleweed as his legal and official given name.

For reasons he could no longer recall, though perhaps for the purpose of selective service registration, Tweed had been required to obtain his birth certificate, thus necessitating a trip to the municipal hall of records. However this brush with bureaucracy was not as daunting as he had at first feared. After negotiating a labyrinthine grid of hallways, departments and offices he had joined the queue at the proper window and waited his turn to speak with a pale elderly woman whose dour demeanor represented the public face of the city. For some thirty years her osteoarthritic hump had been perched upon a swivel stool in the municipal office from which she had issued thousands upon thousands of birth and death certificates. But when Tweed arrived at her station she looked up his record and with a kindly note of surprise and delight in her voice she informed him that officially he had no name. More accurately, his birth certificate had been issued in the name "Boy-child Kelley". She added that omissions of this type were relatively rare, and suggested that perhaps his parents had difficulty deciding on a name in the time prior to the issuance of the original birth certificate.

"I'm afraid I can't make up a copy of your birth-certificate until you get this straightened out!" she said softly.

"How do I do that?" he asked, more than a little exasperated.

"Well, you'll have to appear before a judge, and ask him to change your name."

"I don't need a name change, I just need a birth-certificate!" he protested.

"Yes, I understand. But as far as the city is concerned, you have no name. Therefore you must petition the court to grant you one. Think of it positively- you now have an opportunity to select any name you'd like!"

"I have to go to court? Where? Municipal court house?"

"Fortunately for you there is a judge here on the premises. If you are prepared to proceed you may go to his office, schedule a hearing and resolve this matter today if you like. But you may want to go home first and think about this carefully. There are a lot of nice names from which to choose. I'm rather partial to Theodore myself. Wouldn't you like to be a Theodore?"

As he gazed into the kind face of the same clerk whose wan visage had intimidated him from afar, Tweed wished that she would simply correct the bureaucratic snafu in his favor and send him on his way. He would gladly pay for her trouble. But that vain hope was dashed when she cried, "Next!" and asked him to step aside.

Later that day, after becoming hopelessly lost in the bowels of the municipal building; after finding his way out and having lunch in the adjacent plaza, he boldly reentered to find the judge's chambers. Having gained a rough grasp of the layout of the building during his earlier incursion, he was able to reach his destination without too much delay and was fortunately able to secure an early afternoon appointment.

Before long he found himself standing in front of the judge, nervously asking for a ruling on a name-change request.

"Now, son, it says here that you have selected 'Tumbleweed' to be your name, is that correct?" the judge began after perusing Tweed's petition. His Honor looked like maybe he was getting a little something on the side. For an older dude, his hair was too dark and his skin too tan.

"Yes, your honor," Boy-child Kelley replied, remembering a bit of advice Mrs. Col had once given him about addressing judges.

"But, unless I am mistaken, that was your previous, rather um, unorthodox name," he frowned.

"Yes, that's correct, sir. See, I was sent here by the records clerk..."

"I understand why you're here, boy, what I don't understand is why, when you have an opportunity to pick the name you wish, as opposed to the one I assume your parents selected for you, that you should pick the very same name you've had all along. Have you thought this through? You might consider Philip; my name is Philip."

"No thanks, your honor," Tweed smiled.

"What's the matter? Don't like Philip?"

"No, it's OK, it suits you. But I have thought about it..." Indeed he had, but in the end reason had outweighed the temptation of novelty. "...and I realized that even if I were to choose another name now, everybody knows me by Twee- uh, Tumbleweed. If I change it now it'd just screw everything up."

"I'm glad that you take it seriously; but don't overestimate the significance of this procedure, my boy. You have the right, the means and the opportunity to make a change. Don't let what others may think sway you. This is your decision alone. Would you like to reschedule? Take some time to think it over?"

Tweed felt insufferably nervous now. It frustrated him that he had spent all day trying to get a blasted piece of paper, and yet somehow he would rather that the judge wasn't so damn considerate! There were other people waiting to see him as well.

"No thanks, sir, I appreciate your advice, but I would like you to officially name me Twee- Tumbleweed so I can get my birth certificate and get out of here!"

"I understand. I'd like to get out of here myself soon. Your name change request is hereby granted. Take this slip to the clerk to get your certificate, and the record shall be amended."

So Tweed's one big chance to become a Kirk Kelley, or a Cuchullain Kelley or a Shelley Kelley had gone by unexploited, like the magic fish in the fairy tale.

After fumbling the phone back into its fangled receptacle Tweed leaned back on his side of the futon bed with his torso propped up on his elbows and his leg with the swollen ankle extended and elevated.

He wore only a pair of boxer shorts with a ragged checkerboard waistband. Parallel lines of dark curly hair ran a symmetrical course from his lower abdomen up to a dense mat of chest hair that seemed to blend like a half-tone fade into the coarse steel-wool whiskers on his neck and face. His beard in turn met a curly mop of auburn hair that clearly hadn't seen, and for that matter hadn't seemed to need a brush or comb in months. The hirsute appearance however only seemed to define and accentuate his muscular frame, making him look taller and trimmer than his actual height and weight might otherwise suggest.

Again the phone rang, startling him and causing LaGloria to mutter obscenities in her sleep. It was Des.

"Taweed, my boy! I thought I might find you up and at it."

CHAPTER 6

Des was well aware that he was calling at what any reasonable person would consider to be an inopportune moment. Not only was it earlier than common courtesy would normally condone, but it was also the morning after what may well have been the worst day of LaGloria McManus' life, the day on which he, Des Kelley, had both witnessed and had a hand in the execution of her brothers. However, whatever reticence the old man could or should have felt about disturbing his son and his grieving girlfriend was vastly overshadowed by his visceral need for information. Whether he admitted it or not, the boy had answers to important questions- questions that must be resolved as soon as possible! Nevertheless, Tumbleweed was an independent lad, not one to volunteer help or information unless asked first. In addition, stubbornness was virtually a part of his genetic makeup. Des would have to push firmly, but gently.

"How is my future daughter-in-law? Is she holding up?"

Tweed felt a sudden urge to wrap his arms around LaGloria and protect her. It chilled his blood to speak with Frank's executioner, and the reminder of his father's deed kindled an impulse to flee or better yet, to hold firm and defend his lover.

"So, you heard about what happened, then?" Tweed recalled the bogus claims Des had made during their last telephone conversation.

"Well, Tumbleweed, I think the whole town knows about it now, heaven help us."

Heaven help you, Da. "Yes, LaGloria's asleep, finally. It was a long, hard night." *And you don't know the half of it.*

"Fine. I'm glad. She'll need all the rest she can get."

"Um, Dad, what's on your mind?" *I know you're not calling to confess,* he thought bitterly.

"I was worried, son; I mean, they got the boys…I'd hate to think someone was after LaGloria, too."

If anyone made a move on LaGloria, thought Tweed, *I'd know where to look for retribution.*

"Yeah, well, thanks. I'm keeping an eye on her and the police have already been here to speak with her."

"I'd like to have a word with you myself, Taweed, in fact, I'd like to talk to LaGloria, too."

How dare you! "Oh? What about?"

"Why don't you come down here and we'll discuss it, OK? Be a good lad?"

"Where? That di- um, bar you hang out in?"

"Yes…the biz club." He made it sound as if he were agreeing to a suggestion Tweed had made. "We can talk over coffee."

"I don't think so, Dad, I'd best stay with LaGloria."

"Let her rest, son, let her rest. You come down here and we'll talk, and I'll see what I can do to help."

He had to be joking. Tweed had never set foot in the biz club in his life and he didn't intend to. That was where Dapper Ferguson hung out, and Hard-Ass Storer, and of course, the Kelley gang, or whatever they called themselves. He'd sooner drop in and swap stories with the boys at the regional DEA headquarters. There had to be more to it, perhaps a deal in the offing. But why would he want to deal? Unless…either he knew that Tweed had been involved, or he had something on LaGloria. Shit. He never would have expected the old man to be so blatantly conniving. What did he have up his sleeve?

"You're right, Dad, LaGloria doesn't need me hanging around while she's resting. I'll come see you but I can't stay for long. It's not just because I'm worried about her, you see, but I sprained my ankle yesterday and really shouldn't be hobbling all over creation." It was remarkable how he slipped into his old man's speech rhythms whenever he talked with him.

"That's grand, Taweed, you do me proud."

I'd do you like you did Frankie if I had the chance, thought Tweed, surprising himself with his own rancor. *Of all the blasted pains in the ass…*He was committed now that he had agreed to go and he had better get it over with.

Dressing quietly and leaving the bedroom where his sleeping lover lay was a skill at which he had had much practice, but he had never before tried it with the equivalent of one foot in a bucket of sand. Thrashing about like Slew Foot Sue, cursing under his breath, unable to find his pants and then unable to put them on over his wrapped foot.

"Where are you going?" asked LaGloria, speaking into her pillow in a voice slurred with sleep.

"Gotta go out for a little while, love," he answered, expecting resistance.

"Better take the crutches then."

"Oh, yeah, I forgot we had those!"

The crutches had once belonged to her father, who had left them behind when he moved into a continuing care community. LaGloria had insisted upon keeping them, claiming with her usual inscrutable logic that they would serve as a good luck charm to ward off injury, and if that failed then they would come in handy should anyone become injured.

"They're down in the basement. You better let me get them for you."

"No, babe, you should sleep some more. Keep that bed cozy and I'll crawl back in as soon as I get back."

"You going to get the gun?"

"No…well, not now, anyway. I'm still working on that. I'll go downstairs and grab the crutches on my way out. You gonna be alright while I'm gone?"

"Oh yeah. You know how you took PCP last night? Well, I took half a 'lude I been saving since Christmas."

"Holy shit- well you better stay in bed then. I'll be back soon gorgeous. I love you."

It was much more difficult getting down the stairs than he remembered it had been going up. Before departing he had slugged down a quick breakfast of warm Pepsi with a handful of aspirin tablets and a couple of Darvons.

The crutches, along with a set of chrome Cragar rims and a couple of boxes of old LPs were in his share of the meager storage compartment that the landlord had created for his tenants by subdividing a section of the basement. For this convenience Tweed paid an extra premium on top of his rent.

However, although the crutches were adjustable they were far too large for Tweed. Mr. McManus stood well over six feet tall whereas Tweed was a mere five ten. Normally it wouldn't be a problem to simply cut them down to size, but his saw, and all of his other tools for that matter, were in the trunk of his car, and his car was in the shop.

How we take our legs for granted! thought Tweed as he limped along the access road that led into the apartment complex. He had shouldered the oversized crutches, and carrying them made him resent them all the more. Wasn't there a fable about a man who was forced to carry his donkey? At least he could lug his ass around, while the throbbing in Tweed's ankle caused him to doubt whether he'd be able to do the same for much longer. In order to keep his mind off the pain he started to plan and plot his day.

His primary goal was the bus stop, located at the point where the access road intersected with the main street. If he reached the bus stop, he would collapse and pray for the intervention of a passing Samaritan. It was laughable- what a wimp. So- he could dish it out but he couldn't take it. It was at times of trial and adversity like this when he summoned his spirit guide, the ghost of Carmine Gunther.

"What's the matter, Tweed? Got a boo-boo? Little Tweedie want big old Carmine to kiss and make it better?"

"Ah, fuck, Carmine; it's not the ankle, it's this friggin' sneaker- it keeps chafing my heel!"

"Chafing your heel! What's that, a Converse All-Star? You ever heard a basketball player complain about chafing?"

"I can't lace the thing- and my damn foot is the size of Larry Bird's!"

"Buck up you pussy! You're almost at the bus stop!"

Sure enough, there it was, a prefab aluminum and lexan sweat box, suddenly looking like the promised land. Well then, he had made it this far, so the rest of the journey would be a piece of cake.

The main street ran straight through Rossie as if somebody had gone up to Westbury Heights and unleashed a flood of macadam that flowed down the gradual slope of the terrain leading to Jamaica Center, leaving a dry road bed behind. The bus route followed this path, passing directly by the biz club. But Tweed wouldn't ride the bus that far. Instead he would disembark at Metropolitan Ave and pay a visit to his old friend Gary, younger brother of Wayne and owner of Gary's Rod and Custom.

In the back of Gary's shop, under a painter's tarp and a quarter-inch of body-filler dust sat Tweed's red 1978 Saab 99. He loved the car so much that he rarely drove it, and rather than park it outside his apartment he came up with one pretext after another to keep it in the shop. The quaint Swedish sports car had been in relatively good shape for a 7 year-old car when he acquired it, but he was determined to make it last forever. So he brought it to Gary.

First he had the interior gutted, and had actually paid to have the inside of the car refinished, sealing it with an epoxy paint that hadn't been invented when the car itself was first built. Then, with all of the wiring, dash, console, seats and upholstery reinstalled he ordered a refit of the undercarriage and chassis. Beefed up suspension, reinforced quarter sections and wheel wells, armor skid plating. Next he tinkered with the engine for both show and performance, with a chrome rocker cover, a modified manifold, aftermarket gauges and an enhanced turbo system that bypassed the stock over-pressure valve and added boost. Finally he had the body refined, lowering the roof profile so that a custom windshield had to be installed, adding flared fender wells and aerodynamic ground effects. He topped it off with a candy-apple gloss finish intended to repel dust, mud, rainwater and bird-droppings.

For months now it had sat in Gary's shop, awaiting the day of liberation. And though all along he had refused to set or agree to such a date, he now acknowledged that fate had decreed this should be the day.

Gary's Road and Custom had been in business for almost five years but it still lacked the trappings of an established going concern. Most of Gary's clients first became aware of the place through personal recommendations- and he relied upon the organic, word-of-mouth approach to marketing and expansion. Gary had started the venture primarily with 'seed money' which had come from the triumvirate of dope dealers made up of his brother Wayne, and Tweed and Donal, but he had also invested his life savings into his dream in order to make it into a reality.

Initially he only worked on motorcycle fuel tanks, a specialty that, although his brother Wayne had declined to take on in his own repair shop, had a ready customer base among the motorcycle clubs and gangs of Greater Rossie. Even when limiting himself to tanks he offered repairs, restoration, custom designs and fittings, detail work, graphics, the works.

But when local eccentric and package-store chain heir Lester McNutt entrusted him with the restoration of his cherished '67 13-window VW microbus, he took on the job faithfully and professionally. And when old family friend Wally Scaggs towed in his vintage 1963 Mercedes 190SL and had him replace the rocker panels and floor pans and perform a complete body makeover followed by the replacement of the top, he completed it magnificently. With these jobs and others under his belt he soon gained both a reputation and the confidence to hire an assistant. Frankie McManus had served as an apprentice of sorts to an old traditional body man who had shown him the craft and taught him to respect the ethic of working with his hands. After Frankie enthusiastically accepted his offer Gary proceeded to expand his business and offer additional services.

Before long he was doing frame repairs, custom hot rod soup jobs and the kind of custom body work that enabled him to work almost anonymously, with no signage, no on-street parking and with only occasional use of outside subcontractors.

Gary had been crouching next to a newly painted car, sighting along the fender for defects in the fit or finish. When he saw Tweed enter the shop he stood and hurried over to greet him, unrolling his vast bulk with the lumbering stiffness of a sumo wrestler.

"Ho, ho! Stranger! What's this? What's this?"

Although not afflicted with echolalia like Des' pal Simon, Gary had a habit of repeating himself for emphasis. Not that it was necessary. At 260lbs, with arms like wrecker booms and muscles like rolls of charged compressor hose, he had a presence people tended to notice, and when he spoke, people tended to pay attention, just in case he was talking to them.

"Just call me Gimpy!" Tweed displayed his injured foot prominently.

"What? You stub your toe?"

"Yeah- when I was putting my foot in my mouth!"

"Heh, heh, how's it going, Tweed?" Gary looked into Tweed's eyes for a moment as if he were communicating telepathically.

"It's rough, ain't it?"

"No shit. Gotta tell you Gary, I seen people go before…lost some close friends…but this time I'm a little freaked."

"I don't blame you, man. Any idea what they were doing? The news is making it sound like they were heavily armed and shit."

"Not a clue. I mean, what could they have been doing? Robbing a bank? Trying to become made men?"

It was difficult to lie like this, especially to a good friend, but Tweed knew he'd have to get used to it. Soon enough Det. Storer would show up at his house and by then he'd better have some practice telling his story.

"You know, that's what I can't figure. It's not like I saw them much, but from what I did know, and I've known them for what- ten years? And from what LaGloria told me, I figured they were doing alright for themselves. Working, partying, getting laid. What could have changed? I mean, changed to the point where they were carrying guns in the Arbs."

"No shit, no shit, man," Gary said rapidly. "Frankie was fine last time I saw him, and I'm talking Wednesday afternoon. He was only gonna work 'til Wednesday this week on account of Susan. She had some appointments or something."

Susan? Appointments? Who the heck was Susan?

"You mean LaGloria?"

"Huh? How is LaGloria, man? I guess she' pretty blown away- Oh, sorry- poor choice of words."

"Yeah, she's devastated, but, uh, she's taking it easy."

"I hope so. Like I told Susan, man. But I don't know how she's going to deal with this."

"Susan, Gary? Susan who?"

Gary wiped his hands on a rag and shoved it in his pocket then pushed his long greasy brown hair back on his head.

"You know, Tweed! Susan! Frankie's old lady. She's having his kid, man!"

Tweed felt as if his heart had stopped beating.

"F-Frankie was gonna be a f-father?" Oh Man, Oh man, oh man.

He had trouble getting the words out, and his question sounded more like a statement of disbelief. Did LaGloria know about this? Obviously not, or she would have told him. Or would she? Fuck!

"You know Susan, right?" continued Gary, "She's your friend Bone's older sister, man!"

Bone has an older sister? Tweed was feeling punch drunk. Wait a second- oh, yeah, but she's like, a lot older, right? And off on her own somewhere...

"Susan Cronin? She's like, what? 35 or something? Right?"

"Hey, don't knock it, man. She and Frankie had a good thing going."

"No, no, I'm just sayin'..." That Frankie was banging a broad almost ten years older than him. Why didn't Frankie tell LaGloria? Why didn't Bone say anything?

He was feeling increasingly alarmed, while another sensation that he soon realized was outrage rumbled in his chest. The turmoil ignited a rapid-fire sequence of questions and ideas born of sudden understanding, as well as reactions to feelings of horror, shame and revulsion as he considered the facts newly learned.

LaGloria had persuaded her brothers to be her accomplices on a dangerous, risky mission of revenge and personal vendetta, what Des called 'dioltas' (jilt-us). She had persuaded Tweed, too, but that was different, wasn't it? He was her lover, her boyfriend, her husband-to-be. He was supposed to stick by her through life's gains, losses, joys and adversities. Her brothers on the other hand must have acted out of respect, or loyalty, or because she had inspired something in them. Was it fear? Ambition? Anger? If the venture had entailed anything but murder; if it had meant only a risk of bodily harm, risk of fine or penalty, then Tweed could almost see it. But Frankie had another obligation at stake, a duty to his woman and his unborn child.

One of Tweed's core principles was that a man must ensure that he is strong enough emotionally, physically and financially to protect and provide for the ones he loves. If a man takes a woman to be his mate and lover then he should have the cumulative strength to protect two. If they have a child, his strength must increase to be sufficient for three, and so on. According to this chauvinistic rationale, once Frankie took on the obligation and responsibilities of fatherhood, his duty to his sister should have diminished accordingly. After all, she had a boyfriend of her own.

Tweed looked at Gary, who suddenly appeared older.

Gary looked down, letting his hair fall in front of his eyes again, and he continued quietly.

"I'm going to talk to Susan today, and see if I can help out. You know, since Frankie worked here and I was like his employer in a way, I think I owe it to her. There was no insurance or nothing. They weren't married anyway, and that makes it even harder."

You don't owe her, man, thought Tweed, Des does. And LaGloria does. And I do, too...

"OK, well, uh, let me know how you make out."

Suddenly Tweed's business with Gary seemed of trivial importance. Here they were, talking life and death and he wanted to do something as mundane as settling his repair account.

"I, uh, dropped by actually to, uh,"

"Don't tell me you're finally taking her out? Am I going crazy, or what? Or are you?" His face took on a look of concerned suspicion.

"Hey! I thought you'd want to get it out of here!"

"Well, yeah, but I never though it would actually happen. Don't get me wrong or nothing, it's just there's some people, you know, that never seem to drive their cars. They just want to keep fixin 'em like it's some kind of obsession. Personally I don't get it. Cars are meant to be driven, not put in museums. No offense."

"None taken, Gary. Gee whiz, I didn't think you put that much thought into it."

"Well, look at it this way." He quickly looked around to make sure they were alone. "Weed is meant to be smoked, right? The sooner the better, right? What if you found out they were putting it on a freakin' shelf? You'd think they were touched in the head."

He didn't say who 'they' were, but Tweed got the gist of it.

"All right, alright, no need to rub it in. I'm taking the car. Over the curb,...on the road. Not to the museum,...for a cruise. This baby's only got a hundred K on it. Must have two hundred more in it."

"At least. I hear they go up to 600K. And with what you've put into it that shouldn't be a problem- with regular maintenance."

"Don't worry- you got yourself a customer for life."

"Do your own fuckin' tune-ups, man. I'm a skilled craftsman." Gary pulled the tarp off the dusty 99.

"That's for sure. The usual payment?" Tweed had paid for almost all of the repairs with product. It was a pretty good arrangement considering that Gary's own brother was one of the major dealers in town. The guy had a prodigious appetite for good smoke.

"You know me!" Gary beamed. He caressed the Saab fondly one last time, moving his massive arms over the hood and fenders but only touching the car lightly.

"Alright! I got something new coming in this weekend. I'll have Sharlae swing by."

"Sounds good." He went into his office and retrieved the single black-head key from a locker that was almost concealed in dust and grime. "Take care of yourself, take care of this baby- she's all brandy new! And take care of LaGloria, man. I know what she means to you."

"Thanks, Gary!" You might know, but I'm beginning to wonder.

CHAPTER 7

The Saab was a bit chirpy when Tweed drove down the hill toward the RBC. In other words, the clutch pedal seemed high, the gears tight and the motor so highly tuned that the car left rubber with every shift of the gears. Plus there was an odd sensation of driving down hill, understandable since he was, of course, going downhill. But the feeling Tweed sensed of leaning forward into the road demonstrated to him that the stock 99 wheelbase to which he was accustomed had been planted firmly on the ground, whereas this tweak job, with the raised rear end, the performance gear ratio in the differential, the premium coil-assist load leveler gas shocks and the mini racing steering wheel was flighty and unpredictable. He would have to spend some time breaking it in and training it to accommodate his driving style.

The delight of driving his hot little 99 again after so long compensated to some degree for the lash of pain that accompanied every movement of his foot. Serious driving would have to wait until he was fully recuperated from his ankle injury.

As he rounded the Corinth St leg of the isosceles triangle of streets that made up the 'Square', Tweed began to dread the very idea of walking into the RBC. The friggin' place was so notorious that the cops had a running wire tap on it. But everybody in the square, including people like Tweed who had never been in the place, knew that the phone in the biz club was no good for business. Tweed however knew something else that very few other people knew- that the phone on the corner was also tapped. His source at municipal police headquarters had told him that the detectives monitoring activities at the club were so frustrated that everybody on the street seemed to know about their tap that they obtained an unprecedented order from a district judge to tap the public pay phone as well.

From Tweed's point of view it wasn't hard to understand their frustration, because soon after he found out about the bug on the pay phone he used it to instigate and implement numerous misinformation scams. His original idea was that he could control police activity in his area to some extent and motivate the cops by feeding them tasty donuts of bullshit to chew on. Not empty recitations of false data, but careful and deliberate leaks of info that would cause them to act against his competitors and his enemies, while thwarting any of their attempts to compromise his ability to operate. He also wanted to make them waste time and resources.

For all of his efforts he had never been able to point to any clear-cut evidence of success, no obvious result with which to evaluate the efficacy of the exercise. Were the raids he witnessed carried out per his direction or were they merely evidence of a vigilant local drug enforcement task force? He'd like to come out and ask his contacts in the department for feedback, for any indication that he was having an impact on their work, but that would be both counter-productive and a waste of capital in terms of good will. And yet inwardly he claimed credit for slowing them down and for forcing them to help him gain more control of the market.

His car seized an available spot in front of the bar like a panther taking down a deer; and shaking his head with amazement, Tweed emerged from his beloved red Kombicoupe and approached the red door of the Rossie Businessmen's Club. Now all he needed was a red carpet.

At that moment Des shoved the door open from within and stepped out onto the sidewalk as if he were looking to stretch his limbs and take a walk. A brooding frown momentarily disrupted his poise and then he caught sight of his youngest son. Suddenly he was as congenial as a street barker. Breaking into a smile and flinging his arms wide he cried, "Tumbleweed! My love! You made it, the good man you!"

For the sake of appearances Tweed avoided scanning the perimeter to see who might have witnessed his entrance into the bar. It was also tempting to hike his jacket up over his face like an alleged criminal facing a perp walk. Instead he nodded politely, perched himself on the grips of his crutches and limped like a wounded soldier towards the charismatic geezer who had killed his friends and ruined his life.

"Dad." He paused. "Well, are you?"

"Fit as a fiddle, well, maybe fit as one of them upright bass fiddles, you know," And with that he patted his midsection approvingly.

"Come in son, and let's take a load off that ankle of yours."

Just as easily as Des had opened it from within, he grasped the handle of the heavy door and with a mighty heave-to revealed to Tweed what appeared like the wide maw of a gloomy cave. With a gentle shove and a firm arm round the shoulder Des guided his son across the threshold to his inner sanctum.

"Here he is now, Harris," he bellowed, "I told you he'd show."

"Right-o, Des, I owe you another sawbuck."

"You placed a bet on my arrival?" asked Tweed incredulously as he peered around, trying to adjust his vision to the dark.

"I always bet on a sure thing now, son."

"Don't take it so hard, Tweed, I'm out ten bucks!" shouted Harris from behind the bar.

"Hi, Mr. Toole; no- it's not the first time my father placed a bet on me. Remember Dad, the time with the 'Grant'?"

"Me? I bet fifty bucks? No, I don't recall that…"

"Oh, come on, Dad, I was still living at home at the time and you had Brendan approach me with a fifty."

The warm glow of a fond memory suffused Des' features. "Ah, yes, I do recall now that you mention it. Go on, boy, it's your story, you tell it."

"Alright, as I was saying…I was at home then, sitting in the parlor, reading, when Brendan came in and very calmly and deliberately placed a fifty dollar bill on the coffee table in front of me."

"No kidding?" asked Harris, "A fifty?"

"Yeah, my reaction was pretty similar to yours. I mean, first of all it was fifty bucks, and secondly, we're talking Brendan Tighe, a poor Jesuit…"

"I admit, that was a mistake," said Des, grinning, "I was planning to offer it myself but I bumped into Brendan on my way in and told him what to do."

"So, it was your money, Des?"

"Let the boy tell his tale…"

"So anyway, I'm sitting there, minding my own business, and Brendan comes in and gives me a fifty."

"It was for you, now?" asked Harris.

As if he hadn't been interrupted, Tweed continued, "He says, 'Here now, Tumbleweed, I want you to take this and go out tonight and have yourself a good time.'"

"And what does a Jesuit know about a good time?" scoffed Harris, "Uh, sorry, go on,"

"Of course at this point all of my instincts are telling me there's something wrong here. How often does a monk get his hands on fifty dollars, and if he did, would he then go out and hand it over to a teenage kid? Now, you know Brendan, don't you, Mr. Toole? Anyway, he has a good sense of humor. I mean, the guy can tell jokes until the cows come home. So I played along. I had to, didn't I? I mean, I wasn't going to spoil it for him. So I said, 'Brendan, I'm not taking that money.'"

"He wouldn't as much as touch it!" shouted Des, as if this fact was essential.

"Brendan says, 'What's the matter, Tweed? You must have half a dozen girlfriends you can call right now and with fifty bucks you can have a ball. I just thought you deserved it is all, and I don't mind saying, I'm a little offended that you won't honor a gift from a sincere friend.' Tweed was embellishing; now warming to the role of storyteller.

"So what happened?" asked Harris.

"Well, I stuck to my guns and refused, and he up and cries, 'You bastard!' and throws up his hands. 'You wouldn't take it, would you! You blasted so and so...' and on and on. But by then my Dad had come in, and him laughing his ass off. I knew the game was up, but then I learned what was behind it all, you know, the real joke. You see, the bill was counterfeit!"

Suddenly Des roared with laughter, pointing a crooked finger at his son while Tweed finished his story.

"...See, he was hoping that I'd take it, not realizing that it was bogus, and then the joke would be on me when I ran out and tried to spend it."

Tweed had seen through the ruse instinctively, knowing in his heart that he was intended to be the butt of a joke.

Harris looked disturbed. "Des, don't tell me that was one of the..." and he stopped talking, clearly uncertain about what he might mention in front of the boy.

"Yeah," laughed Des, now coughing and red in the face. "That batch of bad paper we got..." He too suddenly seemed to have second thoughts about letting his guard down and being so candid. Was he really trying to impress the boy? He shouldn't have to do that, but if it was necessary then there were other ways.

"So Tweed, what have you been up to?" Harris asked conversationally. "What are you doing for a living?"

"Oh, my son is a hustler, so he is. Always finds a way to make a buck." Des had taken a seat and it appeared that in doing so he had declared an end to the chit-chat and a commencement to the business.

Tweed took the seat offered to him, but hiked it at an angle, leery about sitting with his back to the door.

"It's so sad, what happened to them McManus boys," Des began. "Local boys, killed in their own home town."

"It is a shame," replied Tweed, "a shame and a tragedy."

The elder Kelley nodded his head in solemn agreement.

"You're worried about LaGloria too, I imagine."

"I don't think she'll be heading to the Arbs with a loaded gun anytime soon if that's what you're saying."

The old man folded his hands and rested them on the table in front of him. "No, heh, heh." His father's wheezy chuckle sounded like the release of pressure from a hydraulic brake system. "I was actually concerned that she might have some idea what her brothers were up to. I'll tell you son, I'm worried about you, too. I'm sure you had nothing to do with whatever shenanigans they had gotten into, but all the same."

"What do you mean? You think LaGloria and I are in danger just because we knew Frankie and Nilvan McManus? I think that's absurd!"

"You can't blame me for worrying, T'weed, and you weren't mere acquaintances. She was their sister, you were practically a brother-in-law. I don't know if you're at risk or not, I was hoping you could tell me. Do you have any idea why they were there? Why they were carrying guns? Had they ever done anything like that before?"

You know as much, if not more than I do, thought Tweed, trying to quell his anger. He told himself to keep in mind he was pretending that he had never witnessed the shocking and horrible event, that he had never seen Des kill Frankie.

"You're interested out of concern for us? Or are you doing detective work for your buddy Storer? Why are you so keen about all of this?"

For a moment anger flared just beneath the surface, but Des held it in check.

"I told you son. Where I come from when a couple of brothers are found dead, the other members of their family start looking over their shoulders if you know what I mean. I'd have been concerned if it was only one of them, Frank or his brother. And no, I haven't spoken to my buddy Storer as you call him, but you can well believe that I shall. I live in this town and I want to know why two of our young men died the way they did. In a way it doesn't matter why they were there so much as it does that they were there. Yes it's a problem when our young men are bringing guns into the park at night, but it's also a problem when neither their sister nor their friends had any inkling or advanced warning about it."

How could he sound so reasonable? The trick was for Tweed to match that performance. And yet as he thought about it, Tweed realized that he had been forgetting his advantage. Fear and intimidation of the biz club and his old man had driven it out of his mind. The fact remained that he knew that Des and his cronies had murdered the McManuses, and now only he and LaGloria knew why the brothers had been there in the first place, that their intention had been to lure Des out and to shoot him down in hot spattering blood. If only it had worked out that way. If that were the case then at worst he would be wrestling with his own complicity instead of staring across a table in some shithole of a bar and mentally jousting with his hateful, smug, lying bastard of a father.

"Why am I so cynical? I should be grateful for your concern. I had no idea that something that affects me so deeply could affect you as well and I should be touched. My girlfriend is at home, in shock, because her brothers were murdered in the park, seemingly out of the blue."

"'Course anyone would be shocked and saddened to learn that their only brothers were dead… but to also learn that they had been armed? Or so it appeared. It could have been made to look that way by the killers. Imagine the shock!

"'Cause these guys, these guys Frank McManus and his brother Nil were just regular, hard workin'," Tweed sniffed back tears with half a laugh, "-shitbums. You know?"

"I didn't hang out with them. I didn't see them very often, but they were LaGloria's brothers, and I knew them pretty well. I can't imagine either of them doing anything remotely like this. That's why it's such a mystery, such a shock! I'm sure you can understand. But let me give you an example.

"A couple of years ago, I guess it was '83, I picked up some tickets to the ball game and asked the brothers if they wanted to come."

"You could have asked your brother," put in Des, randomly.

"I know, I know, anyway, this time I brought Nils and Frank McManus with me. So we head all the way down to the ball park. You know, it's an afternoon game, see, and we're almost there when we run in to this big gang of coons."

"Gang of what?"

"Niggers, Dad, black dudes; and they were looking for trouble."

"Son, your mother and I never taught you to use that kind of language."

"I know, Dad and there should be no exception; except the name kind of suited them, you know? I mean, you know as well as I do that in the old neighborhood in Jamaica Center we were the only minorities. And as a black friend of mine used to say, 'There's niggers and there's niggers.' These were nigger's niggers and there were a lot more of them than there were of us and they were a lot bigger than we were."

"What are you trying to say, Taweed?" Des sounded impatient.

"Don't you want to know what happened, Dad? I mean, I left you hanging there, you know, your little son and his two friends facing certain injury and scary mayhem. No? My point was that we got into a brawl, or I should say, they jumped us. At first I thought we were holding our own. At least I tried to keep from going down, and I was being kicked and punched from all sides. But when I looked around for those two, they were high-tailing it out of there!"

"What were them black fellows after?"

"Lord knows, Dad, I kept my tickets; they got no money…maybe they just wanted to kick some ass. I did get dumped in the river, though, and that kind of ended that, because the gang of them went storming off. In a couple of seconds, Frankie and Nilvan came running back, all scared. But wouldn't you know it, the black dudes saw them, came back and threw them in the river, too. What I'm trying to say is that they weren't 'bad-assed motherfuckers'. They weren't the type to start a fight, and even when confronted with one, they weren't inclined to finish one. Maybe that's why they ended up the way they did. Maybe they got into something too deep.

"As for the guns, I prefer to think that the killers left them. I mean, think of it. Where would a couple of guys like them get guns like those. I think on the news they said an M16 and a shotgun. No way. They didn't even hunt, or fish, or any of that stuff.

"Nil was an asbestos removal tech. He worked mostly in the schools around here. When he wasn't working he liked to take it easy. He was into heavy metal." Tweed didn't want to say anything else about Frankie just yet.

"And what does LaGloria say about all this?" asked Des, as if arising from a reverie.

"She says she's going to bring her father up for the funeral. He lives in Florida now. She says she sensed something was wrong yesterday when I didn't come home when I was supposed to, but she never expected news like this. She says the cops are incompetent and she doesn't think they'll be able to figure out who did it."

"I think she's right there, son. They'll never catch the ones who killed those boys. And that brings me to another thing I wanted to talk to you about. Listen, I think you'd be better off coming and working with me, you know? Like we discussed before?"

What a time to bring that up. He had to be referring to his crazy Irish Republican schemes and theories. For some reason his father thought of himself as a hero of Ireland or something. A son of the sod, a green-blooded Sinn Fein rebel.

Back when Tweed was seventeen, in the spring of the year of his high school graduation, his father had taken him aside and had laid out a proposition that he had immediately rejected. He claimed that there was a family tradition of working to support the cause of Irish liberty, and that he himself had joined the cause when he was seventeen. Without going into specifics, he mentioned working from the US to raise funds, and risking his Visa and citizenship status to smuggle the money and other items back into Ireland. It was time for Tweed to step forth and claim his heritage, he said, time to hitch his wagon to the star of ideology and to work for the goal of a united Ireland and fulfillment of the dream of the revolution.

"My guys are already working on this McManus thing. You might place a bet on me, that I'll have it figured out before my good friend Det. Storer does. And my old friend Makepeace is looking into it. You remember Makepeace, don't you?"

"The old fisherman? The guy who used to sleep in the attic? Why? What has he got to do with it?"

"That old guy is no fisherman, Tweed. He has connections, and he'll put them to use, as a favor to me. I also have connections, and you can be sure I will put them to use. Come and work with me and see how we get this thing licked. Someone's going to wish they never fucked with us, I can assure you."

"With us? With who? With you? You're talking about LaGloria, right? You want to impress LaGloria for some reason, to show her that you have the power to solve the murders of her brothers? Or is it that you want to impress the murderers? Show whoever killed Frankie and Nilvan that you will hunt them down, and find them out? Nobody messes with friends of Des Kelley."

Des shook his head. "T'weed, I want you to come to your senses and to look ahead to your future. I'm getting on in years and for some time now I've been waiting for one of my boys to carry on my work. Buck, as you know, went back to Ireland and he has been working very hard. Keiran threw in his lot with a higher power, and who am I to question a compact with the Lord? But you've been of age for some time now, and there's so much you could have learned."

"To be honest, Dad, learning Irish history is about as relevant as learning Latin as far as I'm concerned."

"You've heard the history your whole life, and if it didn't sink in, what more can I do? Still, these things have a way of boiling to the surface and I wouldn't be surprised if you remembered more of it than you think. But I'm not talking about the past, I'm talking about the future. They're still fighting over there, our people are still oppressed and the nation in still divided.

"Now nobody expects you to work for nothing. Look at our family: We've always had a roof over our heads, plenty to eat, clothes, you name it. I work for the liberation of Ireland, I stand for republican principles and I earn my keep.

"When I say that you have a lot to learn, that's what I'm talking about. Learning how to make it all work." Des meshed his fingers together by way of demonstration.

Tweed humored him, hoping to expedite matters.

"What kind of work, exactly? I mean, day to day, what would I be doing?"

"All sorts of things, T'weed, all sorts. You come and work with us and we'll put you to work believe me, you'll have plenty to do."

"So, you're talking fund-raising, or something?"

Des laughed. "You might call it that. We have businesses to run, people and resources to manage, rents and fees to collect; projects of all sorts."

"And how does this tie into tracking the killers?"

"Ah, yes, well as I said we are already on that one.

"But let me tell you a story, since we seem to be in the mood for storytelling today. I'll start mine the same way you started yours.

"A few years ago, maybe '83 or so, I started hearing some noise, getting some flack from an Italian neighbor, a business neighbor of mine. You see he was all upset, ranting and raving, heh, heh, about how I was in the wrong business. Now, to elucidate, the business we were discussing was book-making, you know, numbers, bets, all that? Harmless, profitable fun. His contention was that we had no business, so to speak, being in the same business. Like there wasn't enough to go around or something. I guess I was supposed to respect the fact that he had been running numbers for years. Well, to make a long story short, we're still making books around here."

"What about the Italian dude?"

"That poor fellow?," Des shrugged, "They found him stuffed in the trunk of his car up on Cummins Highway."

At that moment the door to the street opened and a figure appeared in silhouette like a frame from a movie western when the bad guy enters the saloon. Tweed however saw the entrance as more akin to a scene from a situation comedy, because with a beam of sunlight on either arm and a glimpse of the free open square behind him, Detective William Storer entered the Rossie Businessman's Club, as if on cue.

CHAPTER 8

This had to be the coolest gig that Rick Rose ever worked. Like a private freakin' detective, doin the creep and scooping the low-down on some stiffs. Weed gave him some idea of how he wanted the thing done, but Rick wasn't going to follow no spy-movie script on this one, no way. He was going to follow his nose. Weed wanted to know who the dudes were, where they lived, what they drove and anything else he called pertinent. Rick liked the sound of that word, pertinent. Weed, man, you're giving me a whole range of options with that word. Rick Rose gets to decide what is and what is not 'pertinent'. Then later when Weed pays him for the job, he can decide if any of what he gets is pertinent. This way if anyone asks him what he's doing, he can say, Rick Rose follows his nose. And if they ask him, What for? he'll say, To find out what's pertinent.

First off he called the Sharlae chick and arranged to take her deposition. Rick Rose knew all about depositions because he had been deposed that time when the city was going after his landlord. They wanted damages and money to treat Rick and his sisters for lead poisoning. The deposition wasn't so bad, because folks was paying attention to him, but the rest of the legal bullshit was a mighty bore. After the settlement Rick had undergone years of physical, occupational and speech therapy. His younger sister even managed to finish school. His old lady blew all the damage money, but Rick didn't blame her. If someone handed him fifty grand he'd have done some damage, too. That's some serious cake.

He had also been deposed for another case in which he was the star witness. Rick Rose just described what he saw, in his own words. It happened when his foster brother beat that guy's head in for fuckin' with his shit. He always said that he done it 'cause the guy was fuckin' with his shit, but everybody knew it was because he was fucking his chick. At first Rick had wondered why the case went to court. After all, the matter was settled, wasn't it? But he figured it out later when it turned into such a big deal 'cause by then the kid was born and everybody started fighting again about who the father was. Rick's foster brother was nowhere to be found when his girlfriend delivered her child; and the other guy blew doors for Florida and never came back neither. Rick Rose called the little tyke his nephew, but it wasn't long before the state came along and took him away, too.

Sharlae sounded nice on the phone, a little sleepy though, and she suggested that they meet instead of talking on the phone. It turned out that he was glad they did, because A) it wasn't cool to discuss shit on the telephone, and 2) Sharlae was hot.

If he'd known she was such a fox he'd have worn something better than sneakers, jeans and a hoody. At the thought of changing, he realized that on this gig he was representing, so he resolved to dress to impress from now on.

He and Sharlae hit it off right away, and only partially because he was so blown away by the fact that she owned her own house. Coming from White City projects, Rick hadn't known many people who owned their own homes, except possibly the cops, the lawyers and maybe some of his therapists. Even Weed didn't own his own house. But this chick also had a kick-ass car that she had tricked out to boot.

Ignoring the house was easy for Rick Rose, because in the final analysis it was not pertinent. Though it was real to him in the sense that he was really digging sitting in this hip arm chair that

Sharlae's ex-boyfriend had made for her out of a van seat, it was also abstract, like a restaurant or a mall or any place where he really had no business. But the longer he sat there grooving on the atmosphere and melting into Sharlae's fine green eyes, the less work he was getting done.

"Maybe it would help if you wrote this stuff down?" suggested Sharlae, noticing that Rick had been staring.

"Wrote down what?"

"What I've been telling you, the things you asked me about."

"Oh, no, that's alright, I don't have to write nothing down; I got it all up here."

Sharlae was skeptical, "You do, huh?"

"Yeah, Sharlae, I'm telling you I got this gift for names and faces, stuff like that. I can remember for you people I seen, folks from way back. Let me give you a f'rinstance. When you said your boyfriend was Carmine Gunther? I remembered him. I saw his face in my head."

"You knew Carmine?"

"No, not actually. But I used to see all them kids who went to White City, and sometimes for one reason or another you get to know people's names. From time to time you see them on the street, or on the bus; you see who they're hanging out with, you hear stuff; and the little file up there gets updated." Rick pointed at his forehead and smiled.

"That's cool," said Sharlae, "I do the same thing with words. If I see it in print, I can remember it."

"You see like little picture of the words, the way they looked?"

"Yeah, the same way; but you know what, I can't remember names for shit! You introduce someone to me, and unless I keep repeating their name in my head I forget it immediately. Not only that, I can't remember the names of people I used to go to school with."

"No problem, Sharlae, I can help you there. You can rely on me."

Rick said this with honest sincerity, and he looked in Sharlae's eyes with the intensity of a house-broke pup. She blushed.

It had been a while since she had been close to a man for anything other than business, and it was no surprise that horny ideas started hinting around the periphery of her mind. She sized him up in a series of stolen glances. About her height, maybe a little taller. Skinny though. Wiry arms with primitive, self-engraved Bic tattoos. Looks like he can handle himself. Wonder if he did any time? The lanky hair was kind of, what, retro? A Moe Howard bowl-cut type of style. His thin mustache appeared to droop, but that was a result of the way he set his jaw. In fact it was a straight, narrow, ratty affair, but it complemented his wispy bebop beard, without which he would undoubtedly have looked older. He was a home boy for sure, a genuine product of the projects, but he was cute in a stand up, straightforward way, and his high cheek bones and narrow eyes made him look sort of kung-fu.

Weed had assigned him to ferret out the finks who had pulled the outrageous bump and snatch last night, and that reason alone endeared him to her. He was working for Weed, but he was doing it for her.

"Hey, how'joo meet Weed, anyway?"

"That's a funny story, that is," started Rick, and he leaned back and spread his legs as if this was his story-telling pose.

"Yeah, well, I was hanging on the corner one night down by Mt Hope and Clements? And I seen these dudes come by, and they was looking up at the house there across the street." Rick looked up and pointed as if he were sitting on the same corner and looking at the same house now. "The third floor. That was where it was at, and I knew that was what they was going for. Just something about it." He shook his head solemnly.

"Yeah? And? What happened?"

"Well, this wasn't the first time I seen 'em, and that's how I knew it was the same guys."

"The same guys as who?" Sharlae was getting interested, but exasperated.

"That came back. You know, like I was saying before, about knowing people? Well, it's not like I didn't recognize these guys, I mean, I knew them from somewhere, probably from White City, like Carmine Gunther, but that night, they didn't belong in that place, you know? Then when they came back again a couple of nights later, and they was looking at that same house across the street, and I knew something was gonna happen."

"Like what?"

"Well, first I should probably tell you that I knew the dude on the third floor of that house. He had my pool table up there. See, back when he was cool I brought it up there as a favor, so's he'd have something to do outside of sitting around, dealing weed. Plus, I didn't have no place for it, and it was sitting in the cellar in the building where my old lady lived. Anyway, at one point he says he won it from me, and it was his table, but we played a lotta games back and forth on that table, and I think he cheated me. From then on I stopped going up there."

"OK, so now I'm sitting there, having a smoke, and I realized that these two dudes are gonna make a move; so I went up to 'em."

"It was Weed?"

"You guessed it! One of 'em was, anyway. I told him that I knew what he was up to, and said that I could help. At first they acted like I was nuts, you know, like testing me, so I said, 'You know that dude up on the third floor of the house across the street there? Well, he sells a lot of dope, and I know where he keeps it. Plus, I know the layout of his pad and I can keep watch for you and get you in and out of there pretty quick. What do you say?"

"Why did you want to rip the guy off?"

"Well, actually he was a sleaze-bag all along. His weed sucked, plus, besides ripping off my pool table, he was always trying to con hoodsies into coming up to his place so he could get laid. Oh, sorry,"

"That's alright. What's a hoodsie?"

"A chick,...a girl,...an underage girl."

"Oh, I see. Did they accept your offer?"

"Yep, that's how Weed and me come to be friends."

The Mt Hope raid was one of many that Tweed pulled over the course of his career as he met each challenge to his control of the market head-on and eliminated the competition using whatever means necessary. Usually he would notify the offending target of his redistricting proposal, and suggest politely but directly that they move their operation elsewhere. An emissary, perhaps Og or Bone or one of their minions, would approach the dealer posing as a customer. Some of Tweed's associates relished these opportunities, others found it distasteful. The secret shopper would employ a host of nagging, obsessive, idiosyncratic traits and techniques that might typically be encountered in the worst clients.

"What kind of weed is this?" "Where does it come from?" "Can I try it first?" "Do you have anything buddier?" "Are these bags weighed?" "Will you weigh one right in front of me?" "Can I get it on the cuff?"

Meanwhile depending upon the acquiescence of the dealer, they would bury their noses in the bags, break up the buds with their fingers, take a pinch and taste it, open a number of bags and fail to reroll them, try to cop some when the guy wasn't looking, fuck around with the settings on the dude's scale and intentionally spill shit in his apartment. "Oops, sorry! I knew I should have finished that Coke before I came in!" After the torture they would invariably leave without buying a bag, while promising to tell all of their friends about the guy. "If they say I sent 'em, you can give 'em a discount, alright?"

This particular raid came about because of a request from Carmine, who first had to convince Tweed of the strategic vulnerability of the Mt Hope market. Tweed ultimately went along with the plan when Carmine admitted that he was also trying to help out his friend Kuhn, whom Tweed hadn't met at the time, in a situation that involved Kuhn's girlfriend's sister, and some long-standing beef that Carmine aimed to settle once and for all. How it all centered around the Mt Hope dealer, Tweed never really understood, but the raid itself turned out to be a gas, and lucrative as hell.

"So they agreed to come back later. I told Weed that the guy was gonna go out at 11:30 to go to his friend's sub shop and get a midnight snack. I don't know what he paid his friend, maybe a couple of joints, but he always came back with a steak bomb, a can of Coke and a bag of potato chips.

At the appointed hour Tweed and Carmine met Rick at Mt Hope and Clement. A dusting of snow had fallen earlier in the evening and as the trio huddled on the frigid sidewalk Rick pointed to the clear Vibram-sole footprints heading away from the house.

"Let's boogie!" And they sprinted up the three flights in rapid breathless leaps of two and three stairs at a time. When they reached the top landing Rick said "Check this out!" and removed the decorative wooden ball from the top of the balustrade. Clearly he had expected to find something there. "Shit, the key's gone! Tell you what, let me run around back. I'll climb the porch and pop in through a window...His voice trailed off as he sped off down the stairs.

Tweed turned to Carmine and said, "I was gonna tell him to check the door first."

"Good idea!" said Carmine, testing the knob. "It's locked," and he turned still holding the knob behind his back. "Maybe if I nudge it, like this," and he bumped the door squarely, busting it open and falling through butt-first as if he expected to find a chair there. Tweed stepped over his friend in a vain attempt to be the first inside. He figured that if anyone was gonna get shot for breaking in and stealing someone's stash, it should be him.

But the apartment was empty. Straight away Tweed went to the back bedroom where he found Rick dangling head first from the window frame.

During the next ten minutes a most ruthless and efficient ransacking took place. It seemed that in addition to selling dope, this dude was taking stolen goods in trade and possibly fencing them as well.

Weed took the weed including 2 kilos and assorted smaller bags; there was 1 eight-ball of rock cocaine; 2 scales including one triple-beam; almost $2800 in cash, an assortment of men's watches, a set of golf clubs, a stamp collection, and a couple of ghetto blaster radios. By now each of the thieves were looking like right jolly Santas, with their winter coats bursting at the seams, but Carmine stuffed a handful of dirty magazines down his shirt for good measure. "Hey, don't want him having any consolation."

"Speaking of consolation," replied Tweed, and he hurriedly described an addendum to their plan. Both Rick and Carmine were amenable, so the three of them ran, or fell down the stairs and then flew down to the tracks where they quickly stashed the haul. Just as fast they were back at the house, racing up the stairs. "Grab the booze, and get that freaking pool table!" shouted Tweed as he rounded the corner into the now-familiar apartment.

He had noticed a black and white console television in the bedroom, and this he carried to the back porch, where he quickly tied it to the railing by its cord and flung it off. Now a pendulum, the arc of its trajectory foreshortened by the length of its cord, the television hung in orbit between the second and third levels of the porch. The ever-diminishing period described by the swaying appliance was like a hurry-up timer on the proceedings.

Satisfied, Tweed raced back into the kitchen and grabbed the legs of the now-disassembled pool table, and with Carmine and Rick carrying the top behind him, beat a hasty retreat again down the rear stairs this time. Needless to say Rick and Carmine were sacrificing accuracy in favor of speed, and as a result they took quite a few chunks out of the plaster on either side of the stairwell on their way down.

Now in the back alley of the triple-decker, the guys lugged the slate onto their shoulders while ducking their heads, and as if by magic the green felt covered pool table lurched off toward the tracks to the sound of the bottles clinking in their pockets.

Just as they cleared the alley a high impact crash right on their heels made them jump involuntarily, almost upsetting the load.

"The dude throwin shit at us?" hissed Carmine.

"Nah, sorry, my fault," said Tweed calmly, "...the TV let go."

Sure enough the smashed remains of the television set formed a milk drop circle of debris around a sizable divot in the pavement. Thus originated one of Tweed's favorite subsequent hobbies-collecting used televisions and dropping them from great heights.

The remainder of the operation, including ferrying the items away and divvying up the spoils was a cold business, lasting well into the wee hours. But Carmine had snagged a bottle of Jack Daniels and a Schnapps, Rick had found a Southern Comfort, a Jim Beam and a bottle of vodka, and Tweed had come away with a Courvoisier, a bottle of rum and some assorted nips. Numerous restorative toasts were made in the name of their now busted benefactor. They blessed his health and wished him well, and perhaps it worked, for they never saw him again. Carmine later heard from Kuhn, who heard from his girlfriend's sister, that the unfortunate guy had been threatened with bodily harm for having cuffed, and having lost the equivalent of ten pounds of commercial grade pot.

His name was Stewie Ramos. In the frustration of trying to determine who had ripped him off and put him out of business he hardly could have guessed that he would someday again cross paths with Tweed. For his part Tweed projected a cold remorseless attitude that he would live to regret. He never saw his victim, and he didn't care to know who he was or what he looked like. At this time in Tweed's life he was recusant, an unrepentant scoundrel who would just as readily have accepted defeat in one of his petty struggles if his adversary were worthy enough to make the game interesting.

"No shit!" sighed Sharlae, satisfied with Rick's story at last.

"Nope- that's how it went down, how me and Weed met, and how I got my pool table back."

"Where d'ja get the table in the first place?"

"Sharlae, that story's gonna-hafta wait. It's a long one."

"You do realize, don't you, who the other guy was?"

"Was that your Carmine?"

"Yeah- that was him. I heard that story told once from a different point of view." Almost the same, too, except for the role of Rick Rose, in whose image Carmine had created a larger-than-life street sage, a detail she declined to share with him in case it affected his judgment.

"Like I said, I thought I recognized him from somewhere. So he, uh, he..."

"Passed on, yeah...died right beside me in bed." Sharlae sniffed, wondering that her nose could drip when her mouth was so dry.

Now she truly hoped that something would come of this encounter. She had felt so comfortable in Rick's presence that words she had rarely if ever confided in anyone had come easily. The swan dive of depression that she usually felt in the pit of her stomach when she thought about Carmine, that feeling like being in an elevator when it suddenly drops a few floors, had already passed. The beauty of it was that she hadn't even had to resort to her usual antidotes of eating ice cream or watching Cheers reruns.

CHAPTER 9

Mmmm, Quaaludes are a girl's best friend, thought LaGloria, as she wallowed in the warm bath-water of euphoria. Was there any other way to turn despair into respite, anger into languor, grief into relief? The funereal had become unreal, what was glum was now plum. With the help of the dope she had gone from mope to hope; from all fret to all set.

By now she had accepted the deaths of her brothers. No longer did their return seem a remote possibility. She also accepted her responsibility for their deaths, rationalizing that some must die, some must live. Des Kelley had lived, but she too was still alive.

She would get another crack at him, but this time she would see him brought down on murder charges- humiliated, powerless, and beyond the help of his friends the cops and the politicians.

The business about the shotgun bothered her, but she took it as a minor inconvenience. Tweed would fix that problem. In retrospect it was clear that she should never have allowed him to keep the thing anyway. But Bryan had been so enigmatic, so compelling; and as deviantly original in his idea of a wedding gift as he was handsome. Tweed had treated it like some cursed relic of evil or sorcery, one that would bestow misfortune upon anyone who kept it, and worse luck upon the one who threw it away.

In addition to her lingering concern over the shotgun, there was one other item that troubled her, although in her present state of mind it seemed almost amusing. It was her connection to a live person who represented her only link to a sordid chain of evidence that a cop with enough persistence and ingenuity might unravel in order to expose her. The link was Tommy Toole, a sweet handsome guy whom she had befriended through her work. A weak link in her opinion, yet he represented a potential threat to her, if not in terms of personal safety or liberty, then certainly in terms of her peace of mind.

His participation in her scheme had been nominal and unwitting for that matter, for he did not know how his small commitment of time and resources had been put to use. And yet just as he had become the lynch-pin in her plan to eliminate Des Kelley, he was now also the keystone to her defense from prosecution.

But LaGloria had to give him the benefit of the doubt. Under normal circumstances would he even realize that the information he had given her had helped contribute to the deaths of her brothers? That would require a major intuitive leap. First he would have to know that the incident was a crime gone wrong. He would at the very least have to have some inkling that she hated Des, and she couldn't recall ever giving him the slightest reason to suspect that she bore the old dude any ill will whatsoever.

And yet if it had been Des who died, then Tommy probably would have made the connection. Because then he would have heard the story of how Des was lured to the park, and that he had gone there expecting to meet Bricky. Then Tommy might well have been in for a shock, as he surely would have remembered telling LaGloria stories about Bricky and his relationship to Des. Logic alone would provide a sound conclusion without the intuition.

Whether he had reached an astonishing conclusion about the crime or not, LaGloria still felt compelled to call him for reassurance. But she would have to wait. He would surely call to express his condolences as soon as he heard the tragic news about her brothers. When he did she would gauge both his voice and the content of his words. If he seemed untainted by suspicion, remorse or fear, then she may feel an incentive to tell him how important it was not to discuss their conversations with the police, or anyone else for that matter. However, in doing so she would only arouse his suspicions, although he really was the most genuine, honest guy she knew, and not one prone to think the worst of anyone.

Again she felt that she was left with two options. Either she could wait and see if Tommy spilled the beans, or she could see to it that he never did. The sunny haze of methaqualone would not permit her to imagine or foresee any further consequences along this line of reasoning. Perhaps she had better discuss the matter with Tweed. Maybe if he could get past his general sense of unease about gays then he could think of another way to discredit the evidence, deflect its impact, or to minimize the potential damage.

She still felt that she owed something to Tommy. Among the men with whom she worked he was the most down to earth, the most approachable. And LaGloria believed that was the nature of his personality, that it had nothing to do with the fact that they were both from Rossie and that her boyfriend's family was close to the Tooles. It was a small world after all, and encountering Tommy Toole among the gay men working in porn was only about as weird and coincidental as discovering that Des Kelley had been her mother's lover.

In fact it had been her awareness of all of the coincidences and relationships around her that had led her to concoct her scheme and to put it into action. It was as if one set of equations balanced another and she alone saw that elegant symmetry, or as the case may be, the lack thereof that must be corrected.

CHAPTER 10

"Billy! Just the man I wanted to see!" Des shouted in greeting to the noted detective.
"You're in blues?"

"Des, Harris! Yeah, I'm on my way home so I stopped in at 13 and changed." The policeman was about 5 foot 8, 180 pounds, with graying black hair slicked back from an expansive forehead. In his crisp uniform he looked every bit the authoritarian figure, an impression that was enhanced by his beak-like nose, beady eyes, stern expression and neckless stance.

"You change into your uniform when you're going off the job?"

"Sure; I'll wear this outfit again tomorrow, and change into street clothes when I get in."

"Yeah, yeah, I get ya," mumbled Des.

"Who's this?" asked Storer, staring directly into Tweed's eyes. "Friend of yours?"

"Friend? This here's my son! You remember…"

Storer interrupted, "Tweed? Tweed Kelley? Or should I say Wee-"

"Morning Officer Storer," nodded Tweed.

If he had met Tweed on the street the detective would have wasted no time in establishing the rules of engagement, letting him know that he was in command of the situation and that he expected no less than total deference and respect, including proper forms of address.

Storer had accrued both his reputation and his lifestyle from the patronage and bribes of businessmen and professionals in his precinct. Over the years he had gone to great lengths to gain the attention of people in the community who could help him succeed, and that included people engaged in criminal activities, organized and otherwise. All he demanded was respect, a piece of the action, and a degree of control over the status quo.

The largest landmark in Rossie Square was the railway overpass, across which, in large block letters, someone had spray-painted the words STORER SUCKS. Any other cop so defamed would have called public works to have the graffiti painted over, or had a youngster from juvenile detention work off a sentence by removing the acrylic pronouncement. But it had been there for a decade and Storer was content to let it remain indefinitely, as if it was a form of public acclamation.

However, as proof of the overall modesty of his intentions, he had indeed let it be known that he intended to retire at the earliest eligible age. Once he had left the department he would also leave Rossie and move to the western suburbs where he would someday open a bakery with the proceeds of his pension.

He was grateful for the long-time patronage of good citizens like Des, Pat Fecteau and Joe Harris. He did not however receive patronage from Tweed, although he knew cops who did. He suspected that Tweed was a drug dealer, but there was a possibility that he worked for his father in some less-than-obvious capacity.

"I don't recall ever seeing you in here before," said Storer a bit wearily before sitting down at the bar.

"I don't recall ever having been in here," replied Tweed, trying to be lightly sarcastic.

Des interrupted, "I asked him to come by and discuss the incident; you know the one I'm talking about."

"I suppose you mean the killing of those boys over at the park last night. Why would you want to discuss that, Des? What's it to you?"

"Oh, never mind, Bill. It's not me that's interested, it's my boy here. You see, his girlfriend, LaGloria…"

"My girlfriend is LaGloria McManus," said Tweed, wishing now that he had never come into the club.

"LaGloria; where have I heard that name before? Well, anyway, so LaGloria is, what, some relation? Not the sister of those guys, uhm, Francis and Nilvar McManus?"

"Nilvan McManus. Yes, they were her brothers."

"Yes, that's it! I have her on my list here- LaGloria. Sorry, I just got off and I was going to go home and catch some shut-eye for a few hours. I was gonna call her later. But, while I have you here, uh, say, what were you talking to the old man about?"

"My father only wanted to know if there was anything he could do to help."

"And I'd like to see the killers brought to justice," added Des. "We can't have our young men getting shot, and our parks unsafe now can we?"

"Des, you have a special interest in this case?"

"Billy, they were my son's girlfriend's brothers. That's my special interest. I hope you catch whoever did this horrible thing and put them away for good!"

The detective blew out a long gust of air and scratched his head.

"I will of course do my job, Des, but between you and me, so far it looks like a case where a couple of losers got knocked off by some other losers. Worst comes to worse, I mean, whether I catch somebody or not, at least we're down a couple of losers." He looked at Tweed when he said this, wondering if he would get a rise out of him.

But Harris responded. "Ah, Billy, you know it's not decent to speak of the poor boys like that. They left a grieving sister and I'm sure many other people miss them as well."

"No disrespect intended. Only, I know their records and believe me, we're better off without them. The older one had been in petty scrapes since he was fourteen. He had a couple of raps for larceny, an indecent assault, and an assault with a deadly weapon. The younger one was no angel either by my reckoning. Got a girlfriend in trouble, dropped out of high school, had a couple of minor drug possession charges. Now I know that doesn't sound like much, but in my experience, those are the ones you gotta look out for."

Tweed stood and made as if to leave.

Des asked, "Where are you going, boy?"

"I think I've heard enough. Maybe the police can't deter violence but I had hoped that they would catch the killers and that justice would prevail."

Storer ignored this and said, "Is that your sports car out front there, son?"

"Yes,"

"Oh. OK. See, I have a citation here written out for it-" he pulled a small pad out of his back pocket and waved it in the direction of the door. "But seeing as your Des' son, I think I can let this one slide. Tweed, you know that's a loading zone."

"There was no sign!"

"No, there isn't; there used to be one out there…you know how it is, kids steal them. But in any event it is a loading zone and you are parked illegally.

"Don't worry about it, though." Storer smiled wolfishly.

Tweed had gathered up his crutches and was heading toward the door when he stopped, and fished in his pocket. He pulled out a crumpled bill, smoothed it, straightened it and held it up before the men near the bar.

"I'll place that bet, Dad, only, I'm betting on Detective Storer here. I think he'll find the killers. Here's fifty that says he finds out who did it and what's more, that the killers are in our midst, here in town." He leaned over and released the bill from his fingers so that it floated in two descending arcs to the bar in front of Harris.

"Fifty on the RPD!" confirmed Harris, and he placed a bar bottle on the corner of the bill.

After watching Tweed leave the premises, Des turned to Storer and said, "That was a fine thing to say, about them boys being losers! You had best be following up on this thing!"

"C'mon, Des! That's my job."

"Yes, but you made it sound as if it was police policy to let the bad guys kill the bad guys." The Irishman looked up at the ceiling.

"You gotta admit, it has a certain appeal to it."

"You said it yourself, it's your job, and your duty to find out what happened. The last violent crime you investigated was when that Mrs. Kowalski shot her husband for smiling at a nurse."

"The kid bet fifty bucks," Storer said, almost as a question. "He was pretty confident."

Des met his gaze again, and replied "Must know something we don't."

Storer looked at Des for an uncomfortable moment as if he was trying to figure him out. Then he shrugged and got to his feet.

"You want to know what we found out? Those boys were probably waiting there for somebody to show up, like they were setting up an ambush; but for some reason that we haven't yet ascertained, they were caught by surprise, and were themselves killed.

"This was no one-sided affair. It was a shootout, and they lost. It could have gone another way. It looks as though we could have had more bodies on our hands; or different bodies. It's a puzzle. But don't worry, Des, I am working on it, I just need some sleep before I continue. It was a long night."

After Billy Storer left the biz club Des actually felt relieved. He wasn't accustomed to thinking of his friend and drinking buddy as a peeler. His role as a cop in this town was something that he usually left at the door when he came in, like an actor dropping his guise when he left the stage.

It had only occurred to Des at that moment that in this case Storer was working against him, not for him. And in a very real and threatening sense if Billy did his duty as Des had insisted, then he could at some point come looking for Des and Harris and Simon. Well fuck that. No way was he going to be taken down by a fucking Rossie civil servant. Bigger men than him had tried and failed.

Besides, Des had connections that could conceivably insulate him from a low-level flat-foot like Storer and his lap dog Jimmy Rima. The very existence of the Rossie Businessmen's Club was proof of that.

CHAPTER 11

To Des' recollection, in fact like Des recollection, it had started as an idle dream, a vague concept in his mind.

Back in those days, when he was new to the US, Des would spend many an hour at The Brown Brogan, an historic watering hole in the uptown section of the city. His friend and sponsor was Joe Toole, then a barman at the Brogan. While Des resisted finding honest labor on the streets of town he loitered in the bar and encouraged his friend to have aspirations beyond paying the rent and getting by on his salary.

"You should open your own pub, Joe. Think of it! A lot of hard work, but worth it. You'd be independent, and set for life. I know, because I have a bar back in Ireland."

"You're full of horse shit, Kelley," Joe would say. "If you had a bar of your own you wouldn't be here. And you're a dreamer. It's well nigh impossible to obtain a liquor license in this town."

"Someday you'll accompany me to my pub in my hometown of Boyle, and you'll have your proof; but that will have to wait until you can afford to travel. And the only way you're going to do that is if you open your own business."

"I tell you, crazy Irish bastard, that there are only so many liquor licenses in this town, and they are all in use. When a license becomes available, there's a bleeding feeding frenzy. Bids can go as high as fifty thousand dollars! And even if you had the money there's no guarantee that you'll get the bid, because the system is rigged. You have to know someone who can make it happen. If you want to convince them to help, you have to have something to offer in return, like a plum job for their kid, or a vacation home at the seashore. I'm telling you Des, it ain't easy."

Joe's view on the availability of licenses was valuable to Des only insofar as it captured the essence of the situation in a nutshell. It also represented the prevailing view of other viable candidates for licenses, although their perspectives could be altered by their respective levels of experience and access.

In his quest to obtain a license for Joe, Des would have to speak with city councilors, representatives, licensing board members, various flunkies in the mayor's office; and he'd have to meet with the zoning board and the planning commission and the commission for the preservation of historic sites. Each person in that vast conspiracy of denial had an opinion as to the inadvisability of pursuing such a goal, despite the fact that they were ostensibly there to issue the licenses and to encourage growth in the various competing sections of the city.

Des wasn't daunted. He was an idea man, a pragmatist with a can-do attitude.

So there was inherent difficulty to obtaining a liquor license, and therefore to opening a new drinking establishment. Apparently some well-meaning generation of city fathers had failed to anticipate the potential consequences of limiting the number of licenses in the city.

If Des could see, then anyone could see that the limit begets a backlog and the backlog begets a waiting list. Actually a list and a queue. The official waiting list is posted at city hall for show, but the queue was formed by members of the old families, the heavy hitters and ward heelers who had their fixes in long ago.

With extraordinary luck and patience, plus the unlikely intervention of a war or pestilence, or any combination thereof, one might eventually reach the top of the official list. But getting ahead in the queue would be much more difficult.

Des altered his trajectory to avoid the list entirely. The system and the list were locked together in a death grip on free enterprise. Des intended to bypass not only the system but the old clans, cronies and crooks waiting on it. In order to do this he enlisted the aid of Joe Toole, Pat Fecteau and also Dapper Ferguson, to whom Des had implied that he was distantly related.

Dapper had served in a number of capacities at city hall as he tried to familiarize himself with the workings of the city government. In a career that would eventually span almost forty years he held various positions while working under many different administrations. From the corporation counsel's office to the redevelopment authority, to the inspections department of the licensing bureau, to the traffic commission, to the clerk of the works, all before he ran for elected office. He stood for councilor at large, city rep, city councilor and sheriff.

Pat Fecteau was not a regular at The Brown Brogan, nor was he a friend of Joe Toole or Des Kelley; but Charlie Murphy was, and he knew Pat. So one evening years ago Charlie introduced his friend Pat to his friends at the bar, and a new alliance was forged.

Pat Fecteau owned Cove Corp, a construction company that was based in one of the so-called 'metro-west' communities. His company had grown steadily since he started it as a kid fresh out of high school, and by the time he met Des he owned a sizable fleet of vehicles, including pickup trucks, dump trucks, plows, spreaders and tankers; and heavy equipment including diggers, loaders, and backhoes; tracked vehicles such as dozers and cranes; and specialty construction machinery such as pavers, graders, brush hogs, and cement trucks. At the time when Des approached him his cash flow was at a steady trickle but he was upside down in his financing, and his books were severely out of whack.

Through Charlie Des had proposed a solution that saved Pat, as well as his company, equipment and employees from the hazards and pitfalls of bankruptcy. In a massive staged heist Des would remove all or most of Pat's stock from the yards where they were stored and maintained. Utilizing tractor trailer flatbeds he would take everything Pat owned and let him work out the loss with his insurance company.

Having overcome the last of Pat's objections, Des launched the operation in April of '72. By September of that year Cove Corp had been reimbursed by its insurance company for the loss of equipment incurred during what was in terms of scale one of the largest single thefts in state history. As the local newspaper so aptly put it at the time, "State Police baffled."

The work had all been accomplished over a weekend, with Des himself brazenly leading a convoy of heavily laden and disguised vehicles to a rented parcel of undeveloped land in the northwestern 'sticks'.

Well after the company was back on its feet and operating with some notable new equipment acquisitions, Des sold the stolen equipment back to Pat at a fraction of its value, and returned everything to its original location. The bookkeepers and insurance adjusters were none the wiser and Pat emerged from his difficulties with a stronger, more profitable company with an equitable debt load and a balance sheet showing an impressive list of assets.

Throughout this time Des never stopped working to obtain a liquor license for Joe. Now he had a friendly investor on board, and the core group involved in the plan grew in numbers as well. Pat brought in his brother Simon, and Joe introduced his brother Harris. All of the men, Joe, Des, Pat, Harris, and Simon met regularly at The Brown Brogan to drink and discuss their dream of opening a bar of their own.

Dapper sat in occasionally to update Des on developments at the city level, and it was during one such visit that Des came up with the idea of how to beat the system.

Dapper had been talking about how there was a new effort underway at city hall to purge the voter rolls of invalid, incorrect or inactive names. A study of voter participation in the municipal elections in the fall of '72 revealed that some 1500 deceased voters had cast votes along with 650 infants, 500 incarcerated prisoners, and 380 fictional characters. The mayor may have been a beneficiary of the fraud, but publicly he was fully behind the effort to rid the process of corruption.

The numbers stood out in Des' mind. Some 3000 fake names had slipped by the officials in charge of the election. Surely one name would slip by unnoticed in a licensing issue. It came to Des in a flash: all he had to do was find a license holder who was dead or dying, obtain the license directly from them or their estate, and prevent the city from being notified about the transfer. It would be a simple matter to continue operating under the same name if need be, or perhaps with the cooperation of an inspection official or two, to move the location of the establishment altogether. After all, who was to say that the inspector hadn't looked over such and such a bar at such and such an address.

"Des, you're either a genius or a madman," Joe had said when he heard the plan. "How are we going to find an old, sick, or dead bar owner?"

"Ah, Joe, my friend, you can leave that to me."

Des was confident because he had befriended a good many clerks, secretaries, and low-level functionaries during his many appearances before municipal officials. The information he required surely could be bought for a nominal price from one of these otherwise bored and underpaid city workers.

He put out his feelers, threw a little cash around, and in time he received exactly what he was looking for: the name of an elderly gentleman who owned a failing bar in Dawestown.

Tim McBride's health was also failing and he had few living relatives and no children. Age and illness would soon force him to close his bar The Wet Whistle, but demographic factors had been pushing him out of business for years. Located in a once thriving mixed Irish-German-Italian neighborhood, The Whistle was now alone on the block with a number of closed and abandoned stores, as well as a Hispanic food market, a fast fried chicken joint, and the ubiquitous package store.

McBride's customers had all sold their homes and moved away from that section of Dawestown. In addition, the milkman who used to stop in with his daily dairy order, and the mailman and the cop on the beat who would stop in for refreshment had vanished as well, along with the ice-man and the rest of the vendors who delivered to his business.

The flight of the white working class population had plainly contributed to his problems and may well have been inevitable. However it saddened McBride to witness the concurrent rise in the number of biker gangs, arson incidents, and arrests for drug trafficking.

The grid layout of the streets was the only recognizable feature of the area as Tim remembered it, but everything else had changed during his occupancy of the site.

Recently representatives from the mayor's office of urban redevelopment had been around to distribute fliers concerning an upcoming public hearing. A new interstate bypass project was slated to cut right through Dawestown, and the city along with a cartel of private developers would sweep out any remaining obstacles to 'progress' with a series of property purchases sanctioned by eminent domain provisions in the city and state bylaws.

The construction of the new bypass was welcome as far as Des was concerned, because the resulting activity and disruption would create a smoke-screen, or more literally a dust-screen behind which to hide a fraudulent transaction.

As he prepared to persuade his fellow barman to sell his hard-earned business, to part with a liquor license worth a hundred times its weight in gold, and to cooperate in hiding the deal from the licensing board and the revenue department, he naturally anticipated a hard sell. In truth he was so doubtful as to the likelihood of success that Des contemplated worst-case scenarios that in his imagination looked like something out of a Vincent Price movie.

Yet in the end Des had an edge, the value of which he had underestimated going into the negotiations. That edge was cash. Tim McBride wanted to get out of his business as quietly and quickly as possible, and to enjoy his remaining years "under the radar" as he described it. As his business had taken a dive and his health had deteriorated, his stress had increased and his judgment had suffered, McBride had made a number of deals which were intended to bail him out of his present difficulties, only to sink him in the long run. For this and other reasons he essentially wanted to keep the transaction 'under the table', but he remained dubious and fearful about finding someone willing to carry out the deal in such a manner.

It hadn't been necessary for Des to bring out some of his most carefully considered arguments, for like two strangers who bump into each other only to discover that they are indeed long lost brothers, Des Kelley and Tim McBride were able to reach a rapid and mutually satisfactory accord, and to close the deal forthwith.

The details of the contract were closely held by Des, representing Pat Fecteau, and by McBride himself; and the actual legal terms in which the deal was couched remained a secret known only to the signatories to the agreement. That might not have been the case if for example the scheme was ever exposed by a legal challenge or uncovered by municipal authorities. However, in the course of events the bar and license changed hands again before that happened.

One final item relating to the transfer of the license must be mentioned, for it had the potential of discrediting Des after he had so successfully pulled off the dream deal for his associates. As a last minute response to the cold feet he sensed developing among his associates, Des resolved to simply do away with McBride, thus enabling Pat to keep the money and the bar. He told only Harris, who reluctantly agreed to back him up if necessary. Here it is well worth noting that had he informed his other partners about his intentions, then the long term relationship that Des, Pat, Simon, Harris and Joe so richly enjoyed over the following years would not have come to pass- at least not on the same basis of trust, mutual respect and friendship.

At this point Des was already lining up suppliers and laborers in anticipation of opening The Whistle anew. Pat Fecteau and Joe Toole were delighted but mystified by the manner in which the bar was to change hands. They were handing over a lot of money and taking a substantial risk on his say so that the whole thing would come off as planned.

It was when Des realized how blindly his friends and partners were willing to accept his judgment, and how happy they were to help out old McBride in the process, that he decided against the killing. Not only were they willing to give up a huge investment to McBride, but they also took his word that he would never report them to the IRS, or sell them out to an investigator of any stripe. Des relented, but then he neither claimed nor desired any ownership stake in the bar.

For the sake of brevity, let's just say that the deal went off without a hitch. In exchange for the bar and the license McBride took forty thousand dollars in cash from Pat Fecteau, and Pat had him sign the license over to Joe Toole. McBride left to live happily ever after, which in his case turned out to be about eight years.

At first the group of associates launched themselves heartily into plans for the renovation of The Whistle. However when they visited the site as owners (operating under the previous owner's name) they saw that the boarded up bar fronted a vacant lot that marked the edge of the development zone.

Everything in the neighborhood, including the bar, would be demolished to make way for the highway project, according to a schedule that would be at least partially determined by the number and complexity of legal challenges and obstacles thrown up by community action committees, environmental surveys and the like.

Then a suddenly sober Simon suggested that they run the bar out of another location using the same license, name and everything. In other words, pretend to run the bar from its old location. The old bar would essentially become a mail drop.

Faced with failure or more fraud, the group adopted Simon's recommendation, and immediately leased the first place that became available- a vacant dry cleaner's store in the middle of Rossie square.

Behold, to the trepidatious amazement of all, it worked.

When nosy inspectors came around Des bought them off -with an assurance from Dapper thrown in for good measure. Distributors and vendors became accustomed to delivering to Rossie, and all invoices and business documents were forwarded through the existing legal address.

Not only did they do a bang-up business but they also paid some of the bar's outstanding debts, including back taxes. The decision to take care of the IRS was rationalized as a good will gesture, an attempt to return the company to the government's good graces. They certainly intended to do all they could to withhold payments in the future.

However, in the long run it became clear that it was impossible to keep up the charade indefinitely, and the partners came up with a plan to sell the bar again, this time with professional legal assistance.

In order to make the place legitimate Pat would sell the bar to Joe, and Joe would file for a business permit, an occupancy permit, a business certificate, tax identification and all the rest. It was intended that the irregularities of the prior sale would become apparent during the process of filing for the permits and documenting the chain of ownership and transfer of title. They were in effect placing all of their cards on the table, and risking the possible fines, penalties or arrest that might come of revealing how they had pulled a fast one, copping a license and opening a new bar.

After protracted negotiations lawyers for the city were willing to accept any pretext to avoid a public hearing over the matter. So they dropped it, citing the lapse of ten years and relevant provisions in the statute of limitations. The licensing board was willing to forgo taking action against Pat Fecteau on the condition that he walk away from the liquor business. Meanwhile the sale of The Whistle to Joe Toole was allowed to proceed. McBride's license was also officially reissued to Joe, since he had been operating under it for a decade and the previous owner had made a good-faith assignment in writing that was taken to be binding.

Thanks to friends in the licensing bureau and the assistance of well-paid allies (throughout a system that had been softened up for a politic and persuasive Irishman by generations of infiltrating forebears), Des had accomplished the circumvention of the liquor license backlog stalemate, and had obtained a license previously thought to be unobtainable.

In Rossie square the dive with the red door had been known as the businessmen's club for years, but it was officially rededicated when Joe took legal ownership in '83. Pat Fecteau became the silent partner, Harris became the alternate bartender, Des became the most honored guest and Simon became one of the club's founding members.

CHAPTER 12

When Tweed returned to his apartment LaGloria was sitting up in bed, looking like a person who had forgotten to lay down before falling asleep. She hadn't responded when he called her name upon entering, and her gaze was unfocused.

No doubt she was still in lu-lu-land; but perched in the center of the unmade bed as she was, with her black hair tousled into a fright-wig do, she was stone-cold sexy.

Tweed's preferences aside, it seemed undeniable that LaGloria made clothes look good, and clothes -any clothes, made her look good. Her night-shirt, actually one of Tweed's well-worn oversized t-shirts, draped over her shoulders and emphasized her prominent breasts. Her nipples, like dollops of strawberry sauce atop twin mounds of vanilla ice cream, shone dark against the sheer cotton fabric. Flimsy negligee could not have looked as sexy on her in Tweed's opinion, for he loved a hint of the tomboy.

Her lips were puffy and her nose was red as if she had recently stopped crying. She leaned on one arm with her hand buried in the mattress behind her back. The other hand gripped a knot of sheets in her lap. The bedroom was stuffy with body odor. At first impression it seemed as if she were preparing to follow a lover, sweating and sated, into the bathroom for a shower.

Tweed suddenly felt as if he had never wanted to fuck her so badly. The throbbing in his foot and ankle was rapidly being diminished by the throbbing in his cock and balls.

Oh, man, he thought, What a prick I am! My girlfriend is grieving and I wanna have sex! And only last night I watched her brothers die. What an asshole! And look at her! She's out of it. It would be like taking advantage of her.

But look at her. Tweed practically drooled.

On the other hand what about me? I'm a mess, my ankle's sprained, I'm all beat up...

I sure could use some sweet stuff...and if I could, then so could she, right? (When I get that feeling, I need sexual healing...)

She'd probably think that I'm doing it because of the drugs- not only the shit I took but the shit she took. But fuck that! She's fucking gorgeous, and if this were any other day, we'd be making love right now!"

His anger made his prick ache to the point that he felt like he was wielding a pool cue in his pants.

I'll just snuggle in there, get her all comfy and relaxed, and see about eating her out. She almost never refuses head.

That's it- if she let's me lick her clit, then I'll just take it from there.

He approached the bed with all the demure suaveness of Inspector Clouseau, hopping on one foot while trying to get his pants off and over the bulbous clubfoot wrappings. As he hopped he whirled in an attempt to keep his balance, (Whatever happened to flare-legs? Wrong blasted angle for this kind of work...if I could do this I could suck my own cock!) and he flailed and toppled onto the mattress as gracefully as someone whose hands and feet had been bound.

LaGloria avoided the tumult, and thus the likelihood of being trampolined, by casually stepping out of bed at the moment her lover keeled over. "Gotta pee," she said, before cat-stepping out of the room.

Guess she wasn't so fucked up after all.

She could be doing the go pee and stagger back to bed thing, or maybe she was doing the things women do in the bathroom before they have sex. If she was getting ready, then he'd get ready; and keep the boner he had started as a foundation for a bigger and better hard-on to come.

Sometimes he got a fierce erection just thinking about her, and he almost always did when he looked at her torridly voluptuous body. But on rare occasions when even that stimulation produced flagging results, LaGloria was expert at honing the edge of his desire. While Tweed waited for his lover to return from the bathroom, he fantasized about the way she had taunted him sexually.

Their little love game started not long after they commenced living together. Tweed remembered it as one of those evenings when both of them knew that they were going to end up getting it on, but both of them also felt touchy and irritable in their own ways. One nasty insinuation led to another nasty accusation and before long they were each tossing out sneering, caustic comments such as, "Oh, and I suppose you weren't turned on when I wore that little green dress to the party at your brother's house…" and, "Admit it, you were pissed when she flirted with me…" and, "For you masturbation is punishment; for me it's a reward," and so on. He said that she had an uncontrollable libido; she said that he didn't know what got him off.

Then she started describing some of the men she had worked with, verbally painting images onto the canvas of Tweed's mind so that he could see their clothing and bodies in intimate detail; and when she came to their masculine attributes, she lavished an intentionally rich degree of subjective sensual impressions. LaGloria presented men in their various sizes, degrees of ruggedness and hairiness, their types and colors of skin, ranges of muscle tone and physical fitness as choices on an appetizing smörgåsbord.

She was frank about her fantasies and claimed that she valued different types of stimulation for different reasons and occasions. She might want to dominate a man, or to be dominated, she said, or to make love to a woman if the mood suited her; whereas Tweed, she claimed, was simply excited by the unknown.

At this point she noticed that Tweed had become increasingly agitated and hard as a rock. This provoked more teasing and sexual banter, as she claimed that it was her talk of naked male bodies that had gotten him so horny. He knew in fact that his arousal was caused by hearing his girlfriend talk so openly and unashamedly about sex. Repression and fear and guilt had severely limited his ability to use sexual terms or descriptions, and his ability to understand his own sensuality had been hampered if not stunted altogether during his formative years by religious indoctrination. Catholicism, while encouraging education in almost all other forms, had been pejorative and condemnatory regarding terms and issues of an intimate, sensual, sexual or scatological nature.

As the love play inevitably led to sex, Tweed was willing to go along with it, even though he gradually became accustomed to her filthy tricks and dirty talk. The only thing that bothered him was the realization that over time the excitement he had felt upon hearing the taboo talk was replaced by an edgy thrill caused by anger. The more she pissed him off with her freaky tales of bondage boys, drag queens and burly men, the harder he got, and the deeper and harder he fucked. Inside her he was a smoldering slab of satisfaction, a powerful source of penis-induced pleasure. But in his mind he snarled, "Take that you fucking bitch, and all of your pansy-ass faggy boys too!" They could kiss each other's asses and play do me like a love-doll for all he cared, he was going to pound the cream out of his honey-slut, and make her understand the difference between a gay and a straight to the core of her being.

"Oh, look at you," yawned LaGloria upon returning. "That's what I love about you- always ready to go. What, was my ass hanging out when I got up- and sproing! Up pops your friend and mine?"

"Aw, babe, just showing you how much I love you."

"Aw babe yourself. What did you find out? Where-a you been, anyway? I was zonked!" She stood well out of Tweed's reach at her bureau, where she contemplated her choice of panties.

"Found out that it sucks to walk when you have a sprained ankle. So I picked up the 99 and took a spin."

"Tweed! You got your car back? That's pissa! We should go take a ride, you know? Get the fuck out of here."

"And I saw my old man."

"So he really is alive then. This wasn't all just a nightmare?" For a moment LaGloria appeared to space out, with a look of hopeless apathy on her face.

"No, babe, this was all a nightmare. I just came back from the Rossie Biz Club of all places, and I met Storer there. He's working on the uh, the murder. Your brothers really did die last night, and Storer's gonna call you later to ask a few questions. It's a freakin' nightmare alright."

"Don't get so freaking melodramatic. Why did you go running to daddy, anyway? And you talked to the cops already? Geez, Tweed, I'd think you'd have more sense than that. You have to keep in mind our situation here."

"I am pretty damned sensitive about our situation. I didn't go running to daddy; he called and made it sound like it was in my best interest to hear what he had to say. It was just a coincidence that Storer showed up."

"He just showed up, huh? What did he want?"

"Fucks knows."

"Listen, hon, I think we better go over the evidence again."

"My father said he brought in a guy named Makepeace to help out; supposedly to learn who the killers were. Like he needs to know who they were. Man, this is so fucked up! What's he gonna do when his friend realizes it was him? Evidence? What evidence?"

"You know...things they might have left behind- anything that could tie us to the scene. Makepeace, huh? What a name. Who the heck is Makepeace?"

"I thought he was a fisherman or some shit like that. He's an old friend of my parent's. I remember he lived with us once. Up in the attic. But Des says that he's no fisherman. Made him out to be some kind of heavy, like he's connected or something. I think the only evidence Storer's gonna find will be the bodies, uh, your brothers, that is, and the guns, along with any ejected casings, and just stuff like footprints."

"So this friend of your father is a real cloak and dagger dude, eh? Like, 'Look out, it's Mr. Makepeace!' Don't forget the car." She flitted from subject to subject as if she were flipping through a rack of costumes with one of her clients. "And the shotgun- which you'll remove of course. And any shit that was in the car. 'Course, you guys were all supposed to come back. The only guy that was supposed to die was Des, and he got away clean! I looked the car over before they left, but I wasn't looking too hard if you know what I mean. Just making sure that it looked normal in case they got pulled over. Like a regular working dude's car, you know?"

LaGloria's lower lip was trembling, and she stood facing away from Tweed with her head bowed. She wore only a t-shirt, and she clutched a pair of panties bunched up in her hands, but otherwise her pose reminded Tweed of his mother, whom he had frequently seen in a similar attitude, worrying over her rosary beads.

"By the way, babe, the guys called this morning. They all had good things to say about Nils and Frankie. It was nice of them. Sharlae was in tears."

"Yeah, people always have good things to say when you're dead."

"Well, your brothers are gonna be a lot more famous now than they ever would have been otherwise..." Tweed realized too late how tacky that sounded.

"Dead celebrities. Sounds like the name of a band."

"No shit. You know, this all would have been a lot easier if they had gotten away with it." OK, so what if they had blown away his old man? Guy's an asshole anyway. Wanted to make Tweed's life miserable with his goddamned bullshit Irish politics. How the hell can you make money on people's suffering, anyway?

Des had said, 'We've always had a roof over our heads, food on the table...' Well, so what? Tweed intended to do a lot better than that, and in fact already had. The lease on his apartment was paid in advance, he owned his fully refurbished car outright, he had a stash of cash and plenty in the bank, plus investments. With a hot, sweet loving hunnybun to go along with it all, he had everything he needed right now.

"You think so?"

What? Was LaGloria having second thoughts?

"Don't you? Wasn't that the whole idea? To get rid of Des Kelley and all he represents?"

"Yes, that was my plan. But now I'm wondering about this Makepeace guy, and how many more there are out there like him. What if we killed the old fuck only to unleash a friggin shitstorm? Maybe he is connected."

"Are you serious? Because I'll tell you, I think that we have the advantage here. Only you and I know who really killed Frankie and Nilvan. Des can talk all he wants about finding the killers but all he has to do is look in the mirror. As far as the cops are concerned it doesn't matter anymore why your brothers were involved in a shoot-out at the Arbs, because they were the victims. If they find the killers, that's all only mitigating circumstances. No matter how those guys plead it, they're going down for manslaughter at the very least! And we're the ones who can put them away!"

"No, you're right, and I wasn't really serious, but I was thinking. But still, say we do have the advantage, and I'm not denying that at this point it looks like we do, but what do we do with it? Do we simply hand Des over like you say? Or do we take what we have and play it up for an even better advantage?"

Tweed didn't like the sound of this. When LaGloria started scheming, it was as if he was watching Shiva's dance.

"A better advantage? Like what? Alls we want is to get out this clean. If Des goes away, then the original goal is fulfilled. I mean, you have to accept the losses you've already incurred, but it seems to me like the sum gain is still equitable."

"I'll tell you. Say this guy Makepeace is connected, right?"

"I think you're giving old Makepeace too much credit here..."

"Just say he is somebody, right? What if we convince him that Des had set the whole thing up? That he hired Frankie and Nilvan in the first place."

"For what?"

"Speculation, but say he was gonna move on Makepeace?"

Crazy talk, woman. But Tweed's mind was moving now, too. "What if we convince Storer that Makepeace hired them to kill Des?"

LaGloria smiled, for the first time since her brothers had left her a day ago. "I think you're onto something. Get rid of Des, Makepeace and Storer too, all in one shot!"

"Be pretty tricky to make it work out. I mean, we'd have to do some fast talking."

"Let me think about it." LaGloria pulled on her panties, did a quick aerobic stretch and punched the old one-two into empty air.

Suddenly Tweed's passion drained away. In its place he felt a dull dread as if he'd learned that he had been selected for duty as a juror or as a pallbearer.

CHAPTER 13

He said it before and he'd say it again. This gig was sweet. Rick Rose had done lots of shit work and he had a lot of shit jobs. Mostly day labor, which was fine with him. Only problem with day labor was that unless you got to the labor pool real early, you generally had to wait all friggin' morning for a tag. Once you got your tag, you reported to the crew foreman, and then he made you line up with all of the other day laborers who got the same color tag.

Rick usually ended up with a yellow tag, and that meant he'd be working on a garbage truck. Green tags meant road crew, that is, working out on the county highways; grunt work in the heat or the cold or the what all nature throws at you. Guys stuck with road duty worked right alongside the practically unpaid convicts on the one hand and the overpaid contractors on the other. But at least that was better than blue tags. Blue meant water, or more like sewer, 'cause if you got a blue tag you knew you'd be shoveling shit out of some catch basin, or cleaning the crud out of manholes. White tags went to the dudes that could type and shit like that. Rick never got a white tag, so he never seen any of the places where them dudes worked, but he heard stories. For one thing, they always worked indoors, and for another thing, they didn't handle fish or shit or garbage so they didn't stink after a day's work. Rick hated the blue tags and his chick even said that if he worked in the sewer he could forget calling her when he got off work. The damned garbage trucks were bad enough. Funk stayed with you for hours, but you could wash it off and cover it with aftershave. Rick had heard of blue team workers being kicked off of buses and trains for stinking them up so bad. Imagine spending a day hauling crap out of a culvert, and then having to walk home in the company of your own stench. And we're talking eye-watering odor here, dead critters and rotted vegetation and that acrid ammonia aroma.

Anyway, after a few days working for Weed, Rick would have enough cash to skip day labor for a week. Not that he'd been going there much lately. After the state had declared him disabled, he'd been collecting a bi-weekly stipend that took care of his rent and cigarettes and such. He couldn't afford beer or wine, but he wasn't supposed to drink when he was taking the meds they gave him. It sucked having to put up with the doctors and the tests and all the bullshit, but he had to admit that the pills seemed to help him think clearly. And it had been a while since he had one of his so-called 'spells', the episodes of unaccountable rage and outright mania he had long endured.

His memory was still up to snuff, too, and as a mental exercise he carefully went over the pertinent facts that Sharlae had been able to recall from her ordeal with the kidnappers. Large General Motors sedan, dark blue or black, four doors, with a spotlight next to the driver's side mirror, whitewall tires, and a Dapper Ferguson bumper sticker on both bumpers. When they were following Sharlae, the guys seemed to know their way around, so they were locals, but they weren't anybody she knew or recognized. They picked her up on the Rossie end of the parkway, so it was reasonable to assume they were following her out of the square, or out of Westbury Circle. Nothing peculiar about the interior of the car, the radio was off and she was squeezed in with four big boys, two in the front and two in the rear with her.

First she claimed that no names were ever mentioned in her presence, but when Rick pressed her, telling her to think of the times when her kidnappers were hurrying or yelling, she came up with 'Bo' or 'Mo', she wasn't sure which. He was one of the dudes in the back seat. Then she said that when the driver of the GM yelled to the guy who drove her car, he said something that sounded like "Pissa!" but it could have been his name.

With these facts crowding into the back of his mind, Rick started compiling, allowing a little free association to take place. He had found that when he needed to come up with a solution to a problem or when he wanted to figure something out, the best thing to do was to let it percolate, let it cogitate, and wait for the answer to present itself. Might not be fast, might not be accurate, but it worked.

But even when you're thinking you have to do something, and right now Rick was heading to Rossie square. It was still early in the day but he'd poke around and keep his eyes open and see who was about. Just as importantly, he'd keep his ears open and try to get a sense of the talk on the street.

It was only natural that everybody would be buzzing about the murders in the Arbs, and Rick would have been thrilled if Weed had asked him to snoop out that one. Just goes to show that Weed is all business. Someone offs his girlfriend's brothers and he acts like it's same shit different day. Another thing about Weed that impressed Rick was the way he was looking after Sharlae. He's got murder on his doorstep and yet he's out trying to kick ass and take names for one of his own.

That's respect. If Rick was a businessman like Weed he'd be all over that shit. You can't run a business and let people mess around with your operation. Kidnapping your people? That's disrespect! Rick would teach 'em, same way he was sure Weed was gonna do, as soon as he got all the pertinent information.

Because the payback is a bitch. It goes around and around and it comes around and around. Like they say, you wanna dance, you gotta pay the piper, or he's gonna take his pipe and whack you upside the head. John Lennon said it in his song:

Instant Karma's gonna get you
It's gonna hit you right in the head
Better get your shit together darling
Pretty soon you're gonna be dead

CHAPTER 14

In order to date all of these events, to place them in some kind of temporal perspective, one need only consider that all of the principle actors involved in the conflict between Des and Tweed, and all of the ancillary characters as well, got on the phone at some point early in the action and called other members of the cast. Without overstating its relative importance, it may be observed that the telephone was the medium, the "place" where most of the action took place on Friday morning. Indeed the telephone was the common element of technology that was used, shared and depended upon not only by everybody in Rossie, but in American society.

Other eras had been closely associated with different technologies but the 1980's was defined and put into focus by telecommunications. This was the age of the phone, the fax and the instant credit card transaction, and it was poised on the cusp of the digital era that was soon to revolutionize both commerce and culture.

As an additional reminder of how these events were framed and how they fit against the backdrop of a larger world, it is helpful to examine some of the other key indicators of the times.

Ronald Regan was the President of the United States, his Vice President was George Bush, and from their bastion of power they surveyed a world in turmoil. Favoring 'cowboy diplomacy', Regan, a former movie actor, tended to 'shoot from the hip' in response to international threats and crises. For example, in early 1986 the president ordered a punitive military air strike against Libya for allegedly harboring terrorists.

Elsewhere on the world stage, two tyrants, dictator Jean-Claude Duvalier from Haiti, and kleptocrat Ferdinand Marcos from the Philippines, were taking their final bows. Having abused their power and having plundered their homelands, both abdicated and went into ignominious exile.

In the Soviet Union, the promise of nuclear power turned to deadly peril when an accident occurred at the plant at Chernobyl, resulting in a massive leak of radiation and the eventual melt down of the reactor. People, crops and livestock were poisoned and a broad swath of the northern hemisphere was contaminated.

Meanwhile in the US, the manned space program suffered a severe setback when the space shuttle Challenger exploded shortly after launch, killing all of the astronauts and scientists on board. The tragedy was one of a series of reverses in the latter part of the twentieth century that shook the faith, self-esteem and pride of the nation.

Violent crime, once relegated to the cities, had become commonplace in the US, affecting 54 out of every 1000 people. Unemployment was at 7%, the median household income was just under $25,000, and a postage stamp cost 22 cents. The federal debt reached 2 trillion dollars.

In 1986 the Supreme Court reaffirmed abortion rights, and resumed their work under the leadership of a newly appointed Chief Justice, the honorable William Rehnquist. The other two branches of government became locked in conflict after congress opened an inquiry into the administration's covert program of selling arms to Iran in order to fund the Nicaraguan Contras as part of a CIA-sponsored counter-insurgency effort.

Teams from Boston won the NBA championship and lost the World Series; and in football the New England Patriots humiliated themselves in New Orleans when they lost the Super Bowl. *We Are*

The World was the song of the year, *Out of Africa* was the motion picture of the year, and Nintendo had finally arrived in the US.

From his self-imposed exile in Rossie, Des considered news of domestic and world events to be no more than the background chatter during a performance of the great Irish opera, The Troubles. Since 1974, much had happened in Northern Ireland, and at the same time, very little had changed. Indeed, the signing of the Anglo-Irish Agreement in November of 1985 had failed to assuage the fears or restore the confidence of either Republican/Nationalist or Loyalist/Unionist factions.

It was with mixed emotions that Des heard the news about the recent upsurge in violence by Loyalist paramilitary forces, because much of the violence was directed at members of the Royal Ulster Constabulary. Apparently, although Republicans like Des considered the agreement to be a sell-out and hence would not support it, Unionists were utterly appalled by it.

In November of 1985, 100,000 Unionists gathered at Belfast City Hall under the banner 'Belfast Says No' to hear their leaders condemn the Agreement. Although they complained about a lack of consultation going into the negotiations, their chief objection to the deal that had been signed by Margaret Thatcher, then British Prime Minister, and Garret FitzGerald, then Taoiseach (Irish Prime Minister), was that they felt it threatened their status within the United Kingdom. In response to the Anglo-Irish Agreement, the Ulster Unionist Party Executive voted to end their long-standing special relationship with the British Conservative Party. Furthermore, Unionists launched a strike on March 3 that disrupted life throughout Northern Ireland. Factories and shops were closed; and in a bid to spread fear and intimidation, Loyalists set up barricades on the roads during the day and they rioted at night.

The increase in attacks by Loyalist paramilitaries forced the British into the embarrassing necessity of sending troops to support the RUC against the Unionists. In the month of April, Loyalists firebombed 50 RUC families and 79 Catholic families out of their homes.

During this time a young man named Keith White became the first Protestant to die during the conflict as a result of being shot by a plastic bullet fired by security forces. (Thirteen Catholics were also killed by rubber or plastic bullets during the Troubles, eight of them children.)

All in all, the Agreement was another step in the incremental process of increasing the political as opposed to the military pressure being brought to bear on the conflict. In essence, it affirmed that any change in the status of Northern Ireland would only come about with the consent of the majority of the people living in Northern Ireland. It had been broadly supported as well as partially sponsored by the Social Democratic Labor Party in Ireland, but Sinn Fein leader Gerry Adams said that it only copper-fastened partition and British rule.

Politics may have offered a glimmer of hope, but guns and bombs were still the weapons of choice among partisans operating on the ground. In that regard, Des had plenty of work to do and plenty of opportunities to do it. He saw the Loyalists becoming bolder by the moment and he knew that they were well armed.

By now, money to support the IRA was flowing not only from North America, but also from Libya. In fact, a year and a half later in 1987, a ship headed for Ireland from Libya was intercepted by a French naval patrol in the Bay of Biscay. The freighter Eksund contained 150 tons of weapons including 1,000 AK47 rifles, 10 antiaircraft machine guns, one million mortar shells and one million rounds of ammunition. The interception marked the end of a spectacular run of shipments masterminded by one of Des' contemporaries, ex-IRA quartermaster Michael McKevitt.

Although the scale of Des' operation never matched that of McKevitt's, his contributions were augmented by the efforts of similar enterprising Irishmen throughout the diaspora. Some used commercial ocean liners, some used connections in shipping outfits or they took advantage of military transport options. Some still smuggled the old cross-border routes, arms trails that started at locations throughout Europe and ended in places like Armagh and Eniskillen.

What had been a stagnant pool of arms in the North in 1969 was later refreshed and supplied by a steady trickle of new weapons throughout the early 1970s. In the latter part of the decade and in the early 80's, many tributaries added to the growing river of arms flowing into Ulster. Due to the ever changing dynamics of the situation, Des was forced to adapt. If he was going to continue smuggling "defensive" weapons into Ireland he would have to do it with IRA cooperation. By 1986 he was just one of countless American smugglers vying for the security, manpower and sanctioned access the IRA provided.

Some years ago his friend AD Makepeace had told him that he had become marginalized, that he was irrelevant. Well then he certainly made himself relevant when he started bringing in shipments of arms from the States. However, over the ensuing years a gradual change had occurred in two respects. One was the forfeiture of his independence as he slowly permitted the IRA to dictate the size of the shipments, the type and quantity of items on the manifest, and the timing and coordination of the offloads. The other change occurred when Makepeace made the switch from fishing vessels to passenger pleasure boats. He had done so because despite the proliferation of world-wide fishing fleets it was still too risky and blatantly phony to make repeated transatlantic runs in an Irish fishing trawler before the watchful eyes of the US Coast Guard, the Irish Gardai and the British Navy. Makepeace had been astoundingly fortunate not to have been boarded and searched, but he was prudent to make the transition and operate under the corporate name Trade-Wind Tours with a swifter, less-suspicious class of vessels. Then after the Samhain trip last year, he had returned to the US in his most recent acquisition, a posh luxury liner fit for the Royal family.

Makepeace was his principle supplier, his indispensable ally in the long tedious effort to help bring about an end to the British occupation in Northern Ireland. If they made some money and broke some international shipping laws along the way, then so be it. Des had always believed that most of the people whom he was occasionally required to bribe were secretly in favor of what he was doing, although he also understood that, if asked, all of them would readily deny any knowledge whatsoever of his existence, let alone his cause.

Furthermore whenever Des had needed to interact with the IRA, either at home or abroad, Makepeace had served as his proxy, spokesman and representative, and had proved himself to be more than adequate. Because of his steadfast assistance, Des was able to maintain an image as a retired businessman, one who traveled to his hometown Boyle twice a year as an elder visiting relation from America. Des had no idea what kind of file had been kept on him by the incumbent security forces, but he imagined that it was pretty clean, thanks in no small part to the cooperation of people like Makepeace.

Des' wife Christine had also been his staunch supporter and a promoter of the cause in her own right. But only when his sons took their place either at his side or in his stead would his dream would be fulfilled. He had always envisioned them standing with him, shoulder to shoulder with the courage of the Kelleys to face any challenge.

It might be difficult to objectively understand how Des came to hold his views, or to understand what had inspired him to make the choices he had made. How was it that the son of an honest barman who was no more radical in his politics than the next fellow, should be so extreme and unyielding in his own beliefs?

It was true that his father had kept a framed copy of the Proclamation on display in his bar, but he held no grudge against the British. Some of his best customers were British 'landed gentry', who owned summer homes in the vicinity. He was no table-thumping rabble-rouser, no night-stalking country militiaman.

Much of the republican ideal had drifted into song and folklore, and it was more a matter of quiet tacit approval of the IRA than active participation. Not that he wouldn't welcome the citizen soldiers in his pub, for it had always been there to feed, cheer and sometimes house the gallant boys when needed. But he, like his grandson, had remained rather independent.

Buck Kelley had been working for years keeping the pub going, and establishing his own family in the old homestead. Now he was married and his wife was expecting their first child. A little late by Des' way of thinking, but better than never. Keiran certainly wouldn't be producing any offspring, and Tweed was a playboy, too busy carrying on to think of his future.

Buck had always been careful to avoid any involvement in his father's political and business activities, a decision Des applauded. If the pub was known as a haven for republican activism, it would only draw unwanted attention.

And yet Buck's best friend Diarmaid was just the opposite. He was one of the young firebrands of the movement, who planned and agitated and loudly wore his heart on his sleeve, usually with a mug in his hand. Des had met Diarmaid some years ago, and since then hadn't stopped wishing that his son Tweed were more like him. Diarmaid was the son of one of Des' old comrades from the days of the border raids, one of many in the old brigade who had since been laid to rest. He did his father proud by the looks of him, and Des himself would be proud to call him his son.

The question was what to do about his son, Tweed. There was a time when he would consult with his wife over such a matter, but he and Christine weren't getting along just now. She couldn't seem to forgive him, and heaven help him, he didn't know if it was because of his frequent infidelities, his alcoholism, his failure to stand by her during her frequent illnesses, or all of it combined. Chris and Des, Des and Chris...they had been two sides of the same coin, but now when he flipped that coin it always came up tails. Tweed was his problem and he would handle it.

His gut told him that the best thing to do would be to lean on him hard. Bring the boy in for questioning in the same way that the security units debriefed the ASUs (Active Service Units) back home. Get it all out in the open. Who were the fucking McManus boys and why did they want to kill Des? How did they know to use Bricky's name? Did Tweed know anything about it? Did LaGloria?

But Tweed was his youngest son, his baby boy. He couldn't harm the dear lad. Then again, roughing him up a bit might do him some good. And yet, would it not reflect poorly on Des' authority and leadership if he were forced to interrogate his son in front of his men? After all, what kind of leader doesn't have the support of his own son?

Perhaps he could strike a balance, and instead of coercing, threatening or abusing Tweed, he could simply have him followed? He could easily justify following the boy when there was a chance that he was in danger as well. That's it- have one of his men follow Tweed in the manner of a silent bodyguard, someone who stays at a respectful distance and keeps an eye on the kid. Perhaps Des could discover what he needed to know simply by observing Tweed's movements.

This was just the kind of thing he would usually assign to Bricky. Bricky the gentle giant, the poor son-of-a-bitch who got wrapped up in that business with the RUC. Friends had gotten him out of Ireland in a hurry, and without much time for reflection the best place for him seemed to be with his uncle Tom. Brother Thomas Morris, that is, lately the headmaster of the Xaverian School for Boys.

Morris, one of Des' closest friends, quickly found that he could not abide Bricky, who had an uncannily good-natured way of getting into trouble. Before long Uncle Tom had packed him into an apartment on Mission Hill, which turned out to be the first of many apartments he would inhabit during his extended stay in America.

Bricky, all of 6'4", and 280 lbs, had a congenial, open manner, and the kind of rare sweet face you usually only see in Ireland. Folks he met were always happy to buy him a drink and bring him into their circles. Unfortunately, on more than one occasion the good folks he met were in fact only interested in exploiting his bulk and his apparent gullibility.

The following incident easily illustrates a typical scrape for Bricky: It happened one evening in the Annex section of downtown. He had just completed a one-day brick and mortar job in a condo, one of a dozen subdivided units Des was carving out of an old warehouse. As he walked toward the subway he came upon a familiar looking friendly Irish bar, full of familiar-looking friendly Irish folk. Chatter, drinks, darts, jokes, songs, laughter, more chatter and more drinks, and he emerged with two new buddies. All they wanted, they claimed, was some help getting their car started. The little freckle-faced guy was going to be the designated driver and get his inebriated pal Timmy back home.

The way Bricky tells it, his new friends led him around the streets looking for their car for some time, both saying that they were having trouble finding it because they were so tipsy. Then they came upon a sleek little foreign jobby, and the little guy said, "That's it! That's Timmy's car!" Well, Timmy piled into the passenger seat and Freckles took the wheel and Bricky got behind the rear bumper to give the car a shove. He set his feet, braced himself against the little car and moved it well past the ten yard marker for a first down. A wheeze from Bricky, a cough from the exhaust, and the fancy sports car was yowling around the corner like a frisky bear cub. The two drunks never looked back.

It took only a moment for Bricky to catch his breath, but he was still bent over a bit when the police car arrived at his side, and the two officers that were in it jumped out and grabbed him.

"What's this? Is it a crime to help someone start their car?"

The cops looked at each other and laughed. "Yeah," replied one, "It is when it's not their car."

Some people have that kind of luck, and the fact that more people don't is probably due to the ones like Bricky, who are inordinately unfortunate. If the owner of the sports car hadn't just come out of a restaurant to see his car being stolen, if the guys in the car hadn't immediately gone speeding past a police cruiser, and if another cruiser hadn't coincidentally been in the same neighborhood, then perhaps it wouldn't have looked so bad for Bricky. Otherwise he might have gotten away with it, and if he was really lucky, he might have continued on to the subway thinking that he had done a good deed.

It got to the point when his good-intentioned friends and relations became reluctant to help him for fear of some freak backlash. The old sod was a hot potato in the first place, living without a Visa or green card, and wanted by Interpol, and though he was typically penniless, his only real skill was laying bricks. It was a world of guilds, unions, licenses and insurance, and he worked without credentials or references in a craft that was in decline.

That was why, now that Des decided he needed someone to do the job, he would have called Bricky to follow his son. It was the kind of task that he could do without much risk or effort. But Bricky was in the mountains shooting squirrels, of all things, with his uncle Tom, of all people. So Des would have to find someone else.

CHAPTER 15

"Kuhn- how's it going?"

"Oh yeah, Weed, you said you was gonna call. It's going. What's up? Something you need, something you want me to do?"

"Maybe so…who's on guard duty tonight? P-head?"

"Yeah, Pecker's on, and so is Trudy."

"Alright, do me a favor, will ya? Keep Trudy in the office until, uh, well, as long as you can. Maybe until she has to take a shit. P-head I can handle."

"Almost anybody can handle Peckerhead," said Kuhn with a derisive laugh.

"Yeah, well, depends on what side of the fence you're on, if you know what I mean."

"I take it you'll be on the right side."

"I'll be on the inside," said Tweed.

"That's the right side. What're you after?"

"You don't know nothing, man."

"Nope, and I don'wanna, not me,"

"Right; catch you later. And thanks, man."

Kuhn could be trusted. Tweed wasn't the only one who thought so. Tweed trusted him to sell his dope and to manage part of the sales district. But at Rossie Towing he was trusted with 'the scam'.

In order to understand the scam like Kuhn did, one would have to first understand that Rossie Towing was a firm run by cops; namely, detectives Storer and Rima. Since cops ran the joint, it was only partially legit, and overwhelmingly crooked. A cynical person might want proof. Come now, it was clearly stated that the company was run by Storer and Rima. However, for additional persuasion read on: Most towing outfits made their money on towing and related services. Rossie made its money on back-door scrap sales, wholesale auctions, and retail sales for a select clientèle.

A typical city driver, occasionally subject to parking citations and the threat of towing, might expect that the police were in charge of selecting who gets towed, and why. Not so in the case of Rossie Towing, where it was left to the discretion of the driver to make the determination. They had a token dispatcher, but the free-roaming drivers such as Kuhn were basically instructed to prowl the streets. They towed not only those vehicles tagged for violations, but also a range of other automobiles for a variety of reasons. For example, large cars such as sedans or a station wagons were subject to towing if they were parked parallel to the curb at either end of a row of cars, simply because they were easily removed, and worth more than a tow in scrap.

In this city there were countless legal justifications for towing, such as parking in the live zone of the ambulance entrance at a hospital, blocking the entrance to a driveway or parking lot, or abandoning a vehicle at the side of a road due to mechanical failure. But the drivers at Rossie Towing invented countless more violations. For example, the driver might tow a car because he thinks it's a shit box; conversely, he might tow one because it was included on his special watch list. Vehicles on the watch list were wanted for parts or overall desirability.

As soon as the drivers had the cars safely towed into the Rossie Towing lot located near the tracks in Jamaica Center, they looted them. The drivers reaped a heap of booty at this stage, and management considered the spoils to be a part of the compensation package.

Some of the drivers looked for cash and valuables, but Kuhn wanted items of a different intrinsic worth. First he wanted any emblems of rank or privilege. Police badges, military insignia, hats or uniforms. Secondly he wanted identification such as driver's licenses, proof-of-age, library cards, green cards, corporate pass cards. Sometimes he would come across items that he considered suitable as gifts for special friends. These might include umbrellas, opera glasses, books or records.

Kuhn's license collection, as random a sample of drivers in the greater metro area as might be assembled by any public interest research firm, was proudly displayed on a wall in the living room in his apartment. There on the top center row of the display could be found the driver's license of Dapper Ferguson himself. Apparently when he realized that his car had been towed, Dapper had the presence of mind, despite his considerable inebriation at the time, to call Billy Storer and save his car from destruction, dismemberment or sale. However he was, of course, too late to save his personal belongings, which Storer told him were better written off as lost.

After looting, the cars were sorted in the tow yard for disposition. Some were crushed whole and sold for scrap. Some were stripped for specific parts- such as exterior body panels or electronic control components or flashy non-oem accessories. The remainder of these cars then went into the giant compactor that Kuhn liked to call 'The Recycler'. Special cars were kept intact and sent to a local garage for processing. Serial numbers were altered or removed, locks were changed, and sometimes the cars were painted. Word was that the want-list cars were shipped to a clearing house in Texas and then on to Mexico, Central and South America.

All in all it was a very lucrative operation; as profitable as it was illegal. And yet the owners made no attempt to hide what they were doing from the public. The tow yard looked for all intents and purposes like a tow yard. A small crew of drivers and lot-boys ran the place with added security provided by the two faithful watch-dogs, Peckerhead and Trudy. But Tweed knew how to handle Peckerhead, as he had told Kuhn on the phone.

It hadn't been easy for Tweed to get time on the phone, as he practically had to pry it away from LaGloria. After his father and the dealers had called, LaGloria heard from a number of her girlfriends who called to express their condolences and to help her cry a little.

Detective Rima also checked in with LaGloria, and he promised to stop by with helpful information, "Kind of a rundown for the loved ones of victims of violence crime." The next few days were going to be difficult, he said, and though he had to ask some questions of her, he was also prepared to answer any that she might have.

She would have to face him alone now that Tweed had spoken to Kuhn and confirmed his plans to be elsewhere. First he'd rest up for a spell, maybe a half-hour or so, and then he'd prepare for his late-afternoon excursion to Rossie Towing.

Before he had a chance to place the telephone down it rang, startling him enough to make him drop it. He fumbled the receiver to a position at least somewhat close to his ear, and heard Rick Rose.

"Yeah, Weed, man, I got you some of the information that you wanted there."

"No shit, Rick? That was fast! Man you really get to it! What ya got?" Now Tweed's heart was pounding rapidly for a different reason.

"No, man, I wouldn't fuck with you; I'm serious."

"I know, Rick, I know. That's cool. Just tell me why you called."

"Well, I came down to Rossie, you know, to follow up on some leads that I got from Sharlae's deposition, see?"

"Deposition?"

Rick sounded embarrassed, "I just called it that, dude, to be business-like and all. So anyway, I'm down in Rossie and what do I see?"

Tweed waited. "What did you see? Tell me?"

"The car, man! The car that Sharlae was in. See, I was thinking about the things she said, and I remembered, hey, haven't I seen…"

"Never mind, Rick. Where'ja see it? Where's the car?"

"Right in front of me, man, right in fucking front of me."

"Where are you, then?"

"Oh, I'm at the Fores, Weed, it's down by…"

"I know where the Fores is. Just hang on, I have to think."

Shit. Tweed hadn't considered what he would do when or if he found the people who kidnapped Sharlae. But Rick had only found a car.

"Anybody in that car, Rick?"

"No, man, he's in the bar," he said, as if the fact were obvious.

"So you know who owns it?"

"No, man, not yet anyway."

"Then how do you know he's in the bar?"

"I don't know who owns it, but I do know who's driving it. It's Joey Atkinson."

No kidding? Joey Atkinson? His old man was a regular at the biz club. Tweed wondered where this was headed.

"So what do you want me to do? Should I go in and talk to him?"

"No, man, leave him alone. Wait until you find the other dudes who were involved." It could be a mistake to let this opportunity slide by.

"Tell you what, though. See if you can do anything to keep him there for a while. I don't know, maybe siphon the gas out of his tank, or something?"

"Might be tricky, dude, but I'll see what I can do," replied Rose, sounding cheerful.

"Alright, and call me back in a little while, say, twenty minutes, half an hour. I'm going to check on something, and I'll let you know how I make out."

Now LaGloria was clamoring for the phone again, but Tweed had another important call to make.

CHAPTER 16

AD Makepeace was well aware of the preeminence of the telephone among the tools of modern civilization, but he was also aware that as long as there had been telephones there had been eavesdroppers, and as long as there had been wires, there had been wire-taps. If any of the telephone conversations he held on Friday morning could have been recorded and the transcripts made available, then the district attorney, Det. Storer and Det. Rima, et al. would have snapped them up like bored frequent flyers grabbing the latest juicy bestseller at an airport duty-free shop.

And yet Makepeace was simply initiating an investigation of his own. With all due caution he arranged to make his calls from a secure line at one of the numerous dual-purpose locations held by British interests in the greater metropolitan area. In this instance he borrowed an office from an investment consultant-slash-spook, a lovely woman originally from Stokely-on-Trent.

Not only was she a gracious host but she was also a woman of impeccable taste as reflected in her clothing and her choice of office decor. These qualities, as well as her compelling femininity and the fact of her recent divorce intrigued Makepeace, and helped in no small way to appease the irritation and distaste he felt at having to impose upon her in the first place.

It would not be appropriate to mention the names of the individuals with whom he was speaking because they don't figure into the story in any other significant way. What is of interest to the narrative is what they had to say. For it was only after speaking with some of his contacts that Makepeace realized that although Des Kelley may have been the intended victim of an attack, it was in fact two young men who died in Rossie Thursday night. The two events had to be related, he concluded, because there's no such thing as a coincidental double homicide.

In Makepeace's recollection, Des had only said that someone had tried to kill him. How telling it was that he failed to mention that he left his attackers lying dead in the woods after the supposed assault. He and his men had been a little trigger-happy, or perhaps a little nervous themselves.

Well, at least he now understood the urgency with which Des had contacted him. If it had been a simple case of a personal assault, no matter how serious, Makepeace would have thought that Des could have handled it by himself. But with death on his hands Des could be facing additional retribution, and who knows what consequences.

The more Makepeace learned, the further he refined his tactics and altered his approach. Yet at this point he only knew enough to be as dangerous as a dull knife, and in this environment he would need to know enough to have an edge. He decided that his best bet would be an inside source, because there was no way that he could go and hit the streets personally. As a known associate of Des, he would only arouse suspicion. What he needed was reliable, first-hand information, from someone who was able to observe the situation casually and yet carefully. An informant. Any informant.

Now Makepeace was onto something, teasing the dangling threads of an idea and working them into the fabric of a plan. He called a friend who had solid connections in local law enforcement and told him what he had in mind. Was there any way, he asked, to find out who the feds might be working with in the area? How about the state police, or the municipal organized crime task force? Surely they must have informants on the streets. Couldn't he get the answer from a computer or something? He was told, in response, to wait.

Quickly now, and shrewdly he thought that if only he could recruit Des' youngest son, the rascal Tweed to be his eyes and ears, then he'd have the ideal tool with which to bring an end to his long association with Des Kelley, and to be safely rid of him as well. Thus both Tweed and Makepeace came for a time to occupy a space on the back burner of each other's minds.

For years his deal with Kelley had been based upon the mutual potential for profit, but while Kelley claimed an ulterior motive in defending his homeland, for Makepeace the goal was to gain exclusive access to ranking members of the IRA. Over the years he had become entrenched in his role, always urging restraint on his contacts in British intelligence so that he would not come under suspicion after their periodic successful operations. And though it was true that he had used Des in his bid to prove himself to the IRA, lately he had found himself becoming somewhat of a reluctant apologist for the Irish-American. The ultimate reversal came when Makepeace was forced to help Des prove himself in a manner that demonstrated his value to the effort, all the while protecting him from certain arrest and/or prosecution.

There had been times when he thought that he would expose the whole affair to British intelligence, but he kept putting it off until the right shipment came along. With the proper combination of timing and resources he could deliver the perpetrators, the evidence, and the money, take credit for his coup, and quietly slip out of the picture. But there was always just enough cash in the job for him, just enough danger and risk to entice him, and always the personal elements of faith established and rewarded, and trust bonded and sealed.

He had no idea how to go about recruiting Tweed. First he'd need to know how to approach the boy without scaring him off, and secondly he'd need some form of inducement, some incentive with which to purchase his loyalty. When he was a twenty-something year-old, the need for money was always his primary motivation. But he suspected that Tweed had different priorities. While he waited for a reply about the informants he could nurture this contingency plan.

As eager as he was to get on with the inquiry, he also relished the opportunity to 'kill some time'. His new lady-friend was willing to shut down her office early for the afternoon and accompany him to dinner with a promise of some delightful evening entertainment.

CHAPTER 17

"Hey, Griffin!" As he spoke into the telephone Tweed could picture his friend the info broker leaning against the wall of the social security office building in Rossie square, scanning the streets for familiar cars, and checking the sidewalks for cute chicks.

"Yo, Weed! I was just thinking about you! Remember the time when Bruno and Rat were down at…"

"Yeah, Gerry, listen," Tweed interrupted, speaking right over him, "I gotta ask you something." It was cold shutting him down like that, but when given half a chance the guy could talk a dog off a meat wagon.

"That's cool, man; shoot."

"There was a couple of guys you mentioned to me one time. You said they worked out of a van and they hit up people at the mall."

"Oh, yeah, the body work scam! I remember that one. The guys drive up next to your car when you're parking at the mall and they offer to do body work while you're in shopping. What was that guy's name?"

"That's what I'm asking you, Griff, the guy's name."

"Figures; ahm, let me see…"

"So, you still seeing that chick, what's her name, Karen?"

"Who? Karen? Oh, Karen Fa-,…Mitrano! Those guys you're looking for, they're the Mitranos!"

"Hey! I knew you'd remember!"

"But, ahm, Weed, ahm, they don't really do any body work, you know."

"That's not the way you told the story."

"Oh, so you remember. Alright, cool. You're gonna get in touch with them, huh? Should be interesting!"

"You'll hear all about it, no doubt."

Griffin chuckled as he crunched the receiver in between his chin and shoulder, and he searched his pockets for his 'little black book'.

"Speaking of girlfriends, I was talking to yours recently. Reason I mention it is because it was only the second time I ever talked to her."

"You were talking to LaGloria? When?"

"Wait a second; know when she called? It was yesterday. Shit, so much has happened that I'm losing track of time. She called yesterday, asking me if I'd seen you. Like I say, it was only the second time I talked to her so I didn't know who she was at first. And you know, that first time I talked to her I'll never forget 'cause she told me that her brother was in the IRA."

"LaGloria?" Tweed feigned incredulity.

"I ain't shitting, man, and I almost believed her, too, she was so…real. But I knew her brothers, you know, Nilbar and ah, the older one, the ones that got, well, you know."

Tweed did know, all too well. He'd heard this tale of the long lost brother who lived in Ireland. The rebel hero of her dreams. It was one of many she had concocted and related with seeming utter sincerity to anyone who would care to listen. In some tellings her brother was dead, in others he had recently completed some thrilling mission of strategic importance. But no matter how she portrayed her fantasies she always did so with a straight face, never betraying the slightest hint that she was making it all up.

He had gradually become aware of her behavior when they first started hanging out together, but he never made an issue of it. At first he thought that she had a rational reason to embroider her life with fictional relatives and imagined personal connections. He figured that she was simply overplaying the role of the drug-dealer's girlfriend, blurring the line between what was all too real for her and what she could only understand as utter bullshit. But soon Tweed recognized the figments of her exaggeration for what they were- elements and fragments borrowed from his life.

It wasn't like she was crazy or anything. She held down a good paying job, she had friends and colleagues, and she was articulate, personable and polished. If her 'creativity' didn't interfere with all of that, then where was the harm? Knowing LaGloria, he didn't believe that he could help by pointing out the inconsistencies in her story. And a shrink would only complicate matters by hanging her up with a complex. Why create doubt? The only time she became a problem was when others, people such as Griffin in this case, saw through her.

"By the way," he went on, "Karen's old news. I stopped going out with her ages ago. Now I go out with a little Puerto Rican number."

"No kiddin'? She speak English?"

"Geez, I don't know; I never asked. But we don't do much talking, anyway. Listen, I got your number here. And don't forget to tell 'em; Gerry sent ya!"

CHAPTER 18

Of all the incongruities for which the Fores was noted, the fact that it remained in business without offering any parking was the most striking. A deeply rutted alley alongside the bar led to a courtyard in the rear where the owners barely fit their two compact cars. But for the patrons of the establishment, the availability of parking depended upon a combination of chance, the good will of neighborhood home owners and lax enforcement on the part of the town beat cops and meter maids.

The car Rick Rose identified was a hemorrhage red 1977 Buick Deuce and a Quarter that belonged to Joe Atkinson, Joey Atkinson's father. Converted to diesel because the old man feared another energy crisis and because as a retired trucker he wanted to continue to patronize the same gas station at which he'd serviced and maintained his rig. In all other respects it was the same car Sharlae had described.

Rick Rose looked the car over and noticed that Joey had deliberately parked with the ass-end sticking out into the street, as if he had angle-parked in a parallel parking zone. Man, Rick's grandmother could park better than this- and she was dead! Joey probably thought his father's car would be safer if it was more visible. Rick had to smile, for he half-expected to see some rookie Rossie driver plow into the thing as he came careening around the corner.

OK, this was the car that Weed wanted disabled so that Joey wouldn't be going anywhere for a while. However, removing the gas did not seem to be an option. A modest tank like the one in the 225 might take six or seven minutes to drain, but there was no way Rick was going to double park in the middle of the street just so he could steal Joey's gas.

There wasn't anybody who could suck gas as fast and as efficiently as Rick. Siphoning fuel was what he did. In his custom converted Volkswagen Bug he roamed the streets of Rossie, Roosevelt and Jamaica Center scoping out abandoned buildings and vehicles from which to remove precious fluids.

When he saw a likely prospect such as an apartment unit slated for demolition or an empty municipal or county office building, he swooped, (his term) pulled his car in close, extended a 5/8" diameter fuel-resistant neoprene hose through the opened right hand fly window and inserted it into the filler spout of the selected tank. With a flick of a switch, his jiffy electric fuel pump silently started the siphon into a pair of 55-gallon drums he had installed in his car.

He had dreamed of designing secret compartments that would utilize every void and bulkhead in his Volkswagen, and of installing a pressurized system with gauges and indicators. But for capacity and practical considerations he basically removed the passenger's front seat, the complete rear seat and all of the superfluous upholstery in his bug in order to make everything fit. He lashed the drums in place with chains secured to cradles that he had welded to the floor.

Along with his pumping rig he also carried a tool box loaded with the basic automotive necessities as well as oil filler cap wrenches, an assortment of filler-cap lock keys, pry bars, bolt-cutters and the kind of implements that fall under the category "burglar's tools".

Rick wouldn't let much of anything stand between him and 200 gallons of home heating oil, and if necessary he'd resort to violence short of the bodily physical variety in order to achieve his ends.

In the neighborhood where he lived gas and oil were commodities that people did without if they couldn't beg, borrow or steal them from somewhere. Factoring in labor, Rick wasn't making a lot of money on the deal, but he was redistributing valuable resources, and helping folks in need. Number two oil for the elderly and the families with young children, unleaded regular gas for the folks driving to work or picking up the groceries or delivering the kids to the community clinic.

One might think that storage would present a problem. The fluids Rick collected were foul-smelling, environmentally hazardous and difficult to work with, but he never had a problem storing the shit because whatever he couldn't unload on his friends, relatives or loyal customers he simply turned in for recycling.

The guy at the local recycling center let him browse through the general household junk in exchange for so many gallons of oil. One time he snagged a cool golf-ball retriever. Never played golf, but what the heck? The light-weight aluminum collapsible shaft was equipped with a basket like a mechanical hand poised for plucking, and the stylish handle featured leatherette foam wrap tape and an attached lanyard. The thing was stowed with the rest of his shit in the car right now, but it wasn't going to help him put Atkinson's car out of commission.

The old coil-wire trick would be effective if were able to get under the hood, but he had already checked the door and just as he had expected the car was locked and he didn't have the expertise to remove the grill and the latch cable. A potato in the exhaust pipe? Shoot, no potato in the tool kit and no substitute, either.

Weed wasn't going to wait all day. It was time for Rick Rose to shit, get off the pot or die trying, and in the end he opted for the crude, effective and easy way out.

CHAPTER 19

It gets fun now as the heroic Tweed, suffering from pedal agony that was only somewhat mitigated by a self-prescribed and self-administered dose of Percodan, set out to infiltrate Rossie Towing. At the same time Bone and Og prepared to depart for the northwest suburbs where they hoped to find the house where Tweed had stashed about 80 kilos of pot.

Tweed had a number of reasons for instructing Bone to retrieve a duffel-bag full of dope, that was about 25 pounds, and to bring it back for distribution among the franchisees. First of all he wanted to dispel any notion that his recent personal difficulties would in any way impinge upon his business. Lest there be any doubt about his ability to supply a consistently high-quality product to the streets of the city, Tweed intended to temporarily saturate the market. There was however an apparent contradiction between this purely reactionary strategy and his normal operating procedure. Hadn't he reiterated to his dealers the importance of inventory rotation, and the necessity of establishing a days-supply limit that was based upon historical data, shelf-life, storage capacity and re-order lag time? He recalled the conversation he had with Bone when he had told him what he expected.

"Burple and Bissel? What the..?" Bone's tone implied that he felt his intelligence had been insulted.

"That's just a mnemonic. BRP is Best Reorder Point, and BSL is Best Stocking Level; see, you want to know the point at which you should re-up so that you never run out, and you need to know how much to keep on hand at any time given the re-order lag. You might call me on Thursday and say that you want another kilo, but I can't get to you until Friday. You have to adjust for any possible lag on the re-up."

"Why can't I just play it by ear, you know, go by experience?"

"The only reason that matters is because I want you to do it this way. But I'll explain, because I don't want any hard feelings over this shit.

"See, we're dealing drugs, but one of our most important assets is information. We know our customers, we know the market and we know the product. But we also have to know how to sell and not only how to stay in business, but how to stay ahead of the competition. The way we do that is by keeping track of information. The only way to know how much weed you should have on hand is to know how much you've sold in the past. It's alright to make an educated guess as long as you're educated. You have to keep track of figures like that because after a while it gets hard to remember. You might know how much you're selling this week, how much you sold last week, maybe even how much you sold over an entire season. But you sure as hell aren't going to remember how much you sold at this time last year.

"Information like this helps across the board, too. I'll tell you, I want to know how business is in Jamaica Center and how it is in White City, and who's selling the most. If one guy is doing a lot better than the others maybe I can find out what he's doing right, and get everybody else to do it."

Bone couldn't bitch. Tweed wasn't asking for reports, he wasn't auditing him, and he wasn't going to test him on his knowledge or retention. In fact Tweed had set the bar fairly low. He simply explained his concepts, saw to it that his dealers understood them, and then hoped that they put his theory into practice.

The second reason for sending the unlikely duo of Bone and Og to make a stash grab had to do with Bone.

As the head of this little outlaw conclave of free-market entrepreneurs Tweed would have to be completely insensitive not to have heard the many hints with which Bone had buttered the bread of their conversations. He wanted a bigger stake in the operation, more responsibility, more authority. He wanted to show what he was made of; and he also felt that his age advantage of almost two years over Tweed should somehow earn him special consideration. Tweed could dig it.

Another factor that Tweed had been empathetically led to consider regarding good old Bone was the stress being placed upon him. He knew that he had certainly been personally affected by the deaths of his girlfriend's brothers so it was understandable that Bone would be affected by the death of his sister's boyfriend. And they both knew Frankie; in fact, Bone more so than Tweed.

He was pretty sure that the two of them had grown up in the same neighborhood. He remembered a story Bone had once told him when they were in high school about a kid who could make a standing broad jump to the top of a fire hydrant.

"This friend of mine- you wouldn't believe it! He just kinda crouches a little and- boom! Jumps like a grasshopper- right to the top of the hydrant. I seen him jump over a park bench in one bound! From front to back! And he can jump back again!" The normally unflappable Bone was talking about the amazing Frankie McManus, the human frog.

Tweed saw Frankie do a couple of similar stunts after he started hanging out with LaGloria.

One afternoon in particular everyone in the crowd had dropped tabs of mescaline. They were grooving to the kaleidoscopic patterns cast upon the ground by the late afternoon sun shining through the maple leaf canopy overspreading the lower end of the street. Tweed remembered how Frankie said that he could jump to the roof of a Volkswagen from the ground, starting from a standing position right next to the car.

Volkswagens were 'in' back then because one of Carmine's buddies had recently opened up a repair shop called Bug Love. The cars were parked all around the block in various states of repair. A family of cats had taken up residence in one of them.

So once the claim was made it was of course challenged, with wagers accumulating on the side and a crowd seemingly appearing out of nowhere. For his part Tweed found the proceedings to be insufferably amusing. By the time Frank was ready to jump Tweed was in full hallucinogenic thrall, tripping with an intensity best described as sensory overload. All he recalled of the jump was a rainbow rush of wings as if a flock of colored doves had suddenly launched into the air en masse.

This was an occasion when everyone was looking but only Frank actually saw what happened. However the general consensus was that he made it. He had earned a place in local legend although he never sought any wider recognition or attempted in any way to certify his record.

Shaking off these recollections, Tweed again thought of Bone.

Talk about your cukes…Bone was slab-cool…not only emotionally, but intellectually. Of course, his brain-waves were about as scrambled as they were detached.

Neither Tweed nor LaGloria had the knowledge, compassion, or foresight to have anticipated that Bone would be affected by Frankie's death. Even his token expression of condolence for her loss had hardly triggered their awareness; in fact nothing in his behavior had tipped them off. It was Gary who had filled them in about Frankie, and Susan, and thus Bone.

Sometimes people don't know what's good for them, and in this case Tweed deemed that a substantial mission would be good for Bone.

Demanding work to keep him physically and mentally occupied.

Above and beyond Tweed's concerns for the status and appearance of his business and the health and welfare of his friend and business associate Bone, there was another, overriding reason to send for the 25 pounds of sweet bud. And this reason had to do with Og.

There's only so much exposition the reader can reasonably be expected to tolerate. And yet without the conventional background and character development Tweed's actions in respect to Og could seem unjustifiably cruel and pitilessly inconsiderate. Especially in comparison to his treatment of Bone.

Rather than saying that whatever befell Og he brought it upon himself, we might just as well let the facts stand or fall by their own merits. Following them from one to the next as one might connect the dots on the back of a kiddie place mat, the picture is revealed a little at a time, but from the outset a judgment may be made as to what it represents simply by looking at the outline.

To his friends Og could be frustratingly imprecise about his ethnicity. He neither made assertions nor affirmed the guesses or theories of others, yet he was rather vehement in his denials. He would only say what, in effect, he was not.

His features were no help. In the salad bowl of diversity that was Rossie in the '70s and '80s, he was more of a radish than say, a leafy green. His black hair, dark eyes, dark skin and beak nose were indicators that pointed to his place of ancestral origin as being anywhere from a vast gene pool stretching from Morocco to Pakistan.

Indeed there had been an influx of people from the Mediterranean and Middle Eastern countries since the US immigration quota restrictions were eased in the 1970s. Rossdale welcomed families such as the Mesthenes from Greece and the Jabbours from Syria, while Eban's family immigrated from Israel and Og's came from Lebanon.

As Christian Maronites, religious minorities living in an overwhelmingly Muslim country, Og's parents had been increasingly uncomfortable about raising their children in their beloved homeland in the 1960s.

For the '50s and '60s had been boom years in Lebanon, when Beirut was a capital of international prestige and renown, and construction, trade and tourism were enjoying a period of unprecedented growth. However, the gloss on the jewel of the Mediterranean was marred by political instability, ethnic tension and religious discord. The result was a nation boasting world-class cities and world-class resorts, that was unable to take its place in the community of sovereign and independent nations of the world. Instead, an all-too familiar pattern was repeated as competing factions both internal and external vied for political and religious control of the people, the land and its resources for strategic reasons.

More than 90% of the Lebanese people were Arabs; however, that degree of uniformity did not extend to religion. Just over 20% of the total population were Christians, while an additional 54% were Muslim, and the remainder were Orthodox, Druse and others.

The Christian presence in Lebanon went back to the Roman and Byzantine Empires. Saint Maron, for whom the Maronites were named, was a 4th century evangelist from Antioch who helped spread Christianity throughout the region of Syria and Lebanon.

The predominance of Christianity in Lebanon was especially relevant during the Crusades. Maronites were valued as skilled archers and military men, and Lebanon was considered to be a place of refuge and a crucial part of the line of defense as the Crusaders worked their way from Constantinople to Jerusalem.

However throughout the ages Maronites suffered periodic massacres at the hands of their Muslim brothers, vastly reducing their numbers. In the 19th century brutal onslaughts by Druse, Sunni and Shiite Arabs decimated the Christian communities. As a result European governments applied pressure to the Ottoman sultans to force them to cede control of 'Greater Lebanon', placing it under control of Christian Ottoman officials. Subsequent interventions by the Americans, the British and the French secured the future of the nation, although they could not guarantee peace or stability.

For an example of the turmoil, in 1962 a military coup was attempted and crushed in Beirut. Two years later Bashir Gemayel, head of the Phalange militia and himself a Maronite, ran for president and was defeated. Then in 1967 Lebanon nominally supported the Arabs in the Arab-Israeli War, and in 1968 Israel launched reprisal attacks against Palestinians who had established strongholds in Lebanon's Bekaa Valley. In 1970 Gemayel ran and failed again in his bid for the presidency; and in 1975 the nation devolved utterly into civil war, with hostile conflict raging between armed and entrenched factions of Muslims, Christians and Palestinians.

The purpose of this brief foray into Lebanese history is not necessarily to demonstrate that Og's parents had acted wisely in moving when they did, but to draw a parallel between them and their Irish counterparts the Kelleys. They were worried by the political climate in Lebanon and by the potential for violence, just as Des and Christine Kelley had feared that Irish Catholics -not only in the north but south of the border as well- would be overrun and massacred by the northern Irish Protestants, the loyalist paramilitaries and the British army.

There is a prevailing viewpoint among its citizens that America is the promised land, the land of plenty and opportunity. However, Og's father, hereafter referred to as Mr. Z, readily disputed the notion that he gained any more in coming to the US than he lost in leaving his homeland.

Not so Og. Although he remembered little if any of his preschool days in the old country he equated Lebanon with the ghetto, with the scent of non-filtered Turkish cigarettes, strong coffee and sickly-sweet liqueur on the breath of his eccentric and exotic aunts and uncles.

He eschewed the language, shunned all personal ties to his heritage and ignored the stories and lessons taught to him by his elders. And even though it was in front of his house, he avoided the bench where his father and other Lebanese patriarchs met daily to sit and smoke and talk as if they were back in the old country.

As independent as he wished to be from his parents and his cultural identity, he was further removed and alienated from his peers, classmates and neighbors. Not comfortable with the freaks or the hippies, by no means a jock or a bully, in fact unable to fit in with any of the stereotypes that were promoted and marketed by modern media, Og became isolated and bitter. He would have preferred to be included in the minority groups such as the Italians or the Irish but they too abused him without compunction.

Like Tweed, Og fell in with the dope dealer Wayne Kenney, having become aware of the allure of marijuana and its furtive presence in the community. But whereas Tweed saw pot as a business opportunity that promised a means of making 'easy money', Og saw pot as a source of power. Money changed hands but so what? He chose to have nothing to do with that if possible. The herb possessed psychoactive properties, but who cares? Og believed that the drug was there to test him, and that his ability to ingest it was a reflection of his mental prowess and physical fortitude.

In time Og developed his addiction into a macho ego trip enhanced with rules that ultimately, paradoxically ensured his total lack of satisfaction. Of course, he did not see it that way, but Og was like a nymphomaniac who was unable to achieve sexual satisfaction while demanding more from each and every encounter. More stimulation, more variety, more, more, more. And while he was obsessed with factors such as whether he had smoked pot before or after eating, or the amount and quality of sleep he enjoyed in conjunction with the weed, or the timing and frequency of his bowel movements, his principle concern was with money. Because for Og, the best dope was free dope.

It became his persistent goal to acquire marijuana whether or not he had the money with which to pay for it. Accordingly he developed a number of stratagems specifically for obtaining free weed. Tweed heard about some of these tricks second-hand in a conversation with Nilvan, who at the time had recently been ripped of by Og. Until then he had counted Og among his friends.

"See, he says there's what he calls 'the saps'. These are dudes that can be conned, you know? But not just conned like tricking 'em into giving over money or something, but dudes that are like, almost willing to be duped, you know? Especially when they're looking for smoke. He gets them to go for a ride to get them a bag, then he has 'em wait while he goes in to score the shit. Now, you gotta picture this- first he makes the dude pay too much so he cops a few bucks profit. Now you can imagine he's in there laughing his ass off and smoking a bone with his buddy, whoever's got the dope, making his 'sap' wait in the car. Then he rips the bag off for a bud or two. But get this- when he hands the bag over he has the balls to ask for a bone as a reward for helping the guy out! And you know that when he gets the joint, the bonus joint, he's gonna roll it himself. And this brings up his next strategy.

"Og calls it 'The Pinch'. Dig. 'K- so he's holding your bag like this, see?" Nilvan held up a baggie that Tweed quickly scanned as a nickel A dirty, chafey one at that.

"Let's say he's looking at what you got for sale, or maybe you're lettin' him have a whiff of your bag, you know. Anyway, he's got a bag of pot in his hands like so, and," With the bag suspended between the thumbs and forefingers of both hands, Nilvan made a deft movement with his left hand not unlike flipping a bottle cap, then turned his hand palm outward and showed that he had captured a "pinch" of weed between his ring-finger and palm. "And I exaggerated the move. Imagine that you're not looking', and he's got a lot more practice. Said that he can do it with his ring-finger and palm, his little finger and palm, or between his thumb and practically any finger!"

Tweed's mind had immediately begun searching through countless images of Og holding bags- lids, halfs, ounces, up to his massive honker and inhaling deeply as if to secrete the entire contents of the sack in one immense nostril. Memories of Og greedily fingering buds as if he were sifting clumps of sand in a miner's pan in search of nuggets of gold.

"That's not all, man! Og told me about his 'bone scam'. This one is fucking unbelievable." Nilvan enunciated the word 'fucking' clearly in order to give it more weight.

"I wonder why he told you all of this?" Tweed more or less asked.

"I think for him it was like he was giving out tips; I don't know, giving me the benefit of his experience or something. But let me tell you how he does this bone thing. He gets stoned with a friend, somebody, anyone who's willing to smoke a joint with him. What he does is asks them to roll a joint. That's it. See, he waits 'til they're already pretty high, and for Og that's easy. Then when they roll the joint, he cops it. Just hides it or something, real fast like, and all innocent. Man, I'm saying that he whips the joint into his pocket while the dude is putting his bag away, and then, before the guy has a chance to say anything, he goes, 'Hey, man, when are you gonna roll that joint?'"

Og's ploy in the bone scam was simply to confuse his already stoned mark into rolling two joints instead of one. That way Og gets to smoke one now and one later. Nilvan had continued, "He said that I'd be surprised at how often it works. But you know, I'm really not. Surprised, that is. I mean, I think of all the times I rolled a joint and then forgot that I did it. But fuck me if that isn't the worst of it- he has another scam he calls the 'double roll'."

By this time Tweed was almost nauseated with the realization that he had likely been ripped off repeatedly by his so-called friend and business associate Og. And he understood why Nilvan had seemed to be getting so worked up.

"The way he does this one is pretty sweet, I gotta admit. He gets his 'victim' to let him roll a joint; and you know that a lotta people are freakin' lazy and would just as well let Og roll as do it themselves. Plus since people are pretty much merciless about roll jobs…"

Nilvan was referring to the fact that it was common practice in reefer smoking circles to criticize the tightness, fullness, cleanliness, symmetrical contour and overall aesthetic of a rolled number, and the roller frequently had to endure what amounted to fairly harsh treatment for a creation that was designed to last ten minutes at most.

"Yeah, I know," agreed Tweed, kicking himself for handing his bag and papers over to Og on countless occasions for rolling. "So what does he do when he gets the bag?"

"OK, so he gets the bag and he has this habit of making a little pile of dope in the palm of his hand so he can clean it up close to his face, pick out the seeds, you know…some people use a frisbee or an album cover…So what he's doing is prepping about twice the weed he needs for the joint he's rolling, and dropping the rest into his lap, or a bag that he has stashed in his pocket or someplace. If he cleans the shit on a table he makes sure that there's a little pile left over and he sweeps it all into his secret stash as if he's just getting rid of the seeds and stems. In this way he manages to cop an extra bone here and there and he always has enough for his head.

"Og calls it 'getting over'. It's like his way of getting back at anyone who might've done him wrong. Actually, I guess it's his way of getting back at everyone in general, just on principle."

So Tweed had learned from Nilvan that one of his top level dealers, the one responsible for Westbury Circle and Rossie itself, was a thief, a liar and a scumbag. And what's more, he was apparently indoctrinating others to be like him.

It was easy to get carried away, and to allow anger to sway his plans for a response to this challenge to his operation. After all as he told his 'employees', 'if you steal, you steal not only from me, but from my family, from the rest of the people who work with me, and from their families'. And Tweed would not tolerate people stealing from his family or the families of his friends. Tweed considered theft to be an abomination, and he was known to lecture his associates at length about the evils of larceny both within and outside the 'company'. He also stressed the point that he made no distinction between cash and product.

"Weed is cash," he said, "real money. Don't kid yourselves. Let me show you what I mean. Say you're sitting on $500 worth of reefer. You bought it as an investment. I mean, at $500, we're not talking head stash here, right? OK; so you go out to pick up a box of baggies and when you come back you discover that your roommate stole your stash and split. My question to you is, how much did you lose?

"Now wait a second before you say $500, because let me tell you, you'd be wrong. Think about it: First, you're out the $500 because that's the amount of cash you handed over for a quantity you were going to weigh out and sell for more. Then there's the acquisition fee- including the gas or car fare that you spent when you were going to pick the shit up, plus your ever-valuable time- in phone calls, delays, and actual trips to buy the dope, plus your exposure to risk. How much is it worth to you to avoid being busted? Face it, any one of us could get popped at any time. When you do it's gonna-costcha. Sure, you'll pay when the time comes, or you'll pay along the way for information or protection like some of us do," Tweed flashed a 'you got me' grin. "But either way you have to spread out the cost of your risk over the span of your career. Third, you have to consider storage. In an ideal world we'd all sell out on the first night when we get the shit. But for most of us, in most cases it takes a while to sell out all of your stock. Could be a day, could be a month. But all the time you're holding you're also paying rent and phone and electricity and whatever else it takes to stay in business. It adds up. Now you're talking:

$500 for the pot,

$ 10 for gas,

$125 for risk and rent

"But what about distribution? You have to weigh it and split it up and put it into bags...all cost factors. But if you've been ripped off, you're not gonna be splitting anything up! You're out of business! You missed out on profit! And this last item is worth almost as much as the rest of them put together. Alright, if you sell it whole, to one guy, you might make $50. On the other hand if you had broken it up wisely and marked it up reasonably, then you could have made $500 on the deal. So where are we now? I'm guessing that the total runs to $1200! See, you may have lost only $500 worth of reefer, but your loss in real money, real term is $1200.

"That's what stealing really costs. But let me add something: I catch anyone stealing from me and I'm gonna charge them twice the value. So for that same $500 sack, I'm gonna make my roommate pay me $2400, if I ever catch him. That's right- $2400! $1200 for the reasons I just went over and $1200 again for my aggravation.

"Now, if you say, 'What? You're saying that I have to agree to pay double for any weed that I steal?' The answer is no, I'm saying that you have to avoid ripping me off in the first place".

As far as Tweed was concerned, "getting over" was just stealing by another name.

It was soon after this discussion with Nilvan when Tweed decided that he must keep a closer eye on Og. He knew Og was shrewd, and that was one of the reasons he sold him the territory.

Thinking back, the decision to hand Rossie over to Og had been based upon a number of tangibles, solid facts that Tweed could wrap his hands around. In other cases, such as the sales district Sharlae now controlled, Tweed had wrestled with issues of loyalty, obligation, and duty; ideas, actually, that were real and significant in their own right and yet less qualifiable for a decision's sake and less quantifiable in a business sense. Og had presented a clear-cut business proposition. He was a known commodity, with contacts both above and below him throughout the drug market. Anyone looking for weed would be well advised to ask Og, because it was said that he knew everybody, all the dealers, and all the users, from the movers and shakers to the gram-bag snipe bogarts.

One thing Tweed knew for sure: Og had been looking over his shoulder ever since he first started selling dope. No, it went back further than that- to the time when Tweed first started buying his own bags. It was amazing to think that there might be a one-to-one ratio between the number of occasions on which Tweed had scored some weed and the times that he had gotten Og high. And it was infuriating that on many of those occasions Og might have stiffed him for a morsel here, a bud there, a roach here, a joint there.

Under close scrutiny Og did not fare so well. If he had been a clerk at a fast-food joint then his drawer would have been coming up consistently short. And not only his drawer, but the cash and stash of everyone with whom he came in contact. It did not take long for Tweed to discover that Og had matured in his various strategies for "getting over", that he had graduated from buds and joints to bags and bricks.

It had become necessary to make sure that Og was never present when Tweed split out the bales among his dealers. And though it troubled him to do so, Tweed also told his other dealers, Sharlae, Kuhn, Eban and Bone not to have Og assist them in any bagging or weighing operations, otherwise tedious procedures that were less monotonous with extra pairs of hands and conversation to help pass the time

And then a couple of weeks ago he had nailed Og cold when he caught him skimming a kilo he had sent over for Eban.

In the interest of fairness and objectivity Tweed wanted to confirm his suspicions but it wasn't the best policy to rely upon hearsay, second-hand information or accusations. Fortunately Tweed was in a position from which he could easily arrange to test and observe personally. The first test came with a warning.

In order to ensure objectivity he weighed the kilo to the hundredth of a gram and had LaGloria verify its weight in a triple blind prep for the setup. Then it had been a simple matter to tell Og that he would have to hold a key for a couple of hours until Eban could swing by and pick it up. Since he had no need for the extra key, Eban was told to return it to Sharlae later in the evening. All of this skullduggery meant that a quantity of dope was floating around and increasing vulnerability, but Tweed accepted the risk in favor of proving his suspicions about Og.

Sure enough, between the time the kilo left Sharlae's hands and the time she recovered it, it had lost almost an ounce.

Initially Tweed was surprised that Og had taken so much but then he understood that he wouldn't bother for any less. Og probably figured that there was a better than even chance that Eban would fail to notice. Maybe he'd turn the whole bag over for a profit, or overlook the discrepancy while breaking it up. Even if Eban were aware of the underage, he would likely wait until the next time he saw Tweed before bringing the matter up, and then try to roll it in to his next transaction. Either way, Og gambled that even an amount as large as an ounce would be "absorbed" and that he would therefore successfully "get over" once again.

It was important to confront Og immediately although Tweed had no intention of coming right out and accusing him of stealing. He tracked him down at the South St Market where he was engaged in a game of Missile Command.

"Hey! Og, Man! You still hanging in here trying to pick up hoodsies?"

"Well, you know what they say, if they're old enough to sit at the table…"

"Yeah, just don't tell Vinnie Trementozzi," Tweed laughed.

Nicknamed Mr.T, Vinnie was a former denizen of Rossie now serving an extended sentence at Cedar Junction for child rape.

"Shit, old Vinnie T…I wonder how he's doing…Probably getting bumblasted. So, what brings you around?" Og was naturally suspicious.

For his part Tweed was unsettle by the way Og had linked his visit with prison sodomy. "Oh, I was just stopping by, you know, to see how you're doing. Stopped in on Eban a little while ago, too."

"No kidding? So then you know that he got that little 'present'?"

"Oh, yeah, he got it alright, but you know he was giving me a hard time about it. This is the kind of shit I have to put up with."

"A hard time from Eban? About what? Freakin' sack looked gorgeous if you ask me."

Tweed sighed, "I don't know. Says it was short 26 grams. 'Course he's full of shit because the last thing I did before sending that package out was to weigh it, and I'm talking precision. It was all there -down to the last seed."

"So…what,you think maybe you forgot to zero out the scale or something?"

"Heh, heh, yeah, Og, once upon a time I might have forgotten but the electronic digital scale I have now is self-zeroing."

"So are you gonna make it up to him? How do you handle something like that? Isn't it his word against yours?"

"Ah…no…fuck'im. Let me put it this way. Let's say Mrs. So&So calls the grocery store and asks them to deliver a pound of grapes. Now after the delivery boy leaves she calls back again and complains that she was charged too much because there was less than a pound in the package…"

"Oh, I get it. What you're saying is that the babe, Sharlae did it, am I right? After all, the shit didn't just evaporate. What are you gonna do about it? You gonna bust her?"

"Well, shit, man, you friggin' hit the nail right on the head."

"About Sharlae?"

"No, that the shit didn't evaporate. And I also think that you're right about stealing. You do have to take it seriously. I do. I mean, for me, stealing is about the worst thing a person can do- especially if they're in a group like ours. We have to look out for each other. And if there was any chance, any possibility that someone in the group was stealing, then the whole group would be at risk. We'd be fucked. You bet your ass I'd bust her if I thought that Sharlae was a thief. And I don't mean a pussy slap on the wrist. I'm talking serious sanctions. Ultimate sanctions."

Og shifted his stance from one foot to the other as if he were suddenly uncomfortable. "'Ultimate'? What do you mean 'ultimate'?"

"Well, what do you think, man? Talking hypothetically, of course. I'd take back her territory for starters; and cut her off from sources. And then the usual stuff- breaking her legs, torching her car, you know, the works."

A twisted grin lit up Og's face as if he were privately enjoying a joke that appealed to his base instincts. "Holy fuck! For stealing weed. Wow! Man, you don't screw around!"

"I'm warning you, Og; oh, sorry, I mean telling- you're not a thief...I'm telling you, this is serious shit. Same goes for any of your dealers or your runners or whoever you got helping you. Take my advice and tell 'em that stealing will not be tolerated under any circumstances."

By now the pair had wandered out onto the sidewalk in front of the store. There was construction work in progress up the block near the projects, and a tractor trailer rig was picking up speed on the roadway, cycling through the gears and noisily expounding the principles of inertia and acceleration.

Shouting now, with the April breeze strumming chords on the hairs of his bangs, Og said, "I agree with you a hundred percent, man. You're right- it's the only way to go. Keep them honest and keep them happy. Avoid complications. Nobody needs that kind of hassle."

Looking Og straight in the eye Tweed nodded, gave him a thumbs-up salute and hiked up the street to the Fores for a sandwich.

He had tested Og and now he had no choice but to flunk him. Was the warning too subtle? Should he have been more direct? Said, 'Listen, Og, you're on probation, dude. Better get your shit together. One bad apple and all that'...The problem nagged at him over the ensuing days like a bad tooth in an abscessed gum. But just prior to LaGloria's big night he had come up with a solution, and now he was going to put it into play.

CHAPTER 20

Having worked not merely as if it was a matter of earning his pay but as if his personal pride were at stake, Rick had completed his task, rolled up his tools and hustled back to his car. But where to watch from? This required some calculation, and for a moment Rick sat in study like a head coach plotting the advance of his football team in a 'second and long' game scenario.

Atkinson could be going anywhere, but perhaps Rick could at least make an educated guess by using a process of elimination. He hadn't allowed very much running room as it were, so his area of observation was restricted to a radius of about a quarter of a mile. As he stared at the red Buick in his rear-view mirror Rick realized that Joe really only had two choices, to either go down the street the way he was already headed or to turn around and head up South St toward the square. He was on the verge of removing a coin from his pocket and flipping it to determine which direction he should choose when it occurred to him that this was all related to his boss, Weed. Therefore, there was a good chance that Joey Atkinson was going to head toward Westbury Circle, toward Weed's place, although there was no way to be sure short of asking him. But why else would Weed have asked Rick to create the delay?

His decision was moot, because before Rick had driven up South St extension as far as the ball park he saw Joey's car closing on him from behind. And even from a distance he could see that the car was in trouble. He pulled over to the side of the road to watch the results of his work unfold before his very eyes. His very amused and delighted eyes.

The 1977 Buick's steering geometry was exquisitely engineered so that in principle it relied on the weight of the massive vehicle to hold the front end aligned and true. Idler arms, steering links, pitman arms, control rods, torsion rods and bushings all held the wheels in precise position on straightaways and prevented drag, tow-in or tow-out on curves. The tremendous forces of stress and shear exerted on the axles and bearings were also kept to a minimum due to the proper alignment of the front end. Yet for all of the accuracy of Detroit's engineers and for all of the skill of its technicians, nothing could prevent the damage that Rick had engendered by removing the lug nuts from the front wheels of the Electra.

First the car did a little curtsy like a trained pony dipping to one knee. Then it almost righted itself before falling into a lopsided wobble. The driver, Joey Atkinson, started to realize that something was wrong, and he accelerated suddenly, lurching ahead as if to shake off the queer vibration he felt through the wheel. Wrong idea! Now the car looked like the road runner in the cartoon when it realizes that the cliff upon which it was standing has dropped out from under it. In this case something else was missing, and the car suddenly slumped to the ground chin-first like a clocked hockey player hitting the ice. It didn't move after that, but the two front wheels, bereft of lug nuts and hence free to exploit their considerable potential and kinetic energy, bounded ahead on their own as if in a race to join the traffic on Main St. In moments the two wheels passed by Rick, still rolling as if determined to get away for good. Rick laughed his ass off and as if in tribute rattled the liberated lug nuts in the inverted coolie-hat of a hub-cap he had taken from the car.

The sight of Joey Atkinson and his buddies crawling out of the car clearly stunned but enraged, and then running around as if their pants were on fire reminded Rick of a scene from the Three Stooges. Joey Atkinson as Moe Howard, the perennial wise-guy, in self-appointed command, the grease without which the slap-schtick didn't mesh. His pals Denis Fecteau and Mo Keating were equally suited playing the roles of Larry Fine and Curly Howard.

Rick Rose appreciated good comedy, and he believed that he had a good, basic understanding of it. Prior generations of devotees of comedy had whetted their appetites on Kabuki, Punch and Judy, Max Sennett and Charlie Chaplin. Rick's generation had a taste of all of that plus the Three Stooges, Max Fleischer and Spike Jones, the Harlem Globetrotters and Saturday morning cartoons. In addition, Rick had a personal experience that enabled him to 'get it' on a different level. He remembered it as Nazi D. Figaro, an opera staged for the benefit of the 5th and 6th graders at Rick's school, the Bennet Cerf Elementary.

When the company of college-aged actors and singers took the stage they announced that they were short one performer. Would anyone in the audience, they asked, be interested in playing the part of Cherubino? Rick still didn't know why, but he raised his hand, and out of the thirty or forty kids who volunteered, he was selected.

Backstage an angelic babe breathlessly outlined the plot of the opera to Rick. She was in dishabille and her 19 year-old bosom was packed into a revealing decollete corset so that it appeared to the 12 year-old Rick as though a pair of snowy bunnies were nestled in her shirt.

"See, Figaro wants to marry Susanna, the countess's maid," she whispered, "-but Count Almavina wants Susanna, too. Now, you're Cherubino, the count's page boy, who the count fired for flirting with the countess. You go to Susanna to ask her help getting your job back, OK, when the count shows up, and so you hide, get it? While you're, that is, while Cherubino is hiding, he hears the count making love to Susanna, then Doctor Bartolo comes in and starts talking about how you were carrying on with Barbarina, the gardener's daughter..."

All Rick heard was the sound of his own thoughts: "Look at them boobs! Look at them lips! What a fox! Man, I'm in love" as he rapidly fell into the role more heavily than he anticipated. And yet, although he had paid about as much attention to her as he did to his remedial reading teacher, he managed to get the gist of what was expected of him.

It turned out that the opera company was only planning to perform the one act from Figaro lest they lose the interest of the assembled students. They would follow that up with a question and answer period, and then a finale featuring excerpts from other popular operas, the names of which Rick would no doubt have garbled if he could have remembered them.

One thing Rick would never forget was waiting back stage with the other members of the troupe as if he were one of them; and someone rushing by in the dark and stuffing him into a smock and a floppy beret; the musty, dusty smell of the thick velvet curtain; the floral, sweaty smell of the sopranos and the tenors; the blinding surprise of being thrust on stage where- a play was in progress! And he could see right through it to the audience as if he were looking through worlds in a dream; and the music was loud; and long-hair never sounded so good; and his part came up when he had to crouch with his arms extended, and one of the babes threw a cover over him to make him look like a chair; and the funny-lookin' dude came in singing something fierce; and somebody tried to sit on him, and he jumped up and did the perfect hambone minstrel-show shock pose, and the dude chased him around the other actors for a bit; and then he ran off stage.

That was comedy and the kids in school loved it. For a week afterwards his friends would crack up whenever they laid eyes on him.

As his laughter subsided Rick realized that there would be a trick to preserving the humor of this situation if he were to turn the whole affair into a story. Not having been there, a listener could hardly appreciate the tension and uncertainty that preceded the 'punch line'. The key to the telling would be the set-up, but considering that it would be a while before he could relate the story to anyone else, then he had time to work on that angle.

Maybe he could come up with a full Three Stooges treatment and then pretend that he was describing a rare episode.

CHAPTER 21

"Bone! Sup!" As he approached Bone's car Og swung his arms in an exaggerated power-walk gait that reminded Bone of teddy bears on parade.

"C'mon, Og! Let's get going!"

Bone wondered why Og had to pull this visiting dignitary bullshit. His manner, the way he demanded extra time and consideration suggested an imperious demeanor that his character and reputation simply did not support. Everyone knew that Og was a slob and a bum. His principle ambition in life was to outlive his parents so that he could inherit their home. Someday he too would end up sitting on that bench in front of his house gossiping with the homebodies every day like his father had before him.

He had never held a full-time job and when he did work he insisted that he couldn't start until 10AM because he claimed he was required to stay at home in the morning in order help his elderly mother with her insulin injections. In fact his mother was not diabetic and she was quite self-sufficient, thank you.

For Og it was essential that he be accorded all of the respect due to a man of his stature, as one of the high-volume pot sellers in the greater Rossie area. He considered his occupation to be on a par with that of any career professional in town; a belief reinforced by the fact that many of them were his customers. Even among his peers he reckoned that he was the preeminent dealer in the group due to the central location of his district. Furthermore the fact that he counted people like Weed, Jabbour and Wayne as his personal friends, proved that he belonged in elite company.

Bone thought that Og was a pain in the ass and he resented the fact that Weed had insisted that he drag him along on this most important job. It wasn't like he was going to have trouble carrying a duffel bag packed with choice bud, after all. Knowing what was inside the bag would be incentive enough for Bone. He'd haul his ass and a sack of grass to the top of Pack Monadnock and back.

But privately, he would have welcomed the opportunity to make the dope run alone, since it would have entailed a long ride, with nothing but the radio and his thoughts for company. And Bone had plenty on his mind.

A lot on his mind meant chaos and confusion, a state that made Bone feel acutely uncomfortable. This was a problem he had experienced since he was a youngster. If he had so much as a single unanticipated issue or event on the horizon of his awareness, Bone became troubled and uneasy. He lashed out at others, seemingly seeing the cause of his discomfort everywhere. But when he had everything figured out; when he could live his life according to a schedule that was planned out well in advance, the turbulence in his mind settled and he felt that reason was his guide. Reason and a fat spliff.

Fortunately for Bone his condition had manifested itself early in his academic career, so his teachers and parents were able to recognize and help him deal with it. Treatment included focused therapy, long-term counseling and monitoring, and placement in segregated work groups. The combined treatments were successful although he was forced to grapple with the stigma of being a 'special' child. Now these many years later he still recalled that Og was one of the children who had taunted and stigmatized him.

Maybe he could dump Og out on the highway somewhere.

CHAPTER 22

Evening politely nodded and told the afternoon it had seen enough. Just as the daylight had gathered all of its warmth and charisma it was gently pushed off the stage with, "Don't call us, we'll call you".

Now the lights were down, and the heat was off and yet the scene was marked by a mood of quiet anticipation. Or maybe that was just how Tweed felt as he prepared to make the drop into the Rossie Towing yard.

The compound as a whole had pretty good security. Eight-foot tall fences with coils of razor wire along the top, flood lights to cover the areas the city lights failed to illuminate, and a pair of mean mongrel tow-yard dogs who believed that they owned the place.

Not that there was anything in there that anyone would want to steal. The main concern as far as security was concerned was for the people who invariably felt the temptation to wait until after dark and then go down to the tow yard to repossess their unjustly towed vehicles. It was remarkable how many meatheads would rather take on guard dogs and razor wire than pay a measly fine to get their shitbox off the hook. The temptation was almost understandable in light of the facts that were previously outlined herein regarding Rossie Towing, and because of the attendant reputation the yard had garnered as a place from which cars never returned. Yes, many had tried, but nobody had ever succeeded in beating Storer and Rima out of collecting their towing or storage fees and nobody had ever gotten their car out of the yard without permission.

However there was a flaw in the security apparatus, one that Tweed intended to exploit. Sure it was dangerous, sure it was dark and cold and he had a sprained ankle and was carrying a backpack full of even colder, clanging tools. Most of the negatives were swept aside like opiate-laced dust balls in the corners of his mind. The remainder of his qualms served as the raw material for an alchemical transformation he would perform when he turned his fear into daring and his foolhardiness into ambition.

For now Tweed was climbing the support braces for the pedestrian footbridge that spanned the commuter rail tracks and coincidentally, a corner of Rossie Towing's property. Of course the owners of the place and the designers of the footbridge had anticipated that someone might take advantage of the easy access that the bridge provided to the yard from above. So they enclosed the bridge in chain-link fencing to prevent anyone such as Tweed from jumping. Between the sets of stairs mounted on either side of the tracks the chain-link tunnel enclosed a walkway perched atop four evenly-spaced massive steel girder trestles.

Looking at the whole structure as an oversized jungle-gym, Tweed visualized how he was going to go about getting himself into a position where he could drop or swing himself down into the yard proper.

Good thing he hadn't sprained a wrist, because he was doing a lot of hand-over-hand work. The higher he climbed the more he had to play out the rope of inspiration to which he had secured his courage. Up above his head he could make out a faded graffiti signature done in a style that was reminiscent of the sixties. Some other crazy motherfucker had been up here years before him and they had probably hung from one hand while spraying with the other.

This by comparison was child's play.

For adolescent monkeys, maybe. He must be twenty feet above the ground, and the girders to which he was clinging were slick with condensation as well as being rusty and corroded.

Suddenly Tweed remembered his adventure on the catwalk at his old school, with that chick, what was her name? and then making out in the...hmmm, the useless little thing on the top of the building -the cupola!...cupola nice tits she had.

It was time to go hand over hand. First a brief pause.

There hadn't been any trains in a long while. It would suck to have one go flying under him while he was attempting this next bit.

As he waited a number of different sounds emanated from the blocks of homes and businesses that were crammed in between the train station and the cemetery. Dogs barking, an automobile horn, a torrent of unintelligible shouting, the eccentric wail of a distant emergency siren, the breeze rustling the bushes along the fence below.

He stared at a railway signal that shone a fixed red beacon toward the inbound track, and the old Johnson blues riff came to him,

"The blue light was my baby,

The red light was my mind..."

In the other direction Tweed saw the expanse of the property stretched out below him. It covered about six acres in a fat jagged zee, the tail of which fell under the bridge.

The office shack was visible in the distance, fixed in his field of vision by a light in the window and another illuminating a battered sheet-metal sign that hung over the door.

Tweed imagined Kuhn sitting inside with his feet up on a desk, his eyes glued to a pictorial layout in a men's magazine. If all went well then Kuhn should have no cause to alter his routine. Out on the bridge Tweed might experience thrills and chills, and once he made it into the yard he'd have other exciting challenges to deal with, but the guard and his dogs should rest easy.

Not that he was proud of his record, but let's just say that Tweed had notched a few B&Es on the razor strop of his life. Most of his experiences had been joint ventures with Carmine Gunther, but he did go solo on more than one occasion.

B&E was such a crude term, denoting a lack of skill and/or restraint. Sometimes the only way to gain illegal entry to a given place was to break something. But more often than not if you wanted to gain access to an area from which you would otherwise be restricted, you simply had to take the initiative.

One method was simply to walk in as if you were expected. This worked best in establishments that, as a course of doing business, were required to meet and greet a variety of visitors. Here the key was to exploit the conflicting impulses found in most concierges, security guards and the like to simultaneously please and prevent. These people wanted to put the best face on the corporations they represented while protecting the premises from unwanted intrusion. He ignored them.

However, Tweed found that if ignoring a potential obstacle didn't work, then he was forced to rely upon the two B's: bullshit and bribery. If you can't simply walk in, then the next best thing is to have someone on the inside let you in. In most instances a good story will usually work wonders.

"I got separated from my elderly mother, (my girlfriend, little sister, etc.) and I need to get back in before they start to panic,"

Or, "I thought this door led to the men's room and when I went through it, next thing I knew I was outside and couldn't get back in," That type of thing, with the particulars modified to suit the circumstance.

Sometimes it was impossible to appeal to the nobler, more altruistic instincts in an opponent, and at those times, Tweed used cash. He didn't throw it around in an offensive way, but pressed it into hands and pockets in a sly familiar manner, like an uncle at Christmas, saying, "I'm sorry to put you to any trouble. I know I can't expect special treatment, or anything…"

And as unbelievable as it seems, there were times when it was possible to simply "drop in". For example, one winter evening in 1979 he had heard about a dance party at a local junior college. The event attracted him because it was a chance to meet and dance with college babes, and because the ticket included a buffet with beer and wine. But he really wanted to go because he dug the band and had been looking forward to seeing them perform live.

He arrived at the hall in time for the dance but was turned away when he failed to produce a valid student ID. Then he was almost humiliated when the first two of his three common techniques for gaining entry failed him within twenty minutes. He had attempted a nonchalant saunter in the midst of a group of upper-classmen, but before he crossed the threshold into the hall he was singled-out by a burly campus security guard and ejected. Perfunctory attempts at cajolery and bribery failed miserably but he was undaunted.

He walked away from the hall and surveyed the building from across the quad. Scanning the layout of the windows he realized that there must be a balcony or mezzanine on the second floor and he aimed to find another means of entry that might take him past the dance and directly upstairs. Sure enough, there was a side entrance that led to a stairwell. There was no direct access to the dance hall from here so there was no need for any security. Tweed strolled right into the building and walked up the stairs as if he lived there.

When he reached the second floor he started rapidly searching for a way into the mezzanine that he imagined must be there. He searched closets, conference rooms, an office, an apartment and a kitchen before he found something that looked promising- a pair of glass-paneled French doors concealed behind curtains. Actually they sounded promising because they fairly throbbed with vibrations from the loud music being played behind them.

Stepping through the doorway reminded Tweed of walking into a funhouse. It was dark and disorienting, full of noise and uncertainty. But when he got his bearings he felt gloriously invisible. At first he was unable to discern the layout or purpose of the gallery upon which he was standing. Then he noticed a row of seats and a protective railing and he guessed that he was in a reviewing booth or an executive box. Directly below him was the dance floor, a freaky, flashing, organic mass of upraised arms, thrashing hair and moving feet.

The activity drew and compelled him. He leaned on the railing, gazing over the floor with the satisfaction of a demigod surveying his domain. Having beaten campus security, he had shown the advantage of privilege, bypassing the usual ticketed entry, and rising above those who would forever be to him an underclass.

As he was thus gloating on his superiority by dint of cleverness, he noticed a pair of lovely coeds who were dancing together. Suddenly he became inspired to 'put the drop' on them. Before he had assessed the safety or even the sanity of what he was doing, he had slung his legs over the railing of the booth, dropped to a crouch, and slowly let his body down until all of his weight was hanging from his fingertips, which were gripping the lip of the balcony. He almost laughed.

Hanging there above the dance floor, the soles of his sneakers were still a good three feet above the heads of the unsuspecting dancers below. -And now again, seven years later he was hanging from his fingertips with a goofy grin on his face, his hands cramping in the damp and cold, the distance to the ground greater still than it had been then. How bad was the fall back in '79? He couldn't recall. Mustn't have been too bad.

The guys in the band were hot shits. One of them caught him when he was sneaking a piss out the window into the quad. It was between sets and the lavs were all packed due to the abundant availability of food and drink. The windows, giant floor-to-ceiling jobs, were open to let in the night air, and it looked too good to pass up. How was he to know that there was somebody standing behind the curtain? At the start of the next set he was thrilled to hear the singer announce, "We'd like to dedicate this song to the guy who was pissing out the window just now..."

He stayed for the whole dance, and it seemed that he danced with every chick in the place. Wasn't that the night he ended up hanging out with the weird chick who tried to sneak him into her dorm after the dance? The RA took a fit and refused to let them in, however she did agree to join them and go to the midnight showing of Fritz the Cat. Later, in the theater, Tweed got a hand job from both sides at once, while he held one peach-small hairy-nippled boob in one hand and a big soft pointy-nippled boob in the other.

OK, now ready, set...let go.

Oh, shit; it was further than it looked. As he fell the wind fairly whistled in his ears. He hit the ground, crumpled into a heap and rolled as best he could, kiltered by the knapsack full of tools he had strapped to his back. At 32 feet per second per second he was lucky, having started with only a sprained ankle, to emerge from the fall with no more than a couple of broken ribs, a broken wrist, a shattered collarbone, and a dislocated hip.

Just kidding. Maybe it was the Percs, maybe it was the Darvons, maybe it was the luck of the Irish, or the intervention of a caring deity, but Tweed got up and limped away, bruised like the bottom-most potato in the sack.

The price you pay for such a high-flown opinion of yourself is that sometimes you don't know the most obvious shit because you're so goddamned smart you wouldn't think to ask. For instance when you were on the phone with Kuhn you might have inquired as to the location of Frankie's car. But no, instead you chose to go traipsing about like a blooming tourist. Tourist? You're no tourist! You're more like an old war veteran, hobbling through a cemetery looking for the grave of a fallen comrade. Damn!

Before frustration gained the upper hand Tweed told himself that he had reasons to be hopeful. 1) Given that the car was, in effect, a clue awaiting delivery to the forensics lab it would probably remain strapped to the back of the flatbed truck that had been used to remove it from the crime scene. 2) Also, the car had to be out of the way so as not to impede the flow of traffic, and yet it had be convenient. 3) Car and truck would likely be parked down-wind from the office. As Tweed knew from experience, a burned-out car stinks to high heaven. In fact he might have been able to follow his nose if it weren't for the pervasive junkyard redolence of fresh vulcanized rubber, hot transmission fluid, burning oil, smoldering dumpster, open pools of petrol, corroding heaps of steel and oozing corrosives.

One way or the other he had to move quickly and find his objective. Either or both of the dogs would be patrolling the yard, so he was in a race to reach the truck. The way he figured it, once he climbed aboard the flatbed he should be able to work undisturbed.

Nervously he tapped the contents of his left pants pocket, then his right jacket pocket, and then the rest of his pockets in turn as if he were performing some kind of existential ritual. The tools were in an old standard-issue Munie high school bookbag backpack that had decidedly seen better days. He gathered the straps at the X-stitching and hoisted the bag again as he struggled to negotiate a series of rainwater filled ruts in the road. The bag wasn't up to the task. The straps may have held but the fabric gave way, spilling a jack and crowbar along with a come-along into the mud.

"Of fucking course!" yelled Tweed, as if accusing an unseen tormentor. "I bet this wasn't even my freaking bag!" Now, by some twisted rationale having to do with the fact that he had a choice of two bags when he left the house, he was going to blame LaGloria for dumping his tools.

Should have kept his mouth shut. He was after all breaking into a business, trespassing on private property, carrying implements that were undoubtedly intended to help him commit either theft or vandalism. Wouldn't want to be caught. Not here, not now; not by man nor…beast.

CHAPTER 23

Not a particularly well-traveled man, Rick Rose none the less believed that he was world-wise and street-savvy. He displayed a degree of maturity suitable for his age, his judgment was sound and he made the most of his twelve years of schooling. An education in the municipal school system was nothing to sneeze at, yet for all of its rigor and promise, Rick had not advanced beyond the tenth grade. He had repeated the third and fifth grades, but that was merely a reflection of the fact that in elementary school the teachers worked to monitor and encourage each student's progress, whereas in high school the faculty adopted a sheep-herding mentality. And as every shepherd knows, when you count your sheep at the end of the day you are bound to come up short. Some were lost to the wolves of indolence and drug abuse, some to the lure of the working life, some to early parenthood, sports or the military; and regrettably some were lost to prison, while others were lost to death by accident, murder and suicide.

With four sisters and four brothers, Rick saw his family as a virtual microcosm of the community at large. He had surely witnessed all of the conflicts, joys, traumas and tragedies common to human experience, all within his own extended family.

In short, he thought that he had seen it all; and he was still buzzed from the rush of adrenalin, the excitement and the amusement he got from rigging Joey Atkinson's car to self-destruct. But nothing could have prepared him for what followed next.

When Weed had said, "Sit tight and watch how the shit comes down," he might have expected some prosaic type of activity, such as the arrival of a patrol car or a wrecker, the kind of street scene at which many pedestrians would still gawk, even in this age of cable TV and VCRs. What he did witness was in fact much better than any dumpster fire or geriatric car crash, even better than a sidewalk standoff between the cops and a raving crack pot.

Joey Atkinson's car was stuck in the middle of the South St extension, just where the road widened to join Main St near the municipal ball park. What little traffic there was on South St at this time of day could still get by easily enough, and given the condition of the vehicle, the loss of the wheels and the missing lug-nuts, there was nothing Atkinson could do anyway. So after standing around and swearing, stamping his feet and gesturing angrily, and after a deliberative smoke with his buddies, Joey et al retired back to the Fores bar. There he would make some phone calls and see about getting his father's car towed, reassembled and put back on the road. At this point it didn't look like much was going to happen. Perhaps a tow truck would show up, or maybe some well-meaning individual would place flares or emergency triangles on the street in order to prevent any additional accidents.

Rick had just about given up, and was preparing to start his bug and get moving again so that he could contact Weed and make his report. Maybe he'd call that excellent Sharlae babe and see if she was available for another tete-a-tete.

Suddenly a battered white Dodge van approached from the far end of South St, and Rick saw that instead of passing the Buick it pulled alongside and then stopped, and a group of guys jumped out of the truck, all carrying tools of some sort. These were big dudes, like wrestlers or body builders, and the apparent leader of the group wore a white lab coat and smoked a cigar. He gestured and pointed and shouted and the other dudes worked fast, sliding a floor jack under the Buick and using it to hoist the car in moments onto temporary jack-stands. Rick was impressed, thinking that it was remarkable that a repair crew could arrive so quickly. Had Weed arranged this, and if so, why?

Now that they had the vehicle safely immobilized, each member of the crew rushed back to the van and grabbed more gear. They returned with an assortment of pneumatic tools trailing coiled air hoses that ran into the back of the van where undoubtedly there was a hidden compressor. The petulant whirring noise from the air guns reminded Rick of the sound of tires spinning on ice; and yet the same sound that from an ice-bound car speaks of impotence, in this case spoke of power. In short order they had removed the remaining wheels, the doors and hood, the windshield, starter motor, alternator and radiator, and were starting on the interior of the car. Then the guy in the lab coat whistled on two fingers as if he was hailing a cab, and everybody scrambled back to the van hauling as much of the Buick with them as possible.

By now it was obvious, if it hadn't been before, that this was no road service crew and that these guys were hardly concerned with repairs. Rick also gathered that there was more than profit motivating them as he had plainly seen the leader duck in and reduce the upholstery of the Electra to shreds with a large gleaming Buck knife before he had his crew lower the car to the pavement. Talk about'cha prejudice!

Rick hadn't been timing them, although it was obvious that their crew chief had, but he would later swear that they had spent no more than four or five minutes stripping the car. After they drove away the Buick was barely recognizable. Now firmly planted in the middle of South St on bare wheel hubs, the ravaged car look like the gutted shell of a crab after a seagull has pecked it clean.

He too whistled, in awe and amazement. So this was the payback; this was how Weed answered the bozos who had kidnapped Sharlae. Holy shit! Note to self, thought Rick, don't do nothing to piss off Mr. Weed. 'Cause man, if you rub him the wrong way, he's gonna rub you right the fuck out. Actually, that was the cool thing about it. Weed had arranged the thing so that nobody got hurt. Car was fucking totaled, but nobody was dead or maimed. 'Course, if for some reason they didn't get the message, then Rick imagined that Weed could up the damage accordingly.

Man, and he thought he had a story to tell before! Now he couldn't wait. He spun up the bug's motor, got it kicking and sputtering, then drove off to find a phone.

CHAPTER 24

"You know what your problem is, man? You're too freakin' uptight. You gotta relax a little. That's how you get ulcers, I'm telling you. Learn to enjoy yourself, man!"

Bone's fingers tightened on the steering wheel. Here he was driving a shitbox forty friggin' miles out to the suburbs to get a freakin' shitload of pot, and for the whole trip he had to put up with Og the Dog friggin' Z. What, me worried?

"I'm uptight?" he answered, pitching the question perhaps a bit high. "Well, fuck you, man! Look who's talking! I mean, how the fuck would you know? Don't think I've ever seen you smile. Come to think of it, Og, do you even know how to smile?"

"Fuck you too! So there! So, what, you gotta go around grinning all the time? I'm talking about living life, you know? Digging the scene; kicking back. That's all. Fucking smiling...Who gives a shit if I smile?"

"Ah, your mother? How the hell should I know? It ain't the fucking smile, it's what's behind it. You start a conversation saying, 'Know what your problem is...' and you're the one who always looks like you just buried your best friend. Alright, if you know so much about 'living life', then how am I supposed to relax?"

"Why don't you get laid, man? For starters. Find a girlfriend, you know, the yang for your yin. We both know that pot is a wonder drug, good for almost any complaint, real or imagined, but there are some things that it just can't help."

"I disagree," replied Bone, without looking away from the road. "Weed can help you get laid. It worked for me on a couple of occasions. On the other hand, you know what they say: that dope will get you through times of no sex better than sex will get you through times of no dope."

Looking at Bone's face Og was surprised to see the trace of a blush.

"Uh, Bone, don't you mean money?"

"Huh?"

"Money, man, money. Dope will get you through times of no money better than money will get you through times of no dope."

"Where-dja hear that? The Rip-Off Press? Let me tell you something- the Freak Brothers are cartoons and cartoons don't get laid."

"Whatever. From what I hear, there's a lot of sex at the place we're going."

To this Bone retorted with a sibilant noise of dismissal.

"What? You don't think so, huh? I hear they film stag flicks there!"

Stag? thought Bone, interesting choice of words.

"I don't stick my nose where it doesn't belong, Og. Weed makes his deals, we make ours. I don't ask questions. I don't wonder, I don't care."

"Yeah? Well, I care. And I wonder if they're making a movie right now. I wouldn't mind seeing 'em make a fuck flick. Must be hot."

Now Bone began to wonder if Og knew that the movies being made at the location were solely male gay porn. He wasn't sure if he was justified feeling even more uncomfortable being alone in the car with Og just yet.

"Look, Og, to the people doing it, it's just a job. I imagine that they'd probably think that breaking up pounds of reefer was pretty glamorous, too."

"You think so? Shit, maybe if I offered to let 'em watch me break up a pound they'd let me watch them do some pounding, you know?"

Now he was distinctly uncomfortable.

"Uh, whatever turns you on, man. I didn't know you went in for that sort of thing, but...I suppose."

"That sort of thing? Who doesn't? Shit, just last night I was at a club, and this chick was dancing on the stage, you know?"

Alright, this was more like it. Bone nodded his head.

"So anyway, she's doing her thing and pretty soon she comes down to where I'm sitting. Tell ya the truth I think my friends put her up to it. So anyway she goes and sits on my lap, can you believe it? I mean, at this point she's not wearing much, you know?"

"Yeah, I can imagine."

"So she's sitting there, kind of squirming around on my lap and you know what I wanted to do? I wanted to stick my finger up her ass. Wouldn't that be hot?"

Holy shit. It figures. The guy is queer for sure. Bone almost did a classic double-take, but held his composure, and asked, as calmly as possible under the circumstances, "Wouldn't you want to touch her pussy, dude?"

"Her pussy? Skanky fuckin' stripper's pussy? No freakin' way, man!"

It was difficult for Bone to put himself in Og's place. If a beautiful woman sat on his lap he'd probably try to cop a feel, and why not? 'Course, these days, a lot of the strip joints don't allow that kind of thing, but just saying...Not that it mattered to him, but he pushed a little further. "OK, Og, let's say that you and this chick are all alone and she's lying in front of you with her legs spread. What are you going to do?" It kind of made him ashamed, asking the classic queer-test question.

"Well," Og giggled nervously, "I'd like to fuck her."

Just as Bone was about to breath a sigh of relief, Og continued,

"In the ass, of course."

This was just too much to bear. "Why in the ass, man? You have her gorgeous, wet, fucking pussy staring you in the face and you want to stick your dick in her ass?"

"Shit, man, I think I'd like it better. Gross, hairy, fucking cunt."

He must have picked up on Bone's look of horror, because he followed that up with, "Hey, there's no accounting for taste, man."

"That's for damned sure!"

"What do you mean by that?" Og sounded genuinely offended.

Not put off for a moment, Bone responded, "Just saying I agree. There's no accounting for taste. I happen to like the taste...of pussy, that is."

"Man, that's just sick! Drop it, alright? Drop the fucking subject."

"You brought it up, dude. Look- we're almost at the place."

After exiting the highway Bone spent several minutes seemingly turning onto smaller and smaller streets. From the highway to the bypass to the parkway to the county lane to the town road to the two-lane main street and now onto a secluded residential road. No sidewalks; street lamps spaced at every tenth of a mile; rural flag-type mailboxes designating the otherwise invisible drives leading off the road to exclusive private residences hidden beyond banks of hedgerows and expansive lawns.

Having made this trip before Bone clearly knew what to look for, and he indicated as much by saying, "Sorry to disappoint you, man, but there's no film crew here now."

"Oh, yeah? How the fuck do you know?" Og was still a little peeved, thinking that his proclivities had been called into question.

"Well, it's too late to point it out now, but from the road you can see a signal that says whether anyone is at the house or not."

"And the signal said that nobody's there?"

"No, I didn't say that. There is somebody here, of course. Weed doesn't leave tons of excellent product sitting there just protected by some freakin' ADT home security system."

"What, don't tell me there's a guard at the house or something?"

"24 hours a day; armed to the teeth."

"That's crazy! How can Weed afford to pay somebody to guard the shit?"

"Man, you should be asking yourself how could he afford not to. Remember, he's protecting your stash and mine. You gotta figure, it's worth the investment."

Bone was busy parking the car now, pulling in close to a garage on the far side of the house so as to conceal his car in the deepest gloom he could find. Og was beginning to wonder about the collective paranoia of his colleagues. Here was Bone, trying to hide his car on a piece of property that was so secluded and so poorly lit that it was unlikely that anyone could see them from the house, let alone from the road. There wasn't a neighbor for a half a kilometer. And now they were going to walk into a house where some asshole was waiting with a gun, or worse?

"I'll lead the way, it gets kind of tricky from here," said Bone, trying to be helpful.

"What, kind of tricky to not get shot? Aren't you going to blow the horn or something? Don't you have a flashlight? What the fuck!"

"It's cool, Og, it's cool. I already signaled on the way in. We're expected. No need to worry. I'm not going to blow the horn and let half the neighborhood know we're here. And there's no need for a flashlight because…"

Suddenly a series of floodlights came on in sequence, apparently triggered by motion sensors. Strategically mounted on the corners of the house and garage the lights helped to quell Og's fears, for now he could plainly see a broad flagstone path bathed in light of almost daylight intensity.

"Follow the yellow brick road, dude," Bone prodded, and jokingly added, "And stick to the path or the munchkins will get you."

Og needed no inducement to stay in the light. For all he knew the friggin' grounds were booby-trapped. All of his prior hopes and fantasies vanished and now he wanted nothing more than to wait in the car.

But then another fantasy started to resolve itself in his mind. There was a ton of weed in that house, and that was something he wanted to see. As he started toward the back door he envisioned a room like a bank vault with vast quantities of golden buds piled from floor to ceiling. He'd go in and run his hands through it, and shower himself in fresh, succulent, cured Jamaican marijuana.

"Looks like a regular house, doesn't it?" asked Bone.

"Any reason it wouldn't?" responded Og, half-expecting to hear that the premises doubled as a day-care center or something.

"No; I'm comparing these homes around here to the ones in the neighborhood where we grew up. For one thing they're all single-family."

"Aw, c'mon, the houses were all single-family on your street."

"No they weren't- the Mc…ah, the McManuses lived on the first floor and the Ronans lived on the second of a two family, and the Vogels and the Reuls lived in that black house with the iron fence, and there was a triple decker on the corner of Hewett street."

"That house was on Hewett."

"Same difference. Point is that I came from a lower-middle class, sort of a working class neighborhood, but this is definitely your upper-class…just look- every house has a two car garage, I mean, seriously."

"Don't mean shit."

"Hey, you don't have to have a chip on your shoulder about it, I'm just saying, this place is different, that's all. You and me, we would have turned out different if we grew up around here."

"How so? What difference could it possibly make? If I had the same father and mother, the same brothers?"

"For instance, we probably wouldn't be selling dope, OK? This town has a polo club, for Pete's sake!"

"I thought they cured polo!"

"Very funny, Og. Polo. With Horses. Now let's go in and get this over with."

The flagstone trail ended at a raised concrete slab platform that served as a rear porch or stoop, at a breeze way in the midsection of the post-modern split-ranch. Ever the gentleman, Bone opened and held the storm door for his companion. As he entered, Og removed his trademark knit hat and muttered in passing, "How the fuck was I supposed to know that horses had polo?"

At that moment it looked like he had been set up for a practical joke, because just as he stepped inside, the resident house sitter, undoubtedly acting out of boredom leaped out at Og and screamed, "Aaargh! Bone, you bastard! I got…you? Bone? Oh, there you are."

By now Og was clutching his chest with one hand and grasping the back of a wrought-iron kitchen chair with the other. A moment of unmitigated terror had instantaneously drained his usual olive complexion to a bleached albino tint. It didn't help any that both Bone and his apparent co-conspirator were laughing hysterically, and that neither of them thought to offer him any assistance. Then, to top matters off, the prankster said, "So, Bone, want a beer? Who's your friend?"

If he had been victimized in this way by anyone else or at any other time Og certainly would have lashed out with scathing retribution. But despite his shock he was still wary of seeing guns, or ninjas, or some high-tech automated home defense mechanism.

"Mickey, this here's Og; Og, Mickey. Mickey and Weed go way back. He comes from uptown… or used to, am I right? Where you living now Mick?"

"No shit, I ain't lived in Mission since the '70s. I live in Hampton."

"Holy shit! Killer commute, huh?"

"Not really. I go opposite the traffic, off-hours, you know. Plus I take the back roads and avoid a lot of the aggravation."

"So, how'joo end up in Hampton?"

"Same old story. Following the pussy…"

Despite himself, Bone looked at Og.

"But seriously," he continued, "I'm living with my girlfriend. Hey, speaking of driving- mind if I go out for a few? I'm going to go get something to eat."

Mickey was already pulling on his jacket and heading toward the door. "Like I said- help yourself to a beer. They're in the fridge."

Judging by his reaction, Bone was not pleased that Mickey had chosen this moment for his breach of protocol. He was certainly entitled to a break, and he enjoyed the privilege of self-authorization for the rare off-campus excursion, but Bone felt imposed-upon nonetheless. And yet, hadn't he just said that Mickey was a close friend of Weed's? As if he would take it upon himself to criticize or second-guess Mickey Byrne. But the trumping truth as far as Bone was concerned was that Bone and Weed also went way back, although few among the "Wizards", the self-appointed local group of dealers, knew it. In fact, Bone had set Weed up with his very first pound of pot; and who knows?...If it hadn't been for Bone, maybe the whole joint never would have gotten rolling. Actually he didn't like to make much of his part in the story because at the time he hadn't made out quite so well on the deal, personally or financially.

Anyway, the real issue bothering Bone wasn't really the matter of Mickey's truancy, but his own ability to deal with spending any more time alone with Og than was absolutely necessary.

However, while Bone may have displayed misgivings or regret over Mickey's departure, Og was all for it. In fact he became positively effusive in his generosity. "Hey, man, take all the time you want. You look like you could use a change of pace. Me and Bone, we got this scene covered, so just leave it to us."

Now given Og's unexpected and uncharacteristic chivalry, Bone had little choice but to practically usher Mickey out the door while uttering half-hearted reassurances. "No problem, man. Catch you on the rebound!"

"Hey, thanks, yeah, later!"

Not one tick after Mickey closed the door, Og spoke up and said, "Alright! Now where's the weed?"

"Ahem! Don't talk about Mickey's cooking like that, Man! I know he's a vegetarian but..."

Og was stymied. "I don't know what the fuck you're-"

Bone cut him off, "We don't talk shop, Buck. Not even in shop, got it?" And he fixed Og with a lowered stare and slowly shook his head from side to side. Then he placed his forefinger over his lips.

"So, let me show you around. We'll come back to the kitchen soon enough."

Og hissed, "What? We can't talk **here?**"

"Sure we can talk, dude. Watcha got on your mind? Just use common sense."

Bone was simply adhering to Tweed's rule of paranoia. As he put it: *Always assume that the place is bugged. These days so many agencies could be listening that you have to figure that at least one of them is listening.*

"I'll tell you what I have on my mind," started Og in a threatening growl.

But Bone merely beckoned and led his surly friend down a short flight of carpeted stairs to a similarly carpeted hallway. There were a number of doors off the hall, all of them closed. In any other house there might be a den down here, and a laundry room, an office and a wash closet, and perhaps a finished bedroom.

Og was looking through the eyes of a television game-show panelist, ready to select the correct door in order to win a fortune. However, Bone had already made the choice and had entered a darkened room at the end of the hall.

If Og's feelings of that evening could be summed up, they might be best reflected in a single reaction- the gut reaction he experienced upon entering the bulk storage room in the stash house. But sometimes mere modifiers can not do justice to the actual sensation, as there is no adjective that can adequately describe a slap in the face, no adverb worthy of of capturing a herniated ulcer.

At the time he was barely coping with an excess of anxiety, dissatisfaction, hostility and resentment, like a Rasta trying to stuff an unruly Medusa-head of natty dreads under a modest tam. Besides, he had a considerable stake in terms of money and reputation riding on this particular excursion. And while he bore a generalized ill-will toward all of humanity, most of his anger and resentment were at this moment directed at Tweed. He hated Tweed's jiffy franchise-style distribution system, and all of the bullshit about developing organic strategies and creating a balance in the market.

Og saw no futility in arguing with success. Granted, Tweed may have been successful, but maybe he could have been more so if he had done things Og's way. For Og believed that the weed business was a most suitable environment for proving the advantage of a modified form of natural selection. A big fan of Mutual of Omaha's Wild Kingdom, Og never missed an episode, seeing it as a metaphor and guide for life in the city. His role models Marlin Perkins and Jim Fowler surely would have told him that in order to sell a lot of dope one had to be "red in tooth and claw".

"What a rip!" said Og disgustedly, as he observed that the room was empty. "I'll ask again. Where's the.., uh, salad?" He looked around as if to underscore his inquiry. Gray indoor-outdoor carpeting, sand-tone paneling with light oak trim. Not a single piece of furniture.

"What did you expect, man? Be cool!"

"I expected to see some freakin' dope, man! Now where the fuck is it?"

"Right in front of you."

"I don't see anything."

"I'm the dope, man, for bringing you with me in the first place. Now shut up and *be cool*."

Bone turned away slowly and pointed to a closet with bi-fold doors. From where Og was standing the closet appeared to be about two feet deep, and full of hanging clothes.

"Don't tell me..." he said incredulously.

"See for yourself," and Bone stepped aside.

Steaming, Og wasted no time swatting at coats, flat-handing the walls, looking like a magician's assistant attempting to prove the soundness of a stage gag.

"Here; check it out-" Bone seized the right door frame of the closet at the point where it aligned with the handle, and pulled. The "closet" swung away from the wall on hinges, revealing the entrance to a full-sized walk-in cooler chest.

With hardly a murmur, Og opened the door to the cooler, and stood transfixed, caught in an out-rush of cool mist that was like a vacuum-pressed promise of fresh delights.

What he didn't see was that the cooler had been situated practically and sensibly and according to a design intended to permit for the rapid storage of bulk quantities. At the other end of the hallway, directly opposite the store room was another empty room with an over sized door leading to the outside.

There on the exterior, well concealed by the landscaping, was a ramp and a trailer-height dock. Thus the drive-up loading zone could accommodate trucks of many sizes, from vans to tractor trailers. However, since it would be too conspicuous to bring large trucks to a residential neighborhood, the massive hauls, those measured in tons were still handled at commercial warehouses, while the stash house processed loads measured in bales. Packed to capacity, Tweed's reefer could hold no more than a few hundred pounds, depending on the density of the product and the packing material. Like any grocer he employed precisely controlled cold storage for his perishable inventory, as opposed to the dope dealer portrayed in literature who typically used a humidor and a cedar closet.

The weed was stacked in bricks of fairly uniform dimensions. That is not to say that the marijuana came that way from the mountainside plantations of Jamaica, Mexico and elsewhere; although the growers and smugglers had their own reasons to minimize the size of their freight shipments. At this end of the distribution chain Tweed achieved uniformity by means of a standard household garbage compactor.

"Yo! Og! You OK, man? You don't look so good."

Indeed a flashlight shining upwards against Og's chin could hardly have made him appear more ghoulish.

"I'm fine, Bone, I'm fine. I was just thinking..."

"Probably not the best thing to do under the circumstances," suggested Bone. At that Og turned with a direct look that implied that he knew exactly what Bone meant.

"Well then, I guess you're thinking what I'm thinking."

"If you're thinking that it's as cold as Khrushchev's Christmas in here, then I agree. Let's get what we came for and book it. In the closet there- pass me the golf bag."

Og rummaged around in the false bulkhead and emerged with a shabby caddy's companion. "What are you going to do with this?"

"Wonders never cease, eh, dude?" He revealed that the club heads sticking out of the bag were merely there for show. The supposed golf bag was actually an artfully disguised cylindrical metal canister ideal for transporting about 25 pounds of compressed pot, odor-free.

While Bone worked stuffing the bag, Og poked around among the bales, then cleared his throat and started a little speech. "No, Bone, I was gonna say that you and me should think about this opportunity we have here and, fuck it, take all the dope. You gotta admit, that's how Weed done it; he just grabbed the stash and made his move. If we took all this we'd be sitting pretty, and he'd be fucked. I'll tell you something, man, I been talking to Jabbour recently and I think he'd back me up on this one. Help me move it, you know? What's Weed gonna do? We'll have all the dope. That's why I wanted that Mick to split. Give me time to case the place, figure how I was gonna do it. Shit, now that he's gone, it's a piece of cake. What do you say?"

It really was clever how the lid flipped back down on the canister, concealing the plastic-wrapped bricks of cannabis within. Slinging the golf bag over his shoulder and grunting as his only comment, Bone closed the chest behind him and sealed the closet door, taking care to leave it as he had found it.

CHAPTER 25

"Hey, boy, I guess I should have known you'd be out snoopin' around. What do you look for, anyway? Rats? Well, I'm no rat."

Tweed maintained a stock-still crouching position as he calmly addressed the approaching dog, which, from his point of view, looked like a knobby pair of black shoulders with a gleaming pair of silvery eyes fixed between them. The shoulders rose and fell as the dog tiptoed toward Tweed on massive paws the size of oven mitts, but the eyes remained at a constant level above the ground. Just about Tweed's eye level.

"What do you say, P-head" huh, boy? I got a treat for you." Then he muttered, "Kuhn! Couldn't you keep this guy inside for a spell?"

The dog growled in response, triggering a nervous reaction in Tweed's stomach.

"Is that you, Peckerhead? I have your favorite here…"

Just in case the dog was on the prowl when he arrived, Tweed had come prepared. In one hand he held a deep meerschaum bowl and a lighter and in the other he offered a bag filled with plenty of hashish. P-head loved to get baked.

To think that LaGloria used to say that it was cruel to get the dog stoned. *"You boys ought to be ashamed of yourselves, giving that dog shotguns!"*

Come to think of it, it *was* kind of twisted, Carmine holding P-head's head between his hands and blowing heavy lungfuls of smoke into his face. But here was no denying that the dog looked happy afterwards. In fact, the dog always looked happy.

"C'mon, boy, come here! I was just thinking about the time you ate all of that lamb's breath, remember? And then you climbed to the top of the old school bus and refused to come down? You sat up there for three days tripping your brain cell out, and we got all worried, thought you were gonna…"

The switchboard of Tweed's central nervous system suddenly lit up on all channels. *Red alert! This is not a drill!* The dog was unnaturally quiet now, and it had dropped even lower onto its haunches as if it was preparing to spring. Despite the abundance of light, the dog's features were obscured in shadow, and as Tweed strained to see he began to suspect that this dog wasn't Peckerhead.

But although fear was telling his sweat glands to flood their surroundings, although his goose flesh was raising and his bladder weakening, Tweed remained still as a stone. If this was Trudy approaching, and not some stranger junk yard dog, some latter-day Baskerville beast, then he might just have a chance. Problem was that Trudy had always hated him. Why? Fucks knows. You take two mutts, both of them working side by side at the lot with Kuhn. One loves you, the other hates you; that's just the way it goes. Maybe it was genetic…maybe Trudy came from a long line of British police dogs or something. Sensed the Irish in him and wanted a piece of it. Weren't dogs driven by their reaction to smells? Maybe he didn't change his underwear often enough; maybe it was too often.

But what was he afraid of? Getting mauled in the mud by 140 pounds of misdirected animal aggression? He'd been bitten before and survived. It was just that what with everything else that was going on it would suck to have to go to the hospital for stitches and rabies shots.

Faced with the primal threat of an attack by a wild animal at night in an exposed area, Tweed did not plan for defense, nor did he look for an escape route. He did not pray or yell for help. Instead, he responded instinctively and uttered two words: "Fucking LaGloria!" Not exactly the stuff for posterity. *(Passersby were said to have heard the dying man's last words. Enigmatic and succinct, they were, "*Expletive deleted* LaGloria.")*

Trudy, by comparison, had ideas, or at least one main goal- to get the guy who was crouching in the middle of her yard. She was singularly unimpressed by his strategy, if it could be called that, of remaining motionless. She had attacked plenty of inert objects in her time. In fact her world was so small that it was her specialty. This one seemed to be goading her, saying, "C'mon, boy" Like some kind of idiot.

It had been a long time since anyone tossed a tennis ball for Trudy, or played tug-of-war with her, or sent her to fetch a frisbee. But she still hesitated a moment as if she were waiting for one of those things to occur, no matter how unlikely. And then, with the kind of decisive brutality that Tweed had witnessed in his own father, she leaped straight at him.

Now, this wasn't a life or death situation for Tweed. He was a well-nourished 26 year-old male, for goodness sakes. Generations of his forebears had dealt with generations of her forebears quite effectively, relying not inly upon innate mental and physical advantages, but upon an understanding that had developed between the two species as a result of a special relationship. For both sides, fear, respect, love and conditioning played a role in establishing the dynamics of that relationship. Only rarely was it necessary for men to resort to weapons or extreme force to defend themselves against dogs, or to enforce the terms of their agreement. So now as Tweed watched Trudy bounding through the air as if in slow motion, with her ears back, her claws extended, her fangs bared and a snarl caught in her throat, his mind was not occupied replaying images of a life cut short, but instead, he was remembering dog bites he had suffered in the past.

As he came up from the bullpen to home plate one fine summer day, he had reached for the bat proffered by Jimmy Donovan, who had just struck out. An onlooker would have seen a filthy ten year-old boy running from a grassy knoll toward a bare spot under a chestnut tree, where another small boy stood reluctantly holding out a baseball bat. The idyllic picture suddenly turned horrific as a large German shepherd that had been idly sniffing in the grass, seemingly mistook the intentions of the child and attacked him, seizing the boy's abdomen in his powerful jaws and pinning him to the ground. Tweed remembered how Jimmy's dog seemed to snatch him out of mid-stride as if he were no more than a chew-toy. The dog, Satan, whom Tweed had admired because he had been trained at the police academy, held him patiently while he waited for a signal of approval from his master.

Satan's panting turned to a gurgle as Tweed's blood welled up around his mouth. He looked at Tweed out of the corner of his eye as if to say, "Sorry, kid, nothing personal."

Rumor had it that Jimmy's dog had eaten Tweed's kidney, but even though it wasn't so, the dog had to be destroyed.

Next, with the near-simultaneity usually encountered only in dreams, visions and mutual orgasms, Tweed saw a friendly collie sitting up in the atrium of the public housing project in White City. Tweed was going door to door selling greeting cards for a school fund-raiser, and he had stopped to pat the handsome wheaten canine. It was an average meet and greet, the kind of thing one does casually, with courtesy and affection. A kind of Rockwellian scene as he recalled; the fresh-faced kid, his pockets bulging with brochures, bending over to pat an eager puppy. He should have known better.

If you're going to turn your back on someone, you try to do it so as not to cause offense. Well, he stood and turned toward the door of the next apartment on his list, and the bastard bit him. He felt a double row of needle sharp teeth puncture his left lower butt cheek deeply and rapidly. He was about 14 at the time, and though he was too old for tears he was still young enough to scream in pain, surprise and indignation. When they realized what had just occurred, both dog and boy scampered off in opposite directions. The dog subsequently escaped the fate of Satan, although at times Tweed wished worse upon him, especially when his mother was applying twin swabs of Mercurochrome to his bare backside.

A kennel full of memories rushed at him in that split second, but ahead of the mist of the past and the rest of the pack came the cruel present, and Trudy's nightmare visage.

Perhaps Tweed was a brawny male in his prime, but he can be forgiven for the feebleness of his reaction to the assault because he was also suffering from a sprained ankle and a likely overdose of pain medication. Never one to flinch, Tweed was still in his slo-mo adrenalin induced lethargy when the dog struck; so for him an incident that might have lasted seconds in real time appeared to be something he could have literally written home about. The hair on his bangs had not yet stopped fluttering from the breeze of Trudy's awe-inspiring passage when he realized that her attack had succeeded and yet he had also survived unscathed.

Let's examine the replay from Tweed's perspective, shall we?

Trudy, totally sure of herself at this point, wasted no time on dekes, fades or feints. Sprinting straight for her target, she covered yards of open ground in mere seconds as her stunned opponent waited for the judgment of the universal thumb. Would it turn up and grant him reprieve enough to anticipate another brutal attack, or would it turn down and crush him to the earth? The dog's instincts were unerring as she propelled headlong toward her goal, and only a photograph taken at right moment could reveal the precision with which she succeeded in seizing the bag of hashish and carrying it off to be consumed.

For, as Tweed himself later explained on the many occasions when he told this story, it was some time before he even realized that the bag was gone. As he put it, "It was like when a magician sweeps the tablecloth off a table without disturbing any of the dinnerware stacked on top of it. Trudy swept that bag out of my hand without even touching my fingertips!"

Puzzled, he was waiting for the next sortie; waiting and getting a bit impatient, when he turned and saw that she had found something to eat. Then he understood what had transpired. In his relief he cursed her greed. "Blasted Trudy! That's a god-damned half ounce of primo blond Lebanese you got there! I hope you're happy! I hope you get good and fucked up! You know how much that little snack cost me?" Indeed, the massive mongrel was munching down a $35.00 morsel of exquisite top-quality hash. Mere possession of that quantity of that type of controlled substance could subject a person to possible arrest and imprisonment in practically any country in the world. And here was Trudy the junk yard dog scarfing it down like it was a Scooby snack.

Needless to say, this little episode worked to Tweed's overall advantage. Within fifteen minutes Trudy was passed out full-length on the ground like a drunk-tank sleepover.

Good thing too, because Tweed may have needed a rest after his earlier exertions; but after a quarter of an hour crouching in wait, his calves were cramping up, he had to take a mean piss and his hands were freezing. So his next move was a bit perverse. Standing and shaking out his limbs in order to jump start the circulation, he also unzipped his fly and let loose with a steaming jet of urine. He rocked stiff-legged to and fro as he peed, and managed to place a moat of urine around Trudy's motionless body. This wasn't mere vindictiveness, for he thought that when she came to she'd undoubtedly freak out over the aroma, and run around in circles to follow the trail. However, if Kuhn had looked out of the office at that moment, he might well have imagined that his friend Tweed had killed his boss's dog and was now pissing on the carcass.

CHAPTER 26

Daylight savings time had gone into effect on the first Sunday of April, and by now, Friday the 18th, the results of the change were as yet inconclusive. With the sun setting at 6:30, the gain in useful daylight was negligible. More noticeable from Des' perspective was the shift in his internal body clock; like a bad mood that had taken almost a week to dispel.

Like some nocturnal creature, Des had emerged from his burrow in the biz club in order to commence the active portion of his day. Soon he would consult and consort with his cohorts, but first he would take some dinner and a drink or two.

On Friday evenings, as a result of an influx of new clientèle, the biz club itself underwent a change that Des, his crew, and some of the other older customers found somewhat distasteful. Any other night of the week, the club's stalwart regulars would stop in after work for a few pops before heading home to face whatever it was that they spent their days alternately earning the money to afford and then altering their perceptions to avoid. Come payday however, they headed right for home. Not that they wouldn't end up getting smashed as usual one way or another; in fact Friday vied with Thursday for the day on which they became most frequently and utterly wasted. But when the younger generation of drinkers showed up on Fridays, they altered that mood, the ambiance and the actual noise level at the old familiar Rossie Biz Club.

Very few of the old timers could take it. These younger fellows had a lot of pent-up energy and they tended to bang around the bar, for example, playing the cigarette machine as if it were a jukebox, and practically humping the pool table. However, they were tolerated as they were the stool-warmers, designated bar-brooms and biz-club alkies of the future.

Among them this evening were some of Des' so-called stooges: Joey Atkinson, Mo Keating, Tru Kennedy, Len Abbisso and Denis Fecteau. Joey had come to the club at the head of his little squad like the front man for a house band looking to demand a cut of the door. He had in fact intended to personally report about the mishap involving his father's Buick. Damnedest fucking thing. From personal experience he knew that his old man was probably too wrecked himself to give much of a damn about the wrecking of his car, no matter how wild and colorful he made the tale. Freaking two-ton car disabled and stripped by a freaking circus act! But then, the car could be burning in the middle of the square with his son in it and still old man Atkinson would remain at the bar sipping his whiskey. He was one patron who was unperturbed by the Friday night crowd.

At least the brick shithouse behind the bar would listen to his story and tell him what to do next. Guy's name was Harry Toole, or some shit like that…hey, Hairy Tool! All's Joey knew was that Denis got jobs from him sometimes, and the latest such job had led to the trashing of his old man's car.

Normally he wouldn't give a fuck; it was just that his father, a retired rail man, was usually incapacitated, so Joey pretty much had the car to himself. So unless somebody made good, he was out a job and a car.

This was the mood and the attitude that had taken him from the Fores bar, his usual hangout on one end of the square, to the biz club, all the way at the other.

Des had departed not a half an hour before Joey arrived, leaving Harris to deal out mugs of beer to the acne-pocked mugs of the stooges and their peers. He crossed Corinth St and stepped into an alley that ran back to tiny Taft Hill Place, one of a handful of postal designations in Rossie that were really no more than single addresses, that is, one unit with a parking space. There was no Taft Hill as far as Des could recall, and he wondered how the original owners of the property had managed to obtain a separate street address when any conscientious zoning inspector or postmaster general would have simply called the place 'Corinth St rear'. It never occurred to Des that Taft Hill Place could have predated Corinth St, and in fact it predated the square itself. In any event, it was here that his current girlfriend lived, and Friday was their regular night for pizza and beer.

It was significant that when Des felt threatened, worried or insecure, for example, on the previous evening after he and Harris and Simon had left the Arb's gate and the scene of the crime, he went directly home to his wife. Now that he felt that he had gained her comfort and a sense of control over the situation, he returned to his regular routine, and the company of someone who provided a different kind of comfort.

Caroline was an attractive woman, fitter and younger-looking than he was at her age. As an added bonus for Des, she was an ex-nun, who, though never cloistered, was spending her retirement trying to round out her experiences while attaining a broader appreciation of her self and her potential. Though a fascinating person in her own right, by necessity she will play as small a part in this narrative as she did during the course of the actual events.

When he was in Caroline's company Des adopted a more cultivated air, he strained his vocabulary and restricted his conversation to books, world events, politics and jokes. He never mentioned Ireland, CAFE, or the biz club in particular, or his work or travel in general. Only rarely did he mention his wife Christine or his children. However, as he ate his meal, and talked casually about the recent flare and fizzle of Halley's comet, inwardly he fumed and schemed and considered a thousand plots and possibilities.

If only Tweed were on his side, then together they could get to the bottom of this thing. Everything seemed to hinge on gaining Tweed's acceptance, or forcing his hand. Perhaps he could influence Christine to have a word with the boy, get him to be reasonable.

This was a vain hope, for although he had hardly spoken to his wife in the past six months, he at least maintained a courteous discourse with her, whereas Tweed had been as distant from his mother as he had been from Des himself. He was odd that way, thought Des, for he would have thought that the boy would surely side with his mother during their estrangement. Well, he had his own life to lead. And wasn't that supposed to be his motivation?

Didn't every man slave away at some task or another so that he might earn the things he desired? Tweed had his vixen, LaGloria there, to keep him going, and looking at her, Des could see the motivation.

But as a potential father-in-law he never trusted her, the dark little bitch, for she was a cunning one. He never forgot how she tried to snow him over with some bullshit story after dinner one night a couple of years ago. What was it now...? Her great-great-grandfather, she claimed, had been a leader of the Fenian Rebellion or some such...she had a name and everything. Made it out all innocent, as if the story was something that didn't really interest her, but she had heard it a thousand times at family gatherings and what not.

She knew that she had piqued his interest, fluttering her lashes at him like some coy colleen, but what she was really saying was that she had better blood than him. He was a common country publican's son, and she came from quality...as much as saying that she had the blood of heroes in her veins. Des knew that it was all a crock...had to be. Like to know where she came up with that act, though...like something out of the movies, it was.

He still felt a strong temptation to have her grabbed off the street and hauled in before some blokes who would find out what she really knew. It galled him that she was playing the victim in this affair. He was the victim. He alone. Her brothers had paid the price for their stupidity; and if the price seemed high, well, that's inflation. Ho, ho! He'd have to remember that one to tell his fellows later. *If the cost of living seems high...that's inflation.* Right!

Well, one thing at a time. Makepeace was still on the prowl, doing God knows what. And Storer was looking into the matter as well. Yet, now whenever he thought of Storer, his stomach did a funny little flip. Sure and you can leave it to the cops, they'll set things straight. My arse. How many stories had Billy told in the club about the mischief he and his fellow cops got into? To hear him tell it, the cops were worse than the crooks, for heaven's sake. And if you looked into the boot of his car on an average day! Steaks from the butchers, and liquor, and clothing, and all sorts of 'gifts' from business proprietors who were 'grateful' for Billy's protection. Once he'd even seen him hauling televisions out of his car, and another time it was fur coats. All in a day's work, he supposed. You don't get nothing for nothing.

He was resolved. To lean on Tweed, to lean on Makepeace and to lean on Storer. His smile of self-satisfaction was well-timed to coincide with the conclusion of a droll item that Caroline had remembered from the newspaper. But the pleasure of the moment was disturbed by the telephone. Des swore that Bell hadn't invented the thing to improve communications as much as he had to disrupt decent conversation. The call was for him, and his lover handed him the receiver with a quizzical look on her face.

"Des, I had to call you..." It was Harris Toole.

"Harris! This is a surprise! Lord Almighty! I'm in the middle of my dinner! Can't it wait?"

"Well, you tell me, Des. Denis and his pals showed up here and they're telling quite a story. It seems that someone dismantled Joe Atkinson's car in the middle of South St."

"What are you saying, now? In the middle of the street? Where were the stooges at the time?"

"That's just it, Des, you might want to hear it for yourself, but they were on their way to look after your boy as you requested, when suddenly the wheels fell off the car. So the boys marched to a pay phone to get someone down to help them with the wheels, but when they come back, the car was wrecked- totally demolished!"

Des spluttered, "Joe Atkinson's car? That's a solid car! A big sedan, right?"

"Not any more. Stripped in a matter of minutes. It's nothing but a shell now."

"Joe must be...If it were me, I'd...Well, tell him not to worry- we'll take care of him." Caroline was fussing with the dishes, yet he was still leery of saying too much in her presence or on her phone. With difficulty he lowered his voice. "Listen, Harris, it sounds to me like we've a rat in our midst," he hissed. "What do you think?"

"I would have guessed as much, Des, but the boys here, they have a different idea. Seems that some people at the Fores told Joey that they saw a character sitting in a car parked nearby. They say this guy must have seen Joe's car destroyed, must'a seen the whole thing- but he took off right after. Even if he had nothing to do with it, he might have some idea who did."

"Right, right," said Des thoughtfully, "I'm sure the stooges can come up with another car. Tell them to go out and find this other...witness. They can look in on Ta'weed after..."

Hanging up the phone Des was livid. What in blazes was going on? It was almost as if a pattern were emerging...he moves on LaGloria and not only do the stooges pick up the wrong girl, but she gets away from them- and who knows what shit will come of that fuck up. Now he makes a move on Tweed, and the blasted stooges can't drive down the street without having their faces rubbed in it. Old Joe Atkinson's car is destroyed and the boys are at the bar crowing about payback. Who's going to pay? He didn't know who his enemy was. But he felt that they were close, and watching his every move.

CHAPTER 27

"So you say you've run into this Kelley guy before, huh?"

Makepeace's contact in the state police, Raymond Chmura, spoke with a two-pack rasp. A.D.Makepeace was wearing his British intelligence hat now. After spending hours on the phone to both local and overseas connections, he had made some contacts, called in some favors and established his authority.

"Oh, yeah, we came across him during an investigation of IRA fund raising in the States back in the '70s. As I recall he wasn't considered to be much of a player back then. What do you have on him now?" He heard a shuffling of papers and as he waited for a response he noticed that there was a ringing in his ears, and his stomach felt hollow.

"Not much, I'm afraid; his record is clean but his name has been mentioned in a number of investigations, everything from bookmaking to attempted murder. Looks like nothing sticks to him. Like you said, he doesn't seem to be a major player, but he's always near the action, you know what I mean?"

Makepeace felt relieved. Now he knew that when the time came to take Des down, he wanted to be the one to do it.

"Yeah, sure do. So what do you have for me?"

"Well, you asked if we had any leads on the street, and lucky for you there is a source that we been working recently." Chmura made it sound like this was a game of 'Fish' and he had been asked for a card he would rather not part with. "This guy, this informant, is right there in the middle of things, keeping an eye on 'em for us. We been getting some good stuff from 'im recently. Pretty sure he has a grudge against this Kelley fella, or against someone in his circle anyway. Name is Brennan, Myles Brennan. Bartender at the Shamrock, a bar in Rossdale. Go ahead and talk to him if it will do you any good. As far as I know, the team working this informant ain't ready to move with anything yet, but still, use your common sense. You blow this source and you're gonna owe me more than a favor."

This was the break that Makepeace had been waiting for. If this source was any good then he should be able to get an idea of what was going on without becoming personally involved.

Des said that he needed help. He'd been attacked, he felt vulnerable, and he wanted reassurance. So he was, what do they call it…pulling his lorries into a circle? Makepeace was no cowboy gunslinger, but he had said that he'd see what he could do to find out who wanted Des dead.

Funny thing though, when a guy like Des needs help. He knows he can't talk to the police, and since the gunmen who attacked him are dead, he has no idea where the threat originated. If it was Makepeace, he'd look to the guys he worked with. When you have no obvious leads you look at the money; and the people around you are usually the only ones who know how much is at stake. Undoubtedly Des would vouch for his colleagues and associates, and they would likely resent any examination.

Chmura had just said that the informant, Brennan, held a grudge. A lot of people held grudges, but they don't necessarily shoot anyone. It would have to be a pretty severe grudge to incite or warrant that kind of violence. Of course, if the police knew that Des had been involved in the attack that resulted in the deaths of those boys, they'd consider a grudge ample reason for suspicion.

Means, motive, opportunity. The key elements to a successful prosecution. A cop who finds one of the three will usually manage to come up with the other two somehow.

Fortunately for Makepeace he wasn't out to prove anything. Des certainly wasn't interested in adhering to the niceties of criminal law procedures. He wanted only a name or names. Des was an old IRA man himself, and he should know, as Makepeace himself understood, that the IRA was by no means particular about observing the type of protocol that would stand up in a court of law. Their investigations were crude, cruel and brutal, their tribunals were swift and severe, and their judgments final. Even those deemed innocent came away from the proceedings shaken and traumatized.

Despite his power in the community and the backing of his motley crew of cronies Des didn't have the wherewithal to arrange or stage an IRA-style investigation. In fact it was probable that he had asked Makepeace to look into the matter purely for show. He couldn't let it be known that he could be attacked with impunity. In order to maintain his position, his respect and his dignity, he had to ensure that not only his friends but his enemies and his business associates as well knew that he responded to threats quickly and decisively.

Des pressed for results, but Makepeace suspected that he did so reluctantly. He couldn't afford to permit anyone, even an old 'ally' like Makepeace to look too closely into his affairs.

Makepeace, however, was already looking.

It was apparent that his first obstacle was to see past his own preconceptions. A relationship like the one he had with Des was forged through time and trials, through persistence and compromise, and through conflict and reconciliation. At every stage in the process he made and then tempered judgments. At times he had spoken freely, and at times he had held his opinions in check. Sometimes he had offered substantial financial support, sometimes emotional support, or merely moral support; while on other occasions he had withdrawn his assistance altogether. He had come to know Des not with genuine regard like a friend, but guardedly. Now he wondered how he could possibly claim to possess objectivity. After all they had been through together, how could he exercise professional detachment? It was as if he were looking through a pair of well-worn sunglasses, ignoring the scratches, blurs and imperfections that would render them virtually useless to anyone else trying to see through them.

His next obstacle was the man himself. His record showed Des to be frustratingly and uncommonly nonconformist. While he may have possessed a passport and a fixed abode, he had no career to speak of, no professional or civic affiliations, no college transcripts, and no credit history. Des Kelley was not a man of extraordinary skill, he boasted no special talents, and he pursued no hobbies.

This was not to say that the file Makepeace had amassed on Des was lacking detail or substance. On the contrary it was voluminous, filled with reports and observations that had been provided for the most part by Makepeace himself. It was as if he had prepared an exhaustive case study on Kelley only to fail in reaching a conclusion or drawing a profile. His only consolation in regards to this shortcoming was the fact that he had personally compiled the bulk of the dossier and that he was in a position to dispose of it.

On the positive side, it now looked as though he had overcome the obstacle of access. First he would persuade Myles Brennan to cough up any relevant information, and then he would go after Tumbleweed, Des' own son, and get him to help flush out his father's enemies.

CHAPTER 28

"The place is too clean. It doesn't smell right. Gonna be like working in a freakin' hospital. Every thing's white, and if you ask me, that ain't right."

Detective Storer talked as he walked quickly ahead of his partner through the parking lot toward his car. Tonight he felt like driving, mainly because he wanted to ensure that he got away from the precinct house as fast as possible. This was the new station in Westbury Circle, still under construction and at this point open only for tours and orientation.

Detective Rima matched his partner's footsteps in a hurried attempt to hear what the heck he was saying.

"I like it. Can't wait. *Because* it's clean. Didja see that lunchroom? You could actually eat in there."

"Yeah?" replied Storer over his shoulder, "How about them cubicles? And they call it 'open architecture' or some such bullshit like that."

"Oh, I suppose you like the squad room the way it is now?"

Storer's colleagues had long been accustomed to hearing him bitch about, among other things, the leaky ceilings, the drafty windows, the creaky floors, the antiquated desks and the archaic cells at the old 13th precinct house where they currently worked.

"Damn right I do! I think I'll put in to stay behind when the rest of yous all move up there in July. They'll need someone to look after the place." Storer was irritated that he had been required to visit the new facility. But the captain had ordered everyone in his command to do so by Friday.

His mandatory request turned out to be for the best. During the remaining months before it opened, the new precinct station was vandalized numerous times. Officers investigating the vandalism, as well as the ones who responded to reports of suspicious activity on the site were grateful to have been given the opportunity to become familiar with its layout.

"I can picture you working all alone in the old hell hole. Dja' remember how hot it gets in there in the middle of the summer? You're not gonna stick me there. I'll be with the rest of them moving up to cool air heights. Anyway, I hear that place is already scheduled for demolition."

The doors of the dark Impala clunked like dented oil drums when they opened and the car sagged appreciably as the detectives climbed in and took their seats. Storer turned the key in the ignition and the starter motor kicked in like a beaver struggling to gain a chew-hold on a frozen log. Suddenly the big Chevy turned over, took a deep breath of fresh air, cleared its throat and surged to life.

Rima fumbled with his seatbelt, always nervous about the way his partner pulled out of a parking space without consulting the rear-view mirror or looking over his shoulder.

"Tear it down? What the heck? They can't take down the old precinct house. It's a friggin' landmark, a, a historical, uh,"

"Relic?" suggested Rima.

"No- they won't let them tear that building down," Storer continued, not elaborating on who 'they' were. "You'll see- if the department don't keep it for a substation like they did to the old 9 over in Roosevelt, then it'll go to the community. They'll do it over for housing or something. You'll see."

In fact, in a striking fulfillment of Billy Storer's prediction, the old Municipal Precinct 13 station house was kept as a police substation for the remainder of the '80s. The department did this primarily to demonstrate that the move to Westbury Circle, a more upscale part of town, was not a withdrawal in the strategic sense. The substation served to maintain a 'presence' until it was indeed converted into a condominium complex for low-income elderly residents. But by then Storer and Rima had retired to the suburbs.

Storer turned onto the parkway heading west. Without conscious intent, he was following a broad looping route that would take them past the Arbs Park, the train station at Jamaica Center, Rossie Towing, White City, the Fores and the Shamrock, and ultimately back to Tweed's apartment complex in Westbury, not half a mile from where they had started at the new 13.

"Let's go over what we have so far, shall we?" said Storer, still a little groggy from his afternoon nap, but determined to get down to business.

"What do you want..."

"Evidence; gimme the evidence..."

"We have two stiffs, both male, Caucasian. One, Frankie McManus, aged 27, the other Nilvan McManus, aged 25. Brothers. Death from multiple gunshot wounds. Both of them were hit by automatic weapons fire, looks like standard US military machine gun fired at about 60 yards; and in the case of the older one, Francis, he was also shot 'execution style' by a handgun at close range."

"What do you mean by 'standard military'?"

"Hey, face it, the slugs are buried in the hillside somewhere. But the casings at the scene came from a regular standard-issue M60."

"M60? The Rambo gun? You gotta be kidding?"

"It's a pretty common gun, man."

"Yeah, but it's *crew-served...*"

"Huh? What do you mean?"

"Never mind. It means that the guy had to be big like Rambo, that's all. Alright, go on."

"Alright, we got blood and tissue samples taken from the scene. We have, uh, a car, one 1972 Chevy Chevelle rust-colored hardtop that was found parked nearby. It was registered to the same Frankie McManus. The car was gutted by fire and forensics hasn't gotten into it yet.

"Then there's the guns. Remington 20-gauge shotgun model 870, formerly registered to a Robert Hedges of Hull, who reported it stolen from his collection in '84; and a mil-spec Colt AR-15 M16. The rifle came from part of a shipment that went missing last September. One in a series of shipments, I might add, that 'fell off the back of the truck' as they say, while on route from Colt after refurbishing. Do you know what they consider acceptable shrinkage? Forget it- you don't want to.

"We also recovered pieces of clothing, actually all shreds from the same jacket, scattered on the hill there, caught on trees, hanging on bushes, and behind the wall near where we found the car. The jacket itself was stuck up on top of the fence. Looks like someone fell down the hill maybe; anyway, our people had a real hard time climbing up. At first I thought that the jacket might have belonged to one of the victims."

"But...?"

"But, we also have a couple of other items that might tie into this somehow. First, a couple of officers on patrol down on South Main logged in an incident not long after the first units responded to the burning car at the park. They broke up what looked like a drug deal and chased down a few of the suspects. One of them, described as 'all beat up and dressed in rags', bolted to the tracks and eluded the officers. As usual, the ones who were caught implicated the one who got away, saying that this guy in torn clothing had suddenly appeared offering to sell them drugs.

"So anyway, then we got the testimony of a driver from Fairview Cab. Said that he picked up a fare at the train platform in the square and drove him to Westbury Circle. All of this was within an hour of the shooting. Claimed the guy was filthy and his clothes were hanging off him. It was only later, when he heard about what happened at the park, that he decided to call it in, in case his fare might have been involved somehow."

"So who was the passenger, and what's this got to do with anything?"

"Not sure yet, but I'll tell you something you might find interesting- LaGloria McManus lives at the same apartment complex."

"What? Where?"

"The place where the cabbie went to, where he dropped off the fare- an apartment complex in Westbury Circle."

"No kidding?"

"No; and I talked to the officers we sent out to notify Miss McManus about the incident involving her brothers. They reported that when they arrived at her apartment, both LaGloria and her boyfriend- Tumbleweed Kelley were there."

"Oh, Jeez! This is getting interesting. You think the jacket belonged to Weed Kelley?" He didn't bother mentioning that he had interviewed Tweed just this morning.

"Yep. Uh, *Weed?*"

"It's his nickname on the street- for all the obvious reasons. You think he was at the scene of the crime?"

"I'll tell you what my gut says, Billy. I think he was the shooter."

"That's a stretch," said Storer, frowning.

"I don't know. There's one more item I was gonna mention. After you and I arrived at the scene you had the perimeter cordoned off, right?"

"Yeah, so?"

"Well, one of our guys was down at South and Bussey redirecting traffic. When a couple of young ladies in a car stopped and asked him a few questions. He says that they were all upset, and they claimed they were out looking for someone and they thought they recognized his car- the one that was burned down there, the Chevelle. Not only that, but one of the chicks said her name was 'LaGloria'."

"No shit! LaGloria McManus was at the scene just after the incident? What is going on here?"

"Like I said, partner, a beef between the boyfriend and the brothers. I've seen it happen before. Ten to one we find out she's pregnant, or they were getting married, or something like that that ticked them off. 'Weed' went down there to settle it with his 'in-laws' and things got out of hand. What do you think?"

"Hmmm. You sure you can place him at the scene...."

"Yeah," Rima didn't sound sure.

"What about help? What about the guns? The only ones we found don't match the murder weapons. Remember, we're talking more than one murder weapon. What did he do, carry a machine gun and a handgun? Doesn't it seem like overkill to you?"

"OK. So the McManus boys went well-armed too. And I admit there was more than one gun, but that doesn't mean he had to have help. But if he did, who's to say that it wasn't LaGloria?"

"LaGloria? Which gun did she use, the M60 or the .44?"

Rima actually blushed. "I see what you mean. Well, it's just a theory now anyway. We can fill in the missing pieces of the puzzle later. I say we go after Weed now, bring him in and see what he knows."

Storer sighed and ran a hand through his hair. "His old man ain't gonna like it. But it's like I told him, I don't really care who gets busted for this thing. Someone's gotta take the rap, and it might as well be a sleaze bag like our young Mr. Kelley."

"So, bring him in?"

"Ah…" Storer sounded like he was mentally flipping a coin. Wasn't Weed Kelley using crutches this morning? He should have asked the kid about his injury when he had the chance. Could be important.

"Why not?" he replied at last. "Just don't charge him with anything yet. Tell you what. Let's head up there right now. We'll separate them. I'll take the kid out for a cup of coffee, and you stay with his girlfriend. See if you can get a feel for what she knows. Maybe we'll get a break and something will shake loose."

"Girl's brothers just got blown away…" Rima put in, both dolefully and doubtfully.

"Yeah, and like you said, she might be one of the shooters," replied Storer, with finality.

Thinking better of replying, Rima kept his mouth shut and studied the manila folder in his lap. He had intended to spend some time with LaGloria anyway, if only to explain the forms and procedures she would have to endure over the next few days.

Processing the remains of one's loved ones had become formalized in an attempt to sanitize and depersonalize the experience for the next of kin. Gone were the days of the in-house wake, an intimate exposure to death that was once part of the fabric of life in American society and a fundamental reality for most families.

As the population shifted from a rural and agricultural base toward urban centers of commerce and industry, the 20th century became a boom time for the funeral business. Successive world wars, a burgeoning birth rate, and a standard of living that was applied unevenly across the social strata, all helped to create a demand for a new way to remove the dead.

Crowded cities incurred and faced particular challenges in the form of disease epidemics, growing numbers of homeless and indigent poor, homicides, industrial accidents, pollution and contamination, and mass immigration.

Under these circumstances the processing of death became rigidly controlled and codified, especially in cases of homicide, suicide and accidental death. It was no wonder that the police had developed a packet of information to help survivors and kin deal with the bureaucratic confusion related to death. However, Rima had learned that when folks are in grief, shock or mourning they typically view this type of official assistance as an unwelcome and tactless intrusion.

CHAPTER 29

It's always one blasted nut, one difficult, ball busting recalcitrant freakin' screw that won't come out. Tweed cursed the bolt, cursed his tools, cursed his bleeding knuckles and his stiff fingers. He cursed the car and the flatbed truck to which it was chained, as well as the night itself and the haughty stars that condescended to twinkle at him in his misery. And man, it sucks when even the stars make fun of you.

Shit work he didn't mind. Even unpaid pain-in-the-ass do-it-cause-you-gotta type of work. But pointless shit work was another matter entirely. You get sucked into doing some stupid job that not only sucks in the execution, and offers squat in compensation, but also serves no worthwhile purpose whatsoever.

Not to say that this job, the job of removing the sawed-off shotgun from its hiding place in the sub-floor of Frankie's '72 Chevy Chevelle SS was pointless; on the contrary, if he should succeed then it was essential in the most crucial respect, in that it affected his welfare and well-being. Life, liberty, happiness and all that. However it was such a nasty, filthy, stinking, uncomfortable job, and furthermore a risky one in terms of its legality and dangerous in terms of his personal safety that its benefits and utility were nearly outweighed.

If he determined that the gun was unreachable, or that the car was too badly burned to attempt the retrieval, then he must proceed with his "plan B": destruction of the car. He would be forced to carry out this step in order to totally eradicate any evidence that the vehicle might conceal. In fact, Tweed would have simply opted for plan B, thereby saving himself a lot of trouble if it weren't for the fact that he needed the shotgun so that he might use it in an another plan, one that he had already set in motion.

So he had made it into the inner sanctum, his strength, skill, daring and stamina carrying him into the mud-puddle arena where seized and stolen vehicles were securely impounded. So he had faced the fanged terror that stalked the junk-heap maze, and having bribed the guard, had emerged unscathed from conflict. So he had limped to his goal unaided by crutches or splints until his injured ankle had practically screamed for him to stop. And he had climbed the greasy flatbed tow truck on a night when the air was a mere 43 degrees and the mud was even colder. That was all just the prelude. Now he was getting to the real work.

Since the car had been put to the torch but then rapidly extinguished, its condition was not as bad as its appearance had led him to believe. Tweed rather liked the back-swept smoke damage look. Black soot streaming from the windows and doors had created a radical two-tone effect that complemented the basic rust primer finish the car had sported before the fire.

Tweed and his friends had enjoyed many good times in this car, and without ever traveling very far from home he had driven many miles, beating the shit out of it all the while before handing the keys and ownership over to LaGloria's brother.

Frankie in turn had quickly forked over the fees to register the car in his name, and after installing his own license plates he was naturally eager to take it for his first spin. But as soon as he got it up to speed on the highway, the right front control arm broke and the wheel seized, stopping the car dead in its tracks. So the car was no stranger to tow trucks. Frank had a taste of high-speed equipment failure, and LaGloria, who had conned her boyfriend into parting with the car in the first place, now complained that he was trying to kill her brother.

Although it croaked him financially to do so, Tweed hadn't minded ponying up for the repairs; but then shortly after Frank got the car back on the road, the timing chain snapped. After another expensive tow, Frank had to install a new chain along with cam shafts and sprockets and a distributor and seals. Since he was already in so deep he went ahead and remanned the head and did a valve job while he was at it.

With many of the engine components renewed, the hardware torqued and tightened and all of the fluids topped off, the Chevelle sang a different tune than the wheezy plaint it had chanted when Tweed owned it. For a while there the sporty 6 was something of which Frankie was so proud that he even occasionally took it out for stock quarter sprints. But then, he didn't know about the shotgun concealed in his trunk.

Of course Tweed had hidden the gun in the car before he gave it to Frank, and then he had conveniently forgotten that it was there, unwittingly reinforcing the adage about sight and mind.

Now things were different, Frank was dead; and Tweed needed to get the gun back before the police found it and somehow used it not only to tie him to Frank's murder but to other crimes as well.

Thank heavens the trunk was already open, saving Tweed the time and effort of popping the lid. As every two-bit thief knows, the trunk is a weak spot on most cars, and when the key isn't available a screw-driver forcefully applied will do. Tweed's tool of choice was an auto body dent-puller (basically a steel shaft with a sliding pump-action weight and a threaded nipple chuck at one end for affixing a sheet metal screw). But Tweed had left his dent-puller at home just in case he were to be detained and searched by the police. The tools he carried were sufficiently incriminating, but these were the days when politicians ran for office on promises of enacting mandatory sentencing. According to recently implemented guidelines, it was a crime to carry a dent puller, and getting caught with one was like picking up a 'Go Directly To Jail' card.

This wasn't the first time that Tweed had crawled into the trunk of the Chevelle. A couple of summers ago he had installed a very warm pair of tri-axial speakers in the rear deck, spending a couple of hours with his head and torso stuffed into the car's butt while his legs roasted in the sun. Then, as now, he had skinned his knuckles and cursed his luck and fought with an uncompromising screw or two. Fortunately, on this occasion he could afford to be sloppy.

Between the spare tire well and the brace for the rear seat there was a broad metal panel that was actually part of the floor. Normally it did nothing more than provide access to certain electrical cables, adjuster links for the parking brake cables, as well as insulation and chassis plates for the fuel and vapor recovery lines. But smack dab in the center of the cavity Tweed had hidden the shotgun, wrapped in a heavy canvas bag and a length of chain. Now the only thing preventing him from lifting the shelf and revealing whether or not the gun was there was a pain-in-the-ass bolt that refused to budge.

Frustrated, cold, sore and tired, Tweed took to wiggling the metal panel back and forth in an attempt to snap the remaining bolt. The stench of burned cloth and fiber insulation, an overpowering wet-ash odor mixed with burned rubber, melted plastic, toasted electrical cables and leaking fluids, as well as the closeness of the small trunk combined to make Tweed gag. Fortunately he had smeared dabs of menthol vapor goo in his nostrils- not in an attempt to clear his sinuses but to stifle his sense of smell. With sooty cheeks and green smeg hanging from his nose he looked the right junk yard waif.

The only clothing suitable for wriggling around in this toxic mixture of fire suppressant foam, charred upholstery, melted rubber, plastic and insulation was full-blown body isolation gear, the type worn by waste-cleanup or biohazard professionals. If he had thought about it beforehand, Tweed might have asked LaGloria to look through Nilvan's stuff and find one of the suits he wore for asbestos removal. Lacking that or any other special preparation, the only protection he had from vile petrochemicals, PCBs and other carcinogenic hydrocarbons was a pair of old corduroys he was willing to sacrifice because he had ruined them while painting his apartment, and a mechanic's jacket that he used reluctantly because it had been a gift from his friend Mickey, whose name was embroidered across the back. There was a half-inch of gritty slime sloshing around in the trunk too, so he was soaked right through the fleece-lined hoodie he wore under the jacket. He couldn't wait to strip off all of the contaminated clothing and jump into a nice sudsy shower. But first he had to remove this blasted stubborn hunk of metal, get at the shotgun and find his way out of the dismal, desolate and inhospitable tow-lot.

How had he gotten into this predicament? How could he allow LaGloria to run his life this way? Here he was, basically crawling in the shit at her request.

What about Frankie and Nilvan? How, he wondered, had LaGloria convinced her brothers to march off to their deaths? Or, to put it in a marginally better light, how had she gotten them to take up arms and go off to commit murder? She was a manipulating, controlling, conniving witch.

Admittedly she was beautiful, but beauty alone couldn't account for the hold she had on him. All of his previous girlfriends had been attractive in an average, girl-next-door way. The truth was that she was the first really gorgeous girl he had fallen for. She knew when and where to use perfume and accessories, how to make herself up with style and restraint, and how to dress fashionably. If there was some glamour, some magic influence that she held over him, then it was powerful stuff, for she was his first real love, there was no denying that.

He and LaGloria never discussed their future, they never planned on marriage, or children, or anything beyond the here and now. Indeed, the joy of their relationship was the way in which they celebrated the moment. Whether they were fucking madly or just holding hands, walking together in the park or skiing in the mountains, watching a movie at the drive-in or snuggling in front of the TV; whether they were sharing a shower or eating dinner together, splitting up a bale of primo sinsemilla, or smoking a joint, the glory of their love was expressed in the myriad instances. It was the tentative promise in a glance, the electric spark of a kiss, the raw hunger of a lusty embrace; but it was also the happy relief he felt when she came home from work, the pride that warmed his chest when she curled up in his arms for protection and comfort, and the confidence of a thousand shared secrets.

But now a new question began to arise in his awareness- could he give it all up to save himself? Could he sacrifice LaGloria, abandoning the object of his love and source of his happiness?

At least he had an inkling that there was peril in their union. She wanted to destroy his father, and for all he knew, there were other names on her list of possible targets. She had sent her only brothers to their deaths. She clearly acted out of ambition and compulsion. Perhaps the day would come when she would see him as an obstacle to her success. And now they were both at risk of arrest and prosecution for the attempt on Des' life.

As of now the facts in the case as they were publicly known did not seem to indicate any conspiracy. The way the press told the story, Frankie and Nilvan had died after confronting nameless adversaries, unknown figures who had vanished into the night. It was not described as an attack upon Des Kelley, and Tweed was sure that he wanted to keep it that way. Despite their concern and caution, he and his lover had no real reason to suspect that the police were on to them.

He had told LaGloria not to worry, saying that the police would only bother her if she appeared to be excessively nervous as opposed to grieving. It was her responsibility to portray herself as such, and not to admit either in conscience or confessional that she was the hidden hand who had ordered the hit.

Likewise he could not allow himself to act out of fear. He had to maintain the perception that he was in control of his affairs, that he had no qualms about confronting the police or his father or anyone else for that matter, including LaGloria. As far as he knew, or acknowledged at any rate, neither his father nor his girlfriend were in any way linked to the episode at the South St gate, and furthermore, he could not conceive of any reason why his potential brothers-in-law might have been. In fact if it weren't for the fact that they were indeed found dead at the scene, he wouldn't have believed that they could have anything to do with violence, mayhem or murder.

Like his mother had always told him, stick to your story. Don't go changing the details as you go along. By no means had she encouraged him to lie; on the contrary she believed that honesty was the hallmark of personal integrity. However, storytelling was another kettle of fish entirely, and especially among the Irish, honor and respect were accorded to anyone who could enthrall, beguile or enchant with a cleverly woven and well-embroidered tale. The degree to which fantasy or exaggeration played a part was inconsequential. What mattered was the fabric of the tale- it couldn't have holes in it; however if imperfections should turn up then a good storyteller may improvise, but sparingly, and only using ingredients from a stock of like tales or elements from the store of his own experience.

There he was again, missing his mother, the pang of remorse and the yearning to see her mixing with embarrassment over his insecurity as a grown man as well as a confusion of anger and shame. Yearning was a natural emotion, but the embarrassment came from his brother, who had berated him for childishness, and the anger was a result of lies his father had told him about his mother.

At age 18 it hadn't been as difficult as he had imagined to move out of his parent's home. Mum had fretted for days over his departure, running him through any tactic she could devise to keep him home.

"For heaven's sake, Tumbles," she had said, "...we spent years trying to get out of Jamaica Center, and now you're going back there. Aren't there any flats available in Roosevelt, Rossie or White City? I hear they got bugs down there now. Lord knows there were no bugs when we lived there. But you know Annie McIlheny still lives there...by the circle, in the big gray house; you remember Annie, don't you, love? She's seen a lot of changes over the years and not for the better, I'm afraid. Bugs! Jesus, Mary and Joseph! Her husband Stevie has to clean them apartments from time to time, and the bugs are awful!"

Through the filter of teen exuberance Tweed heard his mother saying that the family was not long out of JC, that there were friends of the family still living there, and that it was a decent place where the rents were cheap because the neighborhoods were in a period of transition.

"And the trains!" she had added. "We only got the one train now, and it's not so bad, but down there the trains run all day and night. And where you're moving to, the folks on them trains can look right into your bedroom window as they pass. Twice a day! In the morning, going into town they'll say, 'Oh, look! Tweed's still in bed!' And in the evening, on their way back home, 'Ah, there he is now, getting ready to go out!'"

Not above playing the sentiment card, his mother had reviewed some of the previous separation traumas she had suffered.

"Mack, you recall, left me to fight for the bloody US in Viet Nam. I never saw him again. (sniff!) Dear Buck left me to go back home to Ireland, and though it's some small comfort knowing he's there, it's still a long way (sniff!) and the visits are all too few for my liking. I've kept Keiran's room for him, but he never thinks to come home either. (Sob!) When he gets a break from his studies he runs off to help the natives in Ecuador, or teaching the gospel in places where church is no more than a hut in the wilderness!"

Realizing that these and other remarks -about loneliness in her old age, the emptiness of the house, and the unsuitability of JC- were having little or no effect upon him. She had threatened to never visit him.

"Oh, that's alright, Mum!" he had said, "I'll come and visit you!"

But, in truth he had not. Over the past few years he had been as faithful about visiting his mother as he was about going to church or paying his taxes. Part of the reason for his negligence was that at the time before he had achieved real independence, when he was still impressionable to a certain extent, he had been alienated by the conflict that had arisen at home between his parents. A variety of factors including stress had contributed to the deterioration of their marriage, but Tweed didn't understand this until he was in his mid-twenties.

During Tweed's last year in high school his mother became ill. She ignored her condition for months, but when she finally agreed to let a doctor take a look at her she learned that any further delay on her part could have been disastrous. She was suffering from heart disease, liver and kidney ailments, arthritis and back problems. Any satisfaction she might have felt at having permitted a diagnosis was quickly replaced by the distress caused by the prospect of expensive procedures, hospital stays and medications.

It wasn't the illness itself that caused Des to drift apart from his wife so much as it was the factors surrounding the illness.

One factor, for example, was that Des had to endure extended separations while Christine underwent numerous medical procedures and then convalesced in the hospital. While he had thought nothing of going away 'on business' at least twice a year for almost twenty years, this was the first time that he had to deal with her absence while he was at home.

Another factor was her determination to learn all she could about her condition, and about the available treatments, and about the top experts in the field. Although Des may have been concerned about her progress and her treatment, he simply could not share her interest in these vital matters. But then, he felt uncomfortable whenever his intellect was challenged in any way.

Also troublesome for Des was the way in which his wife was increasingly surrounded by well-wishers, including relatives and friends who were willing to shop, cook, run errands or simply spend time with Christine. Their love, compassion and attention seemed to outshine Des' tenderness for his wife. At first he welcomed their presence as it afforded him opportunities to get away for rest and decompression, but gradually he allowed himself to be pushed out of the picture almost entirely.

The changing dynamics of the situation affected him in another way as well. For lack of a better description, he became jealous of his wife and the attention and gifts she received. He figured that if the roles were reversed, that is if he was in hospital, then he would have far fewer visitors and nowhere near the same retinue of care-givers and well-wishers.

As it happened, Des eventually chose one individual to represent the target of his resentment and jealousy, and for reasons best left to a psychologist to determine, the person he chose was Brendan Tighe.

Like many of Christine's concerned friends, Brendan had taken to visiting her both in the hospital and at home, where he tried to make himself useful in exchange for all of the hospitality she had shown him over the years. He assisted in facilitating the conversion of the first-floor spare room into a makeshift bedroom, even going so far as to arrange for a secondhand hospital bed and bed-table to be brought in.

It wasn't Brendan's insistence upon plenty of sunlight, fresh flowers, comfortable pillows and colorful bedclothes that troubled Des, although he had thought of none of these by himself. Rather it was his persistent presence as well as his unflagging devotion to Christine that sparked Des' hostility. He was irrationally infuriated by the young Jesuit's willingness to spend so much time with his wife, to read to her, to give her sponge baths and manicures, to cook simple meals and make sure that she ate them.

The gestures Brendan made out of human decency and Christian love were distorted in Des' mind so that he saw them as usurpation, inappropriate behavior, and improper intimacy. Finally Des simply blew up and railed against Brenda, banishing him from the house, and making up false and sometimes salacious stories about his behavior. To hear Des tell it, his old friend, the humble teacher, a servant of Christ and humanity, was carrying on a torrid affair with his wife while her strength to resist was sapped by her illness and her judgment was impaired by medication. Des made a point of disseminating this slander to friends and to members of the family, but especially among those who had visited and cared for Christine. Though still unwilling to spend much time with her himself, Des wanted help in preventing Brendan from spending any more time with her.

Unfortunately the lies had a greater impact upon Tweed than they did upon Brendan. Christine answered all of her misguided husband's charges but to no avail, other than to assure Brendan that she remained his grateful friend and that she would do all she could to clear his name.

Tweed however felt betrayed, angered and humiliated. Whatever traces he had inherited of his father's madness served to blind him to the truth and to compound his impression of supposed grievance. He no longer spoke to Brendan, he no longer trusted his mother and he basically detested Des.

Earlier in the day when he had swallowed his pride and visited the RBC to see his father, he had refrained from asking after his mother. It wasn't that he didn't care, or that he wasn't genuinely concerned, but that he knew he could never believe anything that his father might say about his mother, and worse, he feared that he would hear more of the accusations and bitterness that Des now levied so casually and cruelly against his wife.

Suddenly Tweed's thoughts and his work were interrupted by the sound of an approaching truck coming through the gate into the compound. Apparently another of the Rossie towing fleet was returning to the yard with a car in tow. He curled up so that he would remain invisible in the trunk, but he kept his head up so that he could see what was going on. In a moment the truck rounded the corner into the storage area of the yard, and the driver, a fellow Tweed knew by name only as Meatball, climbed out of the cab and started removing the chains and tie-downs that kept his load steady on the truck.

Wait a moment- wasn't that- yes! Surely it was the remains of the car upon which Tweed had set the Mitranos, the car Rick Rose had described. Holy shit! What a hack job! They got everything worth anything off of that car- and it looked like they trashed it as well. Nice work. He reminded himself to thank Rick for his diligence, to thank the roving chop squad and to thank Griffin for the recommendation.

Seeing the arrival of the car that belonged to Sharlae's tormentors gave Tweed a boost of inspired energy. It also reminded him that he did not have all night to finish his work. With a figurative flame lit under his ass, he redoubled his efforts to remove the stubborn obstacle.

The new jolt of adrenalin coursing through his veins gave Tweed a sudden insight. Surely there was no need to remove the panel cleanly. He lacked the tools to actually drill out the bolt or to cut the metal itself, but why not bend it? For this he would need no tools, only leverage, so he paused and collected his breath and strength.

Meanwhile Meatball, who was clearly unaware that Tweed was there, completed the task of dropping Atkinson's car into the muck and then he hesitated before climbing back into his truck. Tweed had to stifle a laugh because Meatball was peeing too. Like another junkyard dog he relieved himself on the wreck.

CHAPTER 30

"Hey! Hold up there Bonesy! Let me tell you a question. What the heck are we doing here, anyway?"

Hurrying up the stairs in the stash house, Bone was making a dash for his car, deliberately trying to avoid Og. He replied without turning or pausing. "A favor for a friend, remember? Remember the meeting, and all those things we said?"

"Right. OK, so we help him and we help ourselves, get it? Did you ask yourself, 'What am I getting out of this?'"

"Og, man, you didn't want to come, you should have spoke up. I came because Weed asked me, OK? Personally, I was worried about supply. I was afraid things were gonna dry up around here. Now, I don't know about you, but I can't afford to let that happen. Not when I got people depending on me. I don't intend to let them down."

"Listen; I got just as much business riding on this as you do, if not more. Only, I ain't afraid to tell it like it is, see? And I'm sick of doing thing's Weed's way. Guy thinks he has a freakin' monopoly. Thinks he can split up the town and the business. Like I'm not supposed to have any customers in White City. Why the fuck not? Because that's Kuhn's territory. Only Kuhn don't give a fuck if he sells to customers in the square, and that's supposed to be my territory. And don't tell me you have any hesitation about moving into my territory either."

"Look, Og, I told you that kid said he lived in Fairview. How the fuck was I supposed to know he meant Fairview Heights, not Fairview Ave? I thought we had that straightened out."

"I'm just saying is all. This is a cutthroat business we're in, and it's every man for himself."

"That's just it, Og. I mean, you don't get it, do you? The reason we need Weed. Besides the fact that he built this business. When you think about it, all of the customers were his at one time. We all try to increase our business, but I bought most of my customers from him when I got started. Let me finish. The reason, like I said, the reason we need Weed is because he set it up so that there are no beefs like you're talking. I got my areas, you got yours. We have a hassle, we work it out. You ask me, I think everything works better this way. And don't forget- he has a way of eliminating the competition."

"I ain't afraid of Weed Kelley. I known him since he was a freakin' bookworm at the library."

"Well, shit, Og, I didn't know you could read."

"Fuck you, man. Are you going to help me or not?"

"Oh, you made up your mind, didja? Gonna steal the stash, gonna take the inventory that me and Sharlae-" Bone felt exposed and suddenly paranoid. The houses, the cars; none of these places were safe. Even people could be bugged, or listening. He wasn't supposed to mention names. No more names. "-and everybody else need to make a living?"

"Fuck everybody else, man! You and me! We'll take ours and everybody else can go fuck themselves. Especially Weed."

"Carrying around a little too much hostility, ain'cha there, Oggie Dog?" Bone considered his options. Mickey should be back any moment now; but he had left his shotgun leaning in the corner by the back door. He eyed the gun as he crossed the kitchen.

But Og seemed to have similar ideas. He attempted to hustle past, elbowing Bone aside. Bone responded by swinging the golf-duffel bag full of dope from his shoulder and into Og, as if he were trying to shrug him off.

A wordless, grunting struggle ensued. Both men tagged up at the same time, grasping at the cold blue steel barrel of the rifle. Pulling in opposite directions, they gradually managed to raise and manipulate the shotgun so that they each had two hands on it, until they held it horizontally between them.

"F-fucking Og, man!"

Og's face was turning deep red and he appeared to be struggling with his nerve as he struggled with his opponent.

"What, are you going to shoot me?" Og panted.

"I'm not gonna let you rob me!"

"It's not your shit, man! And I told you! I'm gonna let you have some!"

"You can't give what you don't have, dude. Besides, think about it- if you took all of this stock, what would you do after it ran out?"

"Then I'll have the money to do whatever I want. Somebody will sell to me."

Bone made a mighty pull on the rifle, trying to wrest it from Og's grasp, but Og held on firmly and the two of them fell over in a heap on the floor with the rifle still between them. For a few truly awful moments the men rolled around like a couple of impotent walruses.

In most physical confrontations between adult males one of them has an advantage in terms of weight, strength, size or skill. But in their case neither Bone nor Og had the upper hand due to their common lack of stamina, prowess and endurance. Og had never participated in any sports, basically because he didn't like to sweat. Even as a child, he had never hiked or fished or biked or exerted himself in any way that would build his body or physical aptitude.

For his part Bone had wormed through his adolescence, avoiding physical education and exercise whenever possible, which was quite a feat in itself, considering that his father had been a municipal high school track coach. He alternately felt like he was going limp and losing, and then finding some reserve of strength, and winning. Anger, pride and humiliation each had a hand on the throttle of his adrenalin. Suddenly it was full stop.

Og became still as well. The sight of Mickey's automatic pistol acted like a cold bucket of water to halt the dog fight. Mickey gestured for the combatants to separate, waving his gun back and forth between them. Bone's eyes followed the gun like a subject following the suspended pocket watch of a hypnotist.

"Oooh, boy! You guys having fun yet, or what? Shit! I leave for ten minutes and when I come back you're at each other's throats. Or is this some kind of sex thing? Because I can leave you two alone for a while longer if you want, but I gotta take my shotgun back. By the way, those are custom shells in that gun- loaded 'em myself. And while you wouldn't have blown your heads off, if you had pulled the trigger you would have ended up a whole lot uglier. 'Course in your case, Ug, or whatever your name is, that may have been an improvement."

"Fuck you, man!"

For that Mickey kicked Og sharply in the ribs.

"Feisty fucker, ain'cha? You put up with this shit, Bone?"

"Not any more than I have to." Bone got off the floor, dusting himself off in an exaggerated fashion as if he had been rolling in the dirt.

"Now, you boys gonna behave, right?" Mickey had not as yet lowered the pistol.

"What's that, Mick, a Glock?"

"Glock, shit! It's a Beretta! Want to check it out?" He thrust the gun toward Bone.

"No, thanks, we were just, ah..."

"Hey, you don't have to explain anything. Am I right in assuming that your friend here was giving you a hard time? Things kinda got out of hand?"

Og protested, "Don't assume shit! You don't know what happened. We were just..."

"Yeah, same old story."

"No, you're right, Mickey," confirmed Bone. "Never thought he'd go for the gun."

"Like I said, the shotgun is for noise and shit. I use this-" he patted his Beretta fondly, "-if I want to shoot someone. So, how do you want to handle this?"

"Don't worry. Og's not going to give me any more shit. He's gotta get home, doesn't he?"

"Fuck, man! Make him walk. I would."

Bone laughed weakly. "Now that you mention it."

But Og whimpered, clearly becoming distraught.

"Nah; I think he's got his priorities realigned...Don't you, Og? You know when it's time to quit, right?"

Og glared, but he assented meekly.

"We'll be on our way now, Mickey. Let'cha enjoy your dinner in peace. 'Sides, I gotta get back in time."

"Time for what?" asked Mickey, "Something good on TV tonight, perhaps?"

"Fucked if I know. Man said to return at a specific time, that's all," Bone replied self-consciously.

Now basking in the familiarity that shared crisis or adventure bestows, the three walked to Bone's car. Og stepped carefully on the paving stones leading to the driveway as if the timing and sequence of his steps were integral to his continued survival.

Bone was grateful that Mickey had walked them out, and wished that he would ride shotgun on the way back to Rossie.

Almost as soon as they had said their farewells, Og reverted to the same dour demeanor he had worn earlier. But his mood would take a further dive, because as they left the neighborhood and turned onto the main street they spotted a large black box truck approaching. Emblazoned on the side in silver screen printing was a logo depicting a spectral horse galloping through the clouds past a crescent moon, with the highly stylized words, "Midnight Stallion Productions" in frosty print across the bottom. Og stared as the truck drove past, and then said miserably, "That wasn't..."

"Yep, that was the film crew," replied Bone, with some satisfaction. Og sank into silence, clearly depressed.

But by the time they reached the highway he was talking again as if nothing had happened.

"Still think you made a mistake back there, man."

"Shut up, Og!"

"I should have stayed behind and done it myself."

"Yeah? You never would have found your way home. No public transportation here, no cabs."

"Well, I can always come back, anyway."

He simply did not give up. Bone snapped back, "I doubt it, Og. See, I know that you weren't paying attention on the drive out. You don't know what roads we took, which exit. And anyway, I doubt that you noticed, but Weed removed all of the street signs around the house, just in case something like this ever came up. No, I doubt you'll ever be back."

Could it be true? Og bit his knuckles, trying to recall if he had seen any street signs. Who was he kidding? Bone was right. He had no idea where the stash house was located.

"Fuck, man. I almost had you."

"Yeah, Og? Don't you think I would have called Weed? Or called the cops? I wasn't about to let you pull that kind of rip-off."

The ride continued for some distance in silence. Og rocked back and forth on his seat as if he were moving in time to some music he could hear only in his head. Bone tried not to think about the gravity of Og's crime. And yet, Weed had hinted that something like this might happen.

The road Bone was following approached the city from a commanding elevation that afforded a broad view of the skyline. As he took in the vista he thought about how different this trip had been from the typical stash haul. Usually he was bored, driving at or below the speed limit, trying not to run afoul of the cops, the highway race demons or the slow-poke lane gestapos. On this occasion the miles flew past unheeded, as Bone considered how to mention or describe the episode involving Og's attempted theft. Play it off casually as if it were nothing more than a feeble attempt to determine the efficacy of the security arrangements? Or howl and rage about it, demanding Og's expulsion from the circle of dealers. He had no doubt that if any of the other franchisees had witnessed Og's behavior they would be screaming for blood. Figuratively speaking of course.

Weed would know the best course of action. Maybe put the squeeze on, chipping away at his market while raising his wholesale price; maybe something more drastic.

Distracted or not, Bone should have noticed the blue lights in his rear view mirror before the police who were following were forced to add the siren to get his attention.

"Shit! What the hell were you doing?" demanded Og.

"Nothing!" Bone pulled over on a sandy shoulder. "I don't know. Was I speeding?" Was his signal indicator on? Was a lamp blown out? Smoke pouring from his exhaust?

Two officers emerged from the cruiser as if they had sprung forth organically, their crisp uniforms and polished shoes matching the gleaming chrome and glossy finish of the overpowered V8. With flashlights drawn, the officers approached Bone's car, one going directly to the driver's side and the other staying behind to inspect the vehicle and to watch for trouble from the occupants.

"License and registration…" The cop spoke so fast that it took Bone a moment to realize that he had said three words, not one. But what really startled Bone was the fact that he knew the cop from somewhere. And when he handed over his papers, the cop winked at him! What the fuck!

As the two officers held a private conference behind the car, Og whispered, "Shit, man, we're fucked!"

"Why? What's wrong? Stay cool."

"What's wrong? Stay cool! Are you out of your mind? We got pulled over by the freakin' cops, man!"

"Hey, cool it, Og. I've had about enough of your shit tonight, alright? You paranoid or something?"

Og was apoplectic. "Paranoid! Paranoid my ass! We got twenty-five freakin'-"

"Shut up, man! What, are you trying to get us busted or something? Be cool. You got nothing to worry about. I ain't holding, you ain't holding. That's all that matters."

The cop returned to the window and handed Bone his license. To add mystery to flat-out amazement, the officer made a thumb-and-forefinger 'OK' sign behind the registration before handing it over as well. He smiled and said, "Could you open your trunk please, sir?"

Og groaned, but Bone stammered, "Yeah, sure, no problem. You want the keys, or should I get out and do it myself?"

"No; you get out and open it please," he replied patiently. "My partner and I will keep an eye on you." He smiled again.

It took Bone a few tries to get the lock to cooperate. His hands felt fat and uncoordinated and he could feel his pulse in his left temple.

The golf bag lay on its side in plain sight, alone in the spacious trunk.

"You going golfing?" asked the officer amiably.

"Sure am. Over to the municipal course at Roosevelt. You know, the Audie Murphy Memorial?"

"Oh, yeah, whacked a few out there, myself."

A few what? Bone wondered if he was hinting at something. He stammered on. "Golf's not really my game. I do it just to get in with the guys, you know?"

"I can tell," said the officer, "...those are women's clubs."

Zing! Stupid mistake. Bone's blood pressure climbed as he filed away a note to himself.

The officer's resemblance was unnerving, but to whom? It was as if some acquaintance of his had taken up this radical disguise just to 'zoo him out', as he put it.

"They were cheap, that's all I know," said Bone, closing the trunk. Perhaps a bit precipitously? Had the officer seen all he wanted to? When he lowered the lid however, he saw that other officer had pulled Og out of the car and had him spread against the fender. Now he was sweating, although he knew he was clean.

"Am I bumming you out or something?" asked the cop unexpectedly.

What a question! Bone almost broke out laughing.

"It's me, man, Eban's brother Alan. Remember me? It's cool. I'm doing this as a favor to Weed. I owe him one from way back, and he asked me to pull you guys over. Damn! He said you'd be by, and sure enough! Don't sweat it, though," he added, still speaking in a low voice, "We're only interested in your buddy, the cave man there," and he pointed at the unfortunate Og.

Alan, of course! What a freakin' relief! He had almost forgotten that Eban's brother was a cop. In fact, he clearly had forgotten. Bone almost collapsed.

"Why?" he said, "What's up? He got a warrant out against him or something?"

"No- just watch. If Weed was right, then my partner is about to find some contraband during the pat-down."

"Who, Og? No, I don't think-"

But at that moment the officer searching Og cried out, "Got something here!"

"No kidding?" yelled Alan, clearly acting a part now. "Wha'cha find?" He winked at Bone again, and Bone nodded in reply, still amazed. What the fuck? What was Weed doing? Og knew the rules. He was too smart to carry anything to a stash haul. Was Weed trying to put the fear into him?

"Bag of greenish vegetation, some kind of herbal matter, by the looks and smell of it, marijuana."

"Confiscate it for testing, and book him."

But the officer had already pulled Og's arm back to cuff him.

"Hey, Alan," Bone whispered, "Is this for real?"

"Aw, c'mon, man! You think we planted the shit or something? Weed didn't say what we'd find, he just said to pull you over and to search the cave man. Heh, heh...he does kinda look like a cave man, doesn't he?" He walked away to assist his partner. "Oh, yeah," he added, "...he also said not to go easy on him."

Og meanwhile was putting up quite a fuss, cursing and howling and carrying on, and coming just short of resisting arrest. As the two officers pushed him into the back seat of the cruiser, Alan made sure that Og bumped his head on the door jamb, saying, "Watch your head!" as if it were an afterthought.

The partner approached Bone now. He was a younger guy, with a boyish regulation haircut and sharp, clean-shaven features.

"You can go now, Mr. Cronin. If you want to bail your buddy out, come down to Precinct 5 later. But give it a couple of hours. Your pal is going downtown for fingerprinting and processing. Depending on the quantity, we gotta make a federal case out of it, and by the looks of it, he had more than enough on him for that."

Alan was getting into the cruiser but he paused to flash the bag.

"Yeah," he said, holding a sandwich-style baggie up by the corners, "More than enough!" He smiled greedily as if to say, "We're gonna party tonight!"

Holy shit! The scum-bag! How the fuck had he copped that much dope without Bone noticing? Og's reputation was well-deserved, he thought, but he also chastised himself as he realized what must have happened. When he was packing the pounds into the golf bag, Og had opened a kilo to stick his honker into it, for what Bone had assumed was a quick whiff. At the time he thought nothing of it, since he understood that it was difficult to ignore the abundance and quality of the stash. It was always somewhat overwhelming to see that much at one time in one place. If he hadn't split up hundreds of pounds over the past couple of years, he might have wanted to run his fingers through some of it himself. But hadn't Og done the same?

Fucking Og! What a freakin' loser! He was gazing at Bone through the window of the police cruiser, an imploring expression on his face, washed in splashes of blue light as the car pulled away.

Stunned, shaken, suddenly feeling like laughing out loud, and subsequently doing so long and heartily, Bone stood by this car for a minute or two before hopping in and proceeding to his rendezvous with Sharlae.

CHAPTER 31

Don't sweat it. It's no biggie. It's like sometimes when you check your horoscope first thing in the morning and it says 'Today is your lucky day'. You go to the convenience store and spend a buck on a lottery scratch card. Three pips line up and you hit for a free ticket so you trade it in and win again, this time for a buck. Your luck isn't bad, it's just not as good as you had hoped it would be.

Or like when you go up for the jumper at the last second of the game and bang! You put it away for the win, but the game is just between friends and there's nobody in the stands.

Rick Rose had passed by Sharlae's house twice already and she wasn't home. But the third time's the charm, and now he was coming around again for his third attempt in an hour, crossing his fingers, knocking on wood and praying for intercession from Jimi, patron saint of needy rock fans and hopeless romantics, that she might be home when he got there. In his hand was a sweat-damp note addressed to Sharlae that he had yet to complete, because by writing "Sorry to have missed you" he would be admitting to himself that he had struck out. And yet if she wasn't there then he would have to decide whether he was going to circle around again, or pull over in front of her house and spend a moment to compose the rest of the note.

He glanced at her neighbor's houses, wondering if there was anyone watching who might have noticed his many slow orbits. Sharlae had told him that a lot of old folk lived around here, and he knew how paranoid they could be. No sense giving them anything to worry about. He balled up the note, added it to the ever-growing pile of refuse on the floor of his car, and made a decision. If she wasn't home then he would suck it up, go on his way and leave her alone.

As neighborhoods went, this one wasn't so bad, thought Rick. Far enough off the grid that it had a personally-kept appearance. It was removed from town centers like Rossdale and Westbury, and segregated from Roosevelt proper by a natural wedge of land that rose up along the western side of Stonybrook parkway. In addition it was located near the pond, on the other side of the parkway that shared its name. The pond was noted for its scenic beauty, and it was also a valuable resource for the local reservoir system. From this basin a craggy berm of granite ledges topped with scrub pine and shrub bushes stretched all the way to a wildlife reservation area on the outskirts of town that covered ten thousand swampy acres between the city limits and the ocean. Hence a variety of critters, everything from skunks to possums often made forays into Sharlae's backyard, and deer were frequently seen standing in the roadways, especially at dusk.

It was almost too creepy for Rick to imagine living in a place where the hushed roar of the road wasn't a persistent backdrop to every conversation. For him the steady chatter of sirens, trucks, trains, gunshots, music and shouting was proof of life; it was a necessary reminder that he was part of something greater than himself.

He cruised the parkway toward Westbury as quickly as his rheumatic bug would go. He was low on gas in the fuel tank but heavy with oil in the storage tanks. So the car ran with a peculiar rocking motion, like when you try to carry a large cooler full of melted ice and water, and though you try to walk straight, the sloshing keeps you off balance.

After making the turn onto Main St heading toward Rossie it wasn't long before he noticed a Firebird with a hood scoop and chrome rims, painted eagle and the works, careening after him at breakneck speed. It was full of goons, most likely, yep, the stooges from the Fores whose car he had helped to destroy not four hours ago.

Uh-oh. So much for the complacent feeling of vague disappointment that had stayed with him since failing to find Sharlae. Now he was feeling a bit nauseated. Normally the anticipation of trouble or adventure would give him a thrill, but he had to face facts. It was a car load of angry motherfuckers against one mellow laid-back dude, and worse, it was a street-modified Pontiac Firebird against a decrepit Volkswagen rear-engine one-seater. No doubt this would be great fun if the odds were evened a bit, so to speak; say, if he had his brother's supercharged AMC Pacer, or his cousin's Barracuda. Then he'd have a blast leading the belligerent bozos through parts of town they'd never seen, and would never want to see again. Instead he faced a greater challenge- to lose them or somehow use their speed and power against them.

It pissed him off to think that the lovely Sharlae had undergone a similar frightful experience at the hands of these same shit heads. Don't they have anything better to do than to chase folks around in their cars? Maybe they thought that he deserved this, but after a while it becomes hard to tell your tits from your tats. When will they give up?

Oh to have some cool weapon device installed in his car, a la 007. He'd have knife launchers mounted near his headlights, and pneumatic egg throwers that pop out of the hood, and high-pressure nozzles that squirt precision streams of paint out from both sides of the car. Smoke screens and caltrops and grease slicks. *Grease Slicks!* There was something that he might be able to finagle. Perhaps his liability, the hundreds of gallons of home heating oil he was carrying, could be put to immediate use as the only defense mechanism he had at his disposal.

A half mile down Main St he turned onto Stilson and let the traffic and the course of the road serve as a buffer between him and his assailants. There was no way the goons could pull anything dramatic under these circumstances, that is, while caught in a line of cars on a busy two-lane street. And yet the driver was flipping his middle finger and the guy beside him on the front seat was hanging out the window and shouting obscenities at Rick.

They were right on his ass and still they kept blowing the horn and flashing the high beams. *Yeah, I know that you're there, thanks!*

A right on South Centre, past the church and the fire station and then straight for the commuter rail platform, fully intending to drive through the pedestrian underpass. At seven feet high and ten feet wide the tunnel was more of a storm drain than a walkway, but it had been built to provide a safe way for passengers to get from one side of the tracks to the other. Vehicles were not permitted, but then, only a madman would attempt to take a car through.

Having left himself little choice, Rick sized it up in an instant and went for it. He had always wondered if a bug would fit through there. As he slowly chugged under the tracks a ping-pong echo countered the characteristic chirp of the motor; it sounded like he was at the head of a herd of grasshoppers. *Well, what do you know? Success!*

But the conceit that he had left the Firebird behind vanished instantly. He might have been desperate, but they must have been insane, squeezing through the fifty foot long passageway, barely scraping by the hand rails on either side. While the larger car extruded from the hole in the ground, Rick took off.

Next it was a quick circuit of the square, then up the boulevard by the cemetery so that he could take advantage of the general downward slope of the streets heading toward White City from there. Before he knew it he was on Mt Hope and still trying to get the hose out the window so he could direct a stream of oil onto the street. He had rigged the system to siphon oil out of tanks, and then to reverse the process and pump it again. However, always from one vessel to another. The hose was supposed to have a receptacle, and when it was dangling the way it was now, especially while traveling at 35 mph, it flopped all over the place. Fuck it, there was no way to clamp it down or to make it rigid. The only course of action was to switch the pump on and hope that the force of the flow would counter the eccentric motion of the hose.

He looked ahead at the street and saw Mt Hope descending in a heart-stopping grade all the way to the ball field and beyond. If he let the oil go now his pursuers may be able to drive straight through it without any ill effect. What he needed was another incline so that he could leave them spinning on a slick at the base, or better yet, a curve so that he could make them wipe out.

In the end it was a matter of timing to activate the pump just as he reached the bottom of Mt Hope, because there the road skirted the ball park in a loping irregular curve before it terminated on Main St. The trick was to get the shit on the ground, unlike the first few gallons that ended up covering the side of his baby-shit yellow car with a dirty slick sheen. Once he was sure that he had achieved a siphon, he drove with his right hand and held the end of the hose out the window at arm's length with his left.

The effect was almost instantaneous and it looked so cool in his rear view mirror that he almost lost control as he turned around for a better look. There they were humming down the hill with him leading the way around the first bend by the little league diamond. The Firebird was pissing along right behind at a decent clip, when suddenly it flew straight off the road and onto the field. Rick could actually see the expression on the driver, Len Abbisso's face, as he turned the wheel and nothing happened. His surprise quickly turned to horror as he realized that was taking an unscheduled trip over the curb, onto the grass and down the third base line.

Tsk, tsk. Where is there a cop when you need one? If they can't pull them over for speeding on town streets then at least they could pull them over for driving all over and vandalizing the ballpark!

But no, Rick's adversaries were not detained by the police, indeed they were hardly slowed by their radical detour. If by chance you do drive through an oil slick so that your tires aren't worth shit, then the best thing to do is to find some dirt and sand to spin around in for a while. It was mere seconds before the Firebird regained traction and then came charging across the Pee-Wee football gridiron in order to intercept Rick at the corner.

Oh, man. He felt like hopping out of the car and pushing it to make it go faster. Then again he could always hop out and run, but that would mean abandoning his car altogether. And given what had become of their car he'd hate to imagine what they'd do to his. In any event it wasn't far to home from here. He simply had to make it around the corner and then another mile or so.

Thank heavens! There was a cop- sitting in his car just beyond the bus stop. As Rick passed he beeped his little German road-runner type horn and waved frantically to get the officer's attention. Sure enough the guy looked up from his paperwork or comic book or whatever he was reading and gave Rick a curious stare. Rick pointed over his shoulder at the Firebird and mouthed, "Look at them!" But the cop merely pointed at Rick's car, clearly concerned about the spreading grease stain that coated most of his car as well as the long curl of thick rubber hose that hung out his window dripping black fluid.

Fuck! God-damned stupid shit-for-brains fat-ass donut muncher. Put two and two together for Pete's sake!

Oh, well. Rick had faced these guys alone so far, and now he was a mere thousand yards from home. But by now the driver of the Firebird had taken to playing bumper cars. He would catch up close to the rear of Rick's bug and then give his car a goose to shove the smaller car, like a bully pushing a weakling in the schoolyard. With each kiss Rick's car fish-tailed and rocked violently, but each time he recovered and kept to his course, heading for home in the White City Projects.

There were five entrances to the projects, three of them dead-ends, one of which terminated at the tracks and the other two in cul-de-sacs. It was Rick's intention to get as close to his building as possible, the so-called Douglass unit. Instead of taking Douglass Drive he quickly turned into Washington, the cul-de-sac that served as a courtyard for the Garvey, Tubman and Washington units.

Again he was surprised that a car-load of white boys would pursue him into the projects. White City was a place they usually avoided. The name White City, ironic in the sense that this section of town had the highest concentration of black and Hispanic residents, was a holdover from a pre-existing community that had been incorporated into the Rossdale township before the turn of the century. Within the complex the Roses were, in fact, the last white family; a moot point since one of his brothers had married a black girl, two of his sisters had married blacks, and his mother was currently married to a black man as well.

But the Pontiac pursuing him had been practically glued to his bumper while making the turn onto Booker T Washington Drive, and then as he approached the circle the big 350 gave him a sudden violent push, more of a crash than a kiss. Unable to negotiate the turn while accelerating within the radius of the cul-de-sac, the VW bucked the far curb and tipped. Then, like an unfortunate box turtle, the car flipped onto its roof and skidded across the walk, crushing a park bench and striking a mail box before it toppled over onto its side again and crashed into the Tubman building.

As he scrambled free of his crumpled car, Rick felt like shouting, "Let's do it again!" He hadn't had such a terrific ride since his brother took him for midnight bumper surfing at the super-market parking lot. However, his car was smoldering, which was not a good sign. And on the other hand he still had a bunch of goons to contend with. Luckily for him they were recovering from a mishap of their own, having struck a dumpster as they followed through on the deliberate collision. The heavy metal grappling bar on the dumpster had smashed one of the Firebird's passenger windows and it looked as though some of the guys were suffering from cuts and bruises.

And yet a couple of beefy dudes still managed to jump out of the car, and they immediately started running in Rick's direction. He turned and fled without a second thought, and again fast action saved his ass because just as he ran toward his apartment building his car went up in a brilliant fireball that was preempted by a muffled explosion.

At this time, early 1986, White City Housing Project was under threat of demolition by the municipal housing authority. Originally constructed in 1949, the development was intended as temporary housing for young GIs who had come back from the war eager to earn their degrees, enter the workforce and start families, though not necessarily in that order.

Now two generations later the complex was deemed to be unsuitable for continued use as permanent housing. The apartment walls were thin, the buildings lacked air conditioning and almost every major system from electrical to plumbing needed overhaul. In addition, recent changes in rent control provisions had led to conflicts between tenants and the housing authority, and many of the apartments in the complex were held by illegal squatters.

One of the most legendary of these squatters was Mr. Eddie, an elderly black gentleman who inhabited a suite of rooms in a strategic corner of the Washington unit facing the cul-de-sac. As far as the managers of the complex knew, Mr. Eddie had no utilities and no services in his apartment and they claimed that he lived like a latter day savage. But as all the kids in the complex knew, Mr. Eddie lived like a king up there in his penthouse, for he used the children to run errands and to deliver messages and to serve as his link with the rest of the community.

It was said that Mr. Eddie shot porn flicks in his apartment, that he managed a number of raggedy-ass prostitutes, that he dealt in any number of illicit substances, fenced stolen goods and was a general nuisance. None of his friends would confirm any of those allegations, but they would say that he told wonderful stories, that he tried to mediate disputes and to serve as a kind of father figure in his own right. To Rick Rose he was like a godfather, a very real, very kind mentor and friend who had helped him to make a number of important choices in his life, including staying in school to earn his GED.

It was Mr. Eddie who signaled the alarm when he witnessed what was unfolding in the street below his window. Normally the projects would be relatively quiet at this time of night despite the fact that it was a Friday evening. Late April was still cold and damp enough to induce folks to stay indoors instead of gathering in the courtyard or on the street corners as they might later in the spring and summer. In fact if it had been a typical summer evening and a car chase happened to end up in Washington cul-de-sac, then people might have been hurt. Children often played in the circle at all hours of the day and night.

Now Rick's car was burning just below a first-floor Tubman apartment window, and Mr. Eddie was marshaling his forces. In minutes he had a virtual mob of people out in the street, focusing their outrage on Des Kelley's squad of goons. Joey Atkinson had leaped out of the car first and he led Tru Kennedy in hot pursuit after Rick Rose, who knew the apartment complex inside and out.

It seemed that the explosion of Rick's Volkswagen had mobilized more than the residents of Washington, Tubman and Garvey, for the police and fire engines were also en route to the scene with their sirens blaring.

When the car caught fire the flames were fed by the two hundred or so gallons of oil that Rick had stored in his car at the time. Since he had been pumping fuel out of his window just prior to the accident, the oil had spread over almost the entire surface of the body, as well as the undercarriage, engine compartment and fender wells. With such a vast surface area and a ready supply of more fuel, as well as abundant vapor and fresh air, the bug was ready to burn. The flames were bright, huge and searingly hot, and all the more spectacular for being the real thing as opposed to an effect in a movie, for example.

Joey A and Tru K naturally leapt back from the flames and Rick disappeared into the Garvey building.

At this point a number of things started to happen at once, all of them in one way or another the result of Des Kelley's decision to send thugs out after Rick Rose for revenge.

Len Abbisso had remained in the relative safety of his car. Before he dared to step out into a totally alien environment, he wanted to observe what transpired, especially after Joey and Tru had run off.

Meanwhile Denis, who had been showered with safety glass when the car struck the dumpster, grabbed Mo and jumped out to make a stand next to the Firebird in the middle of the cul-de-sac, even though he was stunned and bleeding. It looked like they were vastly outnumbered by a crowd of people who had emerged from the apartment buildings, clearly responding to the sound of the crash and the threat of fire. A smaller group composed mostly of young men had coalesced out of the crowd and they were advancing toward the outsiders, shouting epithets and threats, and making hostile and obscene gestures. Just then the police arrived, led by none other than the cop who had ignored Rick just minutes ago.

Len had an impulse to drive off and save himself and his damaged car, but the officer pulled in and parked directly in front of him as if to say, "You're not going anywhere."

How do these things escalate? Who knows the definitive cause, the actual moment, event or decision that instigated further conflict and chaos. In this wild scene on Washington Drive in White City Projects, nobody could say where the bottle came from, that is, the one that suddenly smashed on the pavement between the two groups of adversaries. But the moment after it struck, Joey Atkinson went berserk. He waded into the crowd of six or eight project punks, swinging his fists and kicking butts. As he was to later describe it, it was an attack of the guided muscles.

Joey's spell of madness actually bought him some time, but at the same moment Rick was running quickly through the Garvey building, heading downstairs to the boiler room. Even from within the building he could hear the sounds of shouting and sirens and fire engines approaching, and inspired by this sense of turmoil and crisis, he decided to put a long-planned idea into action.

He had secretly installed a booby-trap device in the building's furnace. Lord knows what possessed him to sabotage a building in the very complex that he called home, but there had been much talk of closing the place down. The housing authority had already decided that they would seize and seal off any apartment unit that was empty, and whenever an entire building became empty it would be razed. So Rick had determined that the best way to say goodbye to his old home, when the time should come to do so, was by blowing the building up personally. He had prudently chosen Garvey for practice because very few people still lived there. After months of preparation and gathering the necessary items he had placed dynamite charges, blasting caps and an incendiary device in the hopper of the furnace, as well as a firing mechanism that he intentionally left disconnected. Now that it seemed as though the world was closing in on him, he figured he could hasten the implementation of his plan.

With trembling fingers he quickly wired up the remote detonation device and then he hustled out of the basement boiler room and set it off. There was an appreciable delay that Rick used to boogie up the stairs and out the back of the building, praying all the while that no one in the place would get hurt.

As soon as he had flung himself through the steel exit door he gulped some fresh air outside and sprinted toward the path by the tracks. His purpose was to remain unseen during his retreat. Then when the path was clear, he'd bolt from cover back to the rear door of the next building, Douglass, where he and the rest of the Roses lived.

But talk about luck! As he turned onto the path running full bore, he bumped smack into two police officers who were running in the opposite direction, toward the fire and the riot.

"Whoa! Where do you think you're going?" asked one of them, an officer about the same age as Rick.

"Away from there," he said breathlessly, thumbing over his shoulder. "What do you think? There's a fire, you know, and…"

He was interrupted by a peculiar booming noise that startled the cops and made them both turn and look behind them. Suddenly a blast of smoke and soot came from the rear door of Garvey and huge clouds of black smoke could be seen billowing from the chimney. It felt as though the ground shook, and a number of windows in the building rattled.

"You! Wait here!" said the young cop to Rick. "We gotta check this out. Now don't go anywhere; we'll be right back!" And they ran off toward the source of the blast, vanishing into the enveloping smoke.

"Right! I'll wait here…" and before finishing his falsehood, Rick sprinted in the opposite direction.

Only mere yards to go now along the path beside the tracks and then he would be safe inside his own building. He couldn't wait to tell his story to his brothers and then to sit and watch the drama outside unfold from the security of his window on the third floor.

Rick burst through a gap in the row of scraggly lilac bushes along the pedestrian walkway that linked the buildings in the rear, ready to make his final dash across Garvey Drive to the back door of Douglass. And there in the middle of the street, actually looking a little lost until they saw Rick, stood Denis Fecteau and Mo Keating. They greeted him with smiles and open arms, as if celebrating his last stroke of luck.

CHAPTER 32

What could be taking so God-damned long? LaGloria reminded herself that she had a rule: she waited for no one. Let others wait for her, but she hated to wait for anyone else. Her mother used to make her wait, and it was infuriating. Wait until you're older, wait until after school, wait until your father gets home. Whenever she wanted something, she was told to wait. *Patience is a virtue and virtue is its own reward.* Bullshit!

Momentarily confused by a fun house-mirror impression of imbalance in the apartment, she stumbled into the living room as if to prove that the 'luudes were still present in her system and affecting her perception. It wouldn't have been a problem if she had been permitted to sleep as she had wanted, but God-damned people wouldn't fucking leave her in peace! It took three or four phone calls to penetrate her foggy funk, but she was awake.

Well, she shouldn't be sleeping so late, or early, or whatever it was, anyway. She wanted to be wide awake when Tweed got home. He would probably have a story to tell about his evening, and besides, they had a lot to talk about.

Despite all the shit that was coming down she was primed to have it out with Tweed. She had gotten over the lazy, lethargic, dipped-in-molasses stage and now she was enjoying a mellower phase of the drug, like a picnic of wine and dandelions, patchouli oil and candles.

But her overall situation was starting to become a hassle, and as a result she was actually feeling regret, although it may simply have been a by-product of her over-stimulated neurochemistry. She still viewed her goal as legitimate and achievable. She hated that motherfucker Des Kelley and she wanted to destroy him, but she had executed her plan prematurely and now she was suffering the consequences.

One of the phone calls had been from her father, and the conversation had not gone well. At first she was too groggy to make much sense, and he was addle-brained as usual. Insisting that he would look after himself when he arrived, he said that he intended to stay at his sister's house for a couple of days and then fly back to Florida after the funeral. They really got into it when she replied that there wasn't going to be a 'funeral' with a church service and a burial. When she tried to explain, he got all upset and he started becoming confused, saying that his brother deserved better than cremation. She didn't know how many times she was forced to repeat that it was his sons, Francis and Nilvan who were dead, not his brother, who died years ago. It sucked having to explain everything over and again, especially considering that he was in no condition to travel in the first place. Why couldn't he stay in Pinellas Acres Estates where he belonged?

The fact that he was her father meant little to LaGloria. Now he was the only remaining member of her immediate family, but in her eyes he was a lingering burden. It was a burden she managed with only a modicum of effort, and with a nominal degree of personal involvement. In all honesty she couldn't wait for him to pass away as well.

Back when the kids were all living at home LaGloria had always been her father's favorite. He called her his little pet, although she thought of herself as his little slave-girl. Except for physical proximity theirs wasn't an especially close relationship. As soon as she became old enough she had been required to sit at her father's feet and await his command when he relaxed in the evening. "Be a dear, Red, and put the game on for me," he'd say, "And tune it in the way I like it. You're so good at that. And while you're at it tell your mother to get me another beer." It was a mystery why he called her 'Red' when she had always been as dark as a Romany gypsy. After he acquired a set with a remote control he no longer required her services. By then it was she who was beyond his control.

Perhaps she might have anticipated that her father would want a funeral for the boys. He was a traditional sort who had lost his share of friends and relatives over the years, and during that time he had witnessed a procession of wakes, funerals and services. Although for LaGloria the loss of her brothers was an immense blow, a trauma that threatened to rend the fabric of her self-control, she intended to memorialize them in her own way. A funeral was out of the question. She could conceive of no valid reason to have a mortician doll up her brother's bodies and put them on display. No way would she permit Des and his pals the opportunity to exult over their trophies.

Plus, there was a considerable expense involved in preparing two bodies, two caskets, and burial plots. Better to cremate them and hold a private get-together for any who might wish to participate in a formal ceremony.

It would also probably be best not to comment one way or the other upon her choice of a cremation; although she knew that in lieu of information people tended to speculate. Let them speculate. Objectively speaking, who's to say cremation wasn't the stated preference of Frankie and Nilvan? And then again, it could just as well have been necessitated by the condition of the bodies after the shooting and the autopsy.

Of all of the conflicting emotions LaGloria was experiencing, the hatred and fear and passion and loathing, the dread, the anticipation and anxiety, concern for others was not prominent among them. Her decision was final. Frankie and Nil would be cremated.

Come to think of it, she had neglected to mention any of this to her next caller. But then she had been, and still was, flabbergasted by the call that seemed to come right out of left field. Not only had she never met Susan Cronin, but prior to her call she was unaware of her existence.

As soon as Susan had established that she had indeed reached LaGloria McManus, she calmly and methodically introduced herself, described her situation and why she thought her story might be of interest to the woman who might have become her sister-in-law. She spoke with solace, as a sister in mourning, openly sharing her grief. LaGloria in turn was blown away that a stranger could expose herself so readily and intimately, and at the same time elicit raw feelings in her. It disturbed her that by comparison she had seemed emotionally dysfunctional. And yet, though she remained tentative in her own comments, she indeed felt newly awoken, as Susan's words triggered a series of unfamiliar sensations in her.

The way she spoke about Frankie! Since he died a number of his friends had uttered kind words about him, tributes and condolences ranging from the heartfelt to the merely perfunctory. But it was evident when Susan spoke about him that she loved Frankie, and that affected LaGloria in a profound way.

She hadn't known that her brother was in love. He kept to himself, either fostering, or permitting LaGloria to imagine a persona and a lifestyle that was now obviously a gross misrepresentation of his character. She thought she had known her brother. He worked and partied, watched sports on TV and drank beer. She had wondered from time to time why he wasn't involved with someone, or even married, for after all, he was handsome and gregarious. But he didn't read, he seemed to have no particular interests, he had never traveled and his education was limited. In short, LaGloria had been selling him short.

Now she had heard about him and had seen him from another woman's point of view, and she couldn't help but wonder- could she speak like that? Could she sound like that?

When she spoke about Tweed was it obvious that she was in love? Was it clear that he was a part of her life and that she couldn't do without him? For that matter, could she speak of her brothers in a way that reflected her love for them? How could she when she didn't even know them? Frankie was going to be a father, for heaven's sake. He had a job and a future and his boss respected him.

LaGloria had friends, but would they speak well of her? Beyond all other considerations, what troubled her was the prospect of her own death, and the way in which the event would be received or celebrated. She had no family, she worked alone for the most part, so would her legacy reside in the memories of a small circle of friends? The question lodged itself in the back of her mind like a canker sore that she occasionally massaged.

But in the meantime she must attend to more practical matters. How would she eulogize her brothers if she were called to do so? Maybe the best thing to do would be simply to borrow Susan's words. If she could only paraphrase them somehow, alter the wording. Something along these lines: "It is unfortunate that we must meet under these solemn circumstances. This is a difficult time for all of us, but I hope that we can ease the pain of our loss by sharing our remembrances…"

Of course she would have to balance that with a personal note, some incident that made her brothers appear human and real and heroic.

But what, specifically? Talk about how they used to make fun of her, and humiliate her, and push her around and make her do all of their dirty work? Sure! What better way to show people what her brothers were really like. Describe some of their boyish antics? Like having her sneak into their parent's bedroom just prior to Christmas to search out the secret stash of presents and tell them what they were going to get. Or forcing her to be their apologist and cover person? When they wanted to avoid chores and responsibilities she had to run interference for them, either by placating their mother with a plausible story, or by drawing attention to herself and keeping her mother occupied.

Sure, LaGloria could come up with many anecdotes that might give an insight as to who the boys were and what they had accomplished. How about their loutish behavior? She could tell their friends how her so-called over-protective siblings had taunted her with nasty sexual banter and innuendo, how they had wanted her to be sexy and cheap so that they might use her to attract friends for themselves; how they used her to get drugs.

Of course all that changed when Tweed came along. LaGloria recalled how her brothers used to talk about him, like he was the hottest shit around. The big dealer who always had excellent dope.

She saw him a few times around the square and then on the couple of occasions when he came up to the house. Considering how things turned out it was kind of funny how they used to admire Tweed and at the same time basically treat her like shit. *"Shut up, LaGloria…Get lost, LaGloria."*

Meanwhile they were scheming how to get in good with him. They thought they were so smart when they went and set up that big deal, trying to turn the tables and sell dope to him for a change. She could never be sure, but she suspected that Nilvan stole the money they used for the buy. It was about that time, anyway, when a big flap erupted between the McManuses and their neighbors, the Raffas. Mr. Raffa had come over and reported to Mr. McManus that all of his vacation pay and more cash besides was missing from his bedroom. Furthermore he said that he had been able to determine, to within a couple of hours, when the money was stolen. He claimed that during that time only his son Peter and Nilvan McManus were in the house. Peter proclaimed his innocence. A number of heated discussions ensued between the formerly friendly neighbors, and accusations flew. Nil was never officially blamed for the theft, but LaGloria knew that her father had been obliged to do something to resolve the dispute and keep the matter quiet.

In any case the deal was a disaster. Frankie had some shaky connection for a couple of pounds of commercial red that supposedly helped Tweed through a dry spell. But instead of earning his gratitude and gaining prestige as dealers in their own right, the deal was merely the prelude to a fall. LaGloria was fairly certain that Frankie's connection was Jabbour, and that Tweed had quickly stepped over the boys to get to him directly. Undaunted, the boys immediately arranged to buy another kilo, but this one led to their downfall as dealers.

A paragraph of background may set up the scene and illustrate why the end of their careers as dealers came so swiftly.

Anyone who read High Times magazine that year; and anyone who cultivated, transported or sold marijuana from Mexico; and hence everyone else down the line, from quantity brokers to midnight tokers, knew that the seasonal crops had been contaminated by a US govt sanctioned herbicide called Paraquat. The Mexican and US governments were cooperating to eradicate the marijuana trade, and a generation of Mexican sattiva, indica and sensimilla was ruined by the poison rain. However, some unscrupulous smugglers opted to sell the shit anyway rather than accept a devastating financial loss. Thus tons of Paraquat-laced pot found its way onto the streets of the US- and it was usually sold at full retail.

It was fool's gold, an inferior grade of commercial that was stained yellow by the herbicide. Unsophisticated buyers fell for the deceptive color and greasy resinous consistency of the spoiled buds. When Frankie saw it he "went apeshit" as he later recalled, and sank everything he had into the purchase. He had apparently never heard of Paraquat, or the news that might have prevented him from buying the tainted stuff and causing his ruin. The news had lagged behind the arrival of the weed somewhat, that pot smokers by the hundreds were showing up in hospital emergency rooms and doctor's offices with a new malady soon to be dubbed Paraquat lung. Similar to an allergic reaction, it was an inflammation of the bronchial tracts that had, in some cases, caused serious complications.

Facts led to rumors and then to panic. Word was that kids were dying of Paraquat poisoning. A grass-roots protest arose from concerned parents, medical professionals and pot heads, and before long they managed to convince the government to abandon the crop-dusting program.

But it was too late for Nilvan and Frankie, who were ultimately only able to dump about a quarter of a pound of their golden stash at the going rate. Last LaGloria heard, Frankie had let his last pound of the shit go for $60.00 just to get it off his hands. Having lost everything they had on the deal, they realized that even with hard work (something to which they were not accustomed), they wouldn't make a dent in the local market. Not with dealers like Tweed around. And they knew and liked him anyway, so that was that.

The real change in the way her brothers treated her occurred when she started dating Tweed. He'd seen her around, and he knew she was a fox, but he held off on asking her out because he didn't want any problems from her brothers. Of course it wasn't long before they were encouraging them to get together, since they understood that it could only be to their benefit to have such a close tie to the biggest dope dealer in town.

Likewise it wasn't long before LaGloria realized what power she now had over her brothers. And did she lord it over them! Tweed gave them a discount, she tacked it back on. Tweed would let them cuff, she'd make them wait. Tweed gave them first pick, she gave them the dregs. Not that she screwed them all the time, after all, they were her brothers. But when they wanted bags, they had to go through her. Come to think of it, they accounted for some pretty consistent consumption, and that adds up to bags that wouldn't be going out the door anymore.

Shit! She knew she was still fucked up when she had to tell herself that it was better to be alive and high than dead any day. With a somewhat clearer head she also realized that she was going to miss those regular deals she made with her brothers. When it came down to it, pot was the glue that kept the siblings together. Really, the only time they talked to her was when they picked up their bags. Over time the whole process became a kind of ritual. She'd leave the bag on the table, and they'd leave their money on the table. They picked up their bags and she picked up the cash. Impersonal, but also a sort of demonstration of trust.

When Frankie came around he was always smiling, telling jokes, and making gestures as if to touch her, although he never did. Nil on the other hand always used to come in wearing a nervous scowl on his face, as if he had just fought over a parking space, but he always left the place with a big grin on his face, as if he had been picked to be Grand Marshall of the Rose Bowl Parade or something.

Now Nilvan was no more. Always looked up to his big brother, always wanted to be with him, had to do to whatever it was Frankie was doing, right up until the day he died. But what did she know? Maybe there were surprises in Nil's life, too. Other than the fact that he was going to be an uncle, that is.

Can't imagine Frankie as a father! Wonder if it was planned, or what? Susan hadn't indicated one way or the other, but she certainly didn't make it sound as if the pregnancy was unwanted. Kinda made sense that they'd want to settle down. After all, you get to a certain age and you start wondering about your options, don't you?

At LaGloria's age and situation it was difficult to put herself in the place of somebody Susan's age and situation. The past was easy. Whatever she couldn't remember she simply made up. Whatever experiences she had missed out on she merely pretended that she hadn't. The future on the other hand…it was like driving at night on a foggy highway. The harder you try, the less you can see.

But the idea of having a baby had never entered her mind. She tracked her period, she took birth control pills, but she did these things in the interest of having sex, not children. Conception was something to be avoided. It was important to be careful, especially considering that Tweed was a major horn dog and a freakin' spunk machine. It was a wonder he didn't dehydrate.

Nobody could blame her for neglecting the issue of fertility and motherhood and all. She was young, she dealt drugs, and she occasionally took drugs. She worked with gay men. It wasn't a topic of conversation. Pregnancy and childrearing hadn't come across her radar, so to speak.

Her day was becoming all too real. Before she had even managed to put on the water for her first cup of tea she had hashed things out with her old man, and she had heard from a woman who was going to be a single mother and widow before she even had a chance to marry.

Next she received a call from Tom Toole.

What a relief to talk to him…and she told him so. Again, because of her own anxiety and eagerness to touch base with him, his kind words and sincere concern caught her off guard. He said that he didn't want to disturb her, and that he wouldn't have called, but he couldn't wait until the funeral. He was driven by what he called ulterior motives, but actually, guilt had motivated him to call. He was afraid that LaGloria would blame him for the deaths of her brothers. This, she couldn't fathom. After quickly assessing her mental and emotional state she concluded that while it would be inadvisable to compete on Jeopardy in her condition, she should be able to understand her friend Tommy. However, he wasn't making any sense. Her brother's deaths his fault? By what twisted line of reasoning had he come up with that? Was this going to be one of those murders where people lined up to claim responsibility? I killed them! No, I did! Me, too!

He explained. "When I heard about the guns I said to myself, 'Oh my God! I helped Frank get that gun! LaGloria, I swear to you, I didn't know he was going to use it! I mean, you know Frank- who would think such a thing?"

She had tried to calm him down. "No, Tommy, don't…"

"I'm so sorry, hon, I can't imagine how difficult this must be for you, and here I am calling and crying on *your* shoulder. But…"

"Listen, Tommy, I never, for one instant, thought that you had anything to do with what happened. I'm telling you, don't kill yourself over this thing. Nobody knew. Nobody had any clue. I still don't know what got into them..."

"But I gave him *the means*, LaGloria! I told Frankie about it; I mean, I practically sold him the gun myself..."

"Hey, as I recall, you were just trying to help out your cousin. Don't beat yourself up."

"What happened, LaGloria? Do you have any idea? Who were they fighting? What was going on?"

"I don't know. I really don't. I've been wracking my brains."

At this point it might have been advisable to say as little as possible, but LaGloria felt like she needed practice, so she went out on a limb. "Tweed was out all afternoon and I expected him home for dinner. Well, he was late and I started to wonder what was taking him so long, where he might be. I figured maybe he stopped down at the Fores like he does sometimes when he's coming back from JC. Sometimes Frankie goes there...used to go there too, after work. So I thought, maybe they'd hitch up, maybe he'd give Tweed a ride home. But I had a feeling I should go out and look for him; you know, it sounds silly, but I had a feeling something bad was going to happen."

"A premonition, like?"

"Well, I was all nervous and worried...it's not like I 'saw' something or 'knew' something, but I usually don't get so worked up when Tweed's late like that."

Tommy waited for her to go on.

"So, anyway, I thought I'd go to the Fores, you know, take a peek."

"I don't blame you."

"So I had a friend give me a ride down there, and we checked but he wasn't there. Turned out he was in a cab heading home."

"You're kidding!"

"I didn't know it at the time, of course, but yeah. So anyway, we-ah, me and this girlfriend of mine- we were down there by the Arbs, heading back, when we saw Frank's car on a flatbed."

"Oh, my God!" Tommy interjected, breathlessly.

"It looked terrible! Like it crashed and burned or something. So...we asked the cop who was there directing traffic, and he said there had been a shooting. That's when I really started to worry."

"Oh, LaGloria!"

"Yeah.

"When did you last see...I'm sorry, I shouldn't be making it worse."

"No; it's alright...I saw Frankie just the other day. Looked...normal, you know."

While she spoke, LaGloria cast about in her imagination for a clue or a hint, some item that she might include in her conversation that would then find its way to the police. Tommy was a nice guy, but he'd probably pass on anything he heard. After all, it was his penchant for blabbing that had led her and Frankie to the gun. The trick was to get him to blab some things and to withhold others.

"But that's pretty amazing in itself," she continued, "because I just learned something, ahm, you're not gonna believe..."

"What? What is it?"

"Frankie was gonna be a father. I just had a talk with his girlfriend- got off the phone with her right before you called."

"Frankie, a father?"

"Yeah, and that's the thing...I hope he didn't do something stupid, you know, lookin' to make some fast cash or something. I hate to say it, but the more I think about it I think that must have been it."

"Oh, man! You're probably right!"

"But look, I don't want people thinking my brothers were crooks or anything. I mean, as far as I know there's nothing to suggest…"

"No, no absolutely not…"

"And that's why I think it would be best if we kept this thing about the gun to ourselves. At least for the time being. I don't want to say that you should lie if anybody asks you, but unless something comes out that shows that they were gangsters or something, I'd appreciate it if you wouldn't make a big deal about it."

"You think the cops will be talking to me?" Tommy sounded almost delighted with dread.

"Oh, I don't know. No reason they should; I'm just saying is all. But it's not like you have to come forward or anything, either."

"Don't worry about me, hon, I don't want anybody getting in trouble either. My cousin is still laying low if you know what I mean. In fact, he's away right now. But I bet if he were here, he'd be bumming about the gun…"

"Forget about the gun, alright?"

LaGloria calmed herself. It wouldn't do to get all snippy with Tommy when he was just trying to help, just trying to be a good friend. She'd known all along that he was the weak link in her plan, and that she had to risk trusting him. Other than Tweed, Bricky, and herself, he was the only one who knew about the transaction.

Plausible deniability was her goal. She had thought ahead and considered the slim likelihood that an investigation of Des Kelley's murder might bring the police to her door. The odds of her being questioned in connection with the case would have increased if, for example, her brothers were caught with guns in their possession.

In that improbable but not altogether unlikely event, she would say that yes, she had heard that her brother had been interested in buying a gun, but as far as she knew, that was as far as it went. At the time it seemed like boasting and speculation. Her friend and business associate Tommy had told Frankie that his cousin Bricky had been looking to pawn off a couple of rifles. (She'd leave out the part about how Bricky, hoping to make some extra cash for himself, had taken the guns from a hijacked shipment he'd been hired to deliver for Des Kelley.) Her brother Frank had said that he'd be willing to purchase a rifle so that he could do some target practice, and maybe accompany his friends on their seasonal hunting expeditions up to the mountains. But she never heard if he bought one. Frankie never mentioned the matter again, and frankly, she had forgotten about it, having blown it off as just so much bullshit.

Now Frankie and Nilvan were the victims, not Des Kelley; and the gun in question wasn't the murder weapon. It was evidence in the murder investigation; not crucial to revealing the identities of the killers, but incidental to providing an understanding of what happened, who the McManus boys were and what they were doing at the scene.

Of course if Tweed had been smart he would have retrieved the guns even if he couldn't help Nilvan and Frank in any other way as they lay wounded or dead in the park. Then LaGloria would have been free and clear. She had dwelled upon this sore spot since the incident but her anger was somewhat tempered by her knowledge of Tweed. Because when the shit hits, he looks out for himself, and covers his own ass.

But what, she wondered, would she have done with the guns…

The first option that came to mind was to keep them, just in case. She had never been happy with the cooperative security arrangement Tweed had with his partners Wayne, Donal and Jabbour.

When any or all of them needed 'enforcement' they tended to work together and pool their resources to hire professional help. LaGloria would prefer that it was every man for himself.

But then if she actually *had* the guns she might be inclined to dump them. She'd have Tweed take the guns, the ammo, any other incriminating evidence, and haul it down to his underwater disposal site. Shit, he buried all of his other problems there. Tie them into a bundle and toss them in the swamp!

Another option, better yet, would be to sell them back to Bricky! That would have been golden! Plead and cry, 'Oh Mr. Bricky, since my brothers died, I have been trying to manage some of the debt they left and I'm forced to sell their possessions for a loss. Would you please give me some consideration?'

Satisfied for the time being that Tommy would keep quiet about the M16, LaGloria relaxed and started putting herself and her apartment in order. During the time it took to drink a cup of tea she cleaned the kitchen and straightened out the living room and prepared to take a shower. She had promised to notify Tommy about the funeral to make certain that he'd attend. It would be her next opportunity to reiterate the importance of keeping his mouth shut.

The apartment was quiet…almost too quiet. She was alone with her thoughts now, the phone silent at last, no radio, TV or stereo providing the illusion of company. The shower always left LaGloria feeling vulnerable unless Tweed or someone else was at home too. She didn't like the isolation that was enforced by the noise of rushing water, as it cut off the sound of her phone, or doorbell. She had argued with Tweed that they needed an extension for the bathroom, but he merely scoffed, saying that a person needed to be able to take a crap in peace. When she was in the shower she frequently heard, or imagined hearing noises that sometimes distracted, and sometimes alarmed her.

She started disrobing in the bedroom, leaving a trail of clothing as she walked toward the bathroom. Tweed hated when she did that, but LaGloria figured that her clothes were dirty anyway, and she loved the sensation of digging her toe into the carpet and scooping up her silky camisole, or her panties, and flinging them with her foot toward the laundry hamper. Plus it made her feel sexy to strip as she walked, like an exotic dancer on a nightclub runway. There- a lacy bra for the gentleman in the first row! A nylon stocking for the imaginary bartender! With a full-length mirror in the bedroom, another in the hall, and a third in the bathroom, she could watch herself transform from a workaday consultant to a bare-bottomed pixy, a racy nymph the likes of which would never have graced the cover of Harper's.

In the bathroom she appraised herself through 'luude-lensed eyes. Her mother used to say that she looked too serious, but it was hard to imagine her radiantly opaque skin, with her blushing cheeks and doll-like chin, her dainty nose and pretty eyes scaring anyone away. Five-eight, 110 pounds; with black hair done up in a cross between a style and a tease; fair white complexion that accentuated her penetrating blue eyes and her full red lips. A slender neck whose contours had been mapped out with trails of hot kisses, from the fuzzy nape to the treacherous cleft leading to the pride of her torso, her perfect breasts. It was no wonder that Tweed found her boobs so fascinating, because she herself had been playing with them ever since they first appeared when she was thirteen. Full but buoyant, evenly-matched and identical, yet independently alluring, teasing with rose-bud nipples that looked off in different directions like bored models at a photo-shoot. They rode high on softly defined ribs, and swelled prominently over her trim but not muscular belly. Her waist was narrow and her hips were hardly noticeable, but her butt was a work of art and her pussy was feminine perfection.

As she turned and admired her naked body in the mirror it occurred to her that many women simply don't understand the power and attraction of a sexy ass. They know that men want pussy, and they know that men consider breasts to be the appetizer before the main course, as it were, but they aren't so confident about flaunting their butts. Maybe she could advise women in the same way that she advised her male clients. After all, it never ceased to amaze her how few of the male models and actors she knew were aware of their sexual potential until she taught them how to exploit it; and it was simply a prevailing stereotype that promoted the view that all women were sluts and whores. In her opinion women had to be trained, taught or inspired to be sexy, for only a scarce minority of women were naturally predisposed to full-fledged femininity. As if to demonstrate her technique she slowly bent over until she could see her reflection by looking between her legs. There- her face was framed by her slim, tight thighs, and the hair on her quim formed an improvised goatee on her chin. Now, who wouldn't want to fuck that? If Tweed were here he'd grab on with both hands and hump her into a frenzy of euphoria. She reached back and placed her forefinger lightly on her damp clitoris with the sensuous finesse of a porn star. And then in a move that would have killed the erotic potential of any exotic strip scene, she straightened up, placed her hand to her nose and said, "Need a shower, alright."

CHAPTER 33

To be fair, it has been established that Des Kelley did not know at this time, that is, late Friday evening, that his wife of 36 years, Christine, was feeling very ill and was contemplating making a trip to the emergency room at Rossdale Hospital. However the record should also show that if he had been at home instead of gallivanting with his pub pals, then he might very well have seen fit to take her to the hospital. As uncomfortable as she was- and it was later shown that she must have been very uncomfortable indeed, she did not feel up to going alone and facing whatever it was that made her suffer so, yet neither would she deign to call Des at the club.

Des would not become aware of his wife's predicament because he was too busy contemplating his own. And the woman who had been his faithful partner and co-conspirator for the many years of his active career was now consigned to abandonment and neglect. So it was for anyone or anything that was no longer useful to him.

Now he was huddled in conference with his core group of friends and colleagues, drawing closer to the ones who, in supporting his ambitions, shared his culpability for a profligate lifestyle, a spate of crimes, and most significantly, murder.

Is it possible for anyone who has not been part of such a group to understand its dynamics? How might reasonable people, average citizens rationalize the presence in their midst of a gang of retirement-age criminals? Weren't these men supposed to be respected elders? Hadn't they fought the good fight, worked hard all their lives and played by the rules? Hadn't they served their country, and voted in elections and paid their taxes and raised their children to respect authority? Were they not God-fearing Christians? Or was the issue more complex than that?

There is no doubt that on the whole, people tolerate a certain degree of individuality and independence from the dominant generation in society. Even in a system that places a high priority on the rule of law. For as much as they admire the steadfast, the resolute and the righteous, they also admire the rogues, the free-thinkers and the eccentrics.

For example, there is undeniable complicity in an electorate that reinstates crooked politicians term after term. Perhaps they are misguided in their judgment, but it seems to be the case that the voters who reelect these legendary scoundrels, (on every level, from town board to county seat to state capital to federal bureaucracy), believe and expect that there is an implicit advantage in knowing how to 'bend the rules'. An honest leader may be able to fulfill promises to his constituents by utilizing consensus-building, compromise, and the prudent exercise of authority, but the crooked leader will always find a way to deliver. Historians delight in studying these rogue leaders and in exposing their strengths and their foibles; and the public adores them as well, almost to the point of encouraging their behavior.

Furthermore there are many examples of criminals who have been given aid and sanctuary by otherwise law-abiding citizens; thieves, killers and con-men who have been venerated and idolized as heroes; and renegades and desperadoes who have been romanticized as great lovers in literature despite the inherent misogyny of their words and deeds.

And yet, Des Kelley and his gang were no legendary outlaws, they had no reputation to speak of, nor did they draw support from the community. Des and his kind merely exploited the fact that there was nobody paying attention to what they were doing. Cops were crooked and lazy, and politicians were bought and sold, and businessmen spent the bulk of their creative energy finding ways to beat the system. Des merely took advantage of the situation.

However he was finally beginning to feel the squeeze, the uncomfortable sensation of pressure being applied from without by forces he was seemingly unable to understand and powerless to oppose. Who had sent two young men out to kill him? Who had prevented his stooges from protecting his son? Who had destroyed Joe Atkinson's car? And why? What had he done to provoke this?

It all went back to that phone call, and the news that Bricky was waiting for him. Where the hell was Bricky, anyway? And those boys- the McManus brothers. Why them? He remembered a night ages ago, when he had taken the family out for dinner to The Pleasant restaurant, and those boys had approached Tweed- he noticed them because their mother worked at the restaurant. A fine woman that Dolores McManus. Des was aware that many of the men who brought their families to the Pleasant on the pretext of a dinner out really wanted to ogle Dolores. For the buxom Spanish beauty was a sight bustling about in her uniform. But Des was also sure that he was the only one who fucked her. Other than Joe McManus, that is, but he had some medical problems, and Dolores was a needy woman.

The boys though, them skinny kids, little Frankie and his kid brother there, they'd been friends with Tweed, for sure. And then he, of course, started going out with young Miss McManus. Like father like son, as they say.

Was that it? Was that the reason they took up guns and called him out to the park that night? To kill him for screwing their mother? For losing their sister? But that was years ago! Water under the dam.

He'd gone over this a dozen times now.

Didn't they all get along, them kids? For fuck's sake, if they had been sitting around and thinking about shooting the old man, wouldn't Tweed have said something? And if he couldn't talk sense to them, then wouldn't he have called and said, 'Keep a look out and cover your rear, Da- there's a couple of crazy fuckers out after you...'?

No, it couldn't be. Not out of the blue like that. Dolores has been gone, what, these five, six years?

The boys must have got up to something. Somebody must have got to them, and convinced them to go after a guy they recognized and knew, a guy they could get fairly close to. That must be it; they needed money, they were in a bind, they were given an option, and they took it. Simple as that.

If Des needed a couple of low-profile shooters, someone who could take orders and do the job, and who were also fairly dispensable and cheap, then wouldn't guys like them fit the bill?

Only if you knew they were available; and only if you had some incentive, the right incentive, to offer.

So he was looking for someone who knew and hated him, and who knew and had something over the McManus boys; someone who either expected them to have no difficulty with the task, or who thought that they were totally expendable in any event. The mystery person was also close enough to him to know about Bricky, to know about the stooges, and to have anticipated his next move.

Des looked around at the patrons in the biz club; like a pack of mutts, all of them, assembled in the kennel and waiting for someone to toss them scraps and bones. And there were his friends...

Joe Toole, a man who made his own way. The son of an Irish immigrant who held the same job with the postal service for forty years, Joe dropped out of school in the eighth grade, and had a rather inauspicious start to his own career. As a young man he had few options until the war began.

He soon enlisted and found that military life suited him regardless of the horror and devastation he witnessed, and he completed his term of service with distinction. By the time he returned to civilian life he had changed, and the country had changed as well. It was a new America with employment for all and advancement practically guaranteed for anyone who was willing to work hard. He married and raised a family, and was fairly settled in life by the time he met Des Kelley. Literally 'just off the boat', Des was unlike anyone Joe had ever known, and he took to the talkative Irishman right off the bat. At first Joe had given Des a leg up, introducing him to and explaining the American system of patronage and access, offering him advice, and bailing him out with loans. Later Des gave him a great deal of assistance in establishing the Rossdale Businessmen's Club, and in return Joe helped with the formation of the regional CAFE organization.

Next to Joe, with the mug of Pabst in his hand, was Simon Fecteau. Younger than his confederates, but earnestly looking forward to retirement. Still a brick shithouse of a man, still honest and simple and hard-working. Self-deprecating, uncomplaining, even in the face of the insults and mockery he endured because of his echolalia. A loyal friend, Simon was always ready to help under any circumstances. Like Joe, he was a family man, but he participated in most of Des' risky endeavors, and he was willing to go to the mat for his friends.

Across the table from Des sat Harris Toole, Joe's younger brother. An independent chap, he was never married, and he had no children. Perhaps that explained why he was always eager for action, and ready to mix it up. He would lay his life on the line for Des, but not because of some self-destructive impulse or fool-hardiness. In fact he had a sincere conviction that he was indestructible, and judging by the looks of him, he was.

None of these men were violent, they weren't sociopaths, they weren't back stabbers. Imagine them guilty of murder; imagine them being arrested for what was essentially a non-crime. No- it was un-thinkable. Des knew that he was thrice-damned for his sins. But in his heart, the same repository of will and emotion from which he had worshiped the Lord Jesus Christ, he believed that there were wars and there were *wars*. Wars of attrition, wars of territory, wars of conquest and greed, wars of ideology. There was killing, and there was *murder*: murder of innocence, murder of convenience, criminal murder, military murder, accidental or premeditated murder. When murder occurs it is the duty and obligation of the state to step in and record the event, describe the circumstances and ascertain and certify the cause. Responsibility and/or blame must be determined, and from this may emerge further legal proceedings, trials and penalties.

In this example, two young men, armed for murder, were killed while lying in wait to kill. Had a crime been committed? Who was to blame? Given a comprehensive account of the facts relating to the incident, the state could certainly make an accurate and judicious decree, and yet facts alone do not bring closure to a murder investigation. Perpetrators must be apprehended, guilt must be assessed and penalties levied.

Surely if Des were to come forward he would receive the full benefit of the doubt as well as all due clemency. But what incentive was there to come forth and expose himself to the humiliation of a public examination, when in truth the proceedings would play out like a poker game, with just as much preponderance in luck as in process? Like many poker players, Des did not consider himself a gambler. When he played a game he brought his skill to bear and made every effort to win. He played his opponents, not their cards. But strength in poker resides in two factors, confidence in the size of the bankroll, and belief in the hand. Right now he wasn't sure of either.

Perhaps it would be different if he were required to appear before a tribunal of military or law-enforcement personnel, or others who had faced death or who had been required to use deadly force. Most citizen jurors were simply ill-equipped, in his opinion, to consider or judge capital cases, since they had no experience dealing with matters of life and death.

"So you spoke to Billy, Des," said Joe, before belching heartily, and smiling as if proud of his accomplishment, "Any clue what he's thinking about, you know, the incident..."

"Sure I did; just this morning. He talked like a fucking cop."

"No kiddin'? He is a cop, now, Des," said Joe apologetically.

"But he doesn't usually talk like one, does he?" Des took a sip from his glass of Guinness. "You know what he said? He said he doesn't care who gets nailed for this thing."

"Well, that sounds encouraging, doesn't it?"

"He said that, uh, what did he call them, oh yes, he said a couple of 'losers' got killed, and other 'losers' would have to take the fall. Apparently now he has a chance to bag a couple of losers, and it doesn't really matter which ones."

"That's alright with me. Let him wrap it up as quickly as possible. Good work, Billy!"

"I don't know, Joe. And I don't like the way he was talking to my boy, either, like he was rousting a common punk on the street corner."

Joe shook his head commiseratively, but he knew that Tweed was in fact a street corner punk and he wondered why Des was making a big deal out of it.

"Don't let it get to you. He's just doing his job. And Tweed can take care of himself. Billy thinks he can push him around because he's not one of them college kids."

"Yeah? Well, he ain't one of them coke dealers, either; I mean, this is Rossie, not Mission, or uptown. I know the boy's a hustler, but he's just trying to stay ahead of the game. At least he ain't out robbing banks."

The newspapers had been full of the latest escapades of the organized crime gangs that operated virtually unchecked in other parts of the city. Sometimes Des read these reports with envy, impressed by the bold, flashy heists those guys pulled and, if the reports were accurate, the fact that they acquired more cash in one job than his operation did in months. But then he considered the risks and hazards of that type of organization, compared to the benefits of his long-term operation. After all, he worked openly, and he interacted with his community, with no fear of arrest, prosecution, or incarceration; whereas the hardcore gangs in Mission and elsewhere were frequently in hiding, or on the lam, and they preyed upon their neighbors. For them doing battle with the local police was a rite of passage, and a record of time in the penitentiary was a mark of honor.

The idea of prison for him or any of his partners in crime bothered Des acutely, especially now that he was considering various ways to preempt the investigation and negotiate with the police.

"So what's bothering you? Sounds like Billy's not particularly interested in this one. He's already got it figured out."

"I don't know, Joe. I guess what bothers me is that I still don't know who planned this thing. Say Billy does make an arrest, say he does put some stiff or stiffs away, that doesn't make the problem go away...I'm saying that whoever it was that put those boys up to it is simply going to wait until the heat blows over before they try again."

Joe shrugged. "Even if that's true, there's nothing Billy can do to prevent it. I say let 'em come on. You were ready for 'em the first time around; let 'em try it again. Maybe this time we'll nail 'em for sure."

Des smiled, but he was frustrated that Joe didn't understand his concern. For one thing he still wanted to bring Tweed into the fold and he was vexed by a notion that somehow this episode might afford him the best opportunity to do so. And another thing, that he wouldn't admit to Joe, at least not yet anyway, was that he was considering turning himself in.

"We're too old for this shit, my friend," he muttered.

Joe yawned, stretched and nodded, "I'm feeling pretty old myself, right now."

"OK, so what? I have to put a couple of rocking chairs in here for you old farts?" Harris sneered. "Geez! You think maybe you're working too hard?"

"You're not so young yourself anymore, Harris," said Joe.

Harris was a big guy, strong as a mule team, but he had developed a tremendous raccoon's belly of a paunch, his hair had gone gray, and he had deep creases in his face as if he had worked in the sun too long.

"Younger than you guys…" And to demonstrate, Harris stood and flexed his muscles.

"What's this, now…?" asked Des, still preoccupied.

"You'll see," he replied, rolling up his sleeves. Harris squatted down to the floor and with one ham-fisted hand grasped the front leg of one of the wooden chairs at the table. After a moment's prep and concentration, he suddenly lifted the chair clean off the floor, level and erect so that if he had placed a glass of beer upon it he wouldn't have spilled a drop. He brought himself up to one knee, then he stood, raising the chair to shoulder height, before lowering it, ever so slowly, back down to the ground.

"How's that, you…geriatrics." His face had colored so deeply that he looked as if he were made up to play Beelzebub.

Not especially generous with praise, Des replied, "Must be real handy around the house, especially when you're doing the vacuuming. "Oh, and look what the cat brought in, now…"

A balmy breeze tinged with the scent of a wood fire blew in ahead and announced the arrival of Pat Fecteau, who strolled in on leaden feet as if he were dead tired. It was late and Pat looked as though he'd rather be home, but he smiled nevertheless and greeted all together and individually. "So what's all the hullabaloo down the street there to old White City?" he asked, expectantly.

"What the 'hullabaloo' are you talking about, Pat?" asked Des, as if he was helping to set up a joke. He felt his spirits lift a little, as if each friend had taken a corner of his mood and were supporting him with their presence and combined strength.

"No, I thought you knew…There's something going on; a big fire in the housing projects; but they also got paddy wagons and TPF out and they're hauling 'em away by the dozens."

"What? Where is this, now?"

"White City projects, you know, a couple of miles down…" and he waved over his shoulder. "Get me a beer, would you, Harris?"

"Is that what smells? Fire?"

"That's right, Des; looks like the whole bleedin' place is in an uproar."

The phone rang as Harris rounded the bar to retrieve Pat's beer. After answering it he too became excited, and he started pacing, speaking loudly and quickly into the phone and waving his free hand. The level of conversation around the bar grew as the patrons sensed the excitement. Some of them actually unglued themselves from their chairs to stroll outside as if they expected to find more information about what was happening.

As soon as he hung up the phone, Harris relayed what he had heard.

"That was your boy Denis. He's down the street at the Fores. Says that all hell broke out when they went after some guy in a Volkswagen. I don't know…we're going to have to get this from him directly, but he said they, you know, him and Joey and their buddies there, were following this guy into the projects…"

"…The Projects! First mistake…" uttered Simon, shaking his head.

"-and he crashed into the building. Guess he lost it and smashed up."

"Jesus, Mary and Joseph!" cried Des, "So the other fellow crashed…but is Denis alright?" He was asking for Simon's sake.

"They're in rough shape from what he says. He's got a broken nose…"

"Nose?" shouted Simon, "A broken nose?"

"Look, Simon, Denis said he's going to Rossdale to get it checked out- he's a big boy. He just stopped in at the Fores for a pick-me-up before he goes to get it set. But for the others, he said…" he paused and looked around the bar for the elder Atkinson.

His brother offered, "If you're looking for Joe, he's gone." He waggled his fingers toward the door.

"-Right. Yeah, he said that Joey Atkinson is already in the hospital. He's all banged up. Plus his friend Mo is missing…"

Now Des was rising to his feet. "I thought the other fellow crashed. How'd them other ones get hurt? What's going on? Two in the hospital and one missing?"

Harris was flustered. "Like I said, we're going to have to get it from the horse's mouth. He was talking a mile a minute there and I got all I could from him. He's all shook up, you know, so he wasn't making a hell of a lot of sense. I mean, he goes, 'the little fuck had a bomb in his car or something', 'cause, when he hit the wall the thing went up in flames. Next, if I got him right, he said that the whole place blew up, and the fire department and police and ambulances all came rushing in."

Pat couldn't contain himself. "Like I said! I'll tell you, when I was coming up past the station- you know, the way I cut over by White City, -I saw a mob scene on the street down there! Lights flashing, people everywhere, and the cops hauling folks off like it was a riot or something!"

The phone again. This time the place went silent as Harris gathered details from the caller. "It was Denis' friend Abbisso. He was driving and saw the whole thing. You're not gonna believe this, Des, but there's a fucking mad scene down there, and the boys are in the middle of it. Now this one says that when the guy in the Volkswagen crashed, they chased him out of his car, you know, to ask him a few questions about Joe's car. Ya gotta admit, it didn't look good that he was running in the first place. But next thing they knew, every spook, spic and spade in the place is out in the street looking to clobber them. Says he doesn't know why, but that things just started exploding- literally. 'S'like a, uh, chain-reaction or something."

"Yeah- they should have broke out the chains and seen what kind of reaction they got," suggested Pat.

"So how about this nut with the Volkswagen? Where's he?" demanded Des.

"The fucker's gone. Vanished at the same time Joey got hurt. Plus, now I hear that another of Denis' friends is up at Rossdale, too. That makes two in the hospital and Joey heading up there to join them now. I hear this one Kennedy is looking at surgery."

Simon tried to sum it all up. "Looks like there was five of 'em altogether. So Denis got his nose broke, Joey Atkinson and his friend Kennedy are both in the hospital, this fella Mo has gone missing, and that leaves this Bisso kid. How's he doing?"

"The one that called? He's fucking scared, I'll tell you that, and only his dry-cleaner will know how much. Nah- he's alright. Wasn't in the scrap, but he stayed around long enough to get everybody out of there in his car. Everybody except Mo, that is. Brought his friends to the hospital."

"What a cluster fuck. SNAFU."

"You said it. And part of a trend, if you ask me," said Des, rubbing his eyes with his knuckles. "Every time these kids go out on the street they come back with their tails between their legs."

"Well, Des, we don't know what happened yet. We'll get the real story when they calm down."

"Tell you what, Harris. Get that kid Bismo to come here and tell us what happened in person. Give him a chance to set the record straight."

Calls were coming in steadily now, each one with a slightly different take on the crisis at White City. Slowly Des and the rest of the bar-bound gained a better picture of what was happening. Simon, Pat and Harris were busy making calls as well, as they tried to locate Denis and to learn the status of his injured pals.

In the midst of the confusion a call came in for Des personally, on his private line. It was A.D.Makepeace. "Ah, Des- you're still there. I didn't know if I'd find you at the 'office' so late."

"Yes, well, there's been some extra excitement this Friday night on account of some action down to the public housing projects outside the square. They're burning the place down or something. The whole town is in an uproar. Now we hear that Simon's boy Denis may have been injured during all the ruckus. I'll be here for a while yet."

"Well, Des, about this affair you asked me to look into for you; before I go any further I thought I should go over what I've learned so far. Is that alright?"

"Before you go any further...Well, don't let me hold you back. What have you learned?"

"First of all, when you called you didn't give me a whole lot of detail; you said you had been ambushed, almost killed, and you wanted to know who done it, who was after you. Am I right?"

"Yes, I thought we'd all want to know who staged the bleeding thing, who made the phone call to get me out there." Des replied, as if it were obvious.

"Right, you implied that this incident might have been related to your activities, to business, as it were, and so you called me. I mean, first you'd want to know if I had anything to do with it. And if I hadn't sent someone to do you in, then perhaps I might help determine if there were IRA assassins, or some kind of hit squad from British army intelligence after you.

"But you didn't tell me that they were lads from your own town there, and you didn't tell me that you killed the SOBs. Let's be realistic; these were kids you might have seen on the street at one time or another. It's pretty damned unlikely that they were hired for their expertise. Not unless your enemies were scraping the barrel.

"You probably have a better idea of why these fellows shot at you than I do, but what we're really talking here is what you're going to do about killing these lads." He was talking rather quickly now.

"I understand that it's a problem when someone tries to kill you, but it goes without saying that it would have been a whole lot easier to deal with if you could have talked to them; if you didn't kill them boys, right?"

"The fact is, Makepeace, that I was called out to an ambush. Yes, I had the sense to go prepared and yes, my guys did take out the shooters. I did the right thing. Now I want you to do the right thing. Experts or not, one of these boys as you call them was carrying an M16 and the other had a fuckin' shotgun. I say somebody went to a lot of trouble to set this up, and they forced, used or hired those two to do the job. Whoever it was can't be that hard to find. Any ideas?"

"Yes, but let me ask you something- you're not officially connected with this incident, correct? I mean, you didn't file any reports or make any statement? I ask because I made a few phone calls to get a sense of where the inquiry was headed, and I've heard your name mentioned a number of times."

A pause. "By who...the feds?"

"We're not talking the PTA..."

"So now you're a comedian...In what context?"

"Maybe coincidental. I heard about an ongoing investigation. They're looking into so-called influence peddling, bribery, extortion, the list goes on. There's a lot of heat right now and it's focused on Rossdale. I think they're shaking the bushes and kicking over the rocks and seeing what crawls out. The pressure's on and people are talking."

Des had been annoyed by Makepeace, now he was angry.

"OK, so I happen to have become a target in more ways than one, is that what you're saying?"

"Well no, you're not the target of the investigation. They're looking at this fellow Dapper Ferguson. I hope you know him, because you've been linked to him."

Des felt strangely disappointed. "Dapper? I didn't know...I mean, I know him, sure, but I didn't know he was in hot water. But I shouldn't be surprised. They go after all of them pols sooner or later. But what's that got to do with this?"

"They only go after the crooked ones, Des. The thing is that your name is prominent in the investigation. I mean, it's almost as if they're looking for you instead of Dapper."

"Huh! I'm no pol and that's plain to see. Let 'em look. I'm not worried. A lot of people helped old Dapper get re-elected."

"Alright, let me just say that I'm following my instincts on this one. Could be that someone sees you as a liability. But don't jump to any conclusions. In the meantime, I have to find out how these guys knew you. Did you know them?"

"Yes I knew them; well, I used to know their mother. And my son Tweed is going with their sister."

Now Makepeace knew that he shouldn't be involved. This was a private matter, a family affair. Let Des and his friends in the police handle this one. He couldn't help Des out of his difficulty, but it appeared that Des could help him.

Des was down, disoriented and beset by problems. There would be no better time to do him in and be done with him.

"So I'm straight on this...you didn't participate in the shooting, you say?"

He'd already said as much. In a flash Des weighed the value and consequence of lying to Makepeace. For the moment he was still inclined to call Billy Storer and come clean; and if he did then the truth would out in any case. And yet his anger outbalanced his honesty.

"I'm still not sure who shot whom, 80, I don't even know if I've got their names straight, but no, I didn't shoot anyone. Why do you ask?"

"I was concerned about the gun, you know? If you should be questioned about this matter, it helps to be sure that you can account for your guns...whether you know how to use them, whether they have been fired recently, and if your licenses are up to snuff."

"Sounds like you're trying to justify a plea of self-defense."

"Justify or manufacture, as the case may be, Des, but yes, I am considering the possibility."

"I'd be kidding myself if I said that I hadn't considered it as well, my friend."

"Well, there you go," he cleared his throat and went on. "I'm meeting with someone tonight-someone who may be able to shed some light on this affair. I'll say no more than that for now, and if it pans out then I'll get back to you all the sooner."

Two half-full cups sat on the table in front of Des, offering a choice of beer and coffee. He had carried the coffee in with him over an hour ago and he hadn't taken a sip of beer in twenty minutes. He poured the remains of the cold coffee into his beer and took a swig.

"That kid Abacus is on his way, Des. Are you going to hang around and talk to him?" Harris picked up the cups and waited for a response.

Hmmm. Mocha-lager. Kind of an acquired taste. He smacked his lips.

"I'm not going anywhere," he replied in a measured cadence. Then he turned to Joe. "Do you think I should talk to Billy and clear the air, you know, tell him what happened?"

Joe's eyebrows went up as if to make room for the idea to penetrate his consciousness.

"Confess, Des? Why would you want to do that?"

"Not exactly. I want…" he groaned, "I want to avoid dragging you fellows or my son into this mess. I thought maybe if I talked to Billy privately then he'd see a way to close the case quietly."

"Now how would you do that? What could you possibly say that would help him to do that? I mean, you'd have to give him something."

Now Simon and Harris and Pat were paying close attention to the conversation.

"Give him something? Doesn't he owe us enough already? You know how it is with Billy. I've given my share."

"That's not what I mean, Des. Think about it. He needs things to close a case like this. Things like evidence, suspects, confessions…and I'm not talking about your crime-show baloney here. I mean that he would have to have the guns, the proof, you know? He's not going to simply drop the matter on your say-so."

Various grunts of assent and approval issued from the others at the table, but they all looked to Des.

"Say I hand myself over, say that I done it, I shot them boys, and, uh, say I give him a gun, something he can use for the record."

"It's not as easy as that, Des," said Joe, patiently. "Him and Jimmy both know that there was more than one shooter. They found two men down, with two types of bullets in 'em. And remember, the dead guys had guns of their own. It doesn't take a genius to see what must have happened."

"I know what you're saying, but it's possible, well let's say it's within the realm of possibility that one person could have taken on two opponents and come out the victor; and it's also possible that he could have had two guns."

His friends looked at each other doubtfully.

"Sure, Des, and would it be fair to say that you could be that someone? I mean, Billy knows you, he's known you for years. Do you expect him to believe that you marched in there loaded for bear and faced down two guys with rifles? If so then maybe he should just pin a medal on you and offer you a job while he's at it."

"Joe's right, Des," offered Pat, "I see what you're saying, you want to protect us, but if you go to Billy and tell him a story that you were involved in this thing to any extent, you'll end up having to drag everybody in anyway. I say let him do his thing. He'll take care of it."

Des struggled to maintain composure, not yet ready to abandon his reasoning.

"I could say that I was a witness. I happened to be in the park that night, maybe taking a stroll, and I seen the thing, right there in front of me!" He was looking at his friends, but he saw the image of Frankie McManus, sitting on the road, waiting for his execution.

"OK, and what do you say happened? What could you say to make him drop the case? Who was there?"

"It doesn't matter!" His mind was racing now. If only he could get a proxy pair of prints onto one of Harris' guns. Maybe one of the shitbums from Mission who owed him money. He'd have to dwell on that…

"I say that I saw a showdown, uh, two on two, and uh, there was a lot of noise, booms and flashes, you know, and then I seen two of them was hit, and they went down," the fiction played itself out like a Saturday morning serial. "Then the two who survived, well they up and ran. But I seen one of them toss something in the swamp down there next to the tracks. -Now here's the part where we give him something. Harris- you give me one of your guns and I'll toss it into the swamp. Then when Billy wants me to show him where, I show him. They find the rifle, and case closed."

They needed a moment to let that sink in. Then Harris spoke up. "And what about the shooters? They just get away? I mean, are you going to point the finger at anyone?"

Well yes, the thought had crossed his mind. "I could, but I don't have to. I just say that I couldn't make out their faces. It was dark, and I was trying to stay out of sight. Anyway, Billy will take the gun and test it, find out that it matches, and he'll work on tracking the killers from there. Good luck to him…"

"Luck to him!" said Simon, "Maybe after a time the case will simply remain unsolved, but effectively closed."

"That's right, and if he insists on arresting some 'losers' to make his quota or something, then at least I can say I did the best I could."

"So I have to give up one of my guns?" said Harris. Clearly that aspect of the plan didn't hold much appeal for him.

"I think it's worth it," said Des, "Hey- where did you get those things, anyway?"

"They're keepsakes, for Chrissakes! I've had 'em for years! My trusty 60's…man!"

"Alright, alright! Maybe I can come up with something to make it up to you. But I can't substitute guns- that won't work."

Harris grumbled, took up his rag and went back to work cleaning the bar; but Des knew he'd come through.

There was a feeling among the group that something had been accomplished, that an unresolved issue had been cleared away. The mood was brightened and enhanced by another round of drinks, and attention turned back to the fate of Denis and Joey and their pals, and the arrival of Lenny Abbisso.

CHAPTER 34

Was it nerves, paranoia, or hallucinations? Again LaGloria heard things when she was in the shower. Not the running water, not the hum of the exhaust fan, not the radio she had left playing in the other room. If she didn't know better, she'd swear that someone was at the door. But the same thing happened every time she got in the shower. She knew the phone wouldn't ring while she was bathing, because that only happened when she was going to the bathroom. It never failed…even if she put off going in order to give whoever the chance to call, the phone would only ring when she finally gave up, grabbed a book and got situated on the toilet.

There it was again- shit! Fuck! Goddamn!

Man- it was just starting to feel good. She cranked the knob and squeaked off the water.

If she found that there was nobody at the friggin' door when she got there then she'd have to seriously consider giving up Quaaludes. Then again, now that she was out of the tub and wrapping her sopping naked body in a towel, she decided that if somebody really was at the door, then, although it might not justify interrupting her shower, at least it would give her a degree of faith in her sanity.

As she twisted another towel atop her head she reminded herself to tell Tweed that it was time to change the décor in the bathroom. This pink and purple shit had to go. The pattern of the floor tiles was particularly annoying. A repetitive sequence of squares and rectangles created a Warhol effect of facial images. Not images of Marilyn, but a celebrity nonetheless. Ever since she moved into this apartment she had been annoyed by the likenesses of Richard Nixon that she saw in the tiles on the bathroom floor. For that reason she always took a book with her when she had to go. She couldn't stand staring at the forty Nixons on the floor. She stepped on one and drowned the fucker in a puddle of soapy shower water.

It was only six meters or so from the bathroom to the front door and she hopped that distance on the balls of her feet, clutching one towel at her chest and another at the nape of her neck. Suddenly a tense persistent rapping commenced and now she knew that she hadn't been imagining things.

On the other hand she was pissed because some asshole had let this person, whoever it was, into the building. What's the point of a security system and intercom if you're not going to use it? Without a sound she drew herself up to the peephole that Tweed had inconsiderately installed for his height. Hmmm. Two guys. Oh, shit! The cops!

"Hello? Who's there?" she quavered.

"Detective Rima, ma'am. Remember we spoke on the phone?"

Wow. He didn't even check to see who she was.

"Oh, yes, Detective Rima. Uh, could you give me a minute? I'm in the shower."

She heard the muttering sound of a quick conference.

"Uh, Miss, uhm, is your boyfriend in there? Perhaps we could talk to him out here while we wait?"

"My boyfriend?"

"Yeah, T.W. Kelley. He lives here, right?"

T.W.Kelley? That's a new one, she thought, not recalling that the mailbox in the foyer was so labeled. The landlord had gone nuts with a label machine one day, tagging everything from the laundry room to the pay phone. *Tumble Weed Kelley* had gotten a chuckle out of the new monogram on his mailbox, and he left it up.

"Oh, Tweed! He's not here. He went out. I think he had an appointment up at Rossdale."

Another conference.

"OK. My partner is going to go and run some errands. I'll just wait here in the hallway until you're ready."

What? The guy is just gonna stand around on the stairs while she finishes her shower? She took another peek. Sure enough, the older guy was leaving. Holy shit! That was Storer! Thank God he's gone!

"Yeah, OK. Uh, tell you what, detective," what the hell was she doing? She opened the deadbolt, slipped the chain and yanked the police brace bar, pulling the door open about 18 inches. "Why don't you come on in," she said face to face now. "You can wait in the kitchen and I'll be with you momentarily." She pointed to the room at the end of the hall.

If she had any doubts as to the wisdom of admitting Detective Rima into her apartment when she was dressed only in a damp towel, she knew she had made a mistake when she turned to close the door behind the officer. It had been her intention merely to secure the latch, but as she pivoted from one leg to the other she slipped on the puddle of water and her foot went out from under her. It happened so fast that it might have looked deliberate as her leg shot out like hockey goalie making a lightning save, however she struck Rima's foot on the side, bringing him down as well.

As LaGloria and her guest collapsed to the floor like some well-rehearsed vaudevillian prat-fall, the startled detective reached out to catch himself. Unfortunately, what he caught instead was the edge of her towel, which he whipped off like a magician in the climax of his act.

Ouches quickly turned to squeals as LaGloria tumbled onto her bare bottom and she ended up facing Rima with her legs spread wide, her breasts heaving and the rest of her still dripping wet.

Mortified but only slightly injured in the mishap, the good detective struggled to scramble to his feet, facing away as quickly as possible. Not quick enough to miss a glimpse of the finest, foxiest, hottest bod he'd seen...ever.

And then she leaped to her feet, simultaneously tearing the towel from her hair and flinging it around her. As she ran for the bathroom he was rewarded with a further glimpse of the cutest piece of ass he'd ever seen as well.

Oops; he shouldn't have looked. He was supposed to behave as a gentleman. Alright, so he was a jerk. A jerk with a throbbing woody. Well, this interview got off to a rough start. It didn't proceed too well, either. She must have spent ten minutes in the bathroom, allowing him to collect himself in the den. Once she had recovered from her fall, her shock and her embarrassment, she remained in a bright pink blush for the duration of his visit. However she did manage to 'entertain' him.

The detective thought he had been thoroughly prepared for this appointment, but somehow all of his preparation had gone out the window, or down the drain for that matter. He was tempted to beg forgiveness and reschedule, but he could just imagine Storer's reaction. "Oh, sure! She flashes her beaver at you and you go running with your tail between your legs!"

It wasn't that hard to get his head screwed back on. All he had to do to regain his composure and to lose his boner was to imagine naked dead chicks. Like the one they pulled out of the river a couple of years ago. Or the one they found in the wildlife reservation after she had apparently been raped and stabbed. However he was afraid that a trick like that, though effective, could come back to haunt him. So once he had dispensed with the formalities he kept his attention focused upon his notes.

She was a smart kid, this LaGloria, and she seemed to understand everything he had to say about the legal, ethical, and financial ramifications, as well as the personal obligations that may result from the death of a loved one. She talked a lot, too, more than was necessary for simply answering his questions. With disarming candor and almost coquettish charm she discussed her brother's lives and occupations, their dreams and their day to day realities.

For example, prior to speaking with her he had not known that Francis had won the Eisenhower school district spelling bee as a sixth grader; or that he drove in the monthly demolition derbies out on the old roundy-round at the fairgrounds. Plus it came as no small surprise to learn that his girlfriend was pregnant, that he had looked forward to becoming a daddy, and that he had solid plans for his future. Nilvan too came across as a decent kid from her recollection. Sweet, generous, a former boy-scout and student athlete who had enjoyed challenging himself. Orienteering in the mountains, skin-diving off the coast. This wasn't the same scum-bag that his partner Billy Storer had portrayed as a drug-addicted thieving reprobate.

She was pained and troubled by their deaths, and shocked and puzzled by the manner in which they occurred. Wanting to be helpful, she had spent some time trying to recall anything that might help the police to determine what the two of them were up to. Nilvan had said something about a side job, and she was struggling to remember the name he had mentioned. A Mr. Do-Good, or something…no, that wasn't it; it was an odd name like something from the roster of the Mayflower. Mayflower? Was that the name? No, she exclaimed with the relief of recovering a lost valuable, it was Makepeace! Apparently both of her brothers had been doing odd jobs for this fellow Makepeace. That was the only thing, she claimed, that had seemed odd or out of place.

But speaking of odd, the rest of what she had to say left Rima wondering if she hadn't been more traumatized by her ordeal than she let on. For instance, without any prompting from him and without any apparent connection to the subject at hand, she told him a story about her uncle. First she described the guy in detail, as if she had known him well and had observed him at length. He worked as a cop, she said, and from her description it sounded like he was a regular municipal beat cop, someone Rima might have known. It wasn't like she misled him or anything, but suddenly it seemed as if the scene shifted overseas and now her uncle was a bobby in Northern Ireland. She went on to say that the guy had been killed in the line of duty by an IRA bomb squad.

And that was why she hated the IRA, and anyone who supported them. Hypocrites, all of them, she said, and that was why she was proud to be British. British? he had asked…Wasn't her name, McManus, an Irish name? Well, she explained, you can find McManuses all over the place, and her branch of the family must have moved to England long ago.

And when he asked about her work, she said that she was a freelance project coordinator working for the big modeling firms in town. When he asked if she kept busy, that is, if there was enough work for a freelancer, she had said something he thought he might have misunderstood, for it sounded like, "It's all assholes and elbows from where I'm standing."

Disturbed, disheveled and disadvantaged, she still came across as either flip or evasive. For all of her openness about her brothers, she was less direct about her boyfriend Kelley. What does he do? *He's a big help.* What are his hours? *He's at his best late at night.* Does he contribute for living expenses and such? *He holds up his end pretty well.* How long had she known him? *How Long is a Chinaman.* Did they get along? *Oh, yeah, she loved him like a henway.* What's a henway? *Oh, about three or four pounds.* And so on, like that. Maybe it was her way of saying 'interview's over.'

Perhaps, and this was bordering on wishful thinking, she was flirting. Rima decided that it was time to wrap it up, but despite his discipline, his professional demeanor and his self-control, he started to envision taking her in his arms and probing the warmth of her body with his tongue. Then, no sooner had he started fantasizing, when *she* appeared to be sending *him* little hints and signals. Storer was gone, or at least waiting in the parking lot, her boyfriend was out for the evening, and he had already seen her naked. When people share a moment like the one they had, it was only natural to fall into a mad embrace and then rush to make lava-hot love. Damn, there he goes again.

Something about this babe inspired lunacy. He could be downright irresponsible for a girl like her.

From LaGloria's perspective, her encounter with Rima was leading to a new and exciting realm of possibilities. What if she got this guy on her side? What if she convinced him to see her as the helpless victim in the whole affair. Someone he'd be willing to protect, and to stick his neck out for. It was a nice neck. Kind of long, with a dull razor rash under the chin. In his cop-tight clean-cut way he was almost as pretty as one of her gay clients. That same assiduous attention to personal grooming and neat, coordinated clothing was something cops had in common with gay men. Explains why so many cops look queer, she thought. Maybe they were. They probably go out with the mousy bank-teller types, or with the 'artists'. Maybe she could fix him up with one of her dancer friends, hell, maybe a cabaret drag queen. No, wait a second, she had to keep this one interested in her.

Guys who have gazed at the promised land of her pretty pink pussy never forget it; though, like Moses, most were destined to remain forever off-limits.

CHAPTER 35

It was later in the evening than he would have liked, but Tweed had finished the execrable portion of his work. His fucking foot hurt, his back was sore, his neck was kinked from holding his head at unusual angles in the trunk of Frankie's death mobile, and he was in a bitter, querulous mood. He was standing at the take-out counter in South St. Market, absent-mindedly chowing a tuna and chopped pickle spuckie, drinking a cup of Rossdale's finest coffee and thumbing through last month's *Poetry Review*. It was difficult under normal circumstances to give proper appreciation to the type of ametrical cathartic crap that passed for verse in the paper nowadays, but right now it was almost impossible. From the window of the store he was witnessing a spectacle that was becoming all too common in Rossie, even in the White City Projects. A line of emergency vehicles was slowly pulling away from the complex, led by the fire chief himself. He must have over-ridden the signal lights at the intersection so his retinue could merge from Booker T Washington Drive onto Main St, and the resulting traffic jam stretched south all the way to Rossdale Square and north heading to Jamaica Center. Anyone out on the street at this time of night was probably drawn to the fire anyway, and now most of the attraction was removing itself. The market, too, would usually be quiet and slow at this hour, but tonight it was thronged with customers.

The owner of the store, Henry Chung, had already had a long day, and though he welcomed the business he was curt and irritable. His twin Doberman pinscher bodyguards had already called it quits, snoozing in a massive black and brown heap on the floor beside him, like a twitching mass of seal fur.

"When you gonna buy that fuckeen paper, Mr. Tuey? Every week you look; you look but you no buy!"

"Can't make my mind up, Mr. Chung. I mean, the quantity is in the *Review*, but the quality is in the *Atlantic*."

"In the Atlantic?" Chung made this sound like "In a cran tick?"

Tweed understood and nodded his head, but Chung apparently did not. "You fuckeen crazy, Mr. Tuey. Paper's a buck. Buy the fuckeen paper."

Tweed stuffed the last morsel of the tuna sandwich into his mouth, daintily folded the paper shut and smoothed out the creases.

"What's going on out there, Chung? They had a fire down there, huh?" Ambulances and police cars had joined the queue at the light.

"I don't know, I hear somebody got shot or something. But someone else say that one of the buildings blew up."

Given the choice of 'blew up' or 'exploded', Chung would probably have preferred, 'go boom'.

"No shit? Blew up, eh?" Tweed figured that Mr. Chung was pulling his leg. From where he was standing he could see the profile of the apartment buildings in silhouette against the purple night sky.

"They're gonna blow them all up one of these days," said Tweed, and as he stared he recalled the great times he had spent partying there with Carmine.

The building in which Carmine once lived was, at that time, simply called Unit 4. This was before the city announced a plan to rededicate the complex in honor of Martin Luther King Jr. It may seem odd that none of the units were called "King", but the city's decision had immediately been opposed by a vocal group of constituents led by Dapper Ferguson. In hindsight it was difficult to see how the names Frederick Douglass, Marcus Garvey, Harriet Tubman, Sojourner Truth, Booker T Washington and Rosa Parks were less objectionable to Dapper and his cadre, and yet this was the compromise they ultimately accepted. After rancorous debate all parties claimed ostensibly to respect King's legacy in so honoring other icons of African-American ascendancy. The buildings and adjacent streets were redubbed and White City unofficially became the MLKII housing projects.

Unit 4, now 'Washington', had one feature that was highly attractive to Carmine and his friends. The main stairway that provided access to all three floors and the maintenance basement also went up to the roof. At the top of the stairs there was a landing right below the drop-down hatch that led outside, and just below the hatch there was a window facing east. It was this landing that Carmine made his own.

In the morning the uppermost portion of the stairwell was illuminated by the rays of the rising sun. Carmine enhanced this effect by decorating the walls with a psychedelic rainbow rendered in day-glo paint, with silver stars and sundry fluorescent celestial objects. Tweed called it the Peter Max landing. Carmine took this as a hilarious sexual reference, since he had no idea who Peter Max was.

There, at Peter Max landing, at dawn, Carmine and Tweed smoked many a bowl of dope while awaiting the sunrise. The shared magic occurred on clear mornings at the moment when the sun rose high enough to light up the walls and Tweed and his soul-brother basked in the amplified glow.

For sunsets they ascended to the roof where they sat facing west in aluminum and mesh lawn chairs. However there was no special effect provided by that vantage point, and the view wasn't all that spectacular, since neighborhood homes, the rail bed, and the bulk of Arbs Park stood between them and the horizon. Still, it was a place where Carmine and Tweed could sit in relative peace and comfort like complacent lords surveying their domain. They both knew that for optimal sunset enjoyment they had to trek up to the top of the hill in Arbs Park and wait there to behold the sun as it sank confidently, like a patient undergoing anesthesia for minor surgery.

Carmine didn't have too many sunsets left to him in those days, and between the time when he and Tweed started hanging out together and when he died, they partied at the projects ever less frequently.

Things pretty much went downhill at White City after that. Tenants like the Gunthers moved out and folks like Mr. Eddie moved in. There were years of racial hostility, primarily incited by the court-ordered integration of the public school system, as the racially segregated neighborhoods in the city played an experimental game of child-swapping. Then after that public debacle caused the largest population drop in the city's history, when residents pulled out and fled to the suburbs in droves, there were years of appeasement, during which a number of municipal real-estate holdings were virtually ceded to the community.

Tweed's reference to the impending destruction of the complex laid bare the underlying strategy in the city's decision. Lacking resources, community agencies ran sites such as White City-MLK and other local former municipal administration buildings (white elephants and decrepit dinosaurs all) into the ground. Then the city stepped in and asserted the right to bull-doze the properties in favor of redevelopment.

And so places like this one, and Mission Estates, and the Liberty Hill projects in Francestown, would soon be replaced by modern efficiency condominiums to be offered for sale at a price guaranteed to exceed the income of inner-city working class residents. Thus, despite the token percentage of units held aside for low-income residents, another round of population exodus and displacement would follow.

Tweed knew that it was not a coincidence that the chairman of the corporation spearheading the redevelopment effort was none other than fain Dapper Ferguson. And surely Dapper would funnel large chunks of the new project money to contractors that were fronted by Des Kelley. In fact, Tweed suspected with justifiable cynicism that whatever damage was done to the complex tonight was probably incited in one way or another by Des in order to push the process along.

It was partly on account of his father, Des Kelley, that Tweed felt so miserable and upset. LaGloria's attempt to destroy Des had failed, and the price he exacted for that failure was far greater than she had anticipated. Now Tweed was on a mission to destroy someone else, and he wished there was a way to know what cost he might incur if he should succeed, for he already knew what result would come of failure.

LaGloria had wanted him to snatch the sawed-off shotgun away from the reach of the police before they discovered it and used it as evidence linking him to the murders of her brothers. Tweed had agreed to go for it because he knew that the gun carried enough history to put him away for consecutive sentences. Though he was still convinced that he was free and clear of the crime, he was also aware that in the worst case scenario, it would be one thing to be named as a witness or as an accessory after the fact. It would be quite another to be linked directly to the crime, especially in the case of a capital offense.

Once he had the gun, however, he had convinced himself to go ahead with his idea. Especially after snipping through the fence to get out of the tow lot, and scrambling through the jagged coal on the ground, limping the quarter mile back to his car along the railroad tracks at night, stashing the gun in his car, and changing his clothes on the sidewalk; and all of the other pains and inconveniences he had endured.

It was one of those times when one conceives of an entirely new and different way to put a common item to use, as people do either out of necessity, or creativity, or because of circumstance. So a ladder may become a bridge, a hubcap may become a wall-hanging, and an engine block becomes a food-warmer. In this case Tweed was using a shotgun- a particularly illegal, ill-used and inelegant gun that had been re-manufactured for murder only.

Even as a murder weapon it was blunt and brutal, suitable as a short-range human meat grinder. Tweed, however, had no intention of firing the thing. Getting rid of it was still his priority, but he would kill two birds at once, as it were, putting it to use and in so doing, also placing it beyond use.

Risk was an issue; on the one hand it was the relative risk of action as opposed to inaction, and on the other, it was short-term risk as opposed to long-term risk. Before he "pulled the trigger" he thought he would stop and seek consultation from his respected friend, mentor and business partner, Donal Harding.

"OK, Mr. Chung, what do I owe you?"

Chung sighed. He had been staring at a trio of teenagers who seemed to be spending too much time in front of the soda coolers.

"Two fiffy, Mr. Tuey."

Chung had been maiming his name for years, but he wouldn't be doing the old man any favors by saying, "Call me Kelley". He handed over a five instead, and said, "I'll take the *Review and* the *Atlantic*- how's that?"

"OK, six bucks!"

"The Review's out of date, Mr. Chung!"

Chung waved him off like a bad odor. "**You're** out of date too, Mr. Tuey."

As he drove up Main St he told himself that he didn't have to put this thing off. He could do it right now and then tell Donal about it afterwards. Might sound better that way, too. Less opportunity for reproach, or criticism. Then again, maybe he needed some criticism. His father always said that he could never take any. Maybe he should hear what Donal has to say first. After all, he never listened to his father. There was plenty of time yet to do what must be done.

The parkway was the quickest route to Donal's. Four tree-lined miles of road with a roundabout every mile or so. The roundabouts were intended to slow the flow of cars but in his custom Saab Tweed sped through each one as if it were a banked racetrack, riding the apex of the arc and popping out the other side like a stone released from a sling. Further up the road he took a detour via the ambulance entrance to the massive Veteran's Administration hospital. Donal's house was at the far end of a street than ran perpendicular to the hospital campus, down where construction of the road had seemingly been abandoned. The sidewalk, for example, ran past his house, which was the last one on the street, and continued right into the woods that bordered the neighborhood.

Though he was situated within a stone throw of the hospital, Donal couldn't see the building directly from his house because the road rose and fell like a camel's hump, and he was in the gully on the far side.

Tweed dropped the car into second and made the run up the slope, thinking about how he'd once asked his friend why he hadn't taken a house on the top of the hill since he had his choice when the neighborhood was new and wide open.

"Man, wouldn't you rather have the view?" he'd asked.

"Huh!" scoffed Donal, "I see enough of the VA when I visit my buddies there. I don't need a constant reminder."

Donal had his young protege accompany him during subsequent visits to the hospital. They'd cruise the wards collecting his crippled companions, and then they'd wheel them out of the hospital and find a private spot under a stout oak tree out on the grounds. Like some Santa of substance abuse, Donal would bestow gifts of whiskey and schnapps and of course he'd pass around primo bowls of potent pot. The dope had to be good, because these guys had started smoking pot while serving in southeast Asia, and the commercial stuff that was available in the states paled by comparison. It was like the difference between the beer one might taste while visiting Germany, and the weak swill that passes for beer at home. Needless to say, though limbless or chair bound, shrapnel-ridden or diseased, the former GIs fairly flew back into their hospital wards.

Some of the men were in rough shape, but when they had visitors they laughed and carried on, trying to resurrect the spirit of old times. But they never told stories about the war. Donal would talk about it if pressed, but he considered the subject to be part of young Tweed's education.

On the other hand, he despised the barroom braggarts he'd met who adopted the wounded vet persona in order to excuse their drunkenness, as well as their lack of accomplishment and ambition. They were easy to spot, especially when they dropped the names of the units in which they had supposedly served and the mythical Vietnamese hamlets they'd raided.

Donal never denied that Nam was a life changing experience for him, but he claimed that he suffered no adverse effects, no nightmares, no guilt or regrets. For him the cause of the war, the way it was prosecuted and the controversy of its conclusion were separate issues from the value of service to one's country, the rigors and discipline of military life, or the demands obedience placed upon one's conscience.

Donal bore plenty of physical scars, but Tweed suspected that he also suffered lasting emotional scars, for he talked of killing in a detached, cold-blooded way, and he rationalized it as if he had no regard for the sanctity of life. For example, with a total lack of passion he described one of his experiences during the war when he had gone out on a search and rescue mission after some of his comrades went missing. His team did locate the men, or what was left of them, tied to a tree with their guts ripped out. It was hard to say if the Viet Cong terror tactic had any impact upon Donal, but it shocked the shit out of Tweed. Then, with equal cool, he talked about how he and his fellow soldiers would exact retribution, perhaps by sniping local village officials, or by rounding up captives and tossing them off a cliff. It was all in a day's work, he said, necessary for survival like any other job.

How could anyone describe these things as matter-of fact? He wasn't a military reporter or a member of the press corps, observing and taking notes, he was an active participant, a combatant. Yet Donal was sensitive to the fact that Tweed had lost his brother in Viet Nam, and it was with that fact in mind that he tried to get across the point that war was a reality, and that one must consider it head-on. Rather than ignoring, or merely wishing it were not so, one must know exactly what is involved, including the suffering it causes.

Military service was somewhat out of favor by the time Tweed turned 18. He was required by law to register with selective service, but at the time the military was an all-volunteer force, and peace-time recruitment was at an all-time high. In fact Tweed had recently received a notice in the mail informing him that as of his next birthday he would no longer be eligible for service. Only in the event of a declared war would men older than 26 be required to enlist. A small degree of regret about his lack of service had nagged him for a time, but it stopped as soon as his father had started bugging him about joining his quixotic effort to drive the British out of Northern Ireland. At least there was a certain logic and balance to his refusal. If he wouldn't fight for the USA, he certainly wouldn't fight for the IRA, either.

Donal said that he had been expecting Tweed to show up.

"Man, you must be as nervous a long-tailed cat. How are you and LaGloria holding up?"

"Nervous? No, ah, we're alright. Why do you say nervous?"

"Well shit, man, I'd be nervous if my girlfriend's brothers just got blown away."

"Hey, don't worry. You sound like my old man. It's not like someone's coming after us next."

"I'm not worried, Tweed. After all, unlike you, I didn't know what they were up to. Not, that is, until afterwards." He sat back in the tremendous arm-chair he kept on his back porch. Tweed sat on the edge of the railing facing him.

"What do you mean? Are you saying that you know what happened?"

Donal was surprisingly aware of current events for a guy who lived like a recluse without a phone or television and seemingly very little contact with the outside world, but he would have to be clairvoyant to know what really happened to Frankie and Nilvan.

"Let me tell you a little story. Your friend Nilvan was an asbestos removal tech, right? Well, a while back he was working at a job site where there was a good deal of construction going on. So much in fact that the contractors always left their tools at the site. No sense lugging everything in every day. Of course they locked all of their stuff up every night in one of those big yellow steel crates.

"For the week or so that Nil worked there he schemed about how to clean out those tools in a way that would not only succeed, but that wouldn't implicate him in any way. So I'll tell you what he did..."

Donal got up abruptly and went into the kitchen. "*Kettle...*" he explained as he walked away, and he returned carrying two cups of hot tea. "Anyway, so Nil comes up with this plan, see, to break into the job site late at night, on the weekend after he finished his part of the work. He gets in no problem. Actually, it took him longer to open the goddamned steel crate to get at the shit he was after than it did to break into the site in the first place. And boy, did he hit the jackpot. Took him a long time to clear everything out of there…there was so many great tools that he had to make a few trips to get them all. So once he got the stash safe and secured, he went back one last time to put on the finishing touches. Spilled glue all over the blueprints, totally tossed the place, tore out all the files and paperwork, dumped trash on the desks, ripped out the phones lines, made it look like totally random punk vandalism. He had fun with this part and in the process he set the project back a good couple of months."

By now Tweed was staring open mouthed, knowing that the story must be true, but truly amazed both at Nilvan's part in it, and at Donal's telling of it. He seemed to really enjoy telling the story.

"Before you ask, no, I didn't make this up. Let me finish and then I'll tell you how I got all this info."

Tweed said nothing, hardly daring to interrupt, but he lit a joint and passed it.

"The best tools were the surveyor's rig, including the level and transit and the theodolite." He coughed and spat, then went on, enumerating on his fingers. "Then there were Ramguns, brad guns, nail guns, power tools of all sorts, I'm talking jig saws, mitre and circular saws and get this…a complete Sawzall kit. He even took the shovels, rakes and brooms.

"So once he got all of the loot stored away he had to find a way to make some money for his hard work. He basically had no choice but to get rid of the shit, because it was too risky to keep even if he wanted to open his own contracting business, which he didn't.

"Next thing you know he would have blabbed around to everybody he knew that he was looking to unload some hot tools, so it was lucky for him that a mutual friend overheard him talking about it at the Shamrock. When I got wind of his situation I hooked him up with a buyer- someone I knew who could be trusted to come through and to be discrete."

It bothered Tweed to think that Donal had gotten involved purely because of Nil's relation to Tweed.

"As it happens it worked out pretty well. I knew a guy who had been a surveyor for years, and he always said that if he had the tools he could open his own outfit. So now Nil could get rid of that whole batch in one chunk, leaving him with the power tools. Only thing was that by the time they were ready to deal, this friend the surveyor had come up with a scheme of his own. He wanted to know if Nilvan would be interested in guns- real fine pieces, too- in exchange for the equipment. I think he had a Remington shotgun, another hunting rifle, a .357 magnum and a show piece, you know, a replica. The guy kept it all in a big fancy display case in his house but he never used any of it. Now, this was all top quality, a Remington, a Mossberg, the Colt Python…with the mahogany cabinet it added up to thousands of dollars, really not a bad deal for Nil if he liked guns."

He had been gesturing with both hands for emphasis and in doing so he inadvertently knocked the lit end off the joint. It sailed in a blazing arc into the dark yard. Calming himself, he relit the reefer with a one-strike and picked up his story.

"Actually, I was surprised that he went for it, although I had told him myself that he was lucky to get good value for his score. I mean, after all, he'd have to shop that equipment around for a long time before he found another buyer. I figured he was looking to make some money, fast cash. I think what happened was he got the cash he needed selling the power tools to another friend of his, and then the rest seemed like icing on the cake. In any event they did the swap.

"Only later did I find out, when I really should have known all along, that the guy with the guns filed a theft claim with his insurance company. Messed up his own house to make it look like a break-in. And wouldn't you know it? He did get a check out of them, though I don't know for how much."

"I don't remember seeing any mahogany case at Nil's..." mused Tweed, shaking his head.

"Well, take a hit and pass it back."

Friggin' Donal- always hassling him to smoke faster. His theory was: the hotter the reefer the higher the hippie. On more than a few occasions Tweed had argued that he enjoyed the smoke more if he took it slowly, claiming that his pace was regulated by the temperature of the snipe in his hand. He handed off the joint, glad to let Donal suck it down. It was cold out here on the back porch, and Tweed had had enough of the cold for one night. Donal's back yard was basically an extension of the adjacent tangle of woods. In the dark the brush seemed to encroach upon the house, breathing a chill vaporous exhalation down his neck.

"I was wondering about that shotgun..." he said, rising and tossing the remains of his tea out into the darkness.

"I should think you would be," said Donal as if an answer had been expected.

"It's just that when the cops came by they said he had a 20-gauge, and the one I thought he had was a 12-gauge, so I was wondering," he paused, unsure if he should bring up the subject he had come to discuss, or wait and let this one play out first.

"Oh? I thought you'd be concerned because you were probably in on whatever went down that night. Don't look so shocked. Nil didn't tell me anything."

"Alright, Donal, man, I see you have your theories, but that's not the reason I came down here tonight."

"So you're saying that you had nothing to do with what happened?"

He hesitated before responding. It was kind of irritating, to be backed into a corner like this. Not that he didn't trust Don, or that he didn't want to confide in him. It was just that he had something else on his mind that he wanted to resolve, and he didn't want to drag his old friend into any situation that might lead to trouble. Maybe it was the proximity of death, but this whole business spooked him, and he was superstitious about speaking about it.

"What do you think? You have an idea, right? Let's hear it. But then let me run something by you."

"Sure, whatever you say. I just thought you'd want to talk. See, first there was the thing with the guns, and then I hear that they found the shotgun beside Nil's body. I knew he had to be up to something, to take a brand-new 20-gauge to the park. I mean, he wasn't quail hunting. Then I was talking to the Griff, and he tells me that your girls LaGloria and Sharlae were out looking for you at about the time that uh, you know. That kinda sounded funny."

"Look, the main thing is that if you're in trouble in any way, or if you think you might be soon, then, by all means, let us know. We want to help."

He was referring to himself and Wayne Kenney.

In a flash Tweed suddenly saw how everybody was linked in a series of events, contacts, chance sightings. How many people now knew that he had his car back from Gary's? Or that Rick Rose was out snooping around on his behalf? He was going to have to be more careful and think all of his actions through from now on.

"You know, I was thinking about how stories can come back to haunt you. Like the story you just told me for instance, the one behind the shotgun. I think of all the people in that story who could do what you did, connect the dots. Next thing you know somebody's getting brought in by the cops to be held for questioning, or they're arrested on suspicion."

"You're right, Tweed, but sometimes you gotta trust people. Here, come on inside."

Donal generally did not like to discuss matters of substance when he was in the house, which was why they were out on the porch. So Tweed was a bit puzzled, but he followed, happy to get out of the raw weather.

The kitchen was not especially bright, illuminated by a sole reading lamp shining on the sideboard where Donal took his meals. Perhaps that explained the ghost that Tweed momentarily saw seated there. At second glance it was gone. He instinctively blessed himself, and blessed the house, and thought again of Carmine.

A clock ticked loudly from a dusty hiding place atop the refrigerator, and the smell of burnt coffee and overused kitty litter tainted the air. Donal hated cleaning the litter box, and when it got this bad his Siamese, a sleek seal-point called Furbush, refused to use it. The cat had been growing increasingly feral from being forced outside to do his business.

The only rooms Donal used on the first floor were the kitchen, the so-called dining room, and the back room, or den. But it was to the parlor in the front that Donal now proceeded, nudging open the seldom-used door with a hip-check.

"Like I said," said Donal, pointing toward the far corner, "you gotta trust people." There stood a tall conservative-looking mahogany gun cabinet, trimmed with ornate carved moldings and brass hinges and handles. It looked empty.

OK. So the story was true. Not that Tweed didn't believe his good friend. And as far as he was concerned, trust formed the basis of their relationship. Donal had trusted Tweed with his wisdom, his experience, and the benefit of his business acumen. He trusted him to move hundreds of pounds of marijuana each year. To hold thousands of dollars, to run his business in a way that did not threaten the overall health of the enterprise or the welfare of any of its principals.

"You should hear the story of how Frankie got his gun," said Tweed at last, deciding that he couldn't go wrong if he relied upon the right back-up. Thus far his only support had come from LaGloria, and he had reasons to suspect her strength and resolve. He hadn't known her as long as he had known Wayne, but he understood that different relationships always had different dynamics.

"No kidding?" said Donal, placing an unnecessary finger to his lips. He had made his point, and now he returned to the porch.

Now fortified against the night with the snack of hot tea and savory reefer, Tweed described how Frank learned about Bricky's M16s from Tom Toole. Then he explained Bricky's situation, and how he had ripped off Des Kelly on a hijacking run.

Donal tried to make sense of what he had learned. "OK, Nil had a shotgun and his brother had an M16. What happened next? C'mon man, you must know how they ended up dead when they had all this firepower..."

"Why should I know? You know me, I sell dope, I don't friggin' shoot people."

"I'm not saying you do. But I'll tell you, one of the reasons Nil went after that construction site was because it was the advance location for the White City Corridor project. You know, Dapper Ferguson's scam. Did that have anything to do with it?"

"You're asking me? You assume that I know all this shit."

"Your old man handles most of the contracts for them. I think Nil had a hard-on for your old man. Not literally, of course, I mean, I heard all that bullshit about the, (double digital ditto) "psych center.""

"OK, so Nil deliberately destroyed the place now? I thought you said he did it for the money? What, then him and his brother get a couple of guns and say let's go out and kill...who? Dapper Ferguson? What are they, hit men, now? I don't get it. Did you know that Frankie's girlfriend is gunnahava baby? I mean, does that sound like a guy who'd go out and shoot someone?"

Donal pivoted about in his chair as he handled Tweed's questions.

"No, I didn't. Good for her. Good for Frank. Shit, I wouldn't think he'd do anything like that. Gary sure didn't think so, and he's known Frankie for years."

"So have I, so have I…" Tweed was quiet for a moment. He wasn't used to talking so heatedly with Donal, whom he deeply respected.

"Dapper Ferguson had nothing to do with it. At least not that I knew. They were after my old man, Mr. Des Kelley."

"Shit!" was all Donal could say.

"Don't ask me why; all I know is LaGloria asked them to do it, and they did, only he got wind of it somehow and had his guys waiting there. It was no contest. You're right," he looked out into the darkness, "I was there."

"Your father? No kidding! For Pete's sake!"

"Yeah, well, like I said, for LaGloria's, anyway."

"Well, what happened? Tell me all about it."

And Tweed did, including everything from when they parked on Bussey St, to the burning of the car, to his escape on the tracks.

"What I don't understand is why you were so god-damned confident that I knew about all this?" he asked, finally.

"Well, I didn't mention this before, but I got this buddy, see, another disabled vet. He drives a cab down the square. Said he picked you up not a half hour after he first heard the fire engines heading over to the Arbs. I hate to tell you this, man, but when he smokes dope he gets all paranoid, you know?"

"Yeah, so?"

"Well, the thing is, this dude went and told the cops about you too."

"What?"

"Hey, at first he didn't know it was you, man, until I told him, and, like I said, he gets paranoid."

Shit- and LaGloria had got all pissed off that he didn't sell the guy on becoming a customer.

They talked for some time about the crime, the circumstances, and about Tweed's chances for emerging from the conflict free and unscathed.

Donal was harping on the political angle, saying that the reason he had helped Nil in the first place was because he knew about the Dapper Ferguson connection. Wayne and Donal had dealings with Dapper themselves, because they owned a bar located in his district. He had a shakedown routine that was almost comical in its quaintness, but none the less effective. For Donal and his partner, and for many other business owners around the square, the fact that Dapper saw himself as some kind of old-time influential politico, a ward boss who could bestow favors, was no reason to patronize him. It wasn't like he had muscle, although he implied that he did. In fact, an unofficial chamber of commerce had been formed to settle the 'Dapper problem' once and for all.

"What are they going to do?" asked Tweed, suspiciously.

"They ain't gonna shoot him, that's for damned sure. Sorry. No; they turned their complaint and any evidence they had over to the state police. I hear there's something coming down, a sting or something. But they're gonna bust him, you can bet on that."

You learn something new every day, thought Tweed. But should he now go ahead and teach the teacher? Might be a little too much for one night.

"So, what was it you wanted to talk about? Or were you really serious?"

Somehow he didn't think it appropriate in light of all that had been said, to tell Donal about his problem with Og, and his proposed solution. This was not the time to say that he was about to plant evidence, in the form of a sawed-off shotgun, on Og Z's property and set him up for a fall.

First he intended to bail Og out of jail personally and give him one last chance to come clean about his thefts and 'one-overs'. It was unlikely that Og had experienced a jail house conversion, and seen the error of his ways. But if he got no satisfaction from his old neighborhood friend, no confession, no apology, then he'd notify contacts in the department and have them come and put Og away for real.

And then once he was inside he'd have him shanked for good measure.

CHAPTER 36

"What's this now?" muttered the Griff, as a big-ass truck pulled up on the sidewalk right in front of the park bench where he was seated. A wash of hot diesel fumes rolled over him, removing the fresh spring air like a Guatemalan death squad eliminating innocent peasants.

"Some retard thinks he's gonna park on the field?"

He had selected this secluded spot because he needed privacy for a moment. An envelope of coke had been burning a hole in his wallet all evening. Now finally it lay open in his palm, and he was delicately poking around in the meager pile of dust within, as if he were looking for lima beans in a bowl of vegetable soup. He didn't want an audience, so he was further irritated when the driver turned his motor off as if he was planning to leave the truck there. Griff knew better.

"Now the cops'll show up any second…" He would have to move on and find some other place to do his business. Heck, maybe he should just go home. It was late anyway, and now that the excitement at White City had died down the streets were quiet.

"Holy shit!" Now another truck was parking on the curb, right behind the first one! What was this, a convention? Griff reluctantly folded his stash and returned it to his wallet, then he tugged on the bill of his cap, shoved his hands into his pockets and started to walk away.

The driver of the lead truck was climbing down from his cab. He tried to get Griff's attention. "Hey, buddy! You got any packies in this town?"

"'S Rossie, ain't it?" replied the Griff, "Packy on every corner…"

"Any open, like, now?" prodded the trucker.

"Sheesh;" shrugged Griff, "Ah, yeah, the Hilltop- just over the tracks behind you there." He pointed down the foul line across the ballpark toward a row of trees about a hundred yards distant. "Uh, you better watch out," he added, indicating the sloppy parking job, "-the cops around here are pricks." He stared as a curl of vapor rose from the grill on the front of the truck's hood, obscuring the word 'International'.

The second driver had also disembarked from his rig and he was strolling toward Griff on the sidewalk. "Dat's right, boss. All cops preeks! Fuggaht malakas!"

"Alright, Peter, cool it…" said the first trucker, who now stood on the sidewalk before Griff, unbuckling his belt so as to adjust the ride of his pants. "Thanks, but we ain't worried about the cops. This outfit comes through here every year, you know, Simonowicz and Kowalski Carnival? We got this here field all next week."

"Oh?" said Griff, "School must be out for vacay. Well then, good luck, guys." He smiled and walked away, thinking about the vast numbers of hoodsies that would flock to the carnival. A veritable some-more-gasborg! A hornycopia!

As the driver watched Griffin leave, he noticed the deep parallel furrows marring the infield, and mistook Len Abbisso's tire tracks for those of his colleagues. "Yo, Peter! We ain't the first after all! Look at the tracks there! Stewie must have got here before us."

"Shit!" agreed his associate, reviewing the evidence. "And he left already?"

"Yeah, well, he beat us here, I guess, and now he's beating us to the booze."

***

The decent folks who were unfortunate enough to live near Spaz Travers knew him only as the pain-in-the-ass kid who periodically hosted huge bashes in his house. Although he had few friends in his own neighborhood, he must have had friends somewhere because his parties were always loud, well-attended and poorly-managed affairs.

This nonsense had been going on ever since his parents passed away back in '84. He inherited their home, thus gaining by default the sum total of all their years of honest labor, scrimping and sacrifice.

Furthermore he lived off of the proceeds from a legal settlement from a worker's comp claim he had filed against a former employer after he had allegedly hurt his back while on the job. A chronic small-time offender and recidivist, he had gotten the job on a work-release arrangement with the state, and had only been employed there for six months prior to his injury. Just long enough to collect.

Municipal Police Officer Bernie Diprizio was aware of all of this, and more, as she responded to the umpteenth noise complaint arising from the latest shindig on Tindale St, at the home of Spaz Travers. She had busted him on a number of occasions over the past couple of years, most recently on charges of driving without a license or registration, possession of narcotics, the relevant probation violations, and resisting arrest. Tonight she had no desire to deal with any of his adolescent bullshit. He seemed to enjoy provoking the police and disturbing the peace, but she was in no mood to play the role of the austere authority figure in one of his staged performances.

She was still fuming over the treatment she had received from her fellow officers at the scene of an incident to which she had responded earlier in the evening.

There had been a number of reports of trouble at the White City housing projects, and she and her partner had been among the first units to respond. They had arrived promptly, and after quickly assessing the situation, Bernie had met with the manager of the projects and with the security detail from the housing authority, while her partner Kinch collected statements from some of the residents of the complex, apparently all of whom who were loitering about in the front courtyard.

The scene was somewhat surreal, for most of the participants and witnesses were highly agitated and seemingly thrilled by the excitement of the event. The area in the cul-de-sac terminating in front of the projects was partially illuminated by halogen spotlights mounted high on the corners of the buildings. However those lights were vandalized, missing, or flickering, and they clashed with the flashing strobes on various emergency vehicles; plus the general noise level bordered on deafening.

It was several minutes before Officer Diprizio had a clear understanding of the nature of the crisis.

One of the residents of the complex had been involved in a car chase that terminated when he crashed his car on Washington Drive. Despite the initial efforts of local residents and then the professional attempts of the fire department to extinguish the resulting fire, the Volkswagen was still ablaze when officer Diprizio had arrived at the scene.

Following the accident, a melee had ensued when the occupants of the second car tried to follow the injured driver of the VW into the complex. Of course, by then, having heard the initial impact of the crash, people had emerged from their apartments. They quickly saw what was happening to one of their own, and they tried to intervene and prevent the pursuers from gaining access to the projects.

At this point it was still unknown what insult or injury had precipitated the incident, or why a car-load of outsiders would even consider forcing their way into the projects. After all, it was like poking a beehive with a stick. But they had persisted, even risking personal injury to do so.

The thing that bothered Officer Diprizio was the way in which other officers who arrived at the scene- fat, older male officers, had stepped in and imposed themselves into the situation. In particular, that bastard White, surely a crooked cop if there ever was one, having the gall to push her aside and say, "We'll take it from here, Miss," with a condescending smile, as if she were a timid librarian.

Damn it, she had been on top of everything; she was organizing the response, she was initiating the investigation, determining the facts, taking the statements, interviewing the witnesses; she was the one working with local officials and community members. And furthermore she had been close to learning who owned the Volkswagen.

It was obvious what was going on- White had a piece of the action in that part of town. He wanted a say in who got busted and why. Plus he wanted to be the one sitting on his fat ass up at 13, filling out paperwork for the rest of his shift- a chore most cops loathed. And although she hated to admit it, there was another factor at work here, the fact that White feared being upstaged by a woman. Even when it was apparent that she was doing a good job. That was it all right- he was afraid that she would make him look bad, so he simply pushed her out of the way. Well next time she wasn't going to budge. If White or any of the other complacent crooked bastards tried to muscle her out of doing her job she would stand pat and tell them, "I'll take it from here, Mack."

Who was it that had sought refuge in the projects? What happened to the guys who were in the wrong place at the wrong time? She didn't know, because she had left to respond to a fucking noise complaint. A complaint about Spaz Travers, of all people. Another shithead who thought he was God's gift to women.

She couldn't quite remember from his record, but he had to be at least 30 years old. Real name Thomas. Only child. Total fuck up. Ah well, she thought, Rossie's full of 'em. Kids who never grow up, locals who never leave town. All of these Peter Pan types made it difficult for a young single woman such as herself to find a suitable, eligible male. Lord knows she wouldn't go out with a cop, especially none of the ones she worked with. Last decent guy she met also turned out to be on the list of do-not-dates: he was a merchant marine. Talk about your long-distance romance- on his shift rotation he was gone for half the year! No thanks.

Bernie parked her patrol car in the middle of Tindale street, made a radio check and gathered her gear. The car would remain unattended, with the windows open and the strobe on. In this way it would send a message of hope to the neighbors who cowered behind their venetian blinds. It also served as a warning to ward off latecomers and to send certain party-goers into a panic, as they scurried to abandon the festivities. They read the blue light code as saying that discretion was the better part of valor.

Neither Bernie nor her partner would waste any time pursuing the ones who ran, not only because it was too much work, but also because it was a distraction from the primary task of shutting down the overall public nuisance. Yet they were aware that it was likely that drug dealers and felons had slipped through their fingers.

The noise from the house seemed to increase as the officers approached on foot, and a steady ostinato bass line from Zeppelin's *Livin' Lovin' Maid* seemed to shake the very paving stones. Until this moment her associate had been acting bored and moody. Personally she didn't think he was very bright, but she knew that it probably bothered him to be bumped off the White City case, too, although for different reasons.

There was no doorbell and knocking would have been useless, so Bernie led her partner to the rear where they entered the house uninvited. Suddenly a chain-reaction ensued as beers vanished, bodies bolted, doors slammed, and the music stopped. There was a profusion of wasted people in the house, all younger than Bernie herself, and she was the youngest cop in the precinct. Some of these kids were so far removed from reality that the appearance of two uniformed police officers in their midst didn't seem to bother them. Probably took it as a hallucination. What would it take to shake them? Drawn guns? Bullhorns? Blue Meanies?

Officer Diprizio summoned her best impression of Sister Mary Elephant and shouted, "Spaz Travers!"

It was a wonder bottles didn't shatter.

In a stoner's moment he appeared, his drugged eyes sunken behind tight high cheek muscles that were frozen in a rictus grin.

"Officer Bernie!" he said genially, "What can I get for you? A beer? What about your friend there?"

"Alright, Travers, cut the shit. We got complaints from here to JC about this party. Tell your friends that it's time to pack it in."

"Aw, fuck! We'll turn it down, don't worry…"

"You know the routine, Spaz, I want everybody out of here in ten minutes."

It didn't end there. Spaz was in the mood for fun, and he persisted, baiting the patient officers with a stream of good-natured, obscenity-laced wheedling.

He shouldn't have challenged her. Not tonight. If he hadn't pissed her off, then she wouldn't have thought it necessary to detain all of his guests for processing on the front lawn. Actually, Bernie had initially intended only to intimidate him, to let her threats sink in for a time and then to back off.

That was before she discovered Hildy hiding in the dining room. Hildy, a ward of the town's "Home for Wanderers" was 17 years of age but significantly less mature than her peers due to mental disability. When Bernie found her in Spaz's house Hildy had just completed a strip tease dance atop the dining room table. An unsuspecting drunk, passed out in the corner, sported her panties stretched across his lumpy shaved head; and a couple of goons goaded her on with chants of, "Go Dildy, go!"

Grinning as always like a pleasant jack-o-lantern, Hildy complied with Bernie's request to quit dancing, and then she quietly gathered her far-flung garments and dressed.

In the meantime, Bernie's partner Kinch had assembled the thirty odd drunks who were too stoned to avoid him in the patio area of Spaz's back yard. The process of forming up an orderly queue and taking their names could have gone a lot more smoothly if the officer hadn't betrayed his anxiety and lost his cool in front of everyone. But one of the neighborhood cats had chosen an inopportune moment to climb down from his perch in a nearby tree, and Kinch, seeing the unexpected activity out of the corner of his eye, had responded by whipping out his sidearm like a gunslinger in a spaghetti western. When he drew the cat down, all of his credibility was lost. Even without the added amusement brought on by the abundant alcohol, marijuana and other mood-altering substances stoking his audience, the performance was hilariously inept. Now Kinch would forever be remembered as the cop who pulled his gun on a house cat.

Officer Diprizio encountered the 'tail end' of this scene as she emerged from the house with Hildy in tow, and whatever remained of her professional detachment also became unhinged as a purple rage suffused her features. It didn't help that the mostly male crowd erupted at the sight of Hildy, as if she had come back for an encore.

Kinch may have pulled his gun in foolish error, but Bernie was vexed enough to follow suit just for the sheer satisfaction of it. If there was ever a time when she would have loved to scare the piss out of a crowd by firing a few rounds over their heads…But she cooled a bit as she envisioned the bureaucratic purgatory into which she would be placed for such an action.

By the time Bernie had returned from securing Hildy in the back seat of the patrol car, calling in support, and composing herself with a brief preen in the rear-view mirror, Spaz and his retinue had set up a viewing gallery on the porch. From there they harangued the cops and the crowd with snide sarcasm, random commentary and laughter. Bernie reminded herself to go upstairs in the house and spray all of Spaz' towels and pillows with mace before she left.

It looked like it was going to be a tough night, with loads of work and little reward. But suddenly something happened that gave her enough incentive to carry on with a slightly more positive attitude.

Without music, drugs, booze, or any other entertainment save Spaz's lame ranting, the captive guests were becoming restless. One in particular started pushing ahead in line, demanding to be heard, trying to get Bernie's attention. Sure enough when she saw and recognized him Bernie immediately pulled the character out of line in order to interview him separately.

"Weren't you down at White City earlier this evening?" she asked.

"That's just what I wanted to talk to you about. I tell you, I gotta get out of here. This is a drag."

"You get around, don't you? What are you doing at Spaz's party, Mr…" she examined the license he had fished out of his wallet.

"Abbisso," they chimed simultaneously.

"I heard about the party a few days ago, and I told Spaz I'd come, but then I got sidetracked with that thing down, you know…"

"That's what I wanted to ask you," she said, "What thing? What were you guys doing down there at the projects, anyway?"

"Look, are you gonna help me out here, or what? I donwanna stand here all night. I mean, if you're gonna pack everybody into the meat wagons, I donwanna have anything to do with it."

"Oh, you don't like our hospitality down at the station? Then tell you what; you tell me what you and your buddies were doing, and I'll see what I can do."

"You're busting my balls! Look, we were just looking after that guy in the bug. Denis said that he had to keep an eye on him, it was like a job he had, helping out that Irish guy Kelley."

"So Kelley asked Denis to keep an eye on the guy in the Volkswagen? And you were just along for the ride?"

"I *was* the ride. Denis don't have no car, and Joey's car got stripped down at the Fore's earlier this after. So they asked me to drive. I guess they thought that the guy in the bug seen whoever it was that stripped Joey's car, so they wanted to ask him about it."

"OK, so they weren't just keeping an eye on him. They wanted to talk to this guy, whoever it was?"

"Yeah, I guess so. See, I don't get involved in this shit. It's them that works for Kelley. They just asked me cause I have a car."

"I understand. So Joey, uh, Joey who?"

"Joey Atkinson; jeesh." Len seemed to regret his decision to talk.

"Right, so Joey is out looking for this guy who may have witnessed his car getting stripped, and he asks you for the ride?"

"Like I said. Only this guy in the Volkswagen, he starts pouring oil out the window and everything, being a real asshole and shit. I'll tell you- it wasn't my fault that the guy crashed. I think he just couldn't steer and pour oil at the same time." Len smiled despite himself.

Bernie failed to recognize the humor.

"So that was it?"

"Yeah, well, I wasn't going to mix it up like them guys. I mean, Joey and Mo and them, they just up and ran right out and started cracking heads. 'Course, they got the worst of it. Tell you, it was a good thing for them that I was willing to stick around and bail them out."

"But you made it out of there alright. Lucky you weren't arrested with everybody else they grabbed down there."

"Yeah, well, they weren't arresting the *white kids…*"

"Alright, so you don't know who the guy was, the guy you were chasing?"

"He was white," said Abbisso, then seeing the expression in the officer's eyes, he hastily continued, "All's I know is they said he was at the Fores when Joey's car got stripped. So Joey thought he might know who done it, you know?"

"OK, he was at the Fores. And Joey got everybody to go out and look for him?"

"Well, like I said, they was doing it for Denis. And he was doing it for Kelley."

"Well, let me tell you something…" Here Officer Diprizio may have overstepped the line of good judgment, when she revealed that, "Mr. Kelley is a suspect in a murder investigation. Bulletin just came over the radio. So take my advice and stay away from anyone that says they're working for Kelley."

Abbisso's eyes were wide as he nodded in agreement. He took his leave as if he were a soldier who had been granted a reprieve from firing squad duty only to be assigned to mine clearing, and he skulked away. He was still confused by the cop's remark, when she said: "Tell your friend to turn himself in if he knows what's good for him." *What did she mean his friend? That old fuck?*

Well, Joey had told him that whatever he did he'd better stop in at the old fart's club before the night was through. At the time, when he had nothing to say, that request had bothered him. Unlike Denis and Joey, he was at nobody's beck and call. But now he did know something. He had spoken to a cop personally and he had been told that Kelley was a suspect in what had to be the McManus brother's murder. Man, this was gonna be golden!

For her part, Bernie Diprizio was also excited. Her mind racing to fit everything together. What did Kelley have to do with Joey Atkinson, and why had he been named a suspect in the murders of LaGloria's brothers? Who was Tweed Kelley, anyway?

After speaking with LaGloria the other night, Bernie had spent some time trying to remember Frankie and Nilvan McManus. In the end she had only been able to pull up fleeting images and fragments of memories. She really hadn't seen any of the McManus family since high school. Even in those days when she knew LaGloria, they never interacted with her brothers, or their friends. Same thing with Tweed. He was a good-looking guy, and she remembered him as one of those kids who always had a girlfriend back in school. But she had no idea how he ended up with LaGloria, who had always been a pretty hot chick herself. But for him to go and shoot her brothers! How could he? Unless…could LaGloria herself have been involved?

She suddenly felt obligated to call her old friend and tell her what she knew, and what to expect. Couldn't hurt, might help. Just don't say that you heard it from me. Then her boyfriend could hire himself a good lawyer and turn himself in on his own terms instead of getting picked up and questioned at a disadvantage. Just trying to give the guy a break.

The deal with Abbisso had been well worth it. But she was still grappling with the bigger picture. What kind of shit was going down? Murder, car chases and riots in sleepy Rossdale? She'd seen that fliers advertising the carnival were popping up all over town, and it seemed fitting to her that it should arrive now. Rossie already had its share of excitement, scams, thrills and entertainment, yet she sensed a freaky parallel, considering the carnival as a metaphor for the town.

***

It was doubtful that many would credit Bernadette's literary acumen. Rossdale residents were for the most part hard-working, working-class folks who had gotten what they settled for. The schools were adequate, the town library had above-average circulation for the district. Thanks to progressive zoning policies and strictly enforced by-laws the community featured clearly-defined residential and commercial areas; and despite the relatively high population density, each house had at least a quarter-acre of land. There were no golf-courses, no luxury apartment units, no department stores or high-line auto dealerships. No art galleries, no reading rooms, cafes or performance centers. Instead, Rossdale offered bars, news-stands and package stores; small family restaurants and convenience stores; bakeries and smoke-shops; a town taxi firm run out of a military-surplus quonset hut; some veterans clubs and fraternal charitable organizations such as the Elks, Lions, and Knights of Columbus.

No indeed, until recently Rossdale lacked the interest and excitement to be likened to a carnival. Its people were too down-to-earth, and for all of their ethnic diversity, they were too colorless. And in order to judge the applicability of the metaphor one must first agree on a definition for 'carnival'. To some, carnival is a time of celebration in the context of rigid holy days and religious observations. Accordingly, some see the carnival strictly as a pre-Lenten event. Yet Easter had come early this year, and traveling outfits such as S&K Family Entertainments set up for as many weeks of the year as the weather allowed.

Regardless of considerable variations in the definition of the word, Rossdale did share at least one trait with the carnival that was setting up in the ballpark. They were both penny-ante, low-class operations most suitable for the common denominator.

***

As Des Kelley considered the news he'd heard from Makepeace, that Dapper Ferguson was under investigation, he knew that no inquiry of wrongdoing in Rossdale could ever amount to much. And that was because there wasn't much at stake. Take the White City Corridor deal that Dapper was trying to push through. Admittedly, Dapper was lining up a real-estate enterprise that would help him personally as soon as it was complete. It was no secret that while he was a councilman serving on the redevelopment board Dapper was working to get the project approved at the city level, so that he could then retire and immediately assume a trustee position on the project board. He was basically ensuring his own retirement, but the money at issue was not 'big bucks', it wasn't millions of dollars. At best he could hope to enjoy free housing and a modest annual salary that would carry him comfortably into old age, as long as he managed his investments properly.

Lord knows how Des' name got dragged in. He was but one of the many loyal constituents who supported Dapper, but that hardly amounted to criminal association by any stretch of the imagination. Perhaps Des had greater visibility than most because Dapper had asked him for a couple of favors here and there, such as helping to persuade some of the more stubborn residents to move out of their old triple-deckers down along the tracks.

Unless…and it couldn't be, but what if? What if they were planning to blame him for the destruction of the project development field office? Naturally he had forgotten about that because he had nothing to do with it. But it was a major setback, and a criminal act at that. Whoever did the job had halted construction and had set Dapper and his partners back months if not more. Furthermore the cost of the damage was almost incalculable- not so much in terms of money as in terms of time and manpower, a tremendous amount of work that would have to be recreated. The corporation had lost all of their payroll records, the site plans, environmental impact studies, utility layout grids, all the work of the engineers and surveyors, as well as the aerial photographs and state and county parcel maps. Plus, the tools the contractors stored on site had of course disappeared, but Des suspected that was merely an opportunistic insurance scam.

In any case Des had nothing to do with it, and whoever was investigating Dapper had better think twice before jumping to any conclusions and blaming him. Dapper was an old friend and Des was no back-stabber.

Makepeace was blowing smoke. No political inquiry was as potentially threatening or damaging as the problems he faced in relation to the killings of the McManus boys.

There he goes again; it was a mistake to think like Storer and Makepeace. His problem wasn't the killings- that was only a problem for the McManus family. His problem was that someone had tried to kill him. And now he learned from that babbling Bisco kid that the police had named him a suspect.

What the fuck had Billy pulled out of his hat? What facts could he have put together that would lead him to suspect Des, of all people? Does Des go around shooting people? Does he have a reputation for trolling the park after dark? No fucking way! What then? Was it something he said? Something he did? In the 24 hours since the shootings occurred Des had done nothing out of the ordinary for an average Friday. Except for the visit from Tweed, that is. Could that be it? Something Billy extrapolated from seeing them together? Well, fuck him. A man has a right and an obligation to speak with his son.

But there was nothing, no evidence that tied Des to the crime. Makepeace had been worried about the guns? Well, his guns were well hidden, and the cartridges were common, and readily available at any number of local retailers. Storer had to be bluffing, trying to get a reaction from some of the other players in the game. Des would call his bluff, and then raise the stakes with Harris Toole's gun. The M60 was no dime-a-dozen piece like Des' pistol, and if the gun wasn't persuasive on its own merits, then surely a forensic match would be.

The sidewalk in front of the RBC was a bloody lonely and miserable place at this time of night. Not one to "close the place," Des was usually home in bed by the time Joe or Harris locked up. Tonight, this morning, or whatever it was, Des waited for Harris to emerge with his coat and keys so he could bid him good night and possibly bum a ride home. This too was out of the ordinary, as all of Des' friends knew that he preferred to walk. But there was a strange mood in the quiet streets of Rossdale tonight, or perhaps Des was projecting his sense of unease.

Then, if anything could amplify that sensation that was so contrary to his nature, it was the sight of Detective Storer rounding the 'square' in his unmarked police car and swinging it over to the curb where Des was standing. He leaned over and rolled the passenger window down as if he were spinning the crank on an old wireless radio unit.

"Give you a lift, old man?"

"Where?" asked Des, suspiciously, "Home?"

Puzzlement showed in Storer's face. "You have someplace else to go?"

"I thought maybe *you* had someplace in mind."

The detective shrugged. "Hop in, I'll give you a lift."

"Thanks, no, Billy, Harris here is dropping me off."

"Suit yourself, but isn't it out of the way for him? C'mon, I have something to discuss with you anyway."

"I knew you would," Des muttered.

"Eh? Get in, Des, get in."

Now, later, what difference did it make? Although he had hoped to go home and get a good night's sleep and discuss things with his wife before turning himself in to police custody. He raised a finger to signify a moment, turned away and pulled the door of the club open, and yelled into the dark, "I'm on my way Harris- see you in the AM!" He waited for the "Right-O!" response before returning to join Billy in his battered Chevy Nova.

The older Irishman plopped his fat arse down into the bucket seat.

"What's this? I thought you guys were driving them nice Caprice Classics?"

"This old baby? It's a leftover from the '70s. Man I used to be able to pack six punks in that back seat."

"In there?" asked Des incredulously hooking his thumb toward the screened divider.

"Sure! I tell you, they'd shit when they saw us coming. The kids used to call it 'getting Nova'd'. Captain called it a 'Nova Sweep'- when we'd clean the streets with these old workhorses. I bet I had your son T'weed in the back seat more than once."

"You don't say? I don't recall hearing about any arrests." Des sniffed.

"Oh, we never arrested them. We called it, *'haul 'em, hold 'em, and heave 'em'.*"

"Nowadays you're after bigger fish, eh?"

"Yeah, well, now I'm a detective, for one thing."

Des delayed, deliberating.

"I know what you're gonna say, Billy."

"You do? Well then you saved me a lot of grief."

"Grief?" Des shook his head as if to say, "You don't know the meaning of the word."

"Tell you what, then," he continued, "I have a proposal for you. Maybe we can strike a bargain. So hear me out."

"Sure…but there's no need, Des."

"I think there is." As far as he was concerned he was bargaining for his life and liberty, after all. "What if I offered you something in exchange."

"In exchange? For what?"

Des was momentarily taken aback. "For *consideration*, man. Listen for a minute, will you? What if I told you where to find the gun."

"The gun? What gun?"

"The one that killed them boys the other night, of course."

Storer had driven only a quarter of a mile and now he was pulling over. Looking out the window Des noticed that they had stopped in front of the drug store, where a neon RX sign flashed disconsolately, casting a bluish tint to ward off the gloom of night.

"What in God's name are you talking about, Des? Have you gone bonkers, or what?"

"I got the word earlier, Billy, about you guys naming a suspect in the case. I just wanted to make an offer before you made any mistakes."

"And you say you have a gun? You want to what, trade a gun? For what?"

"For freedom, for fairness, for justice, for fuck-all, I don't know. Do you want the bloody gun or not?"

"Listen, Des, I don't know what you heard, but if you have information pertinent to this case, then you have an obligation to come forth. It's your duty as a citizen."

"Don't give me that horse shite. I heard you were ready to make an arrest, and I'm trying to make sure that you get the right man."

Storer was silent for a moment, clearly trying to make a decision.

"Alright. Let's see if you have anything worth discussing. What kind of gun are you talking?"

"An M60, like the ones they use in the US military. Am I getting warm?"

Storer stared. He knew that info on the murder weapon had not been released to the press.

"So you have the M60? Where did you get it? Is this for real, or did you call in a favor from some mick friend of yours in the department?"

"What's it worth to you, Billy? If I hand over the gun do I get a little breathing room? Can we negotiate?"

"Obviously it's worth the case to me, Des. If I had the murder weapon I could run tests and see if I could come up with a killer. That is, unless you're saying that you know who the killer was, too?"

"Let's not get ahead of ourselves, here. Before you haul me in for questioning, I want to know if I can get some assurances."

"Haul you in…what are you talking about? Did you think I'd do that? Is that what this is about? Do you really have a gun, or are you just shitting me?" Storer was becoming aggravated.

"I'm trying to protect myself. Does that make any sense to you? Whenever you deal with the cops you have to be careful." He wished he hadn't said that.

"What's going on here, Des? Did your boy tell you where he hid the gun?"

"My boy? Taweed's got nothing to do with this!"

"He doesn't, eh? We already put out an APB for his arrest. As far as we're concerned, he's our number one suspect."

A terrible thud struck somewhere in Des' chest, like a muffled clapper against a warped gong. Sweat broke out on his forehead, and he felt faint.

"You want to arrest my boy for murder? Are you out of your mind?"

"Hah! I don't think so, old man. Sorry to have to tell it to you like this, but there is what we call a preponderance of evidence against him. Now, I am a bit confused, because a moment ago I could have sworn that you were trying to make a deal to keep him out of jail."

That bastard Bisso! He said that the police were looking for *him*, not Tweed. Now he'd done it. Went and opened his mouth before the need even arose. But then, what if he had known that it was Tweed, what would he have done then? Would he have tried to convince Harris to help out? Would Harris have been willing to part with his machine gun? It was too late to think of that now. Now he had to get himself out of the fix he was in.

"Billy, you got me flustered. You think Taweed had something to do with this crime and I happen to know that he didn't. Now, he would likely be able to prove it better than I can, so if you insist after what I have to tell you, then by all means, go for it, as they say. All I wanted was to avoid…was to avoid being a witness, you know? I don't want to have to appear in court. If I, uh, hand over important evidence that helps your case, evidence that for all intents and purposes will probably help prove my boy's innocence as well, then can I have your word that I'll not have to appear before any magistrate or anything?"

Now it was Storer's turn to be flustered. He turned the car on and proceeded toward the north Rossie neighborhood where Des lived.

"Ho boy, you are a wonder, old friend! Alright then. I guess you had some concerns about getting dragged into an inquiry, God only knows why. But that's between you and him, I dare say. I don't know what I can do for you, Des, until I know what it is I'm dealing with. Let's start over. Do you have evidence or not?"

"Let's say I know where it is. You see, I was hoping to tell you my story so that you'd think of a way to keep me out of it. Like, maybe you say you found it yourself, or something."

"So you found something, is that it?" The good detective's patience was wearing a bit thin.

For the remainder of the drive Des related his quickly improvised story about happening upon a strange scene at the park, witnessing the "boom and the flash" and seeing the mysterious suspect discarding what may well be a gun down at South St swamp.

Storer withheld judgment. By the time he pulled up in front of Des' house he was ready to boot him out on his butt in any event. To think that an old friend like Des would pull some cockeyed crap like that. "I'll get back to you tomorrow and we'll check it out together. But Des, next time, if, heaven forbid there ever is a next time, just tell me when you have a problem like this. It always works out better when you just say what it is you have on your mind. Now, go in and get some sleep. I'm heading home, too. I have a feeling that it's going to be a long weekend."

Des climbed out of the rust bucket, rocking it like a cradle as he relieved it of his weight. He'd like to tell Billy what he had on his mind, but there was no sense in losing a friend over what amounted to a misunderstanding. Now to go in and face Christine.

***

Tooling along Turtlepond Parkway, Tweed was near the end of a day he'd sooner forget. It was a straight shot from here to the Westbury Parkway, then another couple of minutes on the state road heading west. Taking this route he came at his apartment in a somewhat circuitous fashion, but at least he avoided the main drag, the new police station, and hence the most heavily patrolled parts of town. On the one hand he felt constrained by his paranoia at times like this, but on the other hand, it was, as he always said, his job to be paranoid.

Not a hundred yards after turning onto the state road, he caught a flash out of the corner of his eye, braked and swerved and almost freaked out. A freakin' chick, wearing like, pink feathers or something, had come bolting into the road, waving her arms. He could have had a heart attack.

Good thing about the 99, modified as it may have been beyond recognition, it could still stop on a c-hair.

The chick pounded, flat-handed on the hood of his car. Tweed was appalled, but enthralled. This girl, all of 19, two years of which was makeup, was practically naked.

So it's two in the morning, 46 degrees out, he is stoned out of his skull, and a fabulously gorgeous naked young woman accosts him on the highway. Thank God it was him and not some perverted old stiff.

"Cool car, dude! Is this yours?" asked a pair of the most pointed tits he had ever seen.

"You need a ride, lady, er, miss…" Tweed craned his head over to to the right side of the car in an attempt to see her face.

"Honey! Yes, we do!"

And then there were two of them. Girls, not boobs, of which there were now four, equally unadorned.

Tweed flipped the door handle at the same time his lovely hitcher did, negating the desired result. They both tried again, yanking the latch from inside and out, and failing to open the door.

"You gonna give us a ride, or what?" said the second one, in a slightly older and chubbier voice. Her belly button was a dark time tunnel, drawing his gaze to distraction.

"Allow me," he called, and pushed the door open. Now if he managed the seat lever correctly, he may end up with the first chick sitting in the front with him, while her companion could "hog" the back. A subtle instinct informed him that it was likely that the cuter chick flagged for rides. Not so. As the two young ladies entered the car with a gallery of mischievous scents in train, Tweed observed that they both possessed delightful qualities and assets. *Go Leor!* As his old man used to say.

"Evening ladies!" He smiled, and they tittered like fawning hookers in a brothel drawing room.

"Chugga," said the auburn-haired beauty in the back seat. This girl was an eight, to say the least, and to paraphrase the old joke, if her breasts were a bit smaller she'd be a ten. It was difficult not to rate the women like so many pedigree show cats, but they were, well, wearing negligee.

The negligee was indescribably scant and erotic, adjectives that were wholly appropriate in light of the fact that Tweed couldn't look at it. Maybe it was his Christian ethic, maybe it was his sense of modesty, but he was unable to look at either of the girls for more than an instant. Then again, it could just as well have been the case that he was afraid of making a fool of himself, or revealing that he had a glorious and massive erection painfully testing the stretch limit of his pants.

"I'm Tum- uh, Tweed. Glad to meet you."

"Bet you are, Sugar. Did you say that your name was Tumbleweed? Aw, man, that's awesome! Man, your father must have been a cool dude. What's his name...Tex?" asked Chugga with another compelling giggle.

"No, my dad's name is Desmond- Desmond Maurice."

"Desmond Morris? Like, *The Naked Ape?*"

Tweed burst out with a snort of laughter. "Yeah, whatever."

On the replay he caught the allusion, but by then it was too late.

"So, where are we going...ah, what were your names again? Sorry, short-term memory loss."

"We call that a brain fart, baby. Happens all the time. I'm Honey, this is Chugga. We ain't *going*, we're *coming*," oozed Honey.

"Sounds good. Wish I could come too."

Honey looked him over, "S'a possibility."

She flung a dainty hand backwards and palm up as if she were pointing to the rear window, and then Tweed saw that she had taken a pint bottle of Southern from Chugga, who had apparently pulled it out of thin air. Honey took a hefty swig, wiped her mouth and said, "Mind if I smoke?"

You're certainly hot enough, he thought, but he said, "You shouldn't smoke, Honey, it ruins your looks."

At that she sat bolt upright to perfect-posture height. Her jutting breasts reminded him, strangely, of Lady Liberty. Kind of a junior-miss version.

"You think my looks have been ruined?" she pouted.

He did another little short-take, trying to compel his neck to turn for long enough to take a good long gander, but again his willpower was insufficient.

"No, no- you look fine to me."

"Alright then!" and she also produced a cigarette as if by magic.

What the-? They don't have pockets, that's for damn sure.

"How far can I take you?" Shit, he couldn't make these lines up; and yet, somehow delivering them made him sound both provocative and naïve at the same time.

"Like I said, we already went to a party, but when we were on our way back, our van broke down, you know, back there, where you picked us up."

"Always knew that piece of shit would leave us stranded one of these days," said Chugga in a sing-song voice.

"Oh, that's alright," replied Honey, "'Cuz this way we got to meet Mr. Tumbleweed, here." She squeezed over and tried to cuddle with Tweed, despite the parking brake console and shift lever between them.

Her hand was in his lap. "Ooh! What have we here?"

"If you don't know, then maybe I should let it be a surprise," he answered, uncertain if he really wanted to proceed. After all, he was on his way home, and if LaGloria had any talent at all, it was for detecting the trace of strange pussy on her man. Always the Catch-22. If you cheat and have sex they can tell, but if you cheat and try to hide it with a shower, they know that you're too clean. When it came down to it, the only way to arrange sex with another woman was to ask his girlfriend for permission first, and he didn't dare imagine her reaction to that request.

"So, your clothes were in the van, too?"

"What do you care, lover? I think you're happy to see us dressed the way we are."

"I'm ha-ha-happy all right." She had taken a handful and was gently tugging, as if she were trying to coax the sword from the stone.

He took his eyes off the road for a moment, only to catch a glimpse of a dark wrinkled nipple, stiff like whipped eggs and sugar.

"A party, huh? What, like a stag party?"

"Questions, questions. How about a drink?" Honey waved the open mouth of the whiskey bottle under his nose. It smelled cloyingly heavy and sweet, in contrast to the myriad musky and floral notes, the raw and refined odors that emanated from the bodies of his angelic passengers.

"No, thanks, uh, I'm going to swing back down toward Westbury Circle, if that's alright with you."

"Is that near Roosevelt?" asked Honey with sudden interest.

"Ah, no, I'm just coming from Roosevelt now; it's back thataway. Why? Did you want to go there?"

"Just thinking; we met someone who lived there recently, and if we were in the neighborhood maybe we could crash with her. But actually, we're going to Franklin."

"Franklin? I don't think I can bring you that far."

No bullshit. After a quick calculation he had realized that the round trip would be 90 minutes, easy. Not that he didn't want to help.

"Not even if we make it worth your while?" pleaded Chugga.

"You wouldn't leave us on the roadside in nothing but our-" Honey plucked at her feathers, "-At this hour?"

Man- she didn't have to talk dirty, the lilt of her voice alone was a turn-on. But then it helped that she had unzipped his fly, and her mouth was a mere inches from the tip of his penis.

"Sorry, gorgeous. I can't." He shrugged apologetically.

Her hand disappeared, leaving his cock feeling cold and exposed.

He shifted in his seat, trying to enclose his crestfallen kubiton inside his jacket. The zippers were a chilly shock.

"If there's anything else I can do for you...?"

"Oh! Look!" cried Chugga, suddenly.

"I see it," said Honey, "Pull over, will ya?"

Tweed scanned the road trying to catch what they had seen. The only place with the lights still on was a VFW hall, a shabby low-rise building on the right.

"You guys sure about this?" he slowed the car and pulled into the parking lot. But although he listed them quickly and with conviction, his concerns went unheeded, and the women of his dreams and fantasies left him cold. Last he saw of Honey and Chugga they were helping each other across the trash-strewn lot of the VFW post in their impossible high-heel shoes. It was almost tempting to go in after them just to see the looks on the faces of any crusty old drunks who happened to be at the bar when the two skinny exotic entertainers strutted into their establishment.

Irritated by irrational guilt, shame and embarrassment as he drove away, Tweed rationalized that the girls knew how to take care of themselves, and that they had probably chosen the post because of the probability that the place had a pay phone.

***

Across town the traffic signal lights switched automatically to late-night flashing mode.

Solitary joggers took to the empty streets for a smog-free run.

Milkmen started arriving at the dairies to load their trucks for their upcoming pre-dawn routes.

Bakers proofed their dough and set up racks of bread and hot rolls for delivery to vendors and restaurants.

The last flurry of activity before the crucial switching hour before dawn, when the new day picked up the baton and carried the spark of life ahead to awaken the world. And those who were already awake felt a primordial malaise as they made the circadian transition.

Raccoons and possums prowled the alleys and backyards of the greater metropolitan area. Rats and other vermin crawled in the gutters and catch-basins; cats and dogs squared off on the streets like rival gangs in a noisy turf war.

Throughout the night a steady stream of trucks, cars, trailers and mobile homes arrived at the ballpark in Rossie Square. Gradually the field acquired the appearance of a mechanized medieval tournament, or like a camp site at a weekend Grateful Dead show.

When the children of Rossdale arose from their ritual Saturday animation saturation they would have an extra treat, a wonder to behold; and then a mass-exercise of apron-tugging, whining and pleading would commence. Mothers all over town cashed in on the opportunity to collect on a backlog of promised chores.

***

Spaz Travers returned to his now-trashed home after posting bail for himself and a few of his less fortunate guests. The bail bondsman had told him to show up at court on Monday morning. From experience he knew that even if he arrived on time his case would be pushed back to second session. He had all weekend to consider the fix he was in. Perhaps he could go to court unrepresented on Monday and get a continuance on his own before deciding how to handle the endangerment, exploitation and lewd-behavior charges against him. There was a good chance his lawyer would demur.

Damn! he thought. That Hildy was a cute kid in her mongoloid way, and she sure liked to take her clothes off. Just think; if they put him back in jail for this, then she'd be legal by the time he got out.

***

The stooges had reconvened at the Fores to nurse their wounds and to see if anyone knew what had become of Mo Keating, or the guy in the VW for that matter. Soon guesses and theories became the stuff of legend; fact and fiction merged as the tale of the White City incident started to form and expand, elaborated and enhanced with the aid of many a pitcher of beer.

***

Bone Cronin slept soundly after handing the 25 pounds of pot over to Sharlae for safe-keeping. In fact there was a good chance that she would lock the stuff up in Tweed's Weld St office for the short term, anyway. He finally had reason to be optimistic about his immediate prospects, having earned Weed's gratitude for picking up and delivering the product even as Og was busted and hauled off to jail.

***

Sharlae stayed up later than usual, thinking too much, eating too much, smoking too much and worrying too much. Bone's story was too incredible not to be true- almost ripped off by that scumbag Og, then to be stopped on the road by the cops when he had beau coup dope in his car. But instead of busting him or taking the dope, the cops had taken the other dope, Og.

Like a good joint, a story like that was something to savor and to pass on, but Sharlae couldn't help wondering what had become of Rick Rose. She didn't want to seem too eager, but she had hoped that he'd come back and spend the evening with her. Maybe she was wrong, but she thought they jived, they clicked. It had been a long time since she had felt attracted to a guy; she'd just have to be patient.

***

Og, about whose welfare Sharlae hadn't given the slightest consideration, was in Municipal jail trying in desperate futility to sleep. His only permitted phone call had been wasted on Tweed's legal-aid contact. So much for the promise he had made to his franchisees that in the event of arrest he'd have them back on the street ASAP. Fucking guy was grinding his stones, and here he was spending his first night in a cell. No shoes or socks, no belt, no pillow, no freakin' privacy. Sub-human drunk moaning in the next cage, moronic cops making noise down the hall. Plus he had to take a shit, but there was no way he was going to do it in that stainless bowl they called a latrine that was cemented into the wall. It was a matter he never discussed, but the truth was that Og had never gone to the bathroom, to be specific, had never voided his bowels, anywhere but in the familiar comfort of his own bathroom at home. Not in his entire life, as far as he knew. He didn't think of himself as obsessive, but on this issue he was utterly inflexible. He would simply have to wait. It was mind over matter, disregard the cramps, the hot flashes and his distended abdomen. He could hold out until Tweed sent someone to bail him out first thing in the morning.

***

And Tweed went home to LaGloria, weary, a bit anxious, a bit blue-balled, but resolved. Maybe he wouldn't feel so god-damned cock sure if he hadn't found the shotgun as he was supposed to, or if he hadn't spoken with Donal, who had reminded him that he had friends, and the advantage that combined strength and intellect provides.

However his confidence suffered a disturbing setback as he walked across the parking lot from his car to his apartment.

The Corvette was hard to miss for a few reasons. Didn't matter how tired he was, Tweed was till plenty keen enough to know that this particular car didn't belong in the lot where he found it. He had taken care to remember the makes and models of all the cars in the complex, even going so far as to make note of license plates. Sure, it was possible that visitors, delivery or sales people or other stray individuals might park in the lot on occasion, but this car was occupied. At first it caught his attention because it looked so familiar that he had to look twice. Chocolate brown 1983 Corvette Stingray- couldn't be the same one that a client had paid him so handsomely to destroy, for the obvious reason. Yet the resemblance was uncanny. His curiosity was rewarded and his suspicions confirmed when he took a closer but casual look. It was that prick Detective Rima, snoring away like some drunken frat boy. What a rookie! Man, you'd never catch Storer sleeping on the job. Then again, how the fuck would he know? Well, he didn't care about Storer anyway, especially when his straight-man Rima was here in front of him, apparently keeping his apartment unit under surveillance. There were sixteen tenants here, and a simple process of elimination would help Tweed determine which of them he might be after. But why bother when his well-practiced function of paranoia provided the answer. Rima was watching him, or LaGloria, or both.

And yet, the discovery of a police officer on stake-out in his parking lot was not the last item of concern for Tweed this night. Although the fact that the cop was doing such a piss-poor job had alleviated his concern somewhat, the real kick in the butt, the icing on the cupcake was the news with which his lover greeted him upon his return.

It had been a trying day of pain, stress and exertion. When he left the house LaGloria had been luuded to the max, and he figured that she would be pacified, sedate, mellow and recumbent. Instead she had stories to tell, and this time her tales were too real to be ignored. First of all her old man was on his way to visit them, fully expecting to witness the funeral of his sons. However there was little chance that LaGloria would cater to the expectations of her father, or anyone else. Then she had outlined her conversations with Susan Cronin and Tommy Toole. Next she had fed Tweed's fears and anger and frustration as she described the visit from the same detective who was now snoozing in his car outside the apartment. She went on at some length, bitching and bawling, demanding and demeaning, complaining and commanding, testing the limits of his love, patience and understanding.

Then she added the cherry garnee to the aforementioned dessert, when, on top of all the crazy crap she had dumped on him, she mentioned, almost as an afterthought, that a strange thing had happened later in the evening. Sometimes it was difficult to know if she was describing reality or going off on one of her wish-fulfillment escapades, but this time, even though the story sounded strange, Tweed knew in his gut that it must be true. She had been looking out the window, checking to see if he had come home yet, and there in the parking lot, instead of a Saab 99 she saw a large truck with a Tilt-a-Whirl in tow. Covered in blinking white and yellow incandescent bulbs, the carnival ride was taking a tour of the neighborhoods, drumming up business for the upcoming vacation week stint in Rossie square.

CHAPTER 37

Missy Columkille was the latest and last inheritor of a 150 paper route that had been carefully built up, nurtured and maintained by her elder siblings over the course of twenty years. She had to be ambitious and enthusiastic simply to have assumed the responsibility for the route and the collections; and in addition, physical fitness, stamina and strength were key requirements. She hauled a canvas sack full of newsprint that on weekdays weighed almost as much as she did, and on Sundays more than doubled her weight. Missy was stronger than many of her peers, boys included, and it was her strength that made all the difference early on Saturday morning, April 19, 1986.

She had been at it for about forty minutes, pumping her single-speed Schwinn from house to house, by the time she turned the corner onto the penultimate street on her route. There, halfway down on the left, at this early hour, she saw a fire truck, a police car and an ambulance in front of the Kelley's house. In an instant it occurred to her that she must call Tweed, even though she knew that it would put her behind on her deliveries.

Fortunately Missy knew the neighborhood as well as any prowling tom cat. Her excitement provided the advantage in speed and her bicycle provided the maneuverability she needed in order to bound through the intervening yards to her own house in less than a minute.

As she rushed inside she wondered why there was so little activity, until she remembered that it was only 7 AM. That, too, was an advantage because it was the only time of day when the phone would be unoccupied. She dialed quickly and was relieved to hear Tweed's groggy voice answering after a couple of rings.

"Tweed! It's Melissa!" she cried.

"What? Who? What do you want?" he mumbled in reply.

"Melissa! Missy Columkille! You know, Jimmy's sister? Megan's sister?"

"Oh! Melissa! Hey!" he cleared his throat, "Uh, what's up?"

"Listen, Tweed, I had to call you right away 'cuz I saw ambulances at your house."

She could tell he was fading. "Tweed? 'Djahearme?"

"Ambulances? Where?"

"At your house, Tweed. I hate to say it, but I think they're taking one of your parents to the hospital!"

Dawn broke. "Oh, shit!" Tweed bolted out of bed, stumbled, then steadied himself on LaGloria's dresser, staring at his reflection in the attached mirror. He looked like a pasty extra in a teenage killer-zombie movie.

In truth he'd been dreading this call for months.

Shit, the phone- he'd left it on the bed. Reality was slow in asserting itself.

"Melissa? Hello, Missy? You there?"

"Yeah, Tweed, I thought you fainted or something. Look, I gotta get back to my paper route now. You do the right thing, OK?"

What a sweet kid…caring and concerned, about him and his parents. He'd have to see what he could do to take care of her.

"Hey, yeah, for sure. I'll let you go. Thanks, Melissa. I owe you one. Say hi to your mother for me. Bye!"

Now what? Missy had done her duty; now it was time for Tweed to do his. Too late to go to the old man's house. Better head straight for Rossdale Hospital.

In the car Tweed felt as though he had left half of his consciousness back in bed. His face felt like putty, his hands tingled as he gripped the wheel. He homed in on his target following the prompting of his nerves, and a trickle of adrenalin kept him on the road, triggered by the anticipation of pain. It was like the moment after a doctor says, "Now this won't hurt a bit..." Or when a friend looks you in the eye and says, "Bro, I got bad news..."

Hospital visitor parking in the garage.

Fuck it; he parked in the outpatient lot and hobbled around the exterior of the building to the emergency room, his swollen ankle begging him to look for a wheelchair. As he jogged he realized that he had been hearing the wail of distant sirens ever since leaving his apartment, but instead of fading they had been getting louder and louder. Sure enough, the ambulance arrived just after Tweed did.

Without saying a word to anyone he strolled into the emergency room reception area and right on through the double doors leading to the ECU.

Des was standing there in the center of the room, looking haggard and ashen. Strands of hair that he usually combed over his forehead hung like cobwebs from his temple. He was wearing a coat over his pajamas and slippers on his feet.

In the fairness of God's will it could have been Des lying on a stretcher right now instead of his wife Christine, for they had both aged badly. But she was the one being prepped and prodded for vital signs. She was to be the football at the center of a huddle of medical professionals who were concentrating on a strategy of saving the game of her life. Des could only look on, worried and bewildered, hoping to hedge his bets.

Christine had suffered illness after illness during the past few years, and her doctors had warned her that if she wanted to reduce the threat posed to her longevity then she must modify her lifestyle. However, she had been unwilling to do anything that she construed as sacrificing her quality of life.

"Taweed," croaked the old man, "It's your mother."

"What happened, Dad?"

"She collapsed. This morning. When I tried to help her up she told me she was done for. I told her not to be foolish. 'Come now, Chris,' I said, 'You'll be back on your feet in no time.' But she insisted she was dying."

He spoke calmly but his eyes were brimming with tears, and his voice was but a whisper.

"Is it her heart?" asked Tweed, feeling acutely uncomfortable at seeing his father so affected.

"I...I don't know, son, I don't know what it is."

"Is she in much pain?"

"I'm afraid so, but the doctors are doing the best they can to help her. They'll save her, so be patient and say your prayers."

The emergency room was too bright and clean, and the morning was too sunny. Tweed scanned the room for a place to sit, at least for his father; but mostly he wanted to get out of the center of the room, where he felt exposed and at the same time in the way.

Other than the beds in the alcoves around the perimeter, the only furniture in the room was the nurse's station, a counter not unlike the bar in the biz club. Behind the counter stood a winsome looking brunette wearing whites under a floral print smock. She smiled at Tweed and then returned her attention to her clipboards and charts.

Suddenly a voice like that of the ship's computer on Star Trek announced a series of names and acronyms over the public address system. Still the men stood where they had met, feeling further alienated and out of place.

Then the doors at the far end of the room flew open, and through them a man emerged wearing pastel scrubs, a surgical bonnet and a mask over his mouth. He hurried into the room, tugging at his mask as he approached Des and Tweed. He spoke urgently.

"Mr. Kelley? Please come with me right away sir. Is this your son? You may come along if you like. We haven't much time. Quickly now."

He rushed back toward the treatment area, beckoning for them to follow. Tweed did so immediately, sensing the crisis and compelled by his concern for his mother. But Des appeared to hesitate, as if afraid of what he might encounter should he proceed.

Tweed had expected the next room to be somewhat larger; maybe an operating room with nurses and doctors and specialists buzzing around the patient like flies around a picnic.

Instead he found his mother in a quiet examination room, swaddled in sheets and blankets and lying flat out on a table that seemed too small for her. She did not respond when he and his father entered the room.

The peace of the moment was swiftly interrupted as medics started to arrive, prompted by what summons Tweed did not know. However the nature of the emergency was evident, as Tweed noticed to his horror that a flow of blood was issuing from his mother's body and soaking into the bedclothes. Still she did not move as a doctor shone a penlight in her eyes, and a nurse started an IV drip in her arm.

The room was far too small for so many people, and Tweed desperately wanted to escape to the outside and fresh air. But suddenly his mother seemed to convulse and moan and his father seemed to collapse in on himself as he witnessed the event.

The doctors now worked with determination and speed, in a sudden burst of activity, as if they were racing against time. And Tweed saw the reason for their alarm, as his mother appeared to disintegrate in front of his eyes.

"Renal failure…" shouted one of the docs, and although Tweed wasn't familiar with the term he assumed that it had something to do with the fact that the poor woman had lost control of her bowels and bladder, and that blood was pouring from her nose and mouth.

No one looked at Tweed, but he stole a glance at his father, who had covered his face with his hands. Perhaps he did not want to witness the moment that had now arrived, but the doctor who had led them into the room turned to him and said, "This is it…" as if answering a question.

Des could close his eyes perhaps, but Tweed could not, nor could he stop praying. Oh Lord, was this his mother who lay before him? By the Blessed Virgin, was this poor creature the same woman whose strength and love had given him birth and whose wisdom had guided him through life? How could God treat her so, and if He had judged her worthy to receive her eternal reward, then what about her loved ones? Jesus Christ, how were they to go on living when their example and motivator, when the woman upon whom they depended was taken from them?

"Time of death…" said the doc, and one of the attendants marked the hour. How utterly final. She was gone.

Now Tweed too seemed to deflate, to sag under the weight of the knowledge that he had seen his mother die. Nurses were now counting the blood soaked sheets, and at last Tweed could not bear to watch as the doctor made some final observations concerning the body.

A heavy object rested upon Tweed's shoulder and he saw that his father had placed a hand there.

"God help her now, son, she's in His hands."

Tears blinded Tweed as he turned to leave the room. He felt an impulse to run, to flee the hospital.

Partly because of his blurry vision he stumbled into the midst of a group of people who were standing in the emergency room waiting area. Joe Toole and Simon were there with their wives as well. He almost failed to recognize his father's friends, but when he did, emotions over-topped the dam of his reserve, and he burst into wracking sobs.

"Anything we can do for you…" said Simon, and the others made similar noises of comfort before allowing him to pass and turning to Des, who had just finished venting his grief upon the doctors. Tweed continued on out into the daylight, numb to the warmth of the sun, blind to his surroundings, lost in the depths of his sorrow.

When he finally found his car he got in and sat with his head bowed to the steering wheel, trying not to think, not to remember the wretched scene he had just witnessed.

A chunk of himself had been torn away, a portion of his heart and soul that he hadn't realized was dedicated to his mother. For almost eight years he had lived away from home, away from her; but in his opinion the separation had only enhanced their relationship. She had accepted him on his terms, as an adult, with no questions or criticism. And he in turn had learned to admire her. Not with childish adoration but in a more mature fashion, with respect for her struggles and accomplishments, for her principles and her forthright certainty in the basic decency of humanity.

He wanted to go home and share his misery with LaGloria, but first he would have to pull himself together, and delay the self-pity long enough to start the car and drive. Yet he also knew that he couldn't stand it if LaGloria displayed her usual perversity, her penchant for cold, hostile deflection of genuine sentiment, her total lack of empathy.

She had tried to kill his father and he had been fool enough to go along with it; but if she were to say or do anything that disrespected the memory of his mother, then he might well choke the living daylights out of her.

In any event, he had to go home. Time to get something to eat, then to call his brothers and share the pain of loss.

As he drove away he remembered that his father had come to the hospital in the ambulance, so he needed a ride as well. He should have stayed to see that Des was alright, and to offer any help or comfort that a son may provide. But Des had his friends and they wouldn't leave him stranded. Besides, Tweed couldn't help feeling that Des was in some way responsible for the death of Christine Kelley.

CHAPTER 38

Francisco McManus

Of Rossdale, died April 18, 1986, at age 27. Son of Joseph McManus, retired, Florida; and the late Dolores McManus. Also survived by a sister, LaGloria McManus of Westbury. Private service. Arrangements by the Metropolitan Cremation Society.

Nilvan McManus

Of Rossdale, died April 18, 1986, at age 25. Son of Joseph McManus, retired, Florida; and the late Dolores McManus. Survived by a sister, LaGloria McManus of Westbury. Private service. Arrangements by the Metropolitan Cremation Society.

Christine Kelley

Of Rossdale, died April 20, 1986, at age 59. Survived by husband Desmond of Rossdale, sons Buck, Tumbleweed, and Fr. Keiran Kelley SJ; one grand-child. In addition to being a homemaker Mrs Kelley also worked as a private secretary. A lifelong advocate for peace in Northern Ireland, Mrs Kelley was a co-founder of CAFE, the Citizens Alliance for Erin, an organization dedicated to promoting civil rights and focusing on the plight of women and children in Irish society. Funeral Mass at Sacred Name, followed by internment at St. Matthew's Cemetery. Donations to CAFE, the Citizen's Alliance for Erin, AKA the Children's Assistance Fund for Erin.

CHAPTER 39

"Which one's yours, Mister?"

Myles Brennan had been attempting to engage his host in conversation ever since he had joined him at his table in the bay side restaurant. He was referring to the boats that could be seen outside the window moored at the adjacent yacht club on the harbor like some vast leisure-class armada.

He wasn't particularly nervous, but the old dude he had come to meet, this guy Makepeace, hardly made any effort to put him at ease. Rather, he just sat there staring out at the water; -and he was the one who had arranged the meeting. Finally he spoke.

"My boat?" he answered, absently. "It's out beyond the point there." He indicated with his gaze.

Brennan squinted into the glare of the salt-etched window. "The one with the sails?"

"Sails?" he grumbled as if insulted, "No sails. Further out. Past the cove."

Outside the cove? There was nothing out there but the blue haze and then the distant blue hills...His eyes widened. Those weren't hills. "Holy!...That's yours? How come we didn't meet on your boat? Man!" Myles looked around, searching for someone to impress with his newfound knowledge.

"You couldn't afford to set foot on my boat, son; let alone hiring a water taxi to take you out there."

"Well, shit, you must have a skiff or something..."

For Makepeace there was no need to look at his guest directly, no need to observe his comportment, decorum, his relative degree of gentility, let alone his dress or presentation; for he could sense in Brennan the funk of death and decay. It had crept up to the table in advance of his arrival and had taken its slovenly posture in his chair, gesturing half-heartedly for coffee, and fumbling weakly for cigarettes. Even now the shade all but covered Brennan's features, making it plain to perhaps everybody but himself that he was dying.

At this moment on Saturday afternoon, AD Makepeace had not yet learned of his dear friend Christine Kelley's passing, so the discomfort he felt, although real and distinct was not so great as to cause him to abandon his inquiry altogether. Furthermore, he had only just met Myles Brennan and he had no idea what ailed him, and if he did it would have mattered little to him beyond mere intellectual fascination.

For the illness from which Myles suffered was one that would soon extend its gloomy reach across the land, touching people of all types, without discrimination for age, gender, race, nationality, ethnic origin, religion or blood type. At this moment neither Myles nor Makepeace would have understood the relevant diagnosis, for Myles was "HIV positive", optimistic sounding words that at that time amounted to a death sentence.

He knew he was sick, that he lived on coffee and cigarettes during the day and on booze and sex and drugs at night. But his gut philosophy was that you put whatever you had into the day you found yourself living, and that was all you could expect.

His boyfriend Tommy Toole was more cheerful, and he took the long view. He said that you had to plan for the future. Recently Tommy had convinced Myles to go with him to march in the St Patrick's Day parade. Down in New York gays were going to march as a separate organization with big banners and everything, and there was all this controversy and legal challenges back and forth; but all Tommy wanted to do was to go down and join the local municipal parade. Overall reluctance and inertia weighed against going, and in addition the memory of being dragged to the parade by his mother when he was six years old made Myles balk. Tommy said that the parade was a tradition, something you had to celebrate every year, for your whole life.

When they marched they didn't carry a banner or anything; they didn't even hold hands for the length of the parade route, but he had a great time nonetheless. They were just two guys in a huge crowd; probably not the only gays marching in the parade, but he wasn't celebrating being gay. He wasn't celebrating being Irish, really, either. It had made him wonder, when it came down to it, was it one day or life itself that mattered?

"I didn't ask you here to talk about what I have, but about what you have; isn't that right? Now our mutual acquaintance in the state police, Detective Chmura, tells me that you have a knack for keeping your eyes and ears open. I call that a real talent, a valuable talent, and I understand that you have been well-compensated for your efforts."

Myles shrugged. The old grouch had an accent like the proper butler in a television situation comedy.

"The difference between me and the fellows in the state police however, is that for them, the more they find, the bigger the case, the more they have on some person or persons, but for me, if I find out what I need, it's case closed, and I go home. Either way, it may depend on what you know."

"I don't give a shit what you want, why you want it or where you're going with it. I'll tell you what I know only if I feel like it. For me, information is a commodity."

Makepeace focused upon the man now, looking past the shadow. Brennan was underweight; pale, with long, thin arms and bony fingers, a pronounced Adam's apple, an irregular shaped mole on his right temple; hair thinning on top but long on the sides. He had an annoying squint of a facial tic.

"Myles, you do care what I want and you'll help me when I ask you a question. Considering my limited interest I'll pay you more than fairly, but you'll perform to the level of my expectations.

"Let's keep things in perspective. You are here enjoying the ambiance of Quincy's renowned Bean and Cod Restaurant, drinking a cup of coffee, free to order a meal. Such a meeting place is conducive to a productive session, no? On the contrary I could arrange to have a couple of my men interrogate you in a fish freezer, eh? As I said, I am trying to minimize my involvement here. If you wish I can get the ball rolling so to speak, and ask a few questions. So please, fill me in on what you've managed to observe about Des Kelley and his colleagues at the gentlemen's club there in Rossdale." His low growl clearly indicated the imperative, as opposed to the rising inflection of the interrogative.

It took only a moment for Brennan to collect his nerve before he began. So he wanted to know about Kelley. It figured. He and Kelley seemed to be cut from the same cloth, although this guy was clearly more hard-core.

"The gentlemen's club? Oh! You must mean the biz club, that hole in the wall up in the square. I work at the 'Rock, down the other end of town, just so's you know…" Myles pointed in opposite directions like the Scarecrow in the Wizard of Oz, but receiving no response, he went on.

"Kelley, huh?" he began again, as if to say, 'So that's your angle.' "I suppose Mr. Kelley will be in for a bit more scrutiny than he's accustomed." The facial tic again.

"Oh? How so?" interrupted Makepeace.

"Well, shit, his son's girlfriend's brothers were killed the other night- and in cases like these the cops look at everybody in the immediate family. But, hey, it's good for 'em. Put the spotlight on people like Kelley and then folks will start realizing who really runs their town."

Judging by the look of incredulity on Makepeace's face, Myles knew that he had at least earned a degree of interest.

"Like, sometimes in books or on TV you get the idea that towns like Rossdale are all crooked, you know? If organized crime isn't running everything from the shoe-shines to the bowling alleys to the protection rackets, then the cops are squeezing them for all they're worth.

"Now in Rossie people like to keep the image of a peaceful place where everybody minds their own business, you know, working hard and playing by the rules. Little League. Pop Warner. Ladies Sodality. Shriners. That kind of thing. And the fact is that I couldn't take you to Rossie and point to any blatant example of organized crime, or patterns of extortion; I mean, Rossie's not known for squads of rogue cops, there's no hanging judges, no turf wars or street gangs." Again his face flash-froze in a wince as if he had been stricken with a sudden cramp.

"But, on the other hand, between the cops like Billy Storer and the pols like Dapper Ferguson and the so-called businessmen like Kelley there, they got all the action covered."

"So, you're saying-"

"Right- I'm saying that it's not like some towns where, like, a trucker might worry about driving his rig through 'cuz he knows some punk is liable to hop his box, pop his locks, and toss all of his freight out to a gang waiting in a pick-up truck, or where some Guinea mafioso is gunna come into every mom and pop on the block and demand 'special rent'; or some places where, if you get pulled over by the police, you just pay your ticket on the spot and you don't have to worry about no court appearances; in Rossie the system is more, uh, subtle, let's say."

"So between them, this officer Storer, this Dapper Ferguson, and Des Kelley, they handle all the hijackings and extortion and bribery?"

Myles smiled. "In a way, yeah. For one thing, it's a matter if scale. Rossdale's a small town, and yeah, they got it covered. For another, it's a matter of uhm, degrees...See Dapper is all about influence. He'll come into your business and tell you, Mister Business Owner, all about how he has been at city hall for x-number of years, and how he can get anything done if he wants. You want to add a sweat-shop out back? No problem, Dapper will change the zoning law for you. You need a permit to sell milk at your corner store? No problem! Dapper will see to it that you get one, and without an inspection! *(Uhm, make that check out to Dapper F-e-r-)* You get the picture.

"Now when we talk about our man Storer, were talking a real Gestapo, a freakin' terrorist." (Tic) "Officer Storer's thing, I mean his reputation, is for saving you the trouble. If he finds some citizen staggering home from the bar late at night, will he take him into protective custody? Will he bring the guy down to the station and let him sleep it off? No! No such trouble. Instead he'll pack the poor bastard into the back seat of his cruiser and drive to the empty parking lot at a supermarket. There he'll whip the car into figure-eights and donuts until he's got his passenger good and green, then he takes and dumps him out onto the pavement so he pukes long and hard. 'Course he leaves the guy there to think about the experience, and how good old Billy Storer saved him the trouble of waking up in a strange jail cell with a bad taste in his mouth.

"As far as extortion and protection rackets are concerned, he saves his citizens from those as well, by providing the services in a combined package. It's kind of like extortion, protection and police all in one.

"And I'll tell you, although I've found it best not to know certain things, if you know what I mean; I've heard that he and his partner there, Reemer, will also do certain things, uhm, a la carte, you dig? I mean, you got a particularly nasty shit-you-ation, and they can make it come out all right."

"Um-hmm," nodded Makepeace, apparently impressed. "What about Kelley?"

"Well, you know, that's a little touchier. It's kinda funny you should ask. I mean, there's no way you would know, but…" He scratched his chin, looking intentfully thoughtful. "See, uh, me and Tommy, uhm, Thomas Toole…See, my friend Tom Toole is Joe Toole's son. That's the only reason I know anything about all *that* stuff in the first place." He waved as if to indicate something apart from himself. "Joe Toole, Tommy's father, nice guy, well he owns what they call the Rossie Biz Club, a little shit hole up the square. Practically nobody ever goes in there. Nobody except that guy Kelley, that is. They say he uses the place as a front, for all sorts of things, but I never really got into it- I mean who knows what they do in there? You know, Tommy doesn't want to have anything to do with any of that stuff, so he does his own thing. Anyway, they have Dan to work sometimes if they need him, but the regular bartender is Joe's brother Harry. Harry and Kelley and buddies, and if you wanted to know more about Kelley, ask Harry. I hear they been together a long time."

"Longer than you and Tommy, I gather?" asked Makepeace, casually."

"Oh, heavens, yes…" Myles stopped short, looking at Makepeace sharply with a fading blush on his face, quickly trying to assess his intention.

"Look," he began, but Makepeace cut him off.

"I didn't mean to offend you. I am not here to make a value judgment. I'll tell you that I've known Kelley for years, and some of the things you say come as a surprise to me, but that is why I asked. I'll have to keep an open mind if I'm going to learn anything, so please proceed."

"Alright, well," he started slowly, as if he had to catch up to speed. "See, I can talk about guys like Storer, 'cuz he's practically a legend in Rossie. And Dapper comes into the 'Rock all the time. I mean, it's like the guy has a stool in every bar in town. And I ain't shitting, either. I mean, whenever he comes into the place, whoever is sitting on his stool has to get up and let the old bastard sit down. But when it comes to Kelley, it's all what you might call hear-say.

"I mean, them guys in the state wanted to hear about payoffs, bribe money, what have you, and I'm not going to make anything up, I have seen cash change hands, I mean plenty of green that my bosses handed over to Dapper for no reason whatsoever that I can figure.

"But, see, I do have a theory that I never told the cops, but if you want to hear it…It's like this: everyone knows that young Kelley, the one they call Weed is the biggest dope dealer in town. Now I figure that he couldn't get away with that without the knowledge and approval of his father, could he? Or Billy Storer? How about Dapper? They been leading this big anti-drug campaign, you know, Drive Drugs Down, or something or other…but I'm thinking, see, I'm thinking that Weed sells the dope, and he pays off the old man, and he pays off the politician and he pays off the cops. It's all one big scam."

Now a ruddy flush had crept into Brennan's face along his neck, and his ears were red.

"Everything they do is a scam. It's like that time Dapper was breaking ground for the new housing. Wait 'til you hear this one. Him and Kelley, the big consultant, or whatever he was. They line up this project for the city to build a massive housing project for veterans, the elderly and low-income families, and they were going to clear out a stretch of so-called blighted neighborhoods to do it. So Dapper takes his proposal to the city and gets the council to sign on, and they agree to buy up all of the properties that are in the way of the new development. Supposed to be good for the housing market, good for the city; everybody makes out! Here comes Kelley with these cover companies he sets up to go and push folks out of their homes, paying below market value, negotiating for less than what the city was willing to pay. He goes and sets up a real-estate company that buys the majority of the homes from the displaced residents, using money, I might add, that he borrowed in a shady investment scheme that itself was later investigated.

"So anyway after the parcel was secured, the homes were vacant for years, ready to be demolished. Excavations were started, some streets were closed, other new ones were built; a couple of the businesses down there barely made it. Then…poof! The whole thing was abandoned! Ran into some kind of federal roadblock. Turned out it was never viable in the first place. And get this- in the end the real estate company sold all of the houses back to the city at a profit, and Dapper and his pal Kelley made out like bandits. Which is what I hear they are trying to do again with this new White City project.

"See, my boss at the 'Rock explained it all to me. He says Dapper owes Kelley from way back. I guess Kelley helped Dapper get elected here and there or something, and like my father used to say, 'One hand washes the other, and both hands, they wash the face.'"

A glass of wine might help Makepeace digest what he had heard so far. There were few surprises in the kid's testimony, but it was pretty high on the malarkey meter. It all seemed too pat, too convenient.

He was still no closer to understanding why Des had killed the brothers McManus, a couple of likely lads who might just as soon have become part of his extended family if Tweed were to marry LaGloria. Des didn't see it that way however, and there was the rub. For him the crucial question was why did the brothers, who seemingly had nothing to gain by doing so, attack him? And the mystery lingering in the possible answer to that question was the exclusive motivating factor that kept Makepeace here in town dealing with this petty situation, talking to this pale, pock-marked informer.

"The way my boss tells it- I have two bosses, this one's Donal, Donal Harding, anyway, he says- see him and Weed Kelley go way back- like I said, this Weed Kelley sells a lot of dope; that's what they say, anyway. I'm not a pot head; I mean, I drink, I snort a line here and there, but, uh- oh, yeah, and I'm not sure who gets it from who, you know what I mean? But it's that kind of thing.

"What was I saying? Right! About Kelley! That the way he operates is to get people to use what they do against them. At first I didn't understand it, but Donal's like, see, Dapper works at City Hall, he has connections, influence, maybe a little power. Kelley gets Dapper to do something that puts him in an awkward position, you know? Donal says he 'compromises' him. Now I understand it pretty well because it turns out that this was just what Chmura and his crew at state police was looking for."

Maybe a whiskey would be a better choice. No longer bored and implacable, Makepeace felt his temper rising, as if he had suddenly become aware that he had been swindled. His resentment toward Des Kelley had been festering inexorably since 1974, when he had allowed him to establish, no, he helped Kelley to establish a smuggling operation, for he now understood himself to be equally responsible. He might have arrested the bloody Irish bastard at any of a hundred occasions over the ensuing 12 years, but the truth was that he should have arrested him back then, immediately, and put an end to him and his shenanigans once and for all.

To hear the simple wit of Kelley's strategy laid out second-hand from another barman, Harding, was almost too cold a slap to take. It was no wonder someone was taking potshots at the bastard; indeed the miracle was that he had survived this long. To his own credit and for the good of his family he had ingratiated himself into a position of comfort and pseudo-respectability within the community that had accepted him; but in the light of inquiry Des started to look pale and petty indeed.

At least Makepeace hadn't deceived himself. He'd had a successful career working with and against terrorists and insurgents, in his own small way reducing their numbers, firepower and effectiveness. In Northern Ireland as well as in other 'local hot spots'.

He had known all along that in Kelley he was running a dead-end operation that would lead to no more arrests, no more IRA operatives, no more smuggling routes or ports or methods. On the contrary, the potential for profit and self-aggrandizement had lured him to 'compromise' his own goals, and the sheer fun and enjoyment of the life of supposedly pursuing Des Kelley had been a major diversion and thus a failure.

Des Kelley was his biggest fuck up. But look at Des Kelley! His youngest son was a drug dealer! And his best friend's son was a queer! There was no doubt he had problems. But instead of helping old Des solve his problems, it was time for AD Makepeace to solve a few problems of his own.

CHAPTER 40

The news of Chris Kelley's death seemed to spread organically, as if it were seeking a level, seeking a ground, tracing out routes to all who had loved or cared for her, and to those who knew or had any interest in her. Hence a movement began, as her children, her friends and relatives, her admirers, associates, and colleagues, pen-pals, volunteers, and others prepared to arrive in Rossdale in time for her funeral.

Tweed had spent the latter part of the morning on the telephone with his brothers and friends, at once trying to offer consolation, and at the same time trying to find it. Whom do you call, who needs to know? Exhausted, angry, distraught, he was now confused, as he discovered to his amazement that others had already heard the sad tidings.

Only later did he realize the extent to which his brothers had assisted him in his distress. There was something calmly reassuring about Keiran's voice, as if he were most competent to deal with death and grief. And when he acknowledged that Tweed had undergone a brutal trial indeed in witnessing their dear mother's death first hand, Tweed felt almost proud of himself. In addition, the mere knowledge that Buck was coming on the next available flight from Ireland gave him a boost. Suddenly he imagined his oldest brother as a warm friendly teddy-bear of a guy, when all his life he'd never been able to get along with him.

Almost immediately after he returned home from the hospital his father had engaged him in a bitter fight. In order to hold his own he had lashed back, and yet since then he had been feeling further isolated and withdrawn, as well as depressed and vulnerable. LaGloria had sought to comfort him, primarily by pointing out Des' cowardice in attacking by phone, but her own wounds were still too raw or perhaps she simply lacked the selfless tenderness to offer genuine condolence. In any event she only managed to reinforce his suspicions about her emotional and empathic deficiencies.

Now that Tweed's mother had died, all plans were on hold. In fact, not only Tweed, but everyone else in his organization forgot about Og for the weekend, and as a result he was forced to remain in police custody.

After a miserable night of "processing" in the federal holding facility downtown, Og was returned to Rossdale police station early Saturday. Now officially facing a federal charge of narcotics possession, he would be arraigned on Monday morning. Bail was set and a bondsman appointed, but he was forced to remain in jail because he was unable to reach by phone anyone who might help him scratch together the required price of his freedom. When he realized his predicament, he fretted and fumed, and pissed and moaned, and howled at the watch officers from one end of their shift rotation to the other.

One can well imagine how it must have been for Og, a classic "mama's boy", who by his own admission had never slept a night away from his own bed, to be bored, lonely, paranoid and lost in an inhospitable and utterly alien environment.

It may be difficult to believe that a grown man could go through his life without having spent a night away from home, but it was his choice, in fact the utmost reflection of his preference. Throughout his childhood his devoted parents had always acceded to his wishes, never even arranging so much as a sleep-over at a cousin's. During adolescence and later life he assiduously avoided the occasional demands placed upon him by school or career, and simply worked around issues involving friends or vacations.

Now for the first time, for reasons far beyond his capacity to foresee or imagine, he was being exposed to jail, and all that entailed, including rude strangers and policemen, foreign inexplicable noises, and a cold, uncomfortable cell. But Og's story must wait, for it deserves a fair conclusion, having been adequately set up during the course of the telling of Tweed's tale.

The Wizards and the Franchisees, the distributors, and agents; the Friday evening four-finger bag buyers, the eighty joint-to-an-ounce schoolyard bone sellers, the casual lid cuffers, the nickel and dime baggers, the hash heads, and even the home growers paid their respects to Tweed over the course of the weekend. And of course, he also received calls from extended family and people who had nothing whatsoever to do with pot.

For all of these folks and many others as well there was a unaccountable bad vibe in Rossie. Everyone agreed that it started with the killings, but some also blamed the carnival for picking a piss-poor weekend to plant a symbol of fun and frivolity smack dab in the center of town. 12 hours a day of blaring music and flashing neon lights. It certainly provided a jarring contrast for those who were proceeding to services for the brothers McManus and/or Mrs. Christine Kelley at funeral homes that were located just up the block.

After the murders of Frankie and Nilvan, and then with the death of his mother, Tweed felt as if he had tripped black kleiglights, advertising death. And as he spoke with the well-wishers and the morbidly curious alike, he mentally replayed the deaths of Frankie and his mother in a poorly spliced Zapruder loop that had his mother sitting in the park awaiting execution from his father while Frankie's body erupted in a bloody flux upon an ironing board of an examining table.

His close confidant and steady friend Wayne Kenney had survived a fire in his home a couple of years ago. Tweed asked him how he eventually managed to get over losing all of his possessions.

"Get over it? Man, there isn't a day goes by that I don't still blame myself for that fire- and you know? I'm blaming myself, when it wasn't my fault, nobody died, and nobody was hurt...It's just that I lost everything I had, and trauma like that replays itself repeatedly like a hopelessly warped record glued to the turntable of my mind."

"So you're still hung up about it, you're still bumming, years later?"

"Hey, you live, you love, you move on, you know? But when I woke up that night flames were roaring through my place so loud that at first I thought the pipes had burst or something, because it sounded like a flood of water more than anything. But then I got up and walked out into a freakin' conflagration. Burned my feet, burned my hands, tried to save stupid shit.

"You never really forget, but sooner or later other things- positive things- push the negative things out. But think about it, man...folks in our society live through all sorts of tragedies. Just look at all the war memorials in every town and intersection; think of the rate of infant mortality, the people dying of heart disease. Crime, cancer and car crashes. Lots of people are dealing with death and trauma and tragedy, but they just don't show it. You could be sitting in a diner having a spuckie and a cup of joe, and every other customer in the place is nursing some secret pain, or recovering from some terror. Man, grief is everywhere.

"I'll tell you one thing though- I don't care so much for material things anymore, and you shouldn't either- it can all go up," he snapped his fingers, "just like that!"

He also remembered the agony his friend Carmine Gunther had suffered back when they were both attending White City. Midway through the eighth grade Carmine was inexplicably missing from school for a few days. When he returned he told only Tweed the reason for his absence: his mother had died suddenly at an early age, before she even reached forty.

Back then grief was like a mask Carmine wore, putting it on and taking it off for effect, but never discussing it or sharing his feelings, even with Tweed. When the mood came over him he was capable of startling departures from character, and it was at those times when Tweed knew that Carmine was feeling the pain of his mother's loss. In addition, like a character out of Vonnegut, Carmine adopted the almost predictable assumption that he himself would not live to see age forty. But since Tweed and all of his friends had constantly been told that because of their poor hygiene, inadequate diet and bad habits they were unlikely to reach age thirty, it was hard to tell if Carmine's claim was a threat, a boast or a promise. In his case, of course, he was the first to beat the prediction of that dire admonition, and by a good eight years.

Carmine's death by drug overdose was a tragic and bitter blow to his friends, especially Tweed and Sharlae; but for Tweed the experience had not been particularly helpful in terms of preparing him to deal with grief. He was stricken deeply by the senseless loss, so much so that he had even considered, though never seriously, following his friend across the great divide. After all, in the biopic about Jimi Hendrix, the late great guitarist's Harlem buddies had speculated that maybe Jimi hadn't meant to die, but perhaps he simply wanted to see what was "on the other side"; and when he went to take a look, he found that he could not return. To Tweed that notion sounded compellingly romantic. And yet Carmine became just one more star on the death walk of fame; one of so many of Tweed's peers who had died before reaching maturity.

It seemed that somehow Tweed had unconsciously made a distinction. He had seen friends die, and had heard people say, "Well, we all die someday." His friends may be gone, but he was alive, and he had his remaining friends and family to help him through his despondency. But there was a difference in losing his mother. Upon her death he recognized his own mortality too, and also realized the cold truth that he only had himself to rely and depend upon. Having drawn the distinction, he concluded that experience might help one prepare to deal with death, but that it can do little to help one prepare to deal with grief.

His father had frequently recited the annual casualties from the northern Ireland conflict, but such statistics had meant nothing to Tweed. He failed to see why it should matter to him when strangers die on another continent, fighting for a cause that he did not understand, representing an ideology that he found totally alien. The fact that he had Irish blood did not help to personalize the tragedy, or add to his appreciation of the sacrifices made by the combatants. If he were to call all Irishmen his brothers, then every Mick and Paddy from New York to Montana would automatically become a part of his extended family.

Ultimately he did find some comfort from what was for him an unlikely source, a book Jimmy Col had recommended. Col was wrapping up work on a graduate degree at the University of Chicago, and when he called to express his condolences he mentioned the book, adding that it had been required reading for one of his courses.

On Death and Dying by author Elisabeth Kubler Ross had become a valuable resource for the bereaved and for terminally ill patients as well as for the health care professionals who treat them since its initial publication in the 1960s. After all the encouragement, the palliatives, and consolations of friends and family, Tweed found that the author's stage theory of grief was a refreshing approach that helped him to come to terms with his discomfort. The research was clearly authentic, and the style of the writing was succinct and direct so that he immediately identified the stages in himself. So far he had only encountered the first two, denial and anger, but he felt strangely relieved to know what he could expect, that bargaining, depression, and acceptance would surely follow as night follows day.

Once again Tweed had found comfort and a sense of informed optimism from a book, and he realized that he used to derive a similar feeling of peace and understanding when he read the Bible.

Now he wouldn't even consider opening the Bible, especially if he was looking for comfort or clarity, because recently all he had found within its pages were contradictions, paradoxes and archaisms. And he was further disturbed to realize that where once he had thought that truth was the leveler, the unequivocal force that resolved conflict, now he considered that truth was the cause of conflict. Some said that first-hand evidence, that actual experience was the only gauge of reality in a world where illusion was commonplace. And yet he had been a witness to the harshest, hardest, most bitter of realities when he had seen Frankie murdered by his father's cruel intent, and then his mother murdered by his father's cruel neglect.

CHAPTER 41

"Tom! Am I glad to hear from you."

Indeed, the ache in Des' abdomen seemed to subside and the tourniquet of tension that had been twisting at his temple eased.

"Where are you?"

"I called as soon as I could, and I must apologize that it wasn't sooner. I'm still up country. You know, I'm damned lucky I got your message. So sorry to hear about Chris, old man, so sorry. You must be in hell."

Even at a distance of hundreds of miles and with the fickle inconsistency of intervening copper cable, Brother Morris' voice came through like a healing salve to Des' ears, as if he alone possessed a post-hypnotic suggestion capable of relieving vast pain, stress and pressure.

"Tom, you can't imagine what it took to get a call through. In the end I had to get help from the…"

"State Police, I know. When they showed up at camp I knew something was terribly wrong, and I feared the worst."

"They didn't give you a hard time, did they?"

"Oh, no…" Tom recalled that when he saw the highway cruiser negotiating the muddy rutted drive to the lakeside camp he had guessed that the police were delivering news of an emergency or death; but he wouldn't admit how relieved he was when he learned that the deceased was not a member of his own family. "They were kind and courteous considering the circumstances. Offered to drive me to the general store in Patterson. One-way, mind you."

"Patterson? That's a long way from your place, isn't it"

"Well, yes, it's a good forty miles from everywhere. We were pretty much dug in at that point, you understand…I mean, if I was to go to Patterson, I might as well pack it up and go home."

"So where are you calling from?"

"Patterson; but I'm on my way home now, I just wanted to call and let you know that I got the message and I was on the road."

"You say you're on the road;…you're still with Bricky, aren't you?"

"Don't worry about it, Des. We worked it all out. I convinced Bricky to stay behind and to try and make a go of it up here. This story can wait until later, but I thought it would be best…"

"You don't understand, Tom. I need that boy here…**now**. Get Bricky and bring him with you if you're coming home." Des immediately regretted his tone of voice. After all, it was good of his old friend to take the trouble to check in and to express his condolences over the loss of Christine. They'd been close for all these, what, thirty years?

"You want me to go back up camp and get Bricky? For what? To bring him to the ah, to bring him to the funeral?"

The pain in Des' gut reasserted itself. He wished he could see his friend's face. As usual Tom was being generous and kind and patient to a fault.

"No, Tom, uh, yes, Tom. I'm sorry. I'm sure you understand. It's difficult right now. If you would, please make the extra effort and get your man…I'd think you could use the company on the ride down anyway."

In fact Tom Morris had been celebrating his final solution to the Bricky problem. The sole purpose behind planning the camping and hunting trip with his nephew was to have an opportunity to spend some time alone with the lad and to convince him to make a new life for himself up north, far away from the rest of the family. He also wanted to get him away from the law, from immigration authorities, and from Des Kelley, who, frankly, was not the best influence on him.

But this was no time to argue, no time to be stubborn, despite the fact that his conscience was still bothering him like the prick of a splinter. Why so guilty now? His nephew, the big Derryman, who was equal parts heart and brawn, had willingly acquiesced, and he had accepted the proposal as a challenge, with no more objection than a few careful questions. Thank heavens Bricky had been content to stay at camp, or it might have been necessary to implement his secondary plan, the one that called for simply leaving the gentle oaf behind, like an unwanted pet.

Sure it was inconvenient to have to return to the biker bar where he had left his nephew. The place was a miserable little tar-paper shack almost an hour's walk from the camp, but that was where they had parted because Bricky said that he wanted to start making friends right away. He began to imagine the awkward backpedaling it would take to get the boy to understand why all of a sudden it was in his best interest to defer his new destiny and return to Rossdale; but so be it. Penance came in many forms, and in order to return to righteousness he would fulfill them all.

Naturally, since Des had insisted, Tom would bring Bricky to see him; but afterwards, when his business was complete, it would be up to Des to find a way to bring Bricky back up to his new home in the woods.

"Sure, Des, I'll get...I'll bring him. Of course there's no way we'll be seeing you until tomorrow..."

"Tom...I'll be glad to see you whenever you get here. You don't know what I'm going through. It's not just Christine, God rest her soul, though I don't know what I'll do without her. It's...well, we'll talk when you arrive. Be careful on the road, now."

It was somewhat strange to feel relieved, when in fact Des' current affliction was caused as much by what was on his mind as by what was not on his mind.

On the one hand he should be consumed by grief and sorrow and remorse, for his wife had just died, and she had died horribly.

Jesus, Mary and Joseph! When I die...Please! he thought, *Not like that!* He should be trying to push away the dark horror of loneliness and pain by engaging in plans for the funeral, and plans for the arrival of his sons and family. But where all of that should be, all that was Chris and was now no more, there was only a void, like a mysterious room behind a door that hadn't been opened in ages. When he summoned his courage and strength in order to consider his situation and how he would handle facing Buck and Keiran, or how he would put his wife's affairs in order, he encountered the dark absence in his mind and it frightened him.

On the other hand he should be angry or worried or defensive or outraged or...what? He wasn't sure. Billy Storer had said that his youngest, Tweed, was a murderer, and that the police intended to arrest him on suspicion of connection with the deaths of Francis and Nilvan McManus.

But instead of furor and outrage and fatherly protectiveness, Des felt only confusion. His son, a murderer? Could it be true? Why would Tweed kill his girlfriend's brothers? Had they gotten into some kind of disagreement? These things happen; you never know. Maybe the boys didn't want Tweed marrying their sister. But violence never solved anything. Just look at the outcome. If what Billy said was true, then the boys came at Tweed armed for trouble and he gave them more than they bargained for.

More than they bargained for? Wait a moment...Tweed never killed anyone...Des knew who killed the McManus boys, didn't he? Again he felt confused. Look in one direction and the dark void deflected his gaze; and yet almost everything else was obscured by the haze of confusion. He was beginning to feel uncharacteristically hostile and withdrawn.

Was it any wonder he felt hostile, when his partner and ally AD Makepeace had called to say that Joe Toole's boy Tom was a poncy fag, as irrelevant a bit of news as any he ever heard; but he added that Tom was almost certainly the one who had blabbed about Bricky, helping to set Des up for the hit. Oh, yes, Makepeace was simply full of news. For he also claimed that Bricky had sold the guns that the McManus boys used in the attack. If any of this were true then things were more fucked up than he could have imagined.

He'd always thought Bricky was a good man. In his simple way he was a better man than his own son Tweed; and it was hard to believe that he'd do anything to hurt anybody.

It was true that he had been hiding in the US ever since friends had smuggled him out of Ireland. As a "terrorist", an "outlaw", and a "wanted man" he would never be able to show his face in the UK again. Regardless of the status of extradition treaties, he had to keep his nose cleaner than the average illegal alien.

But Des knew the actual circumstances of the incident in which Bricky had been implicated as a trigger man. It was the killing of an RUC constable, and Bricky was actually no more than an unfortunate fall guy. Not that he was an innocent bystander, by any means. As Des heard it, the mission had been planned meticulously, the target had been identified, and the members of the patrol were selected carefully. Bricky had his job to do, and he was faithfully prepared to execute his orders. But in the chaos of war, plans are like yarrow sticks that are shaken and tossed. A new pattern emerges, from which different tactical, operational decisions must be made. In this case Bricky, the wild goose, was disguised as a fox and then sent out to lead the dogs astray.

Thus the clever guerrilla commandos kept a killer free to strike again, the British plastered the wrong photograph on a thousand wanted posters, and Bricky became a man without a country, to be foisted upon ungrateful relatives one after the other on both sides of the ocean.

With the benefit of hindsight, Des wished that the information from Storer and Makepeace, no matter how disturbing, had come prior to his conversation with Tweed. Perhaps he might have succeeded better at holding his tongue; but then, if the accumulated wisdom of age and experience hadn't taught him anything then there was little reason to believe that the caution of friendly advice would have done the trick.

Heaven knows why he had lashed out at his son like that, especially after the boy had shared the most poignant, meaningful and devastating moment of his life when the two of them had watched his wife and Tweed's mother Christine die on her hospital bed.

But no, it was as if her departure had robbed him of his senses as well, for he had called his youngest son and he had accused him of being responsible for her death: "Tweed, you scoundrel, I thought you should know that last night the police came to the house and told us that you had been named as a suspect in a murder investigation. You, Tumbleweed Kelley...my son, are to be brought in for questioning, and you may very well be arrested, and held pending arraignment on charges. Now, I know you, boy, and as difficult as it is for me to believe these things the police are saying, to your mother they were the worst lies and defamation. She cried all night, swearing that she would do all she could, and making me swear to do all I could to set the record straight, to clear your name. In the end I'm afraid it was too much for her. Her pain, her illness, exhaustion, and now this- it was the straw, Taweed, the straw that broke her back."

Maybe he had been a little hard on the boy. What had he expected? That he'd come running over to beg forgiveness? That he'd say, "I've seen the error in my ways, Dad, and now that Mum is gone I know that you need me more than ever. From this moment forth you can depend on me." Hardly likely. He still had his woman and she needed him too. Between the lot of them they'd have to deal with a spate of funerals, and it was too much to expect that Tweed would be of much help in planning his mother's. But even if he had offended his son he was not one to take his words back, and he expected, no, he demanded that each of his boys pay due respect to the memory of their sainted mother. Or they'd have him to answer to.

But Tweed, damn him, had come right back and said, "So I'm the one who killed her, am I? All I can say to that, Dad, is something Mum used to say: 'Whenever you point your finger at someone else there's always three fingers pointing back at you.' So unless you want all those fingers pointing at you, then I'd keep my hands to myself if I were you." Oh, he was a pisser, that boy.

Still Des had not relented. "I'm just thinking of you, my boy, you and your lady LaGloria. I mean, she already lost her brothers, heaven help her. How would you feel if you made her suffer even more by ending up in jail?"

"The bet's still on," said he. "I have faith yet that the cops will find their man. Let's not kid ourselves. We both know I never hurt *anybody*." This last he had emphasized with dark undertones.

Who's kidding whom, kid? Billy Storer doesn't give a damn who he puts away for this thing as long as he gets credit for closing the case.

This was a time of mourning, not a time to allow tempers to rise. It wouldn't have done any good at all to tell the boy what Makepeace had said about him, although the words still rang in his ears. "Your boy's a drug dealer, Des, don't you get it? You call him a hustler! Well he hustles on the same streets your pal Storer claims to patrol, the same streets your buddy Dapper claims to represent. Just think of how it would reflect on you, old man, if folks learned that your son was the big pusher in town!"

Always the one to have a card up his sleeve, Makepeace had offered to keep the information quiet- for a price. But in exchange he said he'd see to it that when all was said and done Tweed would willingly come over to Des' side.

Sometimes when the shit gets deep you can just keep walking until it falls off your shoes, and you leave the stench behind. Other times you have to dig your way out, and the odor clings no matter what you do.

Dapper was putting pressure on Billy to wrap up the McManus murder case quickly because he claimed that the reputation of Arbs Park was suffering from negative publicity. The number of visitors would diminish, tourism would suffer, revenues would fall. Furthermore the press was painting the incident at White City as racially motivated and they were hinting at evidence of possible civil rights violations.

"This we don't need!" he had bellowed, and he had a point. If the projects remained in the spotlight then his new housing initiative would be stymied.

His shouting wasn't directed only at Billy, however, because he expected Des to chip in somehow. "This missing person thing is an embarrassment! I can't stress how important it is to find this guy LaRose, or whatever his name is. Been missing since the riot. Put the word out on the street. See if any of your people can help find him. Believe me, it'll help take some of the pressure off."

Well damned right he's missing...the stooges were looking for him first, and when they found him, they scared him away. No use explaining to Dapper, but sometimes a fellow just don't want to be found. Anyway, a guy with a lick of common sense wouldn't be back. But if the bastard was so blasted important, then alright, Des would do his duty and pass the word on to the boyos to look again.

For the life of him Des could not understand why the scuffle at the projects was being described as a racial incident, or a civil rights matter. You had the stooges, white fellows all of them, trying to talk to the one guy, also white, who might know something about Joe Atkinson's Buick, which, incidentally, was red. Alright, so things had gotten out of hand, as they will when tempers rise; and it was probably a mistake to have li'l Joe lead the stooges to find the fuck. It was five against one going in, not exactly fair odds, but that damned well shouldn't make it a federal case. And again, no matter how big or how tough or how old they are, when a couple of fellows square off for fisticuffs when does it become racially motivated? Not that he'd mind seeing the feds prosecute a civil rights case on behalf of a white guy for a change.

This fellow Keating was probably on a bender. And that guy Rose would turn up sooner or later, that is to say, if he wasn't already turning up daisies. But try to talk sense to Dapper and he turns into a bleeding fence post.

Trouble, trouble, trouble! And Des was the victim! The fact that he had survived an assassination attempt was somehow lost in all of this...this *nonsense.*

His son Tumbleweed was a *murderer,* or a *drug dealer..?* Bricky, apparently a *thief* and a *liar..?* Toole, a *queer,* had betrayed him, for what? His wife Christine, dead, *(Oh Lord, no!)* and him alone, insecure, irrelevant? Makepeace, an old friend, a valuable ally, or just another shark circling at the smell of blood? What would become of him?

He needed Brother Morris, he needed his sons Buck and Keiran, he needed a rest and some distance from the cynics and the controversy.

CHAPTER 42

The weekend was unbearable. It represented one of the predetermined delays anticipated in any given play by the rules of the game. There had been losses taken, and it was only proper to pause and bury the dead. The walking wounded would be among those attending the memorial services, out of respect for the fallen, out of respect for the game, and out of zealous determination to demonstrate that they would be prepared to rejoin the action whenever it should commence.

Of course no one, least of all Des Kelley, would have observed any linkage between the death of his wife Christine and the deaths of Francis and Nilvan McManus. No one in their right mind would have suggested that it was some kind of karmic retribution, or the curse of the Arbs or some cosmic payback that had caused his wife to die right after he himself had killed, but the effect was nonetheless the same.

Various forces were held in check for the duration of the weekend, and would remain so in fact, until the funerals of Mrs. Kelley and the unfortunate McManus boys had been concluded. For example, Detective Storer decided that the police could afford to wait and watch and work to further develop their case, given that their principle suspect was unlikely to leave town. Og's status remained frustratingly unchanged. And whether deterred by grief or confusion, Des was as yet keeping his dogs leashed as well. This awkward delay made the train of days seem painfully long and stifling, as if the brakes and the throttle were both engaged, and the wheels were motionless but screeching.

Yet in the midst of this malaise perc'ed the carnival like one of those annoying push and pop toddler's toys.

"For Chrissakes, Harris! Be a good man and stop over to the park and get them carny bastards to knock it off, will ya?"

Des was picking at the wart on his knee through the itchy black pant leg fabric. He had already complained at length about the relative comfort, or lack thereof, of the funeral home chairs.

"What, like how long do you mean, Des?" Harris knew before he finished speaking that he should have kept his mouth shut. No doubt Des' suit was a poor fit, and his collar was a bit tight to start with, but his features were getting darker by the moment.

"Use your judgment, man."

Harris had already been up to see Christine, and in his opinion she didn't look too bad. Not too flat like a cardboard cadaver, not too glossy like a wax pear. Of course she wasn't natural looking, but that was because Chris was a woman of a thousand looks and glares and glances, the soft and the fiery, the harsh and the sensitive. The spark had fled from those pitiless eyes, now closed forever.

In a similar way Des wasn't himself now either. His eyes were open but distant, and he looked as though there were a dark and fearful grip about his heart; his hair was yellowish, he needed a shave, and his tongue darted in and out in a vain attempt to moisten his lips. Harris wondered if recent events were taking too great a toll on his old friend.

"What I mean to say, Des, is, see, the wake and all that, well, no disrespect or anything, but, it'll all be over before the carnival is on its way."

"So? I don't give a damn! That's what I mean. Talk to them, be reasonable. Tell them what the situation is. Ask for some consideration. They're going to be here for a while. We're only talking the wakes, let's see, Sunday, the funeral, Monday, uh..."

"It's just that it's gonna be a matter of money, you know..."

A look of utter distaste came over his features now and Des seemed to sink in on himself. Harris hastily tried to recover.

"What I mean, see, is they come through here each year, right? And they pay for that field there. Now it's a municipal field, but it's Dapper's district, and way back when, well, I don't actually remember when, but see, he had *us* collect the rate on that property. We been doing it ever since. They're good about it, too, and usually come over and have a bash when they're ready to pack it in, so they throw some business to the bar, plus they give us all sorts of free crap from the fair. Now if I was to go and say, alright, now be nice fellows and shut down until further notice, well, you could imagine..."

He thought he sounded reasonable. An argument like that would usually cut it with the flinty Irishman. But Des was silent, still purple, still hunched over as if he were suffering from abdominal cramps. "Harris..." he started, at last, but he paused again.

"What is it, Des?"

"It was Joe's boy Tommy, Harris. It was Tommy that gave me away."

Harris could have rattled his gourd, so startled was he to hear the complete and sudden non-sequitur.

"What about Tommy? Did you say Tommy, my nephew Tommy, Des?"

"Yep." Suddenly Des straightened up and stared Harris full in the face. His eyes were flat and his expression dreadful. "Tommy did me in."

"Now, what do you mean by that? You say he gave you away? He did you in? What do you mean Des?" Harris was permitting anger to control his voice.

"I mean, old friend, that sweet Tommy Toole, that darling boy, sold me out. Why, I do not know. But I have it from reliable sources that **he was the one** who gave away the information about Bricky so those boys would know how to lure me out *to shoot me*. And what's more..." Now Des' voice was cracking with emotion, "I have also been told that he arranged the buy- he helped the McManus brothers buy the guns they used when they, you know, when they went for..." he nodded to complete the thought.

How could one describe Harris Toole at this moment? Beside himself? He was constrained by his presence at a wake for his old friend Christine Kelley, who had died far too young, unexpectedly, undeservedly; and by the presence of his friend Des Kelley, whom he admired and respected, and to whom he was, unfortunately, devoted. Yet Des had accused his nephew of betrayal and what else? His head was still whirling from trying to take it all in. But Des gave him another push so he'd have enough momentum to spin freely.

"The thing that gets me is that he's one of them fairies," he said rather loudly, "you know, the ones that only like other fellas. Now, how that plays into all this, I don't know, but the way I heard it is he knew about Bricky, of course, and somehow he met them brothers through his queer-boy connections." He shifted his voice again, down into the conspiratorial range. "Now what I want you to do Harris...Uh, are you with me, Harris?"

It was Harris' turn to turn colors. He had stopped looking at Des for he was looking for the door. The funeral home was crowded and he had been crammed into the same corner and perched on the edge of the same chair ever since he first arrived. It was time to get some fresh air, to stretch his legs and to stretch his eyes.

The old man appeared to have recovered some of his vigor, but before he could utter another word Harris unfolded himself and fled for the exit heedless of whether Des had opted to pursue him.

Like his own club on a good night, the mortuary was choked with people and cigarette smoke. Simply pushing through the crowd, Harris found that he was obliged to refuse offers of cigarettes.

He desperately needed space to move in and fresh air to breathe, and he held his breath until he was well clear of the building. Once outside he realized that the wake was being swamped by an overflow crowd, and that the line of visitors now stretched around the block. Standing in the parking lot in front of the Cedars of Lebanon Restaurant, he put his hands on his hips, surveyed the scene and whistled, impressed. Groups of people, polite, well behaved and well-dressed, were standing on the sidewalk self-consciously chatting and smoking and waiting for a signal from the ushers to advance to the final queue that was designated by velvet swag ropes.

Inside, from the other end of the reception line, Buck Kelley had witnessed the sudden departure of "Uncle Harris". He turned to Tweed.

"So, all these people; you must know who they are, I guess?"

"Fuck me! I'm beginning to think these idiots are at the wrong freakin' wake. Where are they all coming from, I wonder?"

Upon arriving Tweed had seen to it that he would stand as far as possible from his father. Guessing that the old man would be attended by his usual retinue of bodyguards, he thought that it made sense to stand with his brothers at one end of the casket, and to place Des and his crew at the other.

This was an early wake, and as expected, the full complement of friends and family had yet to arrive. To Tweed's right stood Keiran, dressed in somber Jesuit black and gray, holding a copy of the New Testament in one hand and a tangle of rosary beads wrapped around the other. Due to his prematurely thinning hair and the pair of reading glasses hanging from a chain around his neck, Keiran looked like a man in disguise, as if he felt it necessary to mourn and mingle incognito. In fact, Tweed had looked his brother over repeatedly, from head to foot, for a trace of recognition, some tell-tale give-away clue that proved that this man was indeed his brother. Buck, on the other hand, whom he had not expected to recognize, had over time taken on the spitting image of their paternal grandfather Emmett Kelley. To be more precise, he was a well-fed, somewhat jollier version of the famous late Boyle barman.

"So they're not friends of yours, I take it?" pressed Buck.

In response, Tweed shook his head and frowned, but Keiran answered, "You must understand, Buck, that Tweed doesn't have any friends. Only customers."

"That may be," replied Tweed, hurt to a certain degree by the comment but to a further degree by his brother's willingness to seize any opportunity to zing him. "But my customers are my friends..."

Tweed smiled and made a sign as if to toast Buck with an invisible glass. But Keiran persisted. "Yes, but there's a difference. Your so called friends only like you because you have something they need."

"I can relate to that," said Buck, softly. "Any barman could, but I think you'll find that all relationships are built upon some form of dynamic."

"At least I know where I stand with my customers, Keiran, and the fact is do have a lot of friends. Perhaps it would have been better if I had said a moment ago that my friends are my customers. I appreciate them for that but I also respect their decency and generosity; you know, like calling this weekend, taking a few minutes with me on the phone and trying to make me feel better?"

It sounded as if Tweed had lost his train of thought, but as he became upset and angry at his brother it dawned on him that he rarely saw his biological brothers, and when they were together they frequently fought. The people he saw every day, the *friends* who helped him through his problems and shared his joys, were also his *brothers*. People like Donal and Wayne and Mickey were more like real brothers than these strangers standing before him. And Keiran had the nerve to talk about his friends.

However, Buck's next question came as a surprise.

"Tell me, Tweed, what about Brendan? Is Dad still at odds with him? Last I heard it was becoming serious."

"I was wondering about that myself," added Keiran, suddenly calm and conciliatory. "Does Brendan put up much of a fight against the old man?"

Were they putting him on? On the one hand he had no idea that there was still a conflict until they mentioned it, and on the other he couldn't understand why it should interest them so.

"Does it really matter? I mean, who cares?" he replied, while avoiding their gazes.

"Well, sure it does! Doesn't it? Brendan stood up to the cranky old bastard..."

"Shhhh! He'll hear you!" shushed Keiran urgently.

"You have to understand what that meant to us, to me, anyway. Growing up...in his house... with nothing to look forward to but the glorious revolution..."

"Yeah," chuckled Keiran, derisively, "-the revolution of 1916. I tried to tell you back before I left home. The old man had plans for you, just like he had plans for each one of us growing up. He expected you to join 'the cause' like he did when he was young."

"Did you ever consider-"

"Joining him?" asked Buck. "No way. For one thing it's not about revolution, it's not even a matter of political ideology. Strip away all the Republican slogans, the songs and the rhetoric, the nationalist bullshit, and what you have left is a smuggler, a guy who makes his living running guns."

"A fanatical con artist..." added Keiran.

"All right, now," said Buck, attempting to maintain a level of civility in the discourse, an attempt thwarted somewhat by his overall resemblance to his father. "But you can see why Brendan posed such an appealing alternative to us. He showed that the life that Dad had planned for us, the life of the con-man, the exiled republican agitator, wasn't the only option available to us."

Shaking his head, Tweed had to decide if this was all for real. The story he had been told, or perhaps the story he had chosen to believe- was that his father needed help raising money for Irish relief efforts. He claimed that the funds he raised benefited those who had suffered losses due to the inequities of life under the yoke of Loyalist and British oppression in the north of Ireland. For as long as Tweed could remember the old man had talked about the lack of housing, employment, and health care; about the senseless casualties resulting from the Troubles; the shattered lives and broken homes, and the desperate need for Irish Americans to do all they could to help their brethren in the Emerald Isle.

Had he been so naïve? Or had he been preoccupied by his success in the drug business? Either way he had avoided the truth. In his eyes his father was an operator, a hustler like him, who kept his fingers in as many pots as possible, looking for a taste here or there, and a piece of the action. Besides, the old man seemed to have done alright without his help.

For both Buck and Keiran it was as if by learning more about Brendan's battles with Des they would come to understand more about themselves and their lives. They both identified adolescence as the key period in their lives, a time of turmoil during which they had made momentous decisions affecting their futures as well as their relationship to Des and their place in the family. And they had both run away, independently chasing their destinies, leaving Tweed- the last child at home- himself an adolescent pulled and pushed between separate and opposing adult males.

There was so much emotion in the room, being aired, displayed, bandied about, worn like ribbons, wrung out like sodden kerchiefs, that Tweed didn't even realize at first that his brothers were feeling sorry for him. Perhaps they were motivated by guilt, or regret, or simply love. Buck took his youngest brother by the arm and looked him in the eye. "I'm sorry, Tumbles, I should have been there for you instead of moving back to Ireland. It must have been hell going it alone. At least I had Mack, and you and Keiran, and..." for the first time since arriving tears brimmed his eyes, "...Mum, God rest her soul. She was like a buffer between us and Dad sometimes when the shite really started flying." He smiled again.

Keiran seemed to think that he had abandoned Tweed as well, and that by selfishly seeking peace with the Lord, he had consigned his younger, defenseless brother to a life of probable cruelty, exploitation and loneliness.

"You were the one, bro, you could have been something. Something more than a dealer, that is." From the tone of his voice he might have substituted the word leper for dealer and lost none of the emotional force of his statement. "Everyone expected you to go to college, to become a lawyer or a teacher, a professional...something great. But when we abandoned you, what chance could you have?"

Of course Tweed didn't remember it like that, but, having no reason to doubt his brothers' sincerity, he began to see a twist of logic and truth in their assertions. Maybe things would have been different for him if they had lived at home, if they had maintained the hierarchy that had been established when they were little.

"Do you remember that time, Keiran, when you got so mad at me that you punched a hole in the wall?"

"Me? I punched a hole?"

"Yes! In the bedroom! Right over my head! You were so mad and you were going to wail me in the face, but instead you wheeled back and, -wham! Put your fist through the plaster instead. 'Course I got the message, anyway. I mean, seeing what you did to the wall..."

For the first time this weekend, Tweed saw his brother smile.

"Yes, I do remember! That's right! And, Oh, Jeez! Dad sure was pissed. 'Who put the blasted hole in the plaster?' he roared. Oh, my..." The three brothers laughed together.

"No, I haven't heard what his latest complaint is. And, although I hate to admit it, the truth is that I haven't spoken to Brendan in years."

Their silence spoke as loudly as a gasp, but although they were clearly surprised and disappointed both Buck and Keiran refrained from pushing Tweed too hard on the subject. This was a difficult place in which to hold an intimate conversation. For far too long the brothers had been neglecting the reception line, simply nodding at their guests instead of acknowledging or greeting them properly.

"I hear it's about the flowers-" hissed Keiran, and Tweed, who realized how blind he could be sometimes, suddenly noticed the variety and abundance of flowers in wreaths, garlands, planters, vases, and plain bunches. Once he became aware of the flowers he wondered why no one had considered the simple expedience of removing some of them in order to gain space and comfort for those attending the wake. Tweed had no idea how such matters were decided. Having chosen not to contribute to the funeral preparations, he was willing to abide by the decisions others had made.

As he thought about it he realized intuitively that even in the best of circumstances the business of burying a loved one had to be most difficult for any grieving family member to endure. Any number of peripheral issues may intensify the inherent pain and anxiety of a process for which most people are not adequately prepared. In lieu of specific instructions left by the deceased, it is up to the survivors to make all the funeral preparations and arrangements. Hopefully they do so with respect and dignity, though they may lack sufficient time for thoughtful consideration, and despite the fact that their judgment may be impaired by their emotions. Tweed sneaked a peek at his father.

Little did he know that Des had no idea what he wanted in a funeral, or how best to send his wife off, as it were. Aside from choosing the burial plots, something Des and Christine had done together with some alacrity not long after their friend JC Byrne had died; he had only to select a mortician. And there was really no choice when it came to morticians, because John Sweeney of Sweeney's Funeral Parlor was an old and trusted friend. When he first arrived in the US, following family who had settled in the area, he was taken under the wing of local 'boss' Des Kelley, who had encouraged him to hang his shingle in Rossdale. Thus Des earned the gratitude of another Irishman, businessman and lifelong occasional customer of the biz club.

When Des visited John's office at the funeral parlor late Saturday, he was in rough shape, emotionally drawn and visibly discomposed. If there was any other way...to settle these matters by proxy, or to wait until he was in a better frame of mind. But some things must be dealt with in their time, and the task was his alone.

He had waved off conversation, then slowly strolled through the showroom, and with a nod had made his selection of a casket.

"Do your best, John," was all he had said.

Flowers were an afterthought, if he had thought of them at all.

However there was another individual, Brendan Tighe, who had magnanimously honored the memory of the woman he loved with flowers, having no say in the disposition of her remains, or in the selection of the vessel that would help to preserve them, or the location of their final resting place. Unable to participate directly in some ways, Brendan had acted independently and indirectly in others.

Tweed may have questioned dedicating so much space to flowers when there was an urgent need to accommodate more guests. But in fact, after filling the allotted area with Brendan's gift, the funeral director had stopped accepting flowers altogether, ordering that all subsequent deliveries and donations should be routed to the Kelley home instead or placed in cool storage.

For his part Brendan thought he acted with the purest motives. Little did he know that by cleaning out the stock of Rossie's two largest competing florists, he had caused a great deal of grief and hostility for other customers, by forcing them to pay a premium for special delivery mail-order flowers.

Flowers alone were not the cause of Des' hostility, however, for Brendan had also arranged for a private organist at the chapel, as well as a chamber ensemble; and he had invited dignitaries of various ranks and stripes to attend the funeral. He did not do this out of a desire to clash with his old friend Des Kelley, for he saw these matters as trivial. On the contrary, he assumed that they both shared a depth of heartache over Christine's passing.

Looking through the blurry gaze of grief and anguish, Des saw Brendan's deeds as an opponent's grandstanding. It was frustrating to have him buzzing around and practically running the show, when Brother Morris would have things well in hand, once he arrived, that is. Who was the foolish Jesuit trying to impress? Didn't he understand? Christine was dead.

Yet his irrational anger toward Brendan was another stark example of his increasing isolation. Christine was gone, and unless Makepeace could work a miracle, Tweed was slipping away. Billy Storer no longer trusted him, Harris had bolted on him, and it was beginning to look as though everyone he knew was choosing sides.

Only a week ago he had been in complete control. The attempt on his life had changed that. It had been a failure, he had survived, he had prevailed, but he was somehow weaker for the ordeal.

Makepeace had gone so far as to say that it was a mistake to kill the boys who had tried to kill him. Had he hit the nail on the head? Was that truly the source of his weakness? If he had displayed weakness in killing his assailants, then, conversely, by merely wounding and interrogating them would he have shown strength? Des shook his head and groaned, and his comrades Pat Devaney and Tom Connolly drew near to lend an arm.

Nothing one can do about the past.

As if he was reading his thoughts, Tom, the pasty stiff on his right, leaned over and said, "Des, I hear that the McManus shindig is being held right across the street at Blevins'."

This he acknowledged wordlessly. End of story; enough said.

But if everything had gone wrong when he failed to ask questions, then it was time to get on the right track and start interrogating people. First off Tommy Toole. Surely he'd tell old uncle Des whatever it was he'd felt so free to discuss with Frankie McManus.

Next, of course, would be Bricky. Come clean, Brick, my boy; old Des is your father confessor.

Rather convenient to have everybody assembled in one place like this. Simon and Joe would be by later, and Harris had nipped out for a bit, but there were quite a few of the good old bar boys from the north shore,...and the south shore. Des scanned the room. Uh,huh. Woody, the Devaneys, plus reps from the bull labor gangs. You have to know where the muscle is when you're preparing to put the arm on a fellow like Bricky.

If strength was to be had by asking the right questions, then he might as well go the Iron man route and also question LaGloria McManus herself. Between the three of them, Tommy, Bricky and LaGloria, he was sure to turn up something to help satisfy his curiosity.

Ever since his wife died Des had asked himself some questions as well, starting as soon as he arrived in the confessional. Upon leaving the hospital he had longed for the peace and safety of the church and the inner sanctum of the booth. But once inside he had deviated from the normal ritualistic recitation of sins, and had engaged in a one-sided dialogue, virtually ignoring the priest.

"What do I want after this situation is resolved? Christine is dead. She left me young and she left me first, and that wasn't supposed to happen. Sure, once or twice over the dinner table we discussed the unthinkable notion of *my* untimely departure, which, at the time had seemed the more natural probability. Instead, Christine is gone and I can't help feeling that she was taken as punishment for my sins."

Here the patient padre had interceded, saying that she had her own soul to account for, that she might have died anyway, and there was nothing Des could do to change that.

Des admitted that might be true, but he added, "You see, Father, I feel no sense of shame for having killed the cowardly McManus kid. Simply add murder to the list of my sins. I've killed before. Who knows? Perhaps I'll kill again."

It had taken some explaining to bypass the priest's blatant antipathy. And although he had sought out the priest and the confessional, he was in no mood to put his feelings into words. What he did say sounded almost like provocation.

"I no longer question the divine wisdom that grants my continued existence on earth, when other souls, surely more deserving in their own right, have been denied that privilege or had it revoked."

To someone of Des' limited grasp such questions threatened to expose either a certain cosmic pointlessness, or at the very least a lack of fair play.

Indeed the parish priest would not be drawn off topic. This "penitent" had entered the confessional claiming to have murdered, and promising to kill again. Perhaps it was important to point out that there was no revolving door on the enclosure.

"Eh, well, setting the matter of mortality aside, let me ask you this: What is it that you want?"

"That's a good question. After all this time as a husband and the head of a household, I'm back to fending for himself again. I have to understand how that will affect my life."

Who was he kidding?

"Have you ever had to fend for yourself before?"

"Truthfully, no. But I do want to survive well into old age."

That was it precisely. He wanted to live; to live in the manner to which he had become accustomed. Perhaps all he really wanted was longevity.

He had left the confessional unsure of whether or not he had achieved absolution.

Meanwhile, at Sweeney's, Makepeace had stopped in to pay his respects. Freshly shaved but otherwise nondescript, he was dressed neatly in a dark suit that looked as though it had been borrowed or stolen. Whether it was the suit, the shave or the setting, Makepeace seemed ill at ease as if he would much rather be somewhere else. After his cursory viewing, he tarried next to his old partner for a moment, hoping to arrange a meeting for later. Des on the contrary wanted to talk now.

"Did you know, 80, that Ireland is on the rise economically? I hear that Irishmen everywhere are sensing the change; they smell prosperity in the wind. They're making their way back home, you know. For some reason the younger generation of Irish these days seem willing to abide or ignore a certain level of violence. They'll accept a stalemate in the political situation in the north, as if all they have to do is wait for the rising tide to float all boats."

"You want to go home, too, Des, is that it?"

Kelley felt a pang. He realized that yes, he too wanted to live out his days back in the land of his birth, in his hometown, close to his son and his family. "Lord knows there's nothing to stop me," he replied. "I've had enough of playing at man of the world, with secret missions and parallel roles. What a life I've led, with one foot in America, the other foot in Ireland, but never at home in either place. I just have to ask myself, is there anything for me here in Rossie anymore? The house is virtually empty now that the boys are all grown up and moved away..."

Unlike Dapper Ferguson, Des wasn't ready to retire, despite the fact that he hadn't managed any spectacular arms runs recently and had no plans for the traditional Beltaine trip.

He did have plans for right now, however, and the thought of them got his blood moving. He pulled him comrades into a huddle.

As much as has been said and revealed about the man it may still come as a surprise that he could lose interest in his wife's wake and instead pursue notions of personal ego and revenge.

Admittedly, it is only possible to go so far in understanding another man's motives or rationale, but in Des' case it was clear that he thought he acted as much on his late wife's behalf as on his own. To some it may appear unseemly that a middle-aged man would scheme and implement plans of abduction, and clandestine interrogation, and that he would actually contemplate bodily injury to others for the means of coercion, all while observing the niceties of a civil ceremony. Funeral rites or no, Des was obsessed by his own brush with mortality, and the closer he came to understanding why he had been threatened, the more relentless became his pursuit.

Perhaps someone else in his position might have proceeded with more caution. It's only natural to keep one's head down after someone has tried to blow it off with loaded weapons. Maybe natural for any other conventional businessman or professional, but Des was an arms smuggler, and he believed that those who live by the gun shall die by the gun.

He figured to warm up to the subject at hand, and to prepare the men first before asking what it was he wanted of them.

"I'm this close to determining if the threat to my life was in fact connected to my work," he began, pinching his thumb and forefinger together as if to indicate a gap the size of a dime between them. Des was referring to his career in arms smuggling, but the disparity between his gesture and his meaning was as wide as it was vague. "For this moment of truth and clarity I can only thank the efficient detective work of my old friend and associate, AD Makepeace here." His principle contact for weapons. "When I see the results of relying upon Makepeace I know my judgment has been proven to be sound. To think I might have been foolhardy and trusted only Billy Storer and his sidekick to solve the case…"

Unaware that Des and his men had been anywhere near the scene of the crime, the hardest working detectives in the municipal precinct had demonstrated the extent of their work ethic by promising to more or less arbitrarily label the McManus murder incident an open-and-shut case. Lacking witnesses, proof, or direct evidence linking a suspect or suspects to the crime, they still anticipated a prompt announcement of indictments.

Almost writhing in discomfort now from social exposure, Makepeace made excuses and wormed his way out of the home. Looking back, he saw the gang gathered around Des like a street corner a capella group preparing a serenade. Before leaving the room however, he took care to examine Tweed Kelley for a moment, noting the difference between him and his older brothers. It wasn't just a matter of age and appearance but the air of independence and self confidence that set Tweed apart. He could be a tough nut to crack.

With hardly more than a nod for the departing hero, Des continued speaking for the benefit of Pat Devaney, Tom Connolly, Woody and a few other close friends and colleagues.

"Billy and his pal would simply gather whatever circumstantial evidence they had obtained and throw it at the first unfortunate perp they could find who lacked an alibi, and see if they could make it stick." Des was livid. "I do the same thing when I'm cooking pasta, you know, throw it to see if it sticks, al dente. But they aren't cooking spaghetti, they're doing police work, and if the victim of this pathetic police scam had been anyone but my own son Tumbleweed, they might have made it stick and gotten away with it!"

After an appropriate pause to allow for murmuring among his cohorts, Des went on. "Doesn't Billy understand that I need my son? I need Tumbleweed just as I needed all of my boys, but one by one they turned their backs on me. Why?"

The men had never known Des to be completely candid. His honesty, though touching and compelling, also left them feeling uncomfortable. And yet they turned as a unit to stare at the younger men at the foot of the coffin, who were unaware that they were being discussed. Des continued, typically blunt and enigmatic.

"How is it that the same opportunity I leaped at when I was their age seems so repugnant to them? Was the example I provided so inadequate? Call me what you may, at least I'm a man of action, heart, and conviction. Are they not the least bit proud of their old man?"

Tom Connolly had removed a handkerchief from his pocket and was dabbing his eyes with it.

"If I had the chance to raise the boys over again, what could I do differently to persuade them to follow the righteous path I illuminated, while still permitting them the right to choose? I tell you, It's not enough to earn respect if they won't follow you."

Even now, at the time of their mother's death, when he expected a little reconciliation, they were hardly inclined to cut him any slack.

CHAPTER 43

"Holy shit, Uncle Tom, look at all the people! What do you think is going on?" Bricky stared out the passenger window of Brother Morris' LTD Crown Vic station wagon with the enthusiasm of a child gazing at a storefront full of puppies.

"Mrs. Kelley's wake, my boy, that's my guess."

Brother Morris was correct for the most part, but if he were to randomly stop and ask passersby why they were out on the streets or where they were going he might be surprised at the variety of responses. On a balmy spring evening folks needed little encouragement to take a stroll.

"I thought all the shops were closed on account of it was Sunday so it didn't make sense to see so many out..."

Not all businesses were closed. Blevins and Sweeneys would be open for some hours yet; the carnival was aiming to surpass all previous attendance and revenue records for the Rossdale spring weekend; and as a result, the nearby Crullers and Coffee chain cafe was doing as much business on Sunday night as it usually did on Sunday morning.

By now the coffee shop had become a terminal node on one leg of an extended relay route. People who were temporarily tired of the rides and the rip-offs stopped there for refreshment and then proceeded toward the square to expend some of their newly-gained energy. After breezing through and rounding the three cardinal points of the square, they would return to the ballpark again, drawn by the bright lights and pounding music. The addition of these pedestrians to the funeral home visitors and the standard weekend sidewalk traffic created the impression of throngs that had wowed Bricky.

"Well, it's interesting..." began Master Morris. "You know, in many respects Rossdale is no more than a way-station, a pass-through point, a depot; even to the folks who live here."

Inwardly Bricky groaned. As far as he was concerned his pedantic uncle was putting the needle back down to continue a drone that he had begun at dawn the moment after he started the car, when they had left the wilds of the far north woods. Didn't he ever tire of spouting so many lectures and so much bullshit?

"The way the town itself is situated: just one in a row of towns that formed along the principle north-south route leading to the city. The rail lines also cut the town into three distinct demographic sections."

"What do you mean?"

"Well, the wealthy live in their enclaves, the middle class workers own their quarter-acre subdivisions, and the poor folk live in the projects and the triple deckers. Where was I? Oh, yes. If you ask the people around here what they like about their town, more often than not they'll say something like, 'It's so close to major highways,' or, 'Only five minutes to Westbury Circle',"

"So? What's wrong with that?" asked Bricky, more bored than genuinely interested.

"There's nothing wrong with it, son, it's just that instead of loving the town for its own merits they love it for its proximity to other places. This merely explains why the place seems so busy and looks different. I mean, we've driven through quite a few small towns during our trip and after seeing so many you start to draw comparisons."

The lot at Sweeney's was full and all of the adjacent on-street parking spaces were occupied so Morris opted to pull his car directly into the lot and drive straight toward the mortuary.

"Kinda hoping I could leave it here," he said, slowly nosing the wagon into the alley abutting the funeral home.

Sweeney usually kept his hearses parked there, however now there was only a green International Travelall with the rear door opened. The interior of the vehicle was dark but there were clearly men inside and others standing by the side doors of the truck.

"Guess they work for Sweeney," mumbled Morris as he turned off the motor. He was first out of the car, but his nephew Bricky was delayed, as he was busily relacing his boots which he had removed somewhere along the road.

With a stretch the elder gentlemen shook off some of the miles and then wearily he approached the men in the truck that stood between him and the door to the mortuary.

There was something unsettling about the way the strangers appraised him. One of them challenged, "You Morris?"

The not altogether unfriendly tone reminded him of an experience he had during a recent visit to Israel. At Ben Gurion Airport, everyone from the attendants to the guards had employed that same cold and efficient tone of voice, sometimes underscored with a machine gun.

"Yes, what's going on?" he replied, concerned.

"Kelley sent us out to meetcha, perfessor. Go on in, the 7 o'clock's already started."

Morris looked doubtfully at his car, then to the side entrance to the funeral home, then at the man who had greeted him.

Bricky, his shoes tied, hair combed, eyes rubbed, had stepped from the car and he was examining his appearance in a crouch at the passenger door mirror.

"You're fine!" shouted Morris, "Come on, lad!"

"This your nephew, Bricky, right?"

Nervously now, "Ah, yes, and who might *you* be?"

"Oh, I'm sorry, Brother Morris, I'm Woody, a friend of Mr. Kelley. You guys might as well head on in. We'll wait here."

Bricky nodded at the crew with a courteous smile as he passed, and Morris shrugged and followed him into the home, grateful for the company.

Sweeney's Funeral Home. *Why didn't this place look familiar?* The floor was covered in dark blue indoor-outdoor carpeting, the walls were decorated with vertical white wooden wainscotting below deep red faux burnished stone finished plaster. Columns in the doorways, pedestals in the halls, massive cast-iron radiators in the viewing rooms concealed behind art-deco ornamental metal screens that had probably been installed back in the 1920s. Other elements of period architecture, style and décor were evident in the late Victorian town house as well, such as the gas fixture nipples that were still in place on the walls and ceilings, although they were no longer functional. The escutcheon in the center of the ceiling for example. It may have supported a large chandelier in the days when this grand home served the living with far more style and comfort than it now served the dead.

Having attended a seemingly endless procession of wakes and funerals of friends, relatives and colleagues over the last few years, Brother Morris thought he must have been in this funeral home before.

But when he failed to recognize the interior of the mortuary, he felt as though he were at a slight disadvantage; and although it was possible that he had been away in the woods too long, the mood of the place also struck him as inappropriate. With three wakes in progress and a full capacity crowd in attendance, the teeming halls and rooms full of earnest, fine folk all turned out in their Sunday best reminded him of intermission at a community playhouse. It was a sense of a spectacle in progress, an all-ages show distinctly lacking the somber formality that should rightfully have accompanied such an occasion. The facility was equipped to handle four wakes concurrently, however this evening only three of the four rooms were 'booked', and of those, the Kelley party was clearly the busiest and most boisterous.

Even more bothersome to Brother Morris was the notion that there was some flaw in the character of the Irish that ensured that every wake would commence with a modicum of dignity and end up in a shambles. Combining death and drink and melodrama, and lacking restraint, Irish-American mourners concocted a recipe for a metamorphosis. They bottled their response to tragedy and reserved it like the distilled spirits in which they placed so much stock and faith, and to which some ultimately commended their souls. All too often he had witnessed wakes where the mourners, unmanned by grief and forsaking sobriety in favor a communal celebration of the final sacrament, had abandoned the facade of quiet control and lost themselves to the passion of sorrow.

Pushing past a huddle of young ladies whose singular lack of consideration appalled him, for they had chosen the doorway as the site for an impromptu conversation, Brother Morris finally caught sight of Des Kelley. Then, as if to confirm his observation, Bricky muttered, "There's the poor bastard!" hoarsely over his shoulder. Bricky had been following at a respectful distance, trying all at once not to get lost in the crowd, and to preen and tweak his appearance. With almost obsessive and cyclical regularity his hands made the circuit of his clothing, tugging at his sleeves, checking the buttons on his shirt, pushing into his pockets and adjusting his scrotum, fingering his belt and hitching his pants. Shoving a meaty arm out as if to brush a fly from his uncle's collar, he suddenly waved and called out to Des, trying to catch his attention.

Now Morris felt the urge to check his laces, or anything to avoid the embarrassment forced upon him by his uncouth nephew. Nevertheless in moments he found himself clapped in Des' effusive embrace.

"Ah! It's good to see you..." Des appeared to be overcome with emotion as he wiped a tear from his eye. "...But the stench offaya! It's making my eyes water, so it is. What, did you stop to put out a forest fire or something?"

Oh, of course! Morris had hardly noticed the odor since he had been living with it for days. Despite the abundance of fresh air in the mountains, the traces of campfire smoke that had permeated and saturated his clothing had yet to dispel. He had showered and changed prior to leaving the campsite, but Bricky, who had not been given adequate time to prepare for his journey, still reeked.

"My apologies, dear friend, that's a bit of burnt balsam."

"Eh? Incense, you say?"

"Heh, heh, after a fashion, yes...I don't mean burnt offerings..."

"Uncle's been sitting too close to the camp fire, if you know what I mean."

"Bricky," Des nodded directly, scarcely acknowledging the satisfaction he felt at seeing the bruiser standing in front of him.

"Des," he replied. "So sorry about your loss. Mrs. Kelley will be missed."

"Thanks Bricky; but do me a favor, stand down-wind, will ya? Or better yet, be a good lad and skip over to the club and get yourself cleaned up. If you recall, the place is within spitting distance, and you'll be back here in a jiffy. Go out back there and tell Woody I said you was to go to the club to wash up. He'll take care of you. Now be a good lad." He smiled as weakly as his delight would allow, trying to be all the more persuasive with a touch of patent paternalism.

But when Bricky responded with a knowing nod, his expression of profound understanding bridged the gap between them, banishing whatever pleasure Des might have taken from the moment.

"Sure, Des, I'll clean up over there and I'll be back before you know it." The big man tipped half a salute to his uncle as well before turning to leave.

"What, did you install a shower or something, Des? I didn't know you could wash…" Brother Morris abruptly stopped speaking as Des squeezed his arm like a belligerent blood pressure cuff.

"Let him go," he growled lowly, and he bore the questioning look of his older friend in silence.

Almost instinctively, Brother Morris blessed himself with the sign of the cross.

CHAPTER 44

"Ooh my my LaGloria! You are...! I think your name says it all girl! La- gloria! That look is so right! Where did you get it?"

As hostess of a modest memorial service held in honor of her slain brothers Nilvan and Francis, LaGloria was ushering the last guests out of Blevins Funeral Home. Tommy Toole was among the last to leave, and as one of her closest and dearest friends he naturally intended to remain at her side ready to assist her in any way.

Dressed in a soft buckskin sport coat over a blue chamois western shirt with black string tie, jeans and burgundy cordovan loafers, Tommy was stretching the casual formal designation to a tasteful degree. LaGloria, by comparison, defied not only the arbitrary assignment of stylistic genre, but also the legitimacy that society bestowed upon a given fashion or dress. Her appearance suggested that upon getting dressed prior to the event this evening, LaGloria had deliberately chosen items of clothing calculated to offset the uniform of conformity. Her ensemble was a poke in the eye of convention. But in fact her dress was no more than the result of a fortuitous combination of ingredients; for example, the availability of certain items in the laundry rotation, plus her shrewd eye, and her knack for assemblage. Above all else, it was a reflection of her desire to please. For she was certain that her father would expect her to deck herself out as dark as a moonless night. So when she selected the black long sleeve fishnet t-shirt, and the black leather mini-skirt, the black silk stockings, the black ankle boots, black leather gloves and the black brocade bustier, she was simply adhering to an inner hint that black was best.

"I'll tell you one thing," she admitted, "I didn't get it from a magazine."

"Yeah, I hear you. So that didn't go too badly, huh? I mean, you came through all right. Good to see so many people turn out. I didn't know your brothers had so many friends."

LaGloria smiled as if she knew that her friend was kidding.

"It was OK. Even the old man seemed, uh, impressed. But anyway the hard part is still ahead. Now I gotta head over and check in at Tweed's mother's wake."

"At Sweeney's right? What's so hard about that?"

"Well, it's just that I'll have to see that old bastard Des Kelley. You know, I'll go in to pay my respects and he'll be there lording it over everybody and I hate that."

"Tweed will be there, won't he?"

"Yeah, but he's with his brothers and he has to stand in a reception line like at a freakin' wedding or something."

"Tell you what, honey, I'll go with you. My brother and my father are probably there too. Anyway, believe it or not, Mrs. Kelley was my godmother."

"Your godmother? No shit?" LaGloria entertained herself with a brief image of a benevolent matriarch bestowing magical favors and granting wishes. "I appreciate the company, but you don't have to..."

"Oh, never mind- Let's go!" And Tommy Toole offered LaGloria his arm.

It was only about a hundred yards from Blevins to Sweeneys, door to door, and the only reason the walk took longer than a couple of minutes was because LaGloria wanted to go the long way around. By striking out at an oblique angle and then coming at Sweeneys by way of the Cedars' alley, she avoided another scene with her father, who was waiting for a cab at the sidewalk.

Rossie's least likely couple walked on in a stately promenade unimpeded but also seemingly out of season. They had left one funeral service with the grave intention of attending another; and that was only fitting given that a reasonable passerby might think upon seeing them that they were six months late for a Halloween party.

And yet while they walked exhibiting no sense of threat or urgency, others scurried all around them as if they inhabited separate zones in which time flowed at different rates.

Feeling somewhat melancholy, but full of love and admiration for the woman whose brilliance with the pornographic photo shoot layout was legendary, Tommy was practically oblivious to the energies and activities that were at that moment being expended on his behalf.

As soon as his uncle Harris had learned that Des suspected Tommy of betrayal, he had gone into action. First, he had called Joe, his older brother, who was Tommy's father, and one of Des' most loyal friends. Of course the telephone itself imposed restrictions on their freedom of speech.

"Joe- listen, it's time we figured out how we're going to handle this situation with Des."

"Don't worry, Harris, we're dealing with it; we got it under control. Why, what's bothering you?"

"Well, when something like this, this incident the other night comes up, the first thing to do is to make sure that everybody is telling the same story, right? You know, singing the same song?"

"Yeah, so? We did that…"

"Then you gotta make sure that you know who you can depend on…you gotta know who your friends are."

"I'm with you…"

"Well, see, Des tells me that your boy Tommy is a rat. He says that Tommy was the one who sold him out. Now, you know what that means."

This next moment of silence on the telephone would be telling and decisive. More or less the same series of images flashed through the minds of both brothers. Unfortunate Tommy, dragged roughly through a beating and an interrogation, then perhaps another beating, or worse, a swift execution.

"Sure, Harris. It means that Des is an idiot."

Joe loved his son and Harris sure was proud of him. The Toole brothers had good reason to be protective of Tommy. The kid worked hard and kept his nose clean, and he was the first Toole in a generation to earn a college degree. Practically put himself through college working at a prestigious downtown insurance firm. Since graduating from school he'd supported himself and he currently leased an apartment in one of the units his uncle Harris owned in town.

Harris had seen the look in Des' eyes, and he knew that there would be no reasoning with the man. He'd expect blind, impartial, obedient loyalty. For his part, Joe knew from the moment Harris called him that they were working against the clock. Everyone was planning to attend Christine Kelley's wake, so in order to defuse this thing promptly there would be an extra advantage in taking a proactive approach. They'd need help from Dan, and from Simon Fecteau, and from anyone else who would have time to hear them out.

Unfortunately, neither Harris nor Joe were the greatest motivational speakers; rather they were aggressive loud-mouths, better suited to defending their own views. Unless they could get the word out before the wake they'd have to openly defy Des so as to encourage the others to do so as well. Joe couldn't picture the scenario going over without also imagining mass confusion ensuing among his colleagues; and despite the fact that he knew in his bones that Des would call for Tommy to be, for lack of a better word, "debriefed", it was simply bad form to question a man's judgment when he was preparing to bury his wife.

But for fuck's sake! Christine herself had often cared for the kids when they were little, and she was Tommy's godmother! Des was a queer old duck though, and he'd probably jack up his own mother if he thought she'd betrayed him. He'd often made the point himself that a threat to any member of an organization was a threat to the organization as a whole. If any of them sold out then they were all sold out.

Evening had darkened the delta of streets that made up Rossdale square, but the gloom would not enshroud the sidewalks and alleys for long, as the municipal power grid switched over to PM mode and the ghastly halide street lamps automatically awakened to bathe the town in the amber glow of their gaze. Groups of pedestrians, walking briskly, laughing loudly, appeared greenish all of a sudden, and as their eyes adjusted to the unnatural blaze of light they saw the square in black and teal.

Woody's group, with all of the friendly intent of a witch-dunking party, had strolled across the green and into the alley that separated the biz club from the neighboring bistro out back. Bricky accompanied them, not questioning the need to have an additional three large men show him the way to the club; complacently permitting himself to be led although he knew the square well and could have found the club in the dark, blind drunk.

It was funny how ever since he arrived in the States he had a dual impression of the people and what he called 'the situation.' Sticking mostly to his own kind, immigrant Irish, he had seen young women with good educations, as frustrated by the job market here as they had been back home; and young men who after finding work as laborers, also started taking cynicism and despair and alcoholism home with their weekly paychecks. When these immigrants became settled in the States they realized that in exchange for their crack at the American dream they they had lost some of their souls.

Here was a nation that cherished nothing of heritage, or of generation, nothing of lasting value; and coming from a land steeped in history and tradition and lore it was difficult to make the transition. Furthermore, in order to thrive they were forced to accept compromises that were especially hard for people raised in the church. In fact, Bricky's conclusion was that it was almost impossible to be a virtuous American. Spirited out of Ireland in a scheme to protect a 'RA man, Bricky was no longer free to make his own way in the world, but rather his fortune was tied to the generosity of people like Des Kelley, who could open doors and provide employment. But Des, damn him, was one of them corrupt Americanized Irishmen who can't see the forest for the trees.

As he walked with Des' gang toward the RBC, Bricky thought, "Well, I may not be *free* to live here, but Des Kelley doesn't *deserve* to live here. And I may not be free to live back home, but I hope they never let him go back there either."

Less than a quarter of a mile away, walking almost directly toward Bricky from the opposite direction, Tommy Toole and LaGloria McManus arrived at Sweeney's Funeral Home for the wake of Christine Kelley.

Just inside the foyer, an elderly gentleman, whom they otherwise might have ignored, accosted them as they passed.

"LaGloria? Is that you, my dear, LaGloria McManus?"

Although his name had not been mentioned, Tommy took more notice of the man than did his escort. Upon entering a busy establishment LaGloria tended to adopt an icebreaker mode and she forged ahead with the steely prow of her mien, in this instance busting up masses of mourners frozen in knots of conversation. Eddies formed in her wake, as people spun off to form new conversational orbits.

JEFF MOYLAN

Tommy was nervous and he would have welcomed the assistance of some authority figure, even an usher or a maitre d'hotel. Perhaps this guy was a funeral home version.

"Do we have to check in or something?" he asked shyly.

Brother Morris was still following LaGloria's progress with his eyes as if he merely wished to ensure that she selected the correct viewing room.

"Eh, what's that, son?" He glanced quickly at Tommy, and then double-dipped for a more thorough inspection.

"I'm here with Miss McManus..." began Tommy, his slight effeminate lisp coming across like nails on a chalkboard to the conservative sensibilities of the elder educator, "...and to pay my respects to my god-mother, the late Mrs. Kelley."

The schoolmaster's arched eyebrows, rigid body posture, and tone of righteous indignation were leveled by the slightest ripple of empathy.

"Ah, I see, my boy," he said, placing a large, warm hand upon Tommy's shoulder. "Let's go in, shall we?"

Lacking any clue as to his guide's identity, Tommy now felt less comfortable and secure than he had upon entering. He would have preferred not to have been noted, not to have drawn attention to himself. But the old dude was pushing him down the hall as if he was going to enter the room and announce, "The godson of the late Mrs. Kelley!"

Tommy's mouth went dry.

The viewing room was considerably less crowded than it was when the entire network of pub colleagues had been standing vigil with Des. As Brother Morris brought his guest into the room, Des' attention was immediately fixed upon the young man, and a gleam like the reflection of a bonfire blazed in his eyes.

By no means an introvert, Tommy nevertheless had no desire to receive undue attention. There should only be one attraction at a wake. The quicker he could get out of there the better. Somewhat fortunately for him, LaGloria was causing a stir as she greeted her prospective brothers-in-law. Des turned to gaze disapprovingly in her direction and Tommy felt as though the heat had been turned off.

"I tried to stop her, Des..." started Brother Morris, just as Des erupted.

"Good Lord, young lady! You're not parading in here like that! Jesus, Mary and Joseph!"

Suddenly Tommy understood why LaGloria's arrival was igniting such outrage. It was her appearance. The ensemble she wore, that had looked so appealingly appropriate, so extemporaneously suitable at her brother's wake, looked tawdry, vulgar and meretricious here. He felt an urge to check his fly, and was doubly aware of the weight of Brother Morris' hand upon his shoulder.

At first it didn't look as if LaGloria would dignify Des' comment with a response. After disengaging from Tweed's embrace, and deflecting one of Keiran's weakly cast barbs, she was standing at arm's length in front of Buck. He too was appraising her attire, but he did so in the manner of a beaming father, pirouetting his little girl so could fawn over and admire her. Buck's heart was large and unafflicted by the malignant roots and deconstructive veins that had gradually eroded his father's judgment and sentiment. However, having rushed halfway across the globe to be at his father's side for this tragic event, Buck was caught up in a heady rush created partially by the jet lag, and partially by the acuteness and breadth of emotions he experienced as a result of his mother's death. Yet another factor contributing to his whirlwind high was his delightful sense of freedom, which was brought on by the mere fact of being off on his own for the first time in years. The pub, his wife and child, and all of his debts and responsibilities awaited his return in Boyle. And though he loved his wife and missed his child and his home and his pub and his customers, he also felt an indescribable thrill being back in the US. And now, with gorgeous LaGloria twirling in front of him, he was getting horny as well. He winked and said,

"Tell the old fool he can-" but thought better of continuing.

560

LaGloria nodded, smiling, and walked slowly along the casket. As she did so she solemnly traced a cross on her forehead with her right thumb and then crossed her lips and breast. Stepping forward she bowed slightly, again placed two fingers to her forehead, and swept them downward in an arc, then left, and right, and she turned to face the deceased.

"Dja hear me, LaGloria!…" Des was speechless with anger. Brother Morris was there to support him, but at this moment he was unsure of how to proceed. As much he objected to the young lady's dress, she had at least had shown good manners and a lick of Catholic piety. Tommy ducked out and away from Morris' grasp, and proceeded to greet the Kelley brothers. As he flexed his shoulders he felt the fabric of his shirt clinging to his skin where the old man's hand had been. A chill ran down his spine. Now he could look forward to the obligatory condolences, the hand shaking and awkward commiseration, but then he was out of there. He had no desire to be part of the agony this family seemed to be in, especially since he wasn't sure if it was all related to Mrs. Kelley's passing.

He glanced only briefly at the prepared cadaver of Mrs. Kelley, but the image brought to mind a flood of memories. LaGloria had paused, presumably to meditate silently, so Tommy stepped past her and summoned up his courage to greet Des Kelley.

"Sir, I don't know if you remember this, but uh, I have fond memories myself of the times when Mrs. Kelley used to come around and cut my hair when I was a kid."

Des' bloodshot eyes offered no response.

"Guess she probably did all the kids back then. But I looked forward to it. She was good, you know, like a pro. Knew I liked the green lollipops."

"Did she now?" Des grunted, still staring.

"Ah, anything I can do for you, sir, you know…well, good night."

"There is something, Tommy. There is something you can do."

Tommy froze, suddenly regretting his blithe offer.

"You can talk to me, son. You can tell me a thing or two."

He faced the widower with wonder in his eyes, "Talk, sir?"

Now everyone in the room was intent upon Des' words, for his tone of voice sounded all at once accusatory and bitter, sarcastic and resentful. But LaGloria seemed to snap out of her devotion, and she walked over and placed herself bodily between Des and Tommy, looked the old man in the eye and said, "So you'd call on our Savior and the protection of his blessed mother and father, would you? You'd use their names as if you were calling out the favorites at the dog track. How about my brothers? Did they pray before they died? Did they ask for Jesus and Mary to save them?"

Des was stunned. A word may have been in his throat, or on the tip of his tongue, but it got no further than that. He would have been well served at that moment by a hearty slap on the back. Indeed, his sons knew him well enough to see the color deepen in his face while he sought in inner turmoil for a response to this outrageous challenge. It was as if he was flailing through a blinding brain storm.

At last he choked, "How the hell should I know?"

But LaGloria stood her ground, now appraising the shaken Irishman for signs of weakness. She knew that she had managed to claim the high ground in this skirmish regardless of his reaction to her clothing, so there would be no sense in frittering away her advantage. She took Tommy by the arm and walked him out of the funeral parlor.

Tweed remained only long enough to take his leave politely, and then he followed like a jilted lover.

CHAPTER 45

"You want a hand with that padlock, Woody? Your hands are trembling a bit. You must be needing a pint. Is that what you're after in the chest there?"

Bricky's congenial grin and easy tone of voice contrasted with the grim impassive mugs of his escorts. All of the men were grand specimens; broad, big boned, hale and hearty. Crowded among them inside the little plywood shed that housed the walk-in chest in the rear of the biz club, Bricky was like the petunia in the radish patch.

"So, you fellows are the hard guys, eh? Des' enforcers, right?" Bricky didn't wait for a response. Still grinning amiably, he went on. "I did some of that type of work before I came over here. Never suited me, 'specially when you usually know the fellows whose teeth you're bashing. 'S like, 'Eh, mate, how's your sister? Well, seeing how you're going to be laid up for awhile, what with these broken kneecaps and all, she's likely to visit…So what say ya' tell her I was asking after her?'…"

"C'mon, Bricky," replied Woody, self-consciously. He pulled off a dingy gray tam to reveal a hippie's mass of tousled auburn locks.

"Knock it off, will you? We'll just go in the chest and have ourselves a chat." The walk from the wake had left roses in his cheeks that offset the sparkling blue of his eyes. He wore a blue zippered windbreaker with the sleeves pushed up to expose his arms, and the collar was turned up as well. Though he clearly needed a shave his beard was so fair that along with his freckles and his flush his face fairly glowed.

"I thought as much." said Bricky. "The old chilly chat, eh?" He placed a hand upon Woody's arm as if to say, 'Hold up a moment,' and suddenly the others drew up close to deflect the perceived threat.

Seeing their reaction, Bricky chuckled.

"You know, from the moment I grabbed those guns I knew something like this was going to happen."

"Guns?" asked Woody, his eyes rapidly contacting Pat's and then Tom's.

"Oh, to be sure, to be sure," said Bricky, "But even then, I told myself…'Bricky,' I says, 'You should know better than to bite the hand that feeds you; you should know better than to get in trouble, than to do something that will come back to *bite you in the arse* someday,' And today is the day, heaven help us. But let me tell you something. It's no use going into the cooler with all them kegs of beer. I mean, *fuck*, I'll tell you whatever it is that Des told you to get from me, but let's at least be civilized and sit inside like gentlemen, shall we?" He pointed to the rear door of the biz club.

"Instead of freezing our bottoms on them kegs, let's empty one or two, and I'll tell you the whole story. What's more, you can tell Des that yuz took me into the cooler and frosted me backside, and I'll back you up. You know,'*Whatever you do, Des, just don't put me into that beer chest again!*' Do we have a deal?"

Here the absence of Harris Toole and Simon Fecteau was starting to be most acutely perceived. Des had not yet lost the support of his most loyal supporters, but the bonds that united the inner circle were weakening. Each member of the group had been satisfied to share in the benefits of friendship and collaboration, and each had taken profit from their association. However the recent misadventure on behalf of Des Kelley had led some of them to become involved in murder. Then while attempting to protect themselves and minimize any further threat, they had either incited or had been otherwise responsible for related incidents of kidnapping, rioting, arson, and vandalism. It was no wonder that they were now less willing to take any action that could lead to further liability or prosecution. And yet it was undoubtedly true that if Harris had been there, then Bricky's interrogation would never have devolved into a friendly chat over a pint. They never would have fallen for Bricky's corny rabbit-in-the-briar-patch routine. The fact was that the fellows Des assigned to interrogate Bricky were all second-stringers, so to speak.

But guys like Woody had bars and territories of their own, and reputations to uphold. Personally, Woody looked upon this favor for Des as an opportunity to stretch his muscles, and to put into practice some of the techniques he had long admired in friends and foes in his own neck of the woods. He was fundamentally a businessman, but Woody also had a perverse streak, and he craved the kind of action that he read about in the novels of Robert Parker and James Lee Burke. He thought that by opening his bar he had provided a venue for the action he desired, but if it didn't come to him, he was willing to go and find it. He was casual in dealing with the boyish man-mountain, expressing the indifference of an inveterate brawler who had on occasions single-handedly faced and defeated multiple opponents at a time. In retrospect, if Woody could be faulted for anything, it was for failing to give Bricky his due.

Likewise Pat Devaney simply was not prepared for Bricky; and considering the extenuating facts and circumstances, it was clear that for Pat at least, this was a 'wrong place, wrong time' scenario.

Again, he was a big, wide, nose tackle of a guy who was often called upon to perform feats of strength and stamina. Off the charts for height and weight since he left the womb, Pat generally remained good-natured about helping out, and as he matured he too looked forward to earning a premium for the advantages that nature had bestowed upon him. The Devaney boys were a handsome lot and Pat was no exception, all dark hair and dimples, but he was insecure about his looks, especially after a couple of years on the varsity football team, during which some of his best features had been rearranged.

A position in the family business, *Devaney Brothers Moving & Storage -since 1902*, was guaranteed, yet he had no desire to follow his equally massive brothers into a career of throwing weight around. He was saved from that fate, however. When Pat was just 19, during one particularly busy day of grunt work, he and his brothers were taking a break at a local watering hole and the bartender in the joint fatefully suggested, "You guys spend so much money on beer you should open up your own bar..."

Within eighteen months, Pat took him up on that idea, when the opportunity to purchase The Brew and Bard (then the Knot Hole) virtually fell into his lap.

For Pat it wasn't simply a matter of leaving the piano-moving to his brothers, or of making money on beer instead of losing it. Rather, he saw the bar providing a means to secure two objectives. The first was gaining access to power. He was certain that a bar with tasteful décor, well-trained wait staff and meticulously selected stock would attract the elite and the powerful in his community. Thus he would strive to form relationships and associations of mutual benefit, a la Des Kelley. Secondly, he desired to level the social playing field. If an uneducated former high-school athlete like himself could manage a first-class establishment patronized by local real estate developers and town counsels and engineers and doctors and architects and judges and businessmen, then he'd achieve a new paradigm marked by a new common denominator.

It wasn't easy to leave the Bard on a Sunday night, but he had driven the many miles from the south shore compelled by the memory of Christine Kelley and respect for Des. Then, just about the time he was ready to return, Des had thrown the evening wide open, offering a bit of spice and an element of thrill. He had claimed that his pal Morris had found the guy who arranged the notorious failed hit on him. In all sincerity he had asked Pat and Woody and Tom Connolly to see what they could get out of this guy; if they were up to it, that is. All three of them had promptly agreed to take a crack at it. They were each familiar with the biz club from the many meetings they had attended there in the past.

In Pat's opinion, the Rossdale Businessman's Club was a dump. Unlike the Bard, or the Geese, it had no basement, or store rooms, and indeed, the walk-in chest was an auxiliary unit tacked onto the building in the rear alley. Growing impatient, he was grateful to see that Woody had agreed with Bricky and had given up on the 'chilly chat' plan.

Pale, taciturn Tom Connolly was also relieved to see Woody putting away the keys. The guys always brought Tom along when the push came to the shove, for he was the one known and certified killer among them. In the darkness of their hearts others may have wished to experience the satisfaction of utter dominance that they imagined must accompany the theft of another's final breath. They may have envisioned the kind of victory ensured by the willful cessation of another's heartbeat. But Tom, having witnessed the final moments of a number of friends and enemies alike, knew death for what it was: the absence of life, the irrevocable and final abyss.

Perhaps at 12 years of age he had not been too young for his first exposure. By that age many youngsters have already lost beloved pets and some have attended the funerals of grandparents or other elderly relatives. But in the summer of his thirteenth year, death claimed two of his siblings and two of his friends in a brutal car wreck which he alone survived. Sitting between his brothers in the front seat, he was both fortunate to have been protected by their torn and shattered bodies, and traumatized to have been soaked in their blood.

His older brother had been driving too fast, trying to impress the carload of younger kids with a foolish maneuver, when he'd lost control of his full-sized Ford sedan before flipping and rolling it. The last Tom saw of big brother Al was his disembodied head rolling around the floorboards in a sticky slick of blood. Only when rescue crews arrived were they able to free his brother Paul's hand from Tom's knee, where it remained gripped tightly and painfully although Paul himself had been largely eviscerated. The friends in the back seat, boys of 12 and 14, were both ejected from the vehicle and killed instantly.

Nobody would lay any blame or fault with Tom for his part in the accident. After recuperating from his injuries he had enough difficulty convincing himself that he deserved to live although God had chosen to baptize him anew in the blood of innocents.

However at 16, Tom was again to encounter death, again as a result of a supposed accident. On this occasion neither death nor Tom himself were so easily convinced of his lack of culpability. After school one day a class mate had asked him to hold a knife for him "for safe-keeping". Word was going around that the classmate was going to be jumped by rivals, and although he carried a knife for protection, he didn't wish to be tempted to use it. Blond Tom, quiet and serious, would be the sensible choice as a neutral guardian for the weapon.

Sure enough, not long after Tom agreed to take possession of the knife, a gang of kids surrounded and attacked Tom's friend, and before long Tom could see that his friend was getting the worst of it. Who knows what he would have done if he were unarmed, or if he were alone, but in the event Tom drew the knife and stabbed first one and then another of his friend's assailants. One victim survived a punctured lung, the other died on an emergency room operating table after massive blood loss from multiple stab wounds.

Nutshell profiles should be walnut, as opposed to coconut sized, but it may be worthwhile adding another note about Tom. At age 18, he was supposedly mugged while waiting for a train at one of the downtown elevated commuter rail platforms. In order to protect himself, Tom had allegedly thrust his attacker away from him- onto the tracks, into the path of the oncoming train, and in any event, onto the highly charged third rail.

Slow to correlate what may have been glaring real-life examples of pathological behavior, the municipal criminal justice system seemingly ignored Tom's history and permitted him to return to a fairly unregulated routine by the time he turned 21.

On the streets again with a rep, a rap sheet and a black cloud hanging over him worse than Joe Btfsplk's, Tom was a wretched societal pariah until he discovered that he could utilize his notoriety to some effect. Putting in with the then infamous Sunset Hill gang, he found that he could earn a profitable degree of respect among colleagues and clients alike. Of course, depending upon how one looks at the record, the history of the Sunset Hill gang can be read in two ways. It was either a story of one of the most prolific, profitable and persistent criminal enterprises in the city, or a story of remarkably successful infiltration by state police, leading to the eventual break up and dissolution of organized crime in the vicinity.

Shrewd observers may note that Des Kelley became interested in the district not long after the gang apparatus was apparently dismantled, and various members, leaders and personalities went to prison, or were driven underground.

Des sensed a power vacuum when the city cleaned up the old Sunset Hill. He watched while they tore down blocks of the old neighborhoods and erected a new development which was officially renamed Crystal Pond Park. The focus of his interest was the Tavern, the gang's old haunt, still standing on the principle hillside avenue in town. By the time Crystal Park was opened, the area around the Tavern was no longer commercially viable, and it would be many years, successive economic cycles and demographic shifts before it rebounded. In the meantime Des needed a character to run his satellite facility, his dive away from home, and Tom Connolly came highly recommended. Actually, the primary factor in Tom's favor was that the musclebound scrub was already living in the bar, having determined to squat there and await the return of the gang.

As an entity the gang never did rematerialize, but various and sundry members did return from time to time, drifting in to crash, to drink, to borrow cash, to reminisce, to sow paranoia, to get laid. The closest Tom came to the inclusive experience he had with Sunset Hill was with Des' CAFE group, and the regional and district meetings that were held in various venues, including his. Sometimes they met for the purpose of rallying support, or for raising money, sometimes to increase awareness of, or to deal with an issue. Other times the members met for crisis management, and on those occasions the group utilized more of a cell structure.

Over the years a number of items it seemed had been added to the unofficial book of rules that held the group together, and chief among these was: Don't provide a target. Des Kelley never claimed a title because by not claiming the presidency of the group he was less likely to be criticized or commended for his actions. He did not wish to provide a handle by which someone might manipulate or undermine the legitimacy of the organization.

Likewise, all of Des' associates believed that they were granted a certain amount of leeway and immunity as long the actions they undertook together were covered under the rubric of a group resolution.

On a shelf in the biz club Harris Toole used to keep an old Gibley's gin bottle containing the foulest concoction of bathtub moonshine, and occasionally a patron would ask for a shot. Neither the bottle nor the label did anything to improve the flavor or aroma of Harris' throat varnish, yet due to the simple subliminal appeal of a well known trademark, the liquid was slowly consumed. So did the members of Des' CAFE alliance perform deeds ranging from bribery to larceny to extortion and worse because they felt they were protected in a sense by a patchwork of promises, of favors owed and exchanged, and of loyalties sworn and proven. When they united in common cause, the result wasn't shared responsibility, but shared disavowal of responsibility.

CHAPTER 46

Upon leaving the wake Tweed piled Tommy and LaGloria into his car and quickly drove out of the square. Like fleas they would be away before the sting of their presence was felt. Somehow his mother's funeral seemed rushed. She died early the day before, so Saturday was essentially a day of shock and preparations, then Sunday was a day of mourning and wakes. Early on Monday would be the burial. Meanwhile his father was chasing folks away from paying their last respects. If he had ever dared imagine this day, he wouldn't have pictured it like this.

Furthermore this was shaping up to be a long night. Already he'd been forced to blow off the so-called Wizards, his top-notch dope-peddling squad. They had left Blevins after the service for Frankie and Nilvan and then before continuing on to the wake at Sweeney's, they had taken a brief detour to a secluded spot on Taft Hill Court where they stoked up a ritual bone circle. They flared up one joint for each of them: Kuhn, Bone, Eban and Sharlae. After an additional joint in honor of the departed, it was no longer a matter of summoning the courage or the will to enter Sweeney's, it was a matter of overcoming inertia. They finally drifted toward the Kelley wake just in time to see Tweed and company leaving, so Tweed hastily made arrangements to meet with them later in the evening. He also recommended, contrary to his own natural inclinations, that they drop the idea of going into Sweeney's, for he could scarcely imagine his father's reaction at seeing a group of stoners bringing up the rear of the viewing line.

Confident that his Saab could hop up Mt Hope hill easily even loaded, he had taken the back route heading toward Tommy's Met Ave condo. Now that his formal obligations were concluded for the day he could look forward to a long night of special errands as well as business as usual. As he drove he felt he owed Tommy an apology, but while he struggled to find the words he was surprised to hear his guest offer one instead.

"Sorry, guys, I didn't mean to put you to any trouble!" said Tommy from his perch on the center of the back seat of the 99.

In response LaGloria had instantly spun around in her chair and looked at him through the loop in her headrest. "Don't apologize! We should apologize to you!"

"No shit," agreed Tweed from the driver's seat, "You go to a wake, you don't expect it to turn into a mad scene."

"Don't say that. Hey, I thought they did a real nice job on your mother. She looked peaceful."

"Yeah, I thought she looked sweet," added LaGloria. "I always liked your mother. Must be hard to make her look peaceful, I mean, how's she spose'ta get any rest with old man Kelly ranting and raving all over the place. Sorry, Love, no offense."

"You're right. He would have to make a scene. Two minutes and he starts roaring."

"So he didn't like what I was wearing," pouted LaGloria, "He'd complain no matter what!"

"Yeah, well, that's just it, was it what you wore…" looking over, Tweed noticed that LaGloria's lovely legs were luminous through the sheen of her stockings.

"Well, he was mad at me, too," said Tommy, nervously.

"Nah, he just said…"

"He said he wanted to talk…I'm so sorry!"

"Stop apologizing! We got you involved in this and we'll get you out of it! As a matter of fact, you should just forget about it."

"Oh, c'mon, Tweed, your father saying he just wants to talk to you is like Professor Toru Tanaka saying he just wants to give you a hug."

"LaGloria! Tommy doesn't have to talk to anyone! Tommy, listen man, just in case, why dontcha lie low for little while, like, at least for tonight? You know, hang out at a friend's house? Meanwhile, I'll clear things up with the old man, alright?"

He liked Tommy and had known him since White City, but the guy had none of the street-smarts of someone like say, Rick Rose. Come to think of it, he still didn't know what had happened to that guy. He told himself that he should probably visit the projects before the night was through.

"Yeah, alright," answered Tommy. "But tell you what- you can still drop me off at my place and I'll make arrangements from there."

"Are you sure?"

"Absolutely. You said you were going to fix things, so go do it!"

"Cool. We'll see you tomorrow at the funeral, but I just want to remind you that you have nothing to worry about. Remember- your father and mine are best friends." Easy to say, but he could picture one of his father's sleazball cronies knocking on Tommy's door late at night, looking for answers.

So the old man wanted Tommy to talk. What could he tell him? About LaGloria and gay porn? Anything he knew didn't matter anyway, Tweed told himself. LaGloria had used the guy to promote her scheme to destroy his father, and now they had to ensure that he remained an unwitting participant in that scheme. In any event, they had to remind themselves that Des was the bad guy. He was the murderer! Who gives a fuck what Tommy might have said to LaGloria, or what LaGloria might have said to Tommy? Fucking Des Kelley was walking around as if he couldn't hurt a soul. He was presiding over his wife's funeral and acting as if he was trying to figure out what everyone was so bummed out about.

For that reason Tweed had no incentive to criticize his girlfriend for taunting Des at the wake. Anyone who overheard their exchange must have wondered if LaGloria was accusing the old man of killing her brothers. How could her words be interpreted otherwise?

He and LaGloria had agreed not to push matters until after the funerals. Only then would they implement their plan, which was to implicate Makepeace. So Tweed held his peace when he left LaGloria at their apartment. He simply told her, "Babe, I'm gonna head out for a while and take care of a few things. You better take it easy and I'll be home in a few."

She complained until he mentioned the gun. He had tried to casually slip it into a list of unrelated items, but she picked it out and refused to let it go.

"Man...I still have to see Donal...it's gonna be a long night so I think I'll grab a hit of mesc before I leave...and I have to pop in to see Sharlae, and Donal's still got that .357 so I thought I'd snag it while I was there...plus I have to get together with Bone and..."

"Right! I want that gun!"

"Uh, hold on, babe..."

"You said you were going to get the .357!"

"Yes, I'll take it off Donal's hands..."

"Excellent! I'll feel much better with that gun around the house."

Tweed knew better than to argue about the fact that they had no permit for the gun, and it was no use claiming that a gun made the house a more dangerous place. In LaGloria's mind the .357 had already become important and sexy and meaningful. The snubnose python- a purse accessory every woman should possess.

The eve of his mother's funeral was becoming busier by the moment. When he arrived at home there was another piece of paper waiting for him in addition to the segment of blotter containing the mescaline. Makepeace had left a note demanding a late night meeting as well.

Alright, so he was meeting with Donal and Wayne for general business reasons and also to discuss his predicament vis-a-vis Og, and vis-a-vis the old man. Normally he wouldn't mention the matter of Og to his closest mentors and advisors, but in this case the guy represented a challenge.

When Tweed was coming up and making a name for himself he had put a number of other dealers out of business. Now that he was established there was no way that he would permit anyone to shake him down, threaten his business or his well-being in any way without suffering consequences. There was still ample reason to make an example of the Ogs in the world.

It was understandable that Og might bear a grudge against Tweed, for in his twisted reverse rationale he must have thought, "there but for the grace of God go I..." No matter what Tweed had done to ensure the success of all, Og merely saw him as an obstacle to his personal wealth and happiness. He wanted a bigger piece of the pie, but he was going to have to stay hungry. To be fair, Tweed had already given Og a chance. Come Monday, Tweed might hear him out, but he wasn't going to give him any satisfaction. The reality was that if Tweed hadn't seen another way to make use of Og, he never would have given him the time of day.

Sharlae would have a part to play in Og's destruction, so Tweed had to meet with her in order to discuss the scheme in detail. It was a big responsibility for the little woman, but she would be handling even greater burdens soon enough.

Then there was Bone, whose desire for greater profit and power was exceeded only by his fear of change. Like Og he would never stray far from home, but unlike Og, he was loyal to a fault. His role picked up where Sharlae's left off. Later tonight Tweed would have to spell it all out for Bone as well, if only to make sure that he understood the implications of seeing his dream come true.

Since his brothers Buck and Keiran were in town, Tweed also had an invitation to spend some time with either or both of them this evening. And he had an obligation to at least call his father as well and tell him to lay off, in order to fulfill his promise to Tommy Toole. And yet he didn't think he could handle an unstructured get-together with his brothers. God willing, they would have other opportunities to see and speak with each other, opportunities that weren't occasioned by death or misfortune.

In lieu of a call to the old man, well, perhaps he might get all he needed out of a conversation with Makepeace, instead.

Looking at his father and the company he kept, Tweed realized that BroMo was his father's opposite; he was the ethical and just man Des wanted to be; whereas Joe Toole and Simon Fecteau were people with whom he shared certain characteristics; they were his faithful buddies and sounding boards. However this fellow Makepeace was more of a shadow to Des, who was, despite his stridency, himself a man of shades of gray.

CHAPTER 47

For all of his vaunted appreciation of the towns that made up and connected the cities along the coast, Brother Morris was cursing Rossdale under his breath for the lack of a pay phone. When he slipped out of the funeral home in order to call Joe Toole, he had expected to find a phone convenient to the building. But upon trotting his fat arse out to the street corner he discovered that there wasn't a pay phone within sight, and when he stopped a party of young folks and asked them, they confirmed that he would have to walk some distance to reach the nearest one. He might have believed them if they didn't smell so heavily of marijuana masked poorly with tobacco, but he suspected they had indeed told him the truth when he walked almost a quarter of a mile before encountering a phone. And the one he finally found was not enclosed in a booth, so he was forced to contend with the ear-splitting noise of a nearby carnival as he made his call.

"Joe! This is Morris, remember me? Des Kelley introduced us. Well listen, I had to call and tell you that I think your boy Tommy is in some danger. Now don't get upset, but this is…yes, yes, how did you know? No; you understand I was just with Des, and he was saying some pretty strong things, things I imagine he'll later regret, but nevertheless…At the wake, at Sweeney's. Right. I honestly think you should skip it. Take care of your boy, instead. No, I'm telling you that he wanted someone to go out and bring Tommy back for questioning. I met the lad; fine lad. Personally, I've never heard the man speak this way before, and I don't mind telling you it sent a chill up my spine. I just thought I should get to you as soon as possible. Des shouldn't be threatening to…especially before his wife's burial…I mean, I can't imagine…Sure thing; you're welcome, Joe, God love you."

Fine, he had followed his conscience and betrayed Des, but now he had to wonder about Bricky. Des had sent him to get cleaned up at the club, but surely he should have been back by now. The trouble was that lacking his nephew's familiarity with the square, Morris would have little chance of finding the club on his own, and he was not keen on asking Des for directions. It was about time to wrap up the visiting hours anyway. Returning from the pay phone he noticed that the town was more normally quiet. Now the only lines at Sweeney's were the ones formed by cars leaving the parking lot.

Morris wondered who other than Des remained inside, and that question formed the basis for a plan. He determined to return to the wake and to round up as many of Des' cronies as he could find and suggest that they take the poor old sod out for drinks, somewhere away from Rossie. Perhaps if Des were distracted, then his apparent hostility toward Joe's son Tommy and Tweed's girl LaGloria would dissipate somewhat.

First he would have to get over his newfound fear of the man. He had expected that his dear friend would be melancholy, or reflective, or reverent, but to see him seething in anger, and storming over the casket of his dead wife, "Someone go out and bring me that feckin' faggot! I'll teach him respect for his elders! Thinks he can sell me like he sells his own pansy ass does he? Well fook'm. Maybe he'll feel like talking when we've got a blade against his balls. It's either spill his guts or feel a slug burning a hole in his guts, his choice."

When someone had objected that he was Joe's son, Des had practically exploded. "I don't give a shite if he's the only son of God Almighty!" he'd shouted before launching another scathing slander on the boy's dress, morals and personal habits. In response, Brother Morris, a mature man whose distinguished career had included military service in two wars, almost fainted.

Yet there was room in his heart for whatever weakness or foibles his poor friend might display during this time of adversity. Lord knows, Des had suffered in his time: leaving his home so young, losing his son so early, now losing his wife so soon. He responded with an indomitable desire to face an unjust and inequitable world, especially in regard to the British oppression in Northern Ireland. However, Morris suspected that some of Des' schemes were little more than confidence rackets, and that his dreams were no more than the delusions of a fundamentally dishonest man clinging to a bankrupt ideology.

Now his only difficulty was maintaining his composure and his overall attitude so that Des wouldn't suspect him of ulterior motives. He found it easier in that regard to address the remaining guests as a group, rather than approaching Des directly.

When he saw that indeed many individuals had chosen to follow Des out of the mortuary at the conclusion of the wake, Morris cleared his throat and called out. "What say we treat Mr. Kelley to a round of drinks? Those of you who don't have to be anyplace else, perhaps you can stick around and keep Des company this evening. Let's remind him that he never has to be alone."

Various cheers of approval and agreement seconded the motion, and Des was in no position to object. Wise Brother Morris added one important qualification. "Alright, then. Who can suggest a fine establishment? It won't do any good to go to the same place Des goes to every day- nothing against *the club*, Des…but you know what I mean."

Woody was presently preoccupied or he surely would have recommended the Wild Geese, and likewise Pat was not available to suggest the Brew and Bard. However, Morris had come up with a pretext to veto any of the CAFE affiliated clubs, had they been proposed.

The city may not have been cosmopolitan, but it certainly boasted more than its share of taps, taverns, restaurants, hotels and the like, and although the hours of operation were curtailed somewhat due to the day of the week, the availability of drink was not.

All that remained was to explain to Des that his core collaborators, Simon, Harris and Joe would meet up with the group later; and to figure out how to get to wherever it was they were going. So it happened that due to the simple expediency of relocating the whole lot of sympathetic drinkers to a place that met Morris' criteria, the Silver Shamrock was chosen as the designated site for the soirée. Brother Morris had no idea where the place was or who owned it, Des wasn't informed until they had arrived, and other than the one who suggested it, nobody else could give a damn.

Needless to say they could have made a better choice. Yet mysteriously, Des appeared unfazed. Apparently fortified by the contents of a hip flask he had been secretly osculating, he walked into the warm and welcoming White City bar hardly aware of his surroundings.

"That wasn't much of a ride," said the puzzled Morris as he disembarked from the same green Travelall he had seen earlier when it was parked at Sweeney's.

"Shortest distance between two points," replied the driver, a member of the Cu's Pub contingent. No reason to take the scenic route. He had simply loaded up the truck and driven the few short streets to the Shamrock.

His comment only confused Morris all the more. Had they not even left Rossdale?

Successive makeovers had worked a glamour over the facade of the Silver Shamrock. Recently installed copper cladding wrapped the roof in broad vertical strips that were supposed to have weathered to a gaia-green. Instead the metal glowed in the artificial light of the street lamps, and the riveted panels reflected odd highlights just as Abe Lincoln's cheekbones might catch the sun on a burnished penny. Despite his misgivings upon appraising the place, Morris entered, behind all the rest.

Not bad. A small room that hugged the sidewalk possessively, peering over it through two large picture windows that were abuzz with fluorescent beer signs. Clean, old-world, charming. The bartender could have been at home at any Irish-American bar from here to Brooklyn. However, looking more closely at the man, Morris saw that he probably would not have have fit in behind a genuine Irish bar in say, Dublin or Galway. And it wasn't merely his raised-in-Rossie inflection.

Myles Brennan had the closing shift tonight, but since it was Sunday he didn't mind. And it looked like tonight was going to be a treat.

Over the past couple of years he'd been skeptical as he watched the new owners of the Shamrock try to pull a pub out of their asses. Growing up in White City, he'd seen the old bar change hands countless times, and he also knew that if anyone was going to make a going concern out of the dive, they'd have to play the game and pay for the privilege.

This play and pay scheme seemed to have been orchestrated by none other than Dapper Ferguson, Rossdale's rep on the municipal council. Dapper's seat in the bar was warmer than his seat on the council however, and he was occupying it at the moment when Des Kelley and his group arrived.

Myles had been earning extra cash by feeding info about Dapper to the state police task force investigating corruption in the White City Corridor. It was his job as a rat fink to relay whatever items that he might pick up or overhear; a job made somewhat easier by Dapper's frequent visits to the Shamrock. Then more recently, the cops also added Dapper's associate, local Rossdale "businessman" Des Kelley as a focus of their investigation; but Myles unfortunately had only limited and indirect access to Kelley.

Now all of a sudden Des Kelley walked into his bar! Dapper Ferguson and Des Kelley were both in one place! And liquor was involved. He wondered if he should casually sidle on down to the pay phone at the end of the bar and make a quick call to his handlers at the state police. Wouldn't they like to see this?

Ah, but of course! The phone was occupied, by one of the old geezers who came in with Kelley. At any rate Myles was getting swamped with orders and he would have no time to call the police, let alone calling Wayne or Donal to let them know that business was picking up.

The geezer who had claimed the phone, Brother Morris, was responsibly notifying Joe Toole of his whereabouts.

"Did you say the Silver Shamrock?" asked Joe, "Here in Rossie? Whyja go there? Never mind. We'll be right along. The Shamrock, huh? And Des is alright with that? I don't know if you realize it, but I'm practically breathing down your neck."

Left to ponder that statement while he hung up the receiver, Morris immediately turned his attention to Des, who was now the source of the loudest voice in the room.

"That's what I'm saying! You got good strong boys, men with hair on their chests. None of these sissy-fags! And I'm proud of you! You raised 'em right! What's your boy's name again, Ed?"

Des was haranguing a haggard looking white-haired gentleman who, after 30 years as a type-setter, had developed hunched shoulders and a myopic gaze. "My boy? You mean Tru?"

"Yes! Sure, the one who runs with Atkinson, right? Them and the Fecteau boy? Well I got a little job I want them to do for me."

"I don't know, Des…I haven't seen Tru…"

"By the way…" another fellow at the bar had butted in. "My boy Mo hasn't been home since that thing over to the projects there…"

Ed and a few of the others turned to listen, but Des ignored him.

"Thing is, he was with Joey Atkinson and Tru Kennedy."

"What's this, Paul? Why didn't you say anything before?" said Ed.

"Hey, you know how kids are…"

"Yeah, but this thing at the projects- you hear how they played that up on the news? Making our boys out to be some kind of bigots or something."

Dapper was listening intently now. But Des was furious.

"That's just what I'm talking about! They were men- and no fookin' faggots can take it away from 'em; just doin' what's right, I say."

"Des- a word, if I may…" Dapper had taken his old friend by the arm and separated him from the bunch. "Sorry I missed the late wake; you know how it is…"

"Eh, yes, well, what's on your mind, Dapper?"

"This incident at the projects, Des. It's no good, you know. We can't have anyone looking too closely now when the money is about to go through. You know as well as I do that the folks down there can kick and scream all they want, but so long as no one is listening then it doesn't matter- the development will close and my, -our plans go ahead."

Raising a tall glass to his lips, Des took a sip of heavy dark stout. He grunted and wiped his mouth with the back of his hand.

Dapper went on. "See, that's what bothers me about what happened to the McManus boys at the park."

Looking somewhat alarmed, Des said, "I don't follow you."

"Well, aside from the fact that we have violent crime in our community…I mean, you have to admit, it's pretty shocking when a couple of young lads get blown away by automatic weapons fire here in our own neighborhood."

"Who said it was automatic weapons?" Des asked vehemently.

"I don't know…the paper, maybe Billy did…what difference does it make? What I'm saying is that this kind of thing scares away prospective clients. Clients like the *university*."

Ah yes, Des had forgotten. Dapper was working on a deal to bring in investment dollars from a local research university. In exchange for the allotment of acreage in the park for the construction of a horticulture and botanics laboratory, the university would provide ongoing maintenance for the park. Personal honoraria for Dapper and Des were also to be thrown into the bargain. And, of course, Des' firms would be given weighted preference when bidding on labor contracts.

"Don't tell me they're scared away, now."

"Well, not so far, but we're talking damage control. Come to find out this isn't the first time there were bodies found in the park. They pulled a couple of murder victims out of a sewer down there only a couple of years ago."

"That was ages ago! And it was a totally random thing- a fluke!"

"Yeah, well you knew about it and somehow they found out about it, but I didn't know about it. Made it look like I was covering up. Fluke you say! I should hope that the odds of finding a corpse in the park are infinitesimally small!"

"Alright, Dapper, so what do you want me to do?"

"Nothing, Des, old man, just keep up the good fight, like you always do. Hang in there and I'll keep you posted."

"You sound like the fella that fell in the cess-pit up to his neck in shite. In other words *don't make waves.*"

"In a manner of speaking…"

"Well listen to me, Dapper. I learned some disturbing news myself. About someone who tried to set me up."

Responding as if he had been dope-slapped, Ferguson winced and asked, "Doesn't affect me, does it?"

Myles Brennan tried to get close enough to hear the response as well.

"Oh for Pete's sake! No, you're not involved. But I have to react before this kind of thing gets out of hand. Don't worry about the kids at the projects the other night- they were working for me. I'm sending them out again too, to give them a chance to make up for the trouble they caused. But I'll tell you Dapper, as far as I'm concerned if they don't get Tommy Toole for me then they're no more than weak queer boys like him."

Brennan's stomach did a flip and he paused to grab the counter for support before serving up the next order of drinks. Tommy was Des Kelley's target? Holy shit! Now he had to use the phone.

CHAPTER 48

"I promised to tell you about the guns, so I did. Well alright then. It was down in Connecticut, oh, almost a year ago now. I was driving a fairly big rig- not one of them tractor trailers, mind you, but more like a beer truck without the reefer. A Topkick I think it was- a shorthauler. Anyway the job was to take a shipment of rifles that were coming back from the factory. See, Des would be notified when a load of refurbished rifles was ready to ship, and he would send me to..." here Bricky made the patented Curly Fine hand popping noise.

"Now, it's one thing to hijack a load of guns when you have an in and you know it's all going to go down easy. But it's another thing when, like yours truly, you're in the country illegally, you haven't got a driver's license, let alone a clue about the friggin' roads in New York State; when you're sticking your neck out so far, that if you get caught, you're basically on your own.

"See, in that circumstance, you get to feelin' a little used, and I'll admit that I thought I could make the job seem less, shall we say hazardous, if I was to make some more money, you know, a little gravy. So I thought I'd take a few of the guns for myself. After all, Des was stealing the guns, his informant was stealing in a manner of speaking, I was just joining the club and taking my fair share. What was a few M16s? I was trucking crates and crates of them.

"You know, I'll never forget stopping at the side of the highway like I had to take a pee. I scrambled up to the edge of some woods and stashed the rifles there feeling like I had just robbed the Mint. Later, after I finished the run for Des I returned and gloated over my incredible bonus; but at the time I had no idea how I was going to sell the fucking things.

"This was America- didn't everyone have a gun? Didn't everyone want one? Why weren't folks lining up to take the friggin' things off my hands? You know the Colt M16 is a lovely piece of hardware and really a steal at the price I was asking. These were the genuine A2s with the pistol grips and accessories..."

"So you ripped off the rip-off, eh? You stole from Des Kelley?" asked Pat Devaney, now enjoying his third mug of Pabst.

"It's not like I'm proud of it or anything, but yes, that's why we're here. You understand, the way I saw it, Des was like the old hag, you know, 'with me tig and me tag and me old leather bag'."

Seeing the blank looks on the faces of his supposed interrogators, Bricky explained, "Oh, it's an old Irish fairy tale. I'm guessing you never listened to the fairy tales when you were young'uns, but I loved 'em. Oh, sure I remember curling up at bed time and hearing my folks tell the old tales of the little people and their tricks and enchantments."

He stood and stretched, then placed his hands on the back of the chair upon which he had been sitting.

"The thing was- no matter how exciting they were, those stories would always, always," and Bricky quickly swung the chair up into the air in a classic batter's stance, "-knock me out!"

And with that, Bricky brought the chair crashing down on Woody's back, folding him up like a sleep sofa, collapsing him like a bullock at the slaughter. "Sorry about that!" Bricky gasped, breathlessly, tossing aside the shattered chunks of wood that remained in his hands.

Now to square off against Pat Devaney and Tom Connolly, the two he had already decided he would rather take on alone. But Pat's reflexes were dulled somewhat both by the drink and by the shock of seeing how brutally and summarily Bricky had dispatched Woody. If he hadn't made the mistake of looking at Woody to check his condition, then Bricky might not have caught him so easily. But it was as if he had offered his chin for the uppercut that turned out his lights, and from Tom Connolly's perspective anyway, it was embarrassing to see Pat fall like a lead bottle on a carnival pot-shot shelf.

Even one-on-one, Bricky did not assume that he had the upper hand. He had no way of assessing his opponent's strengths or weaknesses. Tom looked fine, fit and well-fed, but Bricky had known scrawny fellows who could best him in arm-wrestling. There was no point in hurting the guy. It wasn't his fault that he was stupid. Bricky had been stupid himself. On the other hand there was no point in explaining his objective. All he wanted was to get out of there, but his blood was up and he couldn't resist trying to rub Des' nose in it a little for dragging him down here, for taking him away from the company of decent people and for not allowing him to pay his respects; and not least of all for insulting him by having his 'goons' try to work him over in the cooler. Always a tough bastard, that Des.

Well, he should have known better and he should have asked.

Tom Connolly's eyes swept the room, from the bodies prone on the floor, to the tables and chairs, to the bar and the exit, and then to Bricky. Adrenalin ramped his system up so high that he stood on the balls of his feet.

"Fuck this," he said, and he reached back into his jacket and pulled out a handgun. "I'm not fucking around. Bricky, is it?"

Bricky in turn took one look at the gun and one look at Connolly's face. Then he said, "Me neither." And in one swift movement he stepped forward and seized Tom's gun hand with his left and pulled it back and away, while following through with his right, packing a bowling-ball momentum that was destined to snap an impact somewhere six inches or so behind Tom's head. Of course it had to travel through his face to get there, and the result was spectacular. From Bricky's perspective it was a vivid eruption of blood, and from Tom's it was an instant of stars, lightning bolts, and then blackness.

"With me tig and me tag, and me old leather bag...Oh well."

Bricky sighed and rubbed his hands together and surveyed the damage. He would have all he needed at hand in a place like this, but first it was important to take precautions.

After gathering up supplies from around the bar, he set about binding the hands and feet of his vanquished foes, and quickly taking Woody's key ring to open the chest in the shed out back.

By the time he had dragged the last of them into the cooler the men were moaning and groaning, but he'd already decided to let them yell.

Perhaps he never was a real terrorist, perhaps he never was real IRA, but like many a street kid from the north, he'd learned how to make a petrol bomb before he'd learned how to drive a car.

For ten minutes or so he trotted around the interior of the biz club, scoffing at Harris Toole's choice of cheap commercial liquor, and wondering if he had missed a cache of good stuff in his cursory search.

"Ah, but ya don't mind spilling the cheap shit like this!" he laughed, as he emptied another bottle of vodka and then prepared a wick and fuse arrangement.

He had pooled the most flammable spirits on the bar and on the floor under the liquor rack, figuring that proper ignition was a matter of surface area, and that a successful fire depended upon the availability of fuel.

Bricky's brow was dripping with perspiration as he leaned over to snag a book of matches from a bowl on the bar. He lit a match and then wiped the sweat from his forehead with the hand that held the matches. Dropping the book, he flicked sweat from his fingertips, then picked up one of the bottles he had prepared, and lit the dangling rag wick.

The rag was soaked in alcohol and it readily accepted the flame, but Bricky did not panic and toss the infernal device, but rather he held it casually while he discarded the match and picked up another bottle, which he lit with the first. Now armed with two bombs both sporting lit, sputtering fuses, he chuckled and lobbed one easily underhand into the middle of the floor, and the other over his shoulder, into the puddle of booze behind the bar.

Each bomb seemed to speak upon reaching its destination. There was an eggshell tinkle and then a moo-ish "Whoof", and then the entire premises was aglow with smoky fire. By then Bricky was on Corinth St, walking toward Sweeney's Funeral Home. As he passed the alley, he looked once over his shoulder to make sure that the path to the walk-in chest was unobstructed, and that he had not failed to leave the hasp unlocked.

The air was fresh and cool and the evening was much darker than when Bricky had left the wake. Approaching the funeral home it was easy to observe that the wake was over with and the place was closed.

"*Hail Mary, full of grace…*" began Bricky in his thoughts, and as he prayed he passed the building and the parking lot, his uncle's car, the Cedars of Lebanon Restaurant, the old police station, the field and the carnival and the projects. When he caught his first ride he was almost down to the Jamaica Center train station, heading north.

CHAPTER 49

"So; you know what you have to do, right Sharlae?"

Tweed took a seat in her living room. From the looks of things, this was going to take a while.

"C'mon, Weed, lemme wake up willya? You just make yourself at home while I get my shit together. See if there's anything on TV-"

Her set occupied the area where the shelves used to be in a hutch built into a corner of the dining room. Sharlae rummaged through a drawer below the television. With her pillow-pressed hair, her floppy slippers, her threadbare purple cotton pajamas imprinted with images of Underdog and Polly Purebred, it was difficult for Tweed to take her seriously and talk business. She was so cute he wanted to bundle her up in his arms and tuck her back into bed.

"What are you doing?" he asked.

She paused as if she had forgotten.

"Oh, I'm trying to find the needle-nose pliers so I can turn this thing on!"

Tweed got up and remonstrated. "Forget it! I don't..."

"That's right! You don't watch television. Alright, so listen to the radio." She plodded zombily into the kitchen and activated her FM unit. "We all got baked after LaGloria's thing at Blevins down at the square earlier. You know me. I can't work fucked up so I came home and crashed."

"Hey, how'd that go, anyway? I hear that even more people showed up after I left."

"Yeah. Alright, I guess. There were a lot more people there than I expected." Sharlae paused from spooning coffee grounds into an electric percolator.

"It was like all the faces you see in a year driving around Rossie, except all in one place, you know?"

"Huh? Familiar faces?" Tweed was raiding the fridge. "Yeah, Nilvan and Frankie were popular guys. They got around."

"I hate to say it, but I think it had more to do with how they died."

"You're saying people showed up at the memorial service because Frankie and Nilvan were shot?"

"No, I mean...people were curious. (*Sorry for yawning...*) In a sick way. I mean the fact that they died violent deaths at a young age; you know. Like, Ethel Voigt was there. Why? I guess she went to high school with them or something. And Timmy Shea. What, was he an old family friend or something? Of course we were all there, and Gary too, and Bone's sister Susan." She made it sound as if Susan's name deserved special emphasis.

"Like, everyone from the field was there; and the whole crew from the Fores, and half of the Cedar's softball team. After you left Wayne stopped in for a while, and after he left Jabbour stopped in, of all people! Then not long after Jabbour, in comes that cop Rima, acting all innocent, like he was just doing his duty or something, but I could'a sworn he was after something, by the way he kept looking at LaGloria."

"No kidding?"

"Yeah, well, there really wasn't much to the actual, ah, service, but it was good. Kind of emotional. I think it made a difference that there were no caskets, you know? No bodies to look at, kinda took away the focus, but on the other hand, it made everybody think, and it made everybody listen to what LaGloria had to say. Other people said some nice things, too.

"Like I said, I never really got to know those guys, but I think they would have got a kick out of hearing some of the things people said about them."

"Like what? What did people say?"

"Oh, you know, what hot shits they were, and how life is too short and blah blah blah."

"C'mon!"

"Give me a break, Weed! I just woke up!"

Strictly business. Items on the agenda. Miles to go before I sleep. *But would you look at her!* Sharlae had tiptoed away down the hall so that she could quickly go to the bathroom, clean up and get dressed. As she walked away, Tweed couldn't help but watch and appreciate how truly lovely and sexy she was. He wondered how he had missed that about her for all this time, although it could be he was seeing her through the filter of the mescaline high.

Then when she flipped the switch, and the light from the bathroom back-illuminated her body as she turned the corner, he saw her clearly in intimate detail. In that moment he felt a hot flash of desire to possess her, but just as quickly he felt a lust-quenching sense of shame for having stolen such an intimate glimpse of his friend. Shared physical intimacy with a lover was a gift, whereas ogling a friend was a violation.

He returned to the matters at hand, withdrawing the .357 from his pocket, and fiddling with it in his lap. His visit to Donal's had been productive in a number of ways. Throughout the years of dealing and territory expansion and consolidation, he had found that he gained valuable peace of mind from his association with Wayne and Donal. The alliance afforded him a certain degree of clout and purchasing power, just as each of the partners derived certain benefits when they combined their efforts and resources. However Tweed believed that he especially gained confidence from the combined wisdom of a couple of heavy dudes.

It was Wayne and Donal, after all, who saw the way through this current difficulty, and Tweed had to admit that their solution was elegant. Left to his own devices he might have simply blundered ahead or brazened it out.

They were aware of his troubles. Now they too knew that his girlfriend LaGloria had attempted to murder his father, and that she had lost her brothers in the attempt.

They also understood the position he was in as sole witness to the killing of Frankie and Nilvan. It was a very small circle of people indeed who knew the identity of the true perpetrators.

Having survived the assassination attempt, his father now believed that someone other than LaGloria's brothers had ordered the attack. Yet he had not come forth and sought the aid of the authorities. On the contrary, he had made matters worse, when, in his 'vigilant' search for answers and retaliation, he had inadvertently kidnapped Sharlae. Following that fiasco he had also inadvertently caused a street riot in the projects.

Meanwhile Tweed was dealing with trouble from within his own organization, with the discovery that one of his franchisees had been ripping him off. He intended to put an end to that problem as soon as some of the other distractions had diminished, when he would reshuffle the deck of his distribution network.

What a time for his mother to die. She was definitely too young. Yet death was shining a spotlight on her life and her activities. Now she was emerging from her husband's shadow, and people were seeing all that Christine Kelley had accomplished on her own. Her passing brought great pain to her sons, but with the pain came insight. It was as if a spell had been lifted and now they could see that they too were free to pursue the course of their own destinies.

Father and mother had been the pillars supporting their lives, but Buck, Keiran and Tweed had to realize that parental support was temporary and somewhat illusory. When mother died, father's authority was in no sense diminished, but his strength was, for he in turn had depended upon mother for support. Furthermore each of the sons had to arrive at their own sense of authority and strength. For example, since Tweed started living independently, he had adopted a moral perspective that enabled him to flout secular laws while he subsisted on Christian doctrine a la carte.

Recently however his father had been pressuring him to pursue what he called the cause of Irish freedom, and to join in efforts he supposedly made on behalf of the Irish diaspora to drive the British out of Northern Ireland.

That cause and others his parents adopted had seemed foreign and irrelevant to Tweed, despite his father's fervor and his family's ties to the old country. But when his mother died, Tweed felt the knife of conscience twisting in his gut, and the resulting pang of discomfort spurred him to act.

He was starting to understand that he had enough moral authority to make judgments, and this led him to a preliminary conclusion: There was no room in society for Des Kelley. Both Buck and Keiran had said that his fund raising was all a cover and a scam, and that his efforts would only prolong the violence in Northern Ireland.

Come to think of it, her reasoning may have been fucked up, but LaGloria was right in her own way. Des had to go. Of course, enlightened society had evolved mechanisms to provide for the removal of cancers like him. There were local and state law enforcement authorities, and federal entities such as FBI, IRS, ATF and Immigration; then there were even private organizations that took a special interest.

The only problem was that if Des was anathema, then so must Tweed be as well. How could society, for that matter, how could *he* condemn the gun smugglers while condoning the drug smugglers? No. Tweed would not be a hypocrite. The more he thought about it, he realized that the plan he had agreed to was indeed the best solution, and he felt satisfied.

His thoughts were suddenly interrupted by Sharlae's return.

"Sorry!" she smirked, "You guys want to be alone?" Sharlae's impudent tone left him speechless.

"I come back in here and I find you stroking your rod, there..."

Oops. the pistol was still in his lap and he was absent-mindedly fondling it.

"Sharlae! I...I," Man! He was never going to live this down.

"Never mind, Weed! Just busting your balls! Hey, is that thing for real?"

"Uh, yeah, here-"

"No thanks!" Sharlae spun on her heels, holding her hands up in surrender. "You should at least wipe the barrel off, don't you think?"

"Let me get rid of this thing..." He felt awkward, having virtually no experience with handguns. Rifles were a different story; and if it weren't for the fact that he had so much ground to cover with Sharlae right now, he'd tell her a story of how he and her late boyfriend Carmine used to lie on the roof of the projects late at night and take potshots at the empty commuter trains as they made the deadhead run.

"Hey, Weed, I was wondering...you heard from Rick? You know, Rick Rose, the guy you sent to uh, look after me."

"Yeah, I was just talking to him..."

"Really!" Sharlae was suddenly all excited, and Tweed knew he'd blown it.

"...the other day. I haven't seen him since, though."

"Oh!" Now she was clearly crestfallen.

"But I was going to visit him later tonight. If you want, I'll tell him you were asking for him."

She looked doubtful. "Yeah, OK. Do that for me, wouldja? I was kinda worried after I heard about what happened down there at the projects. Kinda thought he'd call me."

"Well, he's laying low, you know, keeping an eye on things. I'd be surprised if you didn't hear from him by tomorrow. When I see him I'll say, 'Hey, Rick, don't leave Sharlae hanging, dude. Have a heart- she doesn't know if you're dea- ahm, she just wants to make sure you're alright.'"

"Thanks, Weed," said Sharlae, looking away.

Holy shit, she was blushing. He had no idea that they had hit it off so quickly. Well, wonders never cease. Good for her. In a way he was kind of jealous.

"Now, about the 25 pounds I left you with..."

CHAPTER 50

They met at the water tower on the crest of the broad flat hillside commanding a view of Rossdale all the way down to Jamaica Center and beyond. All of the local cops went there to hide at some point in their shift, when they wanted to catch up on paperwork, or reading, or sleep. It was quiet and the parking area was shielded from the road by a screen of cypress trees. Sometimes more than one unit would camp out there, and over time this practice led to the informal designation of radio codes. Since the parkway connecting Westbury Circle to Stonybrook and points east ran past the base of the tower, officers patrolling the road would sometimes notify their comrades of unique or interesting vehicles they had pulled over. For example, one such code meant "Send backup: Babe with beautiful boobs!" Another was a general "Haul your ass down here, I've got a live one!"

Watch commanders knew to avoid the area, but in any event, Billy Storer *was* acting Watch Commander/Shift Supervisor on a temporary basis until the division moved to the new precinct house. He parked his department-issued Impala cheek to cheek with Rima's Corvette so they could talk without getting out of their cars.

"Got you a coffee, Buck."

"No kidding? Shit, you musta hit the lottery."

"You're a real fuckin' comedian, Rima!"

"What did you do? Slip some chloryl hydrate in it so you could steal my car or something?"

"Why bother spiking it? You're only gonna doctor it up yourself anyway."

"Hey, only if it's black, Billy." Rima pulled the cover off his cup and poured some of the coffee out onto the street. "A little libation, you know, to appease the gods..." He then topped it off again with the contents of a nip bottle he carried in his kit. "Alright; so where we at?"

"I think we can wrap up the McManus case tomorrow. We agreed to let the kid bury his mother, and according to Sweeney, the internment is first thing in the AM."

"Old man Kelley must be a wreck."

"Yeah, from what I hear, him and his buddies are all over to the 'Rock *getting* wrecked."

"The Rock, huh? That's a switch! Makes ya wonder! But that's Dapper's hangout, ain't it?"

"Yeah, which brings up something else. You know Bernie D, the broad from the precinct?"

Rima rolled his eyes. "Yeah, I know her. Nice girl; good cop. What about her?"

"Well, her unit was first on the scene at White City the other night, you know, when all the shit went down?"

"Yeah, so?"

"So, she came to me today with this big story; this theory of hers, about what she thinks is going on over there. Now, she says she got screwed out of the collar, I don't know, but she did a lot of the legwork and she heard a few things on the street. See, she thinks that the guys who started that mess were actually working for Des Kelley, and that the whole thing was orchestrated to help push the remaining tenants out of the projects."

"Huh?" Rima coughed and spluttered over his coffee cup, "Why?"

"It's a fact that Kelley has done that kind of thing before; you know, when they wanted to clear out some old triple-deckers or tenements to start a new development. There's always a couple of die-hards standing in the way of these things. See, Kelley gets paid to make life miserable for the hold outs.

"Now, Bernie says that there's a State Police Task Force looking into this big White City Corridor Development project. And you know who's heading up that project? Dapper. 'Course, Dapper and Des are pals. So she could be onto something. Maybe Des did send some goons down there to roust out the squatters."

Rima looked at Storer over the lip of his cup. "To *burn* them out?"

"Well, maybe things got out of hand. Maybe it was supposed to look like a maintenance problem or something. Maybe it's all bullshit, I don't know. But now there's more noise coming from down there. The management office, it's actually kinda like a security outpost down there- well anyway, they got a complaint from a tenant committee. Seems they're missing one of their own. Ever since the ruckus."

"B.F.D. Let 'em file a missing persons report."

"They know just as well as we do that the department won't even let you submit a report until 48 hours have elapsed, and that frankly, we don't take 'em seriously."

"Oh, well then- kids down there go missing all the time."

"Like I said. But here's the thing. She says that she and her partner were doing a street sweeper and they happened to grab one of the punks working for Kelley. He claims that one of *his* gang went missing down there too."

"Ooh- so we're talking the Black Hole of White City!"

"Are you catching a buzz already? I'm saying that we might not be done yet. There might be two more bodies out there somewhere."

"And to think I took this job because Rossdale has no violent crime!"

"You really are a funny guy, Jimmy. Now get serious- what do you have for me?"

"Heh, heh. Well, I just got back from Blevins where they held the McManus wake, or whatever it was. Very informal. The sister, LaGloria, had her brothers cremated. Kinda like one of those eastern ceremonies, with pictures of the deceased, and the little urns…Anyway, other than that it looked like a normal funeral…Considering that it's still pretty much a mystery why and how they died."

"What do you mean? Weed Kelley killed them for interfering with him and his girlfriend."

"Yeah, right, but you know what I mean. One thing though- afterwards I had a chance to talk to this chick, uh," Rima consulted his notes, "-Susan Cronin. She was Frankie's girlfriend, and get this- she's pregnant with his kid." Rima waited for the news to sink in, but Storer merely waved his hand as if he were directing traffic.

"Alright. So anyway, she was all upset, and I guess she's got it in for LaGloria McManus."

"Why, what's her problem?" Storer asked as if bored.

Rima blew air out of his cheeks. "I don't know. She says she went over to meet LaGloria, to introduce herself after Frankie died. Apparently they had never met. Right off the bat, LaGloria's behavior struck her as odd, as if she wasn't in mourning."

As he said this, Rima suppressed the recollection of his own encounter with the charmingly bereft Miss McManus. He cleared his throat and went on, "Then she says that during the ceremony, LaGloria took the words out of her mouth."

"Ain't that a crime."

"No, literally. She says when LaGloria McManus addressed the folks at the memorial service for her dead brothers, she used the words Susan had used when she met LaGloria. Verbatim. She says it was embarrassing. But she's pissed, 'cause now she thinks this woman LaGloria is some kind of heartless monster."

"That's, ahm, pushing it, isn't it? I mean, who is she? Doctor freakin' Ruth? And this broad LaGloria just lost her brothers, for God's sake! How's she supposed to act? Who knows? -Borrowing her words? Imitation is supposed to be the sincerest form of flattery!"

Rima thought about that for a moment, then said, "Yeah, but you have to know this woman LaGloria, Billy."

"What? So you know LaGloria?"

"No, but I met her. You have to have met her. I tell you, the chick can tell you a story like you wouldn't believe. By the way, I looked into it, and her family does not come from England."

"I never said it did!"

"Nah, just saying, is all…" Rima squirmed again, another hot flash turning his intestines to seawater.

"Speaking of England. Get this- I got a call earlier from this guy who claimed to be a British agent."

"Really? Her Majesty's Secret Service?"

"Something like that. Said his name was Makepeace and he was looking into IRA fund raising here in America. Says that the old micks and paddies like Des are illegally supporting terrorists, and that he's here to put an end to it."

"Well, shit, Billy, we could have told him about the micks and their money, I mean, give me a break! But did you say Makepeace? That was the name LaGloria gave me!"

"Yeah, I know. This just gets wilder all the time. At first it sounded like he thought he was playing me for a fool. Did I know that Des Kelley was involved with smuggling guns? I mean, Des Kelley? Who was he trying to kid? The guy couldn't smuggle a toy popgun! But then he asked, did I know that Des was involved with a politician named Dapper Ferguson and a scheme called, (you guessed it), the White City Corridor Project? Plus, he told me he was working with a state cop by the name of Chmura, and that he had taken a statement from an informant who may have had information pertaining to the McManus killings."

"Hmmm. Was he the sharing type?"

"Well, you know, it's funny you should ask, because he was willing to offer up some intel, in exchange for information we had."

"About what?"

"About whom. Weed Kelley. He said he heard that Des' little boy was the number one drug dealer in town and he wanted to know if it was true. Maybe he figured to use it against Des, somehow, I don't know, but he said that he would be willing to set the Staties on the kid."

"Didja deal?"

Storer reached out as if to clear a smudge off the windshield. "I couldn't see how it would do any good." He paused. "But yeah, I did. I told him that Weed was a low-level street punk we kept our eyes on, that he had no record to speak of, that he seemed to be a pretty smart customer, but fortunately for us, he lacked ambition."

"And?"

"And he told me that there's an ex-IRA gunman on the lam in town, a guy Des brought over from Ireland himself, and this guy sold that M16 to Nilvan and Frankie."

Rima could have fallen off the edge of his seat after sitting on the edge of it for so long. Instead he exclaimed, "That doesn't tell us shit!"

"Oh I don't know. It's kinda like the song. How does it go? 'They say that truth is stranger than fiction, and fiction is the strangest truth of all.'"

"Don't know that one, Billy, must be before my time."

CHAPTER 51

"Look, Joe, I've never set foot in the blasted Five Spot, or the Shamrock, or whatever incarnation it's under, and I don't intend to now."

"Oh, quit whining, will you? Des is there with some of the other guys and we have to show our faces. Especially after missing the wake."

"Fuck it! He's probably half in the bag by now. And on *somebody else's booze!*"

"That's beside the point. With the funeral tomorrow I can see why Doctor Morris wanted him to go someplace, uh, neutral."

"Just drop me off at the club! It's bad enough we're closed, but I should be getting ready for after the funeral. Listen. I don't want to go and drink at the freakin' Shamrock!"

"Alright! Joseph, Mary, and Christ Almighty! I'll go to the club first. But I want you to check in with Tommy for me. I feel better now that he's safe, but I want to be able to rest easy."

"Sure thing," Harris finally sat back in the seat of his brother's car. "But it sucks when you have to protect your own son from your best friend. What are going to tell him, anyway?"

"If he's still crazy about this, I'll tell him that Tommy had to go to work in the city. But then I'm gonnahavta convince him that Tommy is my responsibility, and if he has to answer to anyone, it's gonna be me."

Coming from the suburbs, Joe had tried to effect a sensible loop driving around Rossdale as he picked up first Simon Fecteau and then Harris, cinching the drawstring when he ended up at the Silver Shamrock. Simon had fallen asleep in the back seat of Joe's car as soon as they started on toward Harris' place near Calvary Cemetery because he had worked a double shift the previous night so that he could attend the Sunday wakes.

If after picking up Harris, they had proceeded directly to meet Des as planned, they would have merely skirted the perimeter of the cemetery. But since his brother demanded a detour, Joe was taking him straight on to the club.

From half a mile away they could see that there was trouble in the square.

"Looks like they've got all the streets blocked off! Shoot, Harris! What do you want me to do? The closest I can get is the corner of Main."

Traffic was choking up as a bottle neck caused by the blockage forced all cars to merge onto Main Street.

"Would you look at that! They've got Corinth blocked off- looks like the old PK Snows building is going up. Shit, I wonder if somebody torched the place!"

Snows was a five and dime that had been in business since the days when Rossdale was a rural stop on the stage coach route. It didn't occur to Harris that it also shared the block with the bistro and the biz club.

Harris thanked his brother for the ride and left the car, with Simon still asleep in the back seat.

Hoses snaked across the sidewalk from hydrants toward the source of the smoke and the fire. Engines from Rossdale Ladder One were parked across the main streets, and firemen hurried about, shouting commands to each other and at the growing crowd of onlookers.

Now concern began to eat at his sense of fascination. He pulled the keys to the club from his pocket as he pushed ahead toward the alley that led to the back door. Suddenly he heard a shout: "Got some people trapped in the cooler!" and panic seized him when he realized that his cooler was in the center of the confusion.

Next an amazing sight stunned him before he had the opportunity to consider the wisdom of going in to check his bar. Four firemen, laden with gear and covered in soot, were hauling a four-wheel dolly that looked like it was piled with beer kegs.

Were they trying to save his inventory?

Two of the men pulled from in front and two of them pushed from behind as they tried to negotiate the dolly over cracks in the pavement, their own hoses, and debris with a load that included, now that he could see clearly, not only beer, but also people!

The full reality of the situation had still not struck him, but Harris could now see to his astonishment that three of his colleagues, friends who owned bars in other parts of the city, were bound hand and foot, and strapped to beer kegs on that dolly. They appeared to be unconscious.

What the fuck was going on? Oh no! Not the bar!

He almost rushed straight into the fire as if he were some kind of demented human moth, but he stopped when he overheard a call on the emergency radio. It was a status report, listing the name and address of the club, and a preliminary assessment that it appeared to be a total loss.

Ambulances were being called in, while other units were being dismissed, and the police had arrived as well to enforce crowd control.

Harris bolted back through the alleys toward Main street, hoping to catch Joe in the traffic jam. However, he was no sprinter, and it was well over a hundred yards just to get back to where he had been let off.

The traffic was still there, but Joe's car was not; and a busy evening in Rossdale square had turned into a mess of gridlock and chaos.

Panting, dispirited, sweating and coughing, Harris had to decide what to do. Damn! The club was his resource, his workplace, his home away from home. He wiped a tear from his eye. Wait a second-the pay phone on the corner outside the club!

As fast as his legs would carry him, he worked his way back toward the blaze, aiming to get to the phone so he could notify Joe and Des at the Shamrock about what had happened. He'd have to see if he could find anything out about Woody, Pat and Tom while he was at it.

Holy shit! First the thing in the park, now this! Maybe Des really had pissed somebody off. And other people were getting hurt and killed because of it! Well, fuck that! Now his business was gone! There was nothing that wily old bastard could do to make it up to him. He could only hope that the next time someone aimed for Des Kelley, they actually got the son of a bitch.

CHAPTER 52

Hey, it was no problem for Tweed to drive out to the South Meadow National Wildlife Refuge and Habitat, but he wondered why Makepeace would want to meet there. Especially considering that it was nighttime and you couldn't see shit.

The reserve, a marshy 2,500 acre tract, was, in effect, an alluvial plain adjacent to the mouth of the South River, a waterway that had for over 300 years provided the basic resources of trade, transportation and recreation for the communities that crowded along its shore.

As he awaited the arrival of Mr. Makepeace, Tweed recalled that his neighbor, Mrs. Columkille, had once told him that she actually swam in the South River when she was a girl. Nowadays all access to the river was restricted except by permit, and all of the public beaches, launches and fishing holes were long since closed. Supposedly there was a 20 year timetable in the works charting the potential return of the river to public use. But Tweed hoped that after the years of scouring and pollution removal, when the time came for the engineers to certify the water safe for boating and fishing and what-not, then people would just as soon leave it be.

The proposed meeting place was a scenic overlook midway along the Ponakapo'og Parkway. Six or eight parking spaces carved out of a granite bedrock shelf on the elevation opposite the river bend.

Tweed took the grade in third, then he skidded into the shoulder, bringing his car to a halt in the crushed stone berm. He cut the wheel at the last moment so as to end up not only facing the river, but in the best position for a rapid get-away, should the need arise.

The scenic vista had been dramatically illuminated by the low yellow moon, grabbing his attention on the way up the hill so that he almost missed his turn. Now that he was parked he seemed to have a few inches on the moon; and the river appeared like a mysterious traveler that enjoyed the virtue of being in all three stages of its journey simultaneously.

The river soaked up the moonlight like it was the tail of a linen tablecloth hanging from the clouds. Then to the left and right, the landscape couched the frame in wild and unwelcoming darkness.

Tweed didn't remember this spot being so attractive. How many times had he been by here? As if in response to that question he recalled the first time he ever visited Ponakapo'og. It was during the summer of a brutal heatwave when he was eight or nine years old. Like many of the kids in the neighborhood he was stuck sweltering on the street with little hope for relief from the heat. Wayne's older brother Steve, a guy who later spent years as a prisoner of war in Viet Nam, mercifully gathered all of the little lobsters together and packed them into his beach wagon for a trip to Ponakapo'og Pond. For the remainder of the afternoon the kids swam in the cool silty water of the pond while Steve drank Budweisers and played lifeguard from the shade of a stand of pine trees that grew right up to the water's edge.

Later, when Tweed was a teenager, he would come up to Ponakapo'og with his friends to go bumper tailing or roof-rack riding. There were plenty of dark and dangerous dirt roads through the woods there- perfect for insane activities. Thinking back, it was amazing that he was never seriously injured performing those lame-brained stunts.

The first involved hanging on to the rear bumper of a friend's car while he drove at high speed without headlights. The object was to let go of the car when it swerved to one side, so as to use the acquired momentum in order to 'ski' across the gravel on your sneakers.

Roof-rack riding was simply a matter of holding onto the roof of the car while the driver tried his best high-speed maneuvers, braking and acceleration, to throw off the rider.

In both 'sports' the goal was to achieve a kind of free flight, no matter how brief, and often these bodily trajectories resulted in sprains, fractures and contusions. Tweed supposed that it was all a part of the consciousness and experience expansion that he and his peers sought so avidly, regardless of personal peril. More often than not the kids would prime themselves for their nocturnal diversions by drinking vast quantities of beer, or by inhaling glue vapors, or by smoking hash or pot.

Drugs were a means to an end, despite the conventional bullshit about the journey being as valuable as the destination. Never did Tweed view drugs as an escape mechanism, but rather they were the key that unlocked an alternate way of viewing reality. He believed that when he was under the influence he came closer to understanding the nature of existence and his relationship to the cosmos. Truth or enlightenment would come through the proper combination of drugs, or perhaps simply through a quantity just short of overdose. Legions of drug users had witnessed the tragedy that occurred when heroes and icons of the counterculture such as Jimi Hendrix, Janis Joplin and Jim Morrison had dabbled with the complex mystery of neurochemistry. And yet undaunted, millions would follow their example, as if seeking the fountain of youth, the elixir of life, or legendary riches, and continue to experiment and combine substances whose properties were far from alchemical.

In the year after he graduated from high school, Tweed ingested the following drugs while in the pursuit of an altered-consciousness enlightenment: Mescaline, peyote, hashish, hash oil, opium, THC, crystal meth, PCP, angel dust, Quaaludes, butyl nitrate, nitrous oxide, chloroform, Demerol, cannibinol, LSD, ecstasy, Librium, Percocet, chloryl hydrate, amphetamines, Valium, cocaine, STP, and various forms of marijuana, including lamb's breath, indica, and hybrid sensimilla. At the same time he was also partial to Heineken, Southern Comfort, Old Granddad, and Jack Daniel's. Many of these substances he would combine for effect, and many were taken in altered forms and dosages. He would, for example, try snorting Valium; he would pour powdered PCP on his breakfast cereal, or mix Demerol with his coffee.

While the variety and abundance of commercially prepared drugs had reached an all-time high in the history of the modern industrialized state, Tweed also sought his transformative toxins in the natural environment. With his 'what-the-fuck' pluck, his drugged determination, and his young, cast-iron constitution, he proceeded from one promising fungus, seed, plant or tree bark to the next, often leaving only puddles of vomit to mark his passage. For a time he became a proponent of a vile coca-cola and morning-glory seed mash concoction that he tried to foist upon his friends as a sure-fire two-day trip.

Ultimately he was forced to curtail his extra-curricular recreational drug use because of the intervention of some of these same friends. First Jimmy Col accused Tweed of becoming a degenerate, saying that while he was preparing to go to college and pursue a career, Tweed was becoming a latter-day Mr. Hyde; and secondly, Carmine Gunther warned him in a prophecy that he should have heeded reflexively, that the experiments would do him in. As Carmine fondly quoted Bob Dylan, "Like a fool I mixed them, and it strangled up my mind, now people just get uglier, and I have no sense of time…"

Speaking of time- was this Makepeace? The first vehicle to travel along the road since he had arrived was now speeding down the parkway from the south.

The beauty of his surroundings, the peace and quiet of solitude and the comforting savor of nostalgia were suddenly supplanted by the gnawing doubt of reconsideration. He didn't have to come here. Why had he bothered? Who was this Makepeace? What did he think he was going to accomplish? Why here of all places, and why now? Why not simply wait until after the funeral to speak? Or wasn't Makepeace planning to attend?

The car, a gray Mercedes sporting one of those 100k mileage badges on the grill, swept into the parking area as if all of its power was provided by real horses.

"Thanks for being punctual, lad! I was sure you'd come!"

Well, good for you, you salty old geezer.

"Mr. Makepeace, long time! What can I do for you?" asked Tweed.

"Get in, son. I don't drive much in this country, but when a fellow at the yacht club offered to loan me this beauty, well, I couldn't resist. These seats sure are comfortable."

How did you plan on getting here? By cab?

Tweed was reluctant. This place had accepted him, he had achieved a rapport; it didn't seem right to disturb the vibe. At least that's how he interpreted the mescaline buzz. The drug had come on nice and clean, but it left him slightly on edge. Nevertheless, he got in. Thus, he initially faced the older gentleman with a vague sense of misgiving.

"Tweed, I've been looking forward to talking with you. It didn't seem appropriate at the funeral home, and I didn't want to bother you at home in front of your lovely girlfriend."

"I can appreciate that, Mr. Makepeace, but what is it that you wanted to talk about? By the way- you picked a decent spot. I was just admiring the view when you arrived."

"You're in a hurry, I understand, and I'll try to be brief. Yes, it is a fine spot. I noticed it when a friend was driving me from Rossdale to my place at the beach. I figure it to be about halfway for both of us. And that's all I'm asking, son, that you meet me halfway.

"You remember me, don't you, Tweed? Remember the stories I told you? The records we played on the phonograph?" He smiled beneficently.

"Of course I remember you, sir. If you're asking do I trust you, well, that's a different story. Meeting halfway implies some kind of conflict, or negotiations. What are we bargaining for?"

"Ah, son, I hope that you do trust me, I really do. After all, I've known your father for many years now. I remember when you were born. I've lived in your home. And right now I'm mourning the death of your dear, lovely mother, Christine; God rest her soul.

"Now, I don't know if we can bargain or negotiate, or if we have to. But I do know that your father called me on Thursday night to say that he had been attacked, and almost killed. He wouldn't have called me if he didn't take this threat very seriously- for a number of reasons. Not least of all because you don't ask favors from your friends or worry them unnecessarily. If he could have handled the matter himself, he would have. But you see, a number of issues must be considered when someone such as your father is the apparent target of an assassination. Are you with me so far?"

"I hear you loud and clear, but I'll tell you right off the bat that if what you say is true, then my father apparently does place a lot of trust in you. Because he may have called *you* about a supposed attack, but he never called me."

"He didn't?"

"No! We spoke, but it was about the real and successful murder of Frankie and Nilvan, LaGloria's brothers! He said he was worried about LaGloria and me. He never mentioned any attack, he never mentioned feeling threatened in any way!"

There. Let him chew on that. Tweed had no idea what Makepeace was after, but he intended to keep him off balance and at arm's length.

"You said 'supposed attack'. I assure you, son, the *attempted* attack was very real. It may occur to you that your father did not mention the matter because he didn't wish to worry you. He knew very well that you were already dealing with grave matters of your own. Were you not?"

Were I not what, now?

"Yes, of course. Although I wonder when he planned to bring it up. Because you see, I met him on Friday down at the club, and again, all we discussed was the murders...and the fact that my girlfriend LaGloria was having a hard time handling her grief.

"You know, come to think of it- he did ask me to consider working for him- and he also claimed that he had other people working for him who could help find whoever it was that killed Frankie and Nilvan. Frankly, I admit I am a little confused, because when I heard that you were in town, I thought that you were among those people to whom he was referring."

"Oh! Very good! Might I ask why me? I mean, why did you assume that he asked me to look into it?" Makepeace said this as if it were obvious that he was deaf, dumb and blind.

"Because he said so," replied Tweed, succinctly.

So much for your credibility, chump.

"I see," he hesitated, looking at Tweed's face carefully, "But I don't think you do. Bear with me, because although it may difficult for you to believe at this moment, there may be another explanation for the same facts as you have described them.

"First I have to determine if you are really prepared to discuss this. It may have been a mistake to bring you out here tonight."

Oh Please.

"Oh, really? And how do you do that?"

"I suppose I just ask you. Tweed, I need to know if you can handle this. You know, that's what your father was after as well, when he asked you to work for him. He wanted to ensure that you were prepared to handle whatever the world threw at you. You've got to realize that your dad has seen it all, and he knows the ropes. A young kid coming up could learn a lot from a guy like him.

"Of course, at his age he's stuck in his ways. There's the right way, the wrong way, and there's Des' way, and there's no sense trying to change that. That's one thing about your mother, God love her. She never tried to change him. But she put up with so much...Anyway..."

Tweed turned to the window so as to hide his expression. *Did the old man hire you to soft-soap him, or what?*

"Look, uh, I already told my old man...I'm doing fine...I don't need to join up with anybody right now. You're right. My mother was a good lady, and I'm sure she kept my father in line. But right now I have my own girlfriend to worry about. She just cremated two brothers!"

"I'm not here to influence you to help the old man as you so disrespectfully refer to him. I simply wanted to put that in perspective before I went over what it is I came to tell you. Frankly, I could give a flying fuck about what happens to Des and his bleedin' legacy. Mind you- there was a time when I cared. I think it was your mother's death that ended that for me.

"You know, that time when you were little, when I stayed at your house, I really wondered what kind of con your parents were trying to put on. With their teachers and preachers and sanctimonious crap about the quiet family life. I knew what your parents were really like.

"Looking back, I suspect your father courted your mother to get in good with her father, who was a big wheel in Republican circles back in the old country."

Oh boy, another history lesson.

"Des' family had certain influence, but he could gain more influence through her family, you see.

"Likewise, I courted your father in a manner of speaking, so I could gain access and influence with the right people.

"Nowadays he comes to me for influence. Your father doesn't like to admit it, but he's an American now, and he's been away from the people, the politics and the land for too long. When he thought that someone had tried to kill him, he figured that it was related to his political views, to his involvement in Irish affairs. To be blunt, he was afraid that the IRA or another group like them was trying to get rid of him. But I knew, see, I knew that he wasn't important enough for anyone to want to kill. I mean, in Dublin, in Armagh, in Derry and Ulster, nobody knows Des Kelley, and nobody could give a rat's ass if he lived or died. But I said I'd help, if only to allay his suspicion that I might have tried to kill him."

"Did you?"

"I think you know the answer to that, boy. I said I no longer care what happens to him, I didn't say I wanted him dead. But this leads us to the matter at hand, for I'll be quite honest with you in sharing my discoveries and my conclusions, if you like. In exchange, I'd ask you to be honest with me. Does that sound reasonable?"

Tweed decided that the wisest policy was to assume that whatever Makepeace told him was bullshit. "Sure. But first let me ask you, are you saying that my father is paranoid?"

"Paranoid me arse, he's stark fucking mad! Hee, hee! Sorry, I couldn't resist. It's an old joke…" The old guy laughed heartily, "…you had to know it. I apologize," but then Makepeace started into laughing again, apparently overcome by his own cleverness.

"No, no, it isn't that. I already told you the attack did happen. He didn't imagine it. Now I thought we were going to be honest with one another? Or would it surprise you to learn that the attack upon Des was the same incident that resulted in the death of your friends Nillman and Francis." He fixed Tweed with an intense, penetrating gaze.

Go ahead and stare, you old goat!

The old man's eyes were blue, but they looked cracked and pitted like the oldest shooters in a bag of marbles. Short whiskers like clipped aluminum wires carpeted his face, so that his nose and forehead appeared like rocky outcroppings, barren of vegetation. He smelled of alcohol, tobacco and cheese.

"Are you saying that my father murdered my friends, Mr. Makepeace?"

"Makepeace is fine, son. And that's the question, ain't it? When he called, he didn't tell me that anyone had died. You can imagine how I felt when I come to find out that the whole town was mourning the death of these two fine lads. Not only that, but, like yourself, nobody seemed to have heard of an attack upon Mr. Kelley. The more I learned, the less I was inclined to continue asking questions. If this was a family affair, well, needless to say, it was none of my business.

"Now, I've talked to Des, and I've talked to the police, and I've talked to some friends of mine who might have helpful information. They put me through to an informant working in Rossdale. I decided to meet with him because I still hadn't decided whether I should be involved or not, and I figured that perhaps he could tell me something, anything; enough anyway so that I could at least make the call.

"Now, I don't have much faith in informants. They only talk for a price and they're too eager to please, and you have to spend so much time trying to see if what they tell you is of any use. For example, this fellow told me that you were a big drug dealer in Rossdale, and you can imagine my surprise at hearing that. He also told me that your father was in cahoots with this local fat cat politician named Dapper Ferguson, and that the merchants in town have turned to the state police to put an end to Dapper's shakedowns and influence peddling.

"Now this may be true and it may not, but did it have any bearing on the situation at hand? I had my doubts. You can't fault a fellow for trying to make a living. But next he told me that there were other actors involved in this little drama. One was a guy named Bricky, and the other named Thomas Toole. He's the son of the bar owner, I do believe. Alright, so this informant went on to tell me that Bricky met Frankie through Thomas Toole, and that he was the one who provided the guns that your friends supposedly purchased."

Holy shit. Who was this informant? So there was somebody else out there to worry about now?

"Does any of this sound familiar? Because there's one indisputable fact about the killings of those boys- they weren't simply innocent bystanders caught up in a firefight- they were armed as well."

"Oh yeah, I heard that rumor too," answered Tweed, "but you don't know what to believe when there's so much gossip flying around."

"You think it's gossip- just a rumor? Well, the reason I ask is because you have one view of an incident where the boys are the victims, you know, gunned down in the prime of life and all..."

Man, it was infuriating to hear Makepeace belittling the whole thing.

"...And another view where they come across as the aggressors: armed, ready, waiting in the woods and fully prepared for- for what, though? And how would Des fit in?"

"Yeah, I can see how that might make things difficult for the cops. But that's what they get paid for. Personally- to tell the truth, Makepeace, I always thought that the guns were planted on them. You ask how does my father fit in? Well, how the hell am I supposed to know? I wasn't there."

"But weren't you?"

He could have thrown a hot cup of coffee in Tweed's lap for the same effect. So the bastard was pretty cagey after all. Makepeace went on. "You are aware, aren't you, that the police consider you to be their number one suspect? I spoke with a Detective Storer who says that they have articles of clothing and other evidence that link you directly to the scene of the crime."

"My father told me that Storer wanted to arrest me," admitted Tweed.

"OK, but listen kid, he's not the only one. I've also been talking to the state police, and well, I'm not here to pull any punches; they say that they're going to arrest you for dope."

You sure do get around for a foreign fisherman.

"So is that it, Makepeace? Is that why we had to meet? You wanted to tell me that I'm likely to be arrested on drug charges or worse?"

"No. As I said, I wanted you to meet me half way. I'm asking you to be honest with me."

"Why? You already said that you don't care what happens to Des."

"True, but I do have a personal interest here as well. I've known your father for over 20 years because I've been after him for over 20 years. You see, I originally came across Des Kelley during an arms smuggling investigation. I was working for the British Army, trying to infiltrate IRA smuggling routes into Northern Ireland. Made myself out to be a gun-runner with a reliable boat. Over time I gained his trust and soon we were in business, so to speak. Once I had established myself with your father, the goal was to go on and get closer to the real decision makers, the ones who were using the guns and bombs to kill our people. However, after a while, Des was no longer valuable as a target, nor was he consequential as a threat. And frankly, as his friend, I hoped that he wouldn't do anything to change that.

"I would rather not care what happens to Des, but given that I was already here and looking into his affairs, I wanted to make sure that I was doing the right thing.

"Talking to you is part of that, because I had to know if you could tell me anything that might make it easier to understand what happened."

Tweed shook his head.

"Wow, that's some story. I still don't trust you, but I am guessing that your story is probably true.

"The thing is that here you are trying to decide if you want to help my father, when I haven't been able to decide whether I want to help him or not. One thing I do know is that people who routinely lie and cheat and steal from their own community so that they can buy weapons and smuggle them into another community shouldn't exist. My brothers warned me about Des, my girlfriend hates him and I think that if there is a way to do it, then he should be stopped. For his own good as well as the greater good.

"But I'm not worried about myself. I know that I had nothing to do with the incident at the Arbs Park, and I think that if worse comes to worse I can prove it. For example, I intend to tell Storer that I can produce a witness to the actual shooting. That testimony alone should be enough to clear my name."

"Can you indeed produce such a witness, now? You know, I wondered if you were involved…"

Let him wonder. Tweed went on.

"As far as any drug charges are concerned, again, I'm not worried. Like you I have connections in the various police departments around the jurisdiction. I don't believe that when the pedal hits the metal, people will want to prosecute. Let's just say that when all the facts are in, there will be no incentive to go after me.

"So I think that about wraps it up, am I right, Mr. Makepeace?"

"Well you know, son, if I thought you weren't being thoroughly fair and honest with me, I could try to coerce you. What if I told you that I could have a state police drug squad take you down, let's say right after your mother's funeral tomorrow."

"I'd say that I'm surprised you'd stoop to base threats. If you want to arrest me, Makepeace, then call your friends and send 'em in. If not, then have a life. Now, I have other folks to meet tonight and it's getting late already."

Tweed opened the door and pulled himself out of the car.

The moon was higher and whiter, but also quite small.

"You won't tell me what your witness saw, by any chance?"

"I think we've had enough storytelling for one night, don't you? Tell you what- you can read all about it in the papers when the whole thing is over."

With that Tweed stepped into his car and immediately released the handbrake. The Saab rolled forward, following the downhill slope of the Ponakapo'og Parkway, and gaining speed until Tweed turned the key, slipped the clutch into gear and let the car catch a whiff of the night air.

CHAPTER 53

"Sir, how many fingers am I holding up, sir?"

"Ma'am, all I see is lightning bolts. Just a big field of…electric…yellow…"

"You don't see my hand, sir?"

"I'm afraid not, ma'am." Ever polite, Tommy Toole had no idea who was asking the questions. He spoke from bleeding, swollen lips. "To whom am I speaking? Are you a doctor?"

"I'm a nurse. Are you in any pain?"

"Uh, not really, although I think I'll be sore later."

The nurse looked at Tommy's battered, disfigured face and shook her head. "Oh, yes, sir, you'll be sore alright."

Lying on a gurney while an increasing number of nurses prepared him for examination, Tommy could not recall how he had gotten there. A fierce fire of kaleidoscopic imagery played in his eyes although they were open and they should have served as passively as ever. He felt disconnected from his face and his body, and yet he was quite secure. Somehow he was pleased to know that despite his apparent trauma, he was being well cared for. He struggled to recall all of the events in his most recent past.

Last thing he could remember was leaving his place. That's right…waiting for a taxi. The taxi showed up, the guy blew his horn, and Tommy went down to meet him outside his apartment. Did the cabbie mug him? He couldn't recall ever getting into the car. As a matter of fact, the driver was waiting outside his cab when Tommy got down to the street, as if he had gone to ring the doorbell, or maybe like he was waiting to open the trunk for a suitcase. Tommy ran over to the cab and grabbed the door handle…

"I'm going to shine a light in your eye, sir…"

These folks sure sounded concerned.

"And I have some papers for you to sign in a little bit."

Now two or three people were running back and forth and tugging at his clothing, poking at his face, probing his ribs and his hands and limbs and joints. A doctor joined the group. Tommy corrected himself. A male authoritative figure stepped in.

"How'd this happen, son?"

Tommy attempted to face his questioner. "I, uh, don't know, really."

"You can't describe it; you'd rather not say?"

"No, I don't know! One minute I was fine and the next I was here! I've been trying to piece it together but I was hoping that somebody could tell me how I got here, where I am, why I can't see?"

"You are at Rossdale Hospital Emergency Room. You are being evaluated for multiple abrasions and contusions to the face and body. There may be fractures as well. You are likely in shock. Your vision should clear, I hope."

"So…I was brought here by ambulance?"

"No, a couple of cops brought you in the back of their patrol car."

"Oh, shoot! I need to call people!"

"Sir, settle down. You need to relax. You need to sign these forms. You'll be going into surgery soon. All that will have to wait."

"Surgery? What for?"

"The doctor will be here in a moment to discuss it with you."

Des Kelley's stooges could finally count coup. Although they were still wounded themselves they had finally gone out and done what they had been asked to. And boy, had they screwed up.

Their pride injured, their masculinity insulted, their manhood impeached, Joey Atkinson, Denis Fecteau, Tru Kennedy and Spaz Travers were easily goaded into action, assured with a promise of generous rewards.

Despite the concerned interest of Tweed Kelley and the intervention of Brother Morris, and despite Tommy's calls to his father and his friend, and their precautionary plans, it had been all too easy for the simple minded goons to grab Tommy as he left his apartment and then to stomp him. Much to his credit, Len Abbisso sat this one out, and Mo Keating was still missing.

***

At about the time that Tommy was being evaluated for trauma in the emergency room at Rossdale, his uncle was going through a somewhat similar experience on the sidewalk near Taft Hill Court in Rossie Square.

When the fire erupted at the biz club, throngs of people had emerged from their homes in the vicinity so they might observe the spectacle, and cheer on the Municipal Fire Department's Rossdale Ladder One squad as they tried to save other businesses. Des' friend Caroline lived close enough to the club to be able to watch it burn from her kitchen window. However she too was swept up in the excitement, and she prepared a thermos of coffee so that she could carry it down toward the scene and offer it to the firemen.

In the meantime an auxiliary pump truck had blocked Taft Hill Court so that when Caroline emerged from her home she could no longer see the blaze directly. Sirens blared and voices called over loudspeakers. Emergency lights were flashing and the pump kicked into life with a deafening roar as it fed high pressure water to the connected equipment.

Coming around the corner onto Corinth St, Caroline almost tripped over Harris Toole, who was lying unconscious on the curb. If she hadn't been focused on the bar, and worried about the impact on Des, then she might not have recognized the bartender, whom she had only met once or twice. Yet no matter who it was she would have offered assistance, as she did immediately; and it was fortunate for him as her prompt action may have saved his life.

After checking his vital signs and propping his head with her handbag, she dashed across the street and notified an ambulance attendant, handing off the coffee to the grateful crew.

The EMTs wasted no time in evaluating Harris and stabilizing his condition. Preliminary indications were that the patient may have suffered a heart attack. Additional tests would have to be administered and his condition monitored; and just as he was becoming responsive, the go-ahead was issued to transport him. In the meantime, Caroline set about trying to find Des Kelley and Joe Toole.

***

Caroline wasn't the only person looking for Des Kelley. Brendan Tighe had rolled into town late, hoping to find Des so he could go over last minute details with him. He only wanted the funeral to go smoothly, but he also wished to send his dear departed friend off in style. For she had made such a significant impact on his life that he felt he owed it to her.

Entering Rossdale on Sunday night Brendan was alarmed to see the main street congested with traffic. Apparently the fire department was busy cleaning up an emergency right in the middle of the town square, right about where Des' bar should be. Since the funeral home was closed, Brendan would have thought to check the bar next, but there was no way the bar was open for business in the midst of all that smoke and soot. But what if the bar had burned down? What if patrons had been injured? Could Des have been at the bar when it burned?

Brendan parked his car and set about trying to gather information. As he pushed through the crowds on his way toward the fire department cordon, it didn't take long for him to hear the buzz and to pick up some news. Three men had been found tied up in the beer chest of the old Rossie Biz Club! Tied up? He could understand if maybe they had taken refuge there in an emergency. He heard that they had been rushed to the hospital.

Brendan would have to go to Rossdale Hospital as well, to see if Des was among them.

Passing the field on his way out of the square he noticed that workers were busy dismantling the various rides and attractions at the traveling carnival. Apparently they were pulling out after a lucrative weekend.

It took only minutes to reach the hospital, but it was almost two hours later before he had either the opportunity or the peace of mind to make a phone call. With a cup of weak hospital coffee restoring the warmth to his hands, Brendan tried to get comfortable in a phone booth. Then he breathed deeply and dialed Tweed's number.

"Tweed, it's Brendan Tighe. I'm glad I caught you."

"Brendan! You're lucky you did. I've been out all night and I was just thinking of heading out again."

"Oh, well then, listen...I'm up at Rossdale Hospital, and I'm calling for Tommy Toole."

"Don't tell me Tommy's been hurt?"

"Yes, Tweed, pretty badly. A gang of thugs grabbed him earlier this evening right in front of his house, and I'll tell you, he took a hell of a beating."

"Is he ah...how's he doing?" Tweed stammered.

"Well, he's been in surgery for a broken face. They caved in his nose and his eye sockets. It was delicate stuff, but he'll be OK. Guess he's got cracked ribs and a sprained wrist, too. Plus a mass of cuts and bruises...He ain't pretty, that's for sure."

"Oh, shit!" moaned Tweed, "I tried to tell him. I sent him home, I told him, 'Stay out of sight', but what are you gonna do?"

"So you saw him earlier?"

"Yeah, we were at my mother's wake together. My old man started acting funny, saying that he wanted Tommy to talk to him. So I got him out of there and told him to be careful. I hate to say it, but I was afraid that something like this might..."

"You think Des did this?"

"I don't know. Sounds crazy but it had to be. On the other hand, Joe Toole is my father's best friend, for Pete's sake!"

"Yes, well, Harris is here, too. Did you hear about the bar?"

"Harris? What? The biz club?"

"Yes, it burned down tonight. Get this- Police found three men tied up in the beer chest. They were friends of your father's, guys who were at the wake tonight. Harris had a heart attack, and now he's a patient here at Rossdale too."

"No shit! The biz club burned down! Holy shit! Beg ya pardon, Brendan. A heart attack, huh? That's too bad."

"Yeah, well, he survived. It was minor. They're only keeping him for observation. He's mostly worried about Tommy. But now we got them all here: there's Joe, and Harris, and Simon, Brother Morris and Des and Caroline, a friend of your father's."

They hadn't talked in some time, and Brendan felt that he had some explaining to do. Without recounting the whole conversation, it basically went like this:

Back when he knew Tweed, Brendan had been a Jesuit, but it was apparent, especially whenever he was in the same room with men like Brother Morris, that he was not cut from the same cloth as other men of the cloth. He knew that there were many ways to pursue his vocation, and yet over the years he had wondered if perhaps he could do more good individually in the world if he were to become more personally engaged. There were, after all, many activist Jesuits who believed in a hands-on approach rather than withdrawing into the academic or monastic life.

Yet ultimately it was Tweed's mother, Christine Kelley who convinced him to remove the collar entirely and to enter the world of business and commerce.

She had connections in Ireland for hand-made goods of all sorts, from hats, scarves, woolen sweaters and mittens, to brass doorknobs and wooden staffs, to crystal and blown glass. In order to help Brendan become established as an importer she was pleased to provide the necessary introductions. Over the next couple of years Brendan worked with Christine and her friends creating a cooperative venture among artisans, craftsmen and piece workers. Stateside, Brendan opened stores to market their goods, again relying upon Christine not only for seed money but also for help finding qualified sales personnel. Featuring locations in upscale malls, the concept became an instant success and the venture was profitable for all involved.

The upshot of it was that Brendan felt that he owed Christine a debt of gratitude, one that remained largely unpaid by the time she died. Since she had never divulged her dealings with him to her husband for fear of his surely irrational reaction, Brendan was also bound to secrecy. He would have praised her to the sun and moon, but he was obliged to be wary of what he said in Des' presence, and in the case of the funeral, he restricted his enthusiasm to the gaudy flower displays and the music.

"I understand, man." said Tweed, at length. "It's like this funeral means different things to different people. I'm glad you told me. It's been too long, Brendan. I'll have to check out one of your stores some day."

"Yeah, Tweed, do that; and about Tommy..."

"I...I don't know what to say..."

"It's alright, Tweed, I have a feeling that we haven't heard the last of this thing. Stay out of trouble, man. I'll see you tomorrow."

By the time Brendan returned to the waiting area where Des and company were gathered, Detectives Storer and Rima had arrived as well.

Pat, Tom and Woody had already been treated for minor smoke inhalation. However they declined treatment for their other injuries, and they demanded that the doctors let them go home.

The police wanted to question them. However, Des intervened and convinced Billy Storer that if he absolutely had to speak with any of the gentleman he could do so after they'd recovered from their ordeal. Storer relented only because he wanted to interview Harris as well; and now that he was at the hospital he learned that he also had an assault victim on his hands. This was not your average Sunday night in Rossdale.

***

If only his vision hadn't cleared up. Ever since he regained consciousness at the hospital, Tommy had been experiencing a waking nightmare. But now he seemed to be entering the phase where his legs were stuck in molasses, his voice couldn't be heard, and all sorts of terror was being perpetrated on him.

"Are you sure you have to keep me awake for this?" he asked, tears streaming down his battered face.

"It's like I explained, Tom, it's for your own good. You're going to be draining for a long time. Now just sit still while I pack some more in there." The doctor had just finished winding another massive spool of swabbing. Through Tommy's bleary vision it looked like a cone of cotton candy. Like so many before, it was going up his nose, and he didn't think he could take any more. Each roll of batting had been jammed into his septum forcefully, and then packed into place with a twisted pair of needle-nose pliers. The doctor wasn't a big guy, not much larger than Tommy himself, and each time he jammed another wad in, the whole table rocked, and Tommy felt his neck straining.

"Ah, doc, how many more are you going to shove in there?"

"Oh, don't you worry about that, Tom. As many as it takes. By the way, did anybody ever tell you that you had a deviated septum? Took care of it while I was in there."

Oh, my God, thought Tommy, what, am I supposed to thank you, now?

The pain was one thing, but inside, nagging at his conscience was an acute sense of disappointment. He felt that he had let LaGloria down, and that he had been a fool for not taking Tweed's advice. And yet he couldn't help but wonder why he had been singled out for punishment. Anyone could see that there were strange things happening in Rossie these days, but how did he fit into any of that? Was it because he was gay? Because he knew LaGloria? Did it have something to do with Mr. Kelley? Was LaGloria in any trouble? He wished he could call her.

***

"Oh, Tweed, no! Who did it?" LaGloria had just heard the news.

"I don't know. It's gotta be his…guys…those, freakin' motherfuckin,' pieces of shit that do his dirty work…"

"That miserable son of a bitch! That bastard! Who does he think he is? Picking on poor Tommy! My God, Tweed!" LaGloria was sobbing.

"I know, love, Brendan couldn't believe…I can't believe…What? He just doesn't give a fuck? Is that it?"

"He's not going to get away with this, Tweed. Fuck him. He's not going to get away with it."

"Yeah well, Tommy apparently doesn't even remember what hit him, and he didn't see any faces. Plus, they smashed his face, goddamn it!"

"Doesn't matter," sniffed LaGloria. "Des will get what's coming to him. He can count on it. That bastard is going to suffer."

"Yeah, alright, babe," Tweed hugged his girlfriend and tried to comfort her. It had been a long, taxing day and the last thing he wanted was to deal with one of her vindictive tirades. The mescaline had worn down to a mellow afterglow, so that he no longer had the urge to gaze at every object for moments on end. He closed his eyes and let a flood of emotions wash over him. His mother's death. Og's betrayal. The cops closing in. Tommy beaten. The biz club burned to the ground.

"Hey, babe, who do you suppose burned the biz club?"

"It wasn't me…" she said, slowly.

"I know, it wasn't me either, but it makes you think. I guess they have enemies. Kinda works out for us, dontcha think?"

"How so?"

"I'm not sure. I just think it muddies up the picture. Somebody else went after the bar, somebody else could have taken shots at Des."

***

There was a ponderous mood upon the group of characters facing off in the waiting area at Rossdale Hospital, and as he witnessed the confrontation, Brendan Tighe felt like he was a latter day Brother Juniper, witnessing the collapse of the Bridge of San Luis Rey.

The waiting area in the atrium of the hospital, roughly oval in shape, was bisected by a hallway, an info desk and elevators, and surrounded by floor-to-ceiling windows that were now reflecting images of the interior. Des and Caroline stood at one side with their backs to the windows, Joe and Simon remained near the desk, Brendan took a position alongside Brother Morris, while Storer and Rima closed the box, trying to face the group as a whole.

Storer got off to a poor start. "So Des, I have a hunch it was your delinquent boy Weed who torched the bar. What do you say?"

Des was swaying in the breeze, visibly drunk. His response could be characterized as grunting with a brogue.

"Wuff, he swings and he misses! You can do better than that, Billy, or are you deliberately trying to provoke me? Tweed is not the answer to all of your problems. Since when do you investigate arson, anyway? What are you bucking for fire chief, now?"

"You're right, Des, that was uncalled for. But on the other hand, it seems that every time something happens around here lately, you can bet your bottom dollar that the name Kelley will be tied to it somehow."

"The problem is that you're always betting your bottom dollar. You know, gambling is a sickness..." As he said this, Des belched silently into his sleeve.

"You're a pisser, old friend...Alright, listen, it's late and tomorrow morning's the funeral. I want to get to the bottom of this and find out why somebody wanted to put Joe out of business. No, it's not my job to solve the arson, but this is also a case of kidnapping and assault, and it resulted in Harris having a heart attack. I'd think you'd be pushing me on this, Des."

"You pushed me first, Billy. You must be feeling a little defensive. Tell you what, why don't you let the kid have a crack at it for a change?" Des was indicating Rima, although his aim was poor and he pointed at nothing in particular.

"Glad you have faith in Jimmy, Des. I certainly do. What I was trying to say was that you should go home and get some rest. We'll do whatever we can and we'll get back with you tomorrow. I think we've got enough to go on for now. Although I'll never understand how the only witnesses to an incident can fail to see anything."

As if waiting for an invitation to stay, Storer and his partner lingered for a moment, then they said their farewells and hurried out to the parking lot.

The circle of friends closed in on Des.

"Are you going to explain to me what happened, Des?" demanded Joe, angrily.

"What? He said he'd fill us in tomorrow..." he waved after Storer, speaking with a drunken slur.

"That's not what I mean. What happened to Tommy? You sent someone to beat my boy?" Joe approached to within inches of Des' face, bristling.

"No, Joe, of course not! I only wanted to talk to him. That's all. Didn't touch the kid."

"Then how did he end up in the hospital? Why did a gang of hoodlums suddenly pick on Tommy, Des? Huh? Why tonight? Didn't you send your punks out to pick a fight with him?"

Caroline was horrified to hear this accusation. She was also disturbed to see Des inebriated to such a degree. "Des, is this true? It can't be! You couldn't possibly be involved in such a thing! Tell him!"

"Oh, come now, Joe, can't the kid take care of hisself? What a pussy!"

"What did you say? Do you know what happened to my boy, Des? He's lying upstairs with a broken nose, broken cheekbones, cracked ribs, a broken wrist...You'd call him a pussy! He took a heck of a beating. And for what? Tell me that, Des. You were mad at him, is that it?"

Des backed off a little, intimidated by Joe's hostility.

"No, Joe, he's a great kid! I love him! Are you kidding? Your Tommy? I wouldn't hurt the kid!" He punctuated the sentence with a coughing fit.

"Oh,no? Then how do you explain what happened? So help me, Des, if I find out that you sent those assholes out to hassle my son, then I'll never forgive you. If you wanted to know something from Tommy, you should have asked me. I'm his father. A father is responsible for his son, just like you are responsible for Tweed. Now how would you feel if I went out and beat the living shit out of Tweed, huh?"

Caroline didn't like the twinkle that seemed to appear in Des' eye when he heard the suggestion. "Des, I've heard enough," she said in a scathing voice. "Joe lost his bar tonight. His brother suffered a heart attack. His son was assaulted on the street and brutally injured. And you stand there shamefully drunk, making snide remarks? I can't stand to see you like this. I think you owe Joe and Harris and Tommy...I think you owe everybody an apology!"

With that, she stomped out of the hospital without looking back.

Brother Morris attempted to lighten the mood with a neutral comment, but Des interrupted him, speaking to Simon.

"Simon, you understand, don't you? I thought I explained how Tommy was the one that sold me out. He sold me out. Now, I think I deserve an explanation. I guess things got out of hand. But he'll be alright. Listen, Joe! He'll be alright! These kids get banged up all the time and they pull through. I'm telling you. Huh?" He actually smiled, as if to encourage his friends to do so as well.

"Just look at Bricky. Where is he? Woody went over to the club to question..." And as Des raised his head his bleary eyes met Brother Morris' concerned expression. A spark of explanation seemed to leap between them.

"Des," began Morris, "...you say you sent Woody to question Bricky? Was that it? When we arrived you told Bricky to go and get cleaned up. I think I understand now. You really wanted him to go to the club so your guys could ask him some questions. What was supposed to happen to Bricky, Des? Was he supposed to get the same treatment Tommy got? Oh, my Lord! Well I'll tell you something; I don't think it worked out that way." Brother Morris stared at his inebriated friend for the measure of a moment. Then, disgusted, he said, "You are a hopeless old fool, you know that, Kelley? By the love of Christ! You lost your wife and you had the good will of the community at your disposal. Instead of accepting the best wishes of your friends, you turned to spite, vengeance and recrimination- and it all came back at you.

"You've lost me, Des; I don't understand you." He threw his hands up. "Your friends in the police suspect you, your friends from the club don't trust you, your sons don't trust you, and I don't know who you are. May God have mercy on your soul."

In the end it was Brendan who remained. Like a person who appeared to step forth by virtue of standing still while everyone else stepped back, he was the designated volunteer to give the big guy a ride home.

CHAPTER 54

(Lord be with you...And also with you)

***

The phone rang, startling Des Kelley into the realization that he had not been awake after all. When he raised the receiver to his ear he recognized the voice of the caller immediately. "Tell me, you fat Irish fuck, was it as satisfying watching your wife die as it was watching Frank when he was down and bleeding, when he was lined up with the pistol in your hand, as you squeezed the trigger and blew his head off? Or would it have been better if you could have shot her too?"

But even then he did not put it together.

He wanted to lash out immediately and show that there was a price to pay for this kind of harassment. But what resources did he have at his disposal?

Whether it was fury or fatigue, depression or drunkenness, Des failed to pick up the insinuation that he had been observed, that there was a witness. Therefore he also persisted in confusing his role as victim when he might just as well have stepped up and claimed his role as villain and perpetrator.

The phone in his hand felt reassuring. He hadn't hung it up, so it couldn't ring and disturb him again. Plus, it was solid and heavy and it came with a cord so he could wrap it around that bitch's neck and throttle her with it...Or he could use it to call Billy and ask him for help.

The cops were the enemy and Billy was a cop, therefore...No, Billy was a friend. He knew about phones and such. Maybe he could use it against her. Have him trace this prank call, and get her for harassment. Then maybe he can trace that other call...

Hmmm. Something bothered Des, something played at the edge of his mind. Of course! He had already spoken to Billy once before, when he tried to tell him about the gun. That hadn't gone so well.

And at this time of night he had no idea how to go about finding either Billy, his friend, or Storer, the cop. Let it go until after the funeral. There were scant few hours left until then anyway.

***

(Lord have mercy, Christ have mercy...)

LaGloria tried the number again and again, but it was no use, and she also soon fell asleep. It was just as well, for in her desire to punish Des she had almost rewarded him by revealing that she was a party to the plot on his life. Simply by admitting her awareness of his presence at the crime scene she had placed herself at risk, for he would certainly wish to reduce any potential liability.

First thing in the morning she was at it again. While Tweed showered and shaved and dressed for the funeral and the rest of the day's events; LaGloria called in a bomb threat to Sacred Name, where the funeral was to be held.

Tweed wasn't aware that she had made the call, and she didn't mention it. She could have gone all morning without taking credit for her deed, as long as there was a payoff at some point, either in terms of laughter, applause or sheer disbelief. Like a child seeking attention, all she wanted was a reaction in any form.

In her mind the target of her prank wasn't the church, but Des Kelley, although she had no compunction about attacking churches or religious services per se. In fact, once when she was a teen she had taken a dare from her friends to enter the funeral service in progress for an elderly gentleman whom she did not know. As part of the prank she had marched right up to the coffin of the deceased, where she knelt, crossed herself, then in a loud voice declared, "Oh, he had the sweetest, thickest, juiciest cock! I'll miss it so much!" before wailing and moaning and carrying on right out of the chapel, leaving the mystified congregation to speculate.

(Almighty and everlasting God...)

She didn't let on about the bomb threat until Tweed was trying to park at Sacred Name and he discovered to his frustration that the perimeter of the church grounds had been cordoned off. Municipal police squads were scouting the area with canine patrols. In light of the biz club arson, authorities had taken the latest threat very seriously, as evidenced later by the mounted units patrolling the cemetery as well.

Despite all of the attention and the heightened security, LaGloria took the first opportunity to taunt Des. During the Mass when the priest asked the parishioners to turn to each other and exchange words of peace, LaGloria made sure to reach out to Des in particular.

"Go to Hell old man!" she said, venomously. "I know you killed my brothers. Your hands are cold with their blood, you bastard." Despite all of this, she smiled, sweetly. Looking on, Buck, Keiran and Tweed noticed their father's sudden stricken pallor, and how he appeared unsteady on his feet. More noticeable still was the fact that he did not join the file to receive communion.

(Holy, holy, holy, Lord of power and might...)

If she hadn't yet goaded him to a virulent rage, she made another attempt to burst the blood vessels of his restraint by behaving loud, uncouth and ill-mannered. As the family gathered around the burial site, LaGloria had the nerve to say, "It's a shame when these joint plots go to waste- you know, the wife dies, the husband remarries, and that's that..."

(Our Father, Who art in Heaven, hallowed be Thy name...)

Then when the priest committed Mrs. Kelley's remains to the earth, and Des and others began back-filling the grave, LaGloria appeared to add something of her own to the soil. Somewhat shocked, Tweed took her aside and asked, "What did you just do? That wasn't what I think it was...was it?" With a wicked smile, LaGloria merely replied, "Just getting rid of pocket lint!"

Tweed had learned that overall he preferred dealing with LaGloria when she was lying. She was the living example of the person who said, "I lie when I say that I always tell the truth..."

Although he was disturbed by what he thought he had seen, he could not imagine why she would want to add her brother's ashes to his mother's grave.

(Go in peace to love and serve the Lord...)

However, in the meantime the end of the funeral marked the end of any formal obligation, and people were free to disperse. They were also welcomed to attend a reception at Des Kelley's house, where brunch and refreshments would be served. But a trend seemed to be evident from the attendance at the wakes and the funeral. At first large numbers of people showed up, and then the attendance had declined. Saturday night's wake was over capacity, whereas Sunday night's was light. The mass was full, but the grave-side funeral service was sparsely attended.

Des didn't realize it, but he had alienated his friends, his colleagues, his family and his minions. As folks left the funeral and entered their cars, one by one, or two by two, they recalled the boozy, blowhard Irishman and thought it best to leave him alone, and not to follow up with a social visit to his house. The burial had finally removed the real object of their respect.

Faced with a deadline of his own, Tweed was forced to separate from LaGloria in order to accomplish all that he had set out to do for the remainder of the morning. And yet he wished that he was free to take a drive in the country. It would do him some good to remove himself physically from his usual environment, but at the same time, to fully absorb the impact of recent events. His recent exposures to death had left a palpable sadness clinging to him like the funk of secondhand smoke.

Having been by Og's place earlier in the morning to set the stage for his release from jail, he was now depending upon Sharlae to fulfill her portion of the scheme, for if she should fail, then heaven help them both. While she was doing her bit, he would rescue Og from the courthouse following the arraignment. He had already consulted with his lawyer regarding this phase of the operation, and he had also checked in with clerk of the court, if only to synchronize his arrival with the subsequent actions he had planned. His contact at state police was onboard as well, and just in case, he gave a friend at the local police the heads up, too.

From Og's perspective this was to look like a regular gray Monday morning; perhaps a little brighter than most, for he was being released after his first incarceration. Tweed would personally give Og a ride home, and again, this gesture was to be seen as a way of making amends for leaving him stranded in the jail cell over the weekend, when he, like all of the franchisees, had been assured repeatedly that in the event of arrest, he would be freed promptly. In this case the personal touch was also a way for Tweed to have Og's undivided attention. He could not only explain the unique circumstances that had resulted in the extended jail time, but he could address once more the issue of Og's reliability and culpability.

Thus far, Og had failed all of the 'tests' that Tweed had given him. Still, Tweed was hesitant to throw his old friend and associate to the dogs if he could show a glimmer of remorse or a glint of potential for improvement. Sure, he had ripped off his customers, his friends, his fellow franchisees and Tweed himself, but perhaps he had seen the error in his ways. Maybe a 'jail-cell conversion' had taken place. Tweed felt that he owed Og the benefit of at least that much doubt. But no more.

Pulling up in front of the court house he felt like he was privileged and at the same time vulnerable as all hell. He was being watched, that was for damned sure, but all the same, who was going to hassle him for pulling over in the no-parking lane? The 99 probably looked pretty sharp sitting there all alone in the zone out there in front of the county courthouse, but Tweed wished that Og would hurry up and get his ass out of the damned hearing room.

If there was any place that Tweed hated to be, it was that blasted court house. It was like low-life city, a slice of life you never see anywhere else, even in municipal jail. He remembered the time when Carmine was convicted for stealing a couple of rolls of insulation from a construction site along the tracks in White City. First the initial trial was bad enough, what with the lame testimony of the cops- who patently lied, and the incompetent representation of the court-appointed lawyer, and the case being rescheduled and continued for the convenience of everyone but Carmine. Tweed was only there to keep Carmine company, but during the course of the trial they spent days sitting on benches in long anonymous hallways, waiting for hearings that were invariably postponed, and, while they waited, listening to the most outrageous cases being read, tried, continued and postponed like all the others. For example: *Oye, oye, all in attendance for the case of the people versus George Jefferson Curtis, for the charge of assaulting his five-month old baby boy with a slide hammer…Oye, oye, draw near for the case of the people versus Shamila Washington. Your honor, Miss Washington is charged with possession of a Class A substance, Heroin, with intent to distribute; she is also charged with possession of a nine-millimeter handgun, a military style submachine gun, ten thousand rounds of ammunition, a sawed-off shotgun, two machetes, an axe, a .357 magnum revolver, and a 32 caliber so-called Saturday-night special. At the time of her arrest Miss Washington had on her person an ounce of a Class B substance, cocaine, plus a store of methamphetamines, and a bulk stash of food stamps that she had apparently been accepting as currency…*

After Carmine's own trial he was required to visit his probation officer every other week at the courthouse. So for an additional six months, Carmine and Tweed were exposed to characters and facts of a way of life they hoped they never had to experience with any greater degree of intimacy. Witnessing a genuine cautionary tale was a sufficient taste of the spice of life as far as Tweed was concerned. He developed such an aversion to the courthouse that when he was called to serve on jury duty he copped a plea and begged off.

Finally Og emerged, hunching against the daylight, and, inexplicably, sniffing his fingertips.

"Sup!" he cried, climbing into the car brusquely. "Why didn't you come in? I was waiting for like, ten minutes!"

"No kidding? Well, Og, I don't do the courthouse scene. You wouldn't catch me going in there if your life depended on it. You're lucky I picked you up."

"What? Fuck you, man! Hey, you got a bone?"

Tweed gritted his teeth. "Look, I don't know if anybody told you or anything, but I just came back from burying my mother. She died the other day, you know, and that meant that the situation with you kind of got pushed back on the list of priorities. Believe me, man, it made me sick knowing that you were suffering through the whole weekend down at munie jail, but I've known lotsadudes that done that sitting on their hands…so I knew you'd pull through."

It was only a few minute to Og's place, so Tweed either had to drive slow or talk fast. Og stared out the window, brooding as usual. He repeated, "Hey, you got a bone?"

"Yeah, Og, I got a bone, a bone to pick with you."

"What the fuck are you talking about? A bone to pick?"

"Just what it sounds like, dude. Remember last week when I asked you about the bag I sent over for Eban? Well, to tell you the truth, that was a set up. I baited you with that bag to see if you'd pinch from it- and you did! Like a thieving rat eating away at the grain in a store house."

"Oh ho! You calling me a rat! You calling me a rat!" He turned to face Tweed as if he was prepared to fight.

In return Tweed stared him down.

"Not only that, Og, but when I entrusted you with a re-up mission to the stash house, you tried to convince Bone to rip off all of the bales we had there. As if that wasn't bad enough, when he refused to go along with your idea, you went and sleazed a head stash from one of the sacks. Now, you know the rule- when we move quantity, we go clean. We never tempt fate. But you were smarter than that. You had to steal from me and the rest of your partners; you had to give the cops something to find when they pulled you over. And I'll tell you, man, you can say that these rules are bullshit, but think about it- you guys were carrying more than 25 pounds of primo reefer, but did the cops find it? No! They only found the measly stash you had hidden in your skivvies."

Give him a chance to respond.

"Yeah, well, fuck that. Fuck the cops, fuck Bone, the lying motherfucker, fuck the rules, and fuck you."

"Yeah, alright. So you'd take a record for possession of a fucking dime bag and risk losing a bale in the bargain? That doesn't make any sense whatsoever."

They were almost at Og's house now.

"Who gives a fuck? Because I'll tell you something, I talked to someone while I was in that friggin urinal of a hell hole of a jail cell..."

It was rude to interrupt, but they had arrived, and there was a certain subtext in effect, the flow of which Tweed did not wish to disturb. Og didn't notice it, but there was a collective pause just then, as attention became focused upon the Saab and its occupants, as if fate and consequence depended upon their disposition.

"You mean Jabbour? Yeah, he called me. Said that he might give you a chance as one of his street dealers...conditional, of course..."

"What? You talked to Jabbour?" The pitch in Og's voice signaled anxiety. He had expected that as soon as Tweed started getting all lofty and ideal, he'd lay that name on like a one-ton dose of reality.

"That's not what he told me."

Tweed didn't let him get started. "Oh, I know, he said that you'd be his partner in crime and that you'd have total freedom and all that crap, with the best Lebanese blonde, blah, blah, blah, the best Jamaican green, ganja man...Just thought you should know, Og, that he gets most of his stuff from me. So whatever he charges you is just a markup on the markup I'm charging him.

"You're not happy, hey, I'm not going to argue with you. Better you should go work for Jabbour than keep ripping me off. But I'll tell you, don't try that shit with him, because, and I guess you know this better than I do- the Arabs don't screw around. You know his cousin, right? The guy with one hand?" Tweed raised his eyebrow as if to say, "Think about it."

"Anyway, I thought it might come to this. Like I said, I was talking to Jabbour. He told me that he left something for you in the bench there, in front of your house. Something to get you started. If it's the stuff I think it is, you should be alright."

Og was alarmed. "In the bench? Right there?" He grabbed the door handle.

"Yeah, Og, that's what he said. Look, I'm going back to meet my family. I'll see you around; it's not like I'm going to wish you luck or anything. You been ripping me off for a long time."

"Weed, look, it's, uh..." he looked out at the bench and opened the car door.

That's it, thought Tweed. *Go for it, you shithead.*

"It's the cost of doing business, man." Og said as he left the car.

It made sense to drive away, but Tweed wanted to watch. He revved the motor to 1500 RPMs and started rolling down the street, keeping his attention on Og. A team in mufti from the state police watched from a neighbor's porch on the right, and a team from the Metropolitan Police watched from directly across the street. Local municipal cops were on standby, and they were prepared to alert any additional emergency response units such as ambulance and fire rescue, as the situation warranted. All of these forces were keen on taking down the drug dealer, scourge and threat to the community, Tweed Kelley. He was wanted on suspicion of murder in connection with a double homicide in the town park last Thursday; police also wanted to question him about the disappearance of two local men, Rick Rose and Mo Keating; and about the destruction of a local landmark, the Rossdale Businessman's Club.

Tweed however, had struck a deal. In exchange for his freedom, he would give up Og in his place. In order to sweeten the deal, Og would come with a shotgun that had a verifiable history, and 25 pounds of primo marijuana, all delivered, no-fuss, right into the hands of the cops.

If only Tweed could swing around the block and watch it all unfold.

Practically drooling, and with a single-minded sense of purpose that left him totally unaware of his surroundings, Og walked directly to the old bench that his father had built on the sidewalk in front of his house. It was there that the old man used to sit and talk with his friends from Lebanon, and under that hinged seat where he kept his gardening tools, his spare gloves and hat as well as his lunch box and coffee thermos.

Og threw the seat open and looked with wonder. He reached in and drew out a long burlap bag wrapped in an oily chain, and then quickly unwrapped the chain. The bag fell away and he was left holding a sawed off shotgun, which he stared at stupidly for a moment. He actually started aiming along the barrel and checking the hammer action, pawing the blue steel and the oaken stock with a damning profusion of finger prints. Just as suddenly he dropped the gun and started rummaging in the bench for more goodies and sure enough! There was Sharlae's contribution to the morning's deception. If he had looked around him at that moment he would have seen that among the gathered police, all at once there was a synchronized movement in his direction that halted the moment he lifted the bale. It was as if the threat of the gun had caused a collective indecision, perhaps resolved by leadership, and the sight of the bale ignited a new fuse of delay. Og's nostrils flared as he tore open the top of the bale, exposing the uppermost buds, packed in a dense brick of vegetation. He scratched at the weed and inhaled the aroma, and only then did he turn and check to see if anyone had observed him. Now that he knew he possessed 25 pounds of pot and the shotgun to defend it, he was going to pull it close to his chest and run along inside. There he could examine it in depth and run his fingers through it.

It was difficult to account for the speed of the metro drug task force. Maybe they were afraid of losing credit for the bust, but those dudes practically flew over the hedges to get down in front of Og first and arrest him. There was some initial confusion as the officers referred to Og as "Weed", but as soon as he corrected them, everyone was willing to accept one for the other, and in fact, few actually knew that they had.

Tweed had to walk away. That was the deal. No more drugs, no more deals. No more presence on the streets. After today, Tumbleweed Kelley would join Carmine Gunther and the pantheon of posterity.

As for Det. Storer, he was last to know, but it hardly mattered. Without Tweed he didn't have a case in any event, so he was going to have to think about this one from scratch, or give it up. When he found out about the massive pot bust on his own beat he had to wonder what else was going on that he didn't know about. Og Z a major dealer? Federal firearms charges? Possible links to organized crime and the McManus murder case? Shit, in a world where any of that could be true, who knows, maybe a guy like Des Kelley could even be an arms smuggler?

The story took on a life of its own as it spread around town like a case of Mrs. Mulcahy's marmalade. Some said Og had held the state troopers at bay with his trusty sawed-off while he set up a smoke screen by setting the bale ablaze; some said it took seven cops from two area police departments to bring down the notorious Oggy Z, sodomite, drug demon, serial murderer; others said that the arrest of big Og brought closure to a slew of unsolved cases across the commonwealth.

Little did it matter later, when events in Rossdale had died down somewhat, that the only charges on which Og were finally convicted were for possession of marijuana with intent to distribute (25 years), and a mandatory weapons charge for the shotgun (5 years), bringing his total jail time to a possible ten years, out of which he would likely only have to serve eight.

Of course the real question that only a few insiders might ask, was: What would Tweed have done if Og had been truly contrite, and he had apologized to Tweed's full satisfaction?

CHAPTER 55

"Say, Eddie, this reminds me of old times, you know? Don't it remind you of them times when I used to camp out here?"

"Yeah, Rickie, sure 'nuff, like old times. I remember when you daddy gone and you mama dinno what to do with all you kids. I told her, 'It's alright, Mrs. Rose, you leave this here Rickie with me for awhile and he'll be alright.'"

Mister Eddie's voice sounded like grits and gumbo…like chitlings and gravy. It was like the heavily accented voice of a Tuvan throat singer, except with a distinctly southern accent.

"You don't mind having me here, do you?" Rick had his own room in Eddie's spacious suite, and if he wished he could have stayed as the elder gentleman's guest without ever seeing him. At the moment he was in Eddie's living room so that he could watch television. It was pretty boring hanging out day after day.

"Daz nice thinking of Mr. Eddie; you a real thoughtful boy, son. You know me, I always like to have some help around the house."

Rickie and his avuncular guardian smiled at each other.

Rick imagined getting out of there and telling Sharlae about Mr. Eddie; and as he thought about it, he realized that the ideal way to describe him would be as a cross between Louis Armstrong and Muhammad Ali. His infectious smile was gentle but cocky because of the way he viewed the world. No doubt he saw things as they truly were from his cinder-block penthouse in the projects. There were no lawns outside his window for the peacocks of his pride to strut upon.

And there was precious little history to explain how or when he had arrived, or why he chose to remain, for Eddie was neither philosophical nor expansive on the subject of his situation. "I's here," he'd say, "And I ain't a-going nowhere."

Rick wouldn't have minded running errands for the old man like he once had, because since the crash he had been going stir-crazy merely from staying inside. But like Eddie said, "Deys plenty o'younguns to run around…" Besides, Rick was supposed to 'lay low'.

"Weed said it could be a couple of days," said Rick, well aware that Eddie might not be paying attention to him.

"That he did, your Mr. Weed, that he did."

"It's just the waiting…"

"Ain't nobody likes to wait…nobody. Mr. Eddie don't like to wait, no sir."

Rick picked up on something in the old man's tone. "Are you waiting, too, Mr. Eddie?"

Eddie puttered about the kitchen, humming now. This meant that he wasn't sure he wanted to answer. From the many nights, weeks, was it months? Who knows how much time Rick had spent cumulatively over the years bunking at Eddie's, but he had gotten to know the old fellow pretty well. Surprisingly, he answered.

"Maybe I am."

"Who you waiting for…ah, what are you waiting for?" Rick leaned way over to see his friend, imagining him as an overgrown badger snuffling about in the cabinets.

He got up, walked over and spoke to him face to face.

"You know why *I* have to hide out..." he offered, prompting.

"I still think you should hold out until we make a issue out of this here. Boy, you play like you gone and deys no telling what gone come of it. Dat way we got the whole world on our side."

Rick hadn't seen a lot of the world. He grew up here, and his home was the projects. It was as if the buildings and the playgrounds were a part of his extended family, just as Mr. Eddie was part of his family. His apartment wasn't all that different from Eddie's, with the funky blown-in rubber ceilings, the government-issue indoor-outdoor carpeting, and the cinder block walls; only Eddie had second and third- generation furniture heisted from the nearby senior center and municipal building. Still, overall he had little basis to make a comparative value judgment.

"Oh, you're just changing the subject! So, what...you're saying that if I pretend to be missing for a while then my family and the folks in the projects can make a big stink out of it and get all sorts of media attention and everything?"

"Yeah- you catching on!"

"But what good does that do? Missing person in the projects? So what? Who cares?"

"Now, listen to Mr. Eddie, Rickie. Number one- Mr. Eddie cares. Number two- You think people want to hear that a car load of white boys come down to the projects and make one of our own disappear? No way. Not when the mayor and the folk in city hall want to tear down old White City, no sir. Dad be too much bad press. Thing like that stinking to high heaven! Don't mind saying that it helps what with you being a white boy and all."

"Shit, Eddie! I didn't think you noticed!"

"Heh, heh! Old Mr. Eddie might miss some things, boy! He don't miss much! He miss some things, but..." and he cocked a wiry eyebrow at Rick.

"Yeah, alright, I get the point, but I might be cooped up long enough as it is. I don't think I could take waiting indefinitely, until the press took notice, that is. "

"Well, there you go. I wonder if you would have to wait. Just like I wonder if I have to wait." Eddie rubbed his chin thoughtfully.

"You gonna tell me what it is you're waiting for?"

"Hmmm. Well, alright. See, I been talking to Mr. Dapper..."

"Don't tell me..."

"Yep; you see, he and I kind of came to an understanding."

"You made a deal with Dapper Ferguson?"

"Now, it's not like you thinking, son. Maybe you thinking that old Eddie made some kind of deal for to leave quietly, eh? Well, no such thing! No sir! You might say it's the other way 'round."

"What do you mean? It's not like he wants you to stay?"

Eddie fixed Rick with a shrewd glance. "Oh no? And why not? Can you think of a reason why maybe it's good for old Dapper to have Eddie make a fuss down here?"

Furrowing his brow, Rick pondered, considering both the question as it was put to him and the possible complexity of the answer. He tried to approach it like one of those multiple choice exam questions that used to stump him in school. Now how did that go? Take the answer that seems most outrageous and set it aside, then take the two that seem to have something in common and compare them against the remaining selection. Thoroughly confused, Rick answered after a considerable pause. "You got me, Eddie. I have no idea. I thought he wanted you out of here."

"Oh he did, he did. But only until you got hurt. No, I know you ain't hurt, boy, we're talking pub-liss-it-ee. That's all he understands. If it looks good for us to go, he wants us to go; if it looks better for us to stay for a while, well, then, old Dapper going to have a change of heart. Plain as that."

"He said that?"

"Not in so many words, but yeah. He wants me to stick around and be a, uh, what did he call me? Oh yes, he said he wanted me to be a symbol."

Suddenly sickened by the political depravity of Rossdale's representative on the municipal council, Rick was momentarily thunderstruck. That calculating codger! Taking advantage of Mr. Eddie like that! It was difficult to fathom the political advantage Dapper might gain in using the old man, until Rick remembered something his mother had told him.

After she had worked for some years in the hospital laundry, the janitors and housekeeping staff had nominated her to be union shop foreman. When he heard the news, Rick asked why she had gotten the nod. She replied by saying that 'the squeaky wheel gets the grease'.

Seeing his confusion, she explained that she was known as a loudmouth, someone who could vocalize the concerns of her fellow workers. Not only did they want her to represent them, but management also wanted to deal with her, even if she wasn't particularly skilled or persuasive as a negotiator. Because by negotiating with her, they were removing at least one loudmouth from the workplace.

So instead of a legendary squatter, Mr. Eddie would become a convenient symbol, a municipal mercenary, to be trotted out whenever Dapper needed some PR relief.

"No, Eddie! Man! What are you supposed to get out of it?"

"Now don't go getting upset. Remember that Dapper is nobody. You are somebody. Somebody never let themselves get worried over nobody, no how. You know that the only thing I lack here in my home is a phone. I will admit that I told Mr. Dapper about that particular inconvenience."

True, it was inconvenient. There was no phone service into the projects. It had all been removed per order of the housing development when the complex was first condemned. Squatters weren't paying rent, so there was no sense allowing them to establish telephone accounts in their illegal apartments. Whenever the tenants had to make a call, they used the public pay phone on the corner. In fact one of the primary chores Mr. Eddie hired project punks to perform, was running to the phone and making discrete calls. Some of these missions required returning with a response, others involved waiting by the phone for a return call. Since all of the remaining tenants shared the same single pay phone, a line sometimes formed; and eventually Mr. Eddie got into the business of buying his place in line. Rick could see how the offer might appeal to Eddie, especially over the long run. But how long a run was left in White City?

"OK, so Dapper's gonna put in a phone? Huh! I bet that he'll never do it!"

"Already has, son. Got my new phone installed on the QT. Like one of them black sack jobs. They was up here long about the crack of dawn, drilling holes, fishing wires."

Where was Rick when all this was going on?

"You was sleeping when they came, so I ain't surprised you didn't notice."

"You're shitting! You got a phone?"

"Yea-up, the first phone in White City in…" He started ticking off his fingers, "…in a long time. You want to call somebody? Oh, you can't, can you? I forgot- you is dead! Heh, heh!"

CHAPTER 56

"Look at all the food, Christine. You would have hated to see it all go to waste. Put out a decent spread, you'd think people would have the decency to show up and eat it. Fuck 'em. Fuck 'em all."

Des tugged at the knot in his necktie, pulling it loose from his collar as he surveyed the extensive buffet selection that had been prepared, delivered and laid out in his house while he was at the funeral.

"They got your favorites here, hon, deviled eggs, and shrimp with cocktail sauce. I think you would have liked this funeral..."

But the food looked repulsive. Devil's eggs. Nature's symbol of fecundity sliced and spiced. *The fruit of thy womb, Jesus.* Embryonic shrimps curled in fetal rows, beside the baptismal font where they would be dipped. A wave of nausea passed over him and he held his hand to his forehead.

Christine liked people; where were the people?

With his emotions undulating between hope and bitterness, he tried to mentally replay bits of conversation he had with various people at the wakes and the funeral. Had anyone said that they'd see him at the house? Now that he thought about it he recalled that the universal response to his invitation had been non-committal. Well, shit, they should have come right out and told him, and saved him the trouble and expense of having the reception.

Then again, he had done nothing to prepare for this event; in fact he had not even arranged to let the caterers in- and the whole banquet, chairs and all, was being paid for as a gesture of good will by the Rossdale businessman's association.

Opening the refrigerator in search of a beer, he again spoke to his dead wife, saying, "So it's just you and me, dear..."

But he heard a response before he even closed the door.

"Yeah, it sure looks that way- Oh! You're talking to your beer! I figured you weren't talking to me!" LaGloria McManus stood in the doorway of the kitchen. She wore the same modest lilac pant suit she had worn to the funeral, and she was carrying a rain coat over her arm.

"You!" said Des as if the news came as a revelation.

"It was an open invitation, right? Come all, come one?" She smiled.

"And to think I was actually happy to see you, for a second there."

"That's alright, Des, anyone can make a mistake, right? Isn't that pretty much how you justify what you do?"

Des licked his lips, uncomfortable at the prospect of being alone with this woman. He started to think in terms of escape. Then it occurred to him that the very notion of escaping from his own house was ludicrous.

"What do you mean? What are you trying to say?"

"Oh, c'mon, Mr. Kelley, you can do better than that! I'm talking about my friend Tommy, for starters. Yesterday he was fine. Went to your wife's wake. You remember. You saw him there. Then, last night, I guess you made a mistake, because oops, Tommy's not alright anymore."

"I had nothing to do with that."

"Right! And Ronald Regan had nothing to do with Ollie North, but meanwhile in the world of reality, Tommy Toole is recovering from a vicious beating. Somebody thought he'd be better off with a smashed face and broken bones. You put that idea into their heads. You told them to go out and **fuck Tommy up!**" She was livid.

"By the Blessed Virgin! You think you can come into my home with your lies and your profanities? I'll have none of that! Where is Tweed? Where is my boy?"

"What? Do you deny that you sent some assholes out to stomp Tommy Toole? Because if you do then you're only deceiving yourself. Everybody knows. I know, Tweed knows, the cops know, and Tommy knows. Man, you are a fucking asshole."

At this Des advanced and moved as if to strike her across the face with the back of his hand. But as he did so, she stepped back, or cringed, and showed the pistol she had concealed under her coat.

"Hold it, fucker!"

"Oh aren't you the clever one- now what are you going to do with that? Shoot me?" Des managed a wry smile, but he kept his distance.

"Can you think of a reason why I shouldn't? You bastard! You had Tommy beaten! For what? Because he's gay? And that's not all- you had Sharlae kidnapped...they scared the shit out of her, she had to run for her life...and Rick Rose was forced off the road into a brick wall, his car exploded and he's gone...I mean, who the fuck do you think you are?"

"Now calm down, LaGloria, and put away the gun. Is that what's bothering you? We can talk! Guns never solved anything that talk couldn't solve. This is a misunderstanding. You're taking uh, unrelated, uh, threads and trying to tie them all together. Now put the gun down and let me tell you..."

"You rotten motherfucker! You think you can get away with that? Talk? Yeah, you're a fine one for talk. There's one more thing that's been bothering me that I didn't mention." She raised the pistol level with her line of sight and took careful aim at his chest. "You...killed...my...brother...Frankie!" and she fired. Des froze, struck in the cloud of cordite with a ghastly white expression on his face. The bullet pinged of the wall far to his right, removing a sizable chunk of plaster and obliterating a sign that Mrs. Kelley had cross-stitched years ago. It had said "Slainte" with ornate flowers and filigree around the border.

Finally thawing from his involuntary grizzly bear pose, Des came to and promptly slapped the gun from LaGloria's hand, seizing it and stepping away to inspect it. Giggling hysterically, LaGloria was pointing at the hole in the wall. "Wow, the kick on that thing!" she gasped. "Still, I should have hit you."

"You foolish bitch. My wife worked hard on that hanging."

He removed his bifocals from his shirt pocket and examined the gun. "Hmm. Where would a cunt like you get a nice piece like this?"

"Fuck you!"

"I've got the gun, now, LaGloria. Not that I'd need it for the likes of you."

"Ooh. What's that supposed to mean? You're all scary? Well I'll tell you something, you're still just a stupid mick bastard and you're going to get what's coming to you."

Still looking at the gun as if he might recognize it if he stared hard enough, Des replied, "Big threats from the wee bitch."

"I don't have to threaten you, Des, because I know you'll end up losing like you lose everything else. And you know why you always lose everything? It's because you don't deserve anything. Think about it, you lost your home when you left Ireland, you lost your first son when Mack died..."

"Shut up, you..." and Des struck her savagely.

Unfazed, LaGloria continued, "...you lost your second son when Buck went back to Ireland." She spat blood and saliva, before continuing thickly, "You lost your faith when you stopped believing in God, and then you lost your wife because you didn't deserve her either."

"You, you cold blooded bitch! Was it you? Was it you behind all of this…?" A glimmer of light started to enter Des' mind as he realized that he was facing his true opponent. But she wasn't finished.

"You lost your sons Keiran and Tweed because they saw you as some kind of petty criminal, a sleazy counterfeit Irishman, and you lost your friends because you couldn't trust them.

"See? You don't deserve to have anything, that's why you lose everything."

LaGloria sat on a kitchen chair, her lower lip bloody, her hair messy, and Des stood over her, panting, menacing, brandishing the .357. He appeared to be reluctant to use the gun, for he did not wish to diminish its resale value in any way. He told himself that it would always be valuable to the insurgents fighting in Ireland, so he could fire it as much as he liked. Flipping open the chamber, he whistled, and asked incredulously, "You loaded this yourself? Jacketed Hollow Points?"

Neighborhood noises started to filter in, and LaGloria could hear someone saying, "I thought it came from over here." A dog was barking incessantly, and off in the distance a siren cried.

"Ahem! You cooking again, Des?" Makepeace had spoken before knocking, and he was well inside the house before either Des or LaGloria had noticed him. He stepped into the kitchen, fanning the air in front of his face. "Whew! Stinks in here! What, did somebody light off a firecracker?" He surreptitiously winked at LaGloria, and she froze.

"What are you doing here, AD?" asked Des, suspiciously.

"Hoping for a bit of nosh- it was an open invitation, was it not? I mean, you said, 'Why don't you come by after the funeral', so, here I am."

Halfheartedly trying to conceal the gun, Des said, "Oh, yes, of course, well, make yourself at home. There's plenty to eat."

"I can see that! What a spread! Fruit and salad and breads and cheeses, luncheon meats…very nice, indeed. You and the young lady just having a nice chat then, eh?"

"Oh, yes, very nice."

Makepeace made a show of taking a plate and piling it with items from various trays. "Well, that's good, then you don't need that gun, I suppose."

Des appeared chagrined, "Oh this? No, I guess not," and he tossed it onto the table with a sigh of resignation.

"That's fine," said Makepeace, sidling along the buffet so as to interpose himself between Des and the gun. "Because I like to be the only one holding a gun." He withdrew a pistol from a holster concealed in his coat, and pointed it at Des.

Now holding his dinner in one hand and his gun in the other he gestured for the pair to proceed into the living room.

"Looks like things were getting a little heated between you two, am I right? Now let's see, is that your gun, LaGloria? My, my! And you're here to kill Des? You know, I think it's all starting to make sense."

"Do you need a freakin' road map?" she spat.

"No, no, don't tell me. I'll tell you, because frankly I have had it. I have had enough of Des' bullshit and his antics and his lame cornball schemes."

"Cornball schemes! You don't say that when you're making money off me!"

"Des, I haven't made a sou off of you in years. And don't start talking about money. I'm sick over the blasted money. This isn't about money, Des.

"You know it is rather appropriate you should be here right now, young lady, when you seem to be so instrumental in helping us all come to this moment where we now find ourselves."

"What moment is that, AD?" interjected Des, "You going to shoot yourself? Don't be daft!"

"Hah, hah, Des; I carry a gun for self-protection only. I hope I don't have to use it. No, the moment, uh, of reckoning, as they say.

"You know, this incident of yours caused far more trouble than it was worth. Looking back I think everyone would agree that things would have worked out to a much more favorable conclusion if those boys had simply killed you."

"That's easy for you to say, AD. But I have to wonder why you take the side of the crazy bitch here. And I don't even know what she has against me. Alright, she says I killed her brother, although I find it hard to believe that anyone could find me capable of something so heinous. But why are you pointing a gun at me?"

"As I said, Des, I have had enough. You wanted me to find out why someone had tried to kill you and in good faith I attempted to do so, but in the process I found that it was a wonder that I had never tried to kill you myself. You forced me to look back over all the years and all the deals and to reexamine why it was that I decided to let you go when it was my job to stop you. There was a time twelve years ago when I almost took you down, and I wish to God I had, because I would have been done with you; but I was afraid that you had tied me to the sinking of a certain fishing boat off Gloucester Point.

"And there were times when I gathered information resulting in the arrest of persons who were prominent in Republican circles in Derry and Belfast and Portadown, and I expected you to put it together, or that someone would figure it out and tell you. But in the end that's how I knew that you were no longer relevant- you had nothing to do with those people and they had no idea who you were.

"But you weren't satisfied being an American who smuggled guns into Ireland. You had to exploit immigrant labor, and soak decent hard-working Irish-Americans for money to set yourself up as some kind of petty gangster, with crooked cops and pols on your payroll.

"And in the end you had to hurt people, and even kill. You're wrong when you say I took LaGloria's side, but I do agree with her. I think she's right. You did kill her brother, didn't you? What I can't figure out is why? Was it because she took something from you? Was it because she took away Tweed, that you decided to take away her brothers?"

"That's it!" shouted LaGloria, "I said you lose everything. And you lost Tweed because I took him from you. You couldn't stand the idea of getting nothing in return when a 'wee girl' had taken so much from you."

Des stared at Makepeace and shook his head.

"You've got it all wrong, old friend." Turning to LaGloria, he said, "I got mine, bitch, I got what I wanted when I took your brother's life!"

"I knew you'd admit it!" she cried, and she leaped up and ran over to snatch her gun off the table.

"Don't do it, LaGloria!" warned Makepeace, his gun steadily trained upon her.

But Des took advantage of the distraction and made a grab for Makepeace's gun. This time he had no intention of being caught unprepared for LaGloria's assault.

"Get off of me you idiot!" shouted Makepeace, trying to retain his grip on the gun and his aim on LaGloria. "She's getting the..."

But LaGloria had already picked up the snub nosed .357 magnum revolver and she was preparing to fire it again. This time she wasn't going to miss. The gun went off and...she missed.

Makepeace stomped Des' toe with his foot and elbowed him viciously in the stomach. It was enough to break free, and he too fired a shot, striking LaGloria in the upper torso. She spun and went down.

CHAPTER 57

Tumbleweed had no reason to assume that the cops would take one particular route over another, but his gut told him that he should take the least obvious route, the back route. In his experience, they liked to announce a big arrest with a showy parade down Main St, with their sirens blaring and lights flashing. The problem was that they were all headed in more or less the same direction, toward Westbury Circle, and he didn't want to find himself sitting in his car at a red light beside a police car that was holding Og. There might be potent poetic justice in such a scene, and it would surely make the stuff of cop shows or movie plots, but he would rather simply experience it vicariously in his imagination, than actually live it, however brief the instant. For such an instant would haunt his conscience for the rest of his life.

He selected the so-called parkway extension, a stretch of road claimed by neither the state nor the city. Due to its orphan status, the extension went unplowed in the winter and neglected for the rest of the year. Most locals avoided it because of the rough ride it provided, and because there were at least two alternate routes running roughly parallel to it; and from which, conveniently, the less-attractive extension road could not be seen.

The ride hardly mattered to Tweed, regardless of the fact that he was sitting atop the Swedish automotive equivalent of the fairy-tale-princess' mattress stack. His mind was oddly focused and yet free, as he began to explore the possibilities that were available to him as of this moment. Everything was different now. He was about to embark upon a completely new life, and the sense of potential prosperity versus potential catastrophe loomed in his awareness.

There was much to do. First he had to go home, talk to LaGloria, and gather some things together. The manual said that he could pack some 30 cubic feet of storage into his 99, and he was going to need every cubic centimeter of that and more.

He had to get together with all of the guys, but especially Bone; and he had to spring Rick. Maybe he was moving too fast, maybe it was better this way.

A bone of some mellow Humbolt, named, like a Napa valley wine, after the district in California where it was grown, would serve exceedingly well to quiet his seething anxieties right now. But no-for now he would have to get by on his memories of such things. He would have to remind himself that he already had his share. It wouldn't kill him to withhold drugs from his mind or body for the foreseeable future, despite the fact that he still possessed a sizable stash.

The moment he entered his apartment he sensed that something was wrong. Seeing that LaGloria wasn't home, he immediately searched for the gun. He didn't know what instinct compelled him, but it was correct. Both the gun and the girl were gone, which could mean only one thing.

Planning and packing would have to wait. Damn! He wanted to go now! The phone rang, freezing his blood until his brain came up with the reassurance that it could be LaGloria herself, checking in. He picked it up.

"Hey, dickhead. I heard about your friend, Mr. Z."

Just hang up. It's a crank call.

"Uh, hello, Officer, uh, Detective Storer, uh, pardon me? What did you say? Something about dicking my friend?"

"Listen, punk! I've just about had it with you! I don't know how you sleazed out of this one, but I know you're involved."

"What one? What are you talking about, Storer?"

"Og. Og Z. The Mets just busted him on a major pot haul. Kilos. And they have him on federal gun charges. There's talk this wraps up the McManus case. I'm the freakin' laughing stock of the whole precinct, all because of you."

"Don't blame me, detective, I told you all along, I had nothing to do with these things. You say they got Og, I congratulate them. I think it's a step in the right direction."

It sounded like Storer was strangling himself with the phone cord.

"You! Listen to me. Deal or go down. We will hassle you and your buddies wherever you go, whatever you do from now until...Kingdom come, so help me!"

How refreshing to finally be able to talk to Storer without any fear whatsoever. It was as if they were on opposite sides of a looking glass. But then, the Wizards were still on the other side with Storer.

"Yeah, yeah, Storer, we'll talk. But if I were you, I'd just join the winning team, and share some of the credit while there's still enough to go around, you know what I mean?"

"Kid- kid...let me ask you one thing. There's one thing I have to know right now. Is there really an IRA hit man walking the streets of Rossie?"

Aha. Storer's boogie man. Look at it from his point of view. What if it wasn't over? What if it was never over? Tweed would have to answer carefully.

"IRA hit man? You mean Bricky?" he replied in his most unbelieving sing-song tones, "No wonder you're the laughing-stock of the precinct," and he hung up the phone. Give a little, take a little. Now to get to his father's house as fast as possible.

CHAPTER 58

For some reason she couldn't stop laughing, which sucked, because there was a throbbing pain in her chest that was only exacerbated by her breathing. LaGloria lay face down on the floor of Des Kelley's living room, clutching her raincoat, and glad she had it. It was wet down there, and she was feeling cold, and she probably didn't look too good so at least there was something to cover her with.

She couldn't help being focused on her own condition, and yet she was aware that Des was still fighting with Makepeace.

"Ya ijit! You shot the girl!"

"Bloody well had to, didn't I? She would have shot you, or me for that matter."

"Oh, but she's making a mess, you stupid, fucking,...what are you? A traitor? A spy? Are you British?"

LaGloria gasped to a halt and managed to speak. "You are such a fool, Kelley. He was never your friend! He sold you out like all the rest! And I am so glad to see it all happen- to see you destroyed. Well, I want to tell you something, Des. You fucked my mother and you thought it was alright, that nothing bad could come of it. But you destroyed her. And you destroyed my father. And you destroyed my brothers with your goddamned Christian youth rape center!" She screamed.

"But I got you back. Oh, over time I got you back. You fat, ugly, stupid, fuck. First of all, you know I always wanted to seduce a priest."

"Oh, my Lord! Save it for the confessional, girl!"

"No! You hear my confession! Because when your son Keiran decided that he wanted to become a priest, I had a golden opportunity. Yes, that's right. I'm saying I seduced your son, the so-called virgin priest, the holy-man following the path of Jesus. Well, unless Jesus liked to eat pussy, then Keiran's not so freakin' holy after all."

"Oh, God, no! Stop!"

"Fuck you! And your son Buck, married with a family? Well, I seduced him as well. You saw the way he looked at me yesterday. He was remembering the time we fucked! And I'll tell you, he's kinky!" She coughed and tried to roll over to clear her lungs, but her arm would not support her weight.

"Makepeace, for the love of God! Shut the bitch up, will you?"

"Oh, I don't know, Des, I find it all rather entertaining," he replied, but he was peering out the back door. Neighbors had now responded to the second shot, and the boldest and most curious were standing on the rear porch trying to see inside.

"They say that Irishmen make the greatest lovers but I don't know about you Kelleys," she continued, struggling against her pain. "You always wanted to fuck me, you prick. Even back when you came to my house to screw my mother. I knew by the way you looked at me. But I knew about you, because I saw you with her. You had that ugly wart on your knee. And she told me about you. You know, she had a name for you? From what I saw it was perfect, too: Mr. Inch-high Private Eye. Isn't that funny? Well, it looked funny to me to see a big guy like you with a teeny little dick. Bet it wasn't so funny for you, eh, Des? Eh, Mr. Inch High?"

He roared and lunged, ready to kick LaGloria as she lay bleeding on the floor. Makepeace shoved him back and said, "Let me look at her! For Christ' sake!" And he crouched down to probe her wound and staunch her bleeding.

As he did so he considered how he was going to get out of this predicament. He had only anticipated telling Des what he had learned, and telling him that he would surely be arrested for the murder of Frank McManus. Now that he had wounded LaGloria he wondered if events were on some kind of cosmic trajectory that he was powerless to stop. Undoubtedly the local police were already on their way, responding to reports from neighbors and concerned citizens. If he could only hold out long enough to hand the scene over to them.

Suddenly a car screeched to a halt outside and someone came in at a run. But it wasn't the police, it was Tweed Kelley.

He took in the scene in a glance and made a snap judgment. Makepeace was crouched over the bleeding body of LaGloria with a gun in his hand. Des was cowering in fear across the room, and the place smelled like downwind at a target practice range. Makepeace looked up with a strange expression on his face, as if he was resigned; and Tweed knew what he must do. Years ago, when the fisherman AD Makepeace had been a guest in the Kelley home, he had taught Tweed that if he was ever seriously threatened by someone larger than him, or if he as facing overwhelming odds, then one of the best strategic moves to get himself out of a jam was the open-handed nose-smash.

Of course, Makepeace had been addressing a young boy, anticipating that he would be facing a much larger opponent, and therefore, the strike would be performed overhand, above his head, bringing the flat of his hand into full contact with the nose of his intended victim.

In this instance, Tweed rapidly approached the older Makepeace, who was crouched upon the floor, and with a sudden move that had all of the attendant follow-through built into it, swung his open hand underhand style, like a softball pitcher, grinding the heel of his hand into the bridge of Makepeace's nose. It broke with an audible snap, and gushed gory red like a rotten pink grapefruit.

At that, Des thanked his son, and scrambled for the magnum. Meanwhile, Makepeace clasped his hands to his face, saying, "You broke my nose! You broke my nose! You bastard!" And he dropped his gun to the floor.

How she had the guts, the stamina, the presence of mind to grab that gun, nobody will ever know, but LaGloria did, indeed seize Makepeace's gun and bring it to bear upon the others in the room, firing virtually indiscriminately.

"Holy shit!" cried Tweed, and he started hopping about to avoid being shot, but ultimately having no choice but to seek safety outside.

Inside the house a minor battle erupted, as Des and LaGloria fired at each other from opposite sides of the room. Makepeace also tried to make his way to safety, but whether he caught a couple of stray bullets or whether he was targeted intentionally, he ended up with fatal wounds from both his own gun and LaGloria's, wielded by Des.

It would take a Sam Peckinpaw to describe the carnage that took place when only the two bloodied murderers were left in the room to witness it; or a team of forensic specialists to piece together the sequence and timing of the shots and injuries. And they would have to base their conclusions upon a careful examination of the embedded slugs, the discarded cartridges, and witness accounts of firing patterns. In any event, all of the bullets in both guns were fired, and all of the people involved in the shooting were dead. Another curious fact for the footnotes was that each of the victims had fired each of the guns at least once.

CHAPTER 59

Time had taken on that elastic quality it sometimes demonstrated when trauma was nigh, or when emotions ran high, by slowing down to a virtual standstill so that the sound of the sirens in the distance no longer signified impending rescue or relief, but simply constant annoyance.

And yet, despite the apparent blockage in the hourglass of time, Tweed was aware of his surroundings and aware of the noise of the approaching sirens and the noise of the neighbors crowding around his father's house. But most of all he was aware that no more sound was coming from inside the house.

Soon others began to realize what he had at first understood, and expectantly, they began to watch the door, hoping to witness the emergence of a survivor. Certainly no one wanted to hazard a hail of bullets to check inside the house. Tweed however coveted no such illusions. Having seen what he had seen within, and having heard what he heard from without, he had no expectation that a living soul could survive the hell of blood and hatred that had existed in that house only moments ago. And so he walked away.

Perhaps it really was the slowing of the sands of time, nevertheless Tweed was gone before the first police units arrived; and as he drove off toward White City, he passed a good many ambulances, fire trucks and emergency vehicles as they sped on their way to what was to be the last of this strange series of related critical situations. He could do nothing for LaGloria now, and his father was beyond help as well, although he offered prayers for their salvation.

There would only be a small window of opportunity during which he might be effective in helping anyone at all before he had to make good his own escape and disappear from the scene. If he weren't certain that he could rely upon his brothers Keiran and Buck, then the soul grinders guilt and remorse would rule the day, and force him to remain available for the pleasure of the police.

But he saw no future in making statements and incriminating himself. His best course of action was to avoid any personal association with the event that took the lives of LaGloria McManus, Desmond Kelley, and AD Makepeace. Besides, Detective Storer would have wanted it this way, so that he could manipulate the facts to suit his interpretation, thus ensuring that he and his partner Jimmy Rima would somehow emerge both brilliant and heroic.

Within twenty minutes he had cleaned out his apartment and packed his car, leaving just enough room for himself and a passenger. Then, along with all of the possessions he wished to carry from his old life to his afterlife, he headed down to the White City Projects, where he called on Mr. Eddie and Rick Rose.

Rick almost failed to recognize his friend the former weed dealer. There was a light in his eyes that hadn't been there before, and a burgeoning expression of happiness that radiated self-confidence.

For the entire ride to Sharlae's he never mentioned anything that had transpired during the morning. Instead he kept up a listing of recommendations, such as, "If I were you, I'd..." Some were related to the drug trade, some were related to Sharlae, some to life in general. Rick knew better than to ask questions; the answer was in his face. Tweed was leaving and he wasn't coming back. He had a question, however. "Hey Rick, man, about that dude Mo Keating..."

"Don't worry about him, dude. He's gone..."

"That's what I'm afraid of. What happened to him?"

"Him? Nothing. I told you how my brothers found us jamming in the alley? Well they, uh, broke up the fight and took Keating there and threw him in the back of a van. Thought it would be pretty funny if they hauled his ass out into the middle of nowhere, you know? Took him way the fuck up to Maine. Dumped him out near a place called Fort Fairfield, without a cent in his pocket..." Rick had to stop because he was laughing so hard.

"...but he'll find his way back in a day or two, man. I mean, shit, you or I would, if we were in his shoes."

Tweed delivered on the punchline. "Yeah, well, if he's no good at thumbing, he better learn to dig potatoes."

They got to Sharlae's house and the tearful reunion between the young lovers was embarrassing enough to help drive Tweed out the door even faster than he had anticipated.

"I'm sorry, Sharlae," he started, "I thought I needed Rick to be my insurance. If Storer arrested me, I wanted to have a witness I could bring out who could really save my ass."

Sharlae turned to Rick, amazed. "You never said you saw what happened down there!"

"No, I didn't..."

"He didn't see anything," explained Tweed, "I just coached him on what to say that he saw. Rick's a good man, and I'll never forget that he was willing to stand by me and stand up for me when I needed him most. You two are good for each other, and I wish you both the best of luck, and happiness."

And with that, Tweed embraced each of them in turn, then both of them together; and he left.

Fulfilling the arrangement he had made with the blessings of Wayne and Donal, he ceded control of his entire operation to Sharlae, and he rewarded Bone with the area that Og had vacated. In order to smooth out the wrinkles in the sales map he shuffled Sharlae's former beat into Eban and Kuhn's territories. Thus all of the Wizards ended up with larger pieces of the respective pie, and the roles and responsibilities were left largely intact in the manner he desired. As Tweed had explained to his former partners, it was his intention that after he left, Sharlae would handle 'the books', Rick would support her and work as liaison with Donal and Wayne, while Bone, inheriting a role for which he was suited both intellectually and temperamentally, would see to the growth and continued prosperity of the enterprise as a whole.

***

Where to go? The road stretched ahead of him like the invitation to a grand adventure. Perhaps he would finally go to Alaska and follow the dream he had shared with Jimmy Col so many years ago. Perhaps he would go to Chicago, and look Jimmy up for starters.

The car was packed, he had plenty of cash and a blank slate. But his heart was aching and his mind was reeling from the sights and sounds of a morning he couldn't have imagined in his worst nightmares. What was all this stuff? Did he really need to carry 30 cubic feet of crap with him wherever he went? What about the words Wayne had told him, that he didn't care for material things? It was time to take a detour.

So here he was, not quite full circle, but almost, standing beside the swamp at South St, along the tracks at the Arbs Park. It was here where he had first limped away from the aborted murder attempt on his father. *Perhaps he should have helped the McManus brothers that night, and maybe they would have made a clean sweep of the job.*

He popped open the little opera windows in the rear quarters of his car, and made sure that the vents were fully open. Saabs were known to have welded hollow body panels, but he was sure that he could get his baby to sink. *Ah, but the way things turned out, all the real killers were dead, and he was getting a second chance.* If God wasn't sending him a message then maybe he was just too dumb to listen, anyway; but if He was, then he certainly had gotten it loud and clear. Hmmm, a roll-out might work. If not, he'd just get out and push.

Tweed started the car and put it into first gear. Very slowly he let out on the clutch, allowing the car to roll toward the edge of the swamp. All of his prized belongings were still packed inside. But his savings, his stash and his investments were elsewhere, and he had his wallet and a roll of cash in his pocket. It was now or never. He fell out of the car like a drunk toppling off a merry-go-round. The ground felt cool and welcoming, bouncy and soft. From his prone position he watched as his car took the plunge over the hidden embankment, through a stand of milkweed, and into the watery swamp below. The 99 took to the water like a hippopotamus bathing up to its nostrils, and with hardly a bubble, it was gone. That was what he loved about the swamp.

For a time Tweed felt suffused with a feeling of deep and warm appreciation for the natural world. He rolled onto his back and stared at the sky, and let himself be drawn off into the gray void above his head. For a moment he almost felt at peace. But this was no longer his place. And there was deep sorrow in his heart. He could not afford to be found laying around in the Arbs Park. Not with the bodies of his father and girlfriend recoloring the rugs in a house not two miles from here.

As he pulled himself together he let his mind create a picture of police officers, rolling bodies over, checking for vital signs, and hunting for weapons in the same room where he used to tear open presents on Christmas morning, where he used to sleep on the couch when he wasn't feeling well. Then, following roughly the same route he had taken on the night Frankie and Nilvan died, he headed into town to hitch a ride, clearing his mind as he walked.

There wasn't much happening on Main St. The field had a strange appearance, like the lists at the conclusion of a jousting tournament. Strings of colored plastic triangles fluttered from poles that only last night had marked the commissary row and carny-game alley, and the lines for the rides. So the carnival was gone, or going.

A caravan had formed along the side street, with all of the food trucks and the supply trucks followed by the trailers hauling the rides. The leader of the convoy was apparently ready to pull out. Tweed hustled over to the row of trucks as they revved their engines preparing to move on to the next town. He stuck his thumb out expectantly, and started walking backwards along the row, imploring driver after driver with a simple gesture. Finally he heard a call above the roar of the motors, "Hey, you. Come one, let's go!"

He spotted the open passenger door and made for it, swinging himself up and in just as the truck left the curb. It reminded him of the old days when he used to ride the rails. He turned to the driver with a smile and hesitated. Did he know this guy? "Thanks for the lift, man."

"Happy to oblige, I know what it's like when you gotta get out of this town." He was roughly Tweed's age, but balding, with soft aquiline features oddly offset by a left-skewed cigar-smoker's mouth.

"What's your name?"

"Uh, Theodore, uh, Teddy Philips…and yours?" Tweed asked, hoping he hadn't sounded too contrived.

"Stewie. Stewie Ramos. Glad to meet you. It's gonna be a long ride."

"Yeah, man, same here," said Tweed. "That's alright…let me tell you a story to pass the time…"

END